THE BLACKENED TABLET SERIES

A Crown Forged By VICTORY'S CONSEQUENCE

AARYANNA ABBOTT
MARLAYNA JAMES

FWP
Author Group

FRIENDS WITH PENS AUTHOR GROUP

Published by Friends With Pens Author Group
www.friendswithpensauthorgroup.com

Cover Art © 2022 by Keylin Rivers
www.fantasycoverdesign.com

Hard Cover: 978-0-9918512-9-4
Paperback: 978-0-9918512-8-7
Ebook: 978-1-7386710-0-7

Maps created with Inkarnate
Formatted with Atticus
Bloodlines created with Canva

This complete work is Fiction.
Fantasy > Epic
Fantasy > Action & Adventure
Fantasy > Ancient & Medieval
Fantasy > Romance
Fantasy > Paranormal
Fantasy > Fairies & Elves
Fantasy > Magic & Wizards
Fantasy > Series
Fantasy > Dark

First Edition 2023, Friends With Pens Author Group

Want More Marlayna James?

Check out these titles at any online retailer.
    Sugarverse Series: #1: Arm Candy (contemporary romance)

Playtime companion shorts
Restless Bean Series: #1: The Doctor's In Abigail (Naughty Spice)
Restless Bean Series: #2: Checking You Out Adrienne (Naughty Spice)

We're social and love to connect with our readers:
https://www.facebook.com/groups/fwpvip
https://www.facebook.com/FWPAuthorGroup
Instagram @fwpauthorgroup
Twitter @FWPAuthorGroup
TikTok @fwpauthorgroup
Clubhouse @marlaynajames

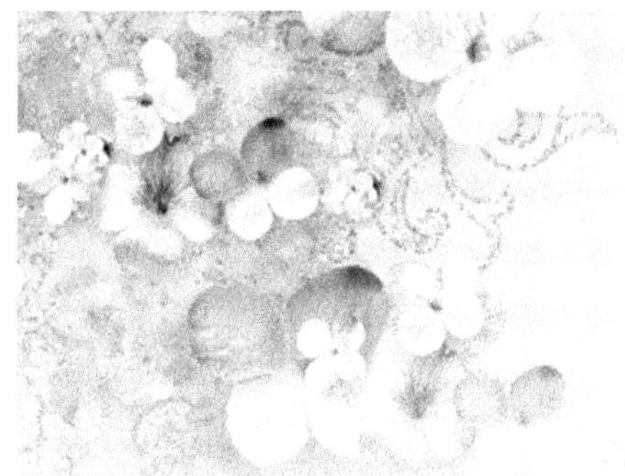

For Ashley—when the water's rising, you will always be my silver lining.

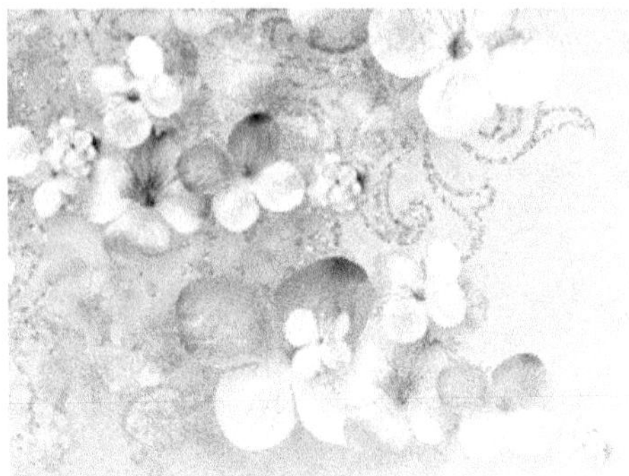

Dear reader,

Thank you for your support and trust. I am truly humbled that you chose my work out of the millions of possibilities, and know the immeasurable responsibility I owe you.

This series' characters came to me as a teenager—many, many years ago. From difficult times, they helped me cope and escape. I won't digress. I am who I am today because of the people I knew and the tragedies which befell me. Without them, I would be a different person—and perhaps not for the better.

I formatted this book with several helpful reference features: character index (back), chronology (back), maps, and bloodlines.

For you, I hope you physically feel every glorious touch, and are torn by each anguished moment, so the ecstasy is made all the more intense. Because if you didn't know pain, you couldn't know joy.

Forever,
Marlayna

Reference Material

Welcome To Speranza

All reference materials are in colour on our website: friendswithpensauthorgroup.com, under Aaryanna's fantasy.

The world of Speranza held nine kingdoms—all connected. Harmonious for nearly three thousand years.

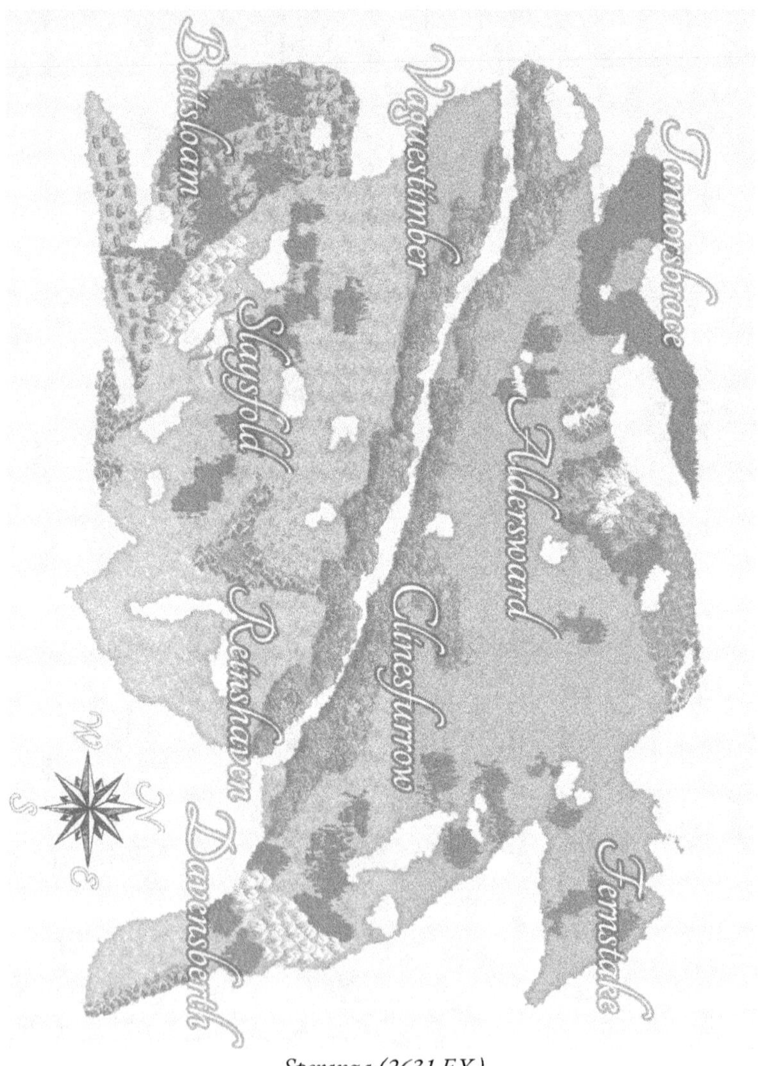

Speranza (2631 F.Y.)

Until the event.

Aldersward (285 N.D.)

Their world was forever changed. Aldersward was all that remained. This series begins 285 years later. Most notable features above include:

The Crystal Lagoon (northeast)

Edson University (middle west)

Rayanna Forest (along the riverbanks)

Lessard (south tip)

Aldersward Castle's Grounds (285 N.D.)

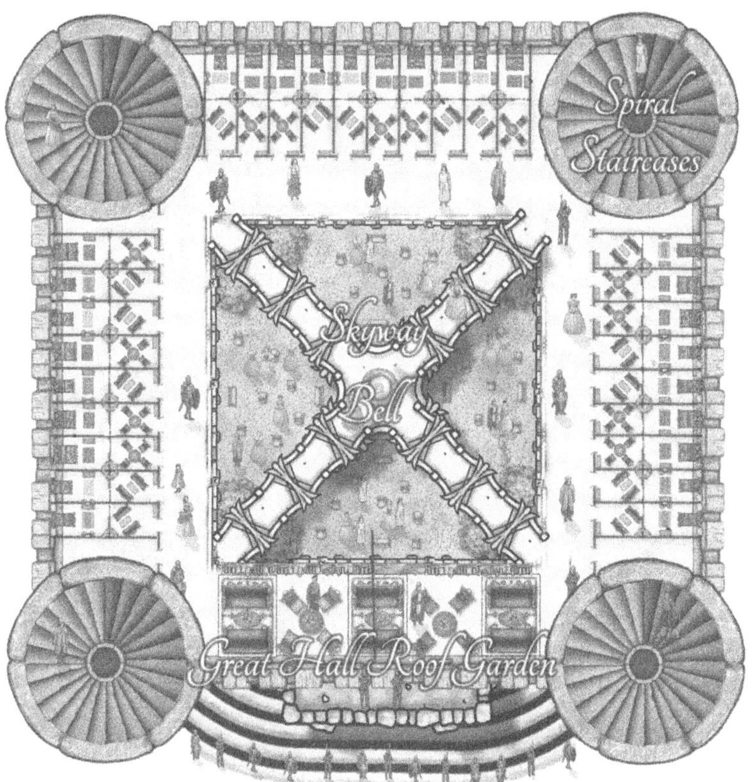

Aldersward Castle (3rd floor)

The third floor is where lesser nobility, dames, knights, ladies-in-waiting, and senior staff will sometimes find themselves assigned. These chambers are smaller than the ones on the second floor. Note the skyway—the bridges which shorten the distance between halls. On the south interior, there is a common area where individuals may socialise. Remember: the halls and skyway are railed but open to the sky/floor above.

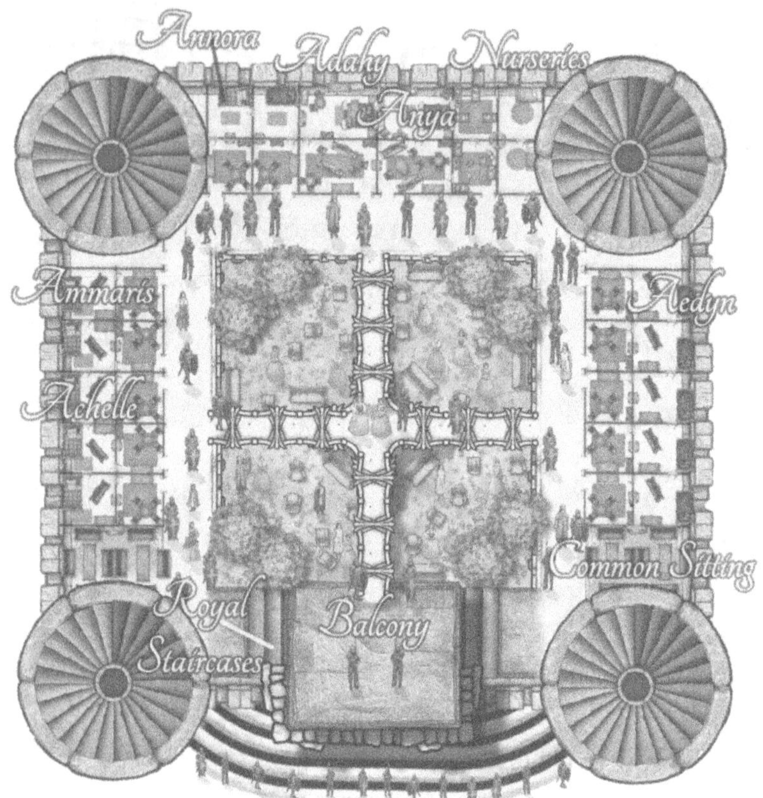

Aldersward Castle (2nd floor)

The royal family is housed on the second floor. Vacant chambers are often filled with dignitaries and honoured guests. The skyway runs differently, north/south and east/west. Next to the nurseries, on the right, there are rooms for nursemaids. There are two straight staircases beneath the balcony, reserved for the royals and those accompanying them. Remember: the halls and skyway are railed, but open to the sky/floor above.

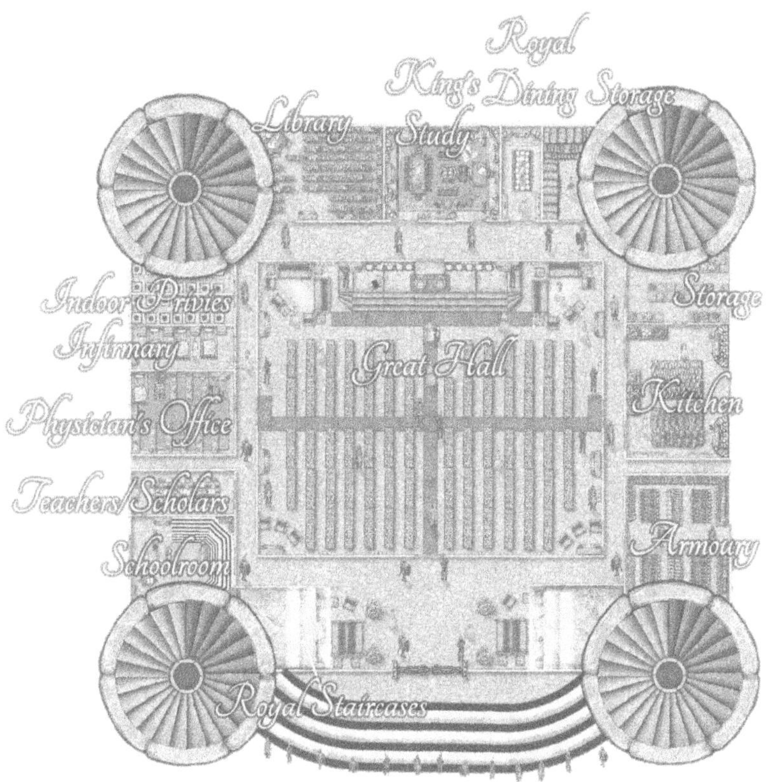

Aldersward Castle (main floor)

Indoor privies are the newest technological advance in this kingdom. Though they didn't plan it very well. The sewage drains from the two rooms on the west-north corner and ends in a sewage pond behind the library. It's a stinky mess. The schoolroom is accessible from the west gardens, so those children in the servants' cottages can attend. The royal staircases were made transparent so you can see what lay beneath them. However, do note, they end a few feet from the large double doors.

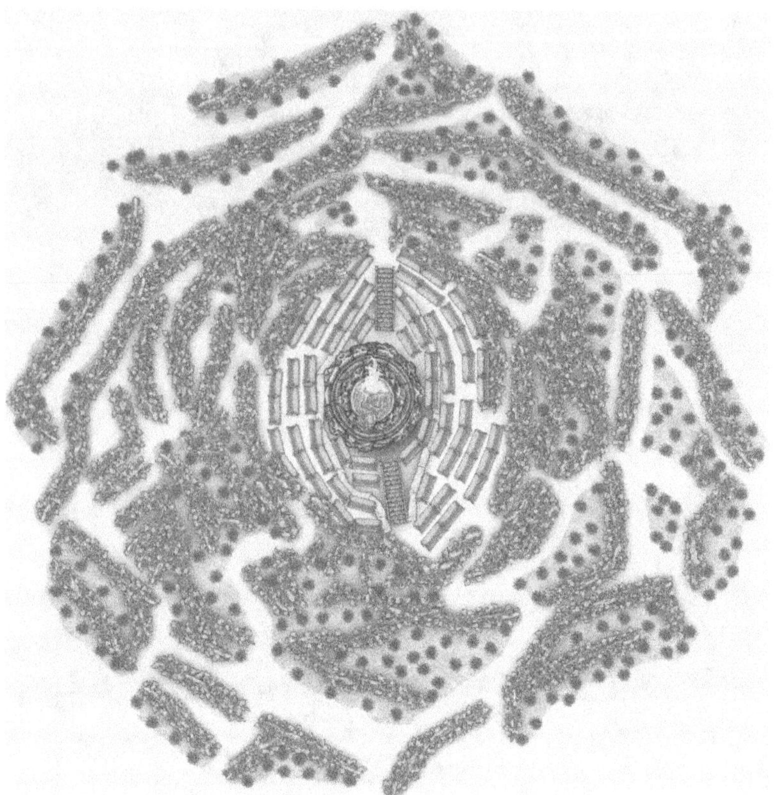

Aldersward City's Dotato Temple

Aldersward's temples look like the image above, but are scaled smaller in other locations. This particular temple is where noughties receive their abilities, where weekly worship takes place, and where royalty wed.

Above shows the kings' bloodline. The two notable generations are: King Asmaud and his children from 2631 F.Y., and the current rulers, King Adahy and his children. *C. P.* means Crowned Prince, future king. *(b)/(g)* indicates gender at birth.

When one dies, a few utilise their own unsullied conscience to measure one's entire character by scrutinising every decision and action, then take pleasure in reducing them to a single word, moral or evil. Does the verdict hold if in hindsight it's revealed another initiated those decisions and actions?

Day 360, 284 N.D. (New Day)
Royal Estate
Wibley Village
Aldersward Kingdom
Speranza

On the kingdom's list of expectations, the king scratched off another on the day of Prince Aedyn's birth. *Replacement.* And the infant checked many of his own; *symbol, employed, betrothed, prisoner, migrant,* and *alone.*

Nestled in Aldersward's Northeast, the farming village of Wibley sloped towards the sea with rust-coloured rocks and sand protected by layers of deep green moss. The serene waves washed the shoreline as the cool sun blanketed the land in light. Across the grey-clouded sky, birds soared and suddenly dove into the water, capturing their feed. Whales in the distance slapped their tails, sending large sprays into the air. Nothing existed beyond the expansive water.

Aedyn reclined on the beach at the edge of the kingdom and their world, Speranza. Bored, he fidgeted with the pendant at his neck—a gift from his mother when he was a young child. Outside of his strictly regimented hours, she had attempted to provide him a loving childhood. Often coming into his room before or after sunset when his teachers, mentors, and scholars left.

The prince was life's spectator. His sisters frolicked and played with few guards or restrictions, attended school with other children, and chose their friends. Since childhood, he had a single companion, Auren, provided by his parents. Imprisoned in the centre of Prince Aedyn's guards, they had no choice but to become friends. Once teenagers, however, Auren, bored with the sedentary routine, sought to experience things the prince could only imagine and accompanied King Adahy on hunts or trips, frequenting the brothels and forming relationships Auren deemed fit.

Shaking off the depressive thoughts, Prince Aedyn discarded his tunic and unbuttoned his trousers, exposing his tapered olive torso to the cool winter breeze.

Guard Asa strode to his side and whispered, not wanting the eleven others to hear. "What are you doing?"

Aedyn's unruly, nape-lengthened black hair fell forward. "It appears I'm going for a swim."

"You cannot. How can we protect you?"

"From what?" his bright blue eyes and hand swept across the open expanse. "There's nothing here."

"Aedyn, please cooperate. I must follow your father's orders."

In frustration, his fingers rushed over his high cheekbone and righted his hair. "Auren cannot return soon enough. At least when he's my Lead, he ignores my father's instructions."

He reminded his liege. "And he can. He has your parents' affection. We are friends, but I don't have the luxury of ignoring my duty. The queen won't save me from the king's wrath."

"Fine, but compromise—you've searched the area. It can't hurt to withdraw the guards higher onto the slope and leave me space to roam."

Guard Asa nodded, ordering the men as Prince Aedyn grabbed his tunic and strode along the beach.

He lapped the shoreline, no longer crowded. From the guards' elevated position, they could maintain watch.

On his third trip, a selkie draped her delicate arms over a partially submerged boulder and pulled her fin onto it as she sat. As a child, he studied the creature. They could choose to remove their pelts and live like humans, or wear them and live like seals. But, no matter their choice, they yearned to be the other. Shifting back and forth, they spent their existence never satisfied. He drew parallels between their plight and his, which left him feeling kindred.

Her long, brown, sun-highlighted hair flowed down her naked back and over her breasts as she removed her pelt and draped it over her lap.

Intrigued by the anonymous opportunity to converse with another increased the beating in the prince's chest. With a raise of his hand and a glance backwards, he stayed the guards in position. She was several yards in the water, unarmed, and not an immediate threat.

"You've changed." Her voice was lyrical as she smiled. "More handsome than ever."

"Are we acquainted?" As he walked closer to the water's edge, Aedyn's thick-lashed eyes narrowed, and he attempted to use his truth magic, uncertain whether it would function on a non-human.

Her expression saddened, and she shook her head. "I apologise, you aren't Abel. Do you know him? Do you bring me a message?"

It wasn't the definitive response he hoped for and cautiously he stepped backwards to a grouping of large rocks. "No, I don't know him."

"We're to meet between sunrise and the sun's highest point."

He vaulted his muscular frame from one rock to another until he reached the tallest, then sat. Nervously, he fingered the small cleft in his chin. "Do you meet him often?"

"Carpenter Abel of Wibley," pain haunted her eyes, "I've waited every day for 167 moon cycles."

"That's nearly fourteen years. Why have you not given up?"

"It's not so simple. Once I offered him my pelt to keep so I could remain with him forever. But with every crashing wave, the sea urged me back. When I struggled against its pull, he watched me suffer. When he could no longer withstand the pain, he encouraged me to take my pelt and return. Eighty-four moon cycles later, he met me here, then the next, but I haven't seen him since. Haven't you loved beyond reason?"

He shrugged. "No. I love my siblings because they are part of me. I love my mother because she is kind and nurturing. I love my father because..." As he searched for the words, he played with the pout of his bottom lip, "it's expected of me."

"Family love bears no resemblance to romantic love. It's painful, exciting, agonising bliss. Your heart can be so full of another's affections you think it may burst. And in an instant, the same lover can shred it into excruciating pieces, leaving you to believe you will never recover from the raw wounds. But in the end, you will do it over and over again."

"I'll take your word for it," his cheek dimpled when he smiled, "as tempting as you make it sound." Prince Aedyn turned at the sound of his name as Guard Asa approached. "I must go, but return tomorrow–"

The selkie stretched the pelt over her legs. "Only every eight-four moon cycles, may we meet the same human. I could meet you then."

"No, I best not promise anything." He watched as the short, grey-haired pelt melded over her legs, and she slipped into the water.

Day 360, 284 N.D.
Leathersmith Daley's Home
Maidstone Village
Aldersward Kingdom

A hired carriage waited nearby, out of sight. Inside it, his younger sister was safe, hidden from her husband's brutalising hands.

Patiently, Lead Auren waited. His body coiled to strike when he laid eyes on his squinty-eyed, scrawny, Daven brother-in-law. Even if he were the last of his race, Auren would kill him for his nature.

A single candle flickered in the large room stacked with dirty dishes, discarded food, and empty kegs. The floor nearly crawled with buzzing insects. Their bodies scurried and their limbs scratched underneath the ankle-deep garbage.

The Daven entered, immediately noting the burning candle and the wide-open bedchamber door. "I don't know how you escaped–"

Lead Auren straightened but hid his solid muscular stature and confidence by dropping his shoulders and relaxing his frame. "I let her out."

His sister's husband, towering over him by a foot, strode forward. "You've no right to interfere in matters of my home and wife."

Lead Auren calmly smiled, his tone conversational and weak. "I've every right. I'm Lead Auren of Maidstone."

"Her big brother returns from his pampering at the castle?" Amused, he laughed. "As head of *your* family, let me welcome you back into the fold and remind you, by law, she's my property." He shoved Auren, and he allowed it, stumbling backwards a few paces.

Lead Auren had promised his frightened sister he would not start a fight. However, he would enjoy provoking him, then ending it. He rubbed his hand over his week's worth of stubble on his head. "Azalea is no one's property."

"It's a brave man who arrives with magic to steal from a *noughty*."

"I need no magic." His brown eyes remained fixated on the man as he lifted the bow and quiver from his back and tossed them aside. "A *noughty* is born without magic. You? You were too stupid to learn."

As Auren hoped, the man's anger ignited, and he attacked. The Lead widened his stance, squared his shoulders, and hardened his frame. This time, when shoved his body did not give.

Day 362, 284 N.D.
Earl Avin's Study
Royal Estate
Wibley Village
Aldersward Kingdom

Like all royal estates, corrals, or fields, depending on soil conditions, lined either side of the drive. The stone and wood buildings purposely formed a clockwise semi-circle, the royal house, privy, washhouse, then the tool shed, staff quarters connected to a cookhouse, staff privy, and the barn so when the royal men visited and drank, they would not lose their way.

The king provided farmhands, groundskeepers, and cooks. Each earl supplied his household staff.

Prince Aedyn relaxed in the study, sipping his whisky. Snapping wood in the hearth warded off the evening chill in the heavily decorated room with its dark woods and bulky furniture, a tranquil place to enjoy after a long day.

Without invitation, knuckles rapped, and Guard Asa entered. He sat in a cushioned chair next to Aedyn, poured himself a drink, and lifted his booted feet onto the rest.

"As requested, I've found the carpenter."

"Is he dead?"

"No, he's married with children."

Aedyn lifted his thick brow and sipped from his mug, hiding his empathetic expression. The selkie longed for a single thing but would never see it realised. Without a word, the prince crossed to the desk and penned a note.

After our meeting, I enquired about Carpenter Abel of Wibley on your behalf.

It pains me to inform you, he died many years ago, and his mother told me on his deathbed he spoke solely of loving you.

I hope you find comfort in these answers.

Aedyn of Aldersward Castle

He folded and poured wax on the parchment, then planted his ring's insignia in the centre, sealing it. "Find someone to deliver this. We'll leave for the castle in the morning."

The guard stuffed it into his long coat as he stood. "Wise decision, I heard several people fell ill last night. We shouldn't risk your health by staying any longer."

Day 362, 284 N.D.
Den's Mercantile
Aldersward City
Aldersward Kingdom

"You don't belong in a whorehouse. I'd rather you stayed on the castle grounds, closer to me." Lead Auren, over six-feet, dwarfed the sparsely furnished room.

The bruises on Azalea's face ached when she spoke. "I listened to no one's warnings, married a Daven, and suffered by his hands. I stayed because of my pride."

"You didn't leave because of a barred door. No one need know the circumstances." His brown eyes reasoned with her.

She held her broken ribs as she sat on the bed. "If you arrive home at the castle with me in tow, there will be questions. Our relationship will be known. People will want answers and, if they don't get them, they will invent their own. I can't allow my condition to scandalise your position."

"When the remaining Davens learn of Daley's death, they'll look for you. They'll want answers. It's why I didn't leave you in Maidstone with Mother."

"Without Daley, there are only seven Davens left throughout Aldersward Kingdom. They meet rarely. Let me recover and decide what I wish my life to be. I'm damaged. No one may want me if I tell them of my interracial marriage."

"You're only twenty-two and attractive. Whom you shared your bed with prior is no one's business. And when it's time, I'll ensure you have another dowry." He stepped aside when the proprietor's wife entered carrying a food tray. "I've known the owner for many years. You'll be well looked after here."

Day 5, 285 N.D.
Great Hall
Castle's Ground Level
Near Aldersward City

A soft peach coloured lizard zigzagged the man's arm and along his shoulder, investigating his actions.

"Settle, Stinger." Lead Auren cocked his head and grinned at the axolotl with its hairy mane of dark pink gills. Its webbed fingers reached to hug the human's face, examining him with blue eyes. It smiled, mimicking its master's expression.

Auren's chuckle vibrated through the long room as he strode inside. A servant observed the pair while her hands animated and orchestrated several feather dusters. By magic, they cleaned the banner-lined walls, empty tables, and chairs, avoiding the open flames of the candelabras and torches.

She smiled. "He's adorable."

Lead Auren quickly inspected the servant, nearly twice his age, and his brow raised in mock indignation. "He's not adorable. He's fierce—deadly even." His hand dipped into the water pouch at his waist, then drizzled it onto his pet as he walked to the woman, temporarily abandoning his duty.

She laughed and pressed her back against the wall when he leaned closer and placed his hand above her. His other pushed her dishevelled hair aside.

"Here, inspect him yourself." He dropped his shoulder.

She glanced at the pet as Lead Auren placed his hand on her cheek. His thumb rubbed her bottom lip. "Why have I never had the pleasure?"

Flattered and not at all uncomfortable by his closeness, the servant giggled. She knocked his hand away. "You should stick with inexperienced girls. They know not how you disappoint them."

"Maybe I need an older woman to instruct me on the skills I lack. Perhaps you?" he smiled and ran his hand over her arm.

Her breath played against his jaw when she stepped into him, her mouth a fraction from his. "I worry I would ruin other women for you." She dipped under his arm and flicked her wrist. The feather dusters jumped to the rise at the room's end. They cleaned the throne and the perch displaying Aldersward's blackened tablet.

Interested, he followed. "I'm willing to risk–"

"Auren," an amused Queen Anya, tall and slender, called from the rise where she inspected the hall's cleanliness before others attended. "Stop pestering the staff. I wish her gone so we may have privacy."

"Your Majesty, of course." He exaggerated his bow and limped the room's length to her. "You appear lovelier than ever before." He smiled as he gathered and hugged her tightly.

"And your leg appears injured. Must I always worry?" Though her eyes clouded with concern, her grey and brown shoulder-length hair swayed when she laughed.

"It's nothing. I merely ended an argument." He rubbed his palm over his stubbly cheek, unhappy with the secret he kept.

She clicked her tongue in dismay. "Why can't you marry and settle down, so I may be left in peace?"

"I believe my antics keep you young and beautiful." His eyes surveyed her laugh lines, the only evidence she neared sixty.

Footsteps paraded through a side door. The dusters jumped from the rise and landed in the servant's hand. Queen Anya lowered herself onto her throne as she waved the staff out and answered Auren. "I'm willing to sacrifice myself for your happiness."

As his guards closed the numerous entrances, Prince Aedyn climbed the rise and kissed his mother's cheek. "It's interesting you would sacrifice your happiness for Lead Auren's, but not for mine."

"Shush, Aedyn, your jealousy is showing. You know I love all my children equally." For a fraction of a second, she winced, then leaned back in her chair. "Tell me about your journeys."

From farther along the rise, Auren brought two chairs forward as Aedyn reported. "Uneventful. A few townsfolk became ill as we left. It took longer than expected to collect my betrothed and return because the women accompanied us. I did not wish to cause them discomfort." The prince accepted a chair.

"You missed the new year celebration." Auren grinned mischievously—unable to elaborate with the queen present.

"*Boring* festivities I'm *obligated* to attend. Where sober, I'm *paraded* and expected to act proper while I converse with ranked subjects I *do not know* or care about. I'm thankful Jezabet saw fit to grant me leave."

"It wasn't our god who granted you leave. You should thank your father." She rubbed her temple. "I've felt quite weak the past few days. Perhaps I've contracted whatever ails the Wibley subjects."

Aedyn clasped her hand in his, inspecting it. Her age-spotted flesh was cold, and he rubbed it to offer her warmth.

"How did you find your mother?" The queen turned her attention to Auren.

"Pretty easily—I remembered where she lives." He smirked and when her green eyes scolded him, he continued. "She's recovered from my father's death. And she's hardly my mother since it was you who raised me."

The heavy doors behind the rise groaned and King Adahy entered. Time had not been kind. Once the tallest man in the room, age now hunched his form and his muscles deteriorated to fat around his middle.

The two younger men carried their chairs onto the floor below, then stood before him as he sat, kissed his wife, and inspected her face. "How are you feeling?"

"Unwell, but I did not want to miss welcoming them back. I'll return to my chambers shortly."

Satisfied, King Adahy addressed the boys. "You aren't presenting Lady Ammaris to us in private?"

Aedyn squared his shoulders, preparing himself for his father's anger. "I saw no reason to subject her to our gathering."

The queen laid her hand on her husband's, stopping his temper. "Of course she should be included. She will be your wife and one day Aldersward's queen."

The king gripped his armrest. "Our gathering wouldn't be difficult if you spoke less and accepted what is. While you fight this betrothal, I remind you, Auren was once a stranger. This is no different."

Lead Auren watched the queen's troubled expression. Knowing these arguments between father and son upset her, he sought to lighten the exchange. He nudged his princely brother and winked, "You *loovvee* me."

Prince Aedyn crossed his arms. "Love, no. Perhaps *tolerate*?"

"There are more important matters than love." King Adahy said.

The prince's voice echoed, "Hypocrite! You married the woman you loved."

Queen Anya bit her lower lip. "Our love grew. Yours will do the same."

"But he *chose* you from a line of women. Chose," Aedyn ruffled his hair in frustration. "He was forced by no one."

King Adahy strode off the rise, coming face to face with his son. "Unlike you, I accepted the responsibility of my position. And I wish my father had forced my marriage, so now I would be young enough to give you the thrashing you deserve."

Queen Anya's heart split as she rushed to stand between them. The father and son ignored her, their eyes locked in a heated battle.

"I wish you would try, if only once. You–"

Lead Auren observed when suddenly the queen's expression paled ghostly white. As her eyes rolled backwards and closed, she collapsed, and he rushed to catch her before her body hit the floor.

Day 30
Princess Achelle's Chambers
Castle's Second Level
Near Aldersward City

As she slept soundly in the comfort of her bed, her mind visited others in their dreams.

The light from the warm hearth shadowed the two girls' frames while they sat on the furs, cross-legged, facing each other. A four-posted bed dominated the room behind them. In a childish game, Princess Achelle and her best friend,

April, chanted the silly words as they clapped their palms together. When they lost the rhythm, they fell over in a fit of giggles and playfully embraced.

Princess Achelle's green eyes sparkled. "I believe Guard Augustus wishes to please me. As we passed by yesterday, I mentioned my favourite colour is blue. Today, his hair was tied with a blue ribbon."

"He's so handsome. If you hadn't claimed him, I would have. I noticed the ribbon, but still he plays oblivious when you're around."

She tucked her long brown hair behind her ear. "He's a masterful man of twenty-five, not a boy. He realises we must hide our relationship. It would be reproachable if he allowed my presence to jeopardise my father's safety. When he held the door for us this afternoon, his slightly longer bow was most affectionate."

Her friend shrugged. "I must take your word for it. I've never indulged in a secret relationship before."

Achelle sighed and rose, righting the short train of her ivory nightgown behind her. "I'll leave so you may sleep peacefully now."

As the princess's physical form dissipated, April nodded goodbye and was left alone in her dream.

Achelle returned to the elaborate groaning hallways, creaking staircases, and echoing drops of nothingness in her mind. Everything shifted like an unexplainable chain reaction—dragging upwards, downwards, and sideways without reason, causing her to tread carefully through the blinding white paths contrasted with murky, black, empty spaces. White doors, invisible except for their protruding ivory handles, appeared along the hallways, and muffled, desperate voices called from behind them. Even though she attempted to enter each, they were often locked. Over the years, she had acclimatised to the cold, isolated atmosphere, understanding this was the price she paid for her ability.

The bannister under her fingertips was icy as her slippered feet climbed the stairs. She recognised the tell-tale shifting sound when it began. Using both hands, she held firm when butterflies pitched in her stomach and a feeling of weightlessness flooded her senses. The staircase vibrated as it twisted and rubbed against another hallway's end. Her mind fell quiet, and she rushed upward, uncertain when the next shift would occur.

Like nothing she had experienced here before in seven years, her eyes were instantly drawn to a pastel blue door farther down the hall and she approached, fascinated by its colour. She ran her hand over its smooth surface as she listened to a wispy, feminine voice chant from within.

A little frightened, Achelle lifted its handle. The door swung inwards, and she was comforted by the familiar blinding light. When she stepped through, her body melted away, then reformed elsewhere, and she surveyed her surroundings.

A beautiful, crystal clear lake embedded in golden sand and lush pastel-coloured flowers stretched out before her. The mesmerising sunset in the distance was hampered by a large mountain with a twisted horn. She felt comforted, warm, and peaceful in the serene dream.

Behind her, chanting voices invited her and when she turned, she was surprised by the strange paler-skinned women whose hair was varying degrees of black and white. Their loose bulky robes nestled them where they knelt around another lying in a bed of grass.

The loudest woman dragged her fingers over the unconscious, injured woman's face, then raised her eyes to the sky. As if the wounds on the woman had never existed at all, they closed. The black of the chanter's hair rushed away, replaced by white. When her chant ended, her body collapsed as if its energy was spent. The other women divided their attention between the pair.

As the unconscious woman opened her eyes and sat up, Achelle rushed forward. But when she neared them, her form dissipated, and she found herself back in her mind's hallways. The blue door was gone.

Who were those women? How had they cured the injured? Can they heal my mother? She wondered as she raced along the corridor, feeling each door she passed. Sometimes, when she searched for a specific person, it took several hallway realignments before she discovered them. When she mounted another staircase, she found only a dark black void beyond it. She sat and gripped the bannister with both hands, waiting for the next shift to occur.

A groaning rumble started and, as all the parts rearranged, the staircase swung sideways, positioning itself against another. At the silence, she descended and entered another long corridor. She ran her fingertips over several doors before she found the one she was looking for.

She fixed an innocent smile on her lips as she opened the door easily and walked through. Prince Aedyn would be angry. He had forbidden her from his dreams years before. She did not care, needing to confide what she had seen.

Day 43
Great Hall
Castle's Ground Level
Near Aldersward City

At an improper hour before daybreak, Lead Auren lit each hearth, driving out the cool air and mildew scent. Suddenly, a loud roar like a tornado sounded, and he turned as a man emerged from the last darkened fireplace.

"The Lead without his prince? I don't believe it!" Physician Axton of Aldersward Castle jested.

"It's good to see you too." Auren smiled, then tossed a flame into the hearth. Lifting his pet, he dropped him inside the water pouch. "I took well-deserved time elsewhere. The distraught women in Aldersward City wept, missing me." His eyes danced with naughtiness. He unbuttoned his vest, puffed out his tunic-covered chest, and rolled his sleeves.

"Ah, I understand now." Physician Axton chuckled and watched the boy prepare to demonstrate his masculinity. "There were rumours of one so ugly. He bore diarrhoea-coloured eyes, rat's hair on his scalp and short, almost non-existent whiskers. He frequented the brothels and flashed his large coin purse so women would service him." His enormous belly rolled with laughter. "I should've realised it was you."

"You misunderstood. My virility is legendary. Women pay for my services." He slapped the man's back as many feet approached.

Prince Aedyn gestured when he entered. His four guards and page wandered to the closest fire while he continued towards the two men, who bowed. He towered over all except Lead Auren, who was an inch shorter.

"Your laughs sound through the halls. Does Auren entertain you with tales of his youthful sexual promiscuity?" The prince rubbed his chin's slight cleft as he warmly addressed his father's long-time physician and his best friend.

"They are not tales if they're true." Lead Auren nudged him. "I add, twenty-three does not make us youthful, it makes us experts in mating, and it burdens us with the stamina to *complete* the job *well*."

Physician Axton's laughter howled. "I warn you *boys*. You shouldn't pass by my cottage at night. My wife's moans will put your theory to shame."

Prince Aedyn's blue eyes danced with mischief. "I cannot say Auren lies, but when he's in my company, the women flatten him on their way to me."

The three men finished their laugh, and Physician Axton sighed. "I've come to appreciate these light-hearted moments."

King Adahy of Aldersward Castle and his guards came through a doorway behind the throne. The three men straightened seriously.

The king's unkempt moustache and long beard moved. "Your report, Physician Axton?"

"Your Majesty, more fall ill. The longer they've slept, the more their pain grows. This includes our queen. I am alleviating their symptoms with conventional herbs but don't have a cure to wake them. The sick don't know each other, nor did they have contact. Most fell asleep together, and I still can't identify the cause." Physician Axton waited for the king's direction.

Aedyn responded instead. "What do you make of Princess Achelle's revelation? Do you suppose–"

"There will be no such talk of your sister's dream-walk," King Adahy said. "We don't know in whose dream she walked or if it was only a dream. How can we trust it wasn't a young girl's whimsical fantasy? We'll waste time and experience great disappointment when we cannot make it a reality. And which fool would venture out of our kingdom to seek a cure based on the dreams of an eighteen-year-old girl?"

The king's words did nothing to weaken Prince Aedyn's resolve. "I would."

"You speak nonsense. You are the only son of the throne. Without you, our kingdom has no future ruler."

The overstated, recited verse surfaced; he alone was the most important person in their entire world. Aedyn's temper threatened to snap, held only by a taut thread. "Without me, my mother and the others will die, then what? I watch my sisters, Achelle and Annora, grieve, too young to understand why I did nothing to save their mother." His blue eyes narrowed. "Do you love her so little you'd willingly let her die? Is this what I look forward to in my marriage to Lady Ammaris... her death?"

The king's face reddened, and his voice echoed. "Never assume my feelings. I would rather die than watch her suffer. We've a duty to our people—to put them above everything and anyone!" King Adahy stepped into his son's frame. "If the only part of your marriage you look forward to is Ammaris's death, then I've raised a fool,—and may Jezabet help my countrymen make it through your rule."

King Adahy turned to depart, his boots as loud as thunder, stomping.

Prince Aedyn reached for him but found his movement blocked by his lead guard.

"Let him go," Lead Auren whispered. His lips pursed and with sympathetic eyes turned to his friend. With brotherly affection, he sought to stop the argument from going further, understanding both were passionate in their stance. It would serve no purpose to continue the barbed words, only create a larger rift.

The prince raked his ear-length black hair, and his bottom lip stiffened with frustration. "I have lost. My mother will die, and I've a slave's power to stop it."

"Your father's mind weighs heavy with her illness." Lead Auren hoped to diminish the prince's anger. "If you've the power of a slave, then what of his? He's king, the most powerful man in our world, yet he must stand by, and let her die. It must be unbearable. Trust, we will convince him, it'll just require time."

"Time is something we may not have." Prince Aedyn strode out. And not caring if he woke the entire castle, he shouted. "I want an account of how many are ill, a list of men willing to go with me, and I want to speak to Achelle. Page, fetch me when she wakes."

Day 43
Training Grounds
Castle's East Bailey
Near Aldersward City

A previous king, Acoose, declared any boy over ten would attend combat training every day. They no longer practised out of necessity. Once attached to Aldersward, the other kingdoms perished when they plunged into the sea almost three-hundred years ago.

The king realised the need for his countrymen to relieve their anger and despair over the sudden loss. It was something to focus on, a common goal and pastime. This forced neighbours, the different classes, and families, out from their solitude and into the public where the raw feelings could be shared. It was how he healed his subjects and no other saw reason to discontinue it.

Not a breath of wind existed as the sun climbed higher into the morning sky. Loud percussion sounded in the bailey. Arrows thumped into targets, wooden swords clashed with shields or dummies, while the tunic-less men attacked one another. Their muscular flesh rolled with perspiration, salting their lips, and the heavy odour of their exertion lingered.

Aedyn watched as Lead Auren thrashed his wooden sword against a shield held by adversary and directly advanced, sparring with another until the man's back sprawled in the dirt. Then he smiled and offered his hand, pulling the downed man upright.

The prince walked past a gathering crowd of women. He abandoned his possessions, removed his tunic, then wielded a wooden sword and poked Lead Auren from behind. "Brother, I distinctly remember when you joined our family, a weakling child of five, ravaged by infection from the wolf's attack."

Lead Auren pivoted to meet his new challenger, and they landed blows while they sparred across the grounds. His clawed and bitten scars strained as he jabbed his opponent. The quarter-circle scar under his eye lifted when he spoke. "Not so weak anymore. I laugh when I recall how the queen's gutless, whimpering son clung to her skirts, weeping for protection."

Aedyn forced the suppressed frustration from his body into his movements. His muscles rippled as he swung the weapon. "You were the precipice of my mother's constant concern. She never worried as much about us as she did you. I admired your unrelenting capacity to come out unscathed in any argument with my parents. For instance, when you travelled with my father and returned with the wolf tattoo on your chest."

With a smile, Lead Auren strove to defend himself from the sword and the words. "I was fifteen, ready to accept my rank, and wanted my freedom. I could hardly invite the droves of lustful women into my chambers without displeasing your mother."

Both men concentrated, balanced in strength, as they took turns attacking and defending. Finally, when they spent their energy and sweat rolled down their bodies, they hunched forward inhaling large amounts of air then went to retrieve their discarded things.

"Feeling better?" Lead Auren dried his chest and after redressing, returned his bow, quiver, and heavy belt to his back and waist.

"Much. Beating on you always improves my mood." Pulling on his tunic, he tucked it inside his trousers, then laughed and nodded toward a man who hoisted a wagon loaded with men high in the air. "I see Guard Asa's showing off for the freshly bestowed boys."

Lead Auren patted his friend's back. "Do you remember the pain of being branded? Look at their welts, bright red and burning. I recall my own by merely glancing at them." Each boys' torso bore the insignia from when the king granted them their magic.

The prince grinned, thinking of his own. "Come, you can demonstrate how you shoot your arrows around obstacles and corners."

Day 43
Schoolroom

Castle's Ground Level
Near Aldersward City

A small leaf-coloured gecko ran along the risers where the children sat. The girls shrieked while the boys studied the creature. A boy scooped it into his hands and brought it forward, showing the teacher as he passed to let it go. *It is remarkable,* Emissary Bennet thought. Its limbs resembled broken twigs and its body and tail like scrunched dried leaves. Outside, he was uncertain whether he would recognise the animal or believe it deadfall from a tree.

His brogue accented his words. "Students, while ye combed the king's library of chronicles, letters, diaries and testaments, I expect ye've learnt a great deal about our world Speranza, the nine kingdoms, and the events surrounding Amelia's birthday. Several pupils will present reports over the following year. Today, April will go first." Emissary Bennet of Baitsloam, the 797-year-old scholar, acknowledged the girl, and she approached the podium.

"Aldersward," she sounded bored, "The largest, most central, and powerful of the nine kingdoms. Once an Aldersward King is crowned and given the insignia tattoo, he may bestow a magical ability on anyone. However, he cannot control which talent he grants, and the receiver must discover it for themselves.

"Aldersward had the most balanced landscape. In 2631 F.Y. or Forgotten Years, it shared borders with Tannorsbrace, Vaguestimber, Slaysfold, Reinshaven, Clinesfurrow, and Fernstake.

"As Alders, we pay homage to our original world by naming our children with the letter *a*. Our race has varying shades of brown or black hair, high cheekbones, and olive skin tones.

"In 2631, on the night of Amelia's sixteenth birthday, widowed King Asmaud and his four children: sons Acoose and Arron, and daughters Amelia and Avery, attended Amelia's celebration. Some diaries claim King Asmaud planned to gift each kingdom's emissary an additional ability to commemorate the occasion. I couldn't confirm this. This same night, the other eight kingdoms perished when they plunged into the sea. The king died in the crypt below the great hall when it collapsed. They discovered him lying next to the golden tablet, ever after black. Even though hundreds have tried to return it to its former state, to this day, it remains black. His heir, Acoose, became king the next day.

"Prior to the quake or the *event* as most refer to it, many races lived within our kingdom. However, the majority were women married to Alder men and because children take their father's race and magics, there are few left. Records indicate Emissary Bennet's the last surviving Bait.

"Unlike the other kingdoms, who had one collective magical skill, Alders have individual abilities. Some are transparent," she ran her fingers through her hair and tiny flowers appeared, "while others aren't. Everyone's specific limitations differ. When the other kingdoms existed, Alders couldn't practise their abilities in Clinesfurrow. It's not clear why but I noted each kingdom had a location limitation.

"Today, our patriarchy includes King Adahy, seventy-eight, and Queen Anya, fifty-seven. Their children are Prince Aedyn, twenty-three, Princess Achelle, eighteen, and Princess Annora, fifteen. The average lifespan of an Alder is ninety years.

She glanced at her best friend, Princess Achelle. "Currently, Prince Aedyn is betrothed to Lady Ammaris of Wibley, aged eighteen. And for sixty days, Queen Anya has suffered from a sleeping ailment. The end," her skirts swished as she returned to her seat.

Day 43
Prince Aedyn's Chambers
Castle's Second Level
Near Aldersward City

After his father and sisters retired, Prince Aedyn met with Lead Auren and Guard Asa in the simply furnished through-room of his chambers. His page ensured ale and food were present before he took his leave. The masculine room, decorated in cherry wood with red and gold fabric, contained floor coverings, cushioned chairs, and low tables. No windows adorned the through-room connected to his bedchamber. They would not be interrupted or overheard while they enjoyed each other's company, a testament to their long friendship.

"Where are we with the tasks I assigned you this morning, Auren?" The prince arched his eyebrow as he crossed his arms and propped his feet up, resting his head against the chair's back.

"I sent nine messengers with letters, asking each Earl to report how many subjects are ill. It explains we're exploring an opportunity to cure them and asks for volunteers to go with you. I expect answers back within a fortnight." Lead Auren plucked a handful of green grapes, tossing them in his mouth one by one.

"Good. Asa, I have an errand for you." While Prince Aedyn continued, the man, a few years older, nodded and chewed a bread crust lathered with honey. "You'll take a few weeks off to visit family in Lessard. Once there, solicit the boat builders. Have them improve the previous designs big enough for seventy men with sleeping quarters and galley for thirty-five men, a kitchen and two rooms for my chambers. We'll need stores for an entire moon cycle. I'll speak to Emissary Bennet then provide a detailed list of specifications before you leave."

"Wait. You want them to build you a larger vessel? Like those in the past, which never returned? How many expeditions were granted, then failed. How big were they?" Guard Asa's pulse quickened. "You can't mean to go or for me to accompany you?"

Lead Auren replied. "At last count, I believe twentyish attempts were made with thirty-odd men. Over five-hundred perished. Some failed immediately, rescued just beyond our shores. Others we don't know what happened. Maybe they found sex-starved women and chose to satiate them?" He tried to lighten the mood with a joke. "It could have happened."

Prince Aedyn ignored his friend's remark. "I will go and want you both to accompany me."

"I'll submit a request for leave and depart the day after tomorrow. Do you believe we'll need so much food?" To appear casual, Guard Asa propped his feet on the low table and relaxed in his chair.

"I'm hoping we find individuals to accompany us who can produce drinking water and food by conjuring them. At the moon's midpoint, if we haven't discovered land, we return home." Prince Aedyn sat forward, refilling their drinks. "I need to know if it's conceivable and how long for the build."

Lead Auren drank thirstily, then bit a piece of cheese. "This vessel, it's not a fishing boat for a dozen men. How can you be certain they will have the expertise the previous builders lacked?"

He shook his head. "I must believe Jezabet will provide and guide us. I'm hoping the builders will cooperate, design, and construct it together. Something they have not done in the past. Previously, it seemed like a race for recognition. Also, I hope the builders know someone who has fallen ill. This provides extra incentive to make it a reality. A man, thrown a rope when drowning, will always grab hold." Prince Aedyn opened Princess Achelle's sketchbook. "There's more. Look here."

Day 44
Prince Aedyn's Chambers
Castle's Second Level
Near Aldersward City

Emissary Bennet of Baitsloam did not look a day over seventy. The Baits aged much slower than the other races through their one-thousand year life cycle. This made him the oldest and last survivor of 2631 F.Y. His hand straightened his shoulder-length curly brown hair before he entered.

With a genuine smile, he addressed his former student. "Prince Aedyn." He bowed, signifying his respect for the royal. "Away." He ordered the speckled owl with a frogmouth-shaped beak from his shoulder. The bird landed on a chair's back, then glared at the human pair.

The prince grinned, welcoming him. "No need for ceremony here. Sit, drink with me. I need your advice and counsel." He poured the ale as his childhood mentor sat in a neighbouring chair. "He looks unhappy?" He nodded toward the pet.

"Miserable, ye mean. Norman's been this way since his mate died last year. Like me, he intends to never love again."

"Sometimes I forget your ability to communicate with birds." He shrugged. "I miss your teachings, and the ease of my childhood. We don't see each other enough."

"I have pupils who, like ye, aren't eager to learn, and then others who soak it up. These tasks keep me busy. Ye only need to ask, and I'll come." He bridged his fingers together, his skin pale like a white dove, different from the Alders' natural olive tone.

For a few minutes, they shared companionable small talk before Aedyn broached the reason for his summons. Then, conversational, he spoke of a vessel's design and the emissary added a privy and washroom to the list.

"I want to show you a drawing." The prince pulled the sketchbook from the table. "What do you make of this?"

Emissary Bennet stared at a group of pale women, in long loose gowns with black and white streaked hair, gathered around a sleeping woman lying in a bed of grass. A young woman's fingers dragged over the sleeping one's face. Clearing his eyes, he blinked and searched the illustration again. The background was a pristine body of water edged by pastel flowers and a mountainous horn with three rings protruding from the ground. His mouth gaped as he grabbed the book.

Aedyn remained quiet and watched Emissary Bennet's face, hidden by his moustache and beard, change from mild interest to familiarity, then shock.

After a considerable pause, the emissary looked up. "May I ask how ye came by this?"

"It's a recent drawing. Have you ever shown your students a drawing like this before?"

"There are few sketches from before 2631 and none so elaborate or finely detailed. King Acoose commissioned drawings from the memories of survivors, but they did not produce this image." He shook his head and placed the open book down.

"How can you be positive? Have you seen this place before?"

Emissary Bennet scratched his head as he chose his words. "It's Cobblershorn, I recognise it from the three rings, the water is Snakestongue Lake, and the pastel flowers grow only in one location. It's the kingdom of Reinshaven, and the girl's a healer, the Reins' only ability." He sipped his ale while continuing to stare at the image. "I visited there when I was a young man, perhaps two-hundred years old. In the past, this would not have interested ye. What's the story behind it?"

Bearing complete trust in his childhood mentor, Prince Aedyn spoke freely. Princess Achelle's ability was common knowledge amongst those within the castle. No convincing was necessary, when he recounted each step of her dream-walk, the other pictures in the sketchbook, and finally his plan to go looking for a cure.

The man had stopped listening and wondered aloud. "Could this be real? If Reinshaven survived, then maybe other kingdoms did as well. Could Brielle and our children still be alive?" Emissary Bennet stood and paced, using the movement to release his anxiety while the owl's scowl followed him. "I must go with ye. We must convince yer father. I can't stay here knowing they may have survived."

The prince grabbed Emissary Bennet's shoulders and stared into the man's grief-stricken expression. This was a man he loved and respected, second only to his own father. Before his eyes, the proud, strong man deteriorated in anguish, and it tore at Aedyn's heart.

He cursed himself for being so cruelly selfish, and guilt riddled him for not preparing Emissary Bennet before exposing him to the drawings. "Stop this now. Of course, you can help convince my father and then come with me. I swear, we will go."

Day 50
Prince Aedyn's Chambers
Castle's Second Level
Near Aldersward City

In bed, Aedyn woke and rolled when wood rubbed stone outside in his through-room. Hearing the sound of bare feet slap against the icy floor, he smiled. His guards wouldn't stop the intruder, used to her seeking out the prince in the middle of the night. She pushed his bedchamber door open, then came to his bed.

As was her habit, Princess Annora, fifteen—his youngest sibling, lifted the covers and climbed in without invitation. She rested her head beside his, turning away from him as he wrapped a protective arm over her, pulling her into his warmth.

He kissed the back of her brown unruly locks. "What was it this time?"

"We were in Mother's chambers when we were younger. I may have been four. You and Auren were sitting on the rugs in front of a warm, crackling fire. Achelle sat beside Mother, and I was cuddled in her lap. She sang and rocked me. We were so happy and affectionate. Auren called me to play with him, but when I pushed off of her, Mother collapsed and died at my feet. It felt so real. My tears and cries woke me."

Her nightmares had increased in frequency since their mother fell ill. His heart hurt for his young sisters. They were used to spending their evenings in her company, and he could not imagine how the loss would affect them. He gathered her closer, brushing his fingers through her hair in comfort. "I'm sorry these nightmares plague you. You sleep and I'll remain awake to chase them away."

She smiled against his arm. "Do you believe the promise you gave to me as a child can fool me now? It no longer appeases me." She pressed her frozen toes to his bare leg; his night robe bunched above his calves.

He chuckled, then rubbed his feet against hers. "And yet, once you're here, you sleep without nightmares. It's obvious my protection works. Sleep now."

She nuzzled her cheek against the pillow, finding a comfortable position. As her breathing regulated in slumber, Aedyn stared into the darkened room. His sisters' despair, his mother's deteriorating health, and his plans to cure her kept him awake. His resolve to search for a healer strengthened, knowing his family would know no peace until his mother was restored.

Day 59
King Adahy's Study
Castle's Ground Level
Near Aldersward City

Ancestor portraits in elaborate frames, their weapons, and artefacts from Aldersward's past lined the vaulted walls. The magnitude of history held here astonished any invited person. In its centre was a long bulky table shrouded with lists, designs, and drawings, surrounded by men.

"Give us the room!" Angry, Prince Aedyn bellowed.

Men stood, collected their things, and hurried out. One paused, flicked his wrist, and sent the chairs into neat positions under the table, then closed the door behind him.

King Adahy, red-faced, shouted. "You ignored my direct orders! You employed my staff without permission! You arrogant, selfish prick!"

The prince matched his father's volume as he glared across the table's length. "You offered me no other choice! I'm going with or without your permission. The only remaining question is whether I go alone?"

Taking a moment to allow their tempers to calm, the prince poured two mugs of sweet tea, then walked the length of the table which separated them. He drank from one and pushed the other to his father.

"Father," he began again, his temper now under control. "I deserve your anger, but for the good of our people, and my mother, can you put it aside? We need to speak of this rationally." He gathered several scrolls, then placed them in front of his father one at a time. "These are Achelle's drawings and Emissary Bennet recognised them as Reinshaven. The Lessard boat builders drafted this. It can carry seventy men and supplies for a moon's cycle. Here's a list of men willing to accompany my guard, the emissary, and I on this journey. I'm not a complete imbecile! This gives us a fortnight to search and another to return. I have asked my sister to dream-walk with me every fourth night to keep you apprised of our progress. This is how I would prefer to leave, but if not, I will take Emissary Bennet, and we'll go alone. The decision is yours."

The king lifted his daughter's drawings, taking a few moments before he answered. "You're committed to wed Ammaris of Wibley in a few months. After the ceremony, together you can take these men and go."

His anger resurfaced, Prince Aedyn raked his hair and icily glared. "You know I made no such commitment! You're forcing me to marry the woman with your betrothal agreement. I don't love her, nor do I hate her! I feel only indifference and sympathy. You'd ruin both of our lives by forcing this. I know her future, trapped in a loveless marriage." He took a long, slow breath, and his voice filled with compassion. "In her eyes, I see pain every time we speak—she of love and I of duty. She'll grow to resent you, the crown, and especially me. I don't understand what marrying her and taking her with me will accomplish."

"A wedding now could make it appear to Ammaris of Wibley and our subjects that you're eager and maybe excited. Then, a journey combined with confining quarters should bring you closer together as man and wife. I assure you, appearance will guide your marriage in the right direction."

"So appearance is what you want? An excited groom, who appears smitten with his bride before his wedding and who's eager to share how happy he is." He raised his brow as he mocked his father.

"Precisely, it's imperative you appear happy with your lot in life." The king nodded, pleased his son finally understood.

Prince Aedyn drank while he pondered his father's position. "Then, let's compromise." He paced and speculated. "I cannot wait months to leave. We can't move my wedding closer or it'd seem exactly what it is, you forcing me. Everyone would wonder and be right. However, if you let my men and I leave during the next moon cycle, there will be enough time for the boat's construction, our search, and our return before the wedding."

"But–"

"You wanted a happy groom?" He stopped, his excited blue eyes met his father's dull ones. "To everyone, upon my return, it'll appear I've discovered feelings for Ammaris of Wibley. Absence grew my love. I'll seek her out, lavish her with affection, and marry her without another word. It's more believable than your plan."

King Adahy rested his back against the chair, his hands clasped over his stomach. "Say I agree to this. Your feelings, all of them, need to appear authentic. They can't appear exaggerated or fake. The men with you must also have a narrative to recount your heart's change. I would leave it to you to determine what would seem believable."

"Done!"

"Not done. I have additional stipulations." The king demanded Princess Achelle dream-walk every third day and removed a few men from the trip's manifest. Not out of necessity, but as backup, he added a man whose ability could supply rations. The trip was cut to ten days either way. Any sign of trouble, and directly, they would turn home.

Prince Aedyn readily agreed to the demands and left to make the preparations.

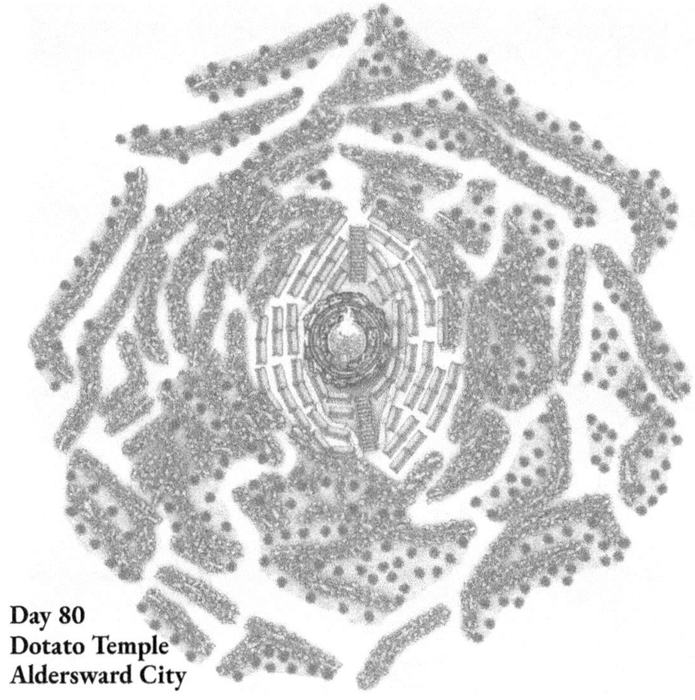

Thousands lined the route to the temple and waited for the royal family, priests, and priestesses to emerge from the castle's gate. Twice a year, the crowds were this impressive. The marking of the new year and this day, the commemoration of the Unification War's conclusion when the kingdoms had established peace. During regular worship, the king bestowed magic onto *noughties*, those aged ten or greater without abilities, and a few who the king, scholars, and priests deemed worthy to hold a second.

The masses hushed when guards stepped through and spread out along the rutted path on either side, securing a clear, wide passage. An elderly priest garbed in long grey robes signalled the pilgrimage's beginning. His navel-length beard moved as he bellowed his hymn.

Behind him, the coal-coloured tablet rested on a wheeled stand, pushed by two young priestesses. They invited the crowd's words by answering, "Receive our praise, Jezabet."

A scholar, Emissary Bennet, and two priests walked with a scroll unravelled between them. From it, two figures emerged, hovered over the scroll, and re-enacted King Abrahin meeting with Jezabet. No sounds were heard, but clearly the pair conversed as the king knelt at the god's feet. Jezabet pulled flattened stones from his robes until there were nine. A dagger struck across Abrahin's hand, then bled over the stones. Jezabet planted one hand on the Alder man's shoulder and raised his other to the sun. Energy poured through King Abrahin and into the tablets, turning them a lustrous gold. Jezabet faded and the Alder gathered the new tablets. The kingdoms' rulers appeared as a battle waged below them. King Abrahin gave one to each, and when he finished, the fighting ended and the men rejoiced together. This represented the end of the Unification War, and peace followed for over twenty-five-hundred years.

Three guards preceded the king, and the crowd quieted, waiting for his speech.

The sunlight played off the gold crown perched on King Adahy's head. It kept his long, wavy curls from the slight breeze. His voice carried as the people genuflected. "Our god bequeathed his son Jordan, this world. Speranza enjoys many years of peace. We are eternally grateful." His moustache and long beard shifted. "He formed an understanding, fellowship, and appreciation among the races. We, alone, could not achieve it without his guidance." He lifted his leathered face skyward. "We offer him this day. Receive our praise, Jezabet." The crowd echoed the sentiment, and his heavy robes dragged when he started forward. His subjects yielded as he strolled by.

Seven guards followed him, then the two princesses, arm in arm. They whispered and waved to the spectators.

"The dress you chose is beautiful, striking on you." Self-conscious of her dusty pink, plain gown, Princess Achelle appreciated her sister's long elaborate green gown with its laced bodice. It covered her collarbone and its sleeves hugged her arms, travelling to her palms.

"I hope it pleases Jezabet, and he rewards me by waking our mother." Princess Annora pulled at the neckline. "It's uncomfortable."

Princess Achelle knocked her sister's hand aside. "It will become natural. These are the clothes of a young lady, no longer a child. Regardless of whether Jezabet rewards you, Mother would be proud."

They shared an affectionate glance and as they drifted, their long hair streamed behind. Another dozen guards, including Guard Asa and Lead Auren, walked in unison behind the girls.

Ammaris of Wibley's arm rested on Prince Aedyn's as they kept pace. Her back was straight and stiff while she held herself carefully away from him. It would embarrass her if the onlookers witnessed his rejection of her familiarity.

The immediate crowd called out to the royal children, hoping to obtain a response. But their calls changed when Ammaris of Wibley's presence became known and they pleaded for her recognition instead.

She ignored them and adjusted her dark blue gown. Pins held her hair at the back, away from her calm face as she stared ahead.

"Lady Ammaris!" A young girl called, her frantic arm waved above.

Prince Aedyn dipped his head to her ear. "They call seeking your favour."

Surprised by his mouth's closeness, her feet stumbled, but she recovered quickly, "Nonsense. They call because I spend my time amongst them. They feel familiar."

"Perhaps they idolise you and envy the reward Jezabet gives for your inspiring deeds."

"Reward?" she lifted her confused blue eyes, not understanding his words, "How so?"

He furrowed his brows. "You will be Queen of Aldersward."

"I see." Her feet stopped, but he drew her forward, unaware of her pause.

"Do you not see your new position as a reward for your selflessness? Someday, you will be the most powerful woman in our kingdom."

"Being decent and compassionate doesn't deserve a reward. These are Jezabet's teachings, and I don't deserve anyone's envy. They could never understand the sacrifices and limitations of our positions."

Prince Aedyn would have questioned her, except no time remained as he steered her through the temple's semi-circled stone maze. Thick leafy vines with white blossoms carpeted the walls and, once inside its centre, there stood four-hundred subjects, gathered like cattle.

He escorted Ammaris of Wibley to the front row, sitting her next to his sisters, then sat beside her. His father stood on the rise next to a large blue fire, which would help provide the noughty subjects with their abilities.

Lead Auren sat next to Prince Aedyn. A place he long held while they listened to the priest govern the worship. He thanked Jezabet for the time of great peace, their abilities, and their lives, then he prayed for the healing of the ill, the men who would journey, and finally, the success of the voyage.

The sun climbed from its midday position to start its descent when the priest bent to King Adahy. The king crossed to the fire as men added more fuel and stirred its embers. King Adahy signalled the guards who barred the south entrance, and they allowed a young, bare-chested boy to enter. He trotted forward and yielded.

"Your name?"

The brave boy replied, "Annoah of Coaldale."

"What draws you to our temple and before Jezabet?"

"I have reached ten. I wish to pledge my life to our god by receiving his brand and gift." He searched the crowd and found his family, who stood proudly watching him.

"Where shall you sacrifice?"

The boy puffed out his chest. "Over my heart, like my father and brothers."

The king expected him to respond, *where Prince Aedyn wore his.* It seemed highly fashionable in recent times.

King Adahy's gloved hand wielded the white-hot iron. Sweat, caused by the intense heat, streamed his face. "Kneel." He instructed him and men seized each of the boy's arms, holding him still. The boy did not flinch when the iron seared and sizzled his skin for everyone to hear. The smell of burning flesh lingered. "I accept your pledge for Jezabet. May he learn from your heart and soul, then deem you worthy to receive his gift." The king withdrew the iron and stuck it into the flames. They hauled the boy to his feet. Skin hung and large blisters covered the red area while blood oozed down his chest into the fabric of his trousers.

Congratulations rang out when the boy grinned widely, bowed, then jumped and raced out the north entrance while a filthy young girl wearing a ragged and too snug dress slowly walked to the rise. A long-matted braid swung behind her.

Bile scorched Ammaris of Wibley's throat at the tiny girl's tears. "I recognise her. She's an orphan from the Alms-house."

Lead Auren turned to her ladies seated behind them. "You–"

"No," she stopped him, "I'll stand."

Prince Aedyn pulled her sleeve. "It's inappropriate. Let your ladies do it."

She ignored him and stepped forward beyond his reach as the young girl genuflected.

"A special friend to Lady Ammaris," the king acknowledged. The young tear-filled eyes turned, and Ammaris of Wibley waved. "What's your name?" The king refocused the child's attention, and Lady Ammaris stepped backward until her legs touched her seat.

"I'm Aila of Aldersward City. I've come to pledge my life to Jezabet by receiving his brand and gift." The nervous girl shuffled her feet and turned to the woman who often cared for them at the Alms-house. Ammaris of Wibley mustered a slight smile of encouragement.

"Where on your body will you sacrifice?" The king sought the girl's attention again.

"Where Lady Ammaris wears hers."

He looked to his son's betrothed. Ammaris of Wibley's eyes widened as she sat and patted her upper arm.

The king instructed. "Remove your arm from your gown."

Lead Auren whispered. "I've never seen a brand on your arm."

She focused cool eyes on him. "It isn't."

"Then, where?"

Prince Aedyn interrupted. "Are you serious?"

"You're right, of course. I apologise, Lady Ammaris." Lead Auren dipped his head in apology, then raised it with a grin and murmured for only the prince's ears. "I have no alternative but to imagine now."

Like brothers, the prince elbowed him hard in the gut and both returned their attention to the rise. The king's voice quietly instructed her to look away while two men held her.

When the white iron touched her soft skin, an unbearable anguished cry escaped the girl's throat, and Ammaris of Wibley swung her gaze elsewhere.

Finally, the young girl fainted, and the men continued to hold her while King Adahy blessed her, then removed the iron. When the crowd cheered, he motioned for one to carry her out. Without an excuse, Ammaris of Wibley followed.

Day 89
Den's Mercantile
Aldersward City

Trading day neared its end when Lead Auren entered the mercantile.

A clever former king deemed it necessary to shift some daytime vendors into nighttime brothels. This was such a place. The kingdom's women, of exceptional quality and standing, frequented the front of the shop, purchasing their fabric, lace, and string. What women assumed were a stockroom and living-quarters were actually a brothel—a well-kept secret from the weak-minded females of Aldersward.

"Auren," the proprietor greeted, as he handed a wrapped bundle to April, Princess Achelle's best friend. Lead Auren recognised her. "Are you here to collect the trousers my wife mended?" The owner stepped from behind the counter, inviting him. "Come to the stockroom. I have them there. You can see if we need to make any further repairs."

Lead Auren studied the room; women browsed, making their purchases, and April disappeared outside before he followed the man behind the curtain. With his palm, the merchant conjured a frame, and a door appeared. They entered, and it vanished behind them.

The room was dim, lit only by candelabras and a hearth in the centre. The smell of smoke, liquor, and sex wafted as a barmaid poured water into a jug. She changed it to whisky with her hand's movement, then splashed it into mugs for delivery to the men while they relaxed and observed the half-naked women.

A nude woman laid on a fur while the fire flashed beside her. She dipped her fingers in strawberry syrup and drizzled it onto her flat stomach. Its contact against her exposed skin caused it to form intricate erotic illustrations for surrounding men to examine. Afterwards, they would take turns licking her clean so she could repeat the process for another. Other men played cards while women perched on their thighs or fondled them from behind.

"Is she all right?" Lead Auren glanced around, disinterested.

"She is. No one knows she's here. My girls see to her every need and when she ventures out she uses the rear staircase, and I or my wife accompany her to guarantee she's not bothered." The proprietor boasted. "Forgive me, the storefront needs me."

"I understand. I'll go visit her." As was customary, he selected a woman and climbed to the second floor. He tipped her, then watched her go inside another room while he tapped on the door at the hallway's end.

The door opened a crack, then widened to grant him entrance. Azalea of Maidstone locked it behind him and without a word walked to a table and poured drinks.

He regarded the woman he hardly knew. They shared the same brown eyes, thick lashes, defined brows, and high cheekbones.

She grinned, and her cheerful personality was evident when she handed him the mug. "I expected you. Sit, so I don't have to continue to strain my neck."

"I cannot remain long. We'll return tonight. I came to say goodbye." He scanned the room with distaste while he sipped. "I despise you being here."

"Brother, you had no choice but to leave me here. In my beaten condition, I didn't want to be witnessed anywhere or have our association known. The proprietor and his wife take good care of me." She sat and reassured him by patting his hand, "The decision is in the past. Aedyn mentioned you'd leave tomorrow."

His voice trembled with angry disgust. "Don't use his name so intimately! He is my friend, but he is your ruler! Prince Aedyn deserves your respect by title." He withdrew his hand from hers and ran it over his face, wiping away his frustration.

"You can't still be angry at me. It was shortly after the new year when I introduced myself to him. Let it go." She made her words sound insignificant and hoped he would get over the subject.

"I want to understand how I'm supposed to reconcile myself to this?" He spat and felt his face flush. "My younger sister peddles herself to the Crowned Prince while he doesn't realise her identity. I'm your protector, and yet I let him crawl on top of you. Tell me how this ends?"

"Stop, you treat me like a young virgin and not the widow I am—caused by your hand, no less. Don't consider me ungrateful, but you don't know me. You left too young." She touched his arm and sat on the floor at his feet. "Auren, I don't want to quarrel. I waited for you to be otherwise engaged, and I approached them. Guard Asa or Prince Aedyn, it didn't matter. They're your friends and so they must be honourable. I don't have to remind you of what my husband did. You saw with your own eyes, but remaining here, in this room alone, fed his power over me. I had to take it back. How it ends? One day, the prince will tire of me or me of him and then I'll take the funds he has paid and disappear. No one the wiser."

Defeated by her words, his anger retreated. He raised her hand and kissed it. "You must be careful. As I have mentioned before, his magic ability is to make others tell the truth. Try to avoid direct questions about who you are." He stepped over her. "I must go. Prince Aedyn will be waiting. While I'm away, should an emergency arise, send the proprietor to find April of Aldersward Castle. She will lead you to Princess Achelle. Come lock the door."

Day 89
North Alms-house
Aldersward City

Prince Aedyn and Lead Auren rode inside a royal carriage, ringed by horse-backed guards, while they travelled through the bustle of the dirty lane to a grouping of rundown cottages. Filthy and half-starved orphan children ran unchecked by the few assigned to aid with their care and with no beds vacant, ailing people laid against the buildings, barely conscious of their surroundings.

"Change the colour of your dress, lady," a merchant called.

"I can colour your lips for a moon's cycle," another offered.

Turn your wooden weapons to steel, a shop sign boasted. It was commonplace to offer abilities for trade or goods.

They came to retrieve Ammaris of Wibley, who, born of a charitable family and newly stationed, devoted herself to eliminating the suffrage of the neglected and less fortunate.

The steaming heat of the clustered bodies fused with the sour stench of death, rotting sick, and the soiled old took Prince Aedyn and Lead Auren aback when they entered the Alms-house. Those who could genuflect did as they stalked through, searching for her. Her ladies withdrew outside as the men passed. They found her standing outside the cottage's rear exit, hauling heavy supplies from a cart into a storage room inside the kitchen. Body fluids, blood, and perspiration coated her simple and modest dress. Her dishevelled brown hair had slipped from its style during the day, but she had not noticed.

The prince lifted the heavy crate from her and placed it inside the cramped closet while Auren walked past to bring the rest inside. As she supervised his Lead, he joined her.

With annoyance, Aedyn's eyes thinned, "Where's the Alms-house staff?"

She bowed, then fanned her hand, striving to cool her body. Hair stuck to her face. "There are too many bodies in need and an inadequate number of people to serve them."

"I concur. You should convey this to my father. Perhaps he can provide a solution to alleviate the shortfall, and you wouldn't have to come here, placing yourself in harm's way where you could become ill."

She nodded her head. Her incessant desire to be acceptable would not allow her to argue. "I will."

Lead Auren finished as the prince took her arm and steered her to their carriage outside.

The driver cracked the reins across the horses' backs and they trudged through the lane toward the castle. No one spoke during the uncomfortable, formal drive, but Ammaris of Wibley wished they could be companionable. Unfortunately, the prince's aloof demeanour wouldn't allow it.

Prince Aedyn's attitude emphasised her mother's teaching. As a child, if Ammaris misbehaved or did not perform to her mother's standards, she would deny her affection. Her mother insisted others would judge them and their household based on how perfect they were. Ammaris blamed herself for the prince's behaviour. Perhaps she was not beautiful or agreeable enough for him to extend anything better than polite courtesy. In the future, she vowed to demand more of herself—focus on her personal appearance, and strive to accommodate his requests above her own.

The second carriage continued on when theirs paused in front of the castle. Prince Aedyn opened the gate, but remained inside as she exited. Clouds formed overhead as she turned around and he nodded his goodbye.

"After this evening's meal, I thought I may perform some harp music to commemorate your departure." Ammaris of Wibley lifted her eyes.

"That won't be necessary. I'm on my way to saddle my horse. I'll depart immediately after our meal."

"Of course," her eyes filled with hopelessness, and she averted her face. "You've a considerable amount to accomplish before you leave."

He knocked on the roof, signalling the driver, and shifted his attention to Lead Auren.

Ammaris was left standing alone. Her gaze followed the carriage as rain fell.

Day 89
Den's Mercantile
Aldersward City

"One last night before we're forced into celibacy, are you reasonably certain we can't take women with us, Aedyn?" Guard Asa's jovial voice asked as the three friends entered the storefront and stepped through the now open doorway dividing the front and the back.

"How would it look to the ladies if we ride out tomorrow with women in tow?" Prince Aedyn sat at a table while Lead Auren left to fetch a round of refreshments. "Trust me, if there were a way to bring them, Azalea would be the first."

An ambitious half-naked woman requested Lead Auren's attention by rubbing herself against him when he returned and sat. "Drink up! There are many women to screw before this night ends." He caught her fingers and dragged her willingly onto his lap, whispering to her as his friends chuckled.

"Men," the owner smiled, greeting them. "I see he's found himself wedded for the night."

Lead Auren lifted his admiring gaze from her body. "Not wedded—it implies one. I intend to employ several at the same time. She and I are discussing price and who else will join us." He gently nudged her from his lap, then held her hand and motioned to three other women as he mounted the stairs.

Prince Aedyn and Guard Asa watched them leave. The merchant sat and Guard Asa questioned him. "Tell us, what do your women say of Auren?"

"He leaves them spent and wanting more, an evil curse to be as handsome as he," the man offered, and they laughed.

Guard Asa eyed the table of men playing cards as someone vacated a chair. "I think I'll enjoy a few hands before I head upstairs. Meet you in a few hours." He joined the game before another could occupy the space.

The proprietor gestured for the barmaid to serve more refreshments to Prince Aedyn and himself. His voice was low, so no one overheard. "Even without your ring, I know who you are." Seeing the prince's jaw clench in irritation, he rushed on. "I intend to make no trouble, only to reassure you. Azalea will remain safe while you're gone." The prince's jaw relaxed as the man boasted. "I'm honoured you have chosen my establishment over all others."

Aedyn fished through his coin pouch. "I intended to pay for her keep while I'm away."

The merchant placed his hand on the prince's arm. "No compensation necessary. I do it out of duty to you."

He nodded as he drained his mug. "I thank you and won't forget your hospitality. I'll see her now. I ask you don't change your mannerisms, they may invite unwanted attention." He stood, threw a few coins down, and then climbed the stairs two at a time, eager to see her.

Prince Aedyn knocked gently, and Azalea drew him inside. She pressed him into a chair with her long fingers, then turned to pour him a drink.

He watched her knee-length skirts swish while she walked. Her hips swayed, and he shifted his position as his trousers bulged uncomfortably.

She was a beautiful whore.

Rather tall, with soft red lips, deep brown eyes covered with thick lashes, and brown curly hair which tickled her ass when she paraded around naked. He'd met her the first night she arrived here and later instructed Lead Auren to claim her by paying the merchant an immense sum.

She knew what he needed—before he knew what he wanted. It was an extraordinary talent.

"Were you expecting me?" He raised his eyebrow, eyeing the pitcher across the room, separated only by her bed and another chair.

She sauntered towards him, her top covered only her nipples, exposing her flat stomach and the rounded bottoms of her breasts. The material slid higher when she raised her arms, deploying her magic. The ceiling vanished and revealed the night's sky. He had no interest in the stars overhead. Her easy teasing pleased him. He was mesmerised by the pointed flesh of her nipples as lust coursed through his veins.

"I'm not caged here. I come and go as I please during the day." She handed him his drink, took a sip of her own, then placed it down, and squatted in front of him. "There are many rumours about your journey, and you mentioned leaving tomorrow. I assumed I'd see you before you left." Her fingers rubbed his chest as she unbuttoned his tunic.

He grabbed her hand and lifted it to his lips, kissing the inside of her wrist. "I shall miss the ease of our arrangement." He pulled her onto his hips, facing him. She ran her fingers up his ribs and through his unruly black hair as she moistened her parted lips, inviting his kiss.

Prince Aedyn claimed her mouth as he wrapped his muscular arms around her, his hands splayed across her back, drawing her soft hot flesh against his firm body. He whispered as his tongue found her lobe. "It unnerves me how good your skin feels against me."

He clutched her long hair, leveraged it to stretch her backwards, causing her torso to arch away from him, and he kissed a path down her throat. She gyrated her hips slowly over his pelvis. His prick thickened against her damp warmth. He drank from her lips as he lifted them both from the chair. Her legs circled his waist, impatient for what was to come. He bent over the bed, placing her back on the mattress, and he settled his firm frame against her lengthy body.

She distracted him. Her tongue glided along his throat, and she rolled him onto his back. He chuckled at her playful manner, and she giggled her triumph when she straddled his thighs with her hips. His hands crept up her midriff, forced the flimsy fabric over her head, trapping her arms temporarily. His palms seized her sides, and he lifted his back. His mouth suckled her breasts while his tongue swirled around her taut nipples.

The desire in her midriff increased feverishly and several times, their fingers tangled as they strove together to remove the barrier of his clothing. His anticipation grew. Her light breath played against his skin as she slid herself down his body. She plunged her wet, small mouth onto his hard cock. His hips arched off the bed at a steady pace while he repeatedly forced his length deeper into her throat. His hand found the back of her neck and held her there, aching with indecision. He wanted her to stop, his agony building, but he needed her to continue as he searched for his release.

She hummed.

The vibration travelled through his shaft into his balls, and her fingers rubbed the point where they met. He felt the loose skin on his balls tighten. He gripped her head firmly with both hands and shot his seed deep inside her throat. After drinking him, she smiled a girlish grin as she crawled her way back up his body and devoured his lips with a passionate kiss. "You're spent?" she teased his ear, and he flipped her onto her back.

"Not even close." He half-smiled. His hand travelled over her breast, his lips tasting it as his hand progressed down the flat plateau of her stomach. He watched her eyes fill with need when he pulled on the knot at her waist and pushed the material of her skirt apart. His hands roamed southward over her navel, and he buried the length of two fingers into her wet valley as he deepened another kiss. She clutched his head in her hands, pulling him more firmly onto her mouth while her fingers threaded through his hair and her pelvis rocked against the steady assault of his hand.

When he had manipulated her opening wider, he shifted his hips between her legs and with a single thrust, plunged every long, thick inch inside her. Her nails raked his back as she moaned, enjoying the pleasurable pain and the fullness she felt. She bit his shoulder, stifling her screams when he rhythmically pushed within her. His breathing laboured, and she bucked her hips upward to encourage his penetration. His desire grew almost unbearable, knowing his savage intrusion pleased her.

Done with the gentleness of this position, he withdrew, flipped her onto her stomach, and mounted her from behind. Her legs laid wide and he pounded his hips forward forcing himself into her hot tunnel, still harder than before. He wedged his hand under her and gently stroked her slick clit with his rough fingers. He knew she was close to completion when he heard her uncontrolled scream stifle into the pillow and he felt her pulsate around his shaft. She tightened like a vice, gripping him.

Her convulsions subsided, and he pulled her back until she was on her knees. Her elbows braced her upper body away from the bed. Aedyn grabbed the bedposts in front of him and used their momentum to launch her repeatedly forward with his powerful heaves as her hips pitched backwards, inviting him to be rougher. He could not go on and tapped a finger on her back—their signal. The prince fell flat on the bed as her mouth fastened tightly over his shaft, sheltering his jerking cock. Her mouth milked him, enjoying the drink his juice provided. Several long minutes passed before he disentangled himself from her, wrapped a sheet around his waist, and freshened their forgotten drinks.

He handed her one and took a few swallows from his own. Looking at the star filled sky, he sprawled on the chair where the evening began. "I'll leave soon, it's nearing midnight. When I return from my journey I don't know if I will see you again." He watched her face for any sign she would take the news badly.

She rolled onto her stomach, bracing herself with her arm under her chin, her legs bent in the air behind her. "No explanations. I'm not a foolish girl with fanciful designs on becoming queen. You pay me to be available and I take immense pleasure in servicing you, but nothing more. I'm a woman with dreams, but they don't include you. We owe each other nothing."

Knowing she could not lie, he put to her a specific question. "What are your dreams?"

She crawled to the bed's edge and sat with her legs parted, dangling to the floor. She braced her arms behind her, the flat of her stomach and round breasts exposed to his gaze. Her pink folds were open and swollen from the forceful beating they had endured. "My eventual dreams, when I have enough money, a small cottage in Lessard, maybe remarry and have children." She trailed her fingers up her leg, then sank them inside her warmth. Her expression changed to one of desire. "My immediate dream is to please you again, make my dream come true?"

Discarding his drink, he joined her. After midnight he departed, leaving his full coin pouch behind.

Day 90
Princess Achelle's Chambers
Castle's Second Level
Near Aldersward City

Well beyond midnight, Princess Achelle paced her chamber, anticipating the guard change. They were an unnecessary chore after the event in 2631. There had been no threats to the castle and its occupants since. She waited for the sound of their voices to quiet and the shuffling of feet to dissipate. She needed to see Augustus, one of her father's guards.

Earlier, in the war room, she discovered his name on a list of men accompanying Prince Aedyn. Her green eyes clouded with tears and they threatened to escape her thick lashes. Her young heart of eighteen sank, and she rushed through the castle and into her bedchamber alone. She had wretched and cried until nothing remained in her stomach. She needed to declare her feelings as badly as she needed air to live.

Finally, the voices faded. She draped a long black cloak over her shoulders and tied it tight, then eased the door open and headed in the opposite direction. She kept to the hallway instead of the busy cross bridge, where discovery would be inevitable. At each window, she peered out, ensuring the skyway bridge remained empty. The secret passage from the queen's chambers would be the safest route.

She passed Ammaris of Wibley's closed door, the only other occupied room in the hallway. When she neared the end, she flattened herself against the wall and listened. She ventured around the corner, passing by Princess Annora's chambers. The outside door stood open, but no one was inside.

She passed her childhood room, certain no one would be inside. Her father's chamber door was closed, and she crossed its path before reaching her destination.

The door was wide and the only light spilled from the bedchamber when she entered. A servant would be inside with her mother, ensuring her comfort. Anyone could walk in and discover her wicked intentions as she tiptoed behind the decorative screen. With meticulous attention, she carefully slid the potted greenery away from the wall. She tried to budge the door without a sound as many feet entered from the hall and carried through to the queen's bedchamber. Princess Achelle held her breath and froze as her father spoke.

"I've brought the musicians to play for us, my darling Anya. I know how much you enjoy them."

A chair dragged across the floor and she imagined her father sliding it closer to the bed. Then the soft sounds of instruments played.

The music created enough noise to mask the groaning sound of the stubborn egress, then she crouched through, and closed it behind her.

It did not take long for her to descend the dark, musty staircase and push outside into the night, behind a growth of bushes along the castle's north wall next to the privy pond. The air smelled of old urine, sour gases, and excrement. She dropped the candle and plugged her nose, then raced along the wall towards the east bailey.

She stayed in the castle's shadows as she proceeded to the staff housing.

Princess Achelle took several deep breaths when she reached the back of the outdoor kitchen, now abandoned. She twisted her hair and lifted her hood over it to cover her identity, then peered along the road she would cross. Guards and men headed south from their living-quarters to the castle, but the distance allowed her to cross without recognition or notice. She tried to appear natural as she walked across the road to the first row of cottages and she sighed with relief when she entered their shadows. The fragrance of vanilla drifted in the air from the night phlox, a welcome change from the previous stench.

She followed the line of buildings until she reached the end, then turned the corner and skirted the three rows. She halted each time she thought she heard a noise. When the shadows ended, her sharp green eyes scouted for another vantage point. She lowered her hood and her dark hair spilled over her back.

One-hundred paces away, the three dormitories in a u-shape housed the unmarried. In their centre was a wide grass quadrangle filled with tables and chairs, all empty, except for one. Farthest from where she stood.

Guard Augustus would be close by. The princess did not see him, but she had come too far to turn back. His shift ended when her own guards changed. She wondered which buildings housed the men and which held women.

A quietness enveloped the evening. The normal hustle and bustle of the daytime was gone, replaced with the quiet sounds of nature and distant hooves.

Footsteps approached, and she had to seek cover or risk discovery. She crouched and ran to a bush eight paces away, then exhaled. The footsteps crunched against the earth as they closed in, and the seated men called greetings to the new arrival. Princess Achelle watched through the leaves as the man waved but carried along a building and out of sight. She could only assume he had entered it from the other end.

Her heart hammered loudly, the anticipation of discovery almost too much to bear.

The vantage point proved useful as others came and went using the west road, their destination the south castle grounds, at this hour.

Her neck hair prickled a split-second before someone's hand covered her mouth and an arm locked her body like a vice.

"Don't struggle," a man's tone insisted as she fought to free herself. "I won't hurt ye, Achelle." She stopped her struggle, recognising his brogue.

Emissary Bennet let her go, then grabbed her arm, lifted her from the crouched position and dragged her backwards to a nearby cottage, pushing her away from him when they stopped.

"How did you see me?" Her eyebrow arched, a habit she shared with her siblings.

"I assume yer father doesn't know ye're here. The bird chirping has sung yer name since ye crossed the road. I couldn't leave ye out here without yer guard." He finished and turned away. "Come, I'll return ye to yer room."

Like a spoiled child, she stomped her foot, requiring him to look at her. "I'm not going anywhere!" She whispered, grabbing his arm. "It's so unfair, I came all this way! I have to meet someone tonight. Please help me, Bennet."

He cursed under his breath. If he didn't aid her, she would attempt whatever this was, alone. Having helped raise them, the royal children easily pulled at his heartstrings, and she was the most hard-headed. He could return her by force, but it wouldn't be peaceful, and it would cause speculation if anyone witnessed them together at this late hour.

The emissary's shoulders slumped, and his words were defeated. "Who are we seeing?"

Princess Achelle smiled and, as she confided in him he covered her hair, took her arm, and led her along the eastside of a long building. Steering her through a door, he checked the first room to ensure it was empty, then pushed her inside.

A single bed, chair, table, trunk, and a small desk furnished the room. Weapons lined the entirety of one side.

"Stay here. Do not leave this room." He forcefully whispered.

She removed her cloak and placed it over the chair's back, then stood motionless against the wall beside the door.

Only moments passed before Guard Augustus walked in, letting the door swing closed behind him. His long hair flowed down his bare back, brushing against his trousers as he fastened them.

She reached out to touch him, anticipating their union for so long, but he spun around and knocked her hand away.

"Princess Achelle," he genuflected in shock and backed away. "What are you doing here?"

He retreated until his back connected with the far, cold wall. Heat radiated from her body when she closed the gap between them. He quickly fastened his trousers, then used his palms to cover his torso.

"Don't leave tomorrow," her fingers reached for his chest.

Guard Augustus, twenty-five, knew this was trouble, and he evaded her hand as if it would burn. He strode out of her range to the bed where he lifted and snapped the sheet, conjuring a tunic, then slipped it on. "Princess Achelle, may I ask what you know? What have you seen?"

"Seen? Oh no, I haven't. Augu–" She glided towards him.

Angry, he forgot himself. "Then what's it like?" What was she doing here in the dead of night, dressed in her nightgown, speaking to him so informally? He strode toward the door and grasped the handle. He had to get out before someone caught them.

"Augustus, I love you. Please don't leave me here all alone." In despair, tears surfaced. She rushed to him, threw her hands around his neck, and buried her face in his back.

He detangled her arms and freed himself as the door swung wide.

Instantly, he wished he were already dead.

"What's the meaning of this?" Lead Auren raged as the door swung shut behind him. He grabbed Princess Achelle and tossed her onto the bed, away from the guard. Grabbing the man by his tunic, he slammed him against the wall. "How dare you use common hands to touch her? I'll kill you myself."

Guard Augustus tried to escape, but the door opened again, and Emissary Bennet cautioned. "Auren, ye've woken half the men. Ye must explain before someone else comes in here."

Lead Auren cursed, took a few deep breaths to calm his anger, and then exited. His words reached her, "men, in my drunken state, I overreacted to a furry rodent." The men grumbled, but accepted his explanation.

Lead Auren returned, and his eyes weighed the situation. Guard Augustus sat on the chair, his eyes cast down, looking at the floor. The princess had righted herself and sat on the bed's edge, her pleading unfocused eyes fixated on the guard while silent tears fell over her cheeks. Emissary Bennet stood between them, his hands crossed behind his back.

"We need to get her out before one of the other guards, servants, or worse, her family finds out she's missing." Lead Auren pointed at her. Fierce loyalty coursed through him for the girl raised as his sister.

"I will go–" Guard Augustus rose.

"Like hell you will!" Lead Auren pushed him back down then crossed the floor and wrenched the princess up. "Let's go, *now.*"

He took a stride and stopped when Emissary Bennet blocked his path. "Ye should both go. If either of ye is caught alone with her, there'll be hell to pay. Together, if ye follow her, like her guards, nay one would question it and it'll give ye an opportunity to discuss this without others overhearing."

Lead Auren thought about this for a few seconds. "Fine!" He begrudgingly agreed as Guard Augustus stood and Emissary Bennet draped her cloak over her shoulders, lifting the hood.

Heading southwest along the road to the main castle entrance, she walked twenty paces ahead. Accompanied and beyond the servant lodgings, there remained no need for her to hide. Now, the night was abandoned, the shift change was complete, giving Lead Auren an opportunity to unload on the man. "What were you thinking, the king's daughter? What's wrong with you?"

Guard Augustus stopped and waited for her to walk farther away. "Do you honestly think me so daft? You've known me for many years. I'm an honourable man. I know how you see her, and I mean no disrespect when I say she acts as a spoiled child who doesn't understand the position this has put us both in. Do you believe I'd tangle myself with an innocent, virgin princess? There are easier ways to relieve myself. I've never uttered a word to her before tonight nor encouraged the feelings she claims to have. She's fabricated them on her own. It's as much a shock to me as it is to you."

She listened as she brushed away her silent tears.

A spoiled child, an innocent virgin, her mortified heart shattered.

Lead Auren grabbed Guard Augustus's tunic, hauling him against him. "Your words are grossly inappropriate! I remind you, I've a brother's anger, and you've done nothing to calm me. I saw you holding her–" He pushed him away and the other fell backwards onto the ground.

"You saw me trying to escape her." He vaulted to his feet and looked Lead Auren in the eyes. His life depended on making the man understand. "You must believe me. I tried as hard as I could to get away from her without drawing attention to your room. I thought she had a premonition about our journey or information from someone else who had."

Unable to bear another word, she ran.

When the men turned to continue their walk, she was nowhere in sight.

"I'll ensure that she returned to her chambers, but we'll continue this conversation later. I'll reserve my judgement until then. For now, this stays between us. I don't want this to postpone Prince Aedyn's journey any longer. We leave at midday." Lead Auren left him.

Women—nothing but trouble, Guard Augustus thought and headed back to his bed. He thanked Jezabet it was only Lead Auren who had discovered them.

By the time they returned, he hoped she would be over this one-sided childhood infatuation.

Day 90
Staff Quarters
Castle's East Bailey
Near Aldersward City

Emissary Bennet retired to his private room, in hopes that this time sleep would come and his shame would ebb, letting him rest. Along the exterior wall, the hearth with its charred wood barely flickered as it gradually burnt itself out, long forgotten. He fidgeted as he twisted on the lumpy mattress, intent on falling asleep, but he couldn't quell the thoughts of his family, who might still be alive. Since his meeting with Prince Aedyn, and the discovery, their memories plagued him.

His hands dishevelled his curly greying hair. He pulled at it in rage and flattened it with regret in alternating succession.

He summoned the last day he spent with them.

Emissary Bennet rolled over to spoon his wife's body, cherishing the feel of her in his arms while he shifted her long blonde hair aside, and with his mouth nuzzled her neck. He placed his hand on her full breast, playing with her nipple, and pressed his erection against her ass.

She snuggled closer, enjoying his warm and strong frame as it enveloped her. She raised her hand behind her and stroked his sandy hair, inviting him to love her as one of their babies suddenly cried. She patted his head and tried to escape, but his strong arm tightly held her against him. Her laugh fluttered as she turned over to examine her husband.

Her blue eyes met his brown, both sets filled with desire. "My love, I must leave. It sounds as though yer youngest son wants his mother."

"Let him cry, it'll strengthen his lungs." He smiled as he rose on his elbow and planted his hand on her thigh, stroking it lightly while his fingertips grazed her nub each time his fingers came close. "I want her now."

She laughed again as her hand miserably failed at deterring his. "He'll wake the others."

His mouth captured hers, then he deepened the kiss by entwining their tongues. He wove his other hand into her hair. Her folds dampened, and her hips raised in response to his fingers between her legs. "Are ye done protesting? Should I love ye now, my beautiful wife?"

"Aye husband, ye should love me now, quickly." She opened her legs, inviting him. He positioned his body, lightly teasing her clit with his hard tip. She wiggled her hips, trying to capture his rod within her as she laughed into his mouth.

"It would not do for me to love ye too *quickly*, wife. My intent is to love every inch of ye, starting with yer ankles." Bennet trudged his mouth down her body until his knees were on the floor and the sheet covering them barely cloaked his ass. He softly kissed her ankles, running his tongue along the back of her leg, and stopped to worship the backs of her knees while his firm hands rubbed her calves.

Brielle softly moaned, enjoying the pleasure her husband was providing. He massaged upwards as he ravished her thigh with his mouth, and left a red mark on her inner thigh.

Focused on his husbandly duty, he did not know anyone had joined them until tiny toes touched the bottom of his foot. He jumped, the moment temporarily broken, as he pushed his head through the side of the covers to face the intruder.

"Papa, what are ye doing?" Their son, sixteen, resembled a four-year-old Aldersward child, stood with his eyebrow raised.

"I'm checking my wife's body to make sure she's healthy." Bennet smiled and shared an intimate glance with his wife while she gripped the covers against her chest, her cheeks flushed in embarrassment.

"And is she?" The young, innocent child asked.

He returned his eyes to his son. "I haven't finished my inspection."

"Will I have to inspect my wife?" The boy rubbed his face, wiping the sleep from his eyes.

He nodded. "A good husband will often inspect his wife's body. Bowan, how about ye go see to yer brother while I finish, then afterwards, when I am done, I'll give ye a gold coin?"

The excited boy ran out and Bennet yelled. "Close the door."

The little feet shuffled back as he captured the high doorknob and slammed it.

"So, ye've come full-circle? Paying for pleasure, like an inexperienced youth?" She laughed as she studied him.

"I'll happily pay for eternity, my love." His head disappeared under the sheet and he continued from where he left off. His mouth clamped over her clit as he cupped his hands under her ass, drawing her more firmly onto his tongue.

Her breathing laboured as her hands gripped the bedding.

"Bennet, come to me?" She begged.

He slithered up her body, placed himself between her folds and braced his arms above her head, then cradled her face to his chest. Her mouth dragged over his throat, gently biting, then licked her tongue over the red marks she created.

He teased her, poking an inch within her, then drew out slowly, torturing her with the promised pleasure. "Do ye love me, wife?"

"More now than ever," she breathed the words wrought with sexual frustration into his neck as she forced her hips off the bed and willed her vaginal muscles to tighten around his shaft.

"Ye can't love me if ye torture me, husband." She chided.

Her movement heightened his desire. Her nails sailed over his back. He was no longer the one torturing but the tortured. "Aye, I love ye more than the grains of sand on our shores. I could lose everything but ye. Ye'd be enough." He drove himself deep inside her. She muffled the unexpected cry against his chest.

His body fell into a steady, slow rhythm as he enjoyed every inch of her body beneath him. Her hands travelled over his back and shoulders, her nails digging into the nape of his neck. Her legs tightened against his sides, her toes curled along his legs, and her soft breasts pressed firmly against his chest. Her hair fanned out over the pillow and her smile dimpled as her eyes stared into his.

He murmured love words inside her ear as he felt her body coil with tension. When her climax came, she moaned and writhed beneath him. He slowed his pace, allowing her to recover.

Once she had, he kissed her breasts and reached his fingers between them to waken her desire again. He patiently waited for the signs, and was rewarded when she tongued his ear, her hands planted on his backside, and she wrapped her legs tightly around his knees.

He increased the tempo, using his elbows to keep his weight from her, aware her second climax would require more diligence and he laboured eagerly toward it. It came suddenly with force as her body rocked uncontrollably against his and he felt her hot, wet sheath grip his rod, draining him. Overwhelmed, he grunted, relaxing his body onto her. His heavy breath was loud as he spilled his seed deep inside her.

He pushed off of her and she turned to drape her leg over his, putting her head against his chest. She melted against him and ran her fingers over his chest as he kissed her forehead.

"Wife, I believe ye're as good as the day I broke ye." He snaked his hand out to grip her breast. "Perhaps, better. Maybe we should try again and I'll determine which statement is truer."

She laughed, then kissed his chest. "Ye need new material, husband. Ye've said it every time since the day we married twenty years ago." She pushed herself away from him, knowing if she stayed, he would convince her. There were children to feed, and he needed to pack.

She left their bed and he laid watching her with his hand behind his head. Her naked body did not look a day over four-hundred and fifty. He appreciated her full, sagging breasts weighed by the milk she carried, and her round ass sagged from the seven children she had given him. Her long hair touched the middle of her back. His body stirred from her beauty, and begrudgingly, he ignored it. He stood tall, stretched, and acquired his trousers.

Emissary Bennet came out of the memory and recalled the numerous women he'd bedded since, then he scrambled to the bucket on the floor and vomited.

His heavily weighted conscience was irrational, but still he was disgusted with himself, and no matter how he tried, he could not escape it.

He assumed his wife dead, and it was natural to carry on and seek comfort in another.

But now he knew she might be alive, how could he face her?

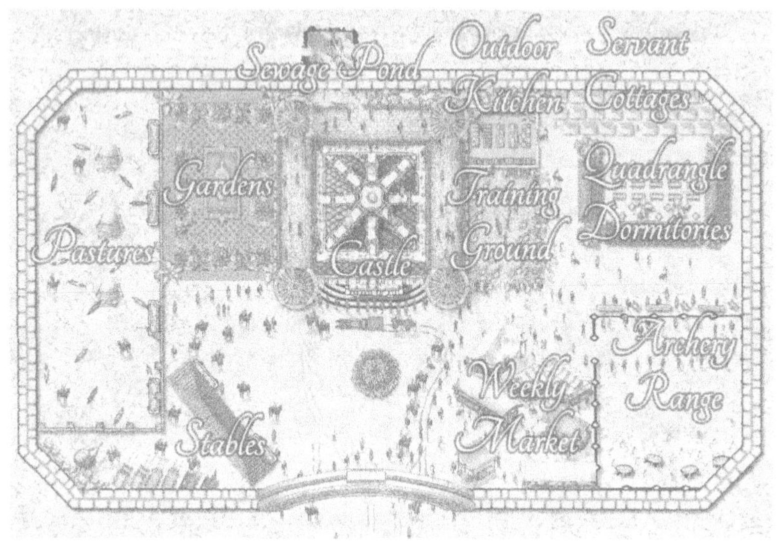

Day 90
Staff Quarters
Castle's East Bailey
Near Aldersward City

They spent the hours before midday ensuring the supplies, horses, and men were ready to embark. Prince Aedyn had one more obligation—his father had insisted—to complete before his departure.

He knew precisely where Ammaris of Wibley would be. Loading the donated clothing, food, and handmade toys, she collected or made with her ladies' help, to deliver to the poorest, most downtrodden people in Aldersward City. In his absence, she would nurse the sick, cook meals in the soup kitchens for the hungry, and spend time with the children in the orphanages. She was renowned, and everyone adored her. He often thought, if not for their marriage, she might find her greatest happiness in life solely devoted to charity.

Prince Aedyn and his guard approached the vacant cottage his father had given her to house donations. The area bustled with activity. Four men carried out crates and loaded them onto a wagon while she sat on the tailgate, and her ladies-in-waiting stood by, supervising how each crate should be loaded and in which order.

Unnoticed, he approached and studied her. She dressed plainly and simple. There were no lacy frills or beads. He imagined she thought it an unnecessary waste she could use to help others.

Ammaris of Wibley was unlike his whore, Azalea.

Azalea's beauty captured her complete confidence, experience, and playfulness. Ammaris of Wibley, though compellingly beautiful and wholesome, was meek, frigid, proper, and lacking any real world experience.

Their faces were the same shape, and their cheekbones high and defined. Ammaris's hair matched the whore's in colour, but instead of a multitude of loose, thick, unruly curls, his betrothed's were much more relaxed, thin and trained with pins secured to her head in an elaborate style.

The whore's mouth was much wider with thinner lips, and her white teeth presented when she smiled. Ammaris's mouth was small with a pouty bottom lip and her smile was reserved. Azalea's brown eyes were bigger, heavy with thick lashes and defined brows, and his betrothed's sultry blue eyes were smaller with sparse lashes and thinner brows.

Attraction was a puzzle. What drew one to another? They were both equally beautiful in his mind.

Her ladies finally noticed him and excused themselves with a slight bow.

With a half-smile, Prince Aedyn watched them join his guards who stood in the shade of a tree a good distance away, allowing the couple privacy. He strode to her, still seated on the wagon's back. "I came so we may say goodbye in private."

Clouds gathered overhead as her mind raced with the things she wanted to say. She wanted to remind him of the flower he had given her when she was eight years old, crying outside the schoolroom. A flower she pressed and still kept in her diary. How she had loved him in the single special moment and more every day since.

How much she would miss seeing or speaking to him. She wished to speak of her many sleepless nights over the last month, worrying he would not return to her. How everything he ever did impressed her, and how she was so proud he would be her husband. And, finally, in the event he did not return, he would be her forever and always. She would never recover and would die loving him.

She did not speak about those things as raindrops gently fell around them. "Aedyn?" Her eyes meekly searched his face for a response. "Will you love me when you return?"

Raking his fingers through his hair, the prince turned from her. "Upon my return, you'll take my side as instructed by my father. We'll have many children and happy years together."

Ammaris of Wibley recognised his words. He spoke them often, never of love, but of duty to his countrymen and kingdom. She had secretly hoped, since their betrothal, her devotion and loyalty would have sparked his love for her but to no avail. She came off the wagon, stepped closer and reached her hand up to caress his shoulder, then moulded her frame to his back, inhaling his scent. "Then I shall impatiently wait for you." She declared as she touched her lips to the fabric of his vest.

Prince Aedyn turned abruptly, breaking the intimacy of the embrace. The rain fell harder as he noted the hurt in her expression. He took her hands and promised. "I will return for you." He delicately lifted her folded hands together and pecked the back of each. He smiled. "Just think, by the time I return, perhaps you will have realised your ability." He did not wait for her response and dropped her hands. "I must leave you now. I want to see my mother." His entourage of guards followed a few steps behind him.

It only took Lead Auren a couple quick strides to reach the prince's side. He walked next to him, his eyes straight ahead, and quietly asked. "Does it bother you to leave her here? Do you worry about her loyalty?"

The prince halted, stopping everyone behind him, then inspected the royal crest on his ring and whispered. "No, I worry I will return because *she is* what awaits me here."

Stunned by his words, Lead Auren fell back with the guards when they continued. She was radiant, beloved, and loyal. It made little sense to him why the prince was so unhappy with Ammaris of Wibley.

Day 90
Queen Anya's Chambers
Castle's Second Level
Near Aldersward City

Prince Aedyn walked silently into his mother's rooms. His escorts stopped outside as he continued through to her bedchamber. Brilliant twirling flowers danced along the walls and ceiling in a continuous motion, a cheerful sight in the otherwise serious atmosphere.

The king murmured in her ear while stroking her hand. Princess Annora stood beside him with her comforting palm on his shoulder. She watched the flowers and escaped into their beauty for a few short moments.

Prince Aedyn stood next to Princess Achelle at the bed's end, watching their mother sleep. He murmured. "The flowers are beautiful."

"April created her favourites."

He whispered. "Have you tried to enter Mother's dreams?"

"Every night," she hugged her arms around herself. "Unsuccessfully."

Prince Aedyn pulled her against him. "I wonder about your ability. How much further it will grow. Have you tried to pull someone out of their dream and into yours?"

"It doesn't function like that. I don't pull someone inside my dreams, but I have brought April out of her dream and into the passages I use to get from one to another. It isn't an ability I have strengthened. It's a quite dull experience. Dream-walking makes me ill for a short time. But pulling April into the space between dreams caused me prolonged suffering."

The king lifted his gaze. "Girls, please allow us a few minutes alone."

The door closed as Prince Aedyn sat on his mother's bed. He took her hand and kissed it gently.

"Father, we have said many words in anger over recent weeks and I don't wish to leave with them hanging over us." He whispered, leaving his mother's hand at her side, and shifted to look at him. "Your love for our mother is undeniable. I regret I challenged it. The anguish you feel as you see her slip further away, I can never understand. I swear, I'll find Reinshaven and bring back the cure for you."

"On occasion, lost in my misery, I forget she is your mother." The king circled the bed as the flowers dissipated. "I can't apologise for your betrothal. These can be loving and satisfying relationships, if we allow them." He placed his arm over his son's shoulder as they walked from the queen's bedchamber. "I should confess, in one of our heated exchanges, I called you a *selfish prick*, I realise you're not, it was unfair."

Prince Aedyn smirked. "I believe you claimed me an *arrogant,* selfish prick."

"I know." The king smiled. "You couldn't be my heir, if you weren't arrogant."

Lead Auren bowed to the pair as he passed them on his way into the queen's bedchamber. For this woman, he felt a son's fierce, devoted love, and he laid his head on her heart and closed his eyes, listening to the steady rhythm as he inhaled deep breaths of her lavender scent. His mind willed her to wake, the need of her embrace strong.

The king leaned against the open doorway, allowing Lead Auren a few minutes. Their relationship was close, the child loved and raised as their own. The royal couple had intended to help the young boy—offer their charity to his parents, but it became so much more as he grew with their own children. Lead Auren gave them his unquestioning love, his adventurous joy, and added exuberance to their lives. He accepted nothing in return.

They planned a title for the son not of their making. An earl, governance of a village and the manor it would entail. But he had made other plans, moved from the castle, and accomplished his way through the ranks until he became Prince Aedyn's lead guard. The queen confided in King Adahy she thought his motives were deliberate so he could maintain close proximity to them.

"My boy," the king warmly spoke with love as he approached. "It's time. Come, let me hug you. You two will return soon with a cure and entertain her with grand, adventurous tales."

Princess Annora raced inside, flung her arms around Lead Auren's waist, and raised her green eyes. "I'll miss you."

"And I, you," he lifted his brow, teasing her. "By the time I return, perhaps you'll be married with children."

"You wish both upon me? Do you hate me so much?" Her face twisted with disgust.

He chuckled. "No, squirt. One day, I will utter those words and they will make you happy."

"Doubtful." Princess Annora's expression clouded with disbelief. "Aedyn and Achelle have gone downstairs. Is it time yet, Father?"

"It is." King Adahy offered her his hand.

"I have one last thing to do before we can leave." Lead Auren lifted the lizard from the water pouch. "I must find someone to care for Stinger while I'm away. I can't possibly take him."

"Oh!" she gushed with excitement. "Could I, Father?"

King Adahy nodded. "It could be your own quest while the boys are away. You would have to check in with the animal scholar every day and ensure you're following his every direction. Auren doesn't want to leave him with you if you will only let him die."

"Of course, I would let nothing happen. He's simply too cute to die." She reached out, but Lead Auren placed the creature on her shoulder.

He unbuckled his belt, freeing the water pouch and handed it to the king, then patted the small lizard's head. "Behave, will you?" He spoke to the creature, but the amphibian had already fixated his attention on the girl's face, trying to replicate her expression. Princess Annora laughed.

Day 90
Castle's South Bailey
Near Aldersward City

The high midday sun emitted its heat onto the active south bailey, increasing the raunchy smell of horseflesh and gathered bodies. Children ran about comparing their talents with one another. One stood in a group's centre and shrank from four feet tall to only one, then, with silliness, danced. The rest laughed as another drew their attention to a straw stack. Lightning cracked from above, setting it on fire. The horses and mules jumped nervously, and men grabbed their ropes to stop their sidestepping. A man strode to the children, grabbed the boy, and marched him away.

Prince Aedyn called to mount, and the men, one last time, kissed their weeping wives and hugged their children, not knowing if they would ever see them again.

A trumpet sounded. King Adahy made a brief speech about duty, the consequences of failure, and bid them the kingdom's prayers. Princess Annora waved to the men on horseback and in wagons as Guard Asa took the first position, leading them out of the castle walls.

Lead Auren, Guard Augustus, and Emissary Bennet lingered beside their mounts, waiting for the prince to finish his goodbyes. Guard Augustus had remained close to both men since the previous evening, and he nervously wondered if the lead would reveal what happened.

Prince Aedyn kissed his father's ring, then hugged him and turned his attention to Princess Annora. He lifted her high in the air and whirled her around while he planted unwanted kisses on her face. She laughed and pushed against him.

Princess Achelle stood behind her father, motionless and hiding. The king stepped aside, exposing her so Prince Aedyn could say goodbye.

"She's there," Emissary Bennet nodded toward the castle staircase. Guard Augustus and Lead Auren turned.

Her complexion was ghostly. Her eyes almost swollen shut from crying. Prince Aedyn misunderstood. "I'll save our mother. Please stop this, it breaks my heart." She did not move. Her body looked numb as he hauled her into his embrace. "See you in three days."

She allowed him to believe his leaving upset her and almost fell from weakness when he let her go. She grabbed her father's arm for support, and he wrapped his hold around her.

Her eyes searched until she found Guard Augustus. She nodded exhaustedly, and he turned away. She wept.

Lead Auren's temper flared and his low tone hissed. "Look what you've done to her!"

Guard Augustus mounted. "Listen carefully, as I'll not say this again. I didn't touch, speak, or glance at her in any manner which would give her the impression she's under." He flicked his wrists and galloped out, eager to leave what happened behind.

"If I might add?" the emissary summarised. "She came on her own to the dormitories. I followed her from the castle. I woke Augustus to speak to her as she refused to leave without seeing him and she would've made a scene, if I had refused." He shook his head, then clasped Lead Auren's shoulder. "I don't know this man as ye do, but I do know a young girl's heart. I've spent the last two-hundred years teaching them. I can tell ye this. Sometimes, young girls form crushes, much like young boys who create fantasies in their minds about grown women they have nay hope of ever conquering. Ye must let this go and I assure ye, the princess will recover by the time ye return. We should mount, Aedyn's nearly finished."

The prince planted a single kiss on Ammaris of Wibley's forehead, then walked to his horse and mounted. The three turned their attention to the people standing on the castle steps, all etching the memory in their minds. Those on the stairs waved their last farewell, praying this would not be the last time they saw each other. Prince Aedyn reined his horse and kicked his heels, sending his mount through the castle gates, his two friends in tow.

The procession marched along the wide path through Aldersward City, and many citizens lined it to wish them luck.

The expedition became daily chatter among the Alders. While Azalea shopped, she heard murmurs of sympathy for their king. According to rumour, his grief had driven him crazy. He was sentencing their future ruler and his brave countrymen on a journey from which none would return. Sorrowful women, their husbands chosen to go, were comforted by the wives whose husbands were ineligible.

Lead Auren spied his sister on the steps. Her hair exotically arranged on the top of her head, with a few ringlets escaping on each side, her lips and cheeks slightly rouged. Excited, she jumped up and down, waving as he recognised her.

He smiled his approval, turning to Prince Aedyn. "She's on the steps of the bakehouse."

"Who?" Aedyn asked as he mindlessly waved in every direction. His thoughts focused on his duty to his people and the love of his kingdom.

"Azalea," Lead Auren no sooner spoken when the prince turned to look for her. He almost missed her, barely recognising the woman dressed in a fine society gown. He waved to her, his face lit with a genuine smile his friend had not seen since they were children.

Prince Aedyn heeled his mount into a gallop, and the pair followed closely behind, making their way to the procession's front, where Guard Asa was waiting for them to arrive.

Day 92
South of Aldersward City

Prince Aedyn wrote in the voyage's journal. *Our journey continues southeast across the land to the village of Lessard, where the boat builders are labouring tirelessly to complete the vessel's construction. I wonder if they have found a crew and trained them yet.*

Over the last two days, our journey has progressed without incident as we cut a direct path through the fields, meadows, and homesteads. We've fallen into a steady routine. The cook rings the morning bell before the sun rises so we may eat quickly and travel until the sun reaches midday. This allows us to rest during the warmest hours, then we set out again before the evening meal and travel until twilight. We're thankful winter has ended. The temperatures are warm, but, at least, it isn't the stifling heat of summer.

We make a crude camp each evening, not bothering to assemble the tent we carry. Each night, men are assigned to patrol, as there are often cottages or livestock within a short distance. I sleep amongst my men under the stars, beside the fires meant to chase away the chill.

The long hours and the minimal camp allow us to travel more than half of the day. Tomorrow afternoon, we'll come within a hundred-and-twenty miles of Cranbrook, reaching the edge of Rayanne Forest. We'll enjoy a lengthy respite before we set out on the most difficult part of our land journey. It'll take us a full day to travel through the north forest, across the river and through the other side before we find an area big enough for us to camp.

I'm eager to reach Lessard, begin our journey's sea-leg, and find Reinshaven.

Day 93
North Shore Camp
Rayanne Forest
Near Cranbrook Village, Aldersward

In the early afternoon, the convoy reached the forest's edge. One hundred foot trees soared into the sky while others were thorny shrubs or vines as thick as a man's arm which tangled and weaved around the other vegetation.

Prince Aedyn rode with Emissary Bennet, Guard Asa, and Lead Auren, their eyes surveying the area and the small trail leading into the woods. He called for a halt where tall grasses grew in a meadow. The wagons circled, and they readied their camp.

They staked the horses and mules where they could graze. Guard Asa procured a pig from a nearby farm and the cook butchered and prepared it for the spit. It would be their finest meal thus far, since time allowed it. Many men who had never met before made acquaintances along the trail and they chatted or relaxed in smaller groups while enjoying the refreshing keg of sweet tea.

At this stop, the erected tent helped hold the perimeter circle. It provided a place for Prince Aedyn to meet with his men and go over their plans. A few thick cuttings of tree trunk were used as stools around a makeshift table of crates.

The prince glanced around the tent. Besides the two guards at the entrance and his page sitting cross-legged in the opening, these were all men he admired, respected, and trusted unequivocally. Lead Auren and Guard Asa leaned against tent poles while Emissary Bennet rested on a crude stool next to him.

"I'm pleased with our progress, but things may get more difficult as we go. We should seriously discuss the leadership and expectations." Prince Aedyn spoke to the others.

"What about it?" Lead Auren felt an uncomfortable conversation brewing as he and Guard Asa took a seat.

"I want to make sure we agree going forward. I'm the Crowned Prince, but we're a team, the four of us. When problems arise, I want each of you to give me your council. If I say *the council*, it means you." He glanced around the table and noted their agreeing nods. "In the event, I can't lead us. I want to make my orders perfectly clear. Auren will take my place then Asa and finally, Bennet." Prince Aedyn put his hand on the emissary's shoulder. "Your journey with us may be short-lived if we find Baitsloam first."

The emissary smiled as a fleeting image of reunion came to mind. "I agree. It makes sense and I've nay experience leading men, only children."

"If I die, on any leg of this journey," Lead Auren and Guard Asa looked as though they would interrupt, but the prince raised his hand to stop them. "I want you to turn home instantly—as I promised my father—with or without my body." His tone clarified he would accept no argument. "There will be no heroic acts to retrieve me. Do you understand?" The others nodded reluctantly and he changed the subject. "Most of these men, we've never met before. It's not unfathomable to imagine there may be those who don't fit in. We've observed them for three days, have seen them as a group, and know some abilities and skills they offer." He paused for a moment to allow them to think about his words. "Are there objections to any man? Or anyone we can utilise in a secondary leadership team?"

Emissary Bennet led the discussion. "There are limited abilities among them. We've one who can change the colour of fabric, and one who can make music. One can make dirty things clean, and another who can animate dolls. The list goes on."

"I don't know about you, but after ten days on a boat, a man who can make dirty things clean could come in handy." Lead Auren made the others laugh.

"Point taken," the emissary conceded. "There's a man, Alonso, who has an enhanced memory ability. He can remember faces, their names, and abilities. I think it'd be wise to use this gift." Not hearing any objections, he resumed. "Yer father sent Apex, one of his trusted advisors, as our food conjurer, pork and beans only, but I think we should seek his counsel."

"Where is he?" the prince asked curiously, realising he had yet to see the grey-haired, chubby man.

"Travelling with Guard Augustus, both are from Edson," Emissary Bennet offered.

Aedyn spoke in thought, "Guard Augustus? We should include him as well."

Auren questioned. "Why? His ability to conjure clothing doesn't seem to fit into our group."

"He's one of my father's personal guards." The prince stated. "We'd utilise him to help supervise watches and such. We can't expect you and Asa to do everything and if we reach land, we may need to split into smaller groups."

"I think the idea is sound." Bennet agreed. "Aidrik, our physician, should ride in the same position every day. His ability is to feel others' pain, convenient for a doctor."

The prince nodded. "Yes. I'd also like him to join our second leadership group. He's an intelligent man with much knowledge."

The emissary mentioned a few more without discussion. "There's Arturo—a human compass, Angelo—needs only two hours of sleep a day, Alberto—can change the wind's direction and Aron – possesses the ability to get along with anyone. Have any of ye interacted with these men?"

Prince Aedyn spoke when no one responded. "I don't think so, but we should consider them. I'll read their names out tonight and tell them to report here immediately after." Then he changed the subject, turning to Lead Auren, "Anything to report?"

"Overall, we fared well. Four men stayed back to replace a wagon's axle and they should pull in sometime this evening." He answered, knowing the state of their men, horses, and supplies.

"Very good, ensure they're reprieved of guard duty this evening as they have had little time to rest. We'll look at dividing the leadership responsibilities between the others as we see fit."

Emissary Bennet studied the map between them. "What's the condition of the trail and bridge?"

Guard Asa responded, the last to cover the trail only a month before. "The trail is narrow, only wide enough for one wagon at a time. The bridge has deteriorated considerably since it was new thirty years ago. I don't know if it can stand the weight of the heavier wagons. The conditions are the same on the other side."

The prince scratched his head. "Is there anyone who could widen the trail?"

"The only person on our list who could is Asa." The emissary offered.

"I appreciate the mention, but no. Even with super-strength, it would take days for me to remove all those trees, and if I could, I didn't bring an abundance of dried snake meat which I must consume to use my strength."

"Then we travel as it is, in single file." The decision made, Prince Aedyn continued. "Is there anyone who can help us with the bridge problem?"

Emissary Bennet scanned the list again. "Perhaps, Ametheus can turn wood into stone, but someone should speak to him about his limitations."

"All right, Asa, discuss it with him and let us know if there's anything he can do. Tonight, my sister will dream-walk with me." He rose, ending the conversation.

The sun set as Aedyn and his friends joined the men around the enormous blazing bonfire. They ate, chatted, and listened to Anthony make lute music with his throat—his ability to imitate musical instruments. Several men danced, competing in the firelight.

A man pulled out a set of dolls and lined them on the ground. He concentrated his mind, wagged his fingers above and the dolls stood without anyone's interference and danced. The men cheered as they watched the tiny inanimate objects dance in time to the lute music. The two masculine dolls in trousers and exaggerated puffy silk tunics vied for the female dancer's attention while she, dressed in a simple blue peasant's dress, passed between them. The small males took turns performing elaborate tricks with her, a flip, twirl, or spin, to outdo the other. As the song ended, one of the two threw her in the air, then caught her on the last note and she kissed his cheek.

When Anthony finished, the entertained men praised him.

"Play it again!" A man named Arlo shouted, then stood with his back to the flames, his posture commanding the men's attention as he sang.

Remember friends, I rhyme in jest,
I'll put your anger to the test,
And beg forgiveness before this story,
About women, their drink, and their glory,

Men clapped as Arlo continued.

My rod's so big with a large pair,
The women flock and easily scare,
Found blessed one day, girl gave me a try,
Nearly destroyed me, when I found her a guy,

Boisterous laughs howled as Arlo strode around the circle. No one dared make eye contact, fearing they would be his next subject. Auren clapped loudly and the prince pushed him forward, inviting the attention.

Volunteered, I see Auren has no panic,
His rod he states is so gigantic,

I came around and spoke to Allie,
Says you didn't fill her valley,
She admitted though he's so handsome,
Confided he held girls' hearts ransom,
It's shameful though about his tiny beast,
But then freely she offered me her feast,

Men danced, enjoying his quick wit as Arlo circled. He rhymed through Guard Angelo, then Guard Augustus, and attacked Emissary Bennet's six-hundred year sex life. Last, he picked on Prince Aedyn.

Prince, it would be unfair to leave you out,
Men here would throw a tantrum and pout,
Aedyn's a big man, a steady string of girls,
When he's enthralled, the whole thing uncurls,
His stamina is a thing of great legend,
The girls come around seeking seconds,
He only leaves when they beg for more,
Dripping with sweat, satisfied to the core,

Arlo finished. The men cheered and mimicked the lines the poet had invented. He poured himself another mug of ale as Prince Aedyn approached him.

"Well done, Arlo. It was very amusing. I'm glad I came out unscathed." He slapped the man's back.

The poet responded. "Your Highness, I sang it purposely for my health. I'm never quite sure how some will receive my jokes. It's better if I tread lightly."

"You needn't worry about me." He jerked his head toward the crowd. "Look at the men. Their spirits are cheerful and raised. I can handle your jests and look forward to more to help pass the time. Excuse me, I must go." He strolled towards the tent where his council, Ametheus, and the eight men gathered inside.

Day 93
North Shore Camp
Rayanne Forest
Near Cranbrook Village, Aldersward

Lead Auren wrote in the voyage's journal. *It is with profound regret I report, among the men accompanying us, I'm still the most handsome. It truly is my lifelong burden. I worry, over time, the others consumed by jealousy, may come to resent me.*

I've formulated a tentative plan to deal with the ageing bridge. Tomorrow morning, Ametheus will travel first with Asa to inspect it.

I orchestrated a test of sorts for the men who joined us this evening in the tent. I set the prince away from where I and the others stood or sat on the ground. I wanted to see how they would interact with him. I and the others took turns interviewing the men and reinforced our prince given authority. Aedyn only engaged those who passed by, or those he specifically asked to converse with.

I and the others found no objections to the behaviours and demeanours of the selected men and, thus, determined the secondary command as follows:

Augustus will supervise the camp guards during our daytime break while Angelo will supervise the night. Both will report to me.

Alonso will be allowed the next couple days to learn the faces, names, and abilities of the men and will report anything of note to Bennet. Alonso will ride in the front position with Prince Aedyn and his immediate men.

Aron, with likeability magic, will make a good Emissary for Aldersward and, to this end, Bennet will train him, and they'll become a team.

Apex, our food conjurer, will oversee our supply inventory. He and Aidrik, the physician, have been assigned the first wagon positions, so they're readily available should anyone need them. They'll report to Asa.

We have determined, while their skills are invaluable, Arturo and Alberto have nothing to offer as we travel on land. However, once we board the vessel, their positions will be imperative. It still makes sense they join the leadership team now, so the other men learn to take commands from them.

Day 93
North Shore Camp
Rayanne Forest
Near Cranbrook Village, Aldersward

After sorting the assignments, the four leaders spread out their bedding inside the tent, fully clothed with their weapons ready, in case they were required during the night.

Nervously, Aedyn laid on his bedding. He wanted to guarantee it was this location and not a brothel he would show his sister. The prince focused his mind on the forest's edge, his first impressions. He concentrated on the tall trees, the smell of the wild grass, and the flowers covering the ground. Birds sang in his mind as he imagined the sun warming his body. Aedyn drifted.

"Aedyn, where are your clothes?" Achelle materialised behind him and laughed.

His eyes glanced downward and indeed he was naked, his clothes laying in a pile nearby. He cursed as she turned away. "I don't know how this happened."

"Don't worry, in the past, April has done the same. What exact thought did you have?" She asked curiously.

"I was thinking about the sun's warmth." He admitted once his tunic and trousers were on. "You can turn around."

She smiled. "You need to learn to focus on scenery and not feelings. It'll probably help if you change your clothes before bed. It's an act April has found useful."

A huge grin covered his face as he looked at her. "It's good to see you." He embraced her tight in his arms then let her go, taking her hand and began walking.

"Must I teach you everything? Stop walking." She giggled as he stopped. "It's harder for you to control where we go if you walk. It strains your mind, filling in blanks, and pulls from your memory. Look!" She pointed. "It's Den's Mercantile from Aldersward City. Why would you think of the fabric merchant?"

His gaze travelled. In the middle of the field, the building stood with cloth in its windows and the sign above, every detail exact. "It is unusual. I pass by it often when I travel to the city. Tell me how things at the castle are?"

"It's been eventful without you to keep Annora honest. I don't think she's completed a single task meant for her. She uses her ability to convince everyone she has, but both you and I know she definitely hasn't." She grinned and arranged her skirts as she sat. "It's peaceful here."

He joined her, lying on his side, his body propped on his elbow. "It is. Aur–"

"No!" She covered his mouth with her hand. "Don't say it. Do not say anyone's name." He lifted his brow, and she explained. "If you say his name, then your mind might envision him here. Depending on how you see him and in what situation, will determine what he wears. Do you want to chance it?"

She dropped her hand, and he laughed, "No, let's not."

"Once you're used to controlling more of your dream, then you can introduce people or we can walk. Let's keep this, although it looks strange with the mercantile there. Try this; close your eyes," once done, she continued. "Think about where it is, the location in the field, then think about how it should look." He concentrated on it, and after a few moments, she proudly announced. "There, you've fixed it. Now, until we've practised, in as little detail as possible, is there a message for father?"

"We've reached Rayanne Forest and will cross in the morning." He finished and grinned, thinking himself quite smart.

"Good, I'll tell him—Oh!" she exclaimed, shock covered her face. "I must leave." She vanished as if the wind had blown her away.

Aedyn rolled over and froze. Azalea, dressed in the fine gown, came towards him.

"Sard," he muttered aloud as he woke. His eyes focused on the tent's ceiling above him. He listened to Bennet's snores and the others' restful breathing. *At least she had worn clothes,* he thought, and he closed his eyes, picturing her otherwise.

Day 93
Princess Achelle's Chambers
Castle's Second Level
Near Aldersward City

Achelle came awake and glanced at the window. It was well beyond midnight. She rolled to her side for a few minutes. Nausea and headaches haunted her after her dream-walks, the price for her ability. The severity depended on how long she was in, how hard she searched for a specific dream, and how she left it—by will or force. The cost of this dream-walk was relatively mild.

She concentrated on the slow draw of her breath.

The forest had been beautiful, everything covered in green while wild flowers grew in a multitude of bold, vibrant colours. She smiled over her brother's undress and the mercantile. For a second, Aedyn's mind must have wondered when the lady appeared. Achelle had not recognised her from the castle. Perhaps someone he met on his travels.

Her stomach settled enough for her to rise and, in darkness, she reached for her robe as she stepped into her slippers. She exited her room and light spilled from her through-room's hearth. It took her vision a moment to adjust before she walked to the hallway.

She opened the doors, and her guards stepped aside. Her father, in his night robe, sat straight in the chair with his chin tucked to his chest. Her younger sister, Annora, slept, curled against him, covered in a blanket. Achelle looked past them to see their guards at either end of the corridor.

"Did you reach him?" Ammaris of Wibley's voice shook as she turned from the rail overlooking the castle's wide centre bridges.

Her voice, though low, echoed through the tall, sparse hall. King Adahy stirred, then woke, "Achelle?"

"Come in," she invited.

The king sent his youngest daughter to her room as Ammaris entered and sat beside the hearth. The castle could be quite cold at night, and she had not noticed the chill until now, wrapping her wool shawl tighter.

"They've reached Rayanne Forest." Achelle sat next to Ammaris.

"They accomplished it quickly. He pushes the men hard." Adahy proudly boasted. "Any problems, anyone hurt or injured?"

"No, I believe everything's fine. Aedyn looked well. He explained they will cross the river in the morning."

"Then I shall retire. This is good news." He rubbed his hands together. "I'm glad you woke to tell us. I wouldn't have slept otherwise." He kissed her forehead. "Good night, darling." He closed the door behind him, forgetting his son's betrothed remained.

Ammaris sat motionless, and Achelle pretended an interest in the hearth's fire. They had spent little time together, these two about to be sisters by marriage. They shared the same meals, but nothing else. When she first came to live in the castle, Achelle had sought to include her in her friendship with April, but Ammaris seemed too mature, more interested in charity than in clothes and jewellery. She spent more time with her ladies-in-waiting outside of the castle than in it.

Finally, Ammaris politely asked. "Was there a message for me?"

"No." Aedyn's sister saw the woman's hurt expression. She tried to comfort her by taking her hand. "Please let me explain. It'll take time for him to learn how to control his dreams while I'm in them. I kept him from saying people's names or thinking of different objects or surroundings. He'll learn, and then in time, tell me things in more detail. I'm certain it will be quite awkward for him to give me a message he intends for you."

Ammaris covered their entwined hands as she stood. "Of course, you're right. How silly, I'm behaving."

"No, not at all, you're in love." The princess smiled widely, imagining what intimate love would feel like.

Ammaris could not confide in her. She would not comprehend the emotionless betrothal. She dropped the princess's hand and left.

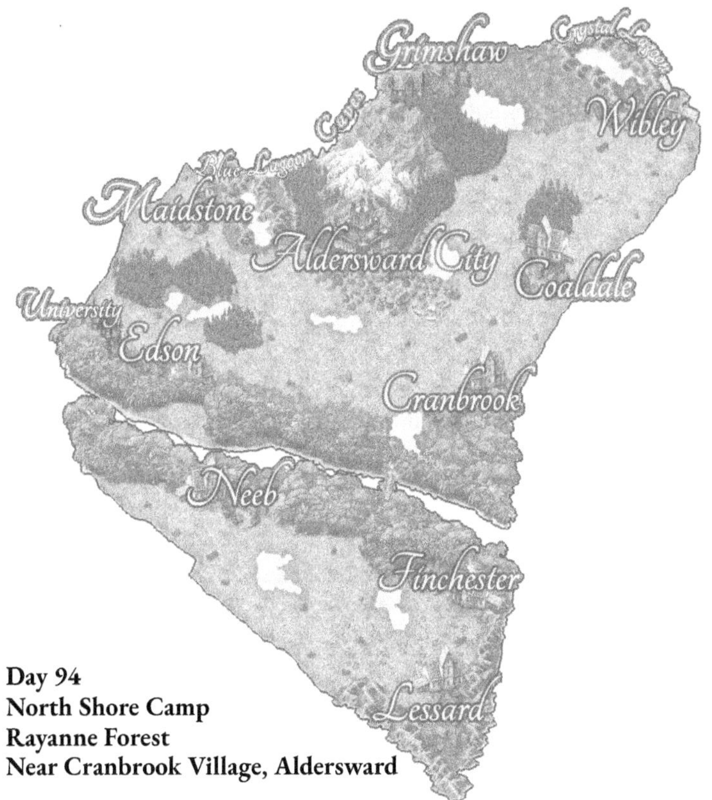

Day 94
North Shore Camp
Rayanne Forest
Near Cranbrook Village, Aldersward

Bennet woke first. His dreams plagued him like nightmares. They were wonderful dreams, but when he came awake, his mind was guilt-riddled. He questioned whether he had done enough to find his family, if he had only stayed, only pushed King Acoose to send search parties into the sea. He had lost the years of his children's childhoods. His last dream had been quite upsetting.

It was their last moments. She stood by the cottage door with their four-year-old infant daughter, Byunca, on her hip while the boys clutched her skirts. As always, when he left his meek, loving wife, she silently cried, hating the times they were apart. He hugged his boys, kissed their daughter's forehead, and then took his wife in his arms, promising he would be back in a few weeks.

A few weeks, he thought. In his mind, he mounted and turned to look at them one more time. He was eager to leave so he could return to the warmth and joy of their small home. His wife blew a kiss as she lifted the baby's arm in a wave while his boys, aged sixteen and twelve, chased after him and stopped at the gate.

Before the sun began its climb, Aedyn woke and laid listening. Bennet no longer snored, but the others, still sleeping, breathed. He rose silently, then grabbed his sword, and exited the tent.

His page, Anik, sat nearby, and the prince held his finger to his lip, gesturing for quiet and motioned him to follow. He walked outside the circle formed by the wagons and tent, not wanting to disturb anyone's slumber.

As he rounded the tent, he saw a small fire in the distance where a group practised their combat skills.

When he approached, the group turned and genuflected. "Good morning, as you were. Come, page." He called and strode to Bennet, who was staring into space. He dropped his sword, then stretched his sore muscles as his page mimicked his movements. "Sleep well?"

Bennet jumped at the sound and shook the memory from his mind. "Hardly, I'm too old to sleep on the ground. Did ye see Achelle?" He bent at his waist, trying to force his head to his knees, unsuccessfully.

"Yes." The prince put his arm behind his head and used his other to stretch it further. After a few more stretches, he spoke, "Enough page, go practice with the others."

"He learns well. Ye've been an excellent teacher." The Bait complimented when the boy left.

"No, Anik's smart, eager, and tries hard. I never stopped to wonder whether he should come on this trip. Perhaps I should have." The prince looked to his page labouring through a series of defensive steps. "I'll speak to everyone this morning before we head out." He walked off to join the others.

Day 94
North Shore Camp
Rayanne Forest
Near Cranbrook Village, Aldersward

Aedyn confidently stood on the empty wagon's back, above the men preparing for the procession to begin, their movements and voices loud as they prepared. His three friends stood behind him, observing the men, as the sun began its rise from the east.

The prince's hand raised, and his page rang a bell. Quiet instantaneously fell over the group.

"Gather around." Aedyn waited, and once he saw little movement, he continued. "Today marks our land journey halfway over. What I need to address is how we proceed going forward. Aldersward has taken for granted our kingdom's harmony. We've become complacent in our training and duties." He paused, taking a drink. "Once we start across the sea and, in the event we find other lands, they may treat us hostilely. If reversed, we would do the same. It's imperative we continue our training. Each of you will train three times daily. This will slow our journey as groups pull out of the procession. While you're training together, get to know each other. If we divide forces, these will be your commanders and men." Aedyn stepped back.

Auren came forward. "There'll be six groups. You'll find your group on this list with your leader's name. Please come forward if I call your name and stand on the second empty wagon. The leaders for these groups will be Asa, Angelo, Augustus, Prince Aedyn, Bennet with Aron, and myself." He watched the others come forward. "The cook will post this list later today." Auren continued, announcing the duties these men would assume, including Alonso, Arturo, Apex, Alberto, and Aidrik. "The vessel has sleeping and dining quarters for thirty-five. This means your groups will combine with one other to sleep, eat, and train."

Asa stepped forward. "Let's speak of today. The forest's path is narrow. This means we'll travel single file and far apart. We don't want any horse to shy or frighten. The forest's thorns can be deadly. If a man in front of you stops, you stop too. Angelo and Augustus will coordinate your departure. It should take you four hours to reach the bridge. Once there, you'll need to cross. Auren, Aidrik, and I'll be there. Once you're over, you'll enter the south forest and ride through for six hours." He glanced at Aedyn, who shook his head, and Asa continued. "Apex and the cook's wagon will be in a clearing. You'll make camp there. Unless you've been otherwise instructed, fall in behind the cook, we begin our departure shortly."

Day 94
North Shore River
Rayanne Forest, Aldersward

Aidrik halted Apex's wagon as he reached the opening onto the riverbank. "Wait here." He returned to the men near the bridge.

Nearby, underneath the rickety bridge, the river raged with powerful intensity. Its ominous roar and hurling speed further added to the tension which gripped the group.

Guard Asa rubbed the back of his neck as he loudly informed the prince. "Your Highness, Ametheus says he can do it. The trouble is, it's composed of stone and wood. He can't meld his rock to those already here."

Each man eyed the nearest damaged footing. Cross braces, several of them gone or broken, zigzagged four posts in varying degrees of fracture. At the footing's centre, rocks filled the empty void. It was impossible to tell if the structure's integrity remained beneath the water.

The unknown tightened the pit of the prince's stomach. "Speak freely. Alonso, any other suggestions?" He asked the man who held the abilities list.

"Once the bridge is turned, we could demolish it using Alvin's stone-shattering scream. Then Guard Asa could fall logs across the river. Ametheus could turn those to stone." Alonso suggested.

"Turn it. Let's test it." Aedyn needed movement to alleviate the tension in his rigid muscles. He crossed to his mount and swung into the saddle.

They watched Ametheus step to the bridge. The man laid on his stomach and reached down to touch a post. Any wood connected to the single piece turned. Except for the slight change in colour and texture, it was difficult to tell anything had occurred at all. From side to side, Ametheus crossed and repeated the action until he reached the south shore.

Finally, he stroked the planked floor and trotted back across to join the group now standing near the prince's mount. "Should I change the railings?"

As if it were a play or theatre company, Aedyn could merely observe—the circumstances beyond his control. It wasn't a familiar feeling. To each, every decision was a risk, with no knowledge of whether one option was wiser than another. Sweat beaded between his shoulder blades and he unfastened the button at his throat.

Guard Asa rocked back and forth on his heels, eyeing the man's work. "We'll see how it holds with a wagon on it before we become too invested in this."

Next to Aedyn, Lead Auren removed a rope from his mount. He tied it to an arrow and shot it into the woods behind them. It wrapped itself tightly around a tree and sailed back, still carrying the line. It landed at his feet.

"What good did that do?" Emissary Aron asked. "The arrow brought the rope back."

"Did you expect it to tie itself into a neat knot?" Lead Auren grinned, then gathered both rope ends and handed them to Guard Asa. "Will it hold?"

After chewing a small piece of snake jerky, he tugged. "It's solid. Ametheus and I will see to the south footings in case we need to devise another plan."

The pair crossed with the line tied around Asa's waist, and when he removed it and gave a thumb's up, it slacked within Auren's reach.

"Lead Auren, take Advisor Apex's wagon across next. Let's see what weight will do." Aedyn dismounted. "Alonso, take watch on the west footing."

The wagon's wheels click-clacked, and the horse's hooves clomped over the rough planks. The bridge remained intact.

As his lead jogged across the distance, Aedyn took a steadying breath, and asked him. "How did it feel?"

"Stable."

He nodded. "Very well. Watch here and move them over."

He mounted his horse to supervise and, one at a time, the procession began.

Halfway through the day, the sun climbed directly above. The glare on the water burned the men's eyes as they struggled to focus on the footings.

"I believe I heard a groan here," Alonso told Lead Auren as the poet, Arlo, led his horse across.

"You *believe* or you did?" He asked, then yelled. "Hurry along, Arlo."

"I–"

The unmistakable sound of cracking wood echoed thunderously above the river.

With Auren's focus completely on the imperilled man, it did not register when the men caught the frightened ground-tied horses.

He witnessed the terror on Arlo's face an instant before he and his horse tumbled into the relentless water as the west footings broke free. His expression showed a horrified understanding—it would be his last breath.

Again and again, the horse rolled, thrashing against the violent water and the wooden debris, making it difficult for him to spot Arlo.

Stable. That single word meant he was solely responsible, and the guilt paralysed him.

"Auren," the prince yelled, urging him to act.

He turned and caught the rope Aedyn threw, then he quickly tied and shot it farther downstream and around a tree on the opposite bank. As the lead jumped into the water, he knotted it around his waist; another man jumped in without a safety line.

Auren felt the taut rope around him slacken, knowing with complete faith that Guard Asa had cut and held it as he searched the water for Arlo, his horse, and the other man.

He would not—could not give up. In an off-channel area, he found Arlo's dead horse where it laid, twisted and mangled against the bank. It renewed his desperation, and he searched the shorelines, then plunged deep into the icy water.

His limbs burned. He could no longer feel his fingers and toes, but still he continued his hunt. His need to recover the missing men intensified as Prince Aedyn and the others joined along the riverbanks and re-examined the areas he had already passed.

It seemed like hours. The distance from where the bridge collapsed was vast.

Guard Asa could see his friend, exhausted from the exertion it took to fight the raging, icy river, and he struggled to resurface each time.

He had to stop him, and he waved to the prince, drawing his attention, then motioned toward their friend, who still desperately dredged the river.

Prince Aedyn saluted and yelled. "Halt the search!"

As Lead Auren fought against his tow, Guard Asa pulled him in. He easily bested him, and by his collar, dragged him out.

His body shivered, and his teeth chattered. "I need to continue. I'm not done."

Preventing his return to the river, he caught the lead's shoulders and gently shook him. "Prince Aedyn says we are."

His breathing was laboured as he reasoned. "I could still find them. I–"

"We have to consider the others and follow the order," Guard Asa said.

The resolve left his friend's body, and when Auren fell limp, he caught him.

Ametheus rode up, leading a second horse.

Asa rolled the unconscious man in a blanket, then lifted his weight and mounted. He held him between his arms as he manoeuvred the horse through a turn, then spurred it into a trot back to where the bridge collapsed.

Lead Auren's body quaked against Guard Asa, yet the man didn't come around in the travelled minutes.

To ward off his awful worry, he instructed Ametheus. "We must start a fire to warm his body, create another bridge, and get the physician from the north side."

When they reached their destination, he ignored the men on the opposite bank, and hauled his friend down, then carried him upriver about twenty feet.

Ametheus found kindling and started a fire, while Asa downed a dead tree, split it with his bare hands, and tossed the chunks into the flames.

Once the fire burned strong, and they were sure it would not travel, Guard Asa ingested more snake meat, grabbed his axe, and downed a swath of tall trees to arrange them across the river. Ametheus followed, changing each to stone. When Guard Asa had made several layers, ensuring there were no holes, he created a crude ramp for the horses and wagons. Prince Aedyn called for a wagon's sides to be stripped and they fashioned another ramp, filling in behind it with more wood so it would not collapse under a wagon's weight.

Ametheus crossed and turned the second ramp. Physician Aidrik and the prince galloped to the other side.

Prince Aedyn came off his horse, ground tying it as he dropped to his knees beside his adopted brother. He was lifeless and tinged blue. When he cradled him, the chill of his body sent a shiver down the prince's spine.

Guilt riddled him. If only he had...

Demolished the bridge and constructed a new one.

Made the initial pass over the bridge.

Continued to stand watch at a footing.

He questioned his every decision.

The physician filled a bowl with water and placed it beside the fire to heat. "Give him this." Aidrik handed him a flask.

As he slowly tipped a bit into Lead Auren's mouth, Aedyn smelled the strong whisky.

The pair tended to the unconscious man while Guard Asa and Ametheus reclaimed their posts.

It neared the evening meal when the final pair, Angelo and Guard Augustus, passed over the bridge.

Day 94
South Shore Camp
Rayanne Forest
Near Finchester, Aldersward

The page took Asa's horse as he dismounted and entered the tent. Bennet and Aedyn drank ale at the table while they watcheda disturbingly still Auren sleep, his body scraped and bruised by the riverbed's stone.

"Your Highness," Asa bowed, then poured himself a drink, and joined them.

Bennet offered. "He woke for a brief time on the ride, but when we laid him here, he fell back asleep. He's exhausted. Aidrik ensured his comfort, then left to check on the others. He offered to return and stay the night."

"Who's the other man we lost? Why'd he dive in?" Asa asked.

"Alonso's checking the manifest as we speak. As for why, some men act before they think." The emissary replied. "Ye should grab something to eat. I fed the men as they arrived. I saw nay reason to wait."

"Have Apex release three kegs of ale." Aedyn instructed Asa as he left. "We'll remain here until I determine what we're going to do next."

Bennet asked. "What are our choices? Yer father ordered us to come back if misfortune struck us."

The prince poured another drink. "That's what he said." He raked his hair. "But he's not here. What happened today was not misfortune. We let it happen. We should have–"

The emissary interrupted him, "Stop. We can't fix this by thinking back. Right now, yer men need ye to lead them. I won't tell ye to obey or disobey yer father. My stake in this differs from yers. My counsel is biassed."

Asa called from outside. "Prince Aedyn, come, you must see."

He quickly crossed the space, and Bennet took extra steps to keep up. They emerged into the black night to see several men crowded by the firelight. As they approached, the crowd backed away, leaving Asa holding a collapsed man who was dirty and ragged while another laid in front of them.

The prince knelt by the other, noting his body was ice cold as he gently turned him over. Even in death, he immediately recognised Arlo, the poet.

Asa covered the man's back with a blanket, and Aidrik came forward as Aedyn spoke. "Tell us."

"Your Highness, there wasn't time to explain. I can travel long distances underwater without breathing. The river carried me as I searched. He was almost one-hundred-and-twenty miles downstream in a pile with the timber from the bridge. I couldn't leave him there. A farmhouse nestled a small clearing with a path to Neeb. I asked for a horse and galloped cross country."

"What's your name?" Aedyn noticed Asa's hands were marred with splinters and scrapes.

"Anders of Maidstone," the man drank thirstily from the mug offered by the physician.

"Aidrik, when he's dry and looked after, take him to my tent and then examine Asa. Bennet, have men wrap Arlo's body then place him inside a covered wagon. Have someone travel to Finchester, hire a messenger, and deliver a letter of condolences to his family." He called louder. "Angelo," as the man appeared, he ordered. "Oversee the digging of a grave to bury him tomorrow. Those who don't dig can take turns sitting with him. He's not to be left alone."

Day 95
South Shore Camp
Near Finchester, Aldersward

Bennet wrote in the voyage's journal. *This morning at sunrise, our men, including Auren, gathered around the chosen burial site. I spoke a few words while they took turns shovelling dirt into Arlo's grave. It's a sobering reminder of our mortality and the dangers we may face ahead.*

I sent a rider to Finchester with the following letter:

"It is with regret, I must inform you of your husband's passing while he accompanied myself, Prince Aedyn, across the land-leg of our journey. We have buried him on the south side of Rayanne Forest and marked the grave with an engraved stone cross. Arlo was an integral part of our group, and upon our return, I wish to extend your family a bereavement allowance. I am forever indebted to your husband. Prince Aedyn"

After some deliberation, Prince Aedyn has decided we will continue. He announced any man who wanted to abandon our mission could return home without penalty. None have left, we leave at sunup tomorrow.

What follows is the list of men, their assignments, and abilities:

Prince Aedyn's group:
Aedyn – by asking an exact question, the person responding cannot lie
Alan – animate dolls
Abraham – make dirty things clean
Andres – recreate music he has only heard once
Ametheus – turn wood to stone
Arjun – make objects glow—five minute limitation
Aryan – instantly create weapons made of wood
Anderson – ability to unlock any lock by touch
Anik – change glass into mirror (Aedyn's page)

Guard Angelo's group:
Angelo – recharge fully on two hours of sleep (Guard)
Arturo – a human compass
Aidrik – feel other people's pain when he touches them (Physician)
Arlo – poetry—he rhymes well
Apollo – create elaborate illusions of gardens—only lasts an hour
Aldo – unbreakable bones
Ameer – duplicate fermented drinks
Alec – change his own legs into arms
Anson – disease resistant

Guard Asa's group:
Asa – super-strength by consuming snake meat (Guard)
Alberto – change the wind's direction

Austin – enhanced hearing, direct line, no barriers
Alcott – conjure any fur as long as he has seen or interacted with it before
Arthur – paint an image from memory, extremely detailed, on eucalyptus paper
Albert – accelerate creating a weapon but must have all materials
Alvin – shatter stone with his scream
Azariah – heat vision

Guard Augustus's group:
Augustus – conjure clothing from cloth (Guard)
Archer – force field for himself only
Alonso – never forgets a face—remembers names and abilities if told
Ashton – enhance another's fire ability and strengthen it
Antonio – enhanced dodging reflexes
Ari – make other people sad
Ahmad – absorbs sunlight, can exude it on command as only heat
Amos – grow his own hair quickly

Lead Auren's group:
Auren – change the trajectory of an arrow forged by his own hand (Lead)
Apex – conjure rations, pork/beans only using rotting meat/vegetables (Advisor)
Anthony – imitate musical instruments one at a time with his voice
Adrian – fire—create flames from his fingertips
Ace – invisibility for himself only—must be naked
Andy – move ink only on hemp paper
Abdullah – speak and understand any language
Anders – breathe underwater for ten minutes

Emissary Bennet/Aron's group:
Bennet – communicates with birds (Emissary)
Aron – instantly likeable—must make eye contact (Emissary)
Alexander – grow any seed by touch
Asher – change the colour of any fabric
Amir – mute any water ability, one at a time
Amari – levitate objects as big as his hand
Armando – disintegrate excrement
Ares – resistant to poisoning, will not die but gets sick
Arvo – marks target's past course (Cook)

Day 96
Prince Aedyn's Tent
Near Lessard Village, Aldersward

When the long, stressful day ended, the others slept soundly. Aedyn needed to decide how much of what happened he would tell his sister. He focused his mind on the tent, the contents, and the men's positions. His breathing slowed as he drifted.

Princess Achelle found him pacing the tent when she appeared near its opening. "I see you've worn clothes this time." She greeted him warmly as she glanced around.

"I changed before bed as you suggested." He hugged her then sat at the table. "I have little to say. We made it across the river. Father should send men to repair the bridge. We stayed an extra day on the south side. We're three days' ride from Lessard. How are things at home?"

She sat, resting her arms on the table across from him. "No change. Mother and the others still sleep. Father spends more time with her, promising her you will return with a cure. I believe he wishes to convince himself more than her."

He wanted her to go, worried she would guess the secret he kept.

"Before I go, any message for Lady Ammaris?" She spoke as if in passing.

Irritated, he asked, "No, why?"

"She wondered after our last visit, and I had nothing to tell her. I only mean to remind you."

"You can tell her, I've thought of her." He instructed.

"Have you?"

He seethed angrily. "I am now, aren't I?"

"I don't think that's exactly what she wished."

"Dammit, Achelle, you've served your purpose. Leave." He ended the conversation.

She vanished.

Day 99
Royal Estate
Lessard Village, Aldersward

Nestled in Aldersward's southern tip was Lessard, a fishing village. From three directions, one could access the sea or make use of the east coast bay. This far south the landscape differed from that of Aldersward City, covered in grey sand, jutting rocks, and rough, sharp land formations.

Prince Aedyn did not take the convoy into its interior. They would overcrowd and cause unnecessary chaos. Instead, they skirted east to the royal estate where Earl Adisa, who governed the community, resided. Guard Asa led them inside the first empty field he found while Prince Aedyn, Lead Auren and his other guards continued to the estate house.

The well-maintained grounds were beautiful, considering there were few trees. In the circular entrance, an elaborate rock garden was the focal point. Vibrant pastel colours painted most rocks, while others formed furniture like benches and tables.

The staff, household, and farmhands lined up, waiting to greet them. They genuflected as Aedyn and his men arrived.

"Prince Aedyn, it's an honour to receive you here once again." Lord Adisa rose from his bow and motioned for men to collect the entourage's horses.

They followed Earl Adisa inside, travelled left through a sitting room, then right into the study. Lead Auren followed the pair and closed the door, leaving the other guards outside. He poured them ale, then leaned against a bookcase behind Aedyn, who sat in the desk's chair.

"What arrangements have you made?" The prince surveyed the heavy, dark furniture, the tan walls, the bulky black beams, and the large hearth, appreciating the room's masculinity.

Earl Adisa was eager to convey his forethought and receive the prince's gratitude. "Your Highness, I've secured additional rations and kegs, hired extra cookhouse staff to prepare your men's meals and grooms to feed and care for your horses. I've installed extra seating in the cookhouse and prepared your rooms upstairs."

Disinterested, Aedyn limited his response, dissuading further conversation. "Well done. Calculate the expenses, and I'll settle the debt before we leave. We'll welcome the change from the less than impressive meals on the trail. In small groups, my men will use the staff washhouse so we don't overcrowd your household and staff. Immediately, I'll go to the village. I'm eager to see the vessel's progress. Should you require anything in my absence, Guard Augustus of Edson will act on my behalf."

Day 99
Docks
Lessard Village
Aldersward's East Sea

Prince Aedyn, Aron, his council, and guards walked the short winding distance to Lessard, set at the bottom of a steeply inclined region. Shops and mercantiles backed the land, lining the north side of the thoroughfare along the water's edge. Behind those buildings, numerous rows of cottages jutted upward with narrow paths between them. Docks marred the water where fishing boats would tie off later in the day. The salty scent of seawater and fish lingered in the air.

Children happily played along the shoreline while women walked the storefronts and men mended fishing nets or boats. The people dipped and lifted like a wave, genuflecting and clearing a path as Prince Aedyn walked by. The enormous, magnificent vessel dominated the water, dwarfing anything man-made. It cast a wide shadow over the new dock at the inlet's southern edge.

Aedyn's group approached with bewilderment, discussing it in awe from their position below while they waited for the designers to learn of their arrival. Three grey-haired men, well past sixty, walked its plank, then bowed.

Guard Asa came forward. "Your Highness, this is Boat Builder Amos of Lessard."

"Your Highness, it's a great honour to be entrusted with building this craft. I would like to introduce you to Engineer Abner and Carpenter Ackley. Together, we created it." His words brought the other two men forward, and Aedyn acknowledged each with a nod. "You and your men must be eager to see it. Come, and we'll show you."

They boarded mid-boat at the tallest mast where men laboured on the vessel's various parts as Amos explained. "Prince Aedyn, this is the vessel's main deck. To our right and upstairs is the navigation deck with a wheel you turn to change directions. Above it, another deck where you can observe. Under the navigation deck, we have your quarters, two rooms; one for sleeping, and the other as your through-room, much like in the castle. To our left, we've put two washrooms, two privies, and the stairs accessing below. Above it, another, larger deck. Below we have the men's sleeping quarters for thirty-five, a dining hall, and a cookery. If need arises, you have holes for oars if you need them to row the vessel. It–"

Emissary Bennet interrupted, astonished. "Ye believe we can row this?"

Engineer Abner answered. "If there's no wind where you go or you get too close to land, then yes, you may have to use the oars. We've tried to address any scenario you may face."

"Very well, continue yer explanation please," Bennet nodded, impressed.

Carpenter Ackley said. "The craft's belly is your storage and cargo hold, for supplies. It took a few days to find someone to calculate how much stone was required to weight the bottom. Th–"

This time, training Emissary Aron interrupted. "You loaded rocks? How are we to float and not sink?"

Carpenter Ackley turned in frustration, but, when he met Aron's eyes, he smiled and answered lightly. "The weight is needed because of the three tall beams you see through the vessel's centre. They hold tied sails, much like the ones on our fishing boats. You'll open them when you're on your way. Without the rocks in the bottom, your craft would tip over."

Emissary Aron muttered as Amos spoke. "Your Highness, shall I show you to your chambers where we can speak more freely?"

They wandered to the stern of the boat and walked through a door. "We've nailed the heavy furniture and cabinets to the floor because they could shift positions and become dangerous, depending on the sea's condition." Amos explained before someone would interrupt.

Aedyn inspected the pleasant room, heavily scented with fresh cut wood. He walked behind a long table to a row of cabinets, then looked to a corner where a round table and four chairs sat empty. Astonished, Aedyn sat at the long table's head which had chairs enough for twelve men. He motioned for everyone to sit as Lead Auren instructed the guards to wait outside.

"It's incredible." Auren said as their men sat at one end and the builders at the other. "How did you construct it so fast?"

"We had men with abilities to help. One felled trees from Rayanne Forest in a single strike of his axe. Another dried the wood, and one manipulated it into any shape we needed, instantly. We only had to provide him with a drawing. It would have taken much longer without them." Amos admitted.

Aedyn spoke. "When can we load and leave?"

"Prince Aedyn, once the cargo hold satisfies you, the men can fill the compartment. We prefer your inspection before anyone makes use of the decks, in case we have missed anything you'd want or need."

Aedyn glanced around, amazed at the crude furniture's detail. "Stay seated." He entered the room behind where he sat, closing the door for privacy. He ran his hand over the wall, then walked about the room: a bed, cabinets, a trunk, several cushioned chairs, and a table. It was complete and masterful.

He came through the doorway and returned to his seat. "I would like a chair installed at every doorway. Bennet and Auren can inspect the rest of the vessel. Apex will come in the morning to inspect the hold. When do the tailors install the cushions, bedding, and tapestries? What about a crew?"

Engineer Abner answered. "Your Highness, they'll install the tapestries and such the day after tomorrow."

Carpenter Ackley said. "Prince Aedyn, men to navigate is something we wanted to talk to you about." Aedyn raised his eyebrow in question as the man continued. "Men to manage the vessel, open the sails, row, clean, and wash, are easy enough to find; your men can do those things. However, finding men who can navigate or understand how the huge masts function then training them, has been an issue. If anything goes wrong, they wouldn't know how to fix it or handle it. If you find land, you'll need your men on shore. We feel that if the craft sinks, we should be on it. It wouldn't be fair to send untrained men while we stayed here."

Aedyn studied the three, but Emissary Bennet spoke, giving the prince time to think. "Would it hurt this vessel if we tied smaller boats to its sides from the railings?"

Amos answered. "No, we can accomplish it without issue."

Emissary Bennet laughed. "Good. Ye speak of going to shore. Without a dock, do we swim to shore?"

Lead Auren scratched his chin. "Did I miss something? How do we stop the vessel?"

Engineer Abner responded. "We found a man with the ability to weave many materials instantaneously. Lord Adisa commissioned him, and after many attempts, he found the strongest to be hemp and the leaf stalks from a banana tree. We rigged a spool of the thick rope to the top deck in the vessel's front. We couldn't determine what we should use as weight other than stone."

Asa offered. "If we took several trees and weaved this rope through them, Ametheus could turn them to stone which would give us weight and the branches the ability to claw into the sea floor."

Emissary Bennet responded. "It's an ideal solution." The men agreed.

The prince rose, "As far as you men joining us," he eyed the old men eager to hear his answer. "I'll stop none of you from accompanying us, if it's your wish. Don't feel obligated to come. You must decide amongst yourselves, the pecking order. I have two men with abilities. Alberto can modify the wind's direction, and Arturo is a human compass. I believe both will be useful."

Aedyn's group withdrew as Carpenter Ackley asked. "Your Highness, one more question, please? What name will you give the craft?"

His eyebrow arched. "Should it have a name?"

Engineer Abner answered. "It's bad luck not to name a fishing boat. I imagine this would be worse."

Emissary Bennet yanked the door wide. "Prince Aedyn, we need ye."

"Let me reflect on it." He strode outside, taking in the scene before him. Aron and Asa ran, nearing the end of the thoroughfare already, as others rushed behind them. The prince's guards and Bennet waited for him near the plank, the last on the vessel.

His powerful legs strode onto the dock. "What's happened?"

"I'm uncertain. Something's happened at the estate. Our man appeared and Asa met him. They spoke and instantly set off."

"I have an uneasy feeling about this." Aedyn increased his pace, leaving Bennet in his wake.

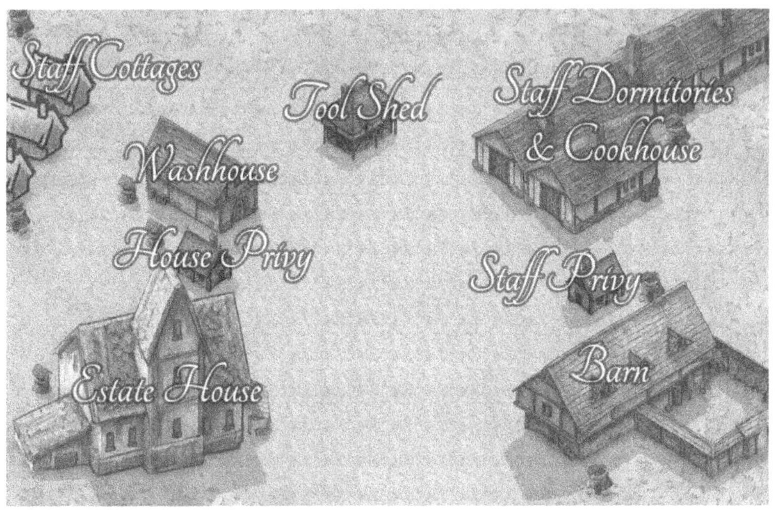

Day 99
Paddock
Royal Estate
Lessard Village, Aldersward

The scene unfolded as the prince drew nearer. He motioned for his guards to stop, and continued alone.

Two groups, eighteen men, stood with their backs against the tent, their weapons drawn. From several vantage points, the rest maintained a close watch on the situation, ready to participate if necessary.

Guard Augustus of Edson blocked the tent's entrance.

Lord Adisa pointed his sword at Augustus while men from his estate waited several steps behind him, carrying makeshift weapons of pitchforks, shovels, and scythes.

"You dare defy me! It wasn't a request. I sent orders to surrender the accused into my men's custody and you outright refused!" Lord Adisa's face reddened and his mouth frothed as he yelled. "I outrank you in every way. I'm Earl of Lessard, appointed by King Adahy. I'm the law here! Who do you think you are? You're nothing but a high-priced thug."

Prince Aedyn, unnoticed, rounded the area to stand with the men furthest away while he observed the exchange.

Augustus, unaffected, spoke evenly. "You're mistaken. You've lingered too long here, away from the castle. In Prince Aedyn's absence, I act in his interest. And I order the man to remain here until I establish what action will be taken." He glanced behind the lord, his eyes roaming each face. Finally, he returned his focus to the sword wielder. "If it's unacceptable to you, then I suggest you ill-equipped farmers take him from us, if you can."

"I'll show you mistaken. If you continue to shield him, I guarantee every one of you will hang. You know nothing of authority. Mine outweighs yours!"

"But it doesn't outweigh mine." Aedyn strode forward to Augustus's side. Propriety was lost on the situation. "You are misguided, Adisa. When I leave one of my men in command, their power does outweigh yours. What Augustus has decided, stands." He stepped closer to Adisa, his voice amused. "You see, I don't even know what he has decided and yet, whatever the decision, it was his alone to make. Now, I do not recall you or your men bending as I arrived." His eyes urged the lord to disregard his order. "Do so, now." The earl hesitated a moment, then he and his men genuflected. "Now, Lord Adisa, if Augustus is finished with you, you may return to the estate, and your men to their fields. Guard Augustus?"

He stepped forward. "Have Physician Aidrik accompany you, Lord Adisa. He'll examine the girl and, once he returns, we'll inform you of what happens next. If any of you come here uninvited again, be prepared to die." He spun and stalked into the tent while the others remained to ensure his orders were carried out.

Aedyn followed and discovered they were not alone. "Can we remove him, perhaps inside a covered wagon?"

"Your Highness, Archer isn't a prisoner. I shoved him inside when we saw them approaching." He said, turning to Archer. "Leave and mingle. Stay close. We may have further questions." As Archer left, he drew a deep breath and exhaled, releasing the pent stress he held, then turned to Aedyn. "Thank you."

"For what?"

"For letting Lord Adisa think you support my decision."

"We've had little opportunity to interact before. It's no act. I left you in command. No different if you were Lead Auren, Guard Asa, or any other out there." The prince ran his hand through his hair. "When you joined me, you became my man. And my men, without exception, have my complete trust. I'll grant you a few moments, and then we'll handle this."

Outside, Aedyn called his page to bring refreshments, and instructed the men away from the tent walls. He motioned to his council, requiring their presence. Once together, they entered and relaxed at the makeshift table, glad someone thought to borrow chairs from the estate cookery.

"Now, what happened?" Their leader crossed his arms.

"Prince Aedyn, Angelo's men returned from the estate washhouse while Bennet's group finished their combat training. As I instructed them, I noticed several estate men striding this way with their tools and one pulled a girl covered with a blanket. They blocked our access to the yard. I approached to learn what happened. The girl was pulled forward—beaten bloody—an awful sight. He ordered her to identify the guilty man, and she pointed to Archer. The man withdrew his hold, and she rushed back to the estate. He demanded I surrender him so they could hang him." Augustus lifted his shoulders. "How could I? They would punish him, without considering the validity of her claim."

Auren nodded. "I agree. He deserves an opportunity to defend himself against the accusations."

Augustus continued. "Your Highness, I informed the earl's man that I wouldn't hand Archer over without questioning, at the very least. Archer would remain here until you returned, and you would handle it. The earl's man walked off, leaving estate men barring our path. I sent someone to advise you and had my men secure the tent while I questioned the accused inside. While we spoke, the earl's man came back with a letter from Lord Adisa. It declared I surrender him into his men's custody. I reiterated my position. I was uncertain of my authority, but I felt allowing a man to be executed was beyond it."

Aedyn sat forward, rubbing his chin. "What does Archer say happened?"

"Prince Aedyn, Archer became agitated—not angry, but scared. He reported seeing no women at the washhouse, and he remained with our men the entire time. Archer and I spoke with Angelo, who confirmed his story. By this point, Lord Adisa was striding over from the estate. I pushed Archer inside the tent and Angelo's men joined mine surrounding the tent. Lord Adisa and his men traipsed straight into the encampment, then he screamed at–"

Aedyn interrupted, "We know the rest."

From outside, Aedyn's page announced, "Prince Aedyn, Physician Aidrik to see you."

"Send him in then return to your group." Aedyn poured the man a drink as he entered and sat. "How bad is it?"

He propped his elbows on the table and clasped his hands. "Prince Aedyn, it's bad. Someone violently violated her. Whomever it was ripped the clothes from her body, beat her severely, and strangled her throat. Her neck's blackening with bruises and her voice is hoarse, barely understandable. She'll survive, but her scars, they will be in her mind. If she were my daughter, I would kill him myself, barehanded, and not seek permission."

"Sard," Asa blurted, then remembered. "Prince Aedyn, this is a mess."

"A mess we do not need nor can afford right now. Did she confide in you?"

"Your Highness, while I examined her, she confided it was Archer. I don't know if I believe her, but it is what she said. While examining her, I noticed she is a noughty." Aidrik informed them she had no magical brand. "I spoke to her father who claimed he discovered her, stumbling along the seashore."

"All right, thank you for seeing her. No one goes near the estate until this is handled."

Loudly, Auren exhaled. "Prince Aedyn, what do we do now?"

"There are so many issues here. First, I'll speak to her. Second, I need to send Lord Adisa to Aldersward castle. He cannot go unpunished for his reaction, nor do I think he'll cooperate any longer with us. Third, Bennet, inform your men they will take the first shift guarding Archer. We'll make further decisions after I see these things accomplished. Augustus, bring him here, to the tent." Aedyn rose, ending the discussion.

Augustus shook his head. "Prince Aedyn, Archer doesn't require our protection, his ability shrouds him in a force field."

"One less task," he turned to his emissary. "Bennet, spread the word, our men are to be more vigilant, and no one goes anywhere alone."

Auren stopped Aedyn, "Including you and your two guards. You'll have a complete set accompanying you. Foremost, I'm your lead. My position is to protect you, and this isn't the castle. It's not open for discussion."

Aedyn nodded. "Assemble the men."

Within minutes, Auren arranged eight guards with formal armour and weapons, including himself and Asa, ready to escort the Crowned Prince.

Aedyn marched to their centre as Augustus returned with Archer. He wasted no time and asked. "Did you do this?"

Archer shook his head. "No."

His answer was truthful, Aedyn knew, as Asa started to the estate house.

Two guards rounded the residence while two stayed out front. Aedyn, without knocking, opened the door and allowed two guards to search the house, then Auren and Asa accompanied him to the study.

Lord Adisa said nothing as the formal guards rushed in and surveyed the room.

Asa announced, "All clear," as Lord Adisa bowed.

Aedyn entered and towered over him. "Where is she?"

Intimidated by the prince's display of force, the lord stammered and sat. "Your Highness, her parents have a staff cottage—the blue one behind the main house."

He strode from the study as Asa bellowed for the guards to follow. They traipsed through the house and out toward the blue cottage. This time, the prince knocked and waited. A woman answered, genuflected, and sidestepped as one of his guards searched the small interior.

Once cleared, Aedyn ordered all to remain outside except Auren.

He found the girl, her face swollen with bruises, resting in a tiny bedchamber where only two feet of walking space divided the bunks on either wall. She struggled to rise, but he gestured, excusing the custom.

He had a hard time focusing on her battered form.

She was not as young as he expected—perhaps seventeen.

While Auren waited outside the open door, Aedyn knelt by her bed.

"Can you speak?" He asked, and she nodded. "You must be in a great deal of pain." She nodded again and tried to shift. He helped by repositioning the pillows behind her, then her back pressed against them.

"I'll be brief, so you may rest. You can appreciate our need to discover what happened. There is much anger and a need for vengeance. Did the man you pointed out do this to you?"

"No," confusion wrought her face, and she hoarsely answered a second time, "No."

He recognised her distraught expression. He was accustomed to receiving it from those who did not know his ability. "Did you think the man you pointed out did this to you?"

"No," she closed her mouth, not understanding her own responses.

He no longer felt sympathy. She had admitted it was not Archer, yet she had maliciously accused him, almost causing his death.

His temper burned under his tone. "Have you figured it out? My ability?"

He sat on the other bunk's edge, needing the distance as he suppressed his now fierce rage. "Let's try another, shall we? Who did this to you?"

"Master Adesh."

The information surprised him, "Lord Adisa's son? Should I continue asking, or do you prefer to fill in what I don't know?"

Giving up, she shrugged. "I found myself pregnant. Not by him. I don't know who the father was. Boredom often strikes me, so I use men to distract me. Master Adesh showed an interest in me, confessed his love, and we were together many times."

"Did you tell him the baby was his to trap him into marrying you?"

"No," she replied, her manner conversational. "I told him it was because I needed help to rid myself of it. Our families and the village would mark me a loose woman, and it would shame my family. His solution was to marry, but I refused. I didn't want a child or husband. I used his affection and eventually persuaded him to beat me. We waited, realising your appearance created the opportunity we needed. Not to accuse someone, but within the chaos, we hoped I might pass unnoticed."

His anger lessened. "Why did he strike your face?"

"It was an accident. I fell as he delivered another blow." She elaborated. "Realising how painful the beating had become, I begged him to strangle my throat until I was unconscious so I wouldn't cry out. When I woke in the barn, he wasn't there and blood covered my body. I left through the back, away from the estate and along a trail to the residence's secluded beach so I could wash unnoticed. I fixated on the water, not seeing the boat coming in with my father on it. He saw me and assumed the worst. I couldn't tell him as he dragged me and estate men followed us. He took me to your camp, ordered me to accuse someone. I pointed and wondered what could my peasant father do to a man protected by the prince?"

Aedyn understood her naivety as a shortcoming of women his sisters' age, "And the blood between your legs? Was it the infant being expelled?"

"Yes."

He used his ability. "Are you apologetic for the situation you have created?"

"Yes." Tears burst from her eyes.

He ran his hand through his hair in frustration as he left. "Stay here."

Aedyn strode to a nearby stand of trees while his guards spread out to protect him. He thought about his options as Auren joined him.

"What do we do?" His lead asked angrily, keeping his voice low.

"We have to defuse this. Right now every estate man is ready to explode. It'd be foolish for us to remain here. If news makes it to the village, there's no knowing how many men would arrive to claim Archer. I'm not worried about them taking him, but several men might die before we could explain." He stomped towards the official residence.

Aedyn and Auren entered the study while Asa waited in the hall. "Where is your son, Adesh?"

"Prince Aedyn, I couldn't say. Perhaps he's out riding." His eyebrow lifted.

Aedyn stepped around the desk. "Auren, order the residence cleared, then deliver the boy and the girl's parents here. Also, send someone to the camp to inform the cook we'll dine there tonight." He stood over Adisa. "I will use your desk. There's much to discuss."

Auren gave the orders to Asa, then returned. Lord Adisa had pushed away and taken a chair facing it.

"This will be hard for you." Aedyn began as the other man's face reddened. "I agree with Augustus, you've been too long away from the castle. Do not interrupt me!" He shouted when Adisa's mouth gaped, then calmly proceeded. "You forget how my father handles the kingdom's problems. You were reckless. You escalated instead of coolly investigating first. Your men could have lost their lives. They may still if we can't manage them." Aedyn clasped his hands together on the desk's top. "I'm ordering you and your household to the castle. I'll dispatch a messenger to deliver a letter to my father. You'll leave the day after tomorrow, stay a few days with the Earl of Finchester and the Earl of Cranbrook, then continue to the castle. It'll appear you journey for pleasure and take your time so your family may rest between stops. My father and your son will know the reason you travel. What you tell your wife and other children is your decision. Before you leave, you'll see to closing the estate and organising the staff."

The lord realised it was unwise to argue, and pulled at the collar of his tunic. "It's time we visited."

Auren opened the door when a knock sounded and allowed Adesh, and the girl's parents, entry. They genuflected as he arranged the chairs, so the lord and his son sat on the desk's right and her parents on the left, enabling them to view each other. He stood between the two parties.

"Show us your hands, Adesh." The prince ordered.

Slowly, the young man of eighteen lifted his hands, covered in welts and cuts, onto the desktop. The others studied them with interest.

"No one violated your daughter—she confessed. She asked him to beat her and he did so because he loves her. She also informed me," he faced the lord's son, "she doesn't love you. Understand," he looked squarely at her father, "No one forced her."

The girl's mother wept as her husband looked dumbfounded and angry.

The boy guiltily averted his gaze.

"I assure you it is fact. Now, we must resolve this." Aedyn addressed her father. "You'll figure out a way to talk the men down. Let them believe she was assaulted but force them to understand she doesn't know who did it. I want no one blamed. I'll leave her reputation intact at this point, but if you can't reconcile the men, I'll have no alternative but to tell them the truth. Are there relatives elsewhere?"

"Your Highness, my sister is in Wibley," her mother dabbed her eyes.

"Good, you'll send your daughter there to live. I'll send a messenger tonight. We'll find her transport with a supply wagon heading there in the morning. Go now to the cottage, pack her things, and calm the men." He dismissed the parents. Auren escorted them out, ensuring no violence between the girl's father and the boy.

The door closed, and Aedyn continued. "I have removed her from the estate." He regarded Adesh. "I tell you the truth. You were her toy. You may love her, but she doesn't love you. I am ordering you to stay away from her. Do you understand?"

The boy nodded.

"Lord Adisa, make your announcements and arrangements. My men will move onto the vessel tonight after midnight. We'll leave the horses in a paddock. Ensure their care while we're away." Aedyn rose and strode from the room.

Day 103
Docks
Lessard Village
Aldersward's East Sea

The vessel became *Anya's Endeavour*, chosen to emphasise what failure risked. An artist painted it on both sides, with *Aldersward Kingdom* underneath. Captain Amos, Prince Aedyn, and his council agreed to devote a few days along the coast to familiarising the men and ensuring no detrimental flaws existed within the design.

Thousands gathered to see the Endeavour make its attempt. Merchants and the gifted wasted no time in monetising the occasion by entertaining and selling things to the crowds.

Vendors sold large amounts of tantalising treats, the pleasant aromas overtook the fishy scent of the previous days. Artists painted animated images, musicians played with no instruments, and glamour artists bestowed simple makeup and flowers. A fire wall blazed, and a man wandered through it uninjured. Others with more advanced abilities, made entire sceneries appear, like mirages—the mountains at Aldersward castle, the lagoon of Maidstone, and on and on.

A merchant stood by a barrel selling small, shrimp-like creatures, their colouring was spectacular in blue, green, pink, and yellow glowing shades. Its stance most resembled a horse and its frame fit inside a child's palm. Two bulging eyes bugged from the top of its tiny head. A set of arms laced with three fingers stretched upwards, as if ready to attack. Two wings covered another pair of arms with four miniature claws. Its shell covered back was long, providing space for four legs on either side. Its tail fanned out behind it.

The children begged for them, then enjoyed tormenting each other with their hideous pets. Some shrieked and shrunk from anyone holding one.

Subjects edged the waterfront, waiting to wave the vessel off.

Aedyn's stance exuded confident dominance as he watched from the observation deck. When he raised his hand, a bell reverberated with deep tones, and all fell silent.

He yelled and paused, allowing his voice to echo through the bay. "It's time—time to explore the sea—to find Reinshaven—to find healers for our people. We could not have undertaken this task without the strong and fearless men aboard. Our kingdom applauds and appreciates your bravery."

He waited as loud cheers from shore rang out, and when they quieted, he continued. "Your faith in our leadership humbles my family. We are aware many question the validity of this journey, but the alternative pushed us forward."

"Aldersward Kingdom is indebted to the boat builders, Earl Adisa, and the citizens of Lessard. Your kindness and cooperation, we can never repay. We ask you one more favour as we go, think of us often, and pray to Jezabet and his son, Jordan, so they may swiftly guide us. By doing so, we hope to return victorious. All clear! Take us out, captain!"

The crowds roared.

As Abner operated the navigation wheel, Captain Amos shouted orders. Men scurried to do his bidding while Asa pulled the heavy lever and hoisted the massive anchor from the sea floor. Alberto changed the wind's direction with a sweep of his hands as the middle sail opened. The vessel drifted out and children raced, following along the shoreline.

As the boat glided the mouth of the bay, Abner manoeuvred it right, parallel with shore. Far enough so it would not run aground. Amos had the men open the other two sails to ensure they functioned, and the Endeavour gathered speed. When satisfied, he ordered them closed. No reason existed to rush while they learnt to perform together, controlling the enormous craft.

Day 105
Prince Aedyn's Quarters
Anya's Endeavour
Aldersward's South Coast

Asa wrote in the voyage's journal. *We've travelled along the coast for two days. We're satisfied with the men's performance and the Endeavour's condition. Tomorrow morning, Captain Amos will turn us south, open all the sails and take us across the sea.*

Sleep evaded all on the first day, but now exhaustion and the cool dampening mist of the sea outweigh the men's excitement and fear. We have settled into a mundane routine of eating, training, watching, and sleeping.

I wonder how long it will take us to find land then return home.

Day 111
Prince Aedyn's Quarters

Anya's Endeavour
Aldersward's South Sea

While his page slept below and his guards remained outside on the main deck, Aedyn requested his council attend his bedchamber.

They sipped sweet tea and sat in cushioned chairs installed around the small, short table. The men knew something weighed heavily on the prince's mind to bring them inside this private space and leave his guards farther away.

After several minutes of awkward silence, Asa offered. "I crave something stronger than tea."

Bennet responded. "Aye, we all do, but we must keep our wits about us."

Asa refilled his drink. "Let's converse, worst fear?" When boredom struck, the question game was a common pastime. "For myself, it would be this journey. I've never wanted to be an adventurer or experience excitement. I wanted to fulfil an uneventful term then return home, marry a woman, and have children."

Aedyn shrugged his shoulders. "I'd say snakes or not being royal. Only because I don't know how to be otherwise. Perhaps it's the unknown."

Auren laughed. "Being common isn't so terrible. We do what we want, how we want, with whom we want. I'd have to say mine is never being ready to settle on a single woman or losing a limb. Though," he scratched his head. "Losing a limb may not be so bad, might make me less desirable—less sought after by women."

The others laughed, then looked at Bennet.

"It amazes me how fears evolve. Ye conquer one and another takes its place. I lived through mine, the loss of my wife and children. Then, never dying replaced it. What if something changed during the event, and now I'm to live forever? But, after Aedyn showed me the illustration, it changed again. Now, never finding my family is my worst fear."

Aedyn raked his hand through his hair and whispered. "I fear I have led you and the other men on a fool's errand. That we will return empty-handed, no closer to finding a cure for my mother. I believe I'm losing hope."

Bennet consoled his ruler. "It hasn't been so many days we have travelled, only six. Originally, ye wanted to travel for fourteen. What's changed?"

"I expected to see more signs of life besides sea creatures, like birds. Honestly, I never imagined it would take this long to find land of some sort." Aedyn spoke freely.

The men sat silently, contemplating his words. Disappointment and failure weighed profoundly on them all.

After several moments, Bennet glanced at each. "I'll not abandon our purpose."

Auren sternly corrected. "No one is abandoning anything. We–"

Bennet walked to the window and stared outside. "Ye're here to find a treatment for yer people—yer Queen. It's truly noble of ye." He let the compliment linger before continuing. "I share in yer quest, but what motivates me differs from ye. I'm here to hunt for my wife, children and kingdom. I can't expect any of ye to understand my desperation for even a mere chance to return home."

Aedyn shook his head. "I don't want to abandon our purpose, either. It's merely my fear—disappointing everyone." More strongly, he said, "We may not understand your desperation, but as your friends and as a secondary mission, we'll do everything within my father's orders to see it a reality." He lifted his mug, and the others followed, drinking deeply. The semi-sweet, tart beverage quenched Aedyn's thirst. "It's these evenings, when I face Achelle with nothing new to say, that are the hardest. I feel my father's scepticism in her manner and words. I struggle to convey the wisdom of this journey."

Auren asked. "Where did you meet in your last dream?"

"Here, in this room. It's the easiest location for me to control."

"Maybe you need to have your meeting on the deck outside." Auren replied.

"It's complicated to explain, but with so many men on deck, it's hard to picture it without. The more people in my dreams, the tougher it becomes to regulate who they are and whether they wear clothing."

"Hold there, Aedyn. Confess which of us appeared naked to your sister? Was it I?" Asa's lips curled into a jovial smile.

"Asa, it was obviously me. Of us, my form is the most enjoyable." Auren slapped Asa's back. "Of course, when we return home, she'll have shifted her ambitions of love to me. Helpless women can't deny the mastery of what I offer them."

As the pair laughed, Bennet fixed his gaze and shook his head in censure for only Auren to see.

"It was none of you ugly mutts." Aedyn chuckled and thought about Auren's words. "What did you mean *shifted her ambitions*? Who were her ambitions set on before?"

Bennet planted his palm against his forehead, then accusingly looked at Auren, "Yer mouth."

Aedyn waited for his best friend to answer, but he placed his hand over his mouth and shook his head. Aedyn's ability made it extremely difficult for him not to answer. The second Auren opened his mouth, words of truth would spew out uncontrollably.

Aedyn turned to Asa without saying a word and lifted his eyebrow.

"I'm as curious as you, I know nothing." Interestedly, Asa replied.

Bennet examined his fingernails, his tone nonchalant. "It's nothing. She had formed a childhood crush on a guard. The night before we left, we both discovered it and thought it wiser not to bring any attention to it while we remained in Aldersward."

In his mind, Aedyn replayed the night. "Auren barely left my side the day before and we enjoyed the city in the evening."

"Her love was unrequited. He had nay notion of her affections. He hadn't encouraged or spoken to her until she revealed her feelings. And when he learnt of them, he squashed them immediately. He was more virtuous than I think any one of us–"

Aedyn smirked. His mentor's avoidance amused him. "You've answered neither question, Bennet. I understand what you're saying. She had a crush, and he didn't know she existed. When and where did this declaration happen?"

Unable to check himself, Bennet blurted, "After ye returned from the city, in the single men's dormitories." Aedyn looked like he would speak, but Bennet asked. "Let me finish? I stumbled upon her, alone outside, hiding in the shadows. When I informed her I was taking her back, she refused and threatened to create a scene if I didn't assist her. What was I to do? I could not let her be discovered and the kingdom would've overreacted, so I helped her. She saw him and declared her affections, and he plainly explained he did not share them. Then Auren and the man escorted her to the castle, appearing as her guards, and left her reputation unscathed. Nay else saw her but us three."

"If it wasn't a significant matter, then why am I only learning about this now?"

"If we had advised ye before we left. Ye may not have allowed us ample opportunity to explain. Ye may have overreacted and initiated an irreversible chain of events; like telling yer father who would've postponed our trip to put the man, who had done nothing inappropriate, on trial. I don't fault yer father for loving his children but sometimes love can be irrational. Auren and I conferred and believe we handled it properly without embarrassing or ruining her."

Aedyn raked his fingers through his hair and knew he could not fault their judgement. "If she saw him the night before we departed, then it must mean he's with us."

"Aye, he is."

"Did he disappoint her tactfully?" Aedyn hoped.

Auren finally removed his hand. "Augustus tried but she wouldn't hear of it. In the end, brutal honesty served."

"Augustus? I should've known. I discovered an image of him she drew. She said it was nothing, practice." Aedyn relaxed against the chair's back.

Auren replied. "Bennet assured me she'll get over it before we return. I'm trusting his assessment, as I'm inexperienced with the innocent."

Realising the discussion over, Asa renewed their previous topic. "You don't have to visualise the vacant decks, Aedyn. I'll confirm with Captain Amos, but I'm certain there's no harm in you being alone on the deck for a short time. It will provide you with a subject to discuss—the Endeavour's operations."

Bennet elaborated. "Offer Achelle the magnitude, the craftsmanship, and the ingenuity of the builders. It may impress yer father. Regardless of the journey's outcome, it's now viable for others to travel, as we have."

Day 111
Prince Aedyn's Bedchamber
Anya's Endeavour

Aedyn took pleasure in the peaceful, empty decks as he wandered about, inspecting certain details he wanted to include in his dream. The night was black. Clouds obscured the stars, blocking his eyes from following their dance across the sky. The craft sounded as it cut through the gentle waves. This is what he would remember to share with her.

As he withdrew, he called for the men lingering in the corridor, and they filed out.

The prince laid down, listening to the water splash against the wood, and felt the soothing rhythm of the boat's motion. He visualised the view from the observation deck above and he drifted.

"Aedyn," Achelle called, her version of dream-knocking, as she materialised beside him.

He held out his palm and grinned. "Let me show you."

"You've grasped the dream-walk well." She accepted his hand, and he whirled her around to face the sea behind them. "It's so desolate and cold."

"No, that's what you feel." He smiled, trying to lift her spirits. "There lies the promise of home— warmth and happiness."

She smiled. "Are you writing verse? Should I inform Father you're homesick?"

"Would it satisfy him if I were?"

"I think it would please Ammaris, but Father, no. He wishes I find you on land. Have I?" she asked.

"No. This was the view earlier this evening. It's calm and private, remarkably different from the normal buzz of activity."

"And dark, can you imagine a lantern?" Instantly, he produced one in his other hand as he spun and escorted her to the ladder. She descended first and when he reached her, he used the lantern to explain the navigation wheel as a light drizzle of rain fell above. They walked down the stairs, and he pointed out the masts as they walked, then climbed the stairs to the anchor deck.

"While Asa holds firm onto the anchor lever, Guard Augustus will set poles in to further break the wheel from spinning." He materialised the two men, and they demonstrated as he studied her.

"I'm rather astonished he's suitable for any duties on this trip." She blandly stated. Disinterested in observing, she turned and watched the rain, occurring more heavily now.

"Oh yes, I forgot you drew him once. It was an exceedingly detailed copy. Did he strike you as inept while he was Father's guard?"

"No, I've never actually considered him effective. He's merely a guard. He stands and waits." The princess explained as the craft rocked, building momentum.

She sought to suppress the spite, but he sensed it. She loved Augustus? Not now. From the tone of her remarks and actions, she despised him. Augustus was clear of her infatuation.

"How is our father?" He shifted the conversation while they peered through the rain at the main deck.

"He prefers you would turn home before—Aedyn, why is the boat swaying so much?" She clutched the railing.

"I'm uncertain." He stepped to the vessel's side, looking out over the sea, and concentrated on smoothing the water. Instead, it roughened. "I can't control it." He yelled.

Waves crawled skyward, as if time slowed, then raced as they heaved savagely onto the decks.

"Aedyn," helplessly, she shrieked and stared.

As merciless water crushed against him, he lost his hold. He groped for another as he flailed and toppled over the side, falling into the churning, murky sea below.

Aedyn's entire body jerked, and he woke immediately. The craft swayed under him as he flew through his chambers and out onto the deck. It was chaos.

"Bring in the sails!" Over the thunderous storm, Amos shouted, and men rushed to carry out his instructions.

The storm was less intense than in his dream. The Endeavour rocked as it was pelted with rain, but no waves reached the decks.

Aedyn tasted the salty water on his lips. "What do we do?"

"There's not much. We bring in the sails, hunker down, and hope this minor storm doesn't get any larger. I'll steer us into the waves. If we turn sideways, we'll capsize. It'll be safest to take the men below. Abner, Ackley, and I can handle the navigation."

Asa joined them. "What if we use Alberto's ability to modify the wind's angle or have it guide us out?"

"I don't know which way is out. As fishermen, we encounter storms. This is no different. Please, take the men and go below. Our biggest risk right now is having so many above."

The volume required strained Aedyn's throat as he yelled across the vessel, so they would hear over the crashing water. He ordered the men to safety. Those closest took sanctuary in his rooms, safer than struggling across the expansive deck.

The drenched men huddled against the walls and sat anywhere available in the prince's quarters while they listened to the worsening storm. Outwardly, each appeared brave, but Aedyn knew, just like him, they shook inside. Heat emanated from their unbathed bodies. The stench made worse by their fear. His throat dried from terror and he closed his eyes, urging Jezabet to intervene.

The storm raged on violently through the hours leading to dawn. Lightening slashed across the blackened sky and for an instance spilled light through the small windows, then complete darkness renewed. Water, whether rain or waves, pummelled the main deck, reaching beneath the door. The sounds were overwhelming—water battered and thunder exploded as wood groaned against the vicious attack. Men, silent and still, surrendered themselves to the expectancy of death.

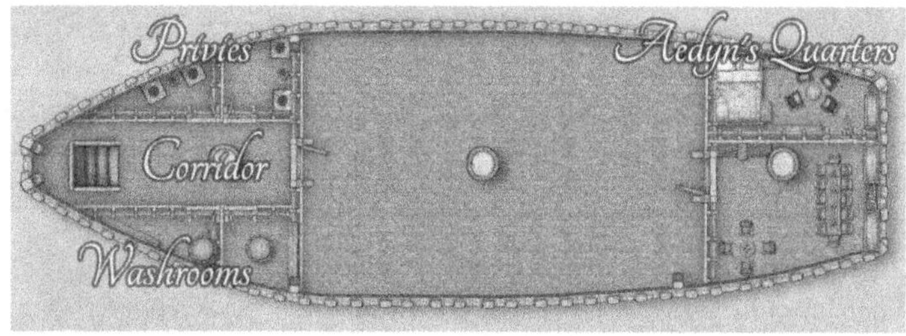

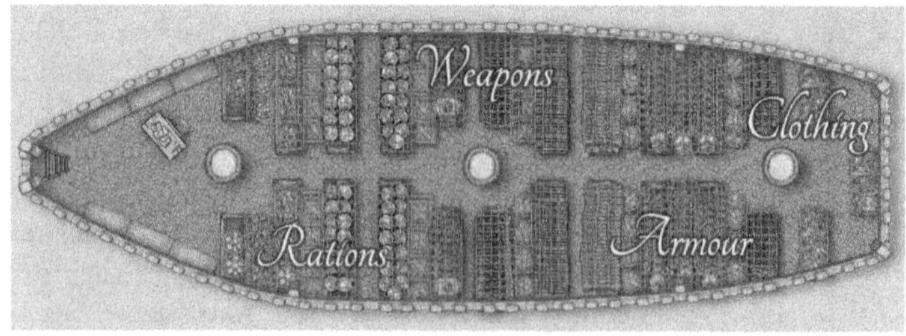

Anya's Endeavour (upper, main, lower, cargo)

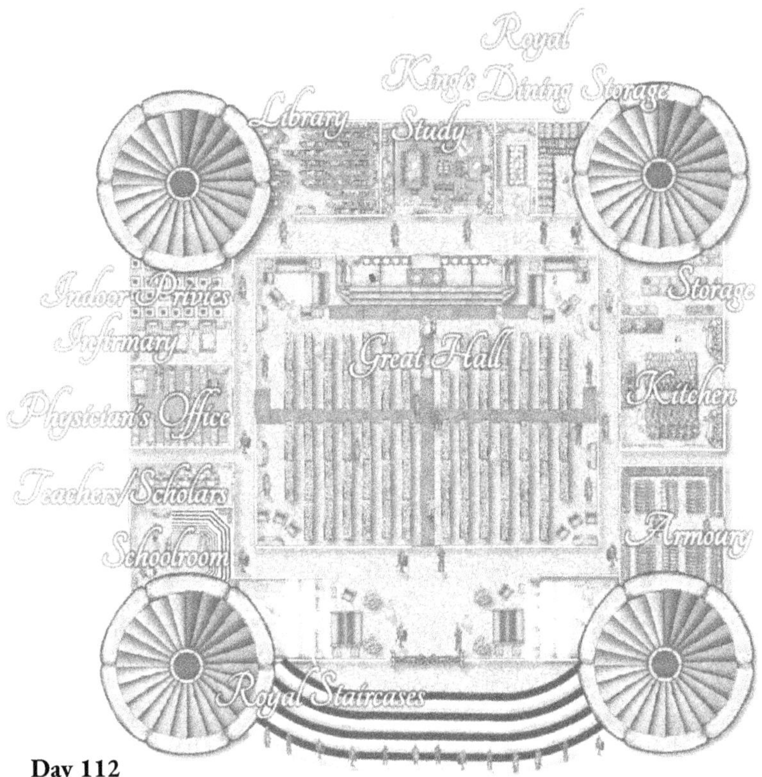

Day 112
Schoolroom
Castle's Ground Level
Near Aldersward City

The children settled on the stone risers as the scholar began. "We will learn now about another kingdom. Abigail."

The girl of fifteen crossed the room and, as she did, her hair changed from black to auburn. She nervously stood before her peers, and her voice faltered when she spoke. "The Slays and the lost kingdom of Slaysfold."

"The kingdom was shaped like a bird's head. The landscape included small forests, tall grasses, flowers, and five lakes. Slaysfold shared borders with Vaguestimber, Aldersward, Reinshaven, Baitsloam, and the sea.

"The Slays, especially the women, were regarded as the most brutal and fierce warriors among the races of Speranza. Their names started with the letter *s*. Compared to us, they were shorter, heavier with muscle or fat, and paler with varying hair colours. Their leather clothing was primarily black and trimmed with furs, spikes, chains, and studs made from the deposits of iron ore in Slaysfold's southwest.

"Most men wore nothing beneath their vests. Occasionally, when they wore a tunic, it had exaggerated puffy sleeves which cuffed tightly at their wrists." As her nervousness ended, her hair turned back to black. "The women wore small half-tunics, bodysuits, trousers, and shorts made of leather with their midriffs and arms often bare. Some women did wear skirts, but they were not long like ours. They were short, above their knees.

"Resting directly above their eyebrows, the race wore leather circlets which would stretch along their jawline in assorted lengths. Each uniquely detailed and accessorised like their garments, but could include animal teeth or bones. Both genders wore boots. Their weapons were often axes, blades, staffs, daggers, and shields.

"The single-level castle was constructed of mud and grasses. They lived simply and without many luxuries, ensuring to preserve their previous world's way of life. Their sole magics were construct creation. It allowed each to conjure objects from specific materials. These abilities were limited to use outside of Davensberth Kingdom. Slays were another race who rarely settled outside of their kingdom.

"On Amelia's sixteenth birthday, the night the Slays perished, King Sofer and Queen Sabah sent Emissary Stephen, aged twenty-one, to attend. After the event, he joined King Acoose's council, married an Alder woman, and settled in Maidstone until his death in 53 N.D. His wife only birthed daughters, and so the race ended with him."

Day 112
Main Deck
Anya's Endeavour
Aldersward's Southwest Sea

Aedyn emerged into the morning's new light as a single cloud drizzled harmlessly above. The world appeared brighter, in sharp contrast to the many hours they had spent locked in his dark rooms. He shielded his blue eyes, allowing them to adjust, then climbed the navigation deck's eight stairs and surveyed the Endeavour as his men cautiously emerged from where they sheltered and began their day.

Abner operated the wheel while Captain Amos inspected the decks, assessing the damage, and directing men to complete the minor repairs.

Aedyn waited for Amos to finish, then waved and strode to meet him on the main deck. "We should talk. Gather those required and join me." He turned, heading back to his rooms.

He found his council tidying his quarters when he entered. He sat at the long table, his back to the cabinets as the men, Alonso, and Aron piled inside and took chairs.

"Damage report?"

"Prince Aedyn, a few railings broke, and we lost a couple of smaller boats. We fared well." Amos shrugged.

"Did we gain any distance during the storm?"

Arturo shook his head. "Your Highness, we're off our previous course. We've travelled southwest instead of south. I estimate it will take a day to get us back and roughly where we were yesterday evening."

Aedyn calculated. "That means it'll be the morning of the eighth day, then only two more days to finish our search." He turned to Amos. "Can we gain speed at all?"

"Prince Aedyn, we could open all the sails at night, travelling as fast as we do through the day. However, we would be blind. We could run aground, hit a whale or something else."

Alonso recalled from memory. "Azariah's ability is heat vision. This should help considerably?"

"Limitations?"

"I'll find out." Asa strode out.

"A couple of you take this crate and the empty keg below. Bring back a fresh supply." Aedyn bent to collect a blanket as Aron and Bennet followed his orders. He took an armload of soaked bedding outside and pinned it to the railings as Auren gave him a hand. Within minutes, his rooms were tidy. Bennet, Asa and Aron returned and the ten men poured themselves a drink and relaxed from the stress-filled night.

Asa wiped the wetness from his upper lip. "Prince Aedyn, the distance of Azariah's heat vision performs within five miles, depending on the grouping size of vegetation, fires, people, or animals. But he suffers from headaches after prolonged use."

Aedyn turned to Bennet. "Can Physician Aidrik offer him any relief?"

"Yer Highness, I'll ensure Aidrik attends him and he's made comfortable."

"All right, let's use Azariah. Open the sails and continue this course. Have three crews sleep until late afternoon and then have the other three sleep until midnight." He glanced over the group. "Anyone have anything else to report or questions?"

Most shook their heads, but Bennet spoke. "Prince Aedyn, do ye intend to turn us around on day ten if we've found nothing?"

As he thought, his palm ran along his jaw, "I've pondered this extensively and have no answer yet."

The men shuffled out, letting the door swing shut behind them.

Aedyn stretched his sore muscles, realising how tired he was. He went to investigate what his page was doing in his bedchamber. He opened the door, glanced around, and spied the boy, deep in sleep, curled on a cushioned chair. The prince withdrew an extra blanket and covered him, knowing the boy had slept little. Aedyn removed his boots and vest, then laid down and closed his eyes and drifted.

Aedyn descended the mercantile's backstairs. Satisfied, he grinned boyishly and turned to watch Azalea close the door.

"Aedyn," Achelle called behind him as she appeared. She ran, throwing herself into his embrace. "It terrified me when you fell into the sea. I tried to get back, but I couldn't find you. Are you all right?"

He held her and focused on the setting. Like a gentle breeze, their surroundings blew away, replaced by the castle garden. "I must be asleep. I intended to only rest my eyes for a short time." He took her head in his hands, looking into her tearful eyes. "I'm fine. A storm came and woke me. It passed, and we're safe."

"Please don't be angry because I've returned unscheduled. I couldn't bear to tell Father what happened. He's already so worried about you."

"I'm not angry." He lied. "Please stop worrying. There's nothing out here. We're in the middle of the sea alone. It was only a storm." He downplayed the severity. "I must wake now, I may be needed."

"All right, but swear you won't die."

"I swear." He half-smiled as she faded away.

Day 115
Observation Deck
Anya's Endeavour
Aldersward's Southwest Sea

Aedyn scanned the sea from the observation deck. As the sun blanketed the world in light, he welcomed its warmth. He scrutinised every direction, including the water and the sky. In frustration, his fingers raked through his hair. The time had come and still he was no closer to a decision. Thoughts of the ill, his father's expectations, and the safety and sacrifice of those aboard weighed on him. He never imagined the journey would be this difficult.

Feet climbed the ladder, and he shifted as Bennet emerged.

Knowing Aedyn, the older man realised his heart and mind were in turmoil. "Should I get someone else, or will I do?"

"You'll do." The prince turned, searching again.

"Do ye see anything?"

"I haven't. Not a bird nor any man-made items afloat in the water."

"Did ye ask Apex about our food stores?"

"For now, we've enough for a couple extra days, but bugs are multiplying and could destroy our stores if Apex cannot stop them. If that happens, he can conjure pork and beans using the destroyed rations. I spoke with Alonso, and he advised me Ameer could duplicate fermented drinks. So, if we continue and turn around in four days' time, we'll return drunk and sick of pork and beans." He chuckled as he glanced at Bennet, and then turned his eyes to the sea, serious again. "If we continue, we're that much farther away when we turn back. It could mean more or worse storms. So I ask myself, is it worth it? And I cannot find the answer."

"Maybe it's the wrong question?" Bennet's eyes skimmed the sea.

Puzzled, Aedyn lifted his brow. "What should I be asking?"

"Do ye believe Achelle dream-walked with the Rein girl?"

"Of course."

"Do ye trust me when I tell ye it was Reinshaven?"

He didn't hesitate. "I've no doubt."

Aedyn turned to his mentor but found himself alone.

He crossed to the main deck's railing and shouted below. "Stay the course. We travel forward until I say otherwise."

Day 118
Anchor Deck
Anya's Endeavour
Aldersward's Southwest Sea

Well after midnight, men intermittently paused to chat or examine the sea from a fresh vantage point. Abner navigated the craft as Azariah watched the path ahead from the anchor deck.

When the sun rose, they would eat breakfast and start the fifteenth day. Azariah's head pounded almost constant, without reprieve. Rest evaded him, waking often to vomit in a bucket by his bunk. He did not know how much longer he could endure, but as long as Prince Aedyn required him, he would try.

Azariah scanned the sea in front of him again, seeing nothing. He twisted his head and called below. "Can one of you bring me a mug–" His eye caught a small glimmer, only for a split-second, and he questioned whether he had indeed seen anything at all. He stepped to the west railing and concentrated. He saw nothing, only his imagination. Someone mounted the stairs, and he turned.

"I heard you." Augustus handed him a drink, then sauntered to the railing Azariah abandoned.

Azariah sat against the anchor wheel, closing his eyelids. "Thank you." His hand travelled to his temple, seeking to rub the ache away.

"How's your head? Do you need me to fetch Aidrik?" His expression furrowed with concern.

Not wanting the attention, he stopped his fingers and opened his eyes. "No, I'm–" Once again, he swore something flickered behind where the other man stood. "Could you come away from there?"

"Would it ease your strain if I sat beside you?" Augustus assumed the upward angle, intensified the man's headache.

"Sure. Yes." He slid over, making Augustus sit on his left, but when he saw another flicker in the distance he leapt to his feet. "I need to be higher, perhaps the centre mast's top. How do I get there?"

"Do you see something?" Augustus joined him but saw nothing through the black of night.

"I'm uncertain, but a higher vantage may help," not prepared to disclose what he saw until he was confident.

Azariah climbed the tall mast's rungs. He rested his dizzy eyes, then blinked several times and looked west. A constant, small orange glow radiated in the distance. He studied it before he descended and crossed to the navigation deck, where Asa and Abner chatted.

He whispered. "I believe something lies west, perhaps five or so miles. Do we wake Prince Aedyn?"

Asa shook his head. "No, we're hours from sun up. Let's change course and once we're a couple miles away, I'll drop the anchor. We don't know what it is or where we've landed. By the time we've accomplished those tasks Aedyn and the others should be awake."

On the anchor deck, Asa waited with Azariah, until he was satisfied with the distance.

"We'll wait for the others wake to decide our next actions." He swallowed the snake meat, then pulled the anchor lever free. The vessel rocked like a pendulum from its weight loss. It hit bottom, and within moments, the boat rocked with a second wave as it grabbed the sea's floor.

So much for letting the men sleep until morning, Asa thought. He clambered downstairs and strode across the main deck as Aedyn, half-dressed, emerged.

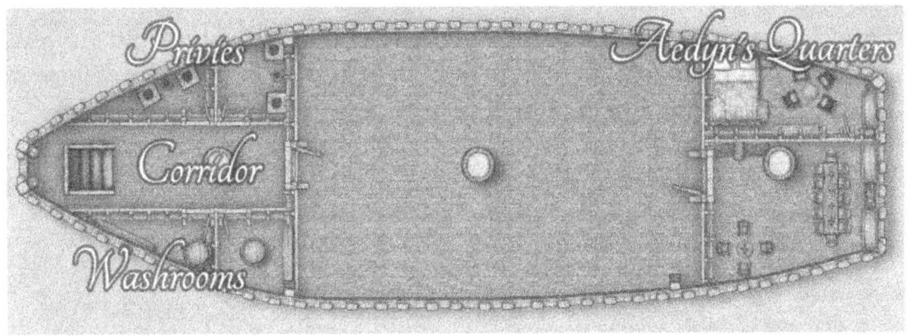

Day 118
Anya's Endeavour
Aldersward's Southwest Sea

In the hours leading to dawn, Aedyn gathered the six leaders and captain to discuss what would happen come sunrise.

"Do you recognise it?" Auren asked Bennet, as the page placed their meals before them.

"It isn't Reinshaven or Baitsloam. I suspect it may be Slaysfold or Vaguestimber." He chewed a thick slice of bottled pork, then elaborated. "Reinshaven had forests, and Baitsloam was much like the landscape at Lessard. Vaguestimber had a forest, but it's possible from this angle we don't see it."

Aedyn cleared his throat. "If it's Slaysfold or Vaguestimber, we'll know soon enough."

"Your Highness, how?" Asa poked a boiled potato.

Bennet laughed. "If they're green with wings, it's Vaguestimber. Slays are paler than yer race but not starkly white like mine."

Auren wiped his mouth with a napkin. "Prince Aedyn, what's your plan?"

Aedyn expelled his breath loudly. "I've no idea. How do we simply go ashore to a kingdom we haven't seen in over two-hundred years? If our places were reversed, and they appeared on our shoreline, what would we do?"

Bennet shrugged. "Yer Highness, yer father would ride out with an army to meet them."

"What if they didn't come ashore?"

Augustus lifted his finger. "Prince Aedyn, he might take men out in boats to see why. But, never seeing a vessel such as this, I believe they would be scared."

"How long would he wait?" Aedyn asked.

"Yer Highness, no more than a couple days."

Aedyn decided. "Let's wait then. Have the three groups who didn't sleep last night take six hours. Angelo, your men will stand watch tonight alone, have them sleep until evening meal."

Auren asked. "Your Highness, is it wise to have so few guard us?"

"It's a foreign vessel. As Augustus said, they'll be more scared than we are and without our ladder, they can't get aboard. Ten men should see them coming and can alert us." Aedyn drank, then continued. "We go about our own business—resting and training. Have our men armed. This evening we celebrate our discovery and wait for them to approach us."

Day 118
Front Room
Castle
Slaysfold City

Midnight neared, the galloping stallion's flanks frothed when it crested the rise and the crude city came into view. The thirteen-hour journey ended as the messenger reached the gate and pounded for admittance.

Made from grass and clay, the long one-storey castle loomed directly in front of her. The iron fire pits flickered and smouldered as the manure fuelling the flames ran low. Its rank stench hung in the air. Urgently, she jumped, not waiting for her mount to halt, and beat her fist against the door.

A disfigured woman in rags with a hunched spine and a protruding limp opened it. The messenger immediately recognised Sahana, the king's slave. At one time, she had been a beautiful, proud, and strong woman until she unwisely refused King Sumner. Then he took pleasure in breaking her—shattered her bones and marred her frame with scars until she was horridly mutilated.

She pushed the servant aside. "I must speak to the king."

The castle had few rooms: the king's chamber, one for his children, and this one, which housed the cooking amenities, tables for one-hundred, and crude benches along the wall where people could sit, sleep, or fornicate. On the far wall, the king's throne rested on a rise with a mess of furs around its sides and back for additional royal entertaining.

Under those furs, several bodies intertwined, their naked limbs visible.

The late night intruder stood at the rise's edge. "King Sumner, I carry news from Ravenwick."

He rose onto his elbows, his eyes filled with desire as he looked upon the messenger's exposed stomach, arms, and legs. She was beneath his station, and he could offer her riches in return for her body. No woman dared refuse him since he had publicly mangled his slave—a lesson to them all.

Under his sexual scrutiny, she proudly raised her chin. "Your uncle, Lord Sabeen, wishes you to bring as many warriors as you can. There's trouble, something in the water."

He watched her face when he tossed the blankets aside, uncovering a much older woman feasting on his manhood. "Mother, wipe your chin and sleep. My uncle has need for his king."

Another well-known story—after King Sumner decapitated his father, King Saul, he kept his mother, Lady Sydni, beside him. Not as his wife, he had one of those, but as a trophy he took from his father. It caused significant discomfort and gossip among his subjects. No one dared question it.

The king stood, arrogant and naked, with his cock swollen and damp. He placed his circlet on his head and sat under the blackened tablet which hung overhead. He placed his leg over one of the throne's arms so the messenger could appreciate the view.

"What do you mean there's something in the water?" He picked at his fingernails, disinterested in the message. He pictured the woman naked and beneath the furs, pleasing him.

Witnessing the incestuous act, she fought the sickening urge to shudder in disgust. "I guess it may be a boat, but two-hundred times larger."

Her words registered and overtook his lust-filled thoughts. He straightened to give the matter his full attention.

His beady eyes sharpened. "Who made it? Where did it come from? How long has it been there?"

"We don't know. At dawn, it was there, a couple miles from Ravenwick's shore." She responded. "Your uncle sent me to fetch you."

"What's it doing there? Did my uncle tell you his plans?"

"No. Unless you have orders, he will wait for you."

Abruptly, he yelled, "Sahana!" The contorted woman cowered forward from a darkened corner. "Have my commander wake the city and sound the bells. We ride immediately."

Day 119
Anya's Endeavour
Aldersward's Southwest Sea

Auren stepped inside the dim interior, where Bennet visited Aedyn at midday. "There's movement on shore. They appear two-hundred strong with several boats. I assume they'll approach soon."

Astonishment laced Bennet's brogue. "All two-hundred?"

"No," Aedyn waved his hand. "They wouldn't be foolish enough to send them all. If we're hostile, we could kill them before they ever board. They'll merely send a few at first. This is exactly how I hoped it would play out. Bennet, instruct the cook to make a large meal for my quarters. I'll invite their leaders to dine this evening if they come before then."

Auren responded. "You'll have an entire guard until we determine if there's a threat or not."

Day 119
East Shore
Ravenwick Village, Slaysfold

After surveying the monstrous and unworldly shape in the water, King Sumner was afraid, but would admit it to no one. He trudged across the yellow sand as the miniscule grains slipped through his boot's stitching and grated against his skin. Once he arrived on the grassy knoll, he strode to the pitched tent.

He wiped the sweat from his nearly baldhead, using the puffy sleeve of his tunic. "Sabeen, anything to report?"

As the king sat on his makeshift throne, Lord Sabeen bowed. "We've seen movement through the prism scope. They're darker than we are. They haven't tried to come ashore, and last night our warriors heard music."

"Take four warriors and go out to meet them." He snapped his fingers, then pointed to his boots. Two servants rushed forward.

"Why?"

"I need to know what they want." Sumner explained, as if he spoke to a young child. "And we can't find out if we sit here, can we?" His sweat soaked feet clung to the boot leather, making it difficult for the women to pull them off.

"You could send younger, less valuable men instead."

"Don't be stupid. Why would I send someone younger? What if they're violent? No, you're useless, old, and the Baron of Ravenwick." King Sumner yelled, ending the argument. "Get on with it." There were more enjoyable things to do than sit in the stifling tent.

Day 119
Anya's Endeavour
Aldersward's Southwest Sea

Asa leaned over the observation deck's railing as the small boat rowed towards the Endeavour. Those aboard came into sharper focus as they neared. However, these were not men, but long-haired women wrapped in leather and metal. They wore less than the women did in Aldersward's whorehouses. Each head held a crude black circlet with an array of studding, long points, and decorations. Tattoos and piercings marred their bodies.

Four women rowed as a man sat idle, scrutinising Asa and the craft. His hair was grey and his skin leathery. Maybe, at one time, the man was virile and feared, but now he was decrepit with age.

Asa entered the interior, knowing Auren and Bennet were inside. He propped his feet on the table and tried to hide his smug grin. "A single boat comes."

Auren noticed right away, "What do you know?"

"Me? Nothing." He concentrated on keeping a bland expression.

Bennet laughed. "Ye look like a dog who just stole food from his master's plate."

Aedyn lifted an eyebrow, wondering if he needed to ask.

Asa gave up. "They're scantily clad women and a feeble old man. Our men have been without women for nearly a month and their behaviour may not be fit given the women's attire."

Bennet chuckled. "Worry more about us surviving those women. There's nay doubt now, this is Slaysfold, and their women are warriors. I must educate ye about the delicate facts yer studies lacked."

Aedyn shook his head in exasperation. "What facts?"

"Ye may have sex with anyone on or below yer station, but ye must gift their authority, whether a husband, brother, or lord."

Auren smiled and rubbed his hands together, "Fine by me. What kind of gift do I need?"

Bennet ignored him. "And there's nay need for whorehouses. The women here are willing, proud of their bodies and abilities to please. It gives them great honour and their husbands many possessions. With others, this isn't an intimate activity. It's a means to an end. And sex isn't an isolated act between people behind closed doors. Ye could be engaged in a conversation during a meal and might find a woman on her knees pleasuring the man ye speak to."

Aedyn rubbed his cleft chin. "So, if Slaysfold's king visited Aldersward, he would expect Ammaris to satisfy his sexual need, then he would gift me according to her skills?"

"Nay, I don't think so. If he visited, I assume they would abide yer customs. It managed that way in the past."

"This could cause problems. Once they've departed, make our men aware of these practices."

Auren rose. "My men will serve your person, and Asa's can guard the main deck. You'll remain here, so it's easiest to protect you. Bennet, have Emissary Aron invite them aboard."

Preparations were complete when Auren placed four guards within Aedyn's bedchamber and closed the door. He placed two behind where the prince sat and an additional pair inside the exterior door.

Lord Sabeen stood as they rowed alongside the Endeavour, staying back about twenty feet in caution. An overwhelming fear caused by the magnitude and uncertainty of the strangers' intentions shook his body. The few who watched them approach had a dark tan to their olive skin. He could not tell if their expressions were those of welcome or hostility.

Emissary Aron studied the old man, who looked angry and perhaps frightened.

The man cupped his mouth, "I'm Baron Sabeen, for King Sumner. Why have you come?"

"Lord Sabeen, I'm Emissary Aron of Aldersward. Your kingdom and race's survival are a wonderful discovery. Prince Aedyn wishes the honour of meeting you and extends you an invitation to board." He smiled, hoping to ease the other's fears and misgivings. "Tie your boat to a ring below and watch above as we toss over our ladder."

A woman replied, "We all come up, or none of us do."

"Of course, we would have it no other way, my lady." Aron bowed in acceptance, appeasing her.

The women laughed as he backed away and allowed the men who guarded the opening to secure the ladder in place.

When the first female boarded, Aron offered his hand, but she ignored it and stood on her own. Her long, curly hair flowed to her ass. A black bodysuit clad her torso, leaving the length of her legs and muscular thighs naked. The bodysuit's front had grommets where a leather strip hung loosely, exposing her round, full breasts, and on her thick belt hung a blade and axe.

Her bracer-covered wrist pulled the axe free, wielding it. The men stepped backward as Aron caught her gaze. "We bear you no harm."

She sheathed her weapon and stood confidently as more men studied her.

Bennet, his skin much paler, came forward and gestured. "It's our pleasure to have ye here. Please move this way so the others may join us."

A second, then a third woman climbed up. They wore similar clothing, but one in a short skirt and the other in tight trousers.

Sabeen took the offered support and pulled himself to stand. He surveyed the main deck, noticing only a dozen men stood scattered, carrying out different duties and relaxed in the knowledge as the last female joined them.

Emissary Aron bowed. "Welcome aboard Anya's Endeavour. May I introduce Emissary Bennet of Baitsloam?"

Bennet genuflected, as Sabeen questioned. "Baitsloam? Your kingdom survived as well?"

"We do not know. On the night the other kingdoms were lost, I attended Aldersward. I've lived out my life with their people. I'm hoping to find my own on this journey. In finding Slaysfold, ye offer me immense hope." Bennet grinned at the thought.

"It would make you hundreds of years old. How is it possible?"

"797 years old. My people live to be near one-thousand and our body's age slowly. How is it ye didn't learn this?" Bennet asked curiously.

"After the event, King Sofer stopped our schooling for more important things, like magic."

The baron smiled at Aron when their eyes met and the emissary spoke. "I hope you're comfortable aboard our vessel. As you can see, we're not hostile. I'll take you to Prince Aedyn."

Sabeen instructed a woman to stay by the ladder and he instructed another to wait outside while he and the others entered.

Aedyn rose as they bowed, and Emissary Aron introduced the guest. "This is Prince Aedyn. Prince Aedyn, Baron Sabeen, for King Sumner of Slaysfold."

Aedyn nodded. "Please sit."

Aedyn's page offered them refreshments. His hands shook as he poured and when he reached to place the mug by a woman, he dropped it. She jumped back, pushing him away.

Aedyn pursed his lips. "I apologise for my page. He's never seen such beautiful, confident women before." He chuckled. "I believe you make him nervous."

Auren came forward to help clean the spill as she sat once again.

"Nervous is the last thing he feels when he looks at me." She said matter-of-factly while sharing a knowing look with her countrymen, then glanced at the other Alders behind Aedyn.

Aedyn focused his attention on Sabeen. "I understand your apprehension over our unexpected arrival."

"Unexpected? We didn't know any other kingdoms survived. Your boat caused much distress. Why didn't you come ashore?"

Aron's eyes met his. "Please use his proper title when you address our Crowned Prince. Either *Your Highness* or *Prince Aedyn.*"

Uncomfortable with the instruction, Aedyn ignored Aron's remark. "I considered it inappropriate, as King Sumner did not invite us. We've travelled twelve days, and your kingdom is the first we've found. If we shored, I assumed you might treat us as enemies."

"Your Highness, wise decision." The lord liked the young prince instantly. Analytical forethought was a trait he admired. "So, what do we do now?"

"I invite you to stay on board and enjoy our hospitality. We have little, but what we do have, we wish to share and joyously reunite."

"Prince Aedyn, it's not my place to stay. King Sumner only sent me to seek your purpose. I must return to shore."

"Of course, but please allow my emissaries, Bennet and Aron, to accompany you. It will allow them to extend my invitation."

"That will do." The baron ended the conversation. The Slays rose and walked out onto the main deck.

Aedyn addressed his emissaries. "Go with him. Extend my invitation."

Bennet responded. "He revealed they nay longer educate their people. Nay teachings, can ye imagine?"

The pair exited.

It was as though the room took a deep breath of relief. Auren dismissed the men, then sat and poured the whisky. After a minute, he let out a low whistle. "I don't know what to say. I've never seen a woman dressed as they were, let alone in daylight, moving about her business." Asa entered as he continued. "It's obscene."

"Pleasantly," Asa winked. "Perhaps we could have your father start a new fashion trend for the women in our kingdom?"

"You both jest unwisely. I admit lust came naturally when I saw them, but make no mistake. These women are warriors and, probably dangerous." Aedyn answered.

Auren joined Asa by the door. "By this night's end, many of our men will beat on something. And it won't be a drum." Both laughed as the door swung closed behind them.

They prepared the craft to receive the guests and Aedyn instructed his two friends to dress and join them. A few guards remained on the main deck, while two other groups observed from the decks above. Elaborate illusions of beautiful bright flowers and vines decorated the vessel's railings and masts. Quiet music played, creating a festive atmosphere.

"They approach," a guard called.

Aedyn checked his buttoned blue silk tunic, leaving the top two open to draw attention to his muscular throat. The black vest and trousers with tall black boots added a mysterious air. His head's tilt, his strong, broad shoulders, and his gait's ease exuded power and complete dominance.

Lead Auren and Asa helped as the emissaries boarded when Aedyn approached. The women from earlier and four more boarded. This time, they spread out, taking various positions along the railings.

Aron watched as one tried to touch a flower, but her fingers passed through it.

Aedyn instructed his emissaries. "You'll both join us inside."

"Prince Aedyn." Bennet nodded, announcing the oncoming couple, "Lady Synnova, King Sumner's sister and, her husband, Lord Sarrell."

Questioning Bennet's strange introduction, Aedyn lifted his eyebrow, and the emissary shrugged briefly as the couple genuflected. Aron led them away as another couple took their place. "Lady Saya, and her husband, Lord Sabeen, the king's uncle."

As the last man climbed aboard, Auren and Asa genuflected and, following their lead, the other guards did the same.

Upon first glance, the man reminded Aedyn of a greasy rat or weasel. He was a foot shorter than Auren, and skinnier than fifteen-year-old Annora, with beady eyes and very little hair slicked-back. He had a small patch of hair on his chin. The circlet with long spikes on the sides and shorter ones in the front had long pieces which ran his jawline. A wide, black leather belt crossed his open tunic, the sleeves puffy and tapered to his wrists. His black metal shoulder pads with spikes and studs made his neck look short. His heeled boots gave him much needed height.

The prince decided the man was a spectacle as Bennet bowed and introduced the royals.

Aedyn waited a few seconds to see if the man would bow. In the past, it was customary for the other kingdoms' rulers to genuflect in the presence of the Aldersward ruler, but he did not.

"King Sumner." Aedyn bowed with respect. "Thank you for accepting our hospitality."

"I couldn't refuse. I saw writing on the boat's side, but I couldn't make it out." He turned for a wider look at the deck.

"Yes, our craft's named after my mother, Anya's Endeavour. Would you like a tour?" Even though Aedyn knew it was necessary, he had no interest in answering an abundance of questions during a tour.

"No, it's a boat. I've seen them before." He waved the offer away with his hand.

"Of course," Aedyn struggled to hide his annoyance at the dismissive words. "Shall I get you a drink?"

"Yes." He continued his interested inspection. Aedyn beckoned for drinks as the king strolled away.

Lady Synnova intercepted them. "How do the flowers grow here?" She sought the Alder prince's attention as she placed her hand on her hip, drawing his eyes to her muscled midriff, her navel exposed.

"They are an illusion, magic." Aedyn offered as the pair turned to inspect them.

He took a moment to appreciate her lengthy legs in her flared trousers and the leather vest belted under her breasts. She was in better shape at forty than most women he knew at twenty. Her hair was an unusual light brown, long, and straight. A tattoo on her backside peaked from her trousers. Her circlet included tangled vines with small blue stones.

Synnova returned her focus to him. "They're stunning."

King Sumner spoke boastfully. "Ourselves, we conjure creations. Remind me, what's the ability of the Alders?"

"Our king gives them to us, and they vary. Could be anything. I have a few creation conjurers on board, like your people."

"What ability do you possess?" She asked.

"There are others far more interesting than mine. Do you hear the music?" He evaded the question, offered his arm to her, and then led them to where Anthony sat. "He can make his voice sound like any instrument." Aedyn stepped away, but Synnova kept her arm wrapped around his.

"It's splendid. We must dance." Her icy blue eyes raised, looking into his as she positioned herself in front of him and settled his hand on the bare skin above her trousers.

"What a useless talent." The king's voice sounded bored.

Aedyn ignored his rude remark, "Perhaps later, Lady Synnova." He dropped his hand, ending the unacceptable contact. "The evening meal is ready. Shall we eat?" He motioned for her to precede him.

Aedyn noted the food's incredible presentation from the limited kitchen and his mouth watered, anticipating the extravagant meal. A welcome change from the simple food they had endured during the voyage.

Bennet explained as the doubtful visitors gazed at their plates. "It's a dish made from an Aldersward native grain called rice with peas, lamb meat, and spices, mostly anise and pepper."

The Alders ate wholeheartedly, and the prince drew his guests into conversation. "May I ask about the night our kingdoms were divided?"

"I've heard tales we lost half of our people, but who can say? It was so long ago." Synnova answered, and the Alder men looked to each other, unaccustomed to a woman offering her words without direct invitation.

"Couldn't you count their graves?"

Synnova shook her head, but Bennet interjected. "Prince Aedyn, they set fire, then float them. Lady Synnova, the Alders bury their dead in the ground or stack them in buildings."

Aedyn placed his mug down. "I would be interested in learning more about this custom. Perhaps one of your religious keepers could explain it to me?"

The king waved his hand in dismissal. "Things changed. Aldersward no longer ruled us. King Sofer decreed no god existed, and no benefit came from education, formalities, or military."

As the Alders thought about his words, Saya smiled. "Ours is a simpler life now."

Sumner did not recognise the ingredients as he chewed. It tasted bitter then sweet with a warming sensation afterwards. He disliked the pungent taste of the meat and he drank what remained in his mug, then refilled it from the pitcher.

Auren washed down his mouthful. "No formalities or military? How is status among your people determined?"

Synnova's husband offered. "The only statuses we have are royal, commoners, or slave–"

Synnova silenced him with a look. "I decide how my husband lives and how he's accepted. There are many families, not titled, who live better than us." Synnova brushed her fingers across her chest. "My body, actions, and skills define our position. I provide the status my family deserves and the things we require. I control my husband and our lives."

"We teach the customs of the lost kingdoms in Aldersward." Bennet said. "Yer beliefs and customs have always fascinated me. In Baitsloam, marriages are a partnership of equals whereas, in Aldersward the men rule their women."

Aedyn could tell as the Slays took small bites that they were unaccustomed to the heavily spiced dish, and he motioned for his page to refill the mugs and pitchers. "Rule—don't ever let my mother or sisters hear you."

The Alders chuckled.

Saya's mouth gaped, shocked by the notion. "Do you mean you decide who your wives have sex with?"

Auren inhaled food into his windpipe and coughed loudly as Bennet pounded his back and responded. "Alder women only sleep within their marriage bed, with their husbands."

As the page replaced their plates, the conversation stalled.

Aedyn offered. "Perhaps this will be more to your liking. It's one of my favourites."

In a petal pattern, pomegranate syrup drizzled across the plate and in the centre rested half a grapefruit while mint leaves decorated the edges. His guests watched as he removed a sliver of the pink flesh and dragged it across the syrup and onto a leaf, then placed it inside his mouth. They copied him, and to Aedyn's relief, they seemed to enjoy it.

When the meal ended, everyone returned outdoors, leaving Aedyn and King Sumner at the table while guards stood around the room.

"How many live in Aldersward?"

"I'm not sure."

"We've over ten-thousand in Slaysfold." He boasted.

"Impressive." He complimented, knowing there were that many in Aldersward castle and grounds alone.

"Why did you travel here?" Sumner asked curiously.

"We didn't have this location in mind. It's a pleasant accident though and a reason for celebration." Aedyn responded cautiously, unsure whether he could trust the king. "We have no expectations. Only to let you know you are no longer alone on Speranza and invite you to have a relationship with us, as we had in the past, before the kingdoms divided."

"You understand how I could be wary of a relationship?"

"I do. It would be unwise to trust a race lost hundreds of years ago. Both kingdoms are in similar situations. I hope with time we'll learn to trust each other. There's no ulterior motive for why we came." Aedyn took a drink.

"Yes, perhaps in time. How long do you intend to stay here?"

"I'm unsure. For transparency's sake, our rations are depleted. We must replenish them or return home." Aedyn answered.

His words dripped with greed. "Will you pay or offer a reward to have your supplies refilled?"

Aedyn noted the man's slimy tone. "Naturally, but it would depend on what you would want as payment."

The king waved his hand, "Another difference. I ask for nothing. You decide what our help is worth. If my wife were present, you would discuss this matter with her. Our women would enjoy a good hunt."

"Our king will reward you greatly."

He rubbed his hands together in excited anticipation. "Then let's spend more time together. We can drink, eat, make plans, and get to know one another better. Visit our castle. Tomorrow night, after the sun goes down, head northwest along our shore until you see a large fire. The next morning, come ashore. I'll have horses and wagons waiting to bring you and your men to the city. It's a much shorter journey from there."

"Are you certain you want to help us?" Aedyn asked specifically.

"Yes. It's as you said. We should celebrate. We can do much for each other."

He recognised the truth in the king's voice and answered. "I accept with my deepest gratitude."

"We'll leave now. It's a long journey back."

The king and Aedyn walked outside where the wood railings and ladder glowed in the darkness.

"Another ability?"

"Yes."

"Prince Aedyn," The king extended his hand to receive Aedyn's lips, but instead, the prince shook it. "Should I ask our women to stay?"

Aedyn chuckled. "King Sumner, your women are exquisitely beautiful, like nothing we have ever seen before. I admit, though interested, I'm intimidated and assume the same of my men."

The king chuckled and followed the others down.

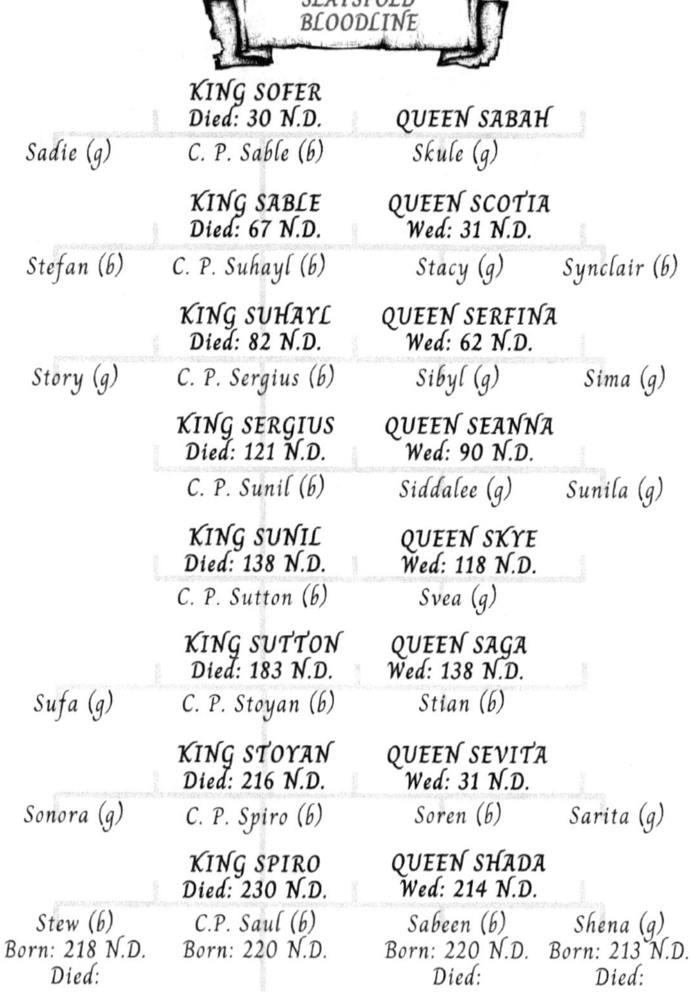

Continued on next page

		QUEEN SYDNI *Wed: 235 N.D.* *Died:*	
	KING SAUL *Died: 271 N.D.*		
	C. P. Sumner (b) *Born: 236 N.D.*	*Synnova (g)* *Born: 241 N.D.* *Died:*	

KING SAUL
Died: 271 N.D.

QUEEN SYDNI
Wed: 235 N.D.
Died:

C. P. Sumner (b)
Born: 236 N.D.

Synnova (g)
Born: 241 N.D.
Died:

KING SUMNER
Died:

QUEEN SOFIA
Wed: 274 N.D.
Died:

Solara (g)
Born: 275 N.D.
Died:

Sorcha (g)
Born: 284 N.D.
Died:

Sile (g)
Born: 278 N.D.
Died:

Svara (g)
Born: 272 N.D.
Died:

Above shows the Slay kings' bloodline. C. P. means Crowned Prince, future king. (b)/(g) indicates gender at birth.

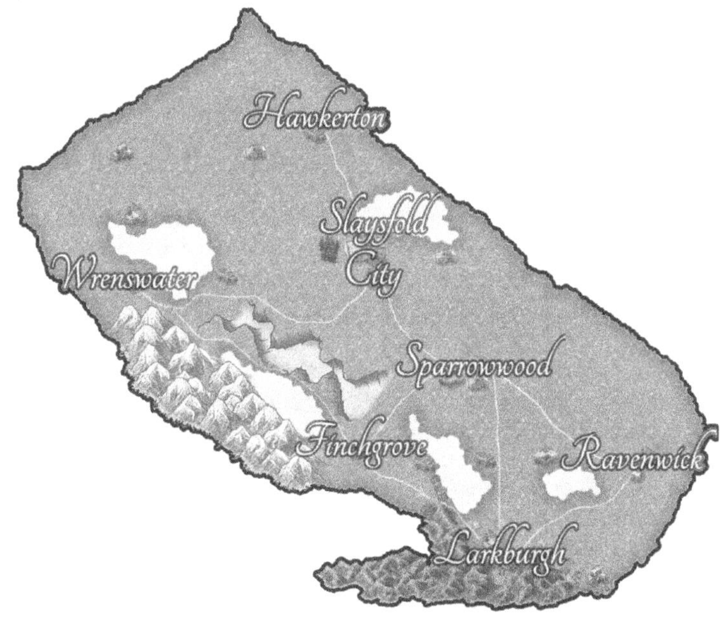

Slaysfold (285 N.D.)

Most notable features above include:
Ravenwick (east)
Larkburgh (southeast)
Slaysfold City (middle north)
Character index page 405.

Day 120
Prince Aedyn's Bedchamber
Anya's Endeavour
Slaysfold's East Sea

Aedyn filled a mug with whisky, then stepped inside his bedchamber, securing the door. The gentle sound of water washing against the vessel soothed the stress from his body and mind. He shrugged out of his vest and removed his boots and belt, then unbuttoned his tunic. He relaxed in a cushioned chair, propped his feet on a footrest, and examined the evening with the Slays.

Not long after, his eyes became heavy, and he drifted.

"Aedyn," Achelle called as she materialised in the craft's bedchamber. She smiled as she sat, moving her feet to join his. "Soon you'll be home."

With all that transpired, he forgot she was unaware of the current situation. *This conversation is going to be difficult,* he surmised. "I've wonderful news to share. We've found land."

"How? Did you miss it on your way?" Her eyes brightened with excitement.

"No. I confess, I didn't turn home on the tenth day. We continued our search."

"You've found Reinshaven? I can't wait for Mother to wake." Her smile widened as she scooted forward onto the seat's edge. "When will you arrive home?"

"No, it isn't Reinshaven but Slaysfold. Come, I'll show you." He crossed, then opened the door, hoping to refocus her attention on something else.

She followed him, inspecting the Slays. "Why are the women not dressed?"

"It's what they wear here. Just as you saw the women of Reinshaven dress differently, so do these women. They're warriors—strong, independent, and dangerous. This is their king, King Sumner of Slaysfold. He tells me they have over ten-thousand people in their kingdom."

"It's bizarre. In Aldersward, it's the men who are handsome and the women sometimes homely. Here it's the opposite, the women are beautiful, and the men are ugly." She laughed as she examined the people she did not recognise. "When will you depart?"

"The king's offered to replenish our food, and we're to spend a few days together. This land is southwest of Lessard's west point, twelve days," he uncoiled the map and showed her.

"Are you worried?"

"No. I want you to relay our location in case something changes. As soon as you leave, draw this, then take it to Father. He'll want to know our exact location."

"I will." She promised.

"I have another message I wish for you to carry."

Day 120
Princess Achelle's Chambers
Castle's Second Level
Near Aldersward City

Achelle ran from her chamber with her robe wrapped around her and paper in hand. Her guards easily kept pace as she knocked on Ammaris's door, then turned the corner to knock on her sister's and continued without waiting for them to answer. She stopped outside her father's chambers, flattening her hair and belting her robe before she knocked loudly and waited.

Her half-asleep father answered as he straightened his nightclothes. She pushed herself inside excitedly, not waiting for his invite. A warm fire burned in the hearth, lighting the area. Annora and Ammaris entered as the guards stood outside.

"They've found Slaysfold." Achelle announced, hugging her sister.

Excited, the guards talked amongst themselves, ready to share the news. King Adahy, shocked, sat on a chair's edge. "Are you sure?"

"Yes, I'm sure. He asked me to give you this. It's so you will know where they are in case anything happens to them." She handed him the paper. "He said they are ten-thousand strong in Slaysfold and their women are warriors." She turned to Annora and Ammaris. "You should see how these women dress. It's indecent. Their arms and legs are bare, belly buttons showing. It's unbelievable when you hear it but more so when you witness it."

Ammaris's expression briefly waived with jealousy, and Achelle noticed it immediately. "Aedyn had a message for you, Ammaris." She hoped to improve the woman's disposition who had moped about since his departure. She took Ammaris's hands. "He said, *tell Ammaris, the lack of her reassuring presence makes me ache for home. Every day brings me one day closer to her and our union.*

This knowledge grants me perseverance as I thwart every obstacle on my way to reach her. Eek!" she squealed. "Isn't he romantic?" She swung Ammaris's hands, and the woman's face beamed with a genuine smile.

"He's something." Adahy finished inspecting the paper his daughter had handed him. Aedyn had continued without consulting him. Adahy saw through his son's appeasing words easily. "Ammaris, Annora, please leave us. I wish to speak to Achelle alone."

Ammaris hugged Achelle, then took Annora's hand and left. The king crossed to the door, closing it from his guards. He lifted his arm, inviting Achelle to his side.

He kissed the top of her head. "I fear in your enthusiasm to deliver Aedyn's message to Ammaris you may have elaborated—unintentionally."

Her chin lifted, examining his face. "No, that's exactly what he said. I'm insulted you would insinuate such a thing."

His anger seethed, but he realised it was not Achelle's fault. He breathed deeply, calming his temper. "No, I apologise. I didn't mean to insinuate. I hoped you did, is all. In the future, I wish to hear any messages for Ammaris before you deliver them."

Day 120
Front Room
Castle
Slaysfold City

The hearth fires burned brightly, illuminating the long tables and side benches. King Sumner relaxed, drinking rum on his throne, while his mother and wife lounged naked at his feet.

"The Alder prince spoke of needing supplies, and I offered our help." He rubbed his foot lovingly against his wife's bulging, deflated stomach. "He promised to repay me."

"Do you trust them?" Synnova's back rested against her husband while he trailed kisses along her shoulder.

"I don't know yet. I suspect they may be a poor kingdom. I said you may be willing to stay, but he passed. Perhaps he had nothing to offer." King Sumner hardened as his wife's hand rubbed his leg.

"Even if they are, they've plenty we can use—trees, for instance. Imagine all you could do with the wood." Lord Sabeen had accompanied Sumner back to the castle, to guarantee his inclusion in any talks about the visitors.

"I agree." The king witnessed his uncle's disgust over Sumner's mother, Lady Sydni, sitting at his feet. The king flaunted his conquest of her to his subjects whenever he could. He lifted her hand to stroke his cock. "Let's play this out. Even if they do mean us harm, there are so few of them. Let's bring them ashore and try to find out what brought them here." Like a puppet master, he raised his wife to her feet, gripped the back of his mother's head, and embedded her face between his wife's pudgy, wide thighs.

Lord Sabeen averted his gaze, pretending to concentrate on his own wife, Saya. She sat behind him, her legs wrapped around his waist while her hand stroked his flaccid member beneath his robe. He grieved for her—who never found satisfaction by her husband's rod—only his hands and mouth.

"The Alders arrive tomorrow. My wife will gather a hunting party and my mother will have them fed for the next week. They'll share the castle's front room for sleeping, which means you four will need to leave." He watched his wife rock her hips forward as she climaxed, grinding Sydni's teeth against her nub.

Sabeen's breathing hitched, pretending his climax neared. "Should we return to our homes or would you like us to rent rooms in the city?"

"A good question," Sumner anticipated his uncle's release coming. "Perhaps, if Saya wanted to join me, then she could return to you with my answer."

Saya, with brown and silver frizzy hair, was a homely woman in her mid-fifties. King Sumner did not want her, but the request gave him an opportunity to prove his dominance.

Sabeen turned and winked for only her to see, knowing inevitably his nephew's greed would prevail. He stayed her hand as he covered his limpness.

"I would like nothing more, Your Highness." Excitement tingled through her body. She disentangled herself, swaying her hips as she walked to the throne.

Sumner pushed his women away and pulled his aunt onto his lap, "Mother, Sofia, go to bed. I have no need for you this evening."

Lord Sarrell sucked on Synnova's breasts, pulling her nipples with his teeth. "When she has satisfied you, perhaps she would like to satisfy me?"

"Why should you wait?" The king spit on his fingers, shoved them under her skirt and into her slit. "Are you able to please us both, Saya?"

Her breath hitched and goose bumps formed on her skin as she felt his rough fingers slide inside her. She lifted her head proudly. "Pretty easily, I imagine." She smiled, happy to increase her wealth and honour with two higher noblemen. It had been months since her last use. She had begun to doubt her feminine abilities, and worried she brought shame to her husband.

"There, you see—the sign of a good wife. Well done, uncle." Sumner cupped her jaw roughly, forcing her mouth open as he kissed her. He meant to draw Sabeen's anger with his comments, but they did quite the opposite.

Sabeen played his part by glaring. "I'm left wanting and will go to bed." He headed in the opposite direction with a grin. He would sleep well, knowing someone was pleasuring her.

Sarrell had only jested when he suggested it. He wanted nothing the older woman offered, let alone join his brother-in-law in his bed, but he had no choice, withdrawing his request would bring shame to their aunt.

Sumner pushed her from his lap. He stood, then playfully shoved her onto the empty furs piled behind the throne as Sarrell joined her. "It's time we all retire."

He took one last glance at his unsatisfied sister as the servant extinguished the fires.

Day 121
Near Hawkerton Village, Slaysfold

As the sun rose, Aedyn and four groups rowed onto the beach. Two groups would swap out every day, providing all a reprieve from the vessel's confinement. Women responsible for the horses' care would utilise an assembled tent next to a makeshift paddock. The men saddled the mounts and rode out, following a Slay guide. Aedyn rode mid procession as they navigated the grassy land toward Slaysfold castle.

"It's monotonous. I see nay trees, merely a mix of grasses and flowers with the odd shrub. Not even around that lake." Bennet surveyed the landscape.

"The meadows appear dead, scorched, and yet the sun is cooler here than home." Aron included himself in the conversation.

Aedyn, puzzled, glanced around. "Where's Auren?"

"His pouch made quite the racket this morning when he disembarked. He was speaking to a woman as we headed out. He must travel behind." Asa twisted, not seeing Auren amongst them.

Hundreds of vibrant blue birds, the colour of the Aldersward blue lagoon, landed playfully nearby, then took flight moments later, seeming to play a childhood game of chase. In the distance, a herd of heavy-framed, large beasts with shaggy coats and hunched backs observed the men's movements. Their heads were wide with a set of horns and bearded chins. Not creatures the Alders recognised.

After a couple of hours, Auren galloped upon them with a wide grin. "This feels much like home. The women here also demand my attention."

"You make a dreadful lead. Remind me to dismiss you once we return home." Aedyn ridiculed as the others chuckled.

He feigned an indignant tone. "I was gaining intelligence. It was strategic."

Amused, Bennet asked. "Strategic?"

He boasted. "While they were busy exercising me, they couldn't kill Prince Aedyn, could they? Furthermore, you're welcome."

They all laughed, aware that Auren's vulnerability was women and someday, not a magical creature, but a woman would be his demise. Emissary Aron poked Asa, then pointed to Auren's purse, which sounded considerably less noisy than it had earlier.

"Did ye learn anything of value during yer, um," Bennet slicked back his hair, "visit?"

"King Sumner executed his father, the last king, and sexually enslaved his mother. They sounded disgusted. They also spoke of another imprisoned slave the king has. Apparently, the king brutalised her until she was unrecognisable and contorted. They were very forthcoming." Auren explained, knowing his information was valuable.

"His people should be disgusted. I imagine we all will be, but let's keep it hidden. It's none of our business. I'm not here to create enemies." Aedyn advised. "Did the women say anything else useful?"

"Trees are rare now and the king has taken the few remaining, planted them together, and now protects them." Auren grinned. "Otherwise, they moaned, cried, and pleaded for me to continue my skilled invasion. I'll spare you your jealousy."

Day 122
Front Room
Castle
Slaysfold City

Aedyn eyed the food while his enthusiastic men rehashed the previous night's entertainment. The rum, mead, and women had flowed easily after so long without the luxuries. They were in great spirits and sat amongst the women, waiting for the king to rouse.

"It was a fine evening." Asa winked at the hungover group. He had remained sober to guard their prince.

Emissary Aron nodded remorsefully, his head in hand. "I can't remember last when I consumed so much."

"You're such a lightweight. You were the first to pass out. No women for you." Asa teased.

"My wife waits back home. None compare to her."

Aedyn trailed his fork over the plate. "Do you know what this is?"

Asa pointed. "They call that a potato. It's like a yam, but not sweet. And that is boiled bear. It tastes fishy. I wouldn't eat it until someone revealed what it was. The bread is good, though."

Aedyn reached for the bread. "How many men will go on the hunt?"

"Not more than ten. I thought Auren would be eager to go but I don't see him." Asa replied.

"He left late in the company of another." Bennet glanced at Aedyn. "I know ye're not leery of this king, but we are. I had Alonso put together a specialised guard for ye today. It's wise to determine if this king is plotting."

"Fine, but he was truthful. I want you, Emissary Aron, and Physician Aidrik here as well. If you require a respite, tomorrow will be soon enough." Aedyn agreed as King Sumner emerged from a doorway and approached.

They stood and genuflected, but the king waved them to resume their activities as he ordered a chair placed at the table end.

"Prince Aedyn, I hope you enjoyed the evening and slept well." King Sumner greeted them as Sahana hobbled over, setting a plate down. "Have you met my imp?" He chuckled as he tugged on her long skirts, making her lose her balance. "Sahana, I don't recall seeing you here last night?"

The young woman raised her head. Scars littered her face, and while one eye stared at Sumner, the other looked in the opposite direction. "Queen Sofia asked me to watch the children until they slept."

"It shouldn't have taken long." The ruler's hand snaked out, clutching her by the hair, and brought her face to his. "Your horrific face will make me no richer, unless they roll you over and poke you in the ass." He hurled her away, and she fell to the floor. Disgusted, he turned to the table. "Would anyone like to take a poke at the ugly? She's open to anyone. Her station is lower than my hound, but even he won't mount her."

Shocked and appalled by the cruelty, the newcomers kept themselves in check, pretending to ignore the exchange.

The vein in Aedyn's neck jumped and, realising the prince barely hung onto his temper, Asa spoke. "King Sumner, it's been a long time since I found a woman's ass to jab. Her face makes no difference. If you agree, I could use her tonight. Our sexual practices are more private, perhaps on our vessel, with your permission. I could offer her to others and see you generously paid in the morning."

"Very well, allow your men to use her as they wish." King Sumner continued eating as the grotesque woman retreated in fear, scurrying into a shadowed corner. The Alders' proclivities were none of his concern. If he could gain wealth from her use, then he would allow it.

"Asa, try not to damage her more than she already is. Ensure whoever uses her pays." Aedyn concluded, then turned to Bennet. "When you find Auren, order him on the hunt with Queen Sofia."

King Sumner wiped the grease from his lips onto the sleeve of his tunic. "You and I will spend the day together. I have business to attend to here."

"Sire, there's no end to your generosity. Perhaps Bennet, my emissary, and my physician can stay. They keep our journey's record and I want exceptional detail added about Slaysfold."

King Sumner finished his meal. "Once the front room clears, I'll introduce you to my children and mother."

Asa's and Auren's men returned to the Endeavour, others accompanied the hunting party, and a few ventured to entertain themselves within the city. The front room became eerily silent after the boisterous voices and liveliness of the morning meal. Aedyn sat with his three men while six Alder guards watched throughout.

The king's arms draped his daughters' shoulders, a few years younger than Annora. "Prince Aedyn, these are princesses, Svara and Solara."

The young girls dressed more modestly than the older women, but still their limbs were bare, wearing short skirts and sleeveless tunics.

The Alders bowed, and Aedyn smiled, "So pretty. You'll break many hearts one day."

Both proudly grinned as they sat on the stairs below their father's throne.

"Prince Aedyn, join me above by my throne. Today I deal with many things but my time is entirely spent here." The king motioned as a woman entered from an adjoining room.

Aedyn turned, stopping as the striking female approached. Only by how she carried herself and her confidence could he tell she was older. Her frame was athletic and solid under the brown leather, legless and sleeveless bodysuit. The front corded binds gaped at the bottom and opened wider as they climbed her torso. Her breasts were noticeably firm under small leather triangles, twined together to hide their bottom halves. Her long, black hair held large ringlets and her skin was flawless, barely wrinkled by age.

On one hip, a long, sheathed blade swung from a wide belt and on the other, a baby cradled against her. A child held her hand, skipping playfully until she spotted the intruders, then hid behind the woman shyly.

"Here's my mother, Lady Sydni with princesses, Sorcha and Sile." The king watched Aedyn's reaction, but it did not change.

While Lady Sydni passed the baby to Sumner, Aedyn attempted to coax the little girl into speaking, but was unsuccessful, and she fled to her older sisters.

"Lady Sydni." He took her hand in Aldersward fashion, but his glance rested a second too long on her.

King Sumner caught it. "Mother, I may see interest bubbling."

Aedyn watched her sit beside her granddaughters. "Her beauty is incredible. I see a resemblance in your daughters." He reminded the king his children were present as he sat.

The king's eyes lit with amusement. "Take the day to think about it. Like your man, if you need someplace more private I can arrange it."

He nodded. "Your blackened tablet," he pointed to it above the king's throne. "It looks like the Aldersward one. How did it turn black?"

His shoulders shrugged. "It was that way ever since I can remember."

"And as long as I can as well." Lady Sydni added.

Aedyn gestured, inviting Bennet to engage in the conversation. "It looks like one of the nine tablets forged by King Abrahin and our god, Jezabet, at the beginning of 1 F.Y." Bennet glanced at the king and he issued an encouraging nod. "The story goes, the war troubled Jezabet. He visited King Abrahin and together they created peace among all the kingdoms in Speranza, but in exchange, our kingdoms would follow the moral guidance laid out by Jezabet. King Abrahin presented one to each kingdom, the Unification War ended, and the kingdoms found peace, the nine kings came together." Bennet weaved the teaching into a tale for the group to enjoy, instead of lecturing them.

"What happened?" Solara, maybe ten, asked.

"For thousands of years, they remained the brightest gold, until Princess Amelia's sixteenth birthday. I can't speak to yer tablet but can of the Aldersward tablet. The night yer kingdom and the seven others vanished, thought fallen into the sea by a tremendous earthquake, King Asmaud was in the crypt. We don't know why he was there, but when his son, Acoose, had the collapse cleared, they found Asmaud lying on the tablet, and it had turned black. Over the last two-hundred years, many have sought to reverse or clean it but they were unsuccessful in their efforts." Bennet finished.

The child's eyes filled with wonderment. "What happened to our tablet?"

He dropped to his haunches, eyeing the girls. "I cannot say what happened to yers. Perhaps it turned black then as well."

King Sumner drew the man's attention with a laugh. "It's an interesting story you have imagined. A god and the Alder king trapped magics inside, then his ancestor broke it. Quite enjoyable, you're a fine storyteller. I'm curious, Bennet, do you still have faith in the Jezabet god of the Alders?"

He nodded, careful not to offend the Slays, "Myself, aye. There's nay alternative to explain how our world came to be. I've spent many years studying the texts in Aldersward. According to them, Jezabet created many worlds from stones in his black garden as experiments for his amusement. He populated our world for his unborn son, Jordan. He plucked his favourite aspects from each world, intricately weaving this one with never-ending possibilities for his son's enjoyment. When Jezabet placed the Alders, his favourite race, on Speranza he met with King Alfred and explained his plans for it."

Lady Sydni clasped her hands in disbelief. "You think we're playthings—toys?"

"Aye, somewhat. But Jezabet's mistake was in the idea we would live peacefully together and before his son, Jordan, grew, we broke into war. If he hadn't intervened and given us the tablets, some races would never have survived."

King Sumner bent forward, resting his arms on the throne's sides. "If our world was such a mess, then why didn't he destroy it and start over?"

"I don't believe the gods can destroy worlds, only manipulate them. In all the passages I have studied, there's nothing about any other world being destroyed."

Sydni asked. "So, what do you think separated us?"

"I cannot say, but the Alders presume it's a test or puzzle Jezabet has given us." Bennet thanked the king, then joined Aidrik and Aron.

"He's the last man alive from that night. Until recently, he taught the children of our castle. Sometimes he lets the story get away from him." Aedyn laughed. To inform the uneducated ruler it was a documented fact within the king's library in Aldersward would achieve nothing.

Day 122
Near Hawkerton Village, Slaysfold

As Asa neared the seashore where the boats waited, he wondered about the disfigured woman stiffly riding in front of him. Earlier when he lifted her, he realised underneath her filthy long skirts, layered tunics, and cloak she was scrawny. He guessed she weighed less than Prince Aedyn's fifteen-year-old sister. He was certain they had deprived her of food. Her matted hair, probably quite long, knotted around her circlet. She smelled putrid, and he struggled not to gag, worrying he would offend her.

It was a silent trip as they galloped across the land. She sniffled, and her body shook with fear, but neither spoke.

She sat motionless, her head down, refusing to look at her surroundings as Asa held the horse's reins tight and dismounted. He imagined she might attempt an escape, and he tried to comfort her with his words. "I can take you willingly, Sahana, or I can simply take you. It's your decision."

She made no response, and he used one arm to drag her from the saddle, then carried her to the boat.

He spoke to her quietly as the others rowed. "Are you not grateful to us for removing you from the castle? We mean you no harm. You can trust us."

Sahana focused on her restless fingers. The chance for escape passed. Her contorted limbs, incapable of swimming, would prevent her from trying. She was trapped.

Asa motioned for her to climb the rope ladder ahead of him. He had not foreseen her difficulty manoeuvring the swaying rungs. After several hampered minutes, Asa rounded her waist with his brawny arm and hauled her to the top, releasing her onto the deck as he climbed the last rung himself.

Crawling, Sahana scurried to the navigation deck's stairs and crouched beside them. She waited, tensely coiled, for someone to grab her, throw slurs, or order her unclothed so they could ridicule her monstrous shape, but none came. She observed her captor standing by the craft's middle pillar as he supervised those arriving and departing. His feet came towards her, and she prepared herself for his hands. Instead, he ignored her as he mounted the stairs and spoke to someone above.

"Captain," Asa patted the man's back. "I thought I would find you here. Shall I relieve you so you may spend time ashore?"

Amos laughed. "I'm too old to keep pace with you younger men, and anyhow, I prefer the water over land. It's peaceful here, no one to disturb me."

"I've brought a visitor aboard. She'll stay in Prince Aedyn's quarters overnight. If I'm required, you'll find me there." Asa descended the stairs, ignoring her as he crossed her path and walked to a door farther along the wall, disappearing inside.

The door swung out and a young boy walked the deck's length, then into a dark corridor. He made several trips back and forth, carrying a pail. She lost interest, ignoring the door swinging open again as she studied her fingernails nervously.

"Sahana," her captor spoke from the doorway. "I request your presence." When she did not acknowledge him, he became irritated. He yanked her to stand and dragged her with him, allowing the door to close before letting her go.

He permitted her eye time to readjust to the darkened interior while he stepped to the right wall and sat on a trunk he had recently removed from the bedchamber. Once he was certain she could see, he spoke. "Sit. No one will disturb us."

Sore from the ride and the exertion of the climb, she went to a cushioned chair far away from him.

He regarded her. "You'll stay in the room attached to this one. No one will bother you. The page brought warm bathing water for you, and you'll give me your clothes so I may have them cleaned." She raised her anxious eye at his remarks. "Understand this. There's a lock on the inside. I'm asking you not to lock it and give you my word—unless you specifically grant permission, no one will enter. If you choose to lock it, know it will only take me a second to eliminate the barrier between us, and I won't be happy when I do. Have I made myself clear?"

The woman nodded in solemn understanding. She realised she could not deny what would happen. Her foul smell and dirty clothes were her tightly clutched defences, which she used to avoid attention. He would eliminate them.

"Once you've finished washing and have dressed, then you may join me here for the midday meal. You may go."

Released from his presence, she hobbled to the room on her left, then turned and distrustfully eyed him as he watched her secure the door between them.

Sahana paused, motionless, staring at the latch, and debated whether she should lock it. She chose not to decide immediately as her gaze travelled over the grand bed, a table with a few chairs, and some cabinets.

Slowly, she limped to the tub, wrestling with another choice. She would be clean or risk this man's wrath and the king's punishment. She striped her clothes away, then begrudgingly savoured the warm water against her skin as she listened for the sound of approaching footsteps. When the water cooled, she washed her circlet-matted hair half-heartedly.

She wrapped herself with the bath sheet, looking at the unfamiliar garment laid on the bed. Sahana struggled with it, pulling it over her body. It was quite large compared to her frame, rolling the sleeves and collar out of her way. She made a mental note not to trip on it.

She pressed her ear against the wall. Her captor's boots thumped against the floor. Voices spoke, and the exterior door closed. The aroma of food wafted through the air and her stomach growled, reminding her she had not eaten since before dawn, and only discarded food she had scavenged. She resolved, if she were to be brutalised then she would take whatever reward she could as she emerged.

Asa rose from the long table set for two. He attempted to suppress his revulsion over her scared and fractured features as she came nearer. "I hope you're hungry. Our cook sent plenty." She nodded as she sat at the other plate with her back to the cabinets.

They ate in silence and he watched her take small bites, wiping her mouth in between. She drank thirstily from the sweet tea after an initial test, ensuring it was not alcohol. It wouldn't serve to have her reaction time slowed further.

When a knock sounded, she flinched, then stiffened at the unexpected noise.

He sought to calm her. "I'll go and will not bring whoever it is inside."

He stepped out, letting the door swing closed.

Sahana had little time. She took the eating knife inside the bedchamber, tucked it under the bed pillow, and retraced her steps as the exterior door opened.

With caution, he walked back inside, searching for changes. He eyed her standing in the doorway. "Are you still hungry, or should I have it cleared?" He would force her to answer with words.

"I would like to eat more if you would allow." She stepped back to the chair.

"Fill yourself. I need to deliver your clothes to be cleaned." Her captor explained as he passed the table and entered the other room. He noted the missing blade, but said nothing.

Asa delivered her clothes outside and within minutes returned, her clean clothes in hand. As she quizzically looked on, he bent them over a chair back. "We have a fellow whose ability is to clean things instantly. I didn't appreciate his skill until now."

She pushed the food around her plate and he realised she was stalling.

"Perhaps you're finished until the evening meal. We could sit more comfortably over there." He nodded to the smaller table and cushioned chairs in the right corner. "Bring your drink." He pretended to pay her no attention. He sat down, propping his feet on the small table.

Unsure of her next move, she scrutinised his actions and words. There would be no harm in joining him. She skirted the room to the chair opposite him, then another knock sounded lightly.

"It's the page coming to clean. May I call him inside or would you rather go to the other room while he's here?"

"I'm fine here if it's only the boy." She answered in another full sentence, and he smiled as he called for the page.

Day 122
Front Room
Castle
Slaysfold City

The afternoon warmth stifled the air in the interior as bodies crowded the room where the king dealt with simple squabbles between his countrymen. Prince Aedyn's father did not handle such trivial matters. He left it to advisors, and they briefed him later. King Sumner allowed each party to explain her concerns, then he reflected for a minute before deciding. Occasionally, he would turn, asking Aedyn's opinion but mostly out of courtesy.

When the children retired after the midday meal, the former queen stayed, sitting on the stairs at their feet. Aedyn found Lady Sydni interestedly peeking at him whenever he spoke. It was quite unnerving, and he unsuccessfully covered his discomfort.

"I'll come out and inspect the animal. Stay seated." King Sumner strode outside and voices murmured in his absence.

Lady Sydni quickly whispered to Aedyn. "I must speak to you. It's of great importance." Her head swivelled front before the king returned.

Aedyn wondered about her words as the king gave his judgement, then ordered the room cleared, leaving a single man before them.

"This is our medicine man. He oversees a population who fell ill a few moons ago." Sumner explained, then addressed the man. "How are the sick?"

"Six moons, and they remain sleeping."

Aedyn leaned forward, giving the man his full attention. "King Sumner, may I ask if your sick knew each other?"

The medicine man shrugged. "If they did, it is unknown."

Sumner laced his fingers together, resting them on his chest. "What do you know of this illness?"

"It struck our kingdom six moons ago as well. It's the reason for our journey. We seek Reinshaven for help."

"I've considered poisoning them. They're a burden to our healers and their families." The king tapped his finger on his jaw. "May I ask how Reinshaven can help, and why would you bother?"

"My mother, Queen Anya, suffers from this illness. Therefore, we travel hoping to find a cure."

"Why Reinshaven?"

Aidrik rose. "The Reins are healers. It's their common ability. We believe they survived the event of 2631."

"It's quite the risk you take to cure your mother. I applaud your loyalty, Prince Aedyn. I'm not so devoted to my family. Isn't that right, Mother?" The ruler nudged her with the toe of his boot, mocking her.

Aedyn ignored the king's action. "Would you consider saving them if you could?"

"Of course, but I won't waste time on a few people. It makes more sense to let them die."

"If we find Reinshaven, I could search out a healer for your kingdom as well."

The medicine man's eyes brightened. "It's most kind of you."

"Nothing is free." The king spoke matter-of-factly, turning to Aedyn. "What would it cost us?"

"My father, regardless, will reward you for the courtesies you've afforded us. Let us speak again later. If I've not thought of anything, then we'll offer it for free in friendship."

Day 122
Prince Aedyn's Quarters
Anya's Endeavour
Slaysfold's North Sea

Sahana studied Asa as he described his kingdom. His short hair was a light, sandy brown and exposed his ears. His shaven face had visible laugh lines. From these, she could tell he smiled often. He was not as tall as his prince, perhaps a half-foot shorter. Earlier, when he lifted her from the horse, she noticed he was fit.

"I've bored you. Tell me of your kingdom."

"I think the king has told you a great deal." She answered blandly.

"Perhaps then it's time for you to retire." He withdrew his feet from their resting place.

"But not everything." She quickly responded, inwardly cringing as she recalled his earlier remarks to the king. "Would you have anything stronger to offer than this?"

He lifted his eyebrow, shocked by her less than stealthy request, then smiled, "Such as?"

"I have no preference. Perhaps you can introduce me to your favourite." She hid her cunning smile while she finished the sweet tea. He crossed to the door and ordered someone to bring whisky.

"You were telling me of your kingdom?" He leaned his back against the wall and crossed his arms.

"Yes, my king's kingdom." She scrambled for something to say. "I wish you would've arrived before he killed his father. It happened fourteen years ago, but his reign of terror started long before then. King Saul tried to redirect his son's boredom by creating a position for him within our warrior ranks, but it failed to dissuade him from his brutalising behaviour. Sumner travelled on the king's business from village to village and wreaked havoc in his wake. As he destroyed livelihoods and girls by raping them, no one dared to tell the king of his son's cruelty for fear he would return, and do more damage."

The page knocked. Asa took the pitcher and returned to sit, placing it between them on the table. She poured the whisky and handed him a full mug.

He noted hers held considerably less. "Is this what happened to you?"

She answered flatly, detaching herself from what happened so long ago. "No. It was much later, after he slit his father's throat. I came to wed in Slaysfold City. My parents had arranged it with King Saul prior to his death. King Sumner spent a great deal of time undoing anything his father had done during his rule. This included any contracts his father had approved which had yet to be carried out. I came to the city on my own, my groom's parents expecting me, but when I arrived they informed me we needed the king's approval again. The king saw us, took one look at me, and asked me to join him that evening. Sex is not obligatory in our culture. I had every right to refuse, and I did. My parents allowed me to remain a virgin, and I intended to stay intact until my wedding night. The king declared plainly, our marriage would not happen unless I agreed, but I did not. The beating I took only lasted for minutes in front of everyone present. But, it felt like hours, and I realised no one could intervene. I understood. I remember the sounds of breaking bones, the unbearable pain as I cried and screamed, but I refused to succumb to the unconsciousness which threatened me. I wanted him to hear me suffer. In the end, his mother, Lady Sydni, stopped him. I don't know why."

Sahana took a small sip, wetting her throat. "She housed me in a neighbouring hut. I was certain I would die, but I wasn't so lucky. No, eventually, I healed to my current state. Later, I found out he had sent warriors to Larkburgh and slaughtered my family while I slept. My betrothed's family no longer wanted me, and I couldn't blame them, as my state was no longer desirable. Lady Sydni and I formed a friendship of sorts. When Sumner found out about it, he took me from her and claimed me as his slave. I became another possession he took because someone else showed interest." She reached for the pitcher and topped his mug while she sipped again. It warmed her suddenly chilled body.

"What do others think about your beating?"

"Often I think they forget why I'm in this state and avoid looking at me all together. Others believe I deserved it and should have given into his demands. But, there are a few who pity me and they will sometimes give me food or clothing when the king is not around to see." She talked and watched him take several swallows.

"You survive off the kindness of strangers?" He said as she raised the pitcher, refilling their mugs.

"No, mostly I live on the scraps left from the evening meal. Unless her son refused her a meal, I can usually rely on Lady Sydni to leave me a portion." She amusingly hid her smile as yet again he drank.

"Why do you think Lady Sydni cares for you?"

Her voice sounded hopeful. "Sometimes, I dream it's because she likes me." Her expression soured. "But I know it's only because she and I are the same—captives."

"But her lot is different. She's not treated nearly as badly as you." He rubbed his jaw, confused.

"No, her position is worse. He takes out his hatred, frustration, annoyance, and anger on me. But she's subjected to his lust, and it comes more often than the others do. He parades and makes her commit those awful acts in front of others, and she must pretend to enjoy them. I can hide from him in the shadows. There are no shadows for her."

He placed his mug down and she lifted the pitcher. He waved her hand away. "You needn't get me drunk." He smiled, and her expression fell with disheartenment as she eyed him. "I drink rather often and have a high tolerance. You've topped off my mug many times, but in my estimation, I've not finished a full mug and it usually takes two or three. I wish to remain sober tonight."

Her hopes died. She took a huge swallow and sputtered, coughing from the burn.

Day 122
Front Room
Castle
Slaysfold City

Men served the heavily burdened trays to their women and the Alders. As they placed each dish, women grabbed for the food without ceremony, using their hands. The scent of fresh bread and roasted meat tantalised their hunger. The continuous drone of chatter echoed, gaining volume as the hunting party returned.

"Prince Aedyn, gentlemen, it was a splendid day." Auren genuflected then sat beside Aedyn and looked about the table. Bennet, Aron, and Aidrik returned his greeting. "Where has Asa gone?"

Bennet ensured his voice carried. "He took the king's gimp to the Endeavour so he could enjoy her." Then more quietly added, "Say something about him liking disfigured women."

"His thirst for uncommon women never runs dry. Do you remember the time he enjoyed the woman born with four breasts?" Auren's loud voice tapered quieter. "She reminded me of a cow. What did I miss?"

The meat's smoky flavour pleasantly surprised Aedyn as he chewed. "The king's treatment of her heated me, so Asa removed her," then raised his voice, "back in the morning."

"My word!" Bennet exclaimed under his breath and fixed his eyes on his plate. "Don't look up."

"Direct your attention to me." Louder Aedyn added. "The king has offered me privacy and his mother." He steeled his expression and lifted his gaze to the throne.

It was empty. Lady Sydni stood behind it with only her head and clutching hands visible. Sumner stood behind her, forcefully pounding his hips into her.

The prince's stomach turned. "Sire, I would like to use her when you've finished."

"Of course, I'll even let her bathe before she joins you." The king shuddered as he climaxed, then pushed away from her and came around his throne, exposing them to his wet and softening manhood. Red with shame, Lady Sydni fell to the ground, making no sound.

Aedyn held his gaze. "Tell me, where and I'll go make myself ready." Relieved to remove this perversion from his countrymen, unsure they could maintain their indifference much longer. "Auren, arrange my guard."

King Sumner smugly grinned as the Alders left. Much sooner than expected, the prince had given into his desires.

Day 122
Prince Aedyn's Hut
Slaysfold City

In the neglected wooden one-room hut, Auren took nothing for granted as he removed the bedding and searched through it, then examined the walls, floor, and ceiling. He found no weapons other than the table and lantern. These things were unavoidable, Aedyn would have to keep them in mind. He arranged for Augustus, Angelo, and Alonso to guard, one standing at each outside corner. Once Lady Sydni was inside, they were no longer protection but prevention from anyone eavesdropping.

She arrived an hour later, entering with a female guard who carried a tray with a pitcher and mugs.

Aedyn feigned a sexual interest as he rose and kissed the back of her wrists. "I desire us to be alone, but we can play with her as well." He stepped closer, eagerly kissing her neck.

She glided into his inviting arms. "She escorted me here. Leave us. Prince Aedyn will see me back when I've satiated his hunger."

When the guard left, Aedyn dropped her hands, moving as far as he could away from her, and Auren stepped forward.

"Lady Sydni, let me apologise in advance. It's necessary for you to undress so I may check you for weapons." As a guard, Auren had trained in searching a woman's body. In Aldersward, they had performed the procedure on well-paid whores. This was entirely different. Lady Sydni was a member of a royal family, but, uncomfortably, he would do his duty.

She stilled. "Then after, I will thoroughly enjoy checking both of you as well."

Auren reddened at the lude comment spoken by a royal tongue, and Aedyn shook his head. "No, you won't. You asked for this meeting. You take it on my terms or you may leave."

She weighed the ultimatum and began by removing her belt, watching Aedyn's eyes as she did. She knew, regardless of the acts Sumner forced on her, she remained a desirable woman. Her bodysuit's style reflected the one she wore earlier, except this one was stone grey. The prince turned his back while she untied the small squares of fabric covering her breasts.

She stopped her movements, her voice sultry in invitation. "If I'm forced to strip, then it's only fair you watch to guarantee a proper search, Prince Aedyn."

He folded his arms and turned to watch her. "I was allowing you the privacy we would normally afford you in Aldersward."

She tossed the squares away. "It pleases me that we're not in Aldersward." She slowly peeled the bodysuit down her midriff, exposing her navel, then slid the leather past her thighs. When it fell to the ground, she stepped out of it.

Auren examined her and could not help but notice her perky youthful breasts, her hard, upturned nipples, and her muscular abdomen. He rotated his position to stand behind her and stepped toward her, removing the pins and circlet as her hair fell in wild curls over her back. He cupped both sides of her head and threaded his hands through it, ensuring no weapons were present.

Aedyn's pulse quickened as gentle heat built in his loins.

Auren cleared his throat. "Spread your legs further apart, bend over, and place your hands on the bed." He waited for her to follow his instruction.

She widened her lengthy legs apart, then she bent forward, her eyes never leaving the prince. She stuck her ass out for Auren to examine.

He stepped back. "Using one of your hands, place two fingers inside yourself to prove there's no hidden weapon."

Unwanted, Aedyn felt himself hardening as she obeyed the command.

She slid her fingers inside, pulling her folds apart as Auren crouched on his haunches to scrutinise it. He smelled her womanhood's musky scent and noted the wetness of her slippery cavern. He moistened his lips, his interest heightened.

"She's clean." Auren gruffly ended the search. He bowed, then collected her blade and withdrew from the hut.

"Get dressed." The prince sat on the bed's edge, hiding his swollen erection.

On all fours, she crawled onto the bed and pushed her ass in the air as she rubbed her breasts against the mattress. "But I've only just undressed. Perhaps you should enjoy my pleasure before I clothe?"

"Unfortunately, I've no intention of using you. I'm betrothed. In our culture, it means we may have no other. So I beg you to dress and state your business." Aedyn happily used Ammaris as an excuse, but knew if she asked again, he could not stop his lust.

She placed the small squares back over her breasts, pulled on her bodysuit, and secured her belt in place, then sat away from him. She offered herself, but she would not beg.

He focused on her expression. "Do you intend to betray your son?"

"Yes," she answered, truthfully.

"I'll let you know, immediately, I'll not involve myself in your kingdom's politics."

"You misunderstand. Your man removed Sahana this morning. I wonder, will he brutalise her?"

"I don't know. What concern is it of yours?"

Her tone softened. "She's my friend. I take care of her."

"I understand," he said, though he did not.

"I brought you this." She walked to the tray and lifted the pitcher. "At the bottom, you'll find my wedding jewellery. I hid it before my son could take it. It would make a fine addition to your future wife's collection."

"Knowing I won't betray your son, what would you have me do for this jewellery?" He arched his brow.

"I wish for you to remove Sahana from the king. Perhaps buy her and take her with you. If she remains here, he will eventually kill her."

"What about yourself, shouldn't I try to buy your freedom?"

"No, he would never allow me to leave, no matter what you offered. The mere mention of it could see us both killed. I've accepted my fate, but he took the girl from me. He beat her until she was almost dead, and I nursed her back to health. She was someone I shared my pain with. When he found out she was recovering in this hut, he took her. My son forced her to live as she does in the castle. I thought that perhaps your man pitied her. Was I mistaken?"

"No." He saw no reason to lie to her. She revealed enough to trust her. "Asa removed her because we're not accustomed to seeing women abused. It's not our way in Aldersward. Men don't raise their hands to women."

"Will you consider what I've asked?" She held her breath, eagerly awaiting his response.

"I will consider it but I make no promise I'll even try." He took the pitcher from her and dumped it out, gathering the jewellery and held it out to her. "If I decide to *buy* the woman, I'll do it using my own means. Keep your jewellery and make plans for yourself."

"I couldn't. It's of no use to me. My countrymen would never betray our king." She shook her head as she tried to give the jewels back to him.

He trapped her full hands in his. "None of your people. But you forget, you're no longer alone. There will be other vessels travelling soon. Not all will belong to Slaysfold."

Day 122
Prince Aedyn's Quarters
Anya's Endeavour
Slaysfold's North Sea

Midnight grew near as Sahana conversed with her captor about any subject to keep his mind from remembering his sexual thirst. She yawned again. The whisky made her sleepy, but she did not intend to go willingly inside the bedchamber.

A knock sounded from outside, and he left to answer it. Someone outside handed him a bundle. The door swung closed as he strode to the long table and unfolded it.

She remained in her chair, curious but not waiting to draw his attention.

He turned. "Are you tired yet?" She shook her head and he continued. "Then we've a problem. I'm exhausted and cannot go to sleep until you leave this room."

She watched him unfold the bedding and arrange it on the tabletop. "What do you mean?"

"I won't sleep if you remain here because you could find weapons, try to escape or one of my men could come in unwanted. Please go to bed. I don't expect to get much sleep."

Shocked, she blurted. "You don't intend to join me in the bedchamber?"

"No. That's why I haven't asked where the knife is." He smiled at her.

"But you said–"

"I said what had to be said. Prince Aedyn was about to lose his temper." He explained.

Tears burst from her eyes as she sobbed. "But you took away my dirty clothes and made me bathe?"

Confused, he stood motionless, unsure of how to comfort a crying woman. "Of course, I provided you with luxuries."

"But those were my defences. They were the reason people avoided me." She tasted the salty tears on her lips.

"Sard," dumbfounded, he cursed. Gratitude was what he had expected. It had not occurred to him she purposely allowed herself to be unclean as a defence mechanism. "Don't cry. In the morning, we'll make you unclean again. No one will be the wiser."

She took several long breaths to calm before she limped away, closing the door between them.

Day 123
Prince Aedyn's Hut
Slaysfold City

Aedyn slept soundly, knowing his guards were outside, and he was alone.

Aedyn opened his eyes and realised he was in Aldersward's stable. What had woken him, he wondered, then realised a warm wet mouth bathed his cock. He smiled as he looked down, expecting to see Azalea on her knees, but he found Lady Sydni naked.

Rhythmically, her head bobbed over his long shaft. Her tongue caressed the sensitive spot under its crown, and his hips thrust upward in response, enjoying the building pleasure. He laid back, draping one arm above him, concentrating on her heated, soft lips wrapped tightly around him. He used his other hand to rub her neck, kneading it gently, encouraging her.

She lifted her eyes and batted his hand away. "You're not permitted to touch me, stable boy. Your station is beneath me."

He played along. "Hmm, yes and how lucky I am *beneath you*." Fleetingly, he wondered where the stablemen were, but quickly forgot about it when she straddled her knees over his thighs.

Her fingers stood his hardened rod upright, and she sank her slickened folds onto him, enveloping his full length. As she bucked furiously against him, her rounded breasts bounced and she threw her head back, arching her torso away. He felt her clit brush against his pubic bone and her muscles clench as she moaned.

His own climax built as his toes curled and anticipation rushed within his body. Suddenly, Lady Sydni was ripped from him as semen spewed from his pulsating tip. Augustus and Angelo held her captive as Auren and Asa hauled him to his feet.

Rage filled Aedyn. "What's the meaning of this?"

No one answered. Auren bound his hands behind his naked body and they marched him inside Aldersward castle. Aedyn, indignant, fought against the restraints as they forced him forward into the great hall where the court waited. Embarrassed, he saw his mother and sisters dressed as Slays, standing along the edge of the parted crowd. His guards led him to the throne's rise. It wasn't his father but Sumner who sat there.

Auren genuflected. "King Sumner, we caught your mother being defiled by this stable hand."

The king, furious, sprang to his feet. "Did you believe your crime would go unpunished?"

Confused, Aedyn's tone held authority. "What crime? We're equals. You offered her to me."

The court laughed, but the king doubled Aedyn over with a forceful blow to his stomach. "You equate yourself to a royal now, do you?" Aedyn shook his head, not understanding what was going on as Sumner addressed the court. "Does this stable boy belong to anyone here?"

His mother and two sisters came forward and bowed.

"I see," the king waved. "Auren, have your guards escort these women to my chambers. I think it's only fair they should service me."

Anya fought the guards who grabbed Annora and Achelle as Aedyn tried unsuccessfully to free himself to protect them. He watched helplessly as the king's men removed them from the room, his young sisters screaming.

The king examined his fingernails, bored. "Hang him immediately. Let him be a lesson to everyone. This happens when you bed someone above your station."

Asa grabbed Aedyn by the neck, pushing him back out into the south bailey's sunlight as Aedyn fought, and tried to speak to his friend who ignored him. A platform loomed in the centre, and Asa marched upstairs and positioned the noose around Aedyn's neck as a crowd gathered to watch.

The floor hatch thwacked when it gave way, and Aedyn's neck snapped by the force of his drop.

Instantly, Aedyn came awake and looked around the dark hut. His breath laboured and his heart raced as he realised it was only a vivid dream and not reality. He began to comprehend the importance and power his position held.

Day 123
Front Room
Castle
Slaysfold City

"King Sumner, good morning." Prince Aedyn, with a pleasant smile, walked into the interior, buzzing with activity as his men ate their morning meal. He genuflected when he reached the throne.

"You're in fine spirits. I gather my mother serviced you well?" The king smiled smugly.

"Indeed, I'll return to the Endeavour, gather a generous sum, and return this evening."

"Will you take all of your men?" He sat forward.

"May I?" Aedyn gestured to the chair next to Sumner placed there yesterday. He nodded, and Aedyn seated himself so they could speak privately.

"Sire, I suppose you think I would leave here without properly thanking and paying you. This is the opposite of what I'm trying to accomplish. Unless you require it, I did not intend to take all of my men with me today. I thought they could remain here, enjoying your hospitality. I merely intend to go back to the craft, ensure everything runs smoothly in my absence, and return with your payment."

"It does make sense. Forgive my distrust." He was already lost in thought over what the prince might offer.

"Nonsense, do not apologise. Ours is a new friendship and trust is something we must earn." Aedyn turned, instructing his men. "Auren, Bennet, and Alonso have horses saddled. We leave with the others who return today. Angelo, Augustus, and Aron, stay behind to ensure our men don't disrupt King Sumner's kingdom."

His men left to do his bidding as Lady Sydni brought a plate to Aedyn.

Day 123
Anya's Endeavour
Slaysfold's North Sea

Aedyn boarded, noting the almost abandoned main deck. Captain Amos waved from the navigation deck while Asa and Abraham stood conversing beside the entrance to his quarters.

"Prince Aedyn, we weren't expecting you today." Asa said, as those present bowed.

"We came so we may make plans in private. What are you two doing?" Aedyn eyed the clothes in Asa's hands.

"Your Highness, Abraham made these clothes clean, and I want them dirty, as they were." He looked at the third man.

"I don't know if it's within my ability. I've never tried to make something dirty."

"Do what you can," Asa dismissed him, and turned. "She's in there."

"I expected as much." Aedyn nodded.

"Let me go in first. Understandably, it will terrify her if I don't explain why so many men are gathering inside."

"She'll need to go back to the castle today. I'll pay for her services. Perhaps four men used her last night?" Aedyn wondered.

"Four serves." He crossed to enter Aedyn's quarters.

Asa knocked on the bedchamber door and waited for Sahana to respond. When she did not, he knocked again, refusing to go inside until she invited him. After a third time, he tried the door, and it swung open.

"Sahana," he stood in the doorway, spying her by the small window.

"You said you wouldn't open the door unless I invited you." She kept her gaze focused on the land.

"Not entirely true. I said *no one would enter*. As you can see I still stand beyond the threshold." He smiled as she turned. "May I come in so we may talk?"

She nodded and hobbled to the small table, then sat down.

"I don't want to upset or alarm you." He sat across from her. "No one on board intends you harm, and I promise if there were such a person, I would guarantee your safety. Do you believe me?" He took her silence as agreement. "Prince Aedyn has returned and requires the use of the neighbouring room. There'll be men coming and going. You may stay here and shut the door so you're not disturbed. If you feel the need to lock it, you may do so, but the rule remains; unless you invite, no one will enter. In a few hours, we'll return to the castle. Prince Aedyn will make the necessary payment and has suggested you serviced four men last night."

"Why does he help me? Why four?"

"He's a man of great integrity. His family is gracious in their power and they strive to ensure their people are happy and healthy." Asa paused. "Four is a generous number to pay Sumner for. If we remain, it may convince him to allow you to accompany men back here again. In case he asks you, you need to match our story. Remember this room and four men." Asa walked to the door. "I'm having your clothes dirtied again. You can change before we leave." Her mouth slightly curled as he left.

Aedyn called for Lead Auren, Emissary Bennet, Captain Amos, Advisor Apex, and Alonso, as he walked inside the now open door. He immediately noticed his trunk in the corner, with things piled on top, as Asa cleared the bedding from the table.

Aedyn lifted his eyebrow, and Asa answered. "I couldn't leave her inside with weapons and I had to sleep somewhere close by. I'll put everything back before we leave Slaysfold."

The page entered with a keg, and Asa filled three mugs while they waited for the others. While passing the long table, he placed one in front of the prince, then continued to the bedchamber and knocked.

She opened it only a few inches and took the mug, then quickly it closed.

Asa sat across from Aedyn as the other men filed inside.

"We've several things to discuss. Thus far, our friendship is one-sided. I worry it looks as though we have nothing to offer him. Are there things to remedy this?"

Alonso offered. "Prince Aedyn, there's a painter, a fur conjurer, and a man who can grow seeds. Those would be the most notably helpful."

Aedyn's eyebrow arched, but Auren asked. "Elaborate."

Bennet tapped his fingers on the table. "Yer Highness, we could offer things their land can't provide. Perhaps their own vessel or bring different varieties of trees or wood from Aldersward. There are also gold, silver, and other resources."

"All right, keep pondering it while we continue. We'll leave here in a few days. Apex and Amos, expect supplies to start loading tomorrow and continue until we leave. Do you require more men or is eighteen sufficient?"

Apex answered. "Prince Aedyn, it's going to be slower loading this time without a dock."

The captain flattened his hand in front of them. "I'll confer with Abner and Ackley to rig a hoist. Eighteen men should be able to lift a full boat together. If not, we'll require Asa."

"I can come back tomorrow afternoon once I deliver the woman back." Asa offered.

"No, I'd rather you stay at the castle with me. I'll need you there. However, I'll leave the checking of the loads to you. If there's something the men can't handle, then you can accompany them."

"Your Highness, what do you need me for?" Asa crossed his arms over his chest.

"I'll get to it." He changed the subject. "I want to purchase the blackened tablet and this slave. What do I offer?"

"Prince Aedyn, ye mentioned ye would bring a healer from Reinshaven." Bennet answered.

"I did, but we can't use that. He doesn't seem to value those who are sick." He dismissed.

Alonso wondered to the others. "How long will it take to reach Reinshaven then bring back a healer?"

"If or when we find it, or die trying, there are too many variables. What was your suggestion?"

Alonso continued. "Your Highness, we know the king's ability relies on wood. We could leave Alexander here to create a forest."

"That's a tremendous ask. If we never return, then we would leave him here alone for his life's remainder." Aedyn looked at the others.

Auren offered. "Prince Aedyn, then we don't leave him behind. How many trees can he grow in a day or two? Is it one seed at a time or many? Is there a way to expedite the process?"

Alonso answered. "I saw him in the city this morning. He stayed behind. We'll find and put these questions to him."

Aedyn nodded. "We'll use it as our first option. Are there others?"

"Yer Highness, if we can't grow him a forest, then we offer him a vessel filled with trees?" Bennet spoke. "It's reasonable to assume we'll build more vessels. We could build an extra, laden it with trees, and deliver it here on the next voyage."

"It will serve if need arises. I don't want him to know of my communication with Achelle yet." He answered. "So we're hopefully trading a forest for the woman and the tablet. We can give gold to the king for the slave's services last night. He wouldn't expect any of you to have possessions here. Auren, go with Apex. Bring back seventy-five pieces and arrange the other three men in case the king asks. The story will be three men paid fifteen each, and Asa paid thirty." Asa knocked and entered the bedchamber when she answered.

"It's wise. Queen Sofia mentioned her ability lies in gold, so it should make the miserable gluten happy. My words are terrible," Bennet's distaste apparent, "but she allows her husband to treat his mother and slave as he does. I can't stand her."

Asa returned. "Sahana has a scar on the inside of her thigh. Tell the three so they can provide proof if necessary."

Aedyn nodded his approval. "Alonso, find the fur conjurer. I would like forty of the most exotic Aldersward furs created, perhaps the zebra or the leopard, something short with a pattern. I've only seen long furs here. We'll utilise it as payment for Lady Sydni's services."

"Prince Aedyn, Lady Sydni?" Asa grinned, the new discovery amusing. "My, my, didn't figure you for one who'd enjoy mother's play."

The men laughed as Aedyn answered. "I forgot you weren't present last night. It was to appear I used her, but I did not."

Auren grinned. "She was naked, willing, and inviting our attention. If Aedyn allowed me, I would have spent many, *many* hours introducing her to pleasures she could never even imagine."

Asa's mouth gaped. "She was naked?"

"But of course." Auren's expression turned serious. "I made her strip to ensure she carried no weapons. I take these matters quite seriously."

Aedyn's eyes glanced at the men. "Asa, stay. I'll explain what I need. The rest of you, see to these arrangements before we leave." The men shuffled out.

Asa called after them. "Someone find Abraham and bring the woman's clothes."

Day 123
Front Room
Castle
Slaysfold City

The sun was setting, turning the sky an array of purples and oranges as they returned to Slaysfold castle. The men dispersed in different directions, to the front room to wait for the evening meal or the nearby drinking establishment. Aedyn, Asa, and Alonso chose the latter to find Alexander. Unlike in Aldersward, where Aedyn's presence passed nearly unnoticed, here every man turned as he entered.

The prince nodded, and the men returned to their previous activities. It seemed too quiet for a private discussion. "Find him, Alonso. We'll wait outside."

Within minutes, the pair came out, and the group strolled leisurely towards the castle.

Asa questioned him quickly, the distance short. "Can you only grow one seed into a tree or several at a time?"

Alexander responded. "Several, if the seeds are on the ground. Using both hands, probably ten and so."

"How long is one process?" Asa asked, as they passed by several street vendors. He watched the crowd, ensuring no one followed or eavesdropped.

"Depending on height, I'd say no more than five minutes."

Aedyn interjected. "How long would it take to grow a good-sized forest?"

Calculating, the man scratched his head. "Prince Aedyn, I could grow seven thousand trees in a day, maybe more."

"Here's what I would like you to do." The prince instructed him as they reached the wagon piled with furs and each hoisted a bundle onto their shoulder.

With enthusiasm, the Alders had accepted the Slays' culture. As they drank and noisily conversed, women sucked their cocks, rode them, or were screwed without caring who witnessed their acts. Their behaviour beyond anything they would do in an Aldersward brothel.

When Aedyn entered, most stood, or bowed where they were as he continued through to where the king sat forward on his throne.

Aedyn placed the furs at his feet. "King Sumner, may I join you?"

The king nodded and looked at the unfamiliar patterns. "What's this?"

"Payment for my time with your mother. Forgive me if it's not enough. I was unsure how much to bring. These are furs from Aldersward." He knew they were more than what the king would require.

"They'll do."

"Then I chose well. They remind me of her." He smiled.

"You had these on your boat?" The king raised his eyebrow.

"No, I have a man who conjures fur. Would you like more?"

"Perhaps you could repay the supplies I gave you by having him conjure more."

Aedyn instructed Alonso. "Have Alcott create another thousand and different varieties from these." He turned back to the king. "Where would you like them created?"

The king called to a woman, and the two walked away as Asa came forward grinning widely, removing the purse from his belt. "King Sumner, I bring payment for the use of your slave."

Sumner visibly shuddered at the thought as he took the purse from the guard's outstretched hand. "Finally, she earns her keep. When I offer her to my own men, they gag. I'll probably make nothing more from her."

Interested, Asa said. "King Sumner, if you're looking to make more from her, then perhaps I can use her again on a different night."

Aedyn laughed and shook his head. "My friend, I don't believe we'll be here long enough." He regarded the king. "We've enjoyed your hospitality, but I've a duty to my people and mother."

"Yes, I assumed you would leave soon."

"King Sumner, I'd be willing to purchase her if you're interested in selling?" Asa offered, as Lady Sydni gracefully mounted the stairs, sitting at her son's feet.

"Why would I sell her?"

"Sell who?" Lady Sydni asked and received a silent reprimand from her son.

"The slave," Aedyn shrugged. "She diminishes the magnificent beauty of the castle and its occupants. With travel possible now, it may be something you wish to consider."

"My son doesn't have the authority to sell her. She doesn't belong to him. She's mine." Lady Sydni whispered sternly.

"No, Mother. You can't own possessions. You're my slave, just as she is." He sent his boot out and connected with her side. Her eyes focused on Aedyn, begging him not to react. "If I decide she goes, then she goes. I could kill her and let you watch."

Aedyn nodded. "Yes, kill her. Although, wouldn't death end her punishment?"

The king refocused his attention on Asa. "What would you do with her?"

"In our culture, there are buildings full of women you can pay to brutalise—do whatever you wish. You could leave them beaten and bloody from every orifice when you're through. I'd sell her to them, I think." Asa shrugged and walked away.

Lady Sydni knelt and begged. "You've taken so much from me already, please don't take her."

The king grasped her jaw between his fingers and brought her face close to his own as he squeezed. "What have I taken from you, Mother? Your husband? Your throne? Your dignity? Remember, I couldn't have taken those things if your husband hadn't been such a weak, simple coward. I'm the one who provides for you, sees you clothed, sheltered, and fed." Forcefully, he pushed her .backwards, and she tumbled down the four stairs, landing on the flat of her back. "You forget how grateful you should be. Leave us. Leave this room. You will not eat tonight. Perhaps, in the morning you will show me your gratitude." She averted her face, scrambled to her feet, and walked to her grandchildren's room with a smile.

The king continued the conversation with Aedyn. "What would they pay for Sahana?"

"Who is Sahana?" He questioned blankly.

"My slave, what would they pay?"

"Maybe ten-thousand gold," Aedyn knew the king could not fathom what it meant.

"So he would pay me ten-thousand gold? Would he, a guard, have the gold to spare?"

"No, I don't suppose he would offer you ten, perhaps seven, or eight, as he would then need to pay me for her keep on the vessel. He may have a good portion of it saved but I imagine he may ask me to invest in her as well."

The king thought about this. "I don't require gold."

"It's the ramblings of an eccentric man. I wouldn't dwell on it." The prince dismissed the subject.

Day 124
Front Room
Castle
Slaysfold City

Aedyn listened to the king as he recounted the stories of his youth, and out of politeness, he laughed. Then turned to find Alexander approaching them.

He genuflected. "Prince Aedyn, a request, if I may?"

"Speak freely."

"I wonder if I may explore the countryside tomorrow. There are some truly exquisite varieties of plants. I wish to collect seeds so I may grow them in Aldersward."

"I take no issue with your request. However, it's King Sumner's decision and he may not want you traipsing through his kingdom alone." Aedyn sought the king's response.

"Where would you go?" Sumner studied the Alder.

"Sire, I'm particularly interested in berry bushes. Perhaps you could direct me." Alexander took a seed from his pocket and presented it to the king. "I found this one along the shore." He placed it on the dirt floor and covered it with his hand. After seconds, he lifted his hand higher as the seed rooted, then grew before their eyes, until berries formed on its branches. Alexander plucked a handful of dark blueberries, ate one, and divided the remainder between the prince and the king.

The ruler sat forward, examining the bush, and Aedyn feigned ignorance while studying the berry. He rolled one through his fingers. "I've tasted nothing like these before."

The king touched the bush, finding it natural and real. "It's quite an ability."

Alexander observed the king's movements. "It's real. I could leave this bush here and it would go through the natural seasons of its life, living for centuries."

Aedyn shrugged. "There are better abilities, but after a village fire, he can instantly grow the wood they need to rebuild. Otherwise, the villagers would trek to the forest and bring it back. Before you go anywhere, Alexander, let me know where we can find you if need be." He strode away as Sahana hobbled along the table, placing dishes.

Alexander stood in front of the king, answering his questions, while Aedyn and the others appeared to ignore the quiet conversation. The prince knew they had set the trap perfectly and now they waited for the king to take the bait.

Finally, Alexander bowed, then gripped the bush, causing it to age quickly, until it crumbled into a pile of dirt, returning to soil.

Just beyond the mid of night, Aedyn, Auren, and Bennet observed their countrymen's interactions and the musicians' entertainment when Asa stumbled inside, weaving and bumping his way through the crowd. He exaggerated his bow, then dropped onto the bench beside Bennet.

The prince eyed him with disapproval. "Are you drunk?"

Asa bobbed his head and slurred his words. "Prince Aedyn, I am."

Auren demanded, his expression marked with disgust. "What is the meaning of this?"

"She haunts me. I imagine her tightly shackled against the walls in the dark cargo hold—scared, naked, and writhing in pain." Asa turned to eye the prince, who watched him carefully. "Aedyn, I need her there. You —you —you and I are friends. I beg you to prove it. Reward me for my loyalty. You owe me this much."

Bennet made certain the king was listening, then averted his eyes and muttered. "Enough."

Angry, Aedyn rose, towering over him. "You forget yourself. Your familiarity with me, in your drunken state, is appalling. Lead Auren, remove him. He may return when he's sober."

Auren motioned men to help. They hauled Asa to his feet and dragged him outside.

Aedyn turned to the king and apologised, then seated himself.

Bennet dropped his voice so only the prince would hear, "Executed well. Where did they go?"

Aedyn pretended blankness. "I instructed them to drink at the tavern. They'll return later, possibly not playing drunk."

Bennet gazed around the room, noting their men and the corners of the room now shrouded in darkness. "I believe the excitement this kingdom offers nay longer outweighs their desire for sleep."

The king, accompanied by his queen, strolled from the throne's rise. Her nakedness hid her womanhood beneath layers of folded blubber. They flailed, slapping against her wide, bulky thighs as she walked.

Aedyn's group stood, and he placed a kiss on the back of her plump hand as the king spoke. "What are your plans for tomorrow?"

Aedyn returned to his seat. "Sire, I thought to stay here. I'll instruct the supply wagons this way, so I may inspect them before they leave."

The king nodded his approval. "Very well. Between loads, you may join me. I have instructed a gatherer to escort your man at dawn to collect seeds. I don't believe it will take long." The king wrapped his arm around his wife, inviting her closer to the table, then cupped her breast in his hand. "We're going to retire."

Queen Sofia trailed her hand along the prince's arm upward towards his neck as she wet her lips. "Would you care to sample my abilities this evening?"

Aedyn hid his revulsion. "Queen Sofia, I'm plain worn out, between Lady Sydni last night and the travel today. These are things I'm not accustomed to. I regret I would not provide you any satisfaction tonight."

Disappointment clouded the queen's expression, and King Sumner answered, "Perhaps another time, then."

When the royals left, Aedyn and Bennet retreated as far from the throne as possible to find benches to spend the night on.

Day 125
Front Room
Castle
Slaysfold City

The morning sky darkened with clouds, threatening to rain at any moment, as Asa and Aedyn examined the wagon's contents. The prince nodded his approval, sending it into motion as another rolled and replaced it, repeating the process.

King Sumner stood in the castle's doorway, and motioned for the prince to join him, then disappeared inside.

Aedyn instructed Asa, then left to answer the summons.

The room was rather empty as the cooking staff prepared the midday meal. The king sat alone at the table where Aedyn usually ate.

"King Sumner," he bowed deeply before gesturing to the bench across from him.

The king nodded as he poured the prince a drink from the pitcher. "I hope the wagons are to your satisfaction?"

"They are, thank you." He took a drink. The unsweetened, bitter tea was not something he enjoyed.

"I hoped to learn more about your seed grower." The king started, his tone conversational.

"What would you like to know?" He remained straight-faced while secretly applauding his men's performance. The king was sniffing the bait.

"He performed the growth quickly. Is it always so fast?"

"Last night, he only grew one seed. Usually he will grow ten or more at a time and it doesn't take much longer. I've seen him create enough wood for an entire village in a matter of a few hours. Why are you so interested in his ability?"

The king stroked his chin hair. "Have you heard about our protected forest?"

His eyebrows pulled as he frowned. "I can't say I have. Why is it protected?"

"Over time, we've decimated our tree population. I had the remaining trees relocated to a guarded area where no one can cut them down. It was three years ago, and they grow well, but it's a slow process." King Sumner tried to keep his voice casual. "Perhaps you would offer his ability in aid."

The hook set. Aedyn raked his hand through his hair in apparent frustration. "I wish we had discussed your issue earlier in my visit. I could have traded his ability for the supplies instead."

"You're still able. Take back the furs and use our women until you're satisfied we've repaid our debt."

"I cannot take them back. They are of no use to us, and I cannot spare the space in our hold. Your offer of women does sound tempting, but we need to leave too soon to use so many." Aedyn feigned regret.

"Surely there must be something I can offer you?" The king swept his arms encompassing the room.

The trap snapped while he surveyed his surroundings. "Allow me to speak with my council. I, myself, don't know of anything. They may have ideas."

"Yes, go speak to them. Your seed grower should be back in a short while. It should grant you the time you need to discuss it."

Aedyn nodded and smiled as he left. For appearance's sake, he gathered Asa, Auren, and Bennet, then stood where they would be observed, but not heard. The prince chatted about their departure the next evening, ensuring they would relay his order to the other men. All were to report to the boat before nightfall.

Once satisfied, Aedyn returned to where the king sat on his throne.

The ruler eagerly asked. "Did you determine a price?"

Aedyn shook his head as he sat beside him. "No, they had ideas, but I realised they were inappropriate."

"Let's discuss them. Even if you don't, perhaps I will find them agreeable."

"It should come as no surprise that my man wanted you to give us your slave and my emissary wondered about the educational value of the tablet which hangs over your throne. He believes it would add to our library." Aedyn shrugged.

"Would either of them interest you?"

"Your slave is not worth the price of a forest. And the tablet is only a piece of rock. We have our own already." Aedyn sounded disinterested.

"My slave infatuates your man. If you don't take her, you may wind up listening to him for the rest of your journey."

Aedyn nodded, his eyes set seriously. "Perhaps, or I might chain him inside the cargo hold until he stopped."

The king tried to convince him again. "The tablet has no significance here. If your emissary believes there's value, perhaps you should consider it. If you think neither on their own is enough, then take both?"

Aedyn feigned consideration as he rubbed his jaw. "Until we speak to my seed grower, it's neither here nor there. I'm not sure how many trees he could provide you before tomorrow evening. Let's talk to him. If he can create you a forest, then I'll consider them."

Delighted, the king smiled. "I'll have the tablet prepared for our bargain."

"I'll see to the wagons and wait for his return."

Day 126
Anya's Endeavour
Slaysfold's North Sea

The sun set as someone helped an exhausted Alexander onto the vessel. Alonso checked the list, then nodded to Captain Amos, who called out, sending the men into action. Guard Asa brought up the anchor, Azariah stood lookout, and the broad sails opened. Alberto changed the wind's direction, and the rocking craft glided along the coastline.

The emptiness of the observation deck welcomed Aedyn. He braced his palms on the railing, closed his eyes, and savoured the water's sound against the boat. Relief and mist washed over his stiff body and tense muscles as he drew deep, steady breaths, replacing the coiled stress caused by Slaysfold.

The cool night air chilled his skin as he retraced his steps to his quarters, calling his council to follow. He chose the intimate smaller table and its cushioned chairs.

Aedyn sipped the whisky, hoping the burn would warm him. "Did you see to their supervision?"

Auren inhaled the alcohol's oak and vanilla fragrance. "I organised the next three shifts. We're free from duty until tomorrow night."

Asa toasted, "To our success."

Bennet smiled. "Ye all could perform with Aldersward's travelling actors. When Alexander explained he could grow over ten-thousand trees, I thought the king would faint."

"He ensured the tablet was in the next wagon before you could even agree." Asa glanced at it, placed on the cabinet behind the long table. It looked no different from their own in the great hall.

Auren shook his head. "Nothing outdid Lady Sydni's sorrowful cries and fight to reach the slave as we rode out. Even I wanted to turn around and reunite them."

Bennet wiped his mouth. "And Sumner, with his cruel grin while he watched the two struggle, as if he had won something."

Aedyn laughed. "We all did well. It played out precisely as hoped. Where is she?"

"She's below in the cargo hold with Apex. I don't think she will trust us all at once. Right now, Apex and I are enough. I instructed her to use whatever she deems appropriate. She'll settle eventually." Asa refilled his drink, then offered more to the others. "What's our plan now?"

"We'll sail in a triangular path, southwest, east, and then north to home. If we encounter nothing, we should be home before the moon starts another cycle." Aedyn passed his fingers through his hair.

"We know the kingdoms are out here. It's only a matter of time before we locate them." Bennet lifted his whisky.

They drank into the early hours of morning. All needed the break, but none as much as the prince who spent the visit watching his men fornicate and celebrate while he tried to remain diplomatic and balance his own morals.

The others retired, stumbling drunk and singing off key, to seek their bunks. Aedyn lingered in the cushioned chair, his trousers unbuckled, and his unbuttoned tunic tugged loose. He threw his boots aside and propped his feet up, then drained the whisky in his hand.

He thought about his mother lying motionless in her bed, sleeping but safe. His mind quieted, and he drifted.

Day 127
Sleeping Quarters
Anya's Endeavour
Slaysfold's Southwest Sea

A shift changed, then another, but the prince's council in their drunken slumber did not rouse. When Asa silently crawled from his bunk, he dressed and gently closed the door so he would not wake the others.

He stretched his sore muscles as he strode upstairs with his natural goofy grin, greeting those he passed as he crossed to the navigation deck where Amos steered the vessel.

He shielded his eyes and straightened his hair, not stubble like Auren's, but not as long as Aedyn's. Asa was self-conscious of his hair's light brown colour because most had darker browns or blacks.

"Good morning, Captain." He spoke quite loudly in his jovial tone, causing a small ache to vibrate through his temple.

"You're first to be seen of the celebrants from last night. You've all missed the morning meal."

Asa stood next to him, surveying the deck. "It shouldn't be long then before the cook announces midday?"

"A couple of hours," the captain followed his gaze. "She hasn't emerged from the cargo hold."

"Has she eaten?" He abruptly answered his own question. "Never mind, I'll go check."

Asa retraced his steps, stopping in the washroom to bathe before he travelled below. Near the kitchen supplies in the hold's front, Apex and the cook conversed. Apex acknowledged him with a shake of his head and pointed to the back.

Announcing his approach, Asa walked loudly to where she was. A blanket looped over a rope, crudely fashioned into a privacy curtain. "It's Asa."

Her hand appeared, pushing the fabric aside. She settled on the pile of bedding where a lantern burned low. In the depressing surroundings, she offered no greeting.

He regarded her. "It can't be comfortable sleeping on this rocky bottom. Prince Aedyn offered you his room. Won't you accept his kindness?"

"No." Her gaze remained downcast as she shook her head. The few pieces of her hair not tightly wound around the broken circlet swayed.

He crouched, then spoke to her like a small child. "Can you offer anything more than *no*?"

"*No*, thank you?" She looked at him and lifted her eyebrow.

"That's not what I meant. Please explain why you've refused?"

"I'm not ungrateful to your ruler." She shrugged. "But I'm not useful to your people on this boat. I've nothing to offer. What's my role amongst you or in your kingdom? I don't understand why I'm here and what I'm to do." She shook her head. "Before today, I knew my every day. They were set out, and now nothing's the same." Her voice sounded defeated. "No, I'm better forgotten here—less trouble. If I haven't been given a role before we reach Aldersward, then I'll leave and find my way through it."

"I assure you, Prince Aedyn has a plan. However, you cannot see him in your condition. You–"

Sahana interrupted, lifting the lantern to force the shadows from her features. "I'll always be ugly and scarred. This is my condition." She put the lantern down, then reached for her hood. "I'll cloak myself so my appearance does not disgust him."

"No. You need to bathe, eat, and be clean before you meet him. It's considered disrespectful in our culture if you go to him otherwise." He lied. "Have you eaten?"

She nodded her head, averting her eye.

His patience was wearing thin. "I'll not continue to beg for answers. If you require anything, you need to ask. If you're hungry, cold, unhappy, or many other things—tell us." He wiped his face in frustration and his voice grew louder. "No one is going to harm you here, throw you from our vessel, or leave you stranded on your own."

She dragged herself backwards and cowered as his angry voice raised. She covered herself with the cloak, only her head exposed.

Giving up, he ordered. "I'll have a bath prepared for you, after which, if the prince is ready, you'll see him. I'll return shortly."

He discovered men's laughter in the dining hall as he passed and entered.

"Augustus, may we speak?" He waited for no response. He climbed the stairs and walked into the washroom as the man followed him.

"What is it?" Augustus closed the door for privacy.

"We require clothing for the woman—preferably modest, with layers of petticoats and skirts. Can you make these?"

Augustus shrugged. "Without looking at her, it may be difficult to achieve the correct sizing."

"She's Aron's height, so roughly six inches shorter than me, and she's much skinnier than him. If they are too big, maybe she'll fill them out with proper food."

"All right, but I've never attempted to conjure women's clothing. I hope they'll be sufficient."

"Make several pieces. Anything you create will be better than the torn, ragged, and filthy clothes she wears now."

Augustus nodded as he left.

Asa followed, but instead of heading below, he crossed the main deck. He spoke to the page, then knocked on Aedyn's quarters.

At the small table, Auren and Aedyn sipped on steaming tea as he entered. Auren pushed one towards him.

"The spirits have you hurting, too?" Auren teased, observing his sour face.

He shook his head and scowled. "No, it's not the spirits. The woman's not responding well to her new lot in life."

"So naturally, I should try?" Auren moved to rise, but Asa gripped his shoulder and pushed him back down.

"No, Aron's best suited. She will have no choice but to like him."

Aedyn asked. "Is she in pain?"

"Even if she was, she wouldn't confide. I've asked Augustus to conjure her clothes. Could I assume you would have no objections if I temporarily bar a washroom for her to bathe?"

"Go ahead." Aedyn nodded, his head aching from the movement. "Perhaps Aidrik could offer her his aid? I'll speak to him. I intend to get something for this headache, anyway."

"Did you indulge more after we left?" Auren smiled.

"Yes. So much so, Achelle was evicted from my dream."

They chuckled.

Aedyn returned to the previous topic, "Back to the Slay. Does she need anything else?"

"Perhaps you could give her reassurance about her treatment once we get back to Aldersward. She doesn't understand what her life will be now. She wants for a purpose."

"I can reassure her." Aedyn combed his fingers through his hair. "But what purpose can I give her?"

"She can conjure from plant fibres. I know little else about her. She was a house slave." Asa shrugged.

"She could clean and such." Auren offered.

"I have my page."

The men thought as they drank their tea. Auren rubbed his chin, Asa rested his head in his hand, and Aedyn pulled at his bottom lip.

Finally, Aedyn broke the silence, rising from his chair. "I'll talk to Anik. Perhaps for now they can split his duties." The men nodded as Aedyn continued. "Tell our men they're to treat her as any noble woman." He flipped the voyage's journal open to the manifest. "What's her conjuring material?"

"Plants." Asa said before exiting.

Day 127
Cargo Hold
Anya's Endeavour
Slaysfold's Southwest Sea

Asa had not returned. It disappointed her, her behaviour had alienated the one person with whom she had been comfortable. Her shoulders slumped, and she cast her welling eye downward.

"Good morning, Lady Sahana. I'm Emissary Aron. You may call me Aron." The man bowed, reaching for her hand.

She hid it and mumbled. "Good morning, Aron."

"It's a dreadful morning until you experience a lovely woman's face. Perhaps you will show me yours?"

She did not wish to alienate another, so she raised her head but did not smile, foreseeing his offended expression.

Aron grinned as he studied her. "There we go. What a splendid morning indeed. Come now, Prince Aedyn requests your presence once you're ready. A private bath waits for you above. It's customary for me to guide you while we walk. Would that be acceptable?"

Unexplained admiration for him travelled through her. She dragged her hood up, then offered her arm.

He draped it lightly on his, then walked, moving at her mangled pace. He tried to maintain distance from her, allowing her body the space to shift, left and right, caused by her misaligned healed bones.

She climbed the ladder and stairs after him, then he led her to the washroom. Her arm fell when he opened the door and stepped aside.

Aron chose his words carefully, not wishing to frighten her. "The water may be too hot still, but hopefully you'll not wait long. There are clean clothes, a sheet for drying, soap, and a comb on the bench in the corner. Generally, many men use this room together, ensure you lock the door so you'll be undisturbed."

She went inside, turned, and lifted her eyes. "Thank you."

"My pleasure. Is there anything else you require?"

She did not want to spend the voyage isolated by her silence. "It's very warm in here. Would it be much trouble to ask for sweet tea?"

"It would be no trouble at all. I'll knock once I return." Aron smiled and bowed.

She slid the wood in place, barring the door, then sat on the bench and combed through her lowest lying hair. She was forced to hold her hair with one hand while tearing out sizeable knots with the comb in the other. After a short time, her arms burned painfully, caused by their elevated position. Four clumps laid in her lap and she had merely passed through the first length. She was grateful for the pause when a knock sounded.

She fisted the knots in her palm, then hobbled to answer. It was the tea, but it was not Aron. The aged, oddly pale man she had seen at the castle waited, holding out the mug.

Bennet smiled and bent his head. He noted the combed patch and the hair she held in her hand. "Lady Sahana, Aron mentioned ye wanted this." When she accepted it, he gestured to her hand. "I'm Emissary Bennet, on this journey, searching for my family. When my daughter was little, I detangled her hair. Perhaps ye would grant me the practice before I locate her again?"

She chewed on her lower lip and thought about his offer as he waited patiently. If she refused, the task would take many hours and without seeing, it would force her to tear out the knots instead of manipulating them free. She surveyed the old man and knew that, even in her contorted state, she could overpower him. She had to agree.

"Yes, I would appreciate your help. Thank you." She let the door swing wider, backing away.

"Perhaps I could sit on the bench and ye in front?"

She agreed by crumpling to the floor, then watched as he crossed the space and sat behind her. He began pulling her hair through the comb. "Prince Aedyn has requested an audience with ye?"

"Yes. What do you think we'll discuss?" Her voice faltered with nervousness.

Bennet knew the extent. "I imagine he'll want to know how ye're faring below and make sure ye're healthy. Perhaps he'll require our medicine man to examine ye." He used the Slay word for physician so she would understand.

Sahana nibbled her lip as the comb pulled through. "I see. Do you think others will be present?"

"There may be."

"Is he a good ruler?"

He finished detangling the few loose strands, then focused on the hair wrapped in knots around her circlet. "He's only our ruler on this vessel, but aye, I believe he'll one day make a great king. His father has taught him well. Ye need not fear, he's kind. Perhaps ye should drink yer tea while I finish."

Her body relaxed, and they settled into a companionable silence.

The monotonous task allowed him to think about his family's milestones, and they flashed through his mind like paintings. He saw his sons, Blake and Bowan, and their various birthdays. The children gathered around as he relayed the grand stories of long ago. Each time his wife laboured with their children, him at her side, comforting her with whispered words of encouragement. But their wedding night was where his mind lingered.

Thousands cheered as King Baeddan, on a balcony, overlooked the arena floor where the combative knights waited for their contest prizes. The joyous noise was deafening as the winners waved to the crowds until the king held a funnel to his mouth, signalling he would speak.

"The tournament champion will be released from service and have first choice of wife from the Queen's ladies-in-waiting." As he made the announcement, an arena entrance opened and six society women, dressed in the standard white bridal attire, a corset, and sheer ground-length skirt walked out. The women's hair colour, eye colour, and attributes varied, but Bennet's gaze never made it past the second. She was breath-taking, and he instantly lost his heart to her. "Applaud our tournament champion, Sir Bennet of Clayview."

The crowds joyously screamed as Bennet, 490, stepped forward and waved wildly to the crowds. *I'm finally free*, he thought. He smiled widely and walked to the woman, not needing to inspect the rest. He stopped before her and surveyed her sky-blue eyes and thick blonde hair weaved in an elaborate style on top. She was the most stunning woman he had ever witnessed and not much younger than himself. It pleased him. He bowed, and kissed her hand, noting its delicate fingers.

He took her arm in his and slowly walked as the crowds cheered again. "What's yer name?"

She whispered. "Brielle of Crow's Pass."

"A beautiful name—it matches the one who bears it." He smiled, hoping to charm her, his long brown curly hair blowing as they walked. "Ye're fortunate, Brielle."

She lifted her questioning gaze to the tall man about to be her husband as a tear slipped from her eye.

His smile radiated. "Sometimes, I see the future, and in yers, I see many years of happiness while yer husband worships ye."

She averted her face, and he understood her dismay. This was the worst way in their kingdom to be married, by trophy. Most often, parents manoeuvred their children into betrothals, usually within the city of birth. The couples were accustomed to the relationship long before their wedding day. But awarded by prize, they could marry any man from any city and not know the family he came from or his nature.

Together, they reached the place in front of the king.

"Sir Bennet, what will be yer city of residence once ye're released?"

He yelled so the king would hear, "Crow's Pass."

His new bride startled, moving her eyes to search his face, and he winked at her.

"Sir Bennet of Clayview, I release ye from the kingdom's service. We appreciate all ye've sacrificed. I reward ye by giving ye a cottage in Crow's Pass and enter ye into a marriage contract with Brielle of Crow's Pass. Yer new name will be Bennet of Crow's Pass. Report to the division estate for yer housing and employment assignment within fourteen days."

The ceremony was complete as long as they appeared in Crow's Pass within the allotted time period.

The crowds cheered as Bennet held Brielle's arm and whisked her outside and to his horse. He mounted first and hoisted her in front of him. He reined his docile mare through the largely populated streets of Baitsloam City, heading north to escape with his new wife. He listened to her muffled cries, and her body shook with fear against him.

They pushed through a stand of trees and reached a cliff overlooking the sea. The setting would allow them privacy he desired. As his wife sat on the cliff's edge studying the sunset, he built a fire and laid out his bedroll. He removed the food packet from his saddlebags and set it between them as he joined her.

Brielle unravelled the package and laid out the contents. He stopped her hand, then laid his other on the side of her face, lifting her eyes to his. "It wasn't much of a courtship." He smiled widely, trying to calm the fear in her eyes. "The wedding ceremony of our people isn't as romantic as the fairies of Vaguestimber Kingdom. Have ye ever travelled there?"

"Nay," she had never travelled outside of Crow's Pass until a few months before, and now, because of her husband's generosity, she was returning home.

He gathered the bundle, then stood and offered his hand for her to take. "I would prefer we start our marriage as they do. May I show ye?"

She placed her shaking hand in his. "Of course. Ye're my husband. If this is what ye want, I'll obey."

He guided her to where the bedding laid next to the fire and she tried to pull away as he reassured her. "We require the fire's heat to perform our ceremony. Sit."

She obeyed and watched as he stood above her.

His voice softened gently. "They're normally naked, but ye should keep yer clothes on." He discarded his robe, exposing the hard flesh of his muscular stomach and sinewy legs. In his loose drawers, he sat facing her. He lifted her palm and kissed it. "I'll stretch out my legs and ye'll place yers over mine and come closer so we're only inches apart." He positioned himself, and she did the same, placing each of her legs on his thighs. He pulled her closer and her breath washed over his bare chest. He glanced behind her, ensuring nothing remained but bedding in case she chose to lie down.

Returning his eyes to her face, he gently whispered with an encouraging smile. "The most important part is that they stare deep into each other's eyes as much as possible, unless ye want to close them. I'll return my eyes to yers between my words. Are ye comfortable?"

"It seems strange they would wed like this," she quietly offered, unsure of her husband's eccentric behaviour.

"To us, it's strange. It's customary for the groom to start and the bride to join in whenever she's ready." He took her hands and placed them on his shoulders, then leaned forward, his mouth close to her ear. He whispered. "I give ye my word. I will never purposely hurt ye." He placed a warm kiss on her neck, then stared into her eyes. He ran his mouth to the other side. "I promise I will never strike ye."

Another kiss—another stare.

He planted his hands on her calves as he watched her eyes. "Ye will want for nothing in this life." He lightly brushed her lips with his.

His hands rubbed her legs as he roamed his lips along her neck, trailing a blazing path of goose bumps on her flesh, and she shivered as her fingers slightly dug against his hot shoulders. "I promise to show ye more love than ye ever imagined possible." He raised his head to look into her eyes. "Are ye cold?"

She shook her head, and he continued the ceremony. He fitted his mouth more fully onto her neck and kissed her softly. Her head rose skyward willingly, and he drew a line from one side to the other with his mouth, sucking on her earlobe when he found it. "My wife, ye will spend every night in the blackened warmth of our bedchamber and never wonder about the stars, because I will create them for ye."

He pressed one of his palms to her face and used his thumb to pull open her mouth. His lips nibbled at her bottom lip, familiarising her with his. Her lips surrendered, and he opened his mouth, gaping it across hers. His tongue lapped inside her mouth, massaging hers. After a few seconds, he returned his hand to her leg, and both his hands crawled up underneath her skirts to cradle her ass. He pulled her closer, their tongues threading together. Her fingers curved around his neck as he trailed his mouth down her throat to the top of her exposed breasts spilling from her corset.

"Brielle, ye will be my only." He ran one hand over her back, allowing her to use his forearm for support as she leaned her torso backwards. He used the other to loosen the tie restraining her peaked nipples.

She did not know when the tie let go. Her body burned from his mouth's assault. Suddenly, she realised her back was on the soft bedding and his tongue was trailing kisses around her navel. She did not care, her body turned liquid as she enjoyed her husband's attention, and she gave into this ceremony. "Husband, I promise to keep a clean house."

He dragged his legs from under hers and placed his waist between her thighs, allowing him to study her face. "My wife, ye will cling to me in ecstasy whenever I touch ye." His hand lifted her skirt, exposing her skin to the cool night air. He moistened his fingers inside his mouth, then placed them on the erect nub between her legs. Gently, his fingers rotated over it. He felt her wetness slick his fingers. His rod hardened, and he pressed it against her thigh as he captured her lips with his. "My fingers will only bring ye pleasure."

Her body writhed under his touch. A touch she had never experienced before, and she softly purred against his ear. "Husband, yer food will always be ready."

He looked into her eyes as he knelt and kissed a trail down her abdomen. "My tongue will worship every inch of ye." His face skipped over her skirt feverishly. He removed his caressing fingers and locked his wet mouth squarely over her secret folds while his tongue dragged across her clit.

Her back lifted as she attempted to push his head away. The sensation she knew improper was more than she could stand. He ignored her hands and concentrated on making her body surrender to him. He enjoyed her musky smell and sweet taste as she settled back down, allowing the new sensations to rush over her. He darted his tongue inside her, testing the temperature and its wetness as he found the thin maiden barrier. She was ready, and as he continued, he loosened his drawers and pushed them down his hips.

He slid up her body once more, granting time for her breathing to slow. He stared into her blazing, want-filled eyes and whispered softly. "Perfection has never been more beautiful than ye." He kissed her mouth and used his hand to rub his shaft against her sex, allowing her to discover him there.

She felt his hard, smooth flesh probe her clit, but did not have time to think about it as his hand cupped her breast and he circled his soft tongue around her hardened nipple. She ran her fingers through his hair, clutching and pulling his mouth firmer against her. "Husband, ye will not break me."

He advanced slowly as he manoeuvred his thick tip in and out, stretching her skin around it. His teeth grit as he fought to control himself. He slicked two fingers again, then placed them on her nub, waiting for her body to respond as he continued to torture his cock with so little of her. When he heard her laboured moans, he knew it was time. He quickly forced his cock through the thin barrier and held himself still as her teeth bit into his shoulder.

She gasped and struggled beneath him, unsure what had wrenched her from the pleasure, now in pain. Her hands pushed against his solid torso, and when he did not respond, she pummelled his back with her fists. She hissed as tears rolled from her eyes. "What have ye done?"

His expression was apologetic. "I've claimed my exquisite bride. Now I will pay yer body homage with my love."

He rubbed and gently pulled on her clit, then trailed his warm tongue along her neck, causing goose bumps to wake on her flesh. His mouth caressed her earlobe, and he flexed the muscles in his cock to twitch within her as he enjoyed the tight folds surrounding him. He waited for her excitement to return.

Her tears turned to soft moans, and her body began to writhe beneath him. He slowly pulled his wet rod out into the cold of the night, then pushed it back inside her heated sanctuary. He repeated the motion continuously until he was sure her body had accepted him, then forced deeper with each thrust. She moaned pleasurably under his assault, and he felt her hands claw his back to the rhythm his hips created. In agony, he waited for her to climax so he could end his own torture. After a lengthy time, he was rewarded. He felt her muscles clench powerfully against his shaft. His hips bucked rapidly, thrusting his swollen cock harder and faster into her sleek cavern. He grunted his completion as his seed poured deep inside her.

She laid motionless and realised the wetness between her legs as he gently pulled himself out, his member sensitive to the warm surroundings. He let it rest against her thigh as he lifted his upper body, removing his weight, and nuzzled her ear. "Brielle, today when I laid my eyes upon ye, instantly, I loved ye and I will love ye for the rest of my thousand years. Never will I have a single regret."

She trailed her fingers lightly over his back as she caressed his smooth muscles. She turned her head so she could kiss his neck and trailed her tongue to his ear. "Husband, I think ye broke me."

The next morning, Bennet rode back to the city alone and hired a carriage for his sore bride. It would take thirteen days, repeating the Vaguestimber marriage ceremony nightly, to travel three-hundred-and-ninety miles to the Crow's Pass Division, where they registered as man and wife.

Sahana regretted the end when it came an hour later, but once finished, Bennet removed her circlet, freeing it from the knots. Her hair laid softly against her back.

"I'm done." He handed her the comb, then offered her his hand. She accepted, knowing her limbs were aching from the long immobility.

"Thank you for your help." She barred the door after he left.

Asa leaned against the exterior wall, waiting for Bennet. When the door closed, he followed him outside.

Asa slapped Bennet's back in jest. "Did you help her bathe?"

"Nay, she was struggling to comb her hair, and I introduced her to the idea of seeing Aidrik. She still has to bathe and may be awhile." He started across the main deck as Asa went to resume his position in the corridor.

Sahana braided a small portion of hair on each side of her face, then one in the middle and secured all three with a loose thread from the belt meant for her dress, letting the rest of her hair hang freely past her waist. She examined her hair-free circlet. It was in terrible repair with crushed or broken vines and where once beautiful roses adorned it, there were now empty voids. She realised it would have to do as she perched it on her head, then swept the cloak around her back and pulled the hood over her hair.

Asa watched as she opened the door and glanced around, unsure what she should do. He pushed himself away from the wall, attracting her attention. Seeing him, she stepped out. Augustus had conjured a dark purple gown with many petticoats, but she had covered it with a black cloak.

She forgot her shyness, glad he had not abandoned her, and smiled. "Hello, Asa."

He strode toward her, noticing her smile, and offered his hand to her. She did not falter. "Good morning, Lady Sahana of Larkburgh." He kissed, then dropped it.

She laughed at his words. "Why do you call me Lady Sahana of Larkburgh?"

He scratched his head, unsure of what she was asking as he eyed her. "It's your name?"

"No, my name is Sahana. Larkburgh is where I was born."

He realised the cultural gap and offered his arm. "In our culture you are *Lady*, it's a sign of respect and *of Larkburgh* indicates where you are from. Your formal title would be *Sahana of Larkburgh*. No one in our culture should address you any other way unless you invite them to do so and only when others of similar affections are about. It's simpler than saying, *I'm Asa and I come from Lessard*. Understand now?"

"I should not have said *hello Asa*. What should I have called you?"

"I hold no title, so you could have said *hello Guard Asa* or hello *Asa of Lessard*, stating my occupation or my origin, but mostly if we've no titles then it's only first names. When you speak to Prince Aedyn, he would be *Your Highness* or *Prince Aedyn*. Your first words while speaking should be one of those. Other than him, there are our emissaries. You may refer to them by their title, *Emissary*

Aron or Emissary Bennet. For the time being, that's enough. Let me escort you to the prince."

They walked slowly while she limped across the open deck. She averted her face but could still see the men slightly bend and heard a few murmured greetings as she passed. When they arrived at the closed door, the page stood waiting. Asa would normally walk past the boy and go in, but instead he waited.

The boy's sympathetic eyes looked at the scarred woman. "Lady Sahana, how should I announce you?"

"I'm Sahana of Larkburgh." She raised her eyes to the boy's face, wanting to see his disgusted reaction to her words. The page's expression never changed as he nodded, then disappeared inside.

Asa gently smiled his approval.

It took only a moment for the boy to return. "Prince Aedyn will see you now." He held the door open for the pair.

Aedyn looked up from the drawing, then rose. She watched as Asa genuflected and she mimicked him. The prince circled the table and greeted her properly. "Lady Sahana. You're looking well. Would you like us to speak alone? I can ask Asa and my page to leave."

"Prince Aedyn, I'm fine with whatever you wish." She could demand nothing of the prince, and remembered the last time she had questioned a ruler.

"I would like to invite our physician and Emissary Bennet, if you would allow?" Aedyn raised his eyebrow.

"Prince Aedyn, if it's necessary." She answered as Asa took her arm, guiding her farther into the room. He whispered to her, and she removed her cloak, handing it to him. He noticed she was not wearing the gown's belt but said nothing.

Aedyn returned, followed by the others. Bennet greeted her, then relaxed in a cushioned chair next to the prince.

Aidrik kissed her hand and pulled her to stand in the open space between the outside door and the long table so everyone could see her. "I promise I won't hurt you. His Highness has instructed me to help you—should you be in pain or need anything. Stay still, please, while I examine you."

Asa sat with the other two, observing quietly as the physician circled her. He pointed to her feet. They were bare, blistered, and infected. Aidrik pulled the fabric of her clothes tight at the back and put his hands around her waist, his hands easily wrapped around her.

"May I ask your age?"

"Twenty-five."

"Can you see from both eyes?" He examined her face, one eye looking at him while the other skewed in a different direction.

"No, one of them moves wherever it wants."

"Does your nose hurt?" The physician studied her nose, beaten flat against her face, like a snout.

"Only when it's cold."

He looked at the scar, which ran from her eyebrow and seemingly through her eye, then down her cheek. It had healed, but without stitches, the scar was deep and jagged. He examined another scar on the right. It started at her nose's midpoint and ran deeply along the bottom of her cheek in a semi-circle. "Do you have pain anywhere else?"

She cackled, nervously, "Everywhere."

"I can provide you with something for pain, and I'll examine your other wounds in private." The physician turned to Aedyn.

Aedyn released the physician with a wave. "Tomorrow you can make use of my bedchamber. The sooner we discover what advances can be made to correct her issues, the better."

Asa rose to guide her to the fourth cushioned chair and helped her sit as Aedyn spoke. "Lady Sahana, I thought it wise if Emissary Bennet provided you with some cultural lessons, so when we arrive home, you'll be comfortable. You could do these every day after the midday meal on the anchor deck."

"Your Highness, I'll do as you ask."

"I noticed while Aidrik examined you, your feet were bare. We will find you appropriate footwear, but before you can wear them, your feet will need to heal. The physician can look at them when he examines you tomorrow. I also observed how skinny you are. It's unhealthy. When women in our kingdom are unhealthy, they eat at least six times a day. I'll expect this of you while we travel. I will not be responsible for your death."

She nodded her head in compliance.

"As far as clothing, Augustus has provided you more. He has carried it to the cargo hold and if you require anything more, you only need ask. You do not have to wear your circlet if you don't want to. It's your choice. I would prefer you did not cover your face or avert your eyes. You've nothing to be ashamed of. What Sumner did to you, you survived. You should consider it a badge of honour." He turned to Asa. "Perhaps you could pour us some sweet tea. I'm parched, as I imagine Lady Sahana is, since she has barely spoken a word."

She raised her eye from her fidgeting fingers. "Your Highness, I apologise. I did not realise you required my input."

Aedyn looked into her good eye as he sat forward and took her hands in his. "You've many decisions to make for yourself. You can become the Emissary of Slaysfold and live on the castle grounds in the single women's lodgings. Perhaps you would prefer to become a woman who serves one of my sisters or mother and live within the castle. You could decide to do neither and stay at the castle, attending the schoolroom and learning. You could be a shop owner who supplies her own wares for sale. Choose to marry or not. Find your own husband or have my father provide you one. Leave the castle or have your own guards and remain. These are the choices you have. Unless you know what you want, you're not required to answer now. You've much time to think about it on our journey." He let go of her hands and sat back in his chair, resting his head on his propped elbow.

Bewildered, she asked. "Prince Aedyn, how would you counsel me?"

His eyebrows raised, unsure how to answer. "Forgive me, I'm a man. I don't know what women want. You should do what you think will make you happiest. If it doesn't, you can always do something else. Except marriage, in our culture you marry for life."

"As in ours," she spoke freely, then remembered, "Your Highness."

The prince smiled. "Bennet may talk these options through with you while you decide. I must ask you a favour, though?" She nodded, and he continued. "I require your services, cleaning and such. My page is inadequate."

"Prince Aedyn, it would please me to be of service to you."

"May I also ask while in the company of my familiars you drop the *Your Highness* and *Prince Aedyn*? If you must, *Prince* or *Aedyn* will do, but not together. Sometimes, it grates my nerves."

"All right, if you will offer me the same courtesy when in the company of familiars, I'm Sahana."

"Our last item to discuss is your sleeping arrangements. I understand you've made the back of the cargo hold quite comfortable and you're welcome to keep the space for your possessions. However, I can have a bunk assigned to you and a curtain installed in the men's quarters below."

She shook her head and her eye jumped, frightened.

"Understand me before you refuse. I speak the truth when I say no man on this vessel or any who would join us will ever speak ill or, by their actions, cause you harm. We're no longer in Slaysfold. You're a part of Aldersward now. You're welcome here, not a burden. There's no reason for you to hide or scurry. You've as many rights here as any other. You'll not be abused in any way, but if it should happen, know I would have any man killed who behaved against my authority."

Asa interjected. "We could schedule one of a handful to remain and sleep in the bunk above her to guarantee her safety."

"I agree. Aedyn deferred, "Sahana?"

She nodded. For all he had given her, she would attempt to trust his words. If she continued to feel unsafe, she would ask him to revisit this.

She spent the rest of the day exploring and staying away from the men's sleeping quarters. Aron came and offered himself to sleep above her if she wanted to turn in on the next change. She agreed and followed him down. No one stared at her strangely, made lude comments, or abused her as she walked through the room to where they had curtained the last bunk.

Aron pulled back the fabric for her. "Augustus conjured a nightgown for you. It's there. You should change once you climb in and close the curtain." She nodded as he used the edge to vault himself onto the top bunk.

It took several minutes for her to figure out how to change in the cramped environment, but she finally managed it and laid listening to the sounds around her. The men breathed heavily, snored, and turned about in their bunks. She smiled, secure in the knowledge Aron was above her. She closed her eyes and fell asleep.

Day 129
Anchor Deck
Anya's Endeavour
Slaysfold's Southwest Sea

Sahana gazed over the main deck. The men laboured, chatted, and joked amongst themselves, but most importantly, they ignored her above. Bennet, carrying a basket, climbed the stairs to the anchor deck. She backed away from the railing, preparing to greet him.

"Good afternoon, Emissary Bennet." She tipped her head, eyeing the aged man.

He dropped the basket and held her hand, chastely kissing the back. "Lady Sahana, ye may call me Bennet as I believe we'll become good friends." He lifted the basket onto the anchor wheel. "I've brought ye another meal, some bread with honey and sweet tea."

A tiny laugh trilled from her. "You may call me Sahana. Before any of you know it, I'll be fat."

"Let's begin. Yer greeting was excellent except ye should offer me yer hand and wait to speak until I take it. It's a formal greeting between a man and a woman in Aldersward. As ye know none, this will be the greeting ye use most. If I were a noble woman, ye would tip yer head and let her speak first. If she had the same social rank, and ye were familiar, then it would be right for ye to grasp her here." His hand cupped her upper arm. He grabbed hers and placed it on his. "Ye would simply pull closer together and kiss the air beside one cheek." He demonstrated. "If ye're unknown, whether man or woman, a simple *good day* or *morning* will do. I see by yer expression, ye're confused. We will practise further and ye'll know it well before we reach Aldersward."

"Thank you." She spoke without hesitation, then struggled to sit, putting her back against the anchor.

He joined her, placing the basket between them. "What would ye like to learn about?"

She removed the bread, tearing a piece, then chewed it. "Perhaps you can tell me about Aldersward castle."

"An excellent place to start," he smiled his approval. "Aldersward castle differs greatly from Slaysfold castle, it's made of stone. It's much wider and four squared, three floors tall. Inside the castle's main level, there's a kitchen and a hall used to hold audiences or meals and dance space for a few hundred. In addition, there's a study, library, schoolroom, armoury, and offices for the king's advisors, physicians, and scholars. I held one before we left where I would study, plan, or meet other officials."

"It sounds much grander than our castle. How many people are in Aldersward Kingdom?"

"Eighty-thousand or so," he continued. "On the second floor, ye'll find chambers. Each includes two rooms. A through-room used for entertaining or study and the second is a bedchamber. These chambers are for the royal family, visiting noblemen and their families, or esteemed guests. I suspect they'll offer ye one upon yer arrival."

Sahana shrugged. "I'm none of those things."

He patted her hand. "Ye're the first foreigner in almost three-hundred years and, therefore, extremely important. It will mean a great deal to King Adahy and the entire kingdom. On the third floor, the rooms are smaller and used for high-ranking officials or the unwed, like dames, knights, or advisors. If ye choose that path, then ye could live there."

Sahana chewed on her lower lip. "Why are the most important people housed on the second floor and not the third? Would it not make more sense to have them higher in case someone attacked?"

He smiled, pleased she was paying attention and participating. "Most naturally, it would make sense. But what if an attack came from the sky? They built it three-thousand years ago when there were wars among our kingdoms—a time when flying men and creatures were plausible enemies. Another reason is the hidden escape routes from the second floor directly outside, if ever required. Under the castle is a royal crypt. The castle's centre has footbridges and is open to the sky. Around its sides are baileys. Where there's room for training grounds, gardens, an outdoor cookery with stone ovens and spits, stables, different outbuildings, and staff living-quarters. Then surrounding those is a high thick wall, where men stand to guard the perimeter and a steep ditch filled with sharp and dangerous obstacles preventing anyone from scaling the wall. The south bailey holds the only entrance and a massive grating covers it so nay one can enter without permission. All together it makes an impressive structure."

"It sounds so." *And cold and scary and confusing*, she thought. "Prince Aedyn has given me many choices for my future. I don't understand what they all mean. Would you explain them?"

He noticed the empty basket and realised they talked for much longer than he expected. "Of course, I'll tell ye of the people and their roles tomorrow. I don't want ye to tire of my teachings." He collected the basket. "Sahana, it has been my pleasure."

Day 131
Anchor Deck
Anya's Endeavour
Slaysfold's Southwest Sea

From where Azariah stood, in the night's cloud-shrouded blackness, it was disturbingly quiet. The water gently lapped against the craft while the men's voices murmured, remembering the previous storm they encountered.

They all anticipated quick orders, but hoped he would lead them to land before it struck.

Seemingly from nowhere, tiny yellow dots of heat appeared in the water deep below, but as they rose to the surface, they grew larger, and orange.

"Asa, Auren," he called below.

Everyone's attention turned at the loud noise in the almost silent night. On the navigation deck, the captain conversed with Sahana and Asa. "Would you wait here while I find out what he wants?" As she nodded, he strode away with a backwards glance. "I'll return shortly."

Auren arrived first. "What's happening?"

"There's an enormous creature alongside us and more, uncountable, in our path."

"Whales?" Auren stared into the dark murky water as Asa joined them.

"No, their shape is unusual, like nothing I've seen. It's as long and broad as our boat." Azariah described while they peered over the railings. "Its limbs look like a magpie's tail feathers in flight, and the fanned digits are long to the centre and get shorter as they near the body. There are six, three on each side. The longest limb on each side is thicker at the base and its individual digits are moving independently. The others decrease in size. Its body resembles a large leech with the head of a bee without antennas. It's magnificent."

His hair blew in the wind, and Asa attempted to right it. "What are they doing?"

"Some float while others swim out of our path."

Auren ordered. "Let's bring in the two smaller sails. We can't risk striking one at the speed we're travelling and run into a storm at the same time. There's no telling what damage, they could do together."

The men hurried to carry out Asa's instructions as he yelled.

Day 132
Schoolroom

Castle's Ground Level
Near Aldersward City

The mischievous teenager bounced from one foot to the other and as he travelled to the podium, a hush fell over the students. He grinned widely with enthusiasm, then spoke. "Mine will not be some mundane, fall asleep report. So pay attention!" He slammed his hand onto the stand, and the children startled or chuckled.

"You may assume you know much about Baitsloam from our Emissary Bennet, but I believe his teaching omitted imperative facts. On the night of Amelia's birthday in 2631, Bennet was here!" His voice accused. "He enjoyed our hospitality while waiting to receive a new ability from our king." He ripped the page from his notebook, crushed it, and threw it onto the floor. "His beloved king, King–" he checked the text, "King Baeddan relaxed in his own kingdom, in his castle with his new queen, Queen Valencia."

He stepped from behind the podium and shielded his mouth from the teacher. "We cannot condemn him. If I were over five-hundred-years-old and had a bride only two-hundred, I know where I would be." The scholar cleared his throat, and the boy stepped behind the stand as the boys laughed and the girls reddened. His chin trembled and his eyes welled. "There were no children." He paused for effect, then chuckled. "But we cannot blame a lack of trying."

"The Baits lived longer than any race, almost one-thousand years and they matured painfully slow. Picture this. Close your eyes." The boy pointed to the children, and they complied. "Imagine her as I paint you a picture. Queen Valencia would look no older than Princess Achelle. She would have flawless skin as pale as the white dove. Imagine her differently with wheat, cinnamon, or fire coloured hair. Her eyes would be blue, grey, or green. She dressed in thin layers of sheer skirts and there would be no top—NO TOP! Only a corset stretched tightly to cover her hips, stomach, and her breasts' rosy peaks." The children opened their eyes as he pumped his fist in the air. "At least this is how I imagine her, late at night in my room when–"

"Do tell, Master Abran, what did the men wear?" The teacher interrupted, and order returned.

He reviewed his notes, ripped the page out, balled it, and tossed it away. He shrugged. "They dressed like Emissary Bennet."

Abran loudly whispered, leaning towards where his peers sat and they copied his antics to listen. "Baitsloam was the fourth largest kingdom, and its shape resembled a whale jumping out of the sea. It even had an eye for a lake, called Braun. On the whale's tail was Baitsloam's castle, it was the westernmost point of all the kingdoms. Rock, gravel, and jutting formations densely covered the land..."

"Now," at his abrupt loudness, the children jumped. "The Baits communicated with animals, but perhaps you didn't know it depended on specific types. Our own Emissary Bennet could communicate with birds, and if a Bait was in Vaguestimber, they had no powers because they wouldn't function there."

"The kingdom fell into the sea in 2631, a tragic loss to all men, and unfortunately, they sent us a male emissary instead of a female." He raised his hand high, and the boys cheered as he bowed deeply. He ran and fell to his knees, sliding to where the girls sat. "Forgive me, Your Highness," he took Achelle's hand, kissed it, then tried to grab the other girls' hands to do the same, but they pulled away, shrieking with laughter.

"Are you quite finished?" The scholar scolded.

He rose and lifted his arms wide, encompassing the room, "The End!"

Abran retraced his steps, bending to collect the crumpled pages. He flattened, then placed them back into the notebook. His hand ran over the cover and when he opened it, the torn and balled pages were immaculate and attached once more. He boasted to the scholar. "That's how you educate a class."

The scholar shook his head. "I cannot wait to see how our children turn out if you're their educator."

Day 132
Anchor Deck
Anya's Endeavour
Slaysfold's Southwest Sea

The clouds dissipated as the sun rose. Sahana stood on the anchor deck, while the men along the craft's main railings examined the exquisite creatures in awe. Their smooth bodies were morning sky-blue with a navy stripe along their back, shaped like a leech, narrowing to a long dark tail. The limbs were contrasts of blue, darkening as the almost-feathers started. The colour faded to white along the length, then darkened to a blue-black point at each end.

Sahana marvelled as they swam out of the vessel's path, flipping over as they dived below or swam away. The next shift of men came on deck, and they repeated sentiments others had already made. The creatures were too numerous and as far as her eye could see. She slowly hobbled from one side to the other, examining them.

She blinked, unsure of what she saw with only one eye. With no way to be sure, she called to the deck below, "Asa."

Instantly, she regretted it when the men below turned. She cringed and backed out of sight.

The three men on the navigation deck looked up, ensuring she was safe.

"Where is he?" Aedyn asked Auren and Abner.

"Below. Should I see to her?" Auren stepped around the large wheel.

"No, we're done here. I'll go, she doesn't know you." Aedyn strode away and Auren followed behind him.

"Well, introduce me, for instances like these."

Abruptly, Aedyn turned around, stopping Auren in his tracks, then narrowed his eyes. "You will behave."

"Of course," he nodded and attempted to continue forward. Aedyn blocked him, putting his hand on his chest.

"It wasn't a question." He let him go, strode across the deck and upstairs, where Sahana sat against the anchor. "Are you all right?" He examined her as he approached.

"Oh, yes. I'm fine. I called for Asa." She lifted her brow as she rose, then genuflected.

"He's below." Aedyn turned as Auren joined them. "Lady Sahana of Larkburgh, may I introduce, my lead guard and friend, Auren of Maidstone."

Auren came forward, grasped her fingers, and bowed deeply as he kissed her hand. He straightened and winked at her. "Lady Sahana. It's a pleasure to meet you."

Her expression gaped, and she took a step back as Aedyn playfully pushed him away, then he turned to face her. "I apologise for him. He has a vulnerability for women. He can't help but get into trouble when they're around. How may we serve you?"

She smiled lightly at his words of reassurance. "I thought I saw something, but I might be mistaken. I confess my eyesight is not perfect, and you may have come for no reason."

"Not for no reason, my lady." Auren shook his head as he anchored his hand to the railing, preventing himself from wandering closer to her while he tilted his head and smiled. "It's a pleasant break from listening to Aedyn drone on about tasks. So, was it a particular sea monster you were looking at?"

She shook her head. "No, I think there may be land behind you."

Auren spun around, and Aedyn joined him.

Aedyn cupped his hands to his mouth and yelled, "Land!" He pointed in the direction, then offered her his hand. "I'll help you down. We'll turn, and it may be difficult for you to hold on."

She took his hand, trusting him while he carefully walked with her to his quarters.

As the temperature rose, the sea creatures disappeared, diving deep into the endless depths and they were forgotten as the boat came alive with action. Abner handled the wheel while he called out orders, and Alberto stood by to change the wind's direction once the manoeuvre was completed.

Aedyn sat at the long table as Sahana filled mugs with sweet tea, ensuring one for the page and herself, then sat at the smaller table. Auren knocked after retrieving Asa, Bennet, Aron, and Captain Amos. They bowed as they entered and sat.

"Let's dispense with the pleasantries." Aedyn began. "Where have we landed, Bennet?"

The emissary's pulse had quickened when Auren had informed them, and his expression gleamed with excitement. "It makes sense this would be Reinshaven or Baitsloam."

Asa scratched his head. "How so?"

Bennet opened a sketchpad on his lap. "I have been examining the position of Slaysfold from Aldersward. Baitsloam was directly west and Reinshaven was directly east." He showed the group. "I only had one variable, so it cannot be conclusive, and it's closer than I calculated."

Auren grinned. "I'm glad you were wrong about the distance. How will we know?"

"I suggest we travel around the kingdom. If there's forest, then it's Reinshaven. If not, it's Baitsloam."

Aron laughed. "We know which you prefer."

Aedyn lifted his eyebrow. "Are we lacking any educational information?"

Bennet's eyes laughed. "Sexually, my people are like yers. Men have mistresses, and the odd lonely woman might have lovers, but not publicly. We have brothels. Maybe the only difference is our women's clothes. They dress much like yers, except their clothes are tighter, often sleeveless, and their skirts are sheer."

Aedyn nodded. "Your plan sounds good. This time we circle until we're ready to go to land."

Sahana listened, observing to ensure their refreshments never emptied. It annoyed her when one refilled their mugs, which could not possibly be empty. It was her job otherwise, why was she here.

"I'll release you now, Captain, so you can communicate our route. Bennet, you might as well stand watch on the anchor deck. Report once you discover which kingdom this is and take Aron with you. You can teach him about Baitsloam and Reinshaven, so he's prepared." Aedyn waited for the men to leave before he spoke again. "Sahana."

Lost in thought, she startled at the mention of her name.

"Have my page send a message to Apex to release three kegs and have the page bring one here with your two afternoon meals. I believe you've missed one, and another is upon us. We'll spend the day in relaxed celebration. You will join us."

Sahana limped outside, unsure what to make of the day ahead. It was true she lived among these men for six days, but never while drink influenced them, and she knew what drink could do.

The three rose and watched her leave, noting her slightly more confident and less introverted attitude. They knew she would require years to get over the emotional scars caused by her residency in Slaysfold castle. They each took a temper-quenching drink and seated themselves as they individually weighed their own feelings on the subject.

Day 132
Prince Aedyn's Quarters
Anya's Endeavour
Slaysfold's Southwest Sea

The pile of sticks Aedyn had purchased and given to Sahana were nearly gone as they taught her a game with five small wooden cubes they called dice. She admitted she was enjoying the evening as the men laughed, joked, and included her. She recalled another occasion when she had happily rolled in the snow with her siblings, playing childishly. Her eye welled at the sudden memory, and she blinked and caged the emotion.

"Lady Sahana, you're most lucky we don't wager drinks tonight, or you would already be fast asleep." Auren's smile widened as Asa handed her the dice.

She shook and poured them onto the table. "I believe you each owe me a stick." She laughed lightly as the men grumbled. The page entered, and she rose to speak with him. The men stood as she left, then immediately sat.

After a whispered exchange, she returned, and the men stood again. Sahana was curious. "Why do you stand every time I move?"

Aedyn's brow quirked as he smiled, "You haven't given us permission not to."

Sahana's eye widened. "You need permission? You're royalty. Surely you don't require my permission."

The men glanced at each other, and Auren covered his smirk with his drink. Educating her would be a long, gruelling process.

Aedyn explained further. "It's a respectful gesture to maintain eye level and I do require an excuse, just as I have waved you from genuflecting or calling me by my title when we're with familiars."

"I give you all permission not to stand. How long does it last?" Sahana sat.

Asa responded. "It's lost after this event. You would have to give your permission again the next time we meet. And, you should never give permission to us when someone you're unfamiliar with is present."

She laughed, a pretty laugh they had not heard yet. "Do you mean to say whenever a woman stands, you *all* stand as well? What if there's numerous women and they stand one after another? Do you spend the entire night bobbing up and down?"

Auren grinned widely. "Now you realise our pain and yes, many times it's like that, but sometimes, we don't stand. If she isn't directly seated with us, we don't. Most times women leave together, so we need to stand only once. If the woman's important or royal, we stand regardless where they sit."

"I still don't understand the reasoning." Sahana threw a stick into Asa's pile as she collected the dice.

Asa ran his hand over his head, mildly embarrassed by the discussion in her presence. "It's lost on you because of where you've come from. If you stand, and I'm seated, with what are my eyes level?" The friends erupted in laughter as the page entered with food.

Day 132
Anchor Deck
Anya's Endeavour
Baitsloam's North Shore

The page cleared the dishes as Aron, without ceremony, rushed inside. "It's Baitsloam. Come quickly."

Bennet's mind spun when all thought left him and he sank to his knees, his strength leaving his body. Uncontrollable sobs blurred his vision and snot trailed from his nose, both drenching his front as he rocked back and forth. Forlorn, anguished sounds ripped from his throat.

The three men followed Aron to the anchor deck, unprepared for what they would find.

The men froze as loud, sorrowful cries escaped Bennet's mouth. He retched under the weight of his emotions, emptying his stomach contents. Sahana heard it as she hobbled up the stairs and recognised them immediately. They were the same noises she had made when she found out Sumner had slaughtered her family. The sour acidic smell of vomit reached her as she pushed through the dumbfounded men, and as fast as her body would let her, she collapsed, then cradled him in her arms.

Sahana continued to comfort him as his bodily fluids let go and covered her. She lifted her chin higher to escape the odour and noted the immobile men. The necessity of action outweighed her fears.

"Asa, drop the anchor. The rest of you leave us." She ordered and, stunned by her assertiveness, they watched her. "Do you believe he would want you to see him like this? I can take care of him."

Aedyn nodded his approval and the other men left, happy to withdraw from the situation.

While Asa prepared himself, the prince came forward. "I won't stay, but I'll help you hold him until the anchor has dragged. I'm uncertain if something goes amiss you alone could prevent either of you from going overboard."

She nodded.

Aedyn knelt beside her and wrapped his arms around Bennet's chest, which laid in her lap.

Asa signalled as he freed the wheel and rushed to where they huddled together, then he trapped Aedyn and Sahana tightly in his legs. He flung his arm backwards, capturing the railing as the anchor hit, then grabbed bottom and rocked the boat powerfully forward and back. None acted until the boat had nearly stopped. They unravelled themselves and found Bennet dazed.

"Now what?" Asa asked her.

"Have a tub prepared. Bring Aidrik and the man who can make things clean. Asa, you'll need to carry him."

Aedyn nodded. "If he hasn't roused after he's clean, we'll place him inside my bedchamber."

Day 132
Bennet's Family Home
Crow's Pass City
Baitsloam Kingdom

It was too quiet in the small five-room cottage. The only disruption, the sound of wood as it snapped and popped in the hearth's fire. The smell of freshly baked biscuits and boiled potatoes lingered, kept in the oven, waiting for her children to return.

Brielle stared into the flames as she caressed the pendant on the chain around her neck, rocking rhythmically in her chair as time turned back and she remembered the day Bennet gave it to her.

In the very late afternoon, the sun beamed through the bedchamber window. Exhausted, she attempted to roll over, but another stomach cramp washed over her and blood gushed between her legs. Her hand ensured the wadded cloth had not dislodged from its position. Her hand came away red. Uncaring, she wiped it on the blankets.

The fence's gate swung shut, then Bennet's boots thudded on the stairs. Any second, he would come.

His heart sank with instant concern as he surveyed the dark sitting room and kitchen where neither hearth burned. Neither she or the aroma of warm food welcomed him, and that was unlike her.

Bennet called as he walked through and opened the bedchamber door, optimism in his voice. "Brielle? Wife? Does our child punish ye with sickness again?" His eyes fastened on the bloodstained bed. He knelt and brushed the hair, stuck in her tears, away from her face.

Her eyes were pinched shut as silent tears ran across her nose and onto the pillow.

A lump rose in his throat, and his voice was hoarse with emotion. "Is our baby leaving ye?"

She nodded as another fierce cramp forced her to breathe through her mouth.

He witnessed her pained expression and placed his head beside hers as he rubbed her shoulder. "It will pass soon, my love."

When her face relaxed and the pain subsided, he kissed her hand, then left to heat water. He filled four large pots, knowing he would need them to remove the blood from his wife, their child, and their bedding. As the physician had instructed when she expelled her previous pregnancies, he poured sweet tea and laced it heavily with sugar; something about replenishing her fluids.

He examined her face as he placed the tea down. "How long?"

She turned onto her back as silent tears continued, "Shortly after ye left this morning. It won't be long now."

He whispered words of encouragement as her face reddened and her breathing laboured. He went to her feet, lifted the soaked bedding, and removed the wadded rag.

She knew the tiny head crowned, but she could not bring herself to push, wanting to hang onto her pregnancy and her denial for as long as possible.

Brielle whispered quietly. "I've failed ye, again."

At the pain-stricken sound of her voice, his eyes welled. He turned to the trunk and removed a small blanket she had quilted for their child's bed fifteen years earlier. The same blanket they used each time she bore another lifeless infant. He realised he should reassure her, but did not want to burden her with his grief.

He positioned himself so he could receive their child, then waited, letting his wife decide when she was ready to let go. The sun was setting when Brielle pushed the blue, partially unformed baby from her body.

Lovingly, he swaddled their tiny, beautiful daughter and set her in her mother's arms, then left to get the water. He would cleanse his wife before he buried their tiny dream next to the others in the yard.

Bennet slowly crawled into bed next to her, not wanting to wake her if she slept. He placed his hand on her back and rubbed, offering her comfort. She tried to shrug his hand away, but he would not allow it. He gripped her shoulder firmly and pulled her onto her back, knowing she was awake. He cupped her face in his palm and pulled it towards him.

"Wife, open yer eyes so ye may see and know I speak the truth." He whispered and ran his hand lightly over her shoulder. He noted her anguished expression, and a tear slipped from his eye, feeling guilty because he could not take the suffering from her.

When Brielle opened her swollen eyes, he continued. "In twenty years, ye've never failed me. Ye've given us four beautiful children who only we enjoy. I've always believed, and still do, yer body doesn't fail but continues to gift me the opportunity to worship ye without interruption. When yer body tires of me, *then* it will grant us many children." He gently kissed her forehead. "We cannot live in our sorrow. Tonight we'll grieve, but come morning, we'll be thankful for everything we have." Bennet pulled a small box from behind him. "Twenty years ago tomorrow, Jezabet gave me ye."

She burst into tears and reached for him. They forgot the box as he wrapped her in his arms and sheltered her body, cradling her while she cried through the night.

The cottage door burst open, ripping Brielle from her memory.
Byunca, their daughter, rushed. "Ye must come see what's happening."

Day 132
Washroom
Anya's Endeavour
Baitsloam's North Shore

A light knock sounded and Sahana, wrapped in a bath sheet, answered it. She attempted to hand the clothing through the cracked door before it swung open, but failed.

"You undressed in his presence?" Asa asked, curiously.

Amazed at his stupidity, she hobbled in front of Bennet, who soaked in the tub, and waved her hand in his face. "He doesn't see me and I stood behind him." She returned to the door. "Bring me the clothes clean, before he realises what has happened."

She bolted the entrance, then washed Bennet's beard, chest, and stomach so he would not know the shame. She pushed him forward and wiped his back and between his buttocks, clearing away the brown mess, then circled to clean his genitals.

A knock sounded again. This time Aidrik, "How is he?"

"Alive. I'm not a medicine man. Is there another tub? This one is filthy." She used her elbow to push the frazzled fallen hair away from her eye.

"There is. I'll have the men bring it. The cook was continuing to boil water."

"Asa can transfer him when he returns with our clothing." She pushed the door closed, but Aidrik stopped it.

"What you do for him is kind, considering your apprehensions and misgivings about people."

"I've known all-consuming grief. He's not a man—a threat. I look at him and see unmeasurable suffering. It would be wrong to turn away and leave him to battle it on his own." She barred the door and stood with her back against it, unsure what to do next.

Day 132
Division House
Crow's Pass City
Baitsloam Kingdom

Heir to the throne, Prince Bryce, the Duke of Crow's Pass, assembled three-hundred of their military, and they waited outside for his orders, as he and his commander listened to the report.

"The craft has *Aldersward Kingdom* scrolled on it."

"How many?" The prince stroked his wrinkled chin and his clouded old eyes viewed the man.

"We're unsure, but there are boats fastened to its sides, enough for thirty men to unload. It's alone, a half mile from shore. If we had a bird, we could send it over."

The commander's muscles tightened as he swung his arm, practising. "Ye're a scout. Do ye know anyone who still has a bird?" The man did not respond. "I didn't think so. There could be other boats following. We should send messengers to the surrounding cities. King Baeddan was right. The Alders survived."

"Are our countrymen gathering at the shore?"

"Aye, they've set a few fires to see, but they stand a couple hundred feet back."

Prince Bryce sat forward, his arms on his knees. "Use them. Have yer men blend in, surround the Alders, and capture them when they come ashore. They betrayed the peace of the nine kingdoms after twenty-five-hundred years. They'll suffer for every person in every kingdom who died. We'll take their boat and wipe their race from Speranza."

Day 132
Washroom
Anya's Endeavour
Baitsloam's North Shore

First, the sensation of warmth enveloped Bennet's body, then the sound of water splashing and finally his mind returned. He dropped his head, recognising a tub, and watched as a hand washed his shoulder.

Sahana, fully clothed, smiled, and circled so he could see her. "You've roused?"

"What happened?" Bennet, suddenly aware he wore nothing, modestly covered himself with his hands.

She chuckled. "You've nothing I haven't seen before. You collapsed. The medicine man thought a bath would help, and I offered to stay with you."

"Physician," he offered as she raised her eyes, stopping her hand from washing his chest. "We don't call them medicine men. We refer to them as physicians."

"Your physician suggested." She corrected.

He batted her hand away. "I'm fine now."

"Are you? Why did you collapse?" She examined him, waiting for his answer.

"I saw the church." He said the words, their meaning took a moment to sink in. "I've seen my home—my village!" His voice grew louder as he repeated the phrase, agitated, and uncoordinated. He seized the bath sheet, wrapped himself, and ran barefoot from the room.

Asa came inside. "Let me help you up." He did and chuckled. "Does he realise he isn't wearing anything?"

She smiled. "I don't think he cares. Imagine your family lost for over two-hundred years, the grief, and the guilt over your survival. Only to have them presented within reachable distance, alive."

He quietly answered. "They may not be alive."

"They live to be one-thousand years old. The odds are, at least one has survived."

Bennet walked across the main deck to the prince's quarters, gathering followers behind him. When he wrenched the door uninvited, the prince looked up from his journal entry.

Aedyn had expected him, but assumed his mentor would wear clothes.

"I'm leaving." His tone challenged the prince to deny him as he crossed his arms over his chest.

"Of course, together we'll make plans to go ashore, soon." He eyed his friend with a shrug.

"I'm going now." His thumb toyed with the wedding band on his finger. His eyes narrowed and met Aedyn's raised eyebrow.

"Naked?" His eyes roved over the old man's body.

Bennet looked down, then returned his gaze to Aedyn, his tone slightly depleted. "Well, nay. I'll dress, but then I'm leaving at once. I will not sit around waiting to make plans."

"We've left the area where the sea creatures were, and we're a half mile from shore. Can I offer you a boat with some men or do you prefer to swim?" He asked, trying to provoke Bennet into seeing the error of his request.

The Bait's voice was serious. "I would prefer a boat but if ye don't offer it, I'll jump overboard and go alone."

"I'm offering, and take Auren's group as yours will go on night duty shortly." The prince's eyes sought Auren. "Make your men ready and have Angelo's lower a couple boats. Be ready in..." He waited for the old man's response.

"Fifteen minutes." Bennet strode out.

Day 132
North Shore
Crow's Pass City, Baitsloam

Darkness fell, and three enormous fires burned along the shoreline about seventy feet from the water. They generated warmth for the milling people, a visible barrier and focal point the enemy would have trouble seeing past. Baits stood back another half the distance to ensure the enemy did not set upon them. The smell of smoke and sounds of excitement lingered as everyone murmured. The opportunity for vengeance had arrived.

As the two boats grew nearer, Bennet could see his countrymen gathered to welcome them. When his boat reached the dock, he jumped off and ran towards the crowd, many more than he expected. The Alders followed ten paces behind while one man stayed behind to secure the boats.

Bennet was in line with the fires and, while his eyes searched the faces, he cupped his hands around his mouth, "Brielle?"

Auren halted the men when Bennet stopped. The people's movements sounded, but only outlines appeared, caused by the firelight's brightness. As the Baits closed around them, Auren realised they were moving as one and too slowly. No one offered themselves in welcome, and there were no flowing skirts in those who came forward.

A woman's crying screams answered and, as Bennet recognised it, he rushed in the direction.

Brielle fought the crowd, tears blinded her vision. Someone held her in place, and she clawed, kicked, and landed blows, desperate to reach her husband. Her blue skirts tore and her corset came loose as her children aided in freeing her.

Bennet focused on finding her.

She surged through the man-made wall and raced toward him with open arms.

He opened his own and took a step towards her. He drank in the beautiful sight of his wife as chaos broke out.

Auren's first instinct was to run, but the Baits surrounded them. No escape existed. The ambush was complete in its design. Even with their powers, resistance would be foolish when the score was ten to a few hundred. He raised his hand, signalling his men to surrender.

Bait men grabbed Bennet's body and hauled him backward, but he reached over their shoulders, frantic with desperation to grasp her outstretched hand only inches from his, shouting her name.

As the couple's fingertips met, someone yanked Brielle by her white hair and threw her to the ground.

Their momentary contact was severed.

The hand Auren held high was grabbed and wrapped behind his back, forcing him violently to the sand. Unable to move, he watched as a man came forward, smashing the butt of his sword into Bennet's head.

His body collapsed.

Helplessly, Lead Auren witnessed his unwilling men fall.

From his position on the dock, Ace turned at the commotion as three men rushed toward him. He dove into the water and propelled his body deeper, stripping away his clothing.

Arrows rained from above and through the water as he finished disrobing and vanished, undetectable. He surfaced at the northernmost point of the beach. His breathing laboured as he gulped air and crawled onto the sand to determine what became of his comrades.

Day 132
Anya's Endeavour
Baitsloam's North Shore

Bennet's group, on night duty, listened to the commotion. But between the dark night and the distance, it was impossible to see. Aron fled the deck to retrieve the prince. Ignoring the guards, his fisted hands pounded on the bedchamber door.

Aedyn's eyes flew open as he startled and sat upright. Now, wide-awake, the urgency of the beating reached him as he strode to the door and flung it open.

"What's happened?" He tied his boots as he grabbed his vest.

"We heard struggling noises, shouting, and angry voices from shore, then suddenly nothing. Quiet."

The prince raced onto the main deck to examine the shore as one of Bennet's men offered. "They've extinguished the fires. There were three."

Waves of guilt consumed Aedyn as his jaw tightened, and his fists clenched. "Wake Asa and Azariah now! I want to know what's happening."

Day 132
North Shore
Crow's Pass City, Baitsloam

The commander ordered the area cleared, then instructed his men to extinguish the fires as they bound, gagged, and stripped the prisoners of their weapons.

Three men came forward.

"One made it into the water."

Auren fleetingly wondered who. His hope rose and instantly plummeted when the man continued.

"He never resurfaced. We believe we killed him with our arrows."

"Go back and stay there! Stay there until ye witness his blood, his body washes ashore, or ye find him alive. If ye haven't found him by morning, we'll assume he escaped."

Nearby, Ace wandered unseen among them, but avoided where they could accidentally bump into him. Although invisible, he still had mass.

The youngest, perhaps 280 years old, offered. "Won't the blue dragons take care of him?"

The commander stepped to his face and spat, "Nay, ye idiot! Now they feed at the bottom and even if he dove to that depth, he would have to touch one, then they would deliver their stinging venom. Go!" He turned to those holding the Alders. "March yer prisoners back to Crow's Pass."

Ace had little choice; either follow the captured and risk being trapped ashore or swim back and hope the creatures didn't surface until he reached the craft.

He begrudged his decision, wading into the water a distance from where the three watched.

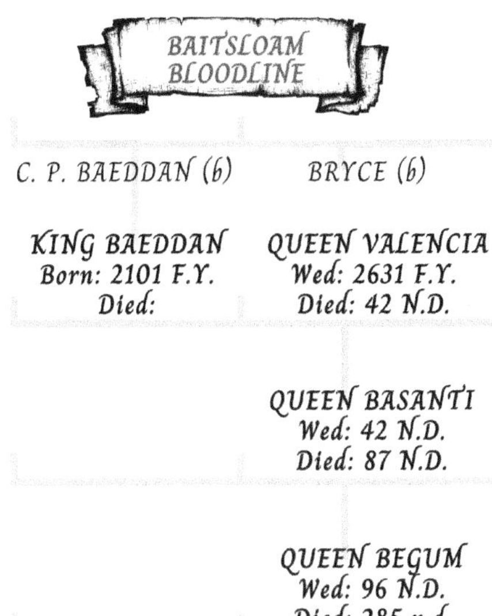

Above shows the Bait kings' bloodline. C. P. means Crowned Prince, future king. (b)/(g) indicates gender at birth.

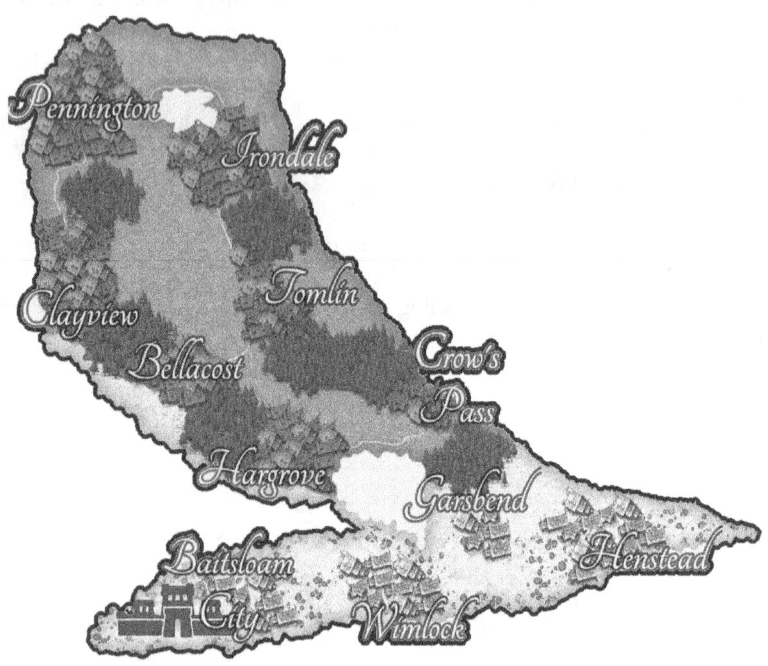

Baitsloam (285 N.D.)

Most notable features above include:
Crow's Pass (middle north)
Baitsloam City (southwest)

Character index page 405.

Day 132
Anya's Endeavour
Baitsloam's North Shore

Prince Aedyn and Asa stood beside Azariah on the observation deck.
"There are three on the dock and more lining the woods along the shore."
Asa squinted through the darkness. "Can you see our men?"
"No, there's nothing else. Should I stay here?"
Aedyn nodded. "Yes. We'll wait. If we don't go ashore by tomorrow evening and nothing's wrong, then Bennet or Auren will come to see why."
Aedyn followed Asa down the ladder and onto the navigation deck. The entire crew stood on the main deck, murmuring and waiting. His hand raised and their voices stopped.
He spoke clearly but tried to keep his voice from carrying. He averted his eyes, unable to face them directly. "We must assume the Baits met our men with malice, and they are either dead or captured. Once we know more, we will act accordingly. Everyone stays below except our guards, who must stay vigilant, quiet, and use bows to kill any animals which approach. The Baits communicate with them; giving away any information may jeopardise those on shore. If you must attend my quarters, then move quickly. Asa, Alonso, and Aron, on me."
Aedyn stormed to his chambers, ripped open the door and, with unmasked violence, swiped the table's contents onto the floor. He grabbed the last mug, hurling it at the wall. It exploded into pieces before falling. He started to turn but stopped, noticing Sahana curled and trembling in the corner. Her hands clamped over her ears as the others came in.
He groaned as he fought to control his guilt, anger, and shame. He shook his head and approached her, going to his knees to soothe her.

"I apologise. I lost my temper and threw a tantrum like a child. It would make me feel less ashamed if you took a chair." He offered his hand, and she took it, still shaking. He helped her stand while the other men collected the thrown items, ignoring the prince's interaction.

Aedyn turned from her, his voice commanding. "Dispense with the pleasantries. Who'd we lose?"

Alonso cleared his throat. "Besides Auren and Bennet, we lost Apex."

He lifted his brow. "Our food conjurer?"

"Yes. As well as a musician, a flaming man, an invisible man, an ink manipulator, a multi-linguist, and Anders, the water breather."

Aedyn sat, and the others joined him. "Aron, how many people can you manipulate at once?"

His shoulders stooped. "One, I require eye contact."

"Alonso, I need to check the complete abilities list."

Alonso downcast his eyes, "Bennet carried it, but I'll recreate it."

Asa interrupted. "I believe he copied it inside the voyage's journal."

The outside door swung open, but no one entered as wet footprints appeared and a puddle formed on the floor.

An unfamiliar voice spoke into the room. "Prince Aedyn." Those present were used to such happenings in Aldersward, but the woman jumped. "There's news. May I have a blanket?"

She had witnessed nothing so astounding. Mesmerised, she limped toward the sound, grabbing a throw from a chair as she passed and held the blanket out.

Fingers tugged. She let go and stepped back when it flung through the air.

It wrapped the form, then secured under his armpit. Ace's corporeal body developed before them.

Aedyn eyed him. "Do we need to fetch Aidrik for you?"

He shook his head. "Your Highness. No, I'm cold but unhurt. They ambushed us. There were hundreds of Baits. Auren surrendered, and our men were bound, gagged, and taken into Crow's Pass."

Aedyn sat back, digesting his words, "Injuries?"

"Bennet was unconscious when I arrived. I didn't see how it happened."

"Where were you?" Asa's temper boiled, thinking the man a coward.

Ace's voice defensively rose. "I had trouble tying off the boat. Bennet jumped out as it landed at the dock and our men followed. When the ruckus started, I turned, and three men advanced towards me. I dove into the sea, and used my power to evade them. I returned to the shore and listened. There–"

Aron offered. "Asa, he could do nothing by himself."

"There's more," Ace's teeth chattered from the exercise of the naked swim and the chill of the air. "The sea creatures, the Baits, called them dragons. They sting their victims. One man assumed they would kill me, but another said the dragons were feeding on the bottom. I only had two choices. I made the best one."

"Someone fill him a tub. Get warm and dressed, then return here. We may need more information." Aedyn glanced over the room, his voice so low they strained to hear. "I should never have allowed them to leave."

Asa put his hand on his friend's shoulder. "This isn't your fault."

The prince shrugged hard, shaking Asa's hand from him, then pounded his fist on the table. "Like hell it's not! I let my relationship with Bennet override my better judgement. I knew they shouldn't have gone and yet, instead of one, I sent nine into an ambush."

Aron offered. "We all knew what could happen when we began this journey. We came willingly, and Bennet was determined. He and the others would want you to focus on freeing them now."

"I've just left my dream-walk with Achelle. She once mentioned she thought that the girl from Reinshaven sought her out. I will try to reach her."

Aron, lost in thought, muttered. "I wonder how many Baits there are?"

Aedyn's eyes narrowed. "We learnt when the Unification War ended, few remained. They were no match for the other kingdoms' powers. Their population depleted to under three-thousand. If we assume an even gender split and we use Bennet's three children as an average. They could be over two million now."

Asa crossed his arms, worry compounding his fear. "If we returned to Slaysfold, they only have ten-thousand and those aren't all warriors. We would never have the numbers to beat the Baits. Home can't be an option, it's too far, and the others could be dead."

Aedyn rose. "You're right. Whatever we do, it must be strategic."

Day 132
Division Compound
Crow's Pass City, Baitsloam

The Alders, strung together, were marched through the torch-lit streets as deafening crowds lined any stairwell, rooftop, or balcony. They shouted, spit, and threw food. Auren could see Bennet's lifeless body carried by two men. He focused on containing his anger and scrutinised their surroundings. If any hope for escape presented itself, the information would be invaluable.

"Not as brave here, are ye?" A lanky Bait man stepped forward and spit in Auren's face.

The Alders filled with rage and pulled at the thick restraints wound from their hands to their elbows, wanting to defend their leader, but Auren shook his head, stopping their struggle.

Pointing, children merrily chanted, "We're going to hang the olive monsters!"

"This was too easy, ye cowards."

Someone tossed a pail of urine and excrement over them.

"We're going to kill yer families." Another vehemently called.

"I'll enjoy watching ye swing."

Cackling laughs followed every phrase.

They left the commoners behind as wood rubbing against stone rang out. A massive gate lifted above their heads, and the military men stomped through with their prisoners in tow.

When the gate fell behind them, many Baits dispersed, leaving about fifty to escort the captives. Auren counted the paces as they came to a stone structure. He noted the other buildings and landmarks, then what the building looked like as they pushed him inside.

They planted the Alders, faces first, against a hard stone wall and a wooden door swung outwards, then they tossed Bennet onto the floor.

"Inside." The first man was hauled forward by his tunic, and the others had no choice but to follow.

The door slammed shut on the windowless dark and musty room. The sound vibrating through to their souls. It felt very final as the lock loudly snapped into place.

In the blackness, Auren's men fought against the coarse restraints.

What looked like a candle flickered to life between them as Adrian pointed his finger and held it to the slick-coated binds holding them together. As his flame dried the piss, excrement, and other juices, the stench was putrid. Finally, the rope caught fire and burned.

He rushed to Auren, but his solidly tied binds had no give, and as the other men offered their hands with the same outcome, they sat on the cold, damp floor. The ropes were too tight to burn without injury.

Auren waited motionless for the last one to be checked and an internal battle waged between his vanity, self-pity, and honour.

I can't do this. Wasn't the wolf attack enough? He stretched out his shaking hands in front of him.

Adrian's shoulders slumped in defeat as he turned to face their leader.

Women will never let you touch them again. What would Anya think if she knew you stood by and did nothing?

Understanding their leader's request, Adrian shook his head and escaped backward until his frame was trapped by the wall.

I can't lose a limb. Can't it be someone else's turn to do the right thing? Do this. Auren strode towards him, throwing his bound hands on the man's shoulder.

Animated with fear, Adrian shook his head.

Can your body take any more pain? Everyone will pity you, just as when you were a child. You could be their only hope. The leader pinned the man's eyes with his own.

The pain from it—you'll never want to touch another woman. Sweat built from fear on Auren's skin, but he nodded, persuading the gifted man.

Your men are counting on you. I'll be worthless to our kingdom—to Aedyn. Adrian lowered his hands, holding them farther from his own body.

Isn't your day to day hard enough already? You'll die from this. You'll be a helpless invalid. Auren dragged his hands down, then jumped up and down a few times, forcing adrenalin to rush through his body.

You coward! You're weak. It's no wonder your parents gave you away. He took a deep breath.

You're nothing but a quitter. You could be Aedyn's only hope. He lifted his wrists into the flame.

The sweet smell of burning flesh carried through the small interior. The men focused on the sacrifice their leader made as they listened to the sizzling meat and his muffled cries of pain.

From somewhere in the darkness, someone hurled himself onto the pair—contact and flame broken.

Auren struggled where he fell, his restraints making it impossible to sit. Adrian rolled on his side and relit his finger.

Bennet towered over them, shaking his head as he pulled at his own ropes. Blood seeped from the friction on his wrists, making the restraints slippery. He sat between them, lifted his heel to his wrists, and used his boot to force the rope over one of his thumbs, freeing his hand. He pulled his gag free, then removed Auren's as he surveyed the blistered and broken flesh of his hands.

The old man's voice seethed with anger. "Jordan and Jezabet, what were ye thinking?"

"Getting us out of here. Are you okay?"

Bennet nodded. "Better than ye, I don't know if I can get ye untied without causing ye pain."

"Untie another first. Return to me when the rest are free."

Day 132
Division Compound
Crow's Pass City, Baitsloam

On a gentle knoll, carpeted in grass, stood the stone, two-storey division house. The main floor held a kitchen, a study, and a hall. Black-stained wood etched with delicate gold designs framed the ceilings, beautifully contrasting the tinged beige walls. In the warmer season, they removed the thick, heavy wood and straw meant to insulate the structure from the biting cold so natural light could stream through the windows' iron grating. A cumbersome cushioned chair dominated the hall, where nobility sat in the king's absence.

Prince Bryce, 780, listened as his commander recounted their enemy's capture and grinned. "Well done. I've sent word to King Baeddan. He'll send messengers to the other cities, then attend here. I expect more than a million will congregate to celebrate our victory. We'll use Bailor's fields on the city's outskirts."

Astonished, the commander voiced his apprehension. "It'll devastate those crops. Our population could starve through the snowy season."

"We've nay alternative. There's nay where else to hold those numbers. The residents will have to rely more heavily on the sea, rats, or horses."

The commander could not believe Bryce's words. Overpopulation drove all animals and birds to extinction, except for the protected horses and the diseased rats no one would eat. "It's against Baeddan's rule to kill horses."

The prince waved his hand, uncaring. "Then the king will need to supply us otherwise afterwards. Take two-hundred men and inform Bailor, then construct a hanging platform and a balcony for our king and his guests. Secure the area in case the remaining Alders attempt a rescue."

"Ye'll only have a few hundred to defend the city should the Alders attempt one here. Is this wise?"

The prince shrugged. "We have seventy thousand subjects here, not soldiers. But, if threatened, I'm certain they'll defend themselves. Besides, it would be futile for the Alders to attack unless forced. They've nay understanding of our numbers and would come in blind. Where is Bennet's wife?"

"We escorted her and her children home. I have guards posted there. I don't think she would betray Baitsloam. It was purely shock which drove her to seek her husband. And her children, they believe as society does."

Prince Bryce nodded. "Check our prisoners and arrange yer travel. I expect ye gone at first light."

Day 132
Prince Aedyn's Bedchamber
Anya's Endeavour
Baitsloam's North Shore

For several hours, Aedyn attempted to sleep, but nightmarish visions of his men being mutilated, his mother weeping over Auren's death, and his father's disappointment loomed over him. Each time his eyes closed, he tried to clear his mind, but the thoughts crept in.

He raised the sweet tea to his lips, coating his dry throat, then laid back and recited in his mind. *Sleep, sleep, sleep, sleep, slee...*

When he spotted Azalea nude on the Endeavour, he knew he was sleeping. He erased her and thought of his sister, hoping this would bring her. She appeared, and he rushed to explain but realised it was not her, only an image formed by his imagination. With a curse, he banished her. Repeatedly, he paced and called her name, growing louder as frustration took hold. Hopelessness washed over him as he sat. He held his head in his hands as desperate tears escaped. He yelled for guidance, begging for someone or something to intervene.

"Aedyn?" the door heaved open, crashing against the wall. Achelle rushed inside, knelt down, and embraced him.

Discouraged by the image, he flung her arms aside. "Go away."

He concentrated on washing her from his dream, but she remained and he glared.

"I'm truly here." She followed his sceptical eyes, travelling over her. "Imagine me in my favourite gown." She allowed him a minute as he tried. "You can't. What's happened?"

He wiped his face with his arm as he stood and embraced her. "I need your help."

Day 132
Bennet's Family Home
Crow's Pass City, Baitsloam

Beside the sitting room's blazing hearth, Brielle rocked in the chair her husband gave her before their first baby was born. Her once blonde hair had turned white, and ageing wrinkles marred her face and hands. Losing her husband so many years before had faded her vibrant blue eyes with sorrow.

Fleetingly, in the moment when she had touched his hand, the pain washed away. But it returned excruciatingly raw.

Blake, their second child, sat nearby, brooding over the evening's events as Byunca, his younger sister, prepared tea in the adjoining room.

The exterior door burst wide. Two soldiers manhandled and pushed her oldest, Bowan, inside. They slammed the door as he stumbled to the floor.

Brielle's eyes scanned her son's angry expression as he stood, righting his clothes. "Where's yer father?"

"They're holding him with the Alders. I asked for an audience with Prince Bryce, but he refused. Someone said our father's an Alder sympathiser and will hang with them."

Blake accepted a mug from his sister. "Father can't be a sympathiser. If anything, they've brainwashed him. It'll take time for him to readjust."

An icy chill numbed her, and Brielle sipped from the hot liquid, welcoming its comfort. "Yer father was one of the king's most trusted aides because he was intelligent. There's nay way the Alders could brainwash him. Magic—aye, but not brainwashing. Ye don't remember yer father as I do. I'm devoted to none above him, including Baeddan."

Byunca sat at her mother's feet. "What will we do?"

"Ye'll do nothing. I'll offer to glean intelligence from yer father about the Alders. Perhaps Bryce will allow it. I warn ye, I'm prepared to stand with my husband."

Hatred for the Alders coursed through his body as Bowan shook his head. "If our father's a sympathiser and yer motivation exposes ye, then they'll brand ye a conspirator and hang ye for treason. Yer children—we'll suffer for yer acts."

Brielle stroked her daughter's hair. "I cannot expect ye to understand my devotion or how loyal ye should be to yer father. He loved us. Our relationship was one of fairy tales. I've never loved another, and he's my world. Whatever he should ask, I will do. Ye're old enough to choose for yerselves, but know if ye choose against yer father, I'll have nay choice except to turn my back on ye."

"Mother–" Bowan's voice was angry and sharp.

"Nay. This isn't a debate." Brielle stood, waving her hand. "Ye make yer choice." Disinterested in arguments, she retired to her room and left them to make their decisions.

Day 132
Division Compound
Crow's Pass City, Baitsloam

Auren's wrists were difficult, and he chose to be gagged while four men struggled with his bindings as he heaved and groaned through the pain. As one wrist loosened, the door's tiny slider opened, and he straightened to face it.

The commander sneered through the window. "We realised ye would break free of yer bindings, but they delivered ye here, nonetheless."

Auren placed his face against the opening. "I demand to see your king. Do you know who we are?"

Remembering their abilities, the commander backed away. "Aye, ye're Alders and ye've nay rights here."

"Tell me, why are you so filled with hate? What have we done?"

"Yer people caused the quake which destroyed the other kingdoms. Ye betrayed us all—after nearly three-thousand years of peace. We barely escaped, but, unfortunately for ye, we did."

Bennet pushed aside Auren. "I'm not an Alder. I'm Emissary Bennet, King Baeddan's Emissary—*yer ruler's* emissary. I assure ye the Alder race did not cause it. Why would they appear on yer shore if they had?"

"Arrogance or stupidity, it doesn't matter. And ye, *Emissary Bennet...*" He spat his name with disgust, "ye travel with them. They've conditioned ye into believing their lies. Ye will swing, too. An example of what we do to traitors."

Angrily, Auren pushed Bennet aside. "There are others with abilities you can't fathom. They'll come for us."

"If they do, we'll kill them. They're expendable. We don't need to hang ye all. It's symbolic more than anything." With a short blade, the commander cleaned his fingernails. "How fortunate ye'll outlive the others." He shut the slider.

Auren turned into the black room, lit solely by Adrian's finger, like a single candle. "It's preposterous that they assume we had anything to do with the event."

The emissary shrugged. "Their belief is not so far-fetched. Three races were capable: Alders, Davens, or Clines. I imagine they assume it was the Alders since yers was the ruling and most powerful kingdom."

Joining the others around the light, Auren sat down. "We must make them realise they're mistaken."

Bennet squatted against a wall, away from them. "How? They've had this theory for over two-hundred years. It's impossible, since they don't intend to communicate with us."

Auren turned to the others. "Let's figure this out. What can we use?"

"I was out cold. What happened to my wife? Where are we?"

Auren answered. "I didn't see what happened to her. We travelled along a winding street until we reached wooden gates with a sign above. It read *Crow's Pass Division*. We are just over two-thousand paces east of it. Do you recognise it?"

"Aye, I know the place, but the grounds have probably changed. I don't recognise this building." He scratched his head. "I wonder if I'll meet King Baeddan before they hang us. Perhaps I can make him see reason."

"You heard, you're no better than us. We can't rely on your relationship. Ace slipped back into the water. What's his ability?"

"Invisibility. Maybe they didn't kill him. If they give us poor rations or we kill a rat, I can conjure pork and beans, but without them, I'm worthless." Apex said.

"How long does the flame last, Adrian? Can you make it bigger and burn the door down?"

"A few minutes, but with prolonged use, my energy wanes and I must break to replenish it. It can be bigger, utilising all of my fingers, but burn down the door? No, not without us inhaling the smoke and perhaps suffocating."

Auren scooted backwards, resting beside Bennet. "We must wait for an opportunity or Aedyn."

Day 132
Division Compound
Crow's Pass City, Baitsloam

"Auren," Achelle called as she invaded his dream.

Tunic-less, his body glistened as he stood in the east bailey. His damp trousers rested below his navel, and the wolf's tattooed head on his chest looked ready to attack. Heavily, he exhaled and wiped the perspiration from his stubbly hair.

She frowned as she walked towards him. "I'm here to help you."

"Aedyn sent you? Does he know they captured us?" He tasted the salt on his lips.

"Yes, he knows. Where are you? Are you hurt? Is everyone okay? Perhaps you can show me the room you're in, or the building. How far are you from shore? What happened?"

Overwhelmed, he raised his hand, stopping her. "I'll tell you. Sit."

Day 132
Belinda's Chambers
Castle's Second Floor
Baitsloam City

Though temperatures rose during the days, the cooler nights continued, requiring a fire in the hearth of the timeworn, elegantly furnished chamber. Fur-bare leather showed from the hides covering the stone floors. The curtains, cushions, and bedding were frayed. Little could be done to alleviate the decaying state.

"Should I braid yer hair?" Beatrice, Belinda's maid, passed the comb effortlessly through the fiery red length.

"Aye," disheartened, Belinda watched her adoptive mother, who had raised her since her parents' death during an epidemic, fix her hair in the mirror.

Beatrice wished to lift the woman's spirits. "Perhaps the king will realise ye're more trouble than ye're worth and send ye packing. He can wed the other one—Bethnee."

The sitting one raised her pale white chin and parted her dark red lips. "Ye know it won't happen. She's too old, over six-hundred. She'll never produce a successor."

The elderly woman harrumphed, twisting the hair as she seethed. "Three wives later, chances are nay one is going to provide him with an heir. The stupid fool doesn't realise it's his fault he has nay children? Instead, he blames his wives and murders them."

"Ow," the younger's head wrenched backwards. "Ye're hurting me."

"I apologise." She eased her grip, but continued the braid. "Once he announces yer marriage, we should seek someone to impregnate ye. I'd offer my husband, but we've nay children. Surely, one of us is to blame, and we can't risk ye remaining barren for too long."

"Bret's like my father," Belinda shook her head in dismay.

"Yer beauty, I'm certain, could persuade another who's willing."

"I don't believe anyone would dare. Wouldn't his previous wives have tried if it were viable?"

"Maybe ye can persuade him to allow ye home for a limited time before yer wedding, then we could find someone there?"

"It's too risky. What if someone discovered our motives and reported it?" She rose. "He would execute us—ye, me, and Bret. Nay, it won't serve." Belinda replied as a knock sounded from the hallway. She clutched her robe and walked into the sitting room to identify the caller at this late hour.

Bret, Belinda's personal guard, stood inside. She nodded, then ensured her robe was securely fastened as the door swung wide, allowing her to observe the man standing in the hall.

As he bowed, she recognised the king's secretary. "Lady Belinda, King Baeddan sends a message." She tilted her head, and he continued. "Ye will accompany him to Crow's Pass tomorrow. Please see ye're packed and ready before the midday meal. Once there, ye'll remain at yer family home. Utilise this opportunity to close the house and collect yer belongings."

It was unlike the aged ruler, 815, to travel for any reason.

Belinda's neck prickled, and distrust fluttered in her abdomen. "What is the purpose of our trip?"

With worry, Beatrice gripped the young woman's arm.

"Alders have landed there."

The older woman fanned herself and Belinda stilled, silently astonished.

Bret said. "Ye must be mistaken?"

"I assure ye, I'm not. We leave in the morning." The messenger withdrew, and Bret closed the door.

"Praise Jezabet," Beatrice beamed. "He's heard our prayers."

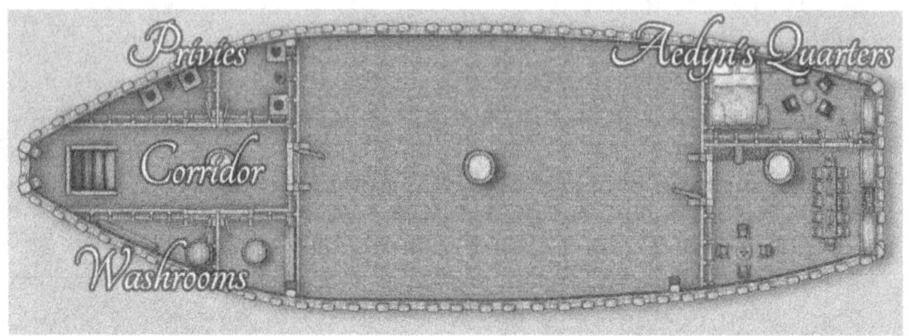

Day 133
Prince Aedyn's Quarters
Anya's Endeavour
Baitsloam's North Shore

Aedyn and Asa studied the list of men's abilities and the map he drew from one Achelle showed him.

"I feel pretty positive about our options."

The prince nodded. "We'll send Ace in first, then create a diversion using Ametheus and Alvin. While the Baits rescue their families from the rubble, Anderson will free our men. Unlike last time, we know they're hostile and we will proceed with the same attitude. No one matters except our men. The Baits created this, and any mass casualty will be their fault. We leave behind those like Arturo, Alberto, and Aidrik in the event anything goes awry. Augustus's men and yours will remain on the craft."

"No, I can't allow you to go while I stay behind. Auren would never forgive me."

"He will understand. Someone must remain. The Endeavour needs a leader." Aedyn responded.

Asa shrugged. "You should stay."

"No, their capture is my fault. I can't expect anyone to endanger himself while I stay behind. I'm to blame and I'll make it right. We wait until dark. Azariah can point out any holes in the defences lining the shores. Most of the Baits should be asleep. We'll use grease and flour to mask our skin. Hopefully, it will be suitable to confuse any wildlife. Angelo's and Aron's groups will go in somewhere over here." Aedyn pointed east, closer to the division compound.

"My group will wait here." His finger slid west. "In case they need a path cleared for their escape."

Day 133
Division Compound
Crow's Pass City, Baitsloam

Brielle waited outside the guard station as the sun rose to its midday position. During regular times, the division was open to the public. The hub where subjects registered for lodgings, employment assignments, or had issues resolved, but now the closed gate and guards barred the entrance. She had whispered her request while everyone shuffled away. But still interested, they strained to listen. Brielle felt ostracised, on display, and alone as hushed voices murmured and hands gestured towards her.

"Lady Brielle?" From a crude door, a man called loudly then motioned for her to follow.

He led her through the grounds, and she noted the minimalistic activity.

"Ye'll meet with Prince Bryce." He informed her as they entered the official house.

The prince observed the milling men from his seat as she entered, genuflected, then waited for acknowledgement. He scanned her impeccable appearance, noting the swollen eyes and tight, thin lips. "My man informs me ye offer to aid us in gaining information from the prisoners. I realise yer husband's appearance shocked ye, but, with time to dwell, what is yer current position?"

A tear welled, and she brushed it aside. "Yer Highness, I appreciate yer understanding. I cry now, only because I know we've lost him. Once I returned home, I examined my beliefs and the consequences of his sympathies." She shook her head, her voice cold. "I realise Bennet is a sympathiser, and he must pay for his betrayal. I wish only to serve our kingdom. I believe myself invaluable and will easily gain answers by questioning him."

His eyes scrutinised her, uncertain of her loyalties. "Ye know, Lady Brielle, if I allow ye to *aid* us, and ye're found to betray our kingdom, ye will not be the only one to suffer. I warn ye, yer children could also pay a price for the traitorous acts of their parent."

She shrugged. "It was my duty to offer. If ye can't trust me, I understand. I apologise for wasting yer time." She bowed and turned to leave.

The guards acted, blocking her escape.

As she turned to face him, Prince Bryce wagged his age-gnarled finger. "It's not that I don't want yer help. I want to ensure my position is clear."

In acceptance, she bowed her head. "I understand and am well aware of the consequences should I choose betrayal."

"Good. Ye can meet in the common yard. I'll have men accompany ye."

Day 133
Division Compound
Crow's Pass City, Baitsloam

Darkness shrouded their damp, chilly prison. Some slept curled on the floor or against walls and others murmured, their remaining senses heightened. They heard people roam around the building's exterior and muffled voices. The odour of unkempt bodies and sour breath lingered.

The harsh squeak of unoiled tracks vibrated as the door's small window slid open, casting a stream of light inside. A man peered through and counted the prisoners; three missing. "All of ye, against the back."

Auren used the wall to rise. Painfully, his cramped, inactive muscles protested.

The guard counted. "Bennet, step out."

Auren blocked his movement. "Where are you taking him?"

"To meet his wife."

The two conversed in a whisper, then the leader dropped his arm, and Bennet stepped forward. The door cracked enough for him to leave, but the guard remained observing from the small window, ensuring no one else moved. In case the Alders attempted an escape, several guards stood outside. But they did not.

Usually smoothed back, Bennet's blood-caked hair was a frizzy mess. A guard spat on his shoulder as they led him outside.

After the long, dark hours, the daylight hurt Bennet's eyes. When they adjusted, he scanned his surroundings. Not much had changed. The stables, the armoury, the dining hall, and the cookhouse remained. Additional lodgings had reduced the common area from ten acres to two.

Prompting him forward, a guard shoved his shoulder, and he stumbled, struggling to regain his balance. Scattered over the grass were crude benches and tables—all empty except for one.

He froze, recognising the angle of her chin and the shape of her body. Automatically, she drew him to where she waited. The guards pushed him opposite her, anchoring his hands to the bench.

She raised her chin to examine his face, but the sun's angle prevented it.

Overtaken by emotion, his vision blurred and his voice rasped, "Brielle."

He noted the white mixed with her long blonde hair, the age lines, and her swollen, tired blue eyes.

Her fingers caressed the necklace at her throat as a single tear slipped down her cheek. "Husband, ye've been gone a long time." She raised her voice in accusation and glanced at the retreating guards.

Bennet's eyes fixated on hers. She lifted her hand to her face and dragged it through her hair. She shook her head ever so slightly, only for him to witness.

"I'm sorry. I'm so sorry." Desperately, he tried to explain. "If I had realised—if I would have imagined—I would have given anything to get here, back to ye sooner."

She fixed a frigid expression and shook her head. "I know." She darted her glance. The guards stood far enough back that, if they whispered, no one would hear. "I'm here to spy and collect information. We, ye, our family, are in a perilous situation. Our people believe the Alders caused the quake, and ye're a sympathiser. After so many years of teachings, our children believe it. We are in danger."

Understanding the consequences his family faced, he nodded. "I realise how our kingdom came to their conclusion, but I assure ye, darling Brielle, it's incorrect. I was in Aldersward. By marriage, races mixed throughout the kingdoms and many died. The grief was intense. It took them a long time to move past it. Each anniversary, they still hold mass services." Bennet inhaled deeply. "Where do ye side?"

"As I informed our children, I side with ye, wherever that may be." Her face shifted from stoic to hatred as a guard passed, and she continued in the same quiet tone, so the guard would overhear. "Yer family, my family disowned ye. Our friends and neighbours have branded ye a traitor. When you hang, we'll rejoice." She continued when the guard nodded and marched on. "Husband, what will we do?"

"Ye should follow my instructions. Tonight, take only what ye may carry on yer body. Ye'll know when. Meet me at the shoreline. Brielle, I beg ye, don't tell our children before the chaos begins. I don't want to afford them the opportunity to betray us. Now, about Prince Bryce…"

Day 133
Division Compound
Crow's Pass City, Baitsloam

When the prison door swung wide, guards pushed Bennet inside. The smell of pork and beans lingered. Eyeing the rations, he sat beside Auren as Adrian's light burned out.

He rested his head against the wall, closed his eyes, and murmured. "My wife, and maybe my children, will meet us tonight."

Auren nodded, then realised his friend could not see him. "You trust her?"

"More than anyone," he paused, taking a deep breath. "I cannot say the same for my children, but I have taken every precaution. They cannot stop what will happen tonight."

"Our kingdom trusts you. If you trust her, then so shall we. Think no more of it. You will be together soon."

Day 133
Division House
Crow's Pass City, Baitsloam

Guards escorted Brielle back into the division house where two commanders and a scholar spoke to the prince. While they finished their conversation, she bowed and waited.

"The king will arrive around midnight. He travels slowly as he brings his intended."

Prince Bryce nodded. "I've instructed the staff to make his rooms ready and complete all preparations before the evening meal. Will his betrothed stay here?"

"Nay, men will escort her to her family cottage. There isn't room, and it would be improper to stay here without her chaperons."

"Fine," when the prince smiled at Brielle his wrinkled skin lifted. "Did yer husband provide ye with any useful intelligence?"

She hugged her arms around herself. "I would prefer ye did not refer to him as my husband. He's long dead to me, but, aye, he did. They're fifty strong and alone in their travels. This was a trip to find Reinshaven. The Alders require a healer. By boat, Aldersward is northeast about sixteen days."

As he scrutinised her demeanour, he stroked his jaw. "Was there anything else?"

She forced herself not to fidget, a habit she had when lying. She worried they would see it. "Nay, he gave me nothing further. However, he asked about their punishment. Details like when and where. It left me the impression he wanted it for a reason."

Interested, Bryce sat forward. "And what did ye offer?"

She shrugged. "At sundown, the day after tomorrow, ye will execute them in the common area. I didn't think ye would care if I lied, and I suppose he believed me."

"They'll waste time planning an escape based on misinformation. They hang tomorrow morning, long before then." Pleased, he rubbed his palms together. "I'll speak to King Baeddan on yer behalf. Perhaps ye can relocate elsewhere, away from this scandal."

Brielle genuflected. "I appreciate yer consideration. Thank ye. I wish to leave and rid our residence of any reminder of him."

Day 134
Anya's Endeavour
Baitsloam's North Shore

In the corridor, the men dressed in heavy bronze armour were weighted with weapons for themselves and those imprisoned. Hours before, the sun had set as clouds drifted across the sky. While Aedyn and Asa waited on the navigation deck for his opinion, Azariah laid on the observation deck, surveying the bank.

He climbed down, crouched, and stared at the map. "There aren't as many as yesterday, perhaps fifty. The north bank is almost clear, ten or so. The further west you travel—the better your chances. On the east, though, I'm uncertain how you get past them."

Asa pointed. "Maybe you all travel west."

"No," Aedyn shook his flour-caked face. "There's too many to fight. Our men advance here, where no one watches." He positioned his finger directly behind the division house. "Let's lower the boats out of sight. We'll place Alvin and Ametheus in the first. When the moon's hidden, they can row east. We'll see how much damage Alvin can create from that distance. Hopefully, enough."

"I'll ready the boats." Asa walked away.

Day 134
Anya's Endeavour
Baitsloam's North Shore

The men waited, and when the moon disappeared, the first boat rowed powerfully. Their oars sliced the water in unison, knowing they must accomplish their destination before the clouds slid clear of the moon and exposed them. Alvin's high-pitched scream was unheard, but loud explosions erupted through the silent night and alarmed voices shouted as those on shore raced to assist within the city.

Suddenly, an enormous limb with slimy feathered digits thrashed the boat which held Anderson. The boat ripped in two, hurling the armoured men into the water to sink. Another boat advanced quickly as the men in the water struggled to discard their heavy weapons and armour. They hoisted four of the water-soaked inside, but no sign of Anderson and Alexander remained. They abandoned the search in hopes the two would return to Anya's Endeavour.

The boats continued. They had no alternative, stopping would jeopardise them all. Their mission was clear. They grounded along the abandoned bank and climbed the steep ridge. The high wall was only half-collapsed when they reached it.

Angelo spoke, unconcerned about his volume, the chaos inside much louder than he would be. "Why isn't the wall entirely collapsed?"

"It was quite a distance and angle. If I were higher, I could have done more damage." Alvin explained.

"What can we expect inside?"

"I collapsed the division house and church for certain. Everything else, I'll take care of as we go. Stand aside, I'll finish the wall and start on the other buildings around."

The leader saw nothing down the sharp slope. The torches they carried were not yet lit. "Bring it down while we wait for the rest."

As the last men clambered over the ridge's lip, someone mentioned. "We lost two, Alexander and Anderson."

"Sard," frustrated, Angelo expelled. "We'll have to improvise without the lock picker. Everyone, light your torches and keep them away from your faces. Alvin and Ametheus, find higher ground, maybe a guard tower. Start by creating a diversion for Prince Aedyn then randomly level swaths. Be mindful of the stone building where our men are kept. We need a constant stream of panic and chaos. We'll start across to where they're held." Angelo commanded as the wall shattered. Alvin and Ametheus stepped through. Alvin opened his mouth and levelled as many buildings as possible, forcing the panicked to run in every direction.

Day 134
Bennet's Family Home
Crow's Pass City, Baitsloam

Brielle sat as her three children played cards. When she finished speaking to Prince Bryce, a guard assigned to her property escorted her back. Pre-emptive, under the guise of cleaning, she had prepared a few belongings—nothing substantial, only a few tiny keepsakes. The children noticed her quiet but assumed she was disturbed by the meeting.

An explosion sounded, the blast rocking their cottage and contents. Each bolted. Brielle stood as her sons pushed outside. The posted guards were gone, their assignment forgotten in the utter confusion. Instantly, Blake and Bowan witnessed the changed skyline—the massive church steeple and division house were no longer.

They hastened inside, stampeded to their bedchamber to gather their weapons, and stalked back as they fastened them to their bodies.

Their mother blocked their path and held her hand up. "Wait. I've something to tell ye."

They stood motionless, but Bowan accused. "Ye knew?"

She shook her head. "I didn't know what the diversion would be, but yer father has escaped and wants us to join him in Aldersward. I've packed things–"

Blain interrupted. "Ye knew they would murder our countrymen, and ye did nothing to prevent it?"

She commanded his silence. "I warned ye. My loyalties are with yer father as yers should be. We want ye to join us, but we will accept if ye can't. Come to my room. We must hurry."

She led them to where the small marked packages laid on the bed. "We can't take much, yer father insisted." As they each collected their own, Brielle lifted her skirt and tied one to her leg. "Let me help, Byunca. Blake, Bowan, put yers in yer vests."

Brielle marched outside, as another explosion boomed in the distance. The scene was surreal. Wanting to lend themselves any way they could, people carried lamps and rushed towards the walled community. She gripped Blake and Byunca's hands and surged with the mob, Bowan a few steps behind.

Another echoing blast ripped behind them. When they approached the division, she fought the crowd's flow to detour around the fence. Not wanting anyone to note their progress in the wrong direction, she tried to remain in the shadows. They tripped in the dark as they stumbled through the trees. She dragged her worried children along towards the seashore where they would not have to manoeuvre any steep inclines, then skirted along the shoreline.

As the clouds shifted and the moonlight illuminated the area, Bowan spoke from behind her, "Ye can't do this, Mother."

Focused on the boats lining the shore, she strode on. "We are doing this." She stopped to stand in the shadows of the trees, waiting for her husband.

"I'm not." Her oldest pulled the sword from his waist as his mother whirled around to confront him.

Brielle pushed Byunca to stand behind her. "Are ye going to hurt me—yer mother?"

Hatefully, he looked upon her and sneered. "I can't let ye betray our kingdom—all kingdoms—because ye believe ye still love him. It's my responsibility as eldest, to ensure our family's loyalties serve King Baeddan. I must stop ye and return with my siblings."

Their mother stepped forward, and ready to defend her, Blake followed. "To stop me, ye'll need to kill me."

"That shan't be a problem." As Bowan struck, the sound of his sword cut the air.

Day 134
Division House
Crow's Pass City, Baitsloam

The massive explosion shattered the stones, collapsing the entry's ceiling, and blocked Prince Bryce's way. He was frantic to find his family above. The air filled with fine dust, coating their nostrils, caking their throats, and blurring their vision as his two guards aided him. They lifted chunks out of the path, but the heavy weight slowed their progress. After fifteen minutes, one guard stopped and motioned toward a window. The three immediately comprehended their negligence, rushing to it as another blast echoed, and the room crumbled around them.

Day 134
North Shore
Crow's Pass City, Baitsloam

Prince Aedyn and those accompanying him pushed through the empty woods. They were not as thick as he had anticipated. A mass exodus streamed towards the division compound as explosions rocked the night, one after another. Suddenly, in front of them, buildings burst. Jagged stones became projectiles and turned into a deadly rain an unlucky few wouldn't survive as their countrymen trampled their bodies.

"We need to move." He motioned the five men to come closer.

Arjun asked. "What do we do?"

"We should head for that wood barn. When Alvin stops, we'll rendezvous with our men as they come out." He stepped beyond the shadows and pushed through the people crossing.

One by one, his men followed.

As Aedyn reached the door, the clouds cleared away from the moon, and light flooded the area.

A man yelled and a dozen or more Baits advanced as other buildings shattered.

Aedyn spurred his group inside, anticipating that an indoor battle would limit casualties.

Two Alders removed their bows and readied for when the door would open. The thump of their arrows hit the targets and enemies fell. This time, as they positioned another set, six rushed forward. The arrows struck true as the other four Baits charged towards them, making it impossible to reload. The archers threw their bows aside and drew their weapons.

The Alders hurried towards their attackers as another wave flooded inside.

Aedyn sparred, his discipline much more advanced than the untrained Baits, obviously not soldiers. He swung his sword through one body while he watched Alan fall to his knees. An enemy ran a blade through his neck.

Abraham yelled above the chaos, "You must leave, Aedyn."

The prince ignored him, cutting open a stomach, then sliced off the arm of another as more men pressed forward.

Anders's head twisted around as a blade cut through his face and he fell.

As the last Bait collapsed, Aryan and Arjun moved to protect their prince.

"You must hide, Aedyn," Arjun demanded.

"I will not hide." He shouted with angry conviction.

As more men advanced, Aryan clubbed Aedyn over the head. The last pair of Alders knocked over a haystack and strode to the opposite corner, hoping no one witnessed what they had done.

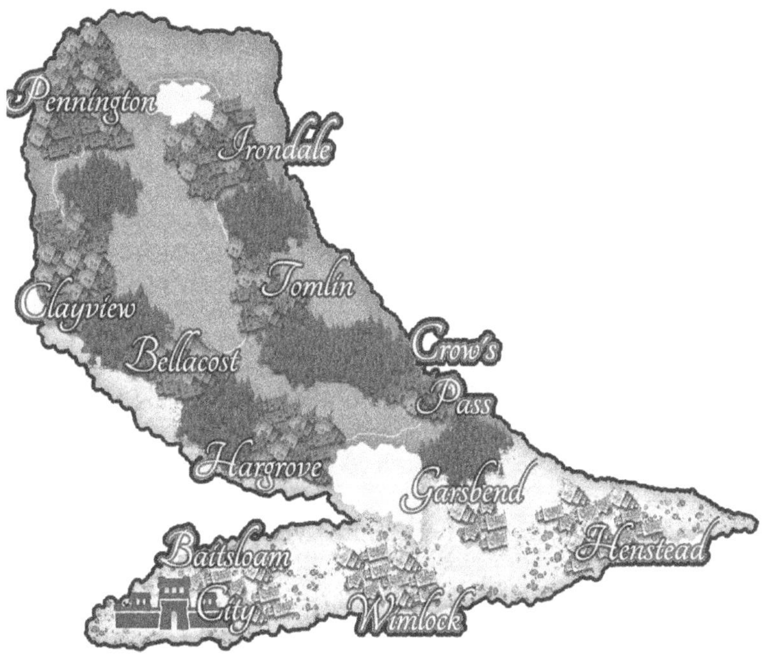

Day 134
Bailor's Homestead
South of Crow's Pass City, Baitsloam

On the Garsbend Road to Crow's Pass, King Baeddan stopped his entourage and surveyed Bailor's fields. Around him, a pair of albino snakes slithered over his torso. The breed, at one time, had been black and red, but when the population declined and he could not introduce new blood, siblings mated. Each generation became more disfigured and lost their colours, until they were white and translucent.

The military ruined the crops as men constructed the gallows platform, high above so thousands could witness the executions.

"Yer Majesty," the commander trotted forward. "We weren't expecting ye."

"Nay, I'm escorting my intended, Lady Belinda, to her family home before I visit the division. The builds are coming along quickly." The king's cataract-covered eyes skimmed the fields, the city skyline in the distance.

"Aye, we started with two-hundred, and now thousands have gathered to prepare for the celebration."

The king nodded. "I will let ye–"

Suddenly a thundering blast sent a fine film billowing above the city. The horses jumped and men seized their reins to prevent their bolt.

Baeddan squinted. "Where's the church steeple? Quickly on with ye, return to Crow's Pass." The king turned. "Have Lady Belinda and her staff escorted home. I'll take the rest and continue."

His advisor's head shook. "Nay, return to Garsbend. Ye're safer there."

The king agreed by yelling his instructions. The carriage and his soldiers swung a wide circle while Belinda continued onward.

Day 134
Division Compound
Crow's Pass City, Baitsloam

As Baits ran by, focused on lending assistance with the collapsed structures, Angelo's and Aron's men drove forward, carrying their torches. The prison's door stood wide, the interior abandoned.

While the others passed to stand behind, Angelo traipsed inside. He slid the door's window open and peered through. The imprisoned were standing and ready to move. "Aren't you a pathetic-looking lot?"

Auren grinned. "I've never been so happy to see someone so ugly."

"Yeah, yeah. Everyone is busy with the explosions. We need a plan." Angelo examined the lock. "I'll be right back."

"What do you mean? Where's Anderson?"

"He didn't make it." Angelo strode to the exit and glanced outside. No one watched as he rounded the backside. "Anyone have a skill to pick a lock?"

No one came forward, but Armando shrugged. "I can swing an axe." He dragged it from his back, entered the prison, and examined the barrier between them and the other Alders.

Finally, after Armando landed six blows against the latch, the door swung free. He turned and stopped. "Next time, search for the keys." He knocked them off a hook as the men exited.

The rescuing men flanked the liberated, handing off their weapons. Auren strapped his arrows to his back and placed the bow across his chest. Brandishing their arsenal would only draw unwanted attention.

The pair in the guard tower overlooked their path. When the others emerged, Alvin's scream destroyed their prison, sending dust skyward so no one would recognise the Alders without flour-caked faces. They joined the stream of Baits, then disappeared through the downed wall. Alvin detonated debris around their escape point to generate further hysteria before he and Ametheus followed.

Day 134
North Shore
Crow's Pass City, Baitsloam

Brielle dropped to her knees and reached for her youngest son who had intercepted his brother's sword, earning a lengthy laceration for his actions.

"What have ye done? How could ye?" Byunca screamed hysterically and rushed at Bowan as he released the weapon and collapsed to the ground beside his mother.

"This can't be happening." His voice faltered with remorse. "I didn't mean to kill him." He attempted to justify his actions. "I had to stop ye. It is my duty." Bowan tore off his long vest and pressed it to his brother's side. Dark, unchecked blood seeped through the grey embroidered material.

With her fists, his young sister struck him. "Ye would have murdered our mother!"

"Stop Byunca. Help me before yer father arrives." Brielle kept calm as she held Blake, wanting to defuse the situation. Her son's death would be the only thing accomplished by escalating it.

Between them, they carried the unconscious body to a boat as Bennet and his men descended the incline.

"What happened?" Bennet slid, using the trees and rocks to slow him.

"An accident," his wife summarised. Now was not the time. "Byunca. Bowan. Climb in. We must go."

"I can't. I can't go." Bowan pointed, his tone hysterical. "Look what I've done!"

Bennet clutched his son's shoulder, examining his eyes. "We must escape now, and we cannot leave ye here alone. Together, we can fix this, if ye come with us." He dragged his son forward as arrows hailed from above, "Ye must come now!"

The pair's robes hampered their movement as they scrambled to the boat where men held shields to protect them. The others rowed with frantic speed, moving out of range.

Day 134
Belinda's Family Home
Crow's Pass City, Baitsloam

As the carriage weaved through the streets, the explosions ended, and Belinda witnessed the devastation. Pandemonium reigned as people struggled to free others trapped inside the collapsed structures. Not every dwelling met the same fate; two or three were downed, but another stood. The pattern continued, unending.

Her parents were long dead, and she had no siblings. She only had the two ancient staff members who were fiercely loyal to her. The carriage rolled, stopping at her home. Its exterior boarded when the king had summoned her.

"Lady Belinda, we should return ye to Garsbend. The conditions here are unsettled."

She stepped out. "Nay, King Baeddan instructed ye to bring me here. Would ye disobey his order?" Belinda argued, then instructed. "Unload our things." She motioned for Beatrice and Bret to follow as she reached the gate.

Triumphant, a man rounded her dwelling and carried a flour-caked head mounted on his spear. "We killed them!"

The king's guards turned, observing the Alder's head. "Where?"

"In the barn—five in total—this was the last."

More men rounded the cottage, their spears dressed the same, thrusting them skyward.

Day 134
Wooden Barn
Crow's Pass City, Baitsloam

The heavy odour of iron registered in Aedyn's mind first, then sounds. The scraping of rock against wood, and distant voices, but nothing immediate. He peeked through the straw which hid him. More than a dozen bloodied, dismembered, and mutilated bodies tangled together on the floor. He struggled, desperate to stand. Knowing at any moment, his enemies could return. He straightened, recognising his men's headless bodies arranged in a tidy row. His stomach twisted violently.

He had to retrain his focus and ignore the sight. Using the wall, he stumbled to the gaped doors and glanced outside.

Several men strolled away, their spears spiked with his men's heads.

Aedyn had to escape. He lurched outside. His temples pounded painfully, and blood gushed from his upper thigh.

In front of him, a boarded-up dwelling loomed like an answer from Jezabet. With a long, deep breath, he prayed for strength, then with revived energy, he stumbled and pushed himself inside as his temporary momentum waned.

He found a darkened room, closed the door, and collapsed, content he would be safe for a time.

Day 134
Belinda's Family Home
Crow's Pass City, Baitsloam

Belinda clutched the fence. The jagged cut necks and severed heads caused her to gag in disbelief. Beatrice caught her.

Bret blocked their view. "Ye see how my lady reacts." He clasped the first's shoulder and feigned a grin. "Ye should present the bodies at the division. Make it known what brave and fierce soldiers ye are. Perhaps the king will reward ye." He encouraged them to vacate.

Belinda started towards the barn, but Beatrice stopped her and steered her inside. "Tomorrow. I'll prepare tea."

The young woman shook her head. "Nay, I'm tired and ye play too well as my maid. I can look after myself–" She stopped as the guards carried her things inside. "Set them in the corner." When the guards exited, she continued. "It's time for ye and Bret to return to yer home. I appreciated yer presence."

"Nay need. Ye're practically our own." Beatrice hugged her as the guards returned with another load.

A guard bowed. "Lady Belinda, we'll take our leave. Those men are removing the bodies as we speak. We'll take the carriage, wagon, and horses to the division stable. They may not go inside a barn smelling of blood."

"Of course, take them." Belinda waved, wanting to be rid of the king's men.

Beatrice closed the door, then crossed to sit on a bench. "Come sit in front of me. I'll remove yer hairstyle." She looked at the thick, flaming red hair which when loose, reached the young woman's knees.

"Nay, we'll worry about it tomorrow. Go home. I want to be alone. I promise to remain inside."

The woman, like a daughter, had decided, and the old woman gave up. "If ye're positive, then we'll see to the damage at our cottage."

She left, and Belinda happily dropped into a cushioned chair. It felt wonderful to be home.

Day 134
Main Deck
Anya's Endeavour
Baitsloam's North Shore

The men climbed the vessel's ladders as those aboard lent their hands, helping them to stand. Happy, jovial voices welcomed them back. Awkwardly, Guard Asa greeted Lead Auren with a relieved hug as Bennet's wife and two children came forward.

"We'll need you to lift a boat. We have wounded." Auren said.

Asa nodded, yelling for Abner to bring a rope.

As they boarded, Alonso checked the manifest against the men and the newcomers to the list.

Sahana crept from the shadows, her cloak's hood pulled tight around her face. Bennet gave her an unwanted hug and introduced his wife and daughter.

Asa followed two men who carried Blake. "Where do you want him?"

The physician came forward. "Put him in the dining room. Sahana, assist me?"

She swiftly limped away, relieved to be out of sight.

Auren smiled as he stood tall, turning in every direction. "Is Aedyn inside pouring us drinks?"

Asa's shoulders slumped. "No, he went ashore to rescue you."

"He what?" The violence in Auren's voice seemed to shake everyone on board.

Asa lifted his palms. "I tried to stop him, but I couldn't."

"All leaders on me," Auren strode inside and the page startled, jumping to his feet. "Fetch some sweet tea and have the cook make enough to feed us all.

Everyone will be hungry." The boy pushed through as the men entered, sitting at the table. "Who's missing?"

Alonso checked. "Eight. The prince's entire group plus two, who we believe drowned at the beginning of the rescue."

Auren fired his questions rapidly. "Where was Prince Aedyn's group headed?"

Asa said. "West of Crow's Pass, to guarantee a clear path out if needed."

"How many men did he have?"

Aron said, "Six, including himself."

"When was he supposed to return?"

Angelo explained. "When the explosions stopped, they were going to head back."

Auren shook his head, unsure how to proceed. The other men sat by, each examining their own thoughts, their consciences weighing heavy.

Day 134
Sitting Room
Belinda's Home
Crow's Pass City, Baitsloam

Belinda relaxed against the chair and closed her eyes, her body exhausted from the long journey. She thought she heard a low moan and walked to the window before she remembered they were boarded over. Disregarding it as her imagination, she pulled her nightdress from the trunks and shrugged into it. She jumped at another noise, a thud.

She lifted the lantern, wandering through the kitchen to her bedchamber. The door was closed, not how she kept it. She retraced her steps and pulled a knife from a small wooden box. Her father had given it to her. She stepped to the door, listened but heard nothing, then quietly pushed it wide, and stared at the sleeping stranger lying on her bed.

She tiptoed back to the sitting room and paced.

Who is he? How seriously is he hurt? What's he doing here? I need answers.

Her mind raced and twice she paced in the direction, but cowardly she stopped herself, frightened.

He may die.

The thought urged her to act, and carefully, she stepped inside. She placed the lamp on the bedside table and knelt, leaving her blade within easy reach.

His large body dressed in bronze armour made rolling him over difficult. His skin was olive-toned—an Alder.

She inspected the flour-caked face, now flaking, and held her finger under his nostrils. Shallow air barely touched her. She noted the gash in his black, matted hairline.

What should I do?

Scared, she hurried into the kitchen. The kingdom's teachings within her were strong. The Alders had massacred so many.

But not this fellow—he wouldn't have been alive then. She reasoned. *It's not my place to choose whether he lives or dies.*

With her decision, she set the water to boil and gathered supplies, then went to aid the man.

She arranged the things she carried on the trunk at the bed's end, then unlaced his boots and tugged them off. Belinda noted the craftsmanship, the intricate details. He was either an accomplished boot maker or someone who enjoyed luxuries. She preferred to believe the first. She could imagine nobody of rank trudging through Baitsloam Kingdom.

Nay, they would be safe on the craft, condemning those of lower stations to death.

Belinda unclasped the back of his greaves and cuisses, noting his thick-muscled legs left little excess strap. Unbuckling the belt at his waist, she lifted the armour from his thighs. The gushing wound on his inner thigh caught her concern. She pulled the ties of his plackart and pauldrons, freeing his shoulders, throat, and chest so perhaps he would inhale deeper.

He never stirred. She planted her hand against his chest and felt it rise.

Forcing modesty aside, she unbuttoned his trousers, noting his slim waist as she stood and rolled them over his hips. Once free of his ass, they slid easier along his thighs, and she cringed, hoping she had not harmed him further. The sight of his testicles and penis, laying flaccid against his unwounded leg, shocked her. No time remained to dwell as she watched fresh blood seep into her straw mattress.

Once, her mother had wrapped a tight string around her father's finger when it was bleeding, and she assumed this would be the same.

She tied the cord from his trousers around his thigh, avoiding his genitals, then rubbed her bloodied hands on her nightdress.

A knock sounded from outside. She protected him with a blanket and carried the lantern out. "Who's there?"

"It's Beatrice. Our cottage is in ruins. We can't stay there."

Belinda unlatched the door and drew them in as she scanned outside. "What happens about?"

Bret cleared his throat. "The Alders escaped. A division commander dispatched the king's men to Bailor's fields to raise makeshift shelters for those in need. We could have gone there."

"Nonsense, ye belong with me. Did we lose many?"

"Not as many as we could have. The initial explosions brought most from their homes. The division house collapsed and is being dug out to find Prince Bryce and his family. If the Alders had wanted, they could have killed thousands. They came in, retrieved their people, and left."

Belinda turned into the sitting room.

Beatrice gasped and hurried toward her. "Are ye all right? Has something happened?" She lifted the nightdress, examining the blood.

She pushed the hands away and passed into the kitchen. "It's not mine. I found a wounded man."

"One of yer neighbours?" The old woman studied the younger's face.

No choice existed but to trust them, she sighed, "Nay an Alder. He's injured and I don't have the knowledge to help him."

Bret's voice echoed loudly, unable to control his temper over her foolishness. "How did ye find him? Was he in the barn? If anyone saw ye—we're in danger. This is preposterous. We must turn him over to the crown." He rose to walk past her.

Belinda blocked him. "Stop! Nay one saw me. As promised, I haven't ventured out. He was here in my room, unconscious." She grasped Bret's arm and pleaded. "As ye said, if they wanted to kill us, they could have. Forget our education. What of Jezabet's?"

Beatrice nodded. "All right, one step at a time. He still may die. Show him to me."

Day 134
Aedyn's Quarters
Anya's Endeavour
Baitsloam's North Shore

Auren broke the pregnant silent. "The king will want to learn if the rescue was successful. Achelle could visit Aedyn tonight, and he may give her a message for us. Maybe the Baits captured them. For now, we maintain our current position, they could yet return."

"If captured, chances are, they'll not survive long enough to be hung. The Baits know we have significant capabilities among us." Bennet offered.

Asa nodded. "And what if they don't return tonight?"

"We have to believe they will." Auren's palm ran over his stubbly scalp. "Your wife and daughter will bunk at the back with Sahana. I'll reassign a few men and revise tomorrow's assignments. You may return to your family. The rest of you, I want two groups on duty at all times."

"My men and Augustus's will finish out the night watch." Asa stood, signalling everyone to leave.

Day 134
Bedchamber
Belinda's Home
Crow's Pass City, Baitsloam

To protect them, if needed, Bret held a sword in hand. He noted the blood on the bed, the knife on the floor, and the foreigner's clothes on the trunk. The sweet, metallic scent lingered.

Beatrice uncovered him and prodded the wound. "Grab yer sewing basket, hot water, and rags. If ye have any herbs or remedies, bring them."

The young woman left to collect the list. She rose on her toes to reach above the kitchen shelves, where she kept unused portions of tonics and herbs, then lifted the boiling water and returned.

The elderly woman accepted the medicine box, riffled through the contents, then pinched a powder into a mug. "This will serve. Bret, raise his head. Belinda, fill this with water and feed him small amounts with a spoon. Hopefully, he will swallow."

Belinda's voice was gentle and encouraging as she coaxed him to swallow. His throat muscles obeyed.

Aedyn's eyes slid open. A beautiful woman with brilliant ivory skin, dark stained lips and piled red hair bent over him. His mind and vision blurred dizzily. His thigh burned, and his body felt heavy. Succumbing to the blissful darkness, he lost focus and his eyes closed again.

"He isn't swallowing anymore." Her breathy tone worried.

"He may have enough. We'll clean and stitch this wound."

Day 134
Main Deck
Anya's Endeavour
Baitsloam's North Shore

As Bennet climbed and emerged from the lower deck, the morning sun rose. With slicked-back hair and fresh robes, his appearance had improved.

The men stationed over the deck were solemn as he joined Asa and Auren.

"Blake rests. The physician said the wound bled a lot, but it wasn't deep. The package he carried took most of the damage."

"We're pleased to hear," Auren said.

From the observation deck, Apollo called. "There's movement on shore."

Asa and Auren raced for the navigation deck's stairs and climbed the ladder.

Baits rolled a wagon onto the beach, then each man removed and planted a spear-mounted head into the sand along the water's edge, ensuring their features faced the Alders.

Acidic bile rose in Auren's throat as he watched. The jagged cut necks and the lifeless faces were more than he could stand. He fought sickening waves as he crossed to the opposite railing which overlooked the main deck. Using it for support, he clutched it in a vice-like grip and bowed his head.

Asa followed him. "There are only five."

"There's no way to know who survived. I couldn't identify them. Could you?"

"No."

Day 134
Belinda's Home
Crow's Pass City, Baitsloam

Perspiration beaded along Belinda's neck as they dragged the unconscious Alder down into the cottage's dugout where they had assembled a straw-filled mattress under the bedchambers. His muscled weight, Belinda's slender frame, and Bret's advanced age made the task challenging.

As the stronger pair gently lowered him, the older woman set a bucket of warm water beside the mattress.

Exhaustion marred Beatrice's expression as she flattened the hair away from her face. "If ye'll leave, I'll clean him."

Belinda knelt on the dirt floor. "Nay, ye both must sleep. I'll do it."

"What if he wakes and attacks ye?" Bret stretched his tired back, feeling his 640 years.

"I have my dagger and with ye straight above, ye'll hear if he wakes."

"Ensure ye slide the chair over the trapdoor when ye've finished." Bret reached for his wife and, with her balance somewhat off, she wobbled. He led her out into the other room and helped her climb the ladder.

Once they departed, Belinda cut the Alder's tunic away, exposing the brand on his left side, then removed his gloves. A gold ring with a large ruby encased in black crystals caught her eye, and she studied it.

A nobility ring, she thought as she wrung the cloth and scrubbed the dried blood from his chest, fallen from his head wound.

She was curious and apprehensive of his almost naked body. His muscled pecs lifted in rhythm with his shallow breathing, and his rib cage tapered to a slim waist where Beatrice had pinned a folded sheet around his hips and genitals. Warming the rag, she washed along his smooth neck and his chin's cleft with the stubble of a day's growth present. She passed her fingers over his pouty lips and high, defined cheekbones.

Belinda wondered what colour his eyes were as she cleaned around them. She moistened the cloth and bathed his black hair.

When finished, she propped his head on a pillow and covered him with several blankets, as she wondered what to do next.

Day 134
Princess Achelle's Chambers
Castle's Second Level
Near Aldersward City

Dawn's light woke Achelle. Pressure thumped loudly in her temples as she opened her eyes. She wondered why she could not find Aedyn. Sluggishly, she put on her robe, and padded barefoot through her rooms into the corridor. In the open-air hallway, the tunnelled breeze and indirect light welcomed her.

Her father, in a chair outside, waited for news. She sat, but when he tried to put his arm around her, she stopped him. "Please, I may vomit."

Concerned, he examined her. "Are you ill?"

"No, it's my cost, a stellar headache." She drew deep, calming breaths.

"You've never mentioned these before."

"They normally aren't bad, bearable, even. This one is much worse."

"Do you know what caused it?"

"I tried to reach Aedyn frequently through the night." She threaded her fingers with his. "Father, I was unsuccessful."

"What does it mean?"

"There could be many reasons. He may have drunk too much, not slept, or bypassed the dream state." Or is *unconscious or dead,* she added to herself. "I will try again tonight."

"My physician will examine you before then. If you can't reach Aedyn, try others like Auren or Bennet. Someone should be sleeping." The king lightly kissed her forehead.

She returned to her bed and pulled the covers over her head, blocking the sun's harsh light.

Day 135
Prince Aedyn's Quarters
Anya's Endeavour
Baitsloam's North Shore

The page set dishes on the long table as Sahana filled Auren's mug with hot tea. They performed in silence, noting the thick tension in their leader's tight, thin lips and gathered brow while he silently consumed his breakfast and wrote in the voyage's journal.

Bennet entered, instantly aware of the mood. He sat and waited for the man to finish.

"Anything?" Auren's sleepless night was made apparent by the dark circles under his eyes.

"A man purchased a special tube of glass from Slaysfold. It can see over long distances. Aedyn isn't among the dead on shore. Achelle?"

Auren shook his head. "Never came to me last night."

"What now?"

"We hold our position until either he returns or Achelle visits me, then I'll decide what further action needs to be taken."

"Is it wise to remain in this spot? Perhaps we should travel the coast back and forth, ensuring King Baeddan can't form a plan against us."

"We can't move. What if a limited opportunity arises for Aedyn to escape and we aren't here? No, we must chance it."

Asa strode through the door, held it open, and motioned for Sahana to leave, then stood behind Bennet's chair.

The Bait felt him at his back. "Aedyn instructed us to return home if anything should happen to him. Asa and I have–"

Auren's face distorted in anger as his eyes flashed and the vein along his neck protruded. "Oh, so *you* have decided, have you? How easy it must be for you both, with your happily reunited family and your gimpy new project? I know what he instructed, but until I'm certain he's dead, we go nowhere. He is my brother and they are my family." His voice bellowed, seeming to shake the room as he stood and pounded his fist on the table. "Fall in or swive off—these are *your only* decisions!"

Asa came over the table, grabbed him by the neck, and pushed him into the cabinet. "You've no right to take your anger out on us. We're your council and we're counselling you." He released him and their new leader fixed his tunic, then stood toe to toe with him.

"Perhaps I should find another council." Auren stomped to the bedchamber, slammed the door, and locked it in place.

When their eyes met, Asa shrugged, then left the interior while Bennet pulled the voyage's journal across the table.

Auren had written. *Seven men from our crew are dead and one is missing. We have yet to determine which one. These men risked themselves to save those captured by the Baits.*

Usually when I write, it is comedic but there is nothing humorous now.

The lives of those on board and those sick back home now depend on me—my leadership and my ability to make swift, precise decisions. I am uncertain of how to make these choices and hope Aedyn or King Adahy through Achelle will guide me.

I

After reading, Bennet dipped the quill in the inkwell, then continued the entry, the handwriting notably different. He struck through the single letter.

~~I~~ Ye will lead in strength and courage with Aedyn's confidence. Ye swore to carry this order through and we will support your decisions as we promised.

We have determined Prince Aedyn is not amongst the casualties. Our hope is in a few hours he will re-join us or Achelle will contact us with a message. Until then, our leader has determined, the best course of action is to remain where we are.

Below is an updated manifest and reallocated assignments.

Prince Aedyn's group:
Aedyn – by asking an exact question, the person responding cannot lie
~~Alan – animate dolls~~
~~Abraham – make dirty things clean~~
~~Andres – recreate music he has only heard once~~
~~Arjun – make objects glow—five minute limitation~~
~~Aryan – instantly create weapons made of wood~~
~~Anderson – ability to unlock any lock by touch~~
Anik – change glass into mirror (Aedyn's page)

Guard Angelo's group:
Angelo – recharge fully on two hours of sleep (Guard)
Aidrik – feel other people's pain when he touches them (Physician)
Arlo – poetry—he rhymes well
Apollo – create elaborate illusions of gardens—only lasts an hour
Aldo – unbreakable bones
Ameer – duplicate fermented drinks
Alec – change his own legs into arms
Anson – disease resistant
Bowan – communicates with frogs
Blake – communicates with squirrels

Guard Asa's group:
Asa – super-strength by consuming snake meat (Guard)
Alberto – change the wind's direction
Austin – enhanced hearing, direct line, no barriers
Alcott – conjure any fur as long as he has seen or interacted with it before
Arthur – paint an image from memory, extremely detailed, on eucalyptus paper
Albert – accelerate creating a weapon but must have all materials
Alvin – shatter stone with his scream
Azariah – heat vision
Ackley – change target's voice to another (Carpenter/Boatswain)
Amos – turns adult to infant—five minute duration (Captain)

Guard Augustus's group:
Augustus – conjure clothing from cloth (Guard)
Archer – force field for himself only
Alonso – never forgets a face—remembers names and abilities if told
Ashton – enhance another's fire ability and strengthen it
Antonio – enhanced dodging reflexes
Ari – make other people sad
Ahmad – absorbs sunlight, can exude it on command as only heat
Amos – grow his own hair quickly
Abner – barrier which prevents teleportation (Engineer/Boatswain)

Lead Auren's group:
Auren – change the trajectory of an arrow forged by his own hand (Lead)
Apex – conjure rations, pork/beans only using rotting meat/vegetables (Advisor)
Ametheus – turn wood to stone
Anthony – imitate musical instruments one at a time with his voice
Adrian – fire—create flames from his fingertips
Ace – invisibility for himself only—must be naked
Andy – move ink only on hemp paper

Abdullah – speak and understand any language
Anders – breathe underwater for ten minutes

Emissary Bennet/Aron's group:
Bennet – communicates with birds (Emissary)
Aron – instantly likeable—must make eye contact (Emissary)
Arturo – a human compass
Alexander – grow any seed by touch
Asher – change the colour of any fabric
Amir – mute any water ability, one at a time
Amari – levitate objects as big as his hand
Armando – disintegrate excrement
Ares – resistant to poisoning, will not die but gets sick
Arvo – marks target's past course (Cook)

Sahana – conjure constructs with plant fibres
Byunca – communicates with butterflies
Brielle – communicates with wolves

Day 135
Dugout
Belinda's Home
Crow's Pass City, Baitsloam

A hand shook Belinda's shoulder. She startled awake, then raised her head from the mattress's edge and straightened, remembering the injured man. He had not woken her, and she turned to the old woman standing behind her.

"Ye must rest, child. There's nay telling how long he'll sleep." Beatrice pulled the future queen's hand.

"What time is it?" Her eyes remained on his lifeless body.

"Mid-morning. I'll take care of him."

Bret's voice called. "Someone's here."

The women rushed to the ladder and climbed.

While she popped a dress over her head, Beatrice hurried to secure its ties, and Bret pushed a heavy chair over the hatch, scraping it noisily across the sitting room floor. Her jaw tensed, hoping whoever was outside had not heard as their knock sounded.

She cracked the door, blocking access to whoever stood beyond. It was one of King Baeddan's guards. Installing a gentle smile on her lips, she stepped outside and closed the door. "Good day, how may I help?"

The soldier bowed and lifted her long, delicate fingers in a proper greeting. "Lady Belinda, King Baeddan wished for someone to check on ye and ensure yer safety."

"How considerate," she placed her arm in his and escorted him back through the fence, wondering if her knee-length hair had fallen out of its style from the previous night. She raised her hand to ensure her ears were covered. "As ye see,

I'm quite well, although fatigued from the considerable chaos of last night." She let go of him, using her arm to shield her eyes, and glanced at the neighbouring cottages now bathed in daylight.

Families, friends, and neighbours laboured together with several substantial piles forming. It was a distressing sight, and she averted her gaze to focus her blue oval eyes on him.

"How is King Baeddan?"

"He's fine. He chose to return to the castle, where it is safer."

"Of course, we must protect him at all costs. How have we managed? Are there casualties?"

"A couple dozen. When they dug out the division house, they discovered two dead guards, but Prince Bryce and his household survived."

"What of the captives? Were they killed?"

"Nay, they escaped."

"Pity. Have they left our shore?"

"Nay, they remain." The guard eyed her curiously. "Lady Belinda, ye ask many questions."

"I apologise. The entire situation is overwhelming. I was going to provide support to my neighbours. Would ye care to accompany me?" She anticipated he would consider it beneath him and bring an abrupt end to their exchange.

"Nay, nor do I think ye should go either while the Alders remain in our sea." The guard skimmed her body with appreciation, then concern. "Yer feet are bare."

"Aye, as I mentioned, I was preparing. It's my obligation as future queen to be amid the community during this tragedy and gain favour for our king. He may require further forces should more Alders appear. Perhaps ye can mention my intentions to him?" She took his hand.

Embarrassed but flattered by her gesture, he withdrew his quickly. "Perhaps it would be better if ye sent a messenger to deliver a written account of yer plans."

"How very astute of ye. Aye, I'll do it, perhaps tomorrow or the day after."

"It would be best, Lady Belinda." He bowed.

Day 135
Anya's Endeavour
Baitsloam's North Shore

Furious, Lead Auren paced the bedchamber, combing his hand through his stubbly hair and stretching his muscles. He used the movement to release his pent rage. An alternative was to drink, and he spied the whisky and guzzled it. He knew he had to calm down before he encountered anyone else, fearing he could kill them with bare hands if one didn't guard their words.

After a while, the whisky produced the desired effect, and he rested in a cushioned chair. Although Asa and Bennet had meant to solidify their understanding, he had driven them away savagely.

Return to Aldersward, with or without my body. The prince's words replayed in his mind.

When was it? He calculated, *just over thirty days ago.*

It seemed greater, though. The declaration was one thing; being the one to follow it through was another.

He closed his eyes and sought comfort in sleep.

Day 135
Anchor Deck
Anya's Endeavour
Baitsloam's North Shore

Sahana's long hair was tied in a heavy braid which fell forward over her shoulder with wide loose sections hanging in her face to shield her scars. She pulled her thick cloak around her body, covering it from sight as someone approached where she sat on the anchor deck with her back against the enormous wheel. She had wedged herself between it and the mast, hoping no one would look for her. A private sunny secret of her own, where she did not wish to be interrupted.

"Sahana," Asa bowed slightly. "What troubles you?"

She did not raise her face to meet his. "Your men have become accustomed to my contorted frame, but I don't want my appearance to upset Bennet's family."

"And you believe it would?" He raised a brow. "Is Bennet a good person?"

She lifted her chin. "Of course. He's most kind. In a number of ways, he reminds me of my father."

He stared into her eye, noting the way it danced when her thoughts turned happy. "I suspect his family will treat you the same."

"I don–" She halted, hearing others climb the stairs. She averted her eye to the sea and pulled her hood forward, creating a barrier no one would see through.

He shook his head and turned. "Lady Brielle, welcome aboard." Asa lifted and kissed her hand. "Bennet," he nodded. "What brings you above?"

"We toured the craft." He draped his arm around his wife's waist.

Brielle smiled. "It's wondrous, isn't it, Guard Asa?"

"Asa, please, I don't respond well to titles."

"I realised it's time for Sahana's lesson, so I brought her afternoon meal in hopes she would share this time with my wife. She also needs educating."

"Yes, perhaps she would appreciate the feminine company after her time trapped with us men. I'll leave you to get on with it." Asa turned to Sahana. "I'll come back later." He bowed and walked downstairs, disappointed their conversation had been interrupted.

Bennet settled the basket next to Sahana, then motioned for his wife to sit beside her. He sat facing them. "What should ye learn about today, Sahana?"

She shrugged and observed her fidgeting fingers.

He reached out, stopping her movement. "Perhaps I should tell ye about the royal family."

When she did not move, he handed a biscuit to her, and she tore a salty, dry piece off, then chewed it.

"I won't bore ye with too much history. In the year 262, King Adahy married Queen Anya when she was thirty-four, and he was fifty-five, three years after he took the throne. He was quite the youth, much like his son, Prince Aedyn. Adahy grew into his leadership position well."

As he told the story, Brielle poured the sweet tea and handed a mug to the young woman as she acquired another biscuit.

"He tasked one of his advisors to interview suitable brides and return with sketches of those who would serve him. I remember, it reminded me of my wedding day, when he walked directly to one. *She'll do*, he said, then grinned foolishly. I recognised his reaction immediately. It was love at first sight. They had a whirlwind engagement, touring the countryside, and visiting the estates. Once they married, it was merely a month before she revealed her first pregnancy. It delighted the king. We drank until the early hours of the morning. It was an extensive celebration."

"What are they like now?" The younger woman asked, lost in his tale.

He had planned it this way. She had an appetite for present events instead of history. "The queen sleeps with this illness, and the king is beside himself with worry. He scarcely leaves her. Back to my story about baby Aedyn, the Crowned Prince. The king was so proud of his son and his constant presence. Aedyn was three when Anya announced her second pregnancy. This time, she gave him a daughter, Achelle—a beautiful, sweet girl. Then when Aedyn was five, Auren appeared hurt, broken, and dying. The royal couple set to aid him. Queen Anya insisted upon his care and placed him inside one of the two nurseries adjoining her chamber. The king would visit this new growing family whenever he could and they would spend the next year or so waiting for Auren to be strong enough to leave the bed."

He reached for a mug as his wife poured it and took a sip. "Once Auren was better, the king had the boys train together, and they grew as brothers. The pair mercilessly pursued the king everywhere. Which left Anya to concentrate on her small daughter, but shortly after, she was pregnant with their youngest daughter, Annora—*the baby*. Everyone spoiled her, including me. I'm afraid fifteen years later we still indulge her." He laughed. "Now Achelle is a beautiful girl of eighteen and resembles Aedyn in several ways. The princesses attend the schoolroom. There's a young woman named Ammaris ye should also know about. She's not a royal yet, but she will be. She will wed the prince once we return."

He stretched his shoulders, then relaxed as his eyes smiled at her memory. "I guarantee ye've met nay one more charitable or selfless than her. Her qualities are unfathomable. I've never known another quite like her. She lives to serve others less fortunate and often returns without her cloak or shoes. She gives them away. I expect ye both will like–"

Asa called from below, "Bennet, a word."

He excused himself, leaving the two women alone. Brielle pushed the basket away and slid closer to Sahana, desperately wanting the Slay to like her as much as she did her husband.

"My husband explained what happened to ye." She looked over the water. "My family's arrival must make ye very uncomfortable. Trust when ye do eventually reveal yerself to us, yer appearance will not disturb us. We'll merely be disgusted with the man who did this to ye." She laced her fingers through Sahana's. "I wish to become great friends."

Uncertain of the intimate contact, the young woman stilled. "We can try. How are yer children?"

Bennet's wife smiled and flattened her wind-blown hair with her free hand. "Byunca's sleeping after worrying about her brother all night, and Bowan lays next to him. He's experiencing extreme guilt, and Blake is using it to his advantage." She laughed, causing a slight giggle from Sahana. "I must admit, I'm frightened of Aldersward. What to expect, if they'll be friendly, and what we'll do?"

Watching the waves rise and fall, Sahana moistened her lips. "Let me tell you of the castle."

Day 135
Kitchen
Belinda's Home
Crow's Pass City, Baitsloam

The injured man slept, and the day passed uneventfully as the evening meal neared.

"Take this blood broth below." Beatrice shoved the mug and spoon into Belinda's hand as she turned, stirring their own meal.

"Blood broth? Where did the blood come from?" She eyed the older woman curiously. Edible meat of any kind was extremely scarce in Baitsloam and had been for many years.

"I had Bret slaughter a couple of rats hanging around the barn. The dead invited them."

Her brow rose. "Ye want me to feed him rat's blood?"

Beatrice shrugged. "Don't be a squeamish child. We must replenish what he's lost."

Belinda crossed the crude dugout, then tested the broth on her wrist before she dribbled the brown liquid into his parted lips. She noted his throat's swallow and, as she spooned it into him, she examined his handsome features and wondered about his character.

He had soft lines around his mouth and a small dent in his chin. She imagined he grinned regularly, and it would cause his chin to dimple further. His bottom lip was full and pouty, probably used to convince those around to give in to his demands.

She envisioned he would be fair and powerful.

Her eyebrows narrowed, and she nibbled her lip. What had driven her to assume he was powerful?

She leaned closer to inspect his face, but no reason came.

She shrugged as she traced her fingers over his eyebrow. He was too handsome, and she supposed he knew it. For a second, she wondered what his lips would feel like against hers. Nothing prevented her but her sense of decency—and it did.

Once he no longer swallowed, she lifted the cloth from his head, wet it, and replaced it, then stepped back.

Powerful, even in sleep, his whole body exuded authority.

As she climbed the ladder, more words came to her. Pompous, arrogant, egotistical, warm, hardened. Again, she wondered about his lips as she pushed the chair into place.

"I'm surprised the noise doesn't wake him." She sat as the old woman set the boiled potatoes in the table's centre.

"It may be some time before he wakes, a fortnight perhaps. I've heard some injured don't remember who they are, or where they came from. It's peculiar." Beatrice shrugged as a knock sounded on the exterior door. She parted the curtain and admitted Bret.

He sat next to Belinda and eyed the pot with distaste. "I miss the castle's abundance of food. How is he?"

"Unconscious. How are matters outside?"

"Calming now. I didn't think ye would mind if I cleaned the barn and stored our possessions in it."

"Of course not. Once I marry, ye could both settle here." The young woman transferred a potato onto her plate. "At least tomorrow we can use the potato water to make bread."

"If things remain quiet with the Alder, I may go fishing tomorrow and bring back something other than potatoes." He pushed the plate away and stood.

Belinda laughed. "It could be rat's blood."

"Don't tempt me." He chuckled.

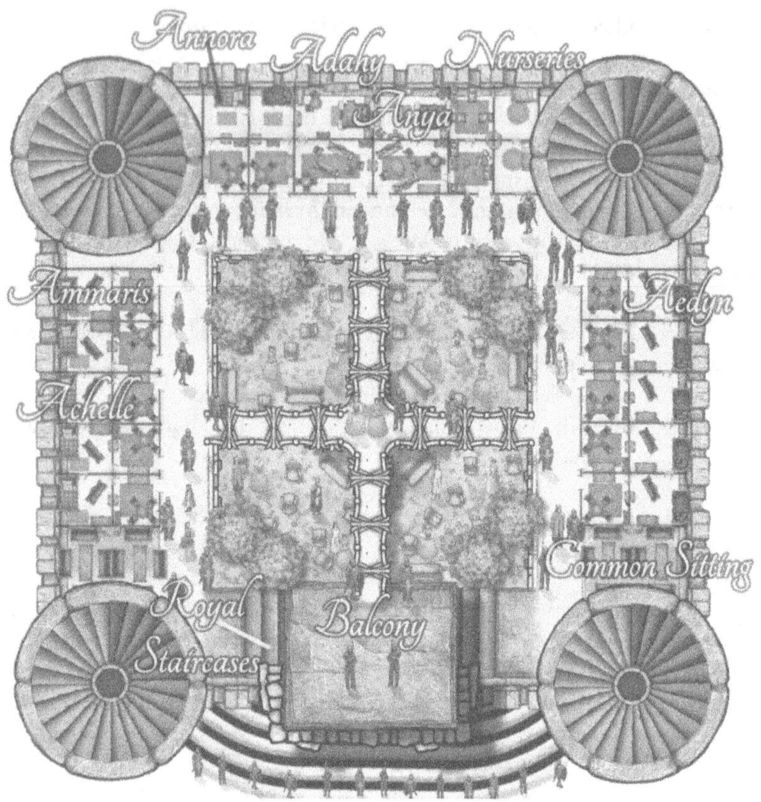

Day 135
Princess Achelle's Chambers
Castle's Second Level
Near Aldersward City

Achelle's head pounded as she tossed and turned. The blankets tangled around her limbs, trapping them. As she sought several times to reach Aedyn, with no success, her headache had intensified significantly. She could not bear to return to her father without news. She concentrated again as she inhaled deeply, willing herself back to sleep, then searched through her mind's winding corridors, hallways, and staircases for Auren and Bennet, but found neither.

Her stomach yanked her out, and she sat upright, vomiting down the front of her nightdress. Wincing, she untangled and removed the soiled garments, separating herself from the sickly stench. She tossed it aside and clutched the table's edge, steadying her imbalance.

Earlier, the physician had given her a tonic to ease her discomfort. She wondered if, while her stomach was upset, she could consume more without expelling it. Her movements slowed as she put on her robe, held it closed, then emerged into the through-room.

"Your Highness?" Her maid, Astrid, rose from where she had nodded off.

"Did my father's physician leave anything for me?"

"Axton left dried herbs for nausea and another for pain. I can prepare them for you. Which do you require?"

"Both—all, everything you have." Her stomach pitched, and she grabbed the basin on the table beside her.

Astrid supported the weak princess, and when she stopped vomiting, guided her back to the bedchamber. "I'll prepare the stomach one first and have something dry brought from the kitchen. You have eaten little today."

The maid noted the wadded nightdress and took another out as Achelle sat on the bed's edge.

"Should I have bath water delivered?"

"No." She shook her head. "I'm too ill."

The maid helped her into a clean garment, then stripped the soiled bed and replaced the covers. After the young woman laid down, the maid filled a mug, removed two packets from her apron, and pinched a tiny amount from one into the water.

"More please." She urged, watching the woman.

Astrid pinched again and added it, then settled her palm over the mug and focused her mind. The water churned into a boil. While she stirred it, a knock sounded from the hallway, and she left to answer it.

The princess sat upright, studying the other packet. It would relieve her agonising headache. She fumbled for it and dumped half its contents into the mug. She lifted the tonic as her maid returned.

"Try to eat while you drink, then I'll make the pain tonic."

"I'll eat. Place it beside me. If the king comes, you must lie. You've not seen me. I don't wish him to worry further. I must reach someone before I meet him. Leave me. I'll call if I should require you again."

"I'll check on you later to ensure you're all right." Astrid bowed.

Achelle walked along the desolate corridor, then mounted a staircase. Typically, when she searched for someone, in particular, she found them easily. It troubled her as she wandered without intuitively knowing where to go. She realised her head no longer pounded, and she was grateful for the reprieve the tonics had offered her. She thought of Auren, then Bennet, but felt no doorway draw her. Her balance wavered, and she stumbled. The teetering was something different from her prior experiences, but she had never striven so hard to contact someone who was unavailable. Time was running out. Her father's patience would grow thin and demand answers.

She inhaled deeply, once, then twice, then three times, calming her body as she wrestled with an idea. As much as she despised him, she could try Augustus. She needed answers and focused on him.

The passageways shifted, and she climbed a staircase, and another, then walked down a hallway as a door drew her. She opened it.

She glanced around. In the past, she would have revelled in joining and observing his dream, but she wanted no part of it now. "Augustus?"

He sat in the crowded, grassy quadrangle between the dormitories and the staff cottages on the castle grounds. His eyes glanced over a table of women as the intense, blistering sun beat down. When she called from behind, he jumped to his feet.

He started toward her, but stopped at her words. "I had no alternative but to visit you. I can't reach anyone else. What's happened? Where's Aedyn?"

Dumbfounded and uncomfortable, he pulled at his tunic's collar and avoided her glare.

Her focus shifted to the noisy crowd. A dull thud began behind her eyes. "Please mute them or take us somewhere less bright without others."

"How?"

"Imagine a different place, perhaps the stables at night."

He closed his eyes and concentrated on the stables, the shuffling sound of horses' hooves and their neighs. The sweet smell of the freshly cut hay stacked along the walls.

"Much better. Now a light?" She spoke into the darkness and a torch flickered, then burned against the wall.

His bewildered eyes glanced around at the wonder—anywhere to avoid her. "I think you should seek Auren."

With suspicion, her eyes widened, and she hugged her body. "I've tried. Was the recovery successful?"

He shook his head and his long hair shifted onto his shoulder. "I can't. You must find someone else."

She straightened, stiffening her back, and raised her chin, then in an icy tone, commanded. "Perhaps in the dark I missed you bend your knee."

He startled, and his eyes found hers. "Am I meant to in a dream?"

"Of course," she lied, waving her hand with authority. As he bowed, she continued. "I'm Princess Achelle of Aldersward Kingdom, daughter of King Adahy, and am sent as his representative to gather the necessary information. Only once more I will ask and if you refuse, I'll inform the king. Were the others recovered?"

He chose his words carefully. "Yes, we were successful. They've returned to the Endeavour."

"What else has happened?" Her chin quivered.

He shook his head, noting the movement, and remembered she was a fragile woman. "I'll say no more. It's not my place. I'll wake and tell Auren you're looking for him."

Her temper flashed as she shouted. "I can't believe I ever thought I loved you! How can you–"

Augustus jolted awake and smacked his forehead on the bunk above. The disturbed man grumbled and rolled over.

"Sorry," he whispered as he collected his things and withdrew.

Day 135
Prince Aedyn's Quarters
Anya's Endeavour
Baitsloam's North Shore

Guard Augustus, one of King Adahy's personal staff, burst through the exterior door to where Auren, Bennet, and Asa sat around the bigger table while Brielle and Sahana relaxed at the smaller, listening to them speak.

At the sudden interruption, the men rose and Auren circled the table to meet the intruder.

Angry, Augustus shouted. "Ridiculous, you do nothing *while* Achelle visited me."

"She what?" Auren hissed.

Bennet gripped his arm, realising where their leader's mind would go.

Augustus paced the floor past him. "How could she visit anyone else? You're all awake. I don't want her contacting me ever again."

"Ye're in nay position to make demands, Augustus." Bennet cautioned him to rein his temper.

Auren shrugged off his friend's hold. "What information did you offer?"

"Not much. She demanded to know if the recovery was successful. I confirmed it, then requested she contact one of you."

"She has no right to demand anything from you. Why would you answer? It wasn't your burden." He yelled.

"She iterated her station and directed me to genuflect."

Her adoptive brother smirked with pride at her cunningness. "And did you?"

"Of course, don't you?"

"It's my dream. Why would I?" He laughed and the other men joined in.

Augustus's temper renewed, and his fist punishingly punched the door wide as he left.

Their leader excused himself and sought sleep, impatient for her to visit.

"Auren," she entered his dream, on the Endeavour, where he sat on Aedyn's bed.

"I'm here." He raised his palm, silencing her. "I'll tell you everything, sit."

He invited her inside the shelter of his arm. Though he chose his words delicately, she wept, and he held her as he explained.

Day 136
King Adahy's Study
Castle's Ground Level
Near Aldersward City

King Adahy's most trusted advisors, commanders, and scholars gathered around the table quietly as he announced. "Lead Auren reported that since the journey's start, eight men have died."

He paused, allowing the statement to sink in.

"The vessel was six days southwest of Slaysfold and travelled east along the land until they found a city on a knoll, visible by sea. This was Baitsloam. The Baits ambushed and captured a group of our men. Prince Aedyn organised a recovery effort, and it was successful."

The men lent their voices of congratulations, but he waved his hand, silencing them. "However, during the retrieval, my son disappeared. They haven't determined if he's still alive or if they hold him prisoner."

When he finished, he slumped back in his chair. Uttering the words made the dire situation undeniable. There existed no rulebook or preparation for a circumstance such as this.

The astonished men murmured amongst themselves. It was a situation none had ever managed before.

Earl Adisa of Lessard's voice boomed with oozing venom. "Sire, we must retaliate. This cannot go unpunished."

"Your Highness," Ainco, the favourite of Adahy's commanders, begged the king's attention, and the room quieted. "I believe we may have an idea." He referred to those with which he conversed.

"Out with it," Lord Adisa ordered.

"The logistics are complicated, but the result remains the same. We build a fleet, travel, then kill every Bait who stands in our way of finding Prince Aedyn." The men whispered to each other, elaborating.

The king waved his hand in dismissal. "It took two months for the original craft to be constructed. It does nothing to help immediately."

"King Adahy, permission to speak frankly?" When he nodded, Ainco proceeded, glancing at each person. "They built the original with very few. We never gave the majority an opportunity to assist with speeding the building process. If we utilise twenty men and send them in pairs to each community, they could conscript those with building or battle enhancing abilities. The men found could report to Coaldale, the central coastline point. We could take hundreds and leave within a few weeks."

As the king contemplated the idea, silence remained while the room waited for his response. "Assemble the teams, have them ride out this afternoon. Instruct the builders to report within four days and battle abilities within seven days to Coaldale. We'll require food conjurers, physicians, and an arsenal of weapons. Prepare twenty boats for one-hundred." He rose. "The Baits shall pay."

Day 137
Main Deck
Anya's Endeavour
Baitsloam's North Shore

As the sun climbed, the men stood defeated. Captain Amos commanded the smaller sail opened and Alberto adjusted the wind's direction. Several scanned the shore in hopes Aedyn would appear in the final moments before the vessel travelled. It weighed heavily on everyone's mind.

Auren shook his head, striving to clear his disbelief. They were leaving Prince Aedyn in Baitsloam alone. He signalled for Asa and Bennet to follow, then strode inside and sat at the long table. Sahana placed the refreshments as Asa joined him.

"When you finish, please sit. I wish to include you in our conversation." Auren's request surprised her, but she sat as Bennet and his wife entered.

"Sahana, I beg your forgiveness. I didn't learn enough during our visit to Slaysfold as I was–" Searching for the appropriate phrase, Auren hesitated.

"Involved in optional trade?" Sahana's lips broke into a slight smile, enjoying his discomfort.

"Precisely." He allowed her description to complete his sentence. "I request your assistance. I need to learn what I may have missed or anything useful going forward. And, Lady Brielle, I need a history of Baitsloam since the divide, anything big or small which may help us find and rescue the prince."

Lady Brielle nodded. "Nothing significant has changed in the royal family. King Baeddan remains childless. He's chosen another bride from two potentials; one nearly two-hundred, and the other over six-hundred. It's rumoured he killed his previous wives. However, our kingdom has changed. Immediately, he ordered population control, only allowing each family a single child. But even though he did this, food and animals became scarce rather quickly. My wolf, Winnie, died eight years after the divide and I never found another. He ordered horses protected. I haven't seen a wild animal other than rodents and bugs for over fifty years. They divided the land carefully into swaths for growing large yielding crops to feed our population. Things like potatoes and wheat. Mostly we survived on those or fish from the sea."

"Can you tell me anything about the sea creatures?"

"Before the divide, maybe they existed." She shrugged. "But we had nay reason to venture into the sea. Afterwards, a few dead washed onto shore and soon we learnt of their powerful stings as they killed several of our race."

"Do any of your countrymen still communicate with animals?"

"Very few. Anything which could be consumed has been. Byunca still communicates with butterflies, but frogs, Bowan's ability, are extinct."

"In your opinion, what will be your people's plan? Has Prince Aedyn survived his capture?"

"I can't imagine there's a plan unless ye return to shore. It's not like in olden times when we commanded dragons, birds, or winged horses in battle. If ye return to shore, I can't speak to what they will do other than kill ye. By now, everyone will observe yer movements. If yer prince isn't dead already, they must have discovered his importance, and they will torture then kill him."

"Where would they keep him if they found out who he was?"

"The castle's dungeon."

"Thank you for your honesty. May I call on you if I have further questions?"

"Of course, anything ye need."

"King Adahy's plan is long term, but what now?" Bennet asked.

"He's ordered us to leave here and suggested we travel along the shore at a snail's pace, in hopes Aedyn is waiting somewhere along the way. After, we return to Slaysfold, where we'll resupply and make the destined vessels known. Achelle will maintain contact with me and she'll continue her attempts with Aedyn." Auren turned to Sahana. "Instead of travelling to Slaysfold City, could a southern community help us resupply? I'm wondering, would it be disrespectful?"

She thought as she sipped her drink. No one had ever sought her counsel. She wanted to ensure any advice she gave would be correct. "We'll be closest to Wrenswater or Finchgrove. Either is quite small and I'm uncertain they would help you without the king's permission. They would not risk his temper. Lady Synnova in Larkburgh may be the answer you're looking for. She doesn't fear her brother as much as the others and may gladly help you. As far as the king, you may wish to send a messenger upon arrival. Inform him of your needs and haste, then invite him to your location. A gift would go a long way."

Auren nodded, his gaze encompassed all. "Let's go there. Any ideas on offerings?"

Asa rubbed his chin. "Sumner, we can offer the same things as before. Lady Synnova though?"

"Sex," Sahana shrugged as Lady Brielle choked on her drink. The men looked at one another, the conversation most inappropriate with current company.

"Lady Sahana," Bennet spoke, using the formality of her name as he patted her hand. "In Aldersward, they do not discuss this topic outside the confines of marriage, the bedchamber, or same gendered friends."

"I apologise." She waved her hand. "But we're not in Aldersward. Synnova is the king's sister. It grants her very few allowances to..." She let the statement die, then continued. "I'm not suggesting it be the only payment, but if someone were to show interest in her, they might gain her cooperation."

Asa wondered. "Doesn't her station require someone above or on her station?"

"But what do my people know of Aldersward stations?" Sahana smiled. "If one was desperate, it could be said, the Endeavour's Commander was enough title to seek her company. *Lord Auren*, wouldn't you agree?"

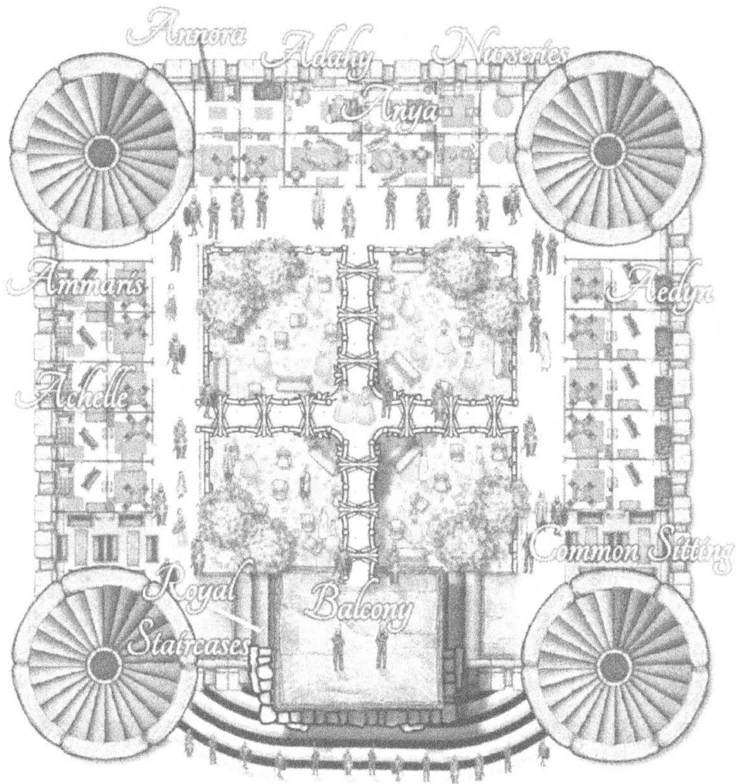

Day 137
Princess Achelle's Chamber
Castle's Second Level
Near Aldersward City

Achelle tripped on the stairs in her mind and she reached to steady herself but missed and tumbled, startling awake when her body jerked. Her eyes glanced at the window where the setting sun smeared the sky with purples, oranges, and yellows. Rising onto her elbows, she noticed the food tray on the small table. Astrid must have brought it in sometime while she slept. Her temples thumped, but not as severe as she had expected. A wonderful side effect of the tonic Axton provided her.

She called for Astrid, and the woman appeared instantly.

"Have you contacted Prince Aedyn?" She scanned her ward's glassy, unfocused eyes.

Achelle's elbows trembled, and she laid down, "No, not yet. I require more tonic."

The maid glided closer. "You took the remainder this afternoon. Once you slept, I sought the physician, but he travels today, tending the ill."

"Go discover if he returned. If not, locate another source. There are other physicians." She closed her eyes, willing herself back to sleep.

Day 139
Bethnee's Chambers
Castle's Second Floor
Baitsloam City

The elegant maiden, Bethnee of Pennington, King Baeddan's rejected betrothed, rubbed the sleep from her eyes as she slipped silently out of bed and secured her robe. She crept to the dressing table, separated the pins from her tousled hair, and combed the tangles free. Dawn's light played off its white and silver shades while she examined her reflection.

Indignation coursed through her. The knowledge of being passed over for someone younger was more than her pride could stand. But she would show both the king and Belinda she would not leave quietly. In fact, she smirked, the circumstances were far better than she had planned.

Unbeknownst to Baeddan, when he and his young betrothed had left for Crow's Pass, she had remained here and sequestered herself in her chamber. By luck's stroke, the young tart had not returned with him and Bethnee seized the opportunity it presented, ensuring she would not be dismissed.

She could not have arranged the previous evening's festivities better. The king hosted a jubilant victory celebration when the Alders had sailed away, obviously no match for the Baits.

Baeddan invited the entire castle to the long hall where musicians played into the night.

The atmosphere was contagiously exciting, generated by the unlimited alcohol being consumed. Bethnee's beauty still enticed attention, over six-hundred years old, but few wrinkles marred her near-perfect complexion. She wore a tight corset, moulding her breasts upward, letting the tops spill out. It complimented her waist and brought awareness to her rounded hips. After hours spent dancing with numerous men in the firelight's glow, which caused her long sheer skirt to become see-through, the king approached her.

She had foreseen it. While she remained under his protection, it was his obligation to see her reputation unsullied. She plied him with liquor as she pretended to be the ignorant virgin, a subtle brush of his thigh or pushing her breasts closer for his inspection.

When he was properly drunk, she inserted accidental comments throughout their conversation which, if misinterpreted, could be naughty. His brown eyes leapt with shock each time, but she continued to make them, playing the innocent role. She lightly sprinkled words of her disappointment over not being chosen his bride as she stroked his ego.

Stifling a yawn with her palm, she requested his escort to her chamber. Her excuse: there were too many questionable characters about for her to go alone. As they entered the wing where her rooms were, she recommended his guards wait so their noise would not disturb the others along the hallway.

Easily, she persuaded him inside, and she dismissed her staff, then began her seduction.

She tinted her lips red as he rolled on the bed behind her, and she noted his confused gaze as it found her.

She ensured her robe gaped as she rose, then bowed. "Yer Majesty."

"Lady Bethnee," he watched her plump breasts plunge forward, her nipples a creamy pink.

Flustered, she secured the robe in place.

Baeddan scanned the floor and found his gown within arm's length, and he clothed himself as he stood. "I must leave. My presence is most inappropriate. Where's yer staff?"

Her staff, those she had handpicked and promised prosperity to for their silence and obedience, over ten years ago.

She bowed her head with feigned embarrassment. Her eyes properly welled with innocent tears as she lifted her gaze to explain. "Ye ordered them away until further notice."

He ran his age-spotted hand over his jaw, struggling to summon the evening's events as he noted her troubled eyes. "I apologise. Don't worry, Lady Bethnee, I'll see my indiscretion doesn't ruin ye."

She nodded sadly, then winced, feigning pain as she stepped backwards, shaking her head. "I seem to be in slight discomfort this morning. Will I continue to be sore each time ye lay with me?"

As he finished dressing, his eyes met hers. His cock twitched at her inexperienced statement. "We'll never lay together again. I'm to wed another, soon."

"I'm ruined. What will become of me?" She dropped to her knees and covered her face with her palms, seeming to overlook the robe's parted folds, exposing the valley between her breasts.

His thoughts raced as he again sought to recall the night before. He had never taken a virgin outside of the marriage bed and was uncertain how to handle it. His old bones protested when he sat on the chair beside her.

"Don't weep. I'll see ye're properly married and yer husband compensated."

She smiled triumphantly beneath her hands for an instant, then replaced it with an anxious expression, pretending to brush away non-existent tears.

He rose, seeing her tears subside. It was an opportunity to flee before she grew upset again. He strode away without a backwards glance. "I'll have yer staff returned."

"May I request ye arrange my marriage immediately? Ye may have planted life within me."

He swung to consider her still on the floor, then walked out.

Day 140
Queen Anya's Chambers
Castle's Second Level
Near Aldersward City

As Princess Annora stood next to Lady Ammaris of Wibley at the foot of her mother's bed, Stinger perched on her shoulder and peered into her gold-flecked, green eyes. The axolotl attempted to mimic her sad expression but failed, then zigzagged along her arm and disappeared inside the water pouch at her waist.

Ammaris aided her by latching its top in place.

King Adahy held his wife's hand as he stroked her hair. He murmured to her alone. "My darling, I must confide before I leave. I miss your counsel and hope I act as you would wish. As you know, our sons journeyed to find a cure. Auren is fine, but I regret to say Aedyn is missing." He searched her face for any sign she heard, but none came. "Have you seen him in your slumber? Do you know what's befallen him? I pray you have kept him safe."

He kissed the sensitive spot behind her ear. "I don't wish to leave, but I must bring our sons home. I promise it. Sleep peaceful knowing my intent. I will return to you."

Seeking his attention, a guard silently came into the doorway as King Adahy placed a lingering kiss on her mouth.

He acknowledged him with a nod as he crossed to where the girls stood.

"I'll perform the bestowals, then leave directly from there. You girls will remain here, excused from temple." He hugged his daughter, then kissed the other's hand. "Look after your mother and each other."

He walked to the door, stopping to regard the two embraced girls consoling one another. Since Aedyn's disappearance, they had grown quite close—near inseparable.

Day 141
Royal Estate
Coaldale Village, Aldersward

A sliver of the sun bathed the land as the procession arrived. The morning meal would be a few hours yet, but the household staff edged the drive as the newcomers rolled to a stop. Like wind against the trees, the people bent. Adahy handed the horse's reins to his page.

"Lord Austen," the king dragged him into a manly embrace. "It's been too long." He wrinkled his nose, studying his friend. "You've grown old."

The man chuckled and playfully poked the king's round belly. "Sire, you're fat." He settled his arm over the king's shoulder and steered him to the entrance. "Your daughters must be grown by now."

The king nudged the man's arm away. "Speaking of daughters, one accompanied me." He crossed to where Astrid waited by a carriage. "Achelle? Come out and attend the Earl of Coaldale."

"Sire," his daughter's maid bowed. "She sleeps."

His eyebrow lifted, his tone hushed. "How can it be? She was asleep when we left the temple. Has she woken at all?"

"Your Highness, a couple of times, but she tries constantly to find Prince Aedyn in order to please you."

"She pleases me plenty. I expect a word with her the next time she wakes. I'll carry her inside. Is she decent?"

Astrid nodded, and the king spoke loudly. "Lord Austen, I regret we must postpone your reunion." He lifted his daughter's unresponsive body, noting she weighed less than he had anticipated. Familiar with the estate's layout, he strode past the earl.

The man followed. "The chamber beside yours should meet her needs."

While Commander Ainco gave them his report, the king and Austen sat side by each in the study.

"Your Highness, we've erected a tent village to the north. It can house one-thousand men. We've ten cooks and helpers. Three hundred builders have arrived from wood manipulators, tree growers, and men of strength. We should be ready to leave within three weeks. I'll assign each commander battle-able candidates as they arrive to evaluate. They'll determine their worthiness, then train together until we leave."

"Well done. Keep me informed of the progress. Once the first vessel's loaded, it must depart immediately."

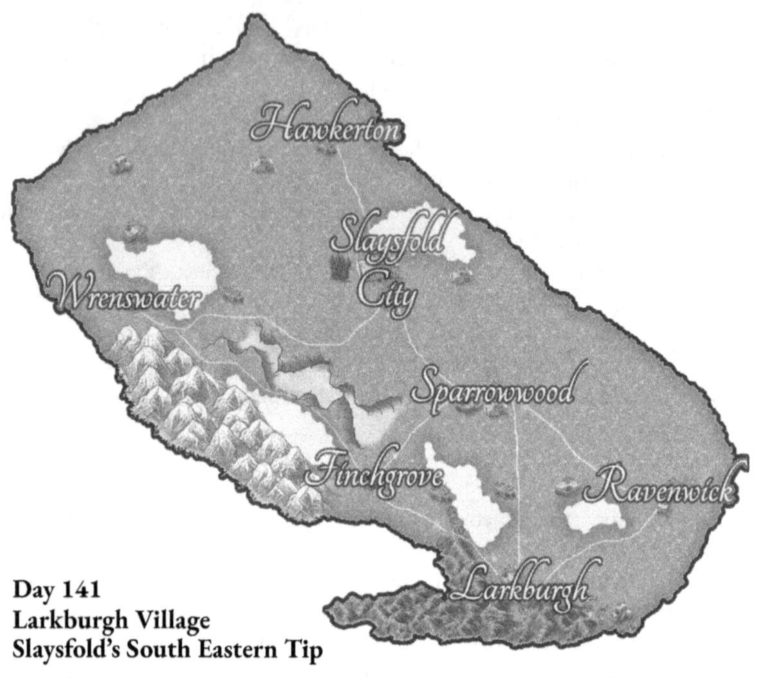

Day 141
Larkburgh Village
Slaysfold's South Eastern Tip

The afternoon temperature felt like an Aldersward winter as the four boats rowed to shore. Auren fixated on the Slays' movements, his instinct scarred with remnants of suspicion from their Baitsloam encounter.

Sahana had educated them at length about the busy mining community of Larkburgh, larger than Slaysfold City. From his vantage point, Auren observed several mining tunnels bustling with activity.

The Slays appeared indifferent to the arrival except for a handful who stood regarding them with interest. Satisfied no threat existed, he studied the group of five striking women. Lady Synnova stood in the centre.

The flare-legged leather trousers dipped to her groin from the axe's weight secured in her belt. He discovered one, then two exposed ribs as his gaze travelled upward over her tight skin. His shaft stirred, excited by his shameless inspection. A taut leather vest inlaid with blue rocks belted across her third ribs and her breasts pushed against the fabric as it climbed to her throat. Her pinned hair nestled against the back of her head, then free-flowed over her spine. Interwoven with shiny fragments of metal, a small braid fell from behind her ear to her abdomen. Her circlet of tangled vines and blue stones rested at her crown. He glanced over her flawless complexion, soft lips, and high, defined cheekbones as she shifted proudly under his scrutinising assault.

As his eyes found hers, his tongue passed over his bottom lip.

Unfairly, she'd been allowed her more beauty than any one man deserved.

He raised his face skyward. *Thank Jezabet, he created her Slay.*

The women drifted closer as the boats touched the beach. Auren, Augustus, Bennet, and Brielle walked forward to greet her as the other men dragged the boats onto the shore.

"Lady Synnova," Bennet dropped his bag and smiled as he bowed and kissed her hand. "It's a wonderful pleasure to see ye again. May I present my wife, Lady Brielle of Crow's Pass."

Lady Brielle curtsied and waited for her to speak, while the other women examined the strangeness of her clothing.

"Lady Brielle, are you injured?" Synnova's expression narrowed.

"I don't believe so." She inspected her bare arms and collarbone. They displayed no sign of injury as Bennet patted her hand, drawing her attention.

"They wonder about yer abundance of clothing." He answered for her. "This is the customary dress in Baitsloam, but we appreciate yer concern." Lady Synnova nodded her proud chin as he continued. "I don't believe ye've met Lord Auren of Maidstone, current ruler of Anya's Endeavour."

Auren strode forward and locked his brown eyes with her blue ones as he grazed his fingers lightly from her elbow to palm. He bowed without altering his gaze, but instead of kissing the back, his lips lingered on the inside of her wrist.

Augustus, who stood beside his new liege, planted his solid grip on Auren's shoulder and pulled him to stand, breaking the embrace.

Auren stepped closer and murmured. "Lady Synnova, I don't believe you've enjoyed the experience of meeting me?"

Her frame stiffened with confidence under his inspection and intimate words. "The enjoyment would be yours, if we had." Her gaze drifted past him to search the Alders. "Prince Aedyn doesn't lead you to shore?"

"I've much to share with you. Perhaps someplace more secluded?" He grinned mischievously.

Her expression flashed regret for an instant. It had been so long since another had satisfied her. She smiled and turned around, but before the other Slays fell in behind her, Auren's gaze met the small tattoo partially visible above the belt at her ass. He imagined her naked on all fours, and he smiled.

The Alders waited for Auren to follow, but when he didn't advance, Augustus nudged him forward.

"Auren, be serious." Augustus hissed, securing his hair with his hand to hold it from the breeze.

"*Lord* Auren." He quietly corrected as he trailed thirty paces behind the Slays. His expression was solemn. "I apologise. I was contemplating the burden of endurance and dedication demanded of me. It became almost too much to bear. Nevertheless, I'll not resent the obligations which have befallen me now." He rested his hand on the man's shoulder as a wicked smile lifted his lips. "Mine's a tremendous sacrifice."

Good-natured, Augustus shrugged off his hand then punched his side. "Your loyalty knows no constraints."

The manor was identical in design to Slaysfold castle, only smaller, a single-storey, long structure and as they approached it, the other four women continued inside, leaving Synnova to wait for the guests.

Bennet strode past the Alders. "Would there be an inn here?"

"As at the castle, you're welcome to dwell with us."

"Aye, my wife and I appreciate yer hospitality. Under ordinary circumstances, we would readily accept, but there is seldom time and space on our boat to be alone. We hope for privacy."

"Sandra?" She called into the dim interior. "She'll guide you. Feel free to join us as you please."

"Most kind," Bennet nodded as Auren and Augustus reached them. "Lord Auren, we'll be at the inn, if ye require us."

"Enjoy yourselves." He dismissed him and stopped next to Synnova. "After you." She turned, and he settled his palm over the small, bared tattoo portion, guiding her inside.

The front room was like the one they'd previously visited, but they wedged the throne in a corner loaded with neglected possessions. It was evident King Sumner had not presented in some time and no one saw the purpose for it otherwise.

Auren's group rested at a table inside the entrance when Synnova and her women returned from an adjoining room. While the others proceeded through the room, past the Alders and outside, she seated herself at a set table furthest from him and his men.

Her voice echoed. "Lord Auren, there's merely a meal for two. Would you join me?"

He murmured to his men as they exited, then he leisurely sauntered to her.

She watched his muscled chest push against the taut fabric of his tunic, admiring his slim, tapered waist. Her gaze drifted over his thick neck, bristled jaw, and settled on his smoky eyes, which had witnessed her hungry inspection.

He cleared his throat. "It looks tempting."

Her curiosity peaked. "What makes you *Lord* in your kingdom?"

Rejecting the opposing bench, he circled the table to sit at her side. He boasted as she repositioned the place setting. "I'm titled by the Endeavour and our king."

"Your title includes property?"

"If you're wondering if we're equals, we are. I'm a lord and you're a lady, both titled by the crown of our kingdoms." He shrugged. The information unimportant. "Is Lord Sarrell not joining us?"

"My husband's in Wrenswater, attending my affairs." As she reached across him, she brushed her breast against his arm.

"Should we seek another chaperon?" He turned his head, their lips only inches apart.

She massaged a large strawberry against her tongue, then bit its end. "You wish to guarantee your safety?"

"No, it's you I wish to protect." He lifted several slices of meat onto his plate and reached for the bread.

A bubbling laugh escaped her as she gripped his forearm and squeezed. "Trust my words, I would adequately dominate you."

"I admit I would enjoy the challenge." He winked, and a devilish grin appeared.

"Perhaps you shall." She placed her fingertip covered with strawberry juice against his lips, and he sucked it clean. "Now then, what's your business here?"

Day 141
The Travellers' Tavern
Larkburgh Village, Slaysfold

"It's not much." Bennet's nervous voice wavered as she stepped inside. He leaned against the doorframe, waiting for her reaction.

Brielle's gaze passed over the table, two benches, and the large bed crafted from bricks of dried mud. She drew back the blanket and inspected the bedding. As she clamped her shaking hands together, she turned and shrugged. "It's clean. Are ye coming inside?"

He shook his head. "Nay, I've a few errands, but ye should remain inside. I'll have a bath delivered for you. Then when I return, we can dine together in my room."

"Yer room?"

"It's been a long time, wife." His pet name for her drew his grin. "I wouldn't presume to share yer bed." He pointed to another door inside. "Our rooms are attached. I'll knock when I return. Keep this one barred."

She locked it, then crossed to the connecting door and opened it. With a barrier between them, they could not renew their relationship.

Day 141
Front Room
Royal Manor
Larkburgh Village, Slaysfold

Their foreplay amused Auren. As they finished their meal, he detailed their encounter with the Baits. "We've conferred with King Adahy. He'll arrive before the next moon with many vessels and supplies, but we require some now. This leads me to why we're here. I hope to gain your help, if you'll lend it?" He dragged his fingers lightly up her arm.

Synnova sipped from her fourth mug of wine, enjoying the touch of his rough hand on her flesh as she thought about his request. "I see no reason not to offer. Our king gave it before. What shall you offer in terms?"

His fingers rubbed the cord in her neck. "Unfortunately, our seed grower died. Would furs interest you?" He waited for her response. Her eyes closed and her hand found his knee. He continued. "I could have any amount created for you." He cursed himself for being exceptional at seduction. Clearly, she was already in a state past reasoning. "Or something else brought from Aldersward?" He turned her body to run his fingers from her forehead down her cheek. Her face pressed into his palm and her eyes drifted open as his settled on her mouth. "Name any price."

She laid her hand against his chest, noting his quickening beat. He expected a desirous, hoarse whisper, but instead, her voice was clear and emotionless. "At one time, a handsome face would have stirred me. But I was your age once, easily excited. You'll have to work harder." His mouth opened, but she placed her fingers over it, silencing him. "In any case, my finest thinking occurs when I'm content. Perhaps we make arrangements, then?"

Day 141
The Travellers' Tavern
Larkburgh Village, Slaysfold

Bennet entered, noting the adjoining door was open as a serving-man set two overfilled platters of boiled meat and vegetables on the small table. He arranged the wildflowers in the water pitcher.

"Husband," Brielle appeared in the doorway.

His pulse raced, and his throat tightened. For a single second, their years apart vanished as, per their normal, she greeted him. He wondered if they would ever restore their previous relationship. He inhaled a slow breath, asking Jezabet.

"Wife," his anxious fingers wound through his curls. "It's time we have a proper discussion about our past and future. Pour us a drink."

Her limbs trembled when she walked to the counter, predicting his words. She was old, no longer a young bride. It seemed logical he would have remarried three times over. Out of honour, she knew he would return to her and their children, but where would his love lie?

The food was more than she had consumed over several months. Yet as she placed their drinks down and sat opposite him, her appetite fled.

"Tell me about yer lives while we were apart." He forked meat, concentrating on it rather than watching her.

"When we lost ye, our kingdom lost many. Changes occurred quickly so we could persevere. We could nay longer afford to bury our dead, but we couldn't waste what they provided either. Baeddan ordered they be fragmented and scattered through empty fields. We nearly starved, and gluttony became rampant. Many nights we spent hungry."

"Yer story tells me what transpired in Baitsloam, but not about ye and our children. I'll begin." He stared at the mug where her hand had been, incapable of meeting her eyes and as he remembered the past, guilt weighted him. "I grieved for many years through six Alder kings. Nightmares and sorrow for our family, for ye, haunted me. At some point, nay matter how much I didn't want to, I had to let go."

Brielle fought to keep her emotions contained as she watched him focus on her drink. She would not cry, beg, or plead. She and their children would conform to any arrangement he made without allowing him to see how it would break her.

"I," she took care in choosing her words, "also grieved, but I had our children to consider and console me." She shrugged. "But I understand, ye were alone. I had nay opportunity to move on as I raised our children."

"Would ye have?"

"I don't know, perhaps someday. The boys worked, and Byunca would have suitors before long. I assumed afterwards, I would find a companion." She sipped the tea, then inspected its side. "Now, our children and I will live however ye wish us to fit into yer life. Understandably, if yer current wife and offspring are distressed by our presence, we could reside farther away from ye."

His eyes skipped to her face. "My current wife? What makes ye think I have one?"

Her gaze narrowed. "Haven't ye? Ye thought us dead, and I recognise yer expressions. Ye look guilty."

"Aye, I'm guilty, but not because I've another wife or children." He wiped his palm over his face, attempting to calm his frustration over the pain he would cause her. "There were other women, but I didn't wed them."

"Oh?" Her voice broke. She sought to shield him from the unfair hurt she felt. She stammered for something to say. "I'm glad ye didn't remarry."

He sat back and crossed his arms. "I need to determine whether ye're angry or hurt."

"It would be wrong of me to be either, wouldn't it?"

He nodded, "Aye. But nevertheless, I expect ye to feel either or both."

She laid her hands in her lap. "Why does it matter?"

"Ye're my wife, and I want our marriage restored. I can't ask ye the same without knowing yer feelings."

She gave up. "I'm unreasonably angry and hurt."

He grinned. "Perfect. Now let's argue about that." He raised his voice. "Ye were dead! Was I supposed to live the remainder of my existence in misery?"

Day 141
Lady Synnova's Bedchamber
Royal Manor
Larkburgh Village, Slaysfold

It was the strangest sensation Auren ever experienced as he followed Synnova into her bedchamber. An intimate sanctuary she shared with her husband. She would be the first married woman he seduced, and his excitement strengthened.

The sound of crackling dung patties in the hearth was the sole break in the silence. She latched the door closed, then circled him. He watched her face as she passed her eyes up and down—inspecting, evaluating—as if he was a stallion she would possibly purchase. Somehow, clothed, she made him vulnerable and insecure.

"What is it you're looking at?" He broadened his smile and reached for her arm, but she flung it off.

"Stay where you are." She backed away and leaned on the bed's edge. "Unbutton and remove your tunic."

He raised his brow. "Wouldn't you prefer we become naked together when our passion overwhelms us?"

She shook her head, her icy blue eyes and expression quite serious. "I would prefer you spoke less."

This was not what he had in mind.

He swept his hands negatively and stepped backwards. "I'm not accustomed to–"

"No, inexperienced, you wouldn't be."

"There haven't been complaints."

"I don't suppose there would be from the *girls* you likely pay." She walked to a side table. "I'm finished. Either discard your clothing and close your mouth or leave." She poured a mug of wine. "I've no interest in what would pass as your expertise."

His mouth gaped, and he stayed watching her. Anger, indignity, disbelief, and the desire to assert himself flowed through his body as he lifted his fingers to the buttons. He would participate in her game and confirm his talents. He vowed, before the evening ended, he would force her to concede.

She lowered the wine from her lips as she turned to see why he still remained.

"I'll take your movements as acceptance." She wrapped her arm around a bedpost while she studied him. "You may finish undressing, but stay there."

He looked at his boots. How absurd. How was he to extract them without tumbling over and making himself a fool? Resigned, he sat on the floor, loosened, and yanked them free, happy his trousers were on. He stood and unbuckled his belt, letting the fabric fall, then kicked them away. His soft cock drooped between his legs. Self-consciously, he pleaded for it to stiffen, knowing without looking that her eyes were fixed on him.

"That's an issue." She tossed her lengthy brown hair over her shoulder and observed the vein in his throat pulsate with anger.

She sauntered around him, running her fingers over his frame, reminding him again of someone interested in acquiring stock. He watched her diminish him to the abundance of muscles on his body and the thickness of his broad torso.

She was aware of his discomfort as her fingers travelled over him, a spontaneous tightening of muscles and tendons under her palm. He was not the strongest, nor the most flexible man she had encountered.

"I imagine you'll do." She passed him the mug and backed away as he took a large gulp of the Slaysfold rum.

She balanced on one leg while she brought her knee up and loosened her boot, then forced her leg to curl inward as she pulled it off.

For the first time, his interest stirred as he appreciated her pliable body.

Her fingers closed over the leather tie holding her trousers secure. It slithered through the grommets when she tugged it free. She turned her ass to him and ran her hands down the bedpost, bending her body in two. She slid her palms up the backs of her legs, then grasped her trousers by the waistline. Synnova dragged them lower and exposed her slit to his gaze. Straightening, she stepped out and crooked her finger for him to follow. She crawled onto the bed, stood, and gripped the two bedposts. She lifted her leg upwards and over his shoulder, curling it into his back, urging him closer.

As she studied his face, she smiled with satisfaction. "You may answer. Did you enjoy your first lesson?"

A musky scent emanated from her, inches from his nose. He shrugged under her leg. "Games, they've never interested me. Either one participates or you find another."

Her smile disappeared.

"My pleasure is never a game. I take it seriously. You," she said pointedly, "should take it very seriously."

When he made the decision to bed her, he knew his skill and handsome, well-built frame would have her spread easily and done before she even knew what had transpired. But she was calculating, and in control, and her less than passionate response made him want to leave.

If it weren't for his duty; he lifted a miffed brow, "What now?"

"Your warm breath caresses me." She cupped her hand to his chin and raised it. "Do you wish to fasten your mouth on me? Like a dog's tongue to water?"

"If it's what you wish." He tried to bend his head, but her grip held firm.

"You've piqued my curiosity. But you should tease me. Run your tongue lazily along my thigh and gently between each fold." She released her hold and transferred her hand to the bedpost.

Inwardly cursing the situation, he pursed his lips. He curled his arm up and gripped her ass, kneading it. Auren turned his head and drew her closer, passing his tongue along the inside of her upper thigh. He angled his face to meet her flesh-covered hole and played his tongue lightly against her, ensuring he granted each piece of flesh ample attention.

After a few minutes, her torso curved away from him, enjoying his thorough exploration.

"Harder and bite," she ordered, her voice slightly broken.

His cock stirred at her words and it inspired him, his tongue pushed harder against her natural pleats. Then he lightly fastened his teeth over her budded clit and tugged. As she moaned softly, her heel dug into his spine, and his mouth curled with a self-assured grin.

He thought she was climaxing when he felt her small jump, but instead, her other leg settled on his shoulder and her hands captured the back of his neck. His palm reached up to join his other on her buttocks, stabilising her there.

Rhythmically, she dragged up and down over his tongue, her thighs trapping his face.

Without warning, she flung her upper body backwards, and the momentum forced him to follow her down onto the bed as she frantically loosened the strap below her breasts, then shrugged out of the leather top, freeing her dark peaks.

"Sink your tongue into my centre." She guided his fingers to her nipple, encouraging him to squeeze and twist. "Hmm, pleasant," her fingers laced with his, and she invited them to be crueller as she arched off the mattress. She pushed his hand over her toned abdomen. "Stretch me open with your fingers, then force them inside." She demanded as her head rolled to the side and she clutched the bedding in her grip.

He dipped his middle and third digits into her and spread her apart, then violently pounded them in and out. In his favour, his annoyance, and her demands served, causing him to forget his usual tenderness. He did as she ordered. He sought to add a third finger inside, but another wouldn't fit. Her hand pushed his head as she grated her clit across his teeth. He increased the pressure and opened his mouth wider.

Her hand let go. The blankets tugged as she balled her fists into them. He felt her upper body twist and her breathing quicken. She was not immune to his technique. His mouth attempted a smile, but she bucked against him, returning his attention to the task.

"That's it." She breathed. "Keep going." She curved her torso upwards, forcing his hand to cover her abdomen and hold her still. Through gritted teeth, she demanded. "Enter my ass."

Her words interrupted his tempo. No, he had misheard.

Her palm cuffed the side of his head, and her voice was louder. "Shove a finger inside my ass."

He felt like a marionette as he dragged out and positioned his two largest fingers at her opening, then slid them inside and rested his third finger over her buttoned anus. It puckered under his finger's pressure. He withdrew his fingers, this time straightening his third, aiming it for the entry she wanted. He buried all three deep inside her as she shuddered under his tongue and thrashed against the bed.

She fixed her feet on his shoulders and pushed herself from his reach as her spasms subsided. He stood and scanned her shaking body.

Her skull arched her neck from the bed, then when her writhing movements ended, she instructed. "Bring yourself over me."

He required no second invitation as he clambered onto the bed and supported himself above her. His shaft was hard and ready to enter her. He spit into his hand, but she seized it.

"No, don't add. Thrust inside me until your hilt grinds against me."

He had never entered a woman without adding saliva or grease to his cock. The thought sent more blood to his engorged member as he directed his tip to her entrance.

He launched his hips forward, feeling his length bounce off her cervix, and she screamed while her nails bit into the flesh on his back. He would have stopped, but her voice encouraged him.

She demanded. "Rougher. Make me bleed."

No woman had ever invited this. His lust turned all-consuming as he settled his body onto her and roughly drove himself into her folds.

As her breathing laboured, she chanted, "Faster, harder."

No matter how cruelly and punishingly his cock thrusted, she demanded more.

He felt her muscles clench around him and let go as she moaned. He waited for it to happen again, then withdrew himself.

As her climax ended, Auren climbed up her body and planted his knees below her armpits. His fingers guided his cock and pressed it forcefully against her lips. Greedily, she cooperated, accepting his head, and he lunged his hips forward, driving his length to the back of her wet throat. He braced his arms against the wall and, in a steady rhythm, he stroked into her slippery, hot mouth. The crudeness of the coupling was exhilarating and, with a grunt of pleasure, he emptied the contents of his balls down her throat as she swallowed.

He rolled off, exhausted, and extremely pleased with his performance.

She sat tall and looked down at him. "That was tolerable."

He opened an eye to see her serious expression. "Tolerable?"

"You'll do better in a few minutes. Care for a drink?" She slid off the bed, walked to the side table, and filled two mugs.

"Perhaps I'm done?" He sat up.

"Perhaps," she shrugged.

Her hand reached for a small bottle and tapped some of its contents into their drinks. As she drank from her own, she turned and handed him the other.

"What is it?" He inspected the dark flakes floating on top and detected the scent of pepper and citrus.

"It guarantees our night's not over. Drink, lover, it won't harm you." She studied him as he obeyed. "I've decided upon terms."

He lifted his brow. "Does your payment come from the use of my body?"

A throaty laugh escaped her. "Hardly. I wouldn't offer you a lame dog for what has transpired thus far." She shook her head. "No, I would like my own craft."

"Easily managed," he tossed back the rest of the liquid.

"Good." She crawled onto the mattress. "Let's determine how done you are."

Day 141
The Travellers' Tavern
Larkburgh Village, Slaysfold

Brielle regretted asking for complete disclosure from her husband as he recounted the acts he had performed. She wiped another tear from her cheek as he finished.

"That's everything. Brielle?" He wanted her to turn her chin so he could see her pain.

She kept her eyes fixated on the opening between their rooms, longing for escape.

"Will ye leave me now?" His whisper struggled, laced with pain. At the same time, he didn't want to hear her rejection, yet he needed to know her intentions.

"I think I shall. I'm exhausted." She walked towards the doorway.

"Nay!" He barked, stopping her. "Do ye wish to live without me?"

She spoke without turning back. "What if our roles were reversed? Would ye want me after so many men had touched me?"

"Ye don't understand—these were transactions, nothing more."

"Ye demand my response, but yet ye cannot answer the question yerself!" She whirled around and accused with narrowed eyes. "Understand? Nay, mine's the only perspective which matters. Logically, I realise my emotions are wrong and still they're what I feel. I cannot simply wish them away. Ye've nay right to demand answers from me. When I know, ye will know." She gripped the door, slamming it behind her.

Day 142
Front Room
Royal Manor
Larkburgh, Slaysfold

The front room was rather quiet as most had eaten then departed to work or search out other activities. Auren wondered momentarily over the words *front room*. In truth, there was no room behind it, so what made it the front? Could it be because it was the place first seen upon entering? Then perhaps, front meant presentation, and yet again, the ignorance of this race astounded him.

He shook off the thought and wrote.

I had scarcely fallen asleep this morning when Achelle visited me. I instructed the princess to deliver Baroness Synnova's terms to our king. I witnessed the toll these dream-walks take on her and wonder if the king has not noticed her pasty, dry skin and weight loss. She continues her search for Aedyn. This morning, most men arrived on shore to gather supplies with the Slays. With urgency, we depart tomorrow at dawn.

He slipped the voyage's journal inside his bag when the exterior door opened. Brielle stepped through, accompanied by Bennet. Waves of tension rolled off the pair, and their stilted body language expressed volumes. They acted as strangers.

Auren stood. "Lady Brielle." He kissed her hand, then turned. "Good morning, Bennet."

They bowed.

"Lord Auren." He spoke as their leader invited them to sit opposite.

She waited until her husband circled to sit next to Auren before she sat.

A young girl placed food trays and Bennet forked thickly sliced moose meat onto his plate.

"I noticed the men. Are we set?" The Bait filled the silence as Lady Synnova stepped from another room.

As she approached, Auren nodded as they stood and waited for her to settle next to Brielle.

Her knowing blue eyes found the lord's as he drank, and she smiled with mischief. "Is it still hard?"

His complexion reddened, and he sputtered a cough into his mug, but recovered quickly. "Yes, Prince Aedyn's disappearance will always be hard."

His glance darted, but Bennet continued eating, oblivious to her meaning, and his wife's expression was distant.

Synnova placed her hand on the woman's arm. "What's become of Sahana?"

Before she could answer, her husband replied. "She knows nothing of the slave." His wife did not understand, and she searched his face. "They've tied her in the hold. She pisses and defecates where she lays. I would not subject my wife to such a grotesque sight."

Brielle covered her puzzled expression. "I wasn't aware there's a slave on board?"

Before anyone could respond, the sound of horses, voices, and activity reached them from outside. The outer door wrenched wide and several women fanned out when they entered.

All but Brielle knew what was happening, and she followed as they straightened to stand in the centre aisle.

Synnova flicked her wrist towards a servant, and the girl rushed to clear the throne of debris.

As he strode through the entrance, King Sumner called a final order over his shoulder.

Those present genuflected as he met his sister.

She held her bow as the rest straightened. He left her in the awkward pose and greeted the foreign group.

"Lord Auren," the king grasped the man's shoulder. "These are regrettable circumstances. I knew I should come to lend my support."

The Alder leader nodded. "Your Majesty, our king sends his appreciation. As I sent yesterday, more of the king's vessels will arrive shortly, laden with payment."

"Sire, may I present my wife, Lady Brielle?" He changed the subject to draw his attention.

"A pleasure." Sumner's eyes skimmed her, disinterested in the aged woman. He turned his attention to his sister. "Rise, I wish for an account of supplies given to the Alders, and where is Sarrell?"

She breathed deep as she stood, releasing her body's tension from the held position. "My husband's away. Their needs are urgent and I've made no account, but the majority is food."

The king nodded. "I'll accompany a load this evening to guarantee we've spared no provisions."

"Your Majesty, it's unnecessary. We're well taken care of." Auren smiled.

"Nonsense, it's the least I can do." Sumner snapped his fingers, and a servant placed a mug in his hand. He strode to the throne with his sister at his heels.

"Sahana," the Alder murmured to the Bait couple, then went to join the king.

Bennet took Brielle's arm in his—their personal circumstances forgotten—and he steered her outside.

He hurried through the street, pulling her behind him. He entered the inn, ignoring the stares his rash movement gained. The woman who greeted them the previous day came forward, and he withdrew a few gold pieces, placing them in her palm. "We require a wagon. Have the packages I left with ye loaded immediately. My wife's ill and wishes to return to our vessel."

He steered Brielle along the hall until they reached their rooms, then he pulled her inside and closed the door.

"We must leave. Gather yer things."

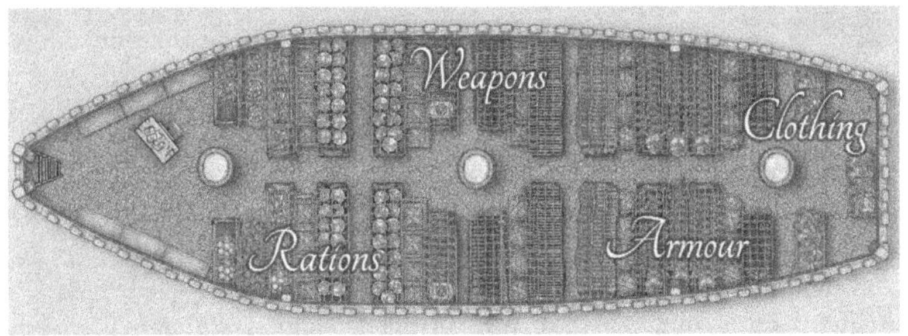

Day 142
Cargo Hold
Anya's Endeavour
Larkburgh's Shore, Slaysfold

Asa wore only his trousers and boots as he ducked under the curtain which partitioned the hidden area of the cargo hold. A crude circle of rocks contained a small flame, casting a dim light. He shoved his discarded clothing onto a shelf, then turned to where Sahana laid on her stomach naked against the sharp stones under a waste-soaked blanket. He studied the transformation she and Brielle had accomplished. Through her circlet, they had twisted and knotted her muddied hair. Soil from the vegetable roots dirtied her face, and her mouth was gagged. He witnessed tears roll from her closed eyes and trickle across her nose.

Wanting to reassure her, Asa crouched, but she made no indication she was aware of him. He placed his hand on her shoulder, and she flinched under his touch.

"As long as I'm here, nothing will happen, I swear." He folded the leg of his trousers and sliced two cuts into his flesh.

She felt his warm wet fingers paint her cheek, temple, and chin, and indignantly she turned her face to evade his touch. She did not open her eyes, but again, his wet fingers traced a path along the other side.

He shifted positions to between her knees, then held the blade against his leg, and listened.

"Lord Auren," Apex signalled.

Asa pushed the blanket high on her back, fixating on his task. The rancid stink of decaying vegetation and piss invaded his nose. Really, there wasn't time to dwell on the decorative-lined tattoo above her scarred ass, but he did, before he gritted his teeth and sliced a large gash along his calf, then held it over her. His blood pooled and flowed between her cheeks.

She cringed when the cool air rushed over her, but when the warm liquid touched her, she struggled against it, pulling at her tied limbs as the stones cut deeper into her breasts and stomach.

The men's voices grew louder, and Sahana sobbed through her gag.

He knew her cries were authentic. Out of time, he could not mention his intentions now. When the volume of blood on her body satisfied him, he cupped his palm over the wound, then stood and dropped his trousers, covering the deep gash. He wiped the blood on the inside of his thighs and over his flaccid manhood.

He remained still with his back to her, affording her privacy. The hair on his neck rose when the curtain dragged open and Sumner stepped into the space with Auren behind him.

Asa turned and displayed his bloodied shaft, seeking to gain the king's attention. He bowed, then motioned, inviting them inside. "Your Majesty, I'm finished. Would you care to use her?"

As his gaze met the man's thighs, the king smiled. "No. No interest."

Auren saw his friend's neck stiffen in anger. "Guard Asa, you're needed above to help unload the last of the boats." He clasped the Slay's shoulder. "King Sumner, let's have a drink in my quarters."

The king nodded and retraced his steps.

Before Auren drew the drape closed, the Alder pair shared a troubled look.

Alone again, he tugged the blanket back over her and belted his trousers. But she did not move. He hoisted the trouser leg, exposed the three lacerations, and secured his tunic around them as he heard the men mount the ladder.

He loosened her gag and whispered. "I'll fetch Brielle to stay with you."

With difficulty, Asa ascended the ladder and paused at the staircase, and leaned against the wall, relieving the burning pressure on his lacerations.

Looking left to ensure he was not cutting anyone's path, Augustus exited the dining hall and noticed Asa's complexion. "Are you unwell?"

"Have Brielle fetched," dizziness spun Asa's mind, "and get Aidrik."

Blackness overwhelmed him.

As she watched the last of the embers burn out, Sahana listened to men hauling and arranging supplies throughout the cargo hold. The sickening stench of spoiled food lingered around her from the dirty blanket sheltering her. She wondered why Brielle had not appeared immediately. Perhaps she did not want to attend to her disgusting, mangled body.

Had the Alders realised she was little more than an animal and left her where she belonged?

The substance Asa had spilled on her body dried, making her itchy. Her misaligned limbs ached from their immobility, and the sharp rocks dug painfully into her flesh.

Tears of humiliation had blocked her from witnessing Asa and Auren's repulsion when they saw her naked, but she could imagine it.

How could she face them now?

Lost in reflection, she missed the sound of light footsteps. When the curtain drew back, she startled, and the rocks scraped against her. She relaxed when the feminine voice reached Sahana through the darkness.

"It's me." As she knelt, Brielle set aside a lantern and swept the hair away from the woman's smeared face. "The king has left. Let's get ye out of here."

She eased the restraints, freeing Sahana's limbs, and carefully helped her to rise as the Slay struggled to retain her hold on the blanket.

"Yer modesty is needless."

She shook her head, wishing she had something to soothe her parched throat. "Except mine looks like the bottom of a riverbed, jagged and marred, now covered in whatever Asa splashed on me."

"Blood," Brielle bent, arranging the woman's shoes in front of her as Sahana tied the disgusting blanket above her breasts.

Her face twisted with distaste, "Covered in animal blood."

"In Asa's blood," she corrected her. "I've had a tub filled for ye above."

After Brielle detangled her circlet, Sahana scrubbed her body with abrasive force—her skin turned angry red, but her arms tired before she could eliminate her humiliation.

The other woman helped her shuffle into the dark sleeping quarters, now deserted, except for Asa, who stretched out on the bunk next to hers. High between them, a lone candle burned in its wall fixture.

His eyes were closed, perhaps in sleep as they passed him. Brielle aided Sahana onto the simple mattress, then closed the curtain over her bunk and left.

He searched for something to say. "This is most improper, us being alone here."

She exhaled with relief and shifted the barrier aside. "How so?"

Wanting the ease of their previous relationship, he turned to study her. "It's our custom. You should never be alone with a man who isn't your husband."

Her lips lifted into a small grin, and she reminded him. "We've been alone together many times."

His cheeks flamed with embarrassment. "I suppose, but this feels strange somehow." He rolled onto his back and ran his eyes along the bunk above.

As feelings of comfort and safety eased the stress from her body, her heavy eyelids closed.

"I'm sorry you endured such treatment." He tried again.

Her lids drifted open. "Don't speak of it or my anger at you will return."

"Don't be angry with us. To keep the peace between our kingdoms, we only did what was necessary."

Her temper sparked and she huffed. "I'm only angry with you—you fopdoodle."

He left the question for another time and rolled as his brows furrowed. "Only me?"

Her quick words scolded. "You wounded yourself to cover me in blood when an animal's would have served as well. Now you lay lame, unable to lead your men because of it. It was reckless. What possessed you?"

As she finished her tirade, he swung to a sitting position. "I didn't wish to demean you further by using animal blood. You had tolerated enough. It was my sacrifice to make, and I'm not lame. I lost a fair amount of blood, but I assure you by tomorrow my leg will only be slightly tender and I'll be ready to resume my duties fully. I appreciate your concern."

Her lips tightened, and he saw anger boiling in her eye. "Your tone does not sound appreciative! *And* I welcome you to forget what my mangled body looks like!" She yanked the curtain closed and flung onto her back.

Frustrated, he threw himself back on the mattress. "There's no need to forget. I took great care to afford you privacy and can honestly say—I never saw *your* body!"

She closed her eyes and turned, seeking her previous feeling of comfort.

He rolled away, not understanding how she could baulk his chivalry.

Day 143
Royal Estate
Coaldale Village, Aldersward

King Adahy settled his forearms against the tower's railing—a perfect vantage point from where he could oversee both the men's training below and the construction of the fleet beyond the village to the south.

As a commander required the enlisted to perform their magic, he observed with interest. More of his military leaders stood near and weighed whether each ability suited the king's purpose.

Adahy fingered his unruly hair. Who could know what would be useful?

Feet pressed against the ladder rungs as they climbed.

Lord Austen joined him, not speaking as he studied his long-time friend. He marvelled at his strength. Positive he himself would buckle under the enormity of his wife's illness, his son's disappearance, and the impending battle—something no one had done in nearly three-thousand-years.

Two men stood below. One directed his power onto the other. The second raised his palms to the six rain barrels, lifting the water out of them high in the sky. He fisted his hands, and the water balled into a single mass. Forcefully, he swung his arms and the water reacted. It crashed into a group of men, felling them.

While those on the ground righted themselves, onlookers clapped and laughed.

Again, the man lifted his arms. This time, he held them longer, and the water droplets rose into the sky, hovering above the wet men. Within minutes, the area and men were dry. He shifted his arms slowly to where the barrels were and poured the water back inside. Once completed, the two men shook hands in triumph, then waited to learn if their talents were acceptable.

"Useful?" Lord Austen wondered.

"I suppose," the king turned as Commander Ainco came above.

"Your Majesty," he genuflected. "Most messengers have returned with the men they chose. We expect the rest before dawn. As you see, the boat frames are being assembled now."

"Has there been a change to the timeline based on their progress?"

Ainco shook his head. "No, we'll be ready in seventeen days."

The king turned back to the railing, not wanting anyone to witness his moment of self-pity.

Austen's voice was stern. "Remind the builders, for every day they take, they leave their prince in the hands of our enemies and further jeopardise his life."

Day 143
Prince Aedyn's Quarters
Anya's Endeavour
Slaysfold's South Sea

The mauve and orange hues of sunset waned as the women retired, leaving the men to discuss more important matters.

Auren refilled his ale, then reclined at the smaller table, propping his feet up. Bennet and Asa followed.

"Since our return, Brielle barely speaks." Auren commented.

"We spoke of my infidelity." Bennet set his back against the cushion.

Dumbfounded, Asa planted his head in his hand. "Why would you confess?"

Bennet eyed the younger unmarried pair, understanding their ignorance. "It was the proper thing to do. I wish to continue our marriage."

"I sense she didn't react favourably?" Their leader sipped.

"She did not. She knows she shouldn't be, but she's angry and hurt."

Asa sat forward. "You can't be serious. You thought her dead."

He shrugged. "That was my defence, but she can't help her feelings. It's better I know, so we may deal with it."

"I'm curious. If you could take back your confession, would you?" Asa emptied his drink and walked to refill it.

"Nay, honesty breeds respect, which breeds love. Ye cannot have a marriage without them." He changed the subject. "Sahana looks unscathed by yesterday."

When he returned, Asa said. "This is how she acts, but I suspect she's worried our opinion of her has changed."

Auren's eyes narrowed as he remembered. "It was difficult for me to see her strung there, covered in blood. I wanted to strangle the smug expression from the pudd-puller."

"As did I," Asa relaxed. "How was Lady Synnova, *Lord Auren*?"

For a moment, he wrestled with whether he should tell them.

"On this subject, I must swear you to secrecy and understand our friendship will depend on it." His manner was serious, and he waited for their agreement.

Bennet barely acknowledged, but Asa eagerly nodded his enthusiasm.

"You both know my reputation with women is superior—nearly legendary in Aldersward—and I embraced the role which burdened me, but..."

"But?" Asa leaned forward.

Incapable of completing his previous sentence, Auren tried again. "She belittled my knowledge and laughed at my experience. Then she forced me to strip. And, while I was naked, she circled and measured my worth. If I have to label it, I'd suggest a lesser man would have felt vulnerable and worthless. I had no power over what transpired. She seized it from me. She directed every touch—its length, firmness, and speed. I did nothing without her permission. Have you ever had a woman instruct you, *squeeze my breast, harder*, or *faster*?"

The Bait man suppressed his chuckle by drinking.

Asa shook his head. "Are you suggesting she *raped* you?"

"No! Finding the words to describe it is difficult. It was degrading, yet with an intensity I've never experienced—I lusted. She measured, scoring every detail, and it drove me to surpass any of my past performances. Then when our initial sex ended, the first of countless, she offered me a potion. I was wary, but she consumed it, too. My cock hardened of its own volition and persisted through many encounters. Her desire's appetite was insatiable, and I lost count of our climaxes. The friction had rubbed my cock raw by the time she dismissed me, finally satisfied."

"You believe she drugged you?" Asa's expression clouded with unease.

He wandered away to pour another drink. "I know she did. But the worst of it—my rod would not soften and in the morning, when you arrived, it was still hard. It wasn't until the midday meal when it disappeared. Do you suppose it's permanently damaged?"

Bennet listened to the genuine concern and realised his immature friend was beyond laughing. "It sounds like Aframomum—a plant. There are many which will produce the effect, but it passes without repercussions. Is it still uncomfortable?"

The younger pair in unison let out a relieved breath, and Auren nodded.

"Aidrik should have an ointment. I'm confident he'll give ye some." He drank as Auren returned. "As far as the rest, ye've encountered the appetites of an older woman. They know what they want and expect it. Whores, as ye're used to, don't have this luxury."

The seriousness faded, and Asa smiled. "The question is, would you visit her body again?"

Day 143
Anchor Deck
Anya's Endeavour
Slaysfold's South Sea

A single torch hung on the mast beside Sahana as she leaned into the railing, listening to the water splash against the craft. Except for the odd voice or shuffling of feet, the night was eerily silent.

As she stole the unobserved moment, she smiled. Invigorated by the sea's mist, she could imagine herself reborn in this instant, and she crooned into the endless expanse before her.

Below on the main deck, a door thudded. She quieted, then listened to Bennet's slurred voice carry as he sang a boisterous tune. The others on watch encouraged him with laughter and jokes as he crossed to go below.

Approaching her position, feet sounded on the stairs, and she turned as Asa appeared.

"Good evening, Lady Sahana." He bowed, exaggerated by his inebriation.

"Good sir." She laughed.

"What became of your companion Lady Brielle?" He swayed as he joined her.

"She retired some time ago. It's late. Perhaps we should turn in."

"I think I'll stay." He turned to the sea and inhaled as the salty mist bathed him. "The air will do me some good."

"I'll leave you." She stepped, but his voice stopped her.

"Nonsense, stay and keep me company. Or I may doze and fall to my death."

"Then let's sit." Worried, she lowered herself against the anchor wheel.

He sat, mimicking her posture. Their legs stretched out in front of them.

His hands rested in his lap as his shoulder pressed against hers. "Let me ask you. Did you ever believe you would escape Sumner?"

She shook her head. "I don't think I did. I, however, hoped to outlive him. Perhaps murder him myself one day." She shrugged. "Or maybe another would have killed him."

He turned and searched her face. "Would you have been free, though?"

She stared past him. "If I killed Sumner, they would have executed me because I was so beneath his station. So, in a way, yes, I would have gained my freedom. If caused by another's hand, I hoped to be released, but who knows if it would have happened at all?"

"This," he swung his arm including the limitless view, then nudged her shoulder with his, "is better than both possibilities you imagined."

"Yes." She glanced at him with curiosity. "Why are you asking?"

He threaded his fingers together and dropped them on his lap. "I forget what freedom feels like."

"You are free." She laid her hand over his.

"No, I confess, I am not." He brought one hand out and settled it onto hers, sandwiching it between his. "It was never my ambition to enter the king's guard or travel on this journey. My dream and freedom lie in a fishing village back home." His chin and volume dropped. "When Auren then Aedyn went missing, this trip became my prison, and I fear it profoundly within me. I quake at the next moment to come." He lifted his gaze, more serious than she had ever seen. "I'm a coward and it's why I didn't go ashore in Slaysfold, and why I intend to stay on the boat for the remainder. When we return to Aldersward, my contract will near its conclusion, and I'll be free."

"My friend, you're not a coward. A coward would never admit his fear." She squeezed his hand. She knelt, using the wheel to pull herself upright. "It's time we slept."

Day 144
Sitting Room
Belinda's Home
Crow's Pass City, Baitsloam

When the king's betrothed, Belinda, wandered in from the kitchen, carrying her steaming tea, Beatrice lowered the trapdoor into place and pushed the loud scraping chair across the floor.

"Leave it, I'm going down. How is he?"

Beatrice's gaze travelled over the young woman's face, noting the tired, blood-shot eyes. "The fever he suffered and the redness of his wounds have left. I assume the combination of herbs and our massaging of his limbs has saved him. Ye should rest today. Get some sleep in a proper bed instead of resting yer head on his mattress. There's nothing to be done."

"I'm fine. I washed the morning dishes and now I wish to read my book." She used the excuse to see the man. Curiosity drew her. Perhaps it was because he was helpless and needed her. She could not imagine how alone he would feel if he woke now.

"Out loud?"

"It fills the silence. It's awkward to sit beside someone so still." Belinda sidestepped to walk past her.

A mischievous light danced in Beatrice's eyes, and her palm wrapped around the other's wrist. "Would ye do the same if he were ugly?"

The younger's milky skin reddened, and a small smile formed on her lips. "I hadn't noticed either way. Compassion is Jezabet's teaching." She pulled her wrist free and descended the ladder.

Beatrice's age lines wrinkled further as she laughed, "Liar. I'll come soon to bathe him."

She popped her head back through the opening. "There's nay need. Call me when the water's ready, and I can do it."

"M-hmmm," the old woman responded to the empty room.

On a blanket spread out next to the stranger, Belinda laid cross-legged. She propped her head on the mattress at his feet with the novel raised above her. The light from the lantern played over the pages.

…The maiden had never encountered the handsome stranger before but, by his single action, she knew her world would never be the same again.

She manoeuvred into a seated position to ask him. "Would ye have jumped in front of a runaway carriage to save a woman ye didn't know?" She examined his face. "Nay, I imagine ye would pay someone to do it instead."

She laid down and flipped the page.

Chapter Seven.

He hauled her to her feet. "Are ye hurt?"

Breathlessly, she shook her head. "Nay, I don't believe so."

The stranger strode away as she watched his broad shoulders, and she realised she did not know his name. "Wait!"

He spun to answer, but she rushed forward and tripped on her dress's hem. His brawny arms caught her, and he lifted an eyebrow. "Are ye always so unlucky?"

The maiden's laugh trilled.

Belinda's complexion reddened with empathy. "I would die of embarrassment."

Tired, she inhaled deeply. Her eyelids drooped, the book slumped, and she fell into an exhausted slumber.

Day 144
Division Compound
Crow's Pass City, Baitsloam

Prince Bryce walked beside Bradley, his most trusted commander, to where the Alders had escaped days before. He stepped through the downed wall and squatted.

"Is this private enough?"

"Aye," ensuring no one was close enough to eavesdrop, Bradley focused his gaze into the division yard. "I've overheard our people."

The ancient prince plucked a blade of grass and examined it. "What's the subject?"

"Many doubt the Alders came to harm us. They possessed great powers. The damage is undeniable, and yet our death toll was minimal. Some even imply our king has been mistaken all along. Perhaps the Alders didn't cause the earthquake."

"This concerns ye?"

"Nay," he shook his head. "I bring the information so ye may consider yer position. I will support whatever choice ye make."

Bryce tore the grass in two. "Ye believe it's an opportunity?"

"With the amount of gossip, I strongly believe King Baeddan should worry."

Day 145
Royal Estate
Coaldale Village, Aldersward

Astrid, Achelle's chambermaid, waited by the estate steps and nodded when the field hands and household staff walked by.

She clutched her cloak tighter. The sun had yet to warm the cool temperature of the morning. He would arrive soon to meet the king, and she needed to intercept him before he entered.

She watched four men emerge from the cookhouse. They said goodbye, and one separated, jogging towards her.

He tipped his head. "Good morning, Astrid."

"Physician Axton?" She reached out as he passed. "May I have a word in private?"

When he saw her, he had the strange impression she had waited for him. He nodded and raised his arm, signalling her to stroll along the deserted drive.

She confided. "Princess Achelle's headaches worsen."

"Perhaps she should take a break from her ability then."

"Oh, she can't." She placed her palm on his arm. "She attempts to reach her brother," then as an afterthought added, "for the king."

"Other than the tonics, the cold compresses, and the dark. I'm uncertain how to help her further." He ordered sternly. "She requires a break."

She walked. "These things are performing well." She inhaled a nervous breath. She disliked being sent on the errand when only two days ago he had supplied the princess. "The tonics have run out."

Furious, he seized her shoulders and glared at her. "What do you mean, they ran out? I left an adequate supply for five days."

As they had rehearsed, the maid covered for Achelle. "While I tidied, I knocked the pouches over and they dropped inside the chamber pot."

He let her go, but continued to examine her expression, wondering if she lied. "I'll provide another small amount. You must understand the danger. Taken too often, one could become dependent."

Astrid could do nothing else but nod.

Day 145
Princess Achelle's Chambers
Coaldale Estate, Aldersward

Staring out the window at the sunrise, Achelle's body trembled where she sat in the chair. Someone entered the through-room, and she knew it would be Astrid. No one else would enter without permission.

Her maid arrived, then closed the door.

The princess's sunken eyes tightened in accusation. "You didn't get it?"

She pulled the pouches from her cloak, and Achelle's trembling fingers snatched them from her.

"Why is there so little?"

"Your Highness, the physician claims it's too dangerous to give you more. He mentioned this must last you four days."

"Four days?" She raised her voice, then remembered she preferred no one else to hear. "This can't be. Does he not understand the seriousness of my task?"

"Princess, he suggests you take a break from dream-walking."

"It's not his decision. If he won't supply more, find another who will."

"But who? I know no one here."

"I don't care who you find," she hissed. "But ensure you have more this afternoon." She poured the pouches into the water and lifted it before the other could boil it.

Achelle's arm shook from the mug's weight. As she drank, it clinked against her teeth, and Astrid held the bottom to aid her.

Day 146
Bethnee's Chambers
Castle's Second Floor
Baitsloam City

Bethnee smiled, checking her seductive appearance in the mirror as she waited for the king. He arrived every morning with the same question.

A knock sounded on the outer door, and she quickly laid down, raised her skirts, exposed her legs, and pretended to sleep.

King Baeddan dismissed her staff and waited until they scurried out, then strode into her bedchamber. His eyes found her waking on the bed.

"Yer Majesty," she startled and scrambled to the bed's side to bow, but he waved her movement aside.

"Lady Bethnee, are ye ill?"

She dropped back onto the bed and stared at the ceiling. "Sire, nay. I'm exhausted and not sleeping well. The hall's noises wake me numerous times through the night."

"Why did ye not confess this before?"

"I didn't wish to bother ye with this trivial matter. Ye've much to look after."

"Not enough that I couldn't fix this. I'll order yer rooms transferred to the south wing today."

"Must I? The warm morning sun heats my body when I wake. It's magnificent."

He shook his head. "I'll instruct everyone else removed so ye may still enjoy the sunlight and sleep soundly."

"I appreciate yer attention. Has yer betrothed returned yet?"

"Nay, she readies for our wedding, but she will soon. Has yer bleed come?"

She covered her face with her hands and bit her lip, bringing instant tears to her eyes as her hands slid away. "I'm worried. What if I carry yer heir and marry another? Whose child will it be? Will ye confide my pregnancy to my husband?"

"I'll deal with it if necessary. Now, nay further tears."

She wiped her face and lifted her lips in a slight smile.

After he left, her servant appeared immediately.

"Arrange for the fellow to be brought inside this evening. And have a large empty trunk placed behind my changing screen, then inform the others to keep the guards clear. While he remains, ensure someone always watches."

"Aye, I expect if he mounts ye several times a day, ye should be pregnant before the next moon." The servant speculated and exited.

Bethnee knelt in the warm sunlight and prayed to Jezabet.

Day 146
Dugout
Belinda's Home
Crow's Pass City, Baitsloam

Except for a single candle next to the stranger and the lantern at her side, darkness shrouded the entire dugout as Belinda, propped against the wall, read.

As the dragon swooped from the sky toward them, he pushed her to the ground and shielded her.

She screamed, watching its movements, and she pulled at his arm, wanting to protect him.

He waited—waited until the dragon reached with its open mouth to capture him. With sudden agility, he ducked, turning at the same time, and swung his sword. It sliced a wide score along the dragon's stomach and it crashed to the ground, its guts spilled, then dragged behind it.

He hauled her to her feet. Quickly, his eyes travelled over her, ensuring she was well. He dragged her behind him as he raced along the path, then pushed her through the doors of a hunting cabin.

From the strain of the run, their breaths laboured. He dropped his sword and wrapped his arms around her, pulling her into the shelter of his embrace.

Belinda studied the sleeping stranger. What would it be like to have his arms folded around her?

It wouldn't be hard to find out. She shook the thought aside as another formed. *Nay one would be the wiser.*

She placed the novel aside and laid against him. Belinda lifted his wrist over her waist. She decided it would probably be different if he were awake.

Embarrassed, her complexion flushed as she hurried back to where she left the book.

Nay one would ever know.

As her body clung to his solid frame, Aedyn had an overwhelming urge to protect the slight woman. The smell of her jasmine perfume wafted in the dark interior of the hunting cabin. He raised his eyes to the hearth, and a fire erupted instantly. When had he developed this power? He wondered. Where had the dragon come from? It had been hundreds of years since an Alder had seen one.

He glanced into her ashen face, and her red lips lifted, inviting his kiss. As tempting as her invitation was, he shook his head. He needed to figure this situation out.

He had memories of saving her from the runaway carriage. And later, they danced at the king's ball, and all the stolen caresses and kisses between.

When he refused, her frightened blue eyes grew bigger.

"How romantic."

Aedyn heard her brogue, but the young woman's lips remained still. He stepped away, but she grabbed his arm.

Concern clouded her expression. "Ye're injured."

Her fiery red hair tumbled forward as she studied his shoulder.

He angled his head to see. Strangely, he felt no pain in his arm, but a bloodstain appeared on his white tunic.

White? Not a colour Aedyn wore.

"It's nothing." He smiled, trying to reassure her and whispered as he pressed his lips to her hair.

Belinda heard the Alder mumble and looked at him. Perhaps she had imagined it. She slid to his head and examined him. But, when he pursed his lips, she startled backwards.

"I'll return shortly." She whispered, then rushed away.

Again, the woman spoke without moving her lips. Her ability was incredible. He had never known anyone who could communicate without the aid of their mouth.

Silence enveloped them—the noises of those who screamed and the chaos beyond fell away. He tested his injured arm. He looked down, but the blood had disappeared. In disbelief, he wiped his hand over his face.

Her eyes fluttered closed as he heard her voice. "Ye must stay here with me."

She sounded terrified, and he stepped to her body, reassuring her with his strength as he answered by claiming her lips. He shuffled her backwards until her frame pressed against the cold wall.

He planted one hand on the hard surface and clutched her side with his other, forcing his body more fully onto hers. Passion ignited between them as he heard her gasp. He reached and lifted the hem of her skirts, dragging them upward, exposing her nakedness to the air. As he unbuttoned his trousers, his heart drummed loudly, then plunged his cock inside her wet, warm centre.

She folded her leg around him as she reached and laid her hand on his forehead.

As Belinda lit another lantern and saw the man's hips lift off the mattress, she gasped. "What's happening to him?"

The old woman grinned and knelt beside the mattress. She waved for her adopted daughter to bring the lantern closer, then placed her palm on his forehead. "He's dreaming."

"Of?" She watched his hips jerk upwards, increasing with tempo.

She reached for Belinda's arm. "If I must tell ye, then ye shall never get pregnant. Come, leave him in private." She doused the candles and lanterns as she left.

The younger woman followed, then extinguished the last flame and hung it from a hook. When they reached the bright sitting room, Beatrice dropped the trapdoor and scraped the chair across the floor.

Aedyn drove himself into her, and her muscles contracted around him. It was his undoing, and he sank to his knees, spewing his seed onto the wall between her legs.

Suddenly, a loud noise woke him. He was no longer in the hunting cabin, and he searched the nearly black area with his gaze.

As he looked around, his head ached. The only light streamed through the cracks overhead.

A basement, he wondered as he looked to the ceiling and saw the floorboards. It was a dugout. *But, where?* Could this be a dream inside of another?

He closed his eyes and sought to remember.

Auren and his men were captured.

The rescuers and he waited on the vessel for the moon to be covered.

How did I get here?

The night was deafeningly silent, and no movement sounded from above. He lifted his hand to his face, exploring it with his fingers. His chin was naked of tiny bristles. Someone had shaved them away. A jagged cut snaked into his hairline, and he winced when he touched it. In the moment, he realised ropes did not confine him. His limbs were free.

He shoved back the blankets and sat up. Except for what looked like an infant's wrap around his waist, he was naked. Dizziness struck him, and he fell back flat against the mattress.

He recognised the sticky wetness around his cock. Though it had been many years, he knew. A vivid sexual dream had deposited his seed into the material. This was embarrassing.

While she listened to the elderly couple speaking in hushed tones, Belinda laid her head on the chair's back and closed her eyes.

Day 147
Observation Deck
Anya's Endeavour
Slaysfold's Southwest Sea

Auren stood beside Amos and Arturo as the sun rose, casting its light over the endless water.

"Where are we?"

Arturo replied, "Maybe five miles from shore. Crow's Pass is straight ahead."

"We remain here until Achelle instructs us otherwise," he ordered.

When the captain called to halt, men rushed over the vessel. Several of the smaller men climbed the masts to bring in the sails, as others below pulled the heavy ropes through the rigging. On the anchor deck, a few men struggled to free the lever before Asa joined them. Then, with the gentlest touch of his finger, the long pole pushed downward, and the anchor fell into the sea.

Day 147
Dugout
Belinda's Home
Crow's Pass City, Baitsloam

It took Belinda's eyes a second to adjust to the almost blackness. Through the floorboards, the tiny streams of light allowed her to discard the things she carried so she could ignite the lantern. She managed to lift it, retrieve her belongings, and walk into the next room.

As Beatrice predicted, the man remained sleeping.

Unworried, she settled next to him and lit a candle beside his head. Its light was sufficient to perform her tasks.

She greeted him cheerfully as she brought the spoon to his mouth, dripping the contents between his lips. "Good morning, my lord. I must apologise for not returning last evening. There's nay decent excuse, but I fell asleep."

Aedyn listened to her melodic voice as he tried to appear unconscious. She spoke with affection, as if they were acquainted.

A spoonful of broth ran down the inside of his throat, then to his astonishment, she rubbed her fingers over the cords in his neck, tickling them while she crooned. "Ye must swallow." The cords performed without deliberate effort and he heard the warmth in her tone. "Well done, keep swallowing."

Whatever the substance, it was vile, and it took all his will to lie unaffected.

It was obvious by her actions and words she had spent considerable time caring for him.

Her voice rang warmly in his ears. "Ye're improving. Ye've never finished the bowl before."

Her eyes studied his full lips again, and she was irritated by her curiosity. She huffed her breath upwards, moving her bangs. *What harm could one kiss do?*

She dropped the spoon into the empty bowl, held her hair, and leaned over him. She settled her lips onto his, as she had seen the older couple do many times.

It was rather strange and not at all what she had hoped, and though her interest ended, still she continued.

Allowing her mouth to match his slightly open shape, she softened her lips. When she tasted the gross blood broth, she hastily drew away.

As she wrung on the soapy water from the cloth, she shrugged, deciding the kiss was not an overly pleasant experience.

When he felt her lips touch him, he nearly flinched, but forced himself to lie still. Was this ordinary practice here, or some sort of healing process?

Her hand tugged the covers downward. It was more than he could tolerate, and he rolled his head.

Alarmed by his sudden movement, she released the cloth on his chest and jolted backwards, scrambling to her feet.

He gripped the cloth and turned his head. His eyes found hers—the ones from his dreams. His voice sounded hoarse, unrecognisable to himself. "Where am I?"

Fear paralysed her throat. Her face flamed with embarrassment, and she opened her mouth to speak, but no sound escaped.

He watched her lips open, then close—the very ones which moments ago explored his mouth.

How had she entered his dreams? What is her magic?

He shifted his arm behind his head and clenched his jaw. The long hours of waiting for someone to come had left his patience thin.

Her tongue moistened her lips, and the lantern's light played off their wetness. "Baitsloam."

"Obviously." He wiped his hand over his face in frustration. The candle beside him reflected off his ring's ruby. "But where in Baitsloam?"

She remembered herself, and in a protective manner, wrapped her free arm around her waist. "My Lord, ye're in Crow's Pass."

Her words lingered while he sought to piece his memory together, but nothing rushed to fill the void. He calculated his course of action.

"I apologise if my sudden awakening frightened you. I admit, I'm confused, waking in this unfamiliar place, disoriented, alone and without memory of how I came to be here." His eyes narrowed to scrutinise her.

Disoriented and alone—But that meant. Nay, he slept while I kissed him.

Her mortified face reddened, but it was best to pretend it had not happened—a part of his dream.

"My Lord, nay," she dismissed his apology, and a nervous trill escaped her throat. "It shouldn't have frightened me. This was the expected outcome of yer recovery." She dropped her arm, stepped a few paces closer, and lifted the lantern higher so she could better see his features. "How do ye feel?"

"My head aches and my stomach's empty. It could eat itself."

Her lips curved into a slight smile. "My Lord, ye've had nothing but blood broth for twelve days."

"Aedyn," he smiled, and his chin dimpled. "I believe you're familiar enough to make *my lord* unnecessary."

She wished to die immediately. *Act natural,* she chided. "Very well, Aedyn."

Instinctively, he knew her name. In his dreams, she had introduced it to him, but he withheld the knowledge from her.

His bladder spasmed, reminding him of its swollen state. "I find myself naked and in need of a chamber pot."

Her eyes widened. "Of course." She did not turn, but walked backwards through the doorway, lacking trust.

Bright girl. Mindful not to act too quickly, he eased onto his elbow, then slowly sat up, preferring to avoid another dizzy spell. He used the single candle to light the others in the candelabra.

Movements sounded above, and dust rained through the floorboards. He heard two feminine voices—hers and another—*perhaps, her mother?*

Before he rinsed the rag, he unfastened the child's cloth. It felt good to have a task, even one as mundane as washing. The water's warmth caused an enjoyable sensation to travel through his body.

Once complete, he stood and wrapped his torso in a blanket. When her feet sounded on the ladder, he took a single candle and went to the farthest wall, hoping his new position would not discourage her.

Her palm settled on the blade's handle in her skirt's pocket and before she entered Belinda peered inside, noting the shadow changes and the mattress empty. "Where have ye gone?"

Leaning his ass against the wall, he stooped forward and feigned a greater weakness than he felt. "Lady, I apologise. I only wished to move, but it seems I'm dizzy."

She drifted within and stopped once he came into sight. She observed his stance and strained features, then decided he spoke the truth. "It is fine."

When she wandered farther inside, he heard the mattress's straw give under the bundle she dropped and the grind of the chamber pot being deposited in the dirt. She shuffled backwards and stood by the doorway.

She filled the awkward silence. "Beatrice stitched the cut in yer trousers and fashioned a tunic from one of Bret's robes."

He lifted his gaze. "My dizzy spell has passed. May I move?"

She nodded, but kept her eyes fastened on him as he stepped to the chamber pot. He used his foot to slide it against the wall, then turned his back to her and let the blanket fall.

Her face heated, and her eyes widened. What had she expected?

The urine splashed against the pot.

Her eyes travelled over his broad shoulders and back, then landed on his backside. As he directed the stream, the candelabra flickered over his tightened muscles, and she decided the high, firm cheeks were pleasurable to look at.

He twisted his neck to see her, noting the crimson colour rise. "Did you not have your fill while I slept?"

He returned his attention to his manhood with a slight smile when he shook it dry, then he stared at the wall before him and cleared his throat. "Lady, should you wish to leave while I dress?"

Could he read her thoughts? She wondered. "And return once ye've better situated yerself to attack me? I think not. Ye've nothing I haven't already seen while I nursed ye."

He shrugged and shook his head. *She's innocent.* Her poor choice of words revealed it. An image of his mouth nursing her breast flitted through his mind. But what would be the harm in playing with her? He rather enjoyed watching her cheeks turn red. "Sadly, I don't recall your breasts but your mouth–"

She inserted, "Nursed ye back to health. And what do ye speak of—my mouth? Nay matter, it must have been a dream. Like yesterday when I observed ye lift yer hips from the mattress. Ye were dreaming."

He nodded, blew out the candle, and dropped it to the ground. He turned sideways, cupped his genitals, then bent, gathered the blanket, and settled it around his waist. When he faced her, his chest rippled and the muscles in his abdomen tightened as her eyes glanced downward.

Again, she blushed, and her long, unruly waves of curls tumbled forward when she dipped her head, interested in the dirt.

This will be challenging. He sat on the mattress and brought the bundle to his side. Propriety demanded he snap another blanket over himself to cover his lower extremities.

His hands tunnelled beneath and released the one around his waist. After sifting through the bundle, he exposed his calves and rolled his stockings on. Then he bunched the repaired trousers around his ankles, covered himself, and laid back on the bed. He reached underneath, pulled them over his knees and onto his thighs. For a moment, his movements stilled—the exertion of the process weakened him, and he closed his eyes.

When he stopped, she curiously looked at him.

"Are ye all right?" She meant to speak it normally, but it came out as a breathy whisper.

"Lady, it would be easier if you weren't standing there, but these are the choices you've made." He opened an eye to peer at her. "Shall I continue to call you *lady*?"

"Belinda will do."

He confirmed her name, and it was good to know a detail without being informed, even something so insignificant.

"Belinda." It rolled from his tongue as a vision of her pressed against the hunting cabin wall flashed through his memory.

He grasped his trousers and raised his hips, then belted them around his waist. To his surprise, the pain in his leg was tolerable.

He bunched the blanket which had concealed him and sat up, tossing it near his feet.

Another set of feet sounded, descended the rungs and across the dirt as he shoved his head through his tunic.

An elderly woman entered and brushed her touch through Belinda's hair as she passed. She eyed their visitor, then met the younger woman's gaze. A silent message transferred, and the first nodded.

More wrinkles surfaced when she smiled and advanced on him. "Right as rain, Lord Aedyn?"

"I'm fine, thank you. Please, I'm not a *Lord*. Aedyn will suffice." He smiled as she lit another group of candles. At once, she reminded him of his mother, and he knew he would like her. "May I ask who you may be, miss?"

Unafraid, she chuckled. "Ye're gifted with an enchanted tongue. I'm Beatrice and I must keep my wits about me or my husband will worry."

His expression shifted with disappointment. "It would be my rotten luck you're married. Confess—do you expect him to live long?" His mouth dimpled with a smile.

"Aye, another several hundred years, shameless boy." She handed him a bowl. "It's not much, but it'll fill yer belly. I'll make more blood broth later."

Distaste flickered across his face as he recalled the horrible flavour, but he said nothing as he lifted a boiled potato to his mouth. Her husband would be six or seven hundred years old, he noted.

"It's vile, but it kept ye alive." Beatrice turned and stopped to study Belinda's expression for distress, then placed a hand on her arm. "When ye're ready, come above, and I'll arrange yer hair."

She covered the wrinkled, age-spotted hand, lightly squeezing it. "Soon."

The feet retreated on the rungs, leaving Aedyn and Belinda alone, but she remained rooted where she was. He imagined she was ready to flee if he made any sudden advance. He realised she carried a weapon inside her skirt, her hand was in her pocket. It made no difference, and he hoped it lulled her.

"I'm getting a neck strain from this angle. Perhaps you would sit while I eat, and we could discuss gaps in my memory?"

To her, the request sounded reasonable. She had equipped herself to gut him if he tried to overpower her. She crossed to the blanket she commonly used at the mattress's foot, and sat, adjusting her skirts. "What would ye like to know?"

He shrugged. "How did I happen here? Where is here? What happened to my people held by the crown?"

She waited for him to spoon another potato. She smiled, delighted, like a mother proud of her offspring's action. "We were almost home, travelling from Garsbend, when explosions thundered through the night. My home lies on the edge of Crow's Pass." She left out the beheaded Alders. "I discovered ye lying on a bed upstairs. Ye were injured and unconscious. After deliberating, we decided it wasn't our place to determine yer fate. Together we closed yer wounds and put ye here." She pushed a thick chunk of hair behind her ear. "It was nearly two weeks ago."

His thoughts reeled. What must his father think? His men? Had this woman somehow blocked Achelle from joining his dream while she was in it?

She continued, unaware he no longer listened. "Yer body overheated and yer wounds turned red. We used tonics to treat the reddening and water to cool ye. Eventually, both subsided."

He demanded to remember the explosions, but nothing came. "Do you know what happened to the Alder prisoners?"

"Aye, they escaped and remained offshore for several days before they fled." *They must think me dead.*

He stared into her eyes. Had she answered truthfully? He couldn't be certain his ability functioned.

Day 147
Kitchen
Belinda's Home
Crow's Pass City, Baitsloam

Tired, Bret entered through the back door and stomped the dirt from his boots as Beatrice shushed him.

"Quiet there. The man's woken."

His eyes searched for Belinda, who relaxed at the table. He pecked his wife's cheeks and handed her a string of fish.

He sat down, "When?"

As she gutted a fish, the older woman looked over her shoulder, "A few hours after ye left. How was yer day?"

"Good, lots of men fishing on the sea's edge. Losing Bailor's fields has everyone concerned about where their next meal will come from."

She dropped the waste into a pail. "T'sk! It was stupid of Prince Bryce to destroy them."

"Many blame the king for it and more."

"Really?" Interested, Belinda sat straighter.

"Today, nay one spoke in quiet murmurs. They were loud and uncaring about who overheard. They're questioning every decision and activity by the king since the divide."

She sliced her knife along a fish's belly. "I wonder what he thinks of it."

Belinda offered with disgust. "He's the king. He doesn't care what his subjects say."

"So, what of the stranger?"

She moved to stand next to her husband. "She spent the day below, and he never tried to attack her."

"Quite the opposite. He ensured my virtue and comfort above his own."

"But he speaks as a charmer." The old woman grinned.

He lifted his gaze. "Should I worry?"

"Aye—for her, not me," she returned to her task.

Resentful of the teasing, Belinda pursed her lips. "Aedyn doesn't recall what happened, and out of sympathy, I offered my assistance." She turned to the man who was like her father. "I filled in the straightforward parts, but ye should tell him about the dead. I could not bring myself to recount it."

"After we eat, I'll speak to him." He left to change his clothes.

Day 147
Dugout
Belinda's Home
Crow's Pass City, Baitsloam

Aedyn had every intention of attempting to reach Achelle in the afternoon, but when he fell asleep, it took only moments before his dream state passed and he slipped into a deep slumber.

Heavy feet crossed the floor above his bed, waking him. He rolled onto his back and stared at the ceiling. He noted the fishy smell, and his stomach growled.

Had the woman called her husband by name? No, but it must be his feet, he heard.

The women are cautious. They have brains or a good man to instruct them. He realised he could overtake them and run. But to where? Nowhere would be safe in Baitsloam.

He inspected his wrists. *It doesn't appear they ever bound me, but they didn't invite me above either. Could this dugout be my prison?*

Until he contacted his sister, he was at their mercy. If this was not his prison, then this cottage and its occupants were. He would have to be careful, gain their trust, and patiently wait until he could form a plan. He needed further answers.

As he took the tray, Bret pecked his wife's forehead. "The soup was tasty."

"Should one of us accompany ye?" She asked with a worried expression.

"Nay, I'm armed and only a stupid man would attack. I can handle stupid. A smart man will know he's trapped." He strode into the sitting room.

Aedyn listened to the scraping sound before the hatch opened. He shifted, resting his back against the wall.

An old man entered, paused at the entrance, and scanned the area. No reason existed for Aedyn to assess him. More damage than good would come from an appraisal and have the man react defensively. He busied his hands, lighting the other candles around his mattress.

Bret saw intelligence in his eyes as he stepped closer. There were questions and conflict, but the man kept quiet. This analytical manner he could appreciate.

"Food," Bret handed it off.

"Thank you." He watched him walk backwards to the opposite wall. Then he slid down, and sat—he moved well.

"It's all we can offer. We should talk. Are ye well enough now?"

"Now is fine. Your wife threatened me with blood broth. Fortunately, this isn't."

The very mention made him shudder. "Aye, the broth is foul. The traps caught nay rats today."

"I'd appreciate if the traps remained empty." His lips curved upward as he broke the bread and dipped it into the bowl.

"What drew yer people here?"

He welcomed the frankness. "We sought a cure for our ill, more specifically—for Reinshaven."

"Aldersward believes other kingdoms survived?"

Aedyn swallowed. "We know they did. We've visited Slaysfold and we're certain about Reinshaven as well."

"How did ye find Slaysfold?"

"Vastly different from here. They welcomed and celebrated our mutual discovery. When we arrived here, a Bait in our company assumed your kingdom would welcome us." Aedyn left the rest unsaid.

"How did Aldersward fare through our world's end?"

"From stories I've heard, the toll was widespread. Other races who made homes in our kingdom took the loss severely. They lost their entire bloodlines. We lost families who had resided elsewhere, and we lost our king. It was a devastating time."

"Do other races remain in yer kingdom?"

Unsure of his education, Aedyn treated the question offhandedly rather than as a lesson. "The father determines race and their children's magic. Most men took their wives to their homelands. But, yes, there are a few." He shrugged. "What about here? Do you still have other races?"

"Nay, seldom did anyone marry a Bait who would live ten times longer."

"No, I don't expect so. Our Bennet never remarried in Aldersward."

"With what are yer people ill?"

"It's not only ours, Slaysfold as well. They suffer from a sleeping disease. Are there any ill here?"

He shrugged. "Not within our circle, but it doesn't mean there can't be. Unless it happened to our neighbours, I wouldn't know."

Done eating, Aedyn set the tray aside and lifted the water-filled mug. "You weigh my character. Have you decided if I'm a threat? How do I measure or prove myself?"

The stranger's candour pleased the old man, another trait he admired. "Tell me yer plans now."

"I wasn't certain I had choices in the matter. I can do little until you turn me over to the crown or decide to kill me."

"Nay, I suppose not. I don't know if either will come to fruition. We should discuss the night we discovered ye."

"Lady Belinda gave me her version, and I would welcome yours. Men speak amongst themselves. I wish to learn what happened that night and since."

"It's mostly how she explained, except for one detail. When we arrived here, men greeted us. The Alders, who we assume ye were with, killed many, but they died themselves."

Who had been with him? How many men? Aedyn thought about the last moments on the vessel. There had been five others, and he named off each in his mind, remembering their faces. How had he survived? He hated that he could not remember his men's end.

Bret granted him a few seconds to process. "The Alders invaded the division. Their magics were destructive. Our temple and the division house collapsed first, then buildings all around sporadically. We didn't lose many. We've wondered if this was calculated. Would ye know?"

Apparently, his captors did not know his ring's significance, and for now, his identity remained a secret. "Unless forced, the orders were to create chaos without loss of life. We assumed the situation was a misunderstanding."

"It grows late. Do ye have more questions before I go?" He stood and his muscles groaned, but he hid his discomfort from the stranger.

"Just one—tell me, am I a prisoner in this dugout?"

"I don't know. It's not my place to decide. There are only two bedchambers above, ye'll sleep here. If ye need anything, ye only need ask." He left less cautiously, an understanding of sorts established. His back exposed as he exited.

Aedyn doused the candles, pitching the room into darkness, and he laid on the mattress. He sought to sleep but could not. His men's faces, including the dead, flashed through his mind. He wondered how close to home the vessel was. He knew he laid awake for hours, but without a window, he could not judge when he eventually drifted to sleep.

It took some time for him to realise he was dreaming. The castle gardens surrounded him and he called for his sister.

She never came.

Day 148
Princess Achelle's Chambers
Royal Estate
Coaldale Village, Aldersward

Those who had accompanied the king were unused to the estate's informality. King Adahy travelled throughout the dwelling without his entourage.

His daughter had not reported for several days, and he decided she would answer to him. If she slept, he would wake her.

Astrid stepped back from the chamber door and genuflected when she saw the king.

He nodded, then walked past and, without knocking, opened his daughter's bedchamber. The morning's harsh light streamed across her face, oblivious to it as she slept.

"Achelle?" His tone carried loudly through the sparsely furnished room then, louder, he tried again.

She stirred, but his irritation over her constant slumber propelled him forward. He clapped, striking his hands hard repeatedly.

She shifted, and he continued to clap and call her as she sat up. Her confused eyes met his.

"Give me an account. What's our men's state, and how often do you attempt to reach Aedyn?"

"Father?" Her voice was small as she willed her mind's drug-induced fog clear. No pain plagued her, only a warm euphoria.

He shook his head. "I'll wait no longer. Where's the vessel?"

Warmth wrapped her mind.

Where is the vessel? She recalled her last conversation with Auren. *What day is it?* She did not know, nor could ask. She would think on this after he left.

Her hand trembled as she lifted the near-empty pitcher, poured water, and drank, buying time to invent a suitable answer. "The vessel nears Baitsloam."

She would need to reach Auren and determine if this were true. She remembered they had spoken when the boat departed Slaysfold.

"When did you last visit Auren?"

"The night before last," she confessed. "Last night, I tried to find Aedyn." Had she tried to reach her brother last night? She must have. She searched her memory but only found holes. When was the last time she had dream-walked? She remembered her last conversation with Auren. But there must have been other times since. How could she not have?

"You'll visit Auren nightly, regardless of your efforts to find your brother. We cannot leave them alone to fend for themselves. Are we clear?"

"Yes, Father. Is there news I should relay?"

"No, but I want updates. I'll not be blind." He strode out and Astrid rushed inside, closing the door.

"Princess?" She bowed, her face marred with concern.

"I'm fine." She waved the woman's worry away. "However, I've lost track of days. What day is it?"

"It's day one-forty-eight."

Her mistress's behaviour and appearance had changed dramatically since she began taking the tonics.

Again, Achelle tried to remember what day she last dream-walked.

Four or maybe five days ago—not that long, was it? She shook her head, uncertain.

"I'll sleep now." Her guilt renewed her determination. She settled onto the pillows.

"Perhaps you should eat. Breakfast is available."

"No. I'll eat when I wake. Leave me." She tossed onto her side.

Day 148
Dugout
Belinda's Home
Crow's Pass City, Baitsloam

Beatrice found Bret slumped in the chair over the trapdoor, sound asleep, when she came out to make breakfast. Last night, he declared, complete trust in the stranger would be foolish. They should take turns staying above the opening.

Aedyn lit the candles and lanterns, hoping to dry the air and add much needed warmth as Beatrice entered with a bucket, bandages, and food.

"Remove yer trousers. I wish to examine yer wound."

"I think not." Aedyn scowled, and a slight pink flushed his skin. He was not a child to be ordered around by his mother. He was a grown man and expected to be treated as such.

"We need to ensure it does not redden like yer face." She chuckled. "Come now, I've seen all ye've to offer a woman."

He snatched the bucket and bandages from her. "Just the same, I'll care for it and let you know should I have concerns."

She shrugged. "Suit yerself. I hate to think we healed ye only to die from modesty later."

Aedyn slipped the tunic over his back, then waited as he listened to what he gathered were Belinda's feet on the rungs.

When she stepped inside, he acknowledged her by tipping his head. "Lady Belinda, good morning."

Her smile widened, pleased by his greeting. A sign he improved. The day before, they had neglected formal manners.

"Good morning, Aedyn. Belinda will do. There's nay need for ceremony in our home."

As she talked, he noticed her hand in her pocket. Today, however, through the sheer, off-white material, he could see the blade's shape.

He offered her his hand. "Should you like to sit and keep me company?"

She hesitated, then placed her fingers on his palm. Such formalities were normal in public, but it was strange to have them here.

When she was ready to sit, he planted his other hand on her elbow and steadied her as she lowered onto the blanket. His eyes followed her down, and he discovered a pleasant flaw between his manners and her clothing. The tight black corset forced her breasts upward. By standing over her, he had an unobstructed view. His libido stirred.

He relaxed on the mattress, rested his back against the wall, and smiled. "I apologise, my current lodgings cannot afford you a chair or refreshment."

She glanced around, seeing the dugout from his perspective. It was dark, rather damp, and smelled of earth. Depressing was a fair description. Out of necessity, they placed him here. In case anyone should happen upon her home but this was not part of her home—only a place to store things, not to entertain visitors.

"When ye feel stronger, ye may join us upstairs during the day. We'll need to ensure ye're not seen through the windows." She checked her hair with her fingers nervously.

The flickering light played against her elaborate up-do. The red-orange colour reminded him of overripe tomatoes, and the thickness could cover at least four women's heads.

"Perhaps your father should determine how free I am?"

She laughed, and the candlelight danced in her blue eyes. "Bret's not my father, nor Beatrice my mother. Although, at times, we feel it's so. Nay, this is my home and they are also guests."

He had wondered about the household hierarchy. "I accept your offer and appreciate your trust. I would like to join you above."

"Has yer memory returned?"

"My memory of the combat has not. I wish to remember how they died, so I may tell their families how brave they were."

"Ye think ye'll escape Baitsloam?"

His eyes narrowed. "Do you plan to keep me hidden or a prisoner indefinitely?"

"Oh—nay, ye're not our prisoner and may leave whenever ye wish. It will be difficult considering yer skin tone and the fact yer boat has left. As far as hiding ye, we'll do so until ye decide against it."

"Then my answer is yes. I'll leave Baitsloam, perhaps sooner than you would expect."

"It's good ye have hope." She shrugged his optimism away. "Do ye remember anything from when ye slept those days?"

"As you said, I dreamt the strangest dreams."

"What were they about?" She spoke without thinking, then suddenly remembered his hips' movements and she blushed.

He wondered if she was testing him, and his brow arched. Did she not remember the dreams she had inserted herself into? "I rescued you from a runaway carriage, then fought against dragons. We found shelter in a hunting lodge. Do you not remember my dream? You were there."

Her jaw dropped, and she rose, crossing to a crate. She pulled out a book, tossed it to him, and returned to the blanket.

"It's what I read to ye while ye slept."

It was his turn to be astonished. Several things made sense, her words without her mouth's movement and her presence by his view of her before he fell unconscious.

He tried to manipulate his mind backwards from when he saw her above him. A vision flooded back. Baits retreated from the barn. He recalled his fear and desperation as he stumbled toward the cottage door.

She watched recognition flit over his expression. "Ye remember?"

"Just now—some."

"Perhaps more will come later," she said with an encouraging smile.

Later, Aedyn came to understand the meagre food offerings when he joined them for the evening meal. It was awkward as Beatrice apologised, setting the potatoes, bread, and water in the table's centre.

He dismissed the words with a smile, placed his hand on Belinda's shoulder, and their thighs brushed as he sat next to her. He complimented the meal, and then a discussion about Baitsloam's shortages covered the stilted pleasantries.

When darkness fell, he reflected as he settled under the blankets. The Baits could have benefited from a relationship with Aldersward. It would have solved many issues if not for their ridiculous king. At least now the Baits questioned their plight. He could not imagine remaining idle while millions who relied on him starved.

His sister never appeared.

Day 149
Sitting Room
Belinda's Home
Crow's Pass City, Baitsloam

Aedyn relaxed in the high-backed chair, which normally protected the trapdoor, as he read the novel. It was a woman's tale, but little else existed to occupy him, and begrudgingly, he found it amusing. He caught his thoughts wandering, more interested in Belinda than reading, and so he reread several paragraphs.

The yard gate closed. From where she sewed, she glanced out the window. "Hide."

He jumped below as she covered the opening. A heavy fist pounded and Beatrice appeared from the kitchen to answer.

"I seek Lady Belinda." The messenger announced, but her eyes settled on the king's guards standing at the gate.

"Sir, now's not a good–" Beatrice began, but Belinda interrupted, palming her shoulder.

"Ye don't hold the authority to make decisions for me." She scolded, then regarded him. "She worries ye'll judge me by my home's condition. We've packed most everything. But of course, ye're welcome inside."

"Nay, there's nay need. I carry a message from the king and a letter." He offered it to her. "Yer to hire wagons, load them, and return to the castle immediately."

So he would not witness her worried expression, Beatrice stepped back.

Belinda opened the letter and it closely resembled his words.

"Please," she smiled, placing her hand on his arm. "Allow me to write a reply."

She closed the door, then crossed to the desk and wrote.

Yer Majesty. Yer eagerness for our union pleases me, as mine is just as great. I have devoted considerable time helping my neighbours, yer subjects, restore their lives. Time has slipped away from me. Has it been so long since together we left the castle?

I will pack and arrive within the fortnight.

Lady Belinda of Crow's Pass

She waxed it with her seal and handed it to the older woman.

As the messenger and king's men rode off, Beatrice watched from the front gate. Her husband crossed from a neighbour's cottage, where he'd lent his carpentry skills to the repairs.

She embraced him and whispered, "A message from the king."

Beatrice threaded her arm with his, urging him inside.

Belinda lifted the hatch before she returned to her sewing as the old man scanned the letter, his wife clinging to his side.

Witnessing the stress in their actions and mannerisms, Aedyn felt his presence was an intrusion. "Should I retire?"

"Nay, why?" a small chuckle escaped Belinda's throat. She meant it to add absurdity to his words. Instead, it sounded stilted. Her hands shook as she punched needle through fabric.

Several times, Bret's gaze passed from the letter to her. An uncomfortable silence held the small cottage.

The prince turned to the ladder. "I am intruding on a private conversation. You may wish to continue without my presence."

"There's nothing we cannot tell ye. What could ye do with the knowledge, anyway?" She motioned for the old man to speak freely, as his wife joined her and covered her hand in comfort.

Bret cleared his throat. "King Baeddan demands her return to the castle for their wedding."

Day 149
Princess Achelle's Bedchamber
Royal Estate
Coaldale Village, Aldersward

Achelle's hand shook as she flattened several stray hairs in the mirror. She wore her favourite dark purple gown laced with intricate white beading. Once a tight, perfect fit, now hung loose from her pale, washed-out frame. She looked sickly.

Her sunken green eyes found Astrid studying the gown. "I cannot attend my father and his men."

The summoning bell clanged outside, signalling the evening meal at an hour's end.

"Princess Achelle, the king ordered it."

She knew. He had visited at dawn and demanded her company. Attempting to diminish the tonic's effects, her maid kept her mind clear of substances and fed her dried bread and tea throughout the day.

"Your Highness, I'll sew the sides together at your back. No one will be the wiser." Astrid crossed to the wardrobe and removed the sewing box.

Achelle turned sideways. Perhaps she would go unnoticed.

This cannot be over soon enough. Achelle settled her hands in her lap. She was weak, and her limbs trembled each time she used her utensils or lifted her mug. She received scrutinising looks from her father's physician, seated opposite her.

Finally, the king invited everyone to the study. When he left without stopping to escort her, she was grateful. She could escape.

As those present left, she lingered, feigning a fascination in a painting across the room. She sought to shift her chair back, but when she stood, weakness struck her, forcing her to brace her palms against the table.

A gentle grip steadied her, and she turned. Physician Axton stood at her side, offering his guidance. She could not refuse and accepted, averting her face from him.

"Princess Achelle," he wrapped her arm in his and slowly guided her.

The other guests had already disappeared. The hall was empty.

"I know your father appreciated your update from Auren. Though, I wonder if you could quell my curiosity. How many days' rations are available before they must return to Slaysfold?"

Her eyes stared ahead. "Seven." The lie came easily.

He checked their steps, turning to her. "Your Highness, is this what Auren told you?"

Indignation brought her eyes to his. "Of course. Why would I state it otherwise?"

"Princess, forgive me. I understood when you delivered Auren's reports to your father, they were verbatim. I didn't realise you withheld parts."

He suspected the truth, and defensively, she answered. "I didn't realise you had a right to question me." She pulled her arm free and turned to climb the stairs.

"Your Highness, you're correct," he caught her arm and said to the back of her head. "However, I wonder how your father would respond if I informed him you're lying about your dream-walks? And you've left our men without guidance to fend for themselves and perhaps die? The tonic you're taking is dangerous. If others haven't noticed yet, they soon will. Your weight loss, colouring, and the hollowing of your cheeks are very apparent. I fear your father's too worried about his sons to even imagine something is wrong with you."

She turned her cold eyes on him. "The tonic you gave Astrid ran out, and I haven't received more from you. There's no danger. You can free your conscience."

He nodded. "Princess, perhaps then shortly, you can clear yours."

As a maid stepped into the hall, he left her standing alone beside the stairs.

Day 149
Dugout
Belinda's Home
Crow's Pass City, Baitsloam

The noise above ended as they retired, then hours passed as Aedyn tossed and turned in the dark.

What a predicament—harboured by Baitsloam's next queen. Of all the cottages to take refuge in. He needed to test his ability on these people. The old king choosing to wed the young woman, almost the same age as Ammaris, disgusted him.

How long after being disobeyed would his own father wait before enforcing his rule? Perhaps two moons, at most, but Adahy was a patient man. By this king's actions, he was not like Aedyn's father. He suspected Belinda had less than a moon cycle.

As bizarre as it was, he was fiercely loyal to these individuals. They had saved and sheltered him. How could he help?

He drifted to sleep and called for Achelle, but she didn't come. After a few hours, he woke with worry. What was going on? Would he ever get home? Doubt sprouted in his heart.

Day 149
Anchor Deck
Anya's Endeavour
Slaysfold's Southwest Sea

Bennet leaned his arms against the anchor deck's railing as he observed Angelo's men train below.

Blake, recovering from his injury, relaxed against a wall. As his youngest son studied the men's exercises, his lips smiled, and Bennet followed his gaze.

The Alders took turns attacking Bowan, measuring his oldest son's worth. Many times, they knocked him down, and Angelo remained near, instructing him how to avoid it.

Light footsteps sounded on the stairs. He turned, expecting Sahana, but it was his wife instead.

They had not spoken since their return. She avoided his sole company and spoke around him when with others. It was frustrating. He had no choice but to wait for her to come to him in her own time.

He treated her as any woman when he bowed and kissed her hand.

She wandered to the opposite railing overlooking the water, affording them more privacy from onlookers. "We must solve this, husband."

He followed her. "Ye only need to explain how."

"I don't know. But we can't have found each other after so many years only to lose what we had. I've tried not to feel the way I do."

"Brielle, turn to me." He gathered her hands, moving them to his mouth as he gazed lovingly into her eyes. He laid a kiss on each wrist, then placed them on his chest. "If I took ye, found each of those women and denounced their meaning and reinforced yer position in my life, would this help? Do ye need me to do this for ye? I'll do anything."

She smiled. "Would these women still be alive?"

"Certainly most would be. I reiterate, I was weak and alone. I only wanted comfort from losing ye. Doesn't the fact I took nay wife prove anything? I didn't seek to replace ye. Remember how ye felt when ye thought I had remarried?"

"It devastated me." She averted her eyes, remembering the pain.

"Why?"

"I didn't want to be removed from yer life or watch ye live with another. I didn't want to live as strangers and become a burden for ye to be saddled with."

He lifted her chin to show his sincerity. "Nay, because ye still love me as I do ye. Regardless of what happened through those lost years. Should we continue to live in pain over something neither of us controlled? Or do we go forward, happy for the years we're now afforded? I swear on our children's lives, I never touched another while we lived as man and wife, and when the possibility of finding ye arose, I never again. Finally, I swear I'll never touch another but ye for the rest of our years. I need ye to understand how truly sorry I am."

"Would ye marry me again?" Feeling foolish, Brielle turned her head, not wanting to see his rejection.

She was on a decision's precipice, and he needed to prove his devotion. "Ye want me to return to Baitsloam and register us as man and wife again?"

"Would ye?" Startled, she eyed him, noting his serious expression.

"I would. But ye know, most likely, I wouldn't make it out alive."

She laughed. "I meant a Vaguestimber wedding, husband."

In answer, he crossed to the opposite railing and joyously shouted. "We're to have a wedding!"

Overwhelmed with joy, he left her there. He strode downstairs, receiving the men's congratulations, then crossed to Aedyn's quarters and entered, interrupting Asa and Auren.

"We're to be remarried." Bennet beamed, but not even Sahana, who sat at the smaller table, offered congratulations. His body stiffened. "What's wrong?"

"She didn't come last night, either. Nine days without a single communication." Asa responded as Auren stared at the journal pages.

Day 150
Earl Austen's Study
Royal Estate
Coaldale Village, Aldersward

The morning sun broke the horizon and promised a better day before intrusions could ruin it. A bird warbled and others replied in song.

Forgetting the lists spread on the desk, King Adahy leaned back and stared outside. He remembered a simpler time when he and his wife had enjoyed dawn from the privacy of his bedchamber's balcony.

The door swung open, reluctantly drawing his attention inside.

His page bowed. "Sire, Physician Axton requests an audience."

When the king nodded, the page stepped aside, and Axton entered.

He genuflected and noted the two guards stationed within. "Your Majesty, may we speak alone?"

"Leave us." He waved his dismissal.

"Sire, permission to speak directly?"

King Adahy smiled. "Old friend, you require no permission. What troubles you?"

Axton sat opposite. "I know you require no further distress, but I must tell you I worry about Achelle."

He raised his brow. "What about her?"

"Last night, I noted signs she may be dependent on the tonic I provided for her headaches."

"Your remarks aren't direct enough. If you have concerns, I'll have them without the delicate wording."

He crossed his arms. "The symptoms are many, weight loss, sunken eyes, and absence of appetite."

"Could these be attributed to her fear for her brothers?"

"Of course." He shrugged. "But there's also the amount of tonic her maid has requested. And, when I questioned Astrid this morning, she revealed her worry and the extensive periods Achelle spends sleeping. The maid also mentioned tremors, weakness, and acute anger. These are further indications of a reliance."

The king rushed toward the exit. "We shall see to this now."

"There's more." Axton stood and Adahy spun around. "I believe she's lied about Auren's reports and her dream-walks. I don't think she's had contact in many days or even tried to reach Aedyn."

The king nearly pulled the door from its hinges as he rushed to her rooms. The physician hurried to the fireplace, but the hearth fire above blocked his magic.

Adahy burst through the bedchamber door and Astrid jumped at the suddenness, dropping her sewing as she bowed.

His abrupt entrance had not woken his daughter, and he bellowed her name as Axton entered, closing the door for privacy.

Her father grabbed her by the arms and shook her, demanding her to wake with his voice.

Immediately concerned, the physician elbowed the king aside and examined her. Her skin was cold and clammy as he checked her shallow breath and weak pulse. He slid her eyelids back, noting the pinpointed pupils. Axton struck her face, then checked her body over.

He lifted her face, pried her mouth open, and pushed his fingers down her throat, but only bile ran over them.

He examined her again, then confronted the maid, who stood nearby, her expression distressed. "What has she taken?"

When she hesitated, Adahy shouted. "Answer him! Damn you!"

She stammered. "When you refused to give her more, she had me find someone who would. A travelling peddler in Coaldale supplied me with another substance. Here," she hurried to the wardrobe and produced the packet. "There isn't much left."

He snatched it and studied the contents. Fear, then concern, flashed over his expression. "I know nothing of this substance. Astrid, prepare a cold tub. Your Majesty, have someone fetch my kit."

Day 151
Dugout
Belinda's Home
Crow's Pass City, Baitsloam

Belinda glanced from the book to the window. It was late and the midday meal would be upon them soon. Aedyn had yet to rise and she worried. *What keeps him below?* She closed the novel, then descended the rungs, lit the lantern and carried it with her.

She tiptoed into the dark room where his mattress laid. "Are ye unwell?"

His clipped, curt voice replied. "No."

She wandered, lighting the various candles. He ignored her presence, fixating on the floorboards.

"We worried," she explained her intrusion. "Should we examine yer injuries?"

"Nothing ails me." His emotionless words held an even tone.

She settled onto the blanket at his feet. He pushed his troubling thoughts away and sat up, resting his back against the wall. He knew he must test his ability, but feared her resentment and lost trust. His survival outweighed her feelings.

"Humour my curiosity?" He concentrated his gaze on her as she nodded. He chose a simple question. "What colour are your eyes?"

Her eyes narrowed in confusion. "Blue."

He swallowed, stealing himself for the difficult ones ahead. "Do you want to marry King Baeddan?"

"Nay."

No dishonesty presented itself. He proceeded further. "Do you wish him dead?"

"Aye," her head shook. "Nay."

His body relaxed. There it was. "How would you kill him?"

"Poison," her mouth clamped shut. She scrambled to her feet and backed away. *What's this?* She asked herself. *What hold does he have?*

"Finally, can I trust you and your household?"

"Aye," but disbelief and fear marred her face.

He ruffled his hair with his hand. "I apologise. I'll ask no more questions. I can force people to speak the truth. It's my magic, and why you answered honestly—even though you wished to keep it from me. I needed to know if I could trust this situation."

She crept to the blanket, her movements cautious. Her tone was hard and her eyes flashed. "Did our actions not speak loud enough for ye?"

"I rely heavily on my ability. I apologise, I meant no harm, but understand your offence. It wasn't my intention." Relieved to confide, Aedyn continued. "There's much I've kept secret. You assumed this is a nobility ring." He raised his hand, and the candlelight played over the gold. "It means royalty." His voice thickened with contempt and guilt. "I commanded the boat. I allowed my men ashore and their capture. And, I who ordered the destruction of Crow's Pass. The deaths, including my own men, were my fault."

Astonished, she asked. "What's yer title?"

"Crowned Prince of Aldersward Kingdom. There's more I want to share." He inhaled deeply. "My sister enters people's dreams. She's my contact with my father and my other men. It's how we communicate when separated and how we orchestrated the escape. I have summoned her only once. I know it's possible, I'm merely uncertain of how. When I stated I thought I would leave here, I based it on our contact." He quieted. "She hasn't come, nor have I reached her. I worry. How long can I remain hidden? Especially with you, the king's betrothed? He could send men or appear himself. I cannot imagine you've much time left before something happens. If I'm found, they'll kill us."

She placed her palm on his leg, offering him sympathy. "I'm sorry ye have nay method to reach yer people, and I appreciate yer concern for my household. However I believe, for the present, I've handled my situation."

He shook his head. "My advice, it's not handled. He'll tire of your excuses. He'll act to force your obedience."

"Do ye have a suggestion?"

He lifted her hand, moving it back to her lap, then stood, towering over her. "No. I only wished to warn you."

Day 151
Prince Aedyn's Bedchamber
Anya's Endeavour
Baitsloam's North Sea

Bennet adjusted the belt at his waist as he examined his reflection. Earlier, he described their original wedding day outfits to Augustus, and with precision, he had conjured them.

When Sahana tapped and entered, he was slicking back his long, wet curls. She smiled. "You look handsome."

"Aye? My hair continues to fall wherever it wants." He dampened his hand and passed it through the locks.

She produced a blade from under her cloak, lifted her petticoat's edge, and sliced a narrow strip from it. She pushed his shoulder, spinning him away from her, then gathered the top layer of hair and secured it back.

"Food and beverages for later." Asa carried a tray inside and placed it on the table as Auren followed.

As he surveyed them through the mirror, the Bait shook his head. "I think we should postpone this. It's inappropriate to celebrate under these circumstances."

"Nonsense. The men require a distraction while we're held in this uncertain state. Are you nervous?" Auren eyed him.

"Nay. Are ye?"

He shrugged. "I've studied the lines you've prepared. Your wedding customs are strange compared to ours."

"Are these not the Vaguestimber wedding rituals? Brielle has rehearsed the words." Sahana's expression clouded with worry.

"Nay, we'll re-enact the Baitsloam traditional wedding march, but the Vaguesmen's ceremony is something we'll perform later—in private."

An elaborate garden of brilliant flowers blanketed the decks, masts, and railings. The illusion reminded Bennet of Aldersward castle's west bailey. While the men shouted from the upper decks, he stood alone on the main deck. They lacked the deafening roars of the original crowd, but they compensated with enthusiasm.

Lead Auren stepped to the observation deck's railing, silencing them.

"Our tournament champion receives a bride from the queen's ladies-in-waiting." Sahana, followed by Brielle, then Byunca, shuffled out from the interior corridor, and crossed to the centre mast.

His gaze lingered on his wife's bridal attire. Possibly more beautiful than ever—she was a fantasy. He recognised the excitement in her eyes rather than the dread from long ago.

He looked to Auren, waiting for his words, but his eyes focused on the three women.

Drawing his attention, Asa nudged him.

"Sir Bennet of Clayview," their leader announced and cheers rang loud.

Like the first time, he walked directly to her. He took her hand, bowed, and kissed it. He brought her forward, placing her arm in his. For a few moments, they stilled while Arthur captured their memory to paint a portrait.

"What's yer name?" He asked, maintaining the serious manner of their initial meeting. He kept his eyes on the artist.

She lifted her gaze, a smile playing on her lips. "Brielle of Crow's Pass."

"Brielle's a beautiful name. It matches the woman who bears it." He winked at her, then guided them casually around the deck. "Ye've lucked out, Brielle. I see the future and, in yers, there are many years of happiness while I worship ye."

Startled, her steps wavered. "Ye remember?" She lifted her eyebrow, and a tear trailed over her cheek.

He whispered. "It's not every word, but is it similar enough?"

"It's incredible." She smiled.

The main deck was much smaller than the stadium they had originally marched through. The Bait emissary had marked a queue point so Auren would know when to continue.

When signalled, he raised his hand, quieting the men again. "Sir Bennet of Clayview, I release you from service. Your new name will be Bennet of Crow's Pass. Report there within fourteen days."

The men shouted congratulations as the groom pulled his bride inside Aedyn's quarters.

He barred the door—both impatient to commence the second ceremony.

Day 151
Main Deck
Anya's Endeavour
Baitsloam's North Sea

Apollo swept his arms wide and the beautiful garden returned, coating the decks and railings once more. Candles flickered from the dozens of lanterns situated throughout. A lively, favourite, festival tune from home escaped Anthony's throat.

Against the various walls, kegs and food loaded the crate-made tables. Men rested on benches or lounged on the floor while others danced and joked. The mood was jubilant and contagious.

Auren and the leaders drank while posted at the anchor deck's railing. To ensure no fights resulted from overindulgence, they held their eyes on the men below and raised their voices to be heard above the music, the stomping feet, and the loud, animated crowd.

Byunca, who first danced with her youngest brother, whirled around the centre mast to the music's beat. Men interrupted often, enjoying the opportunity to dance with her. She laughed as she spun from one to the next, adjusting her steps to each new partner.

Sahana observed the festivities from the observation deck, partially obscured behind the mast so she would go unnoticed. She envied the woman's cheerful, innocent personality and her agile athleticism. She recalled when she would have happily been in the men's midst, sought after and admired.

A shiver crawled along her spine, and her fingers darted inside her cloak an instant before a hand clamped tightly on the back of her neck. Immersed in thoughts and the activities below, she had not heard or seen anyone approach the lower navigation deck.

"I understand ye have yer uses." The voice whispered in her ear. She could not confront the man by turning, her neck held stiff in his grasp.

Shocked, the man's voice did not register. Her eye tightened on the anchor deck. She accounted for the leaders, then ran her gaze over those below. It was pointless to inventory them. She returned her eye to where Auren and Asa stood.

Auren nodded and broke into laughter at something Asa said, then whacked his shoulder. The pair turned, overlooking the deck. They did not see her, which was indeed why she had chosen her location.

She was confident whoever held her remained behind the thick pole, concealed from anyone who looked in their direction.

Sahana was frightened—not for herself—but for the man who held her. She could shout and any number of men would rush to assist, or she could twist her knife into his belly from his present angle. Both would most definitely see his death.

Calm washed over her as she realised the absolute trust she had in the Alders and this environment.

"Come now." She sought to shrug his hand away. "Let's not spoil the occasion."

His breath touched her ear, and his grip tightened. "I could enter ye here, now. Nay one would notice or even care." His wet tongue ran along her cheek to her lobe. "Ye're afraid. Go on, scream."

Her patience held. "An unwise man would dismiss my silence for fear. If I were scared, the rhythm under your fingers would race. Do you feel it? Perhaps initially it jumped, but now it's natural. Even your remarks and actions have produced nothing."

She watched as Asa sauntered down the anchor deck's stairs, paused to fill his drink, and as he sipped, he turned, finding her above. Instinctively, she knew he would approach and realised she must resolve this now.

Under her cloak, she slid her fist along the fabric to where she expected his thigh to be. "I don't invite attention for your benefit. It's certain they would lynch you. Accept this as my warning." She stabbed the blade's tip through her cloak into his flesh and twisted.

His hands grabbed for his leg, and she spun around, then backed against the railing as her friend mounted the ladder.

Asa's eyes flew to her first. She appeared serene and relaxed. Once reassured, he turned his gaze to the man who had his back to them. "Lady Sahana?"

He lifted his brow, bent, and reached for her hand, but she pulled it beneath her cloak, offering her other instead. When he would have let go, she folded her first knuckle against his palm and pulled him to the railing next to her.

"Wasn't it splendid?" She feigned pleasure and smiled.

"It was a joyous occasion."

When the man groaned, Asa peered over his shoulder and watched Bowan straighten his robes and leave.

Sahana shifted to the mast and into the lantern's light, then produced the blade, and wiped it against her cloak's lining. Satisfied it was clean, she returned it to its sheath at her side.

He caught her by the shoulders. "What's happened?"

Her face held no fear or distress, only self-assured calm.

She shrugged free, "An error in judgement."

"And the blade?" His expression narrowed.

"Sometimes these require more than words." Her lips curved upwards, convincing him she was unscathed. "What leads you to me?"

"I hoped you would indulge me in a dance?"

She stammered. "I couldn't. My body moves much slower than the fast pace of these dances. I would look foolish and probably injure myself."

He waved his hand, rejecting her claim, and spun backwards, farther away from the lantern's intensity. "It's dark here and we can slow our movements to accommodate you. Come, no further excuses. You must learn before our return to Aldersward." He stretched his arm in invitation. He mimicked the ritual he had witnessed many men perform when they invited a noblewoman to dance at the castle.

His pleasant voice urged her, and she felt childish declining his offer. She knew he would ensure no harm befell her. She accepted his hand.

"For my education then," she smiled as he settled her palm on his shoulder.

"Rest your elbow on the outside of my arm." He lifted her other, fastening her hand in his grip. He allowed a wide space between them and planted his other palm on her waist. "I can't say I've ever danced before, but as two skilful warriors, this shouldn't prove too difficult if you follow my footsteps."

She shook her head and giggled as they fumbled, careful not to tread on each other. He anticipated when her steps would falter and attempted to make adjustments for them. The couple danced unnoticed as the garden dissipated and the men trickled away to seek their bunks or the crude bedrolls installed in the dining hall.

Only five would guard above tonight.

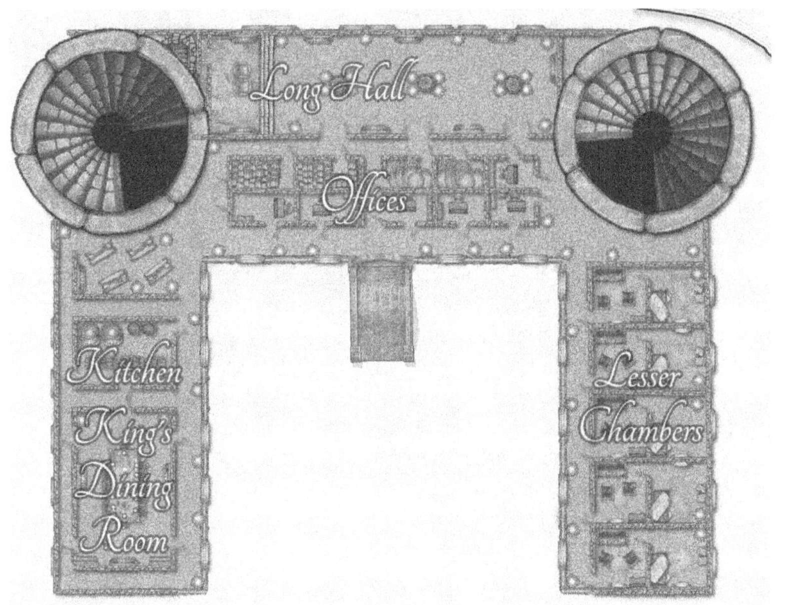

Day 152
King's Dining Room
Castle's Ground Floor
Baitsloam City

King Baeddan relaxed against his chair at the table's head while servants placed fish and vegetable-laden platters between him, his brother, and a third place setting. The king waved, and the staff scurried to the kitchen, then he signalled his secretary to open a side door.

An elegantly aged woman with her hand resting on her stomach entered as the secretary left. They stood as she approached, and after she ran her fingers across the king's shoulders, she sat.

The king introduced, without acknowledging her, "Lady Bethnee of Pennington."

Prince Bryce recognised the significance. "Have ye revised yer preference?"

"Nay, but she'll remain under my protection until further arrangements are made about her future. What matters brought ye here?"

His lips thinned with irritation as he eyed the woman. "I wish to speak freely."

"And ye may." Baeddan waved off his concern.

His tone was even without emotion. "The subjects contemplate the Alders and many of the directives ye've passed since the kingdoms' divide. They're deeply disturbed. There's rumour of an insurrection." Bryce informed before the messages reached his brother from another source. A favourable advantage, in case an opportunity arose where a devoted ally could oust the current king.

Her loud laugh echoed as she touched Baeddan's hand. "Our king can't satisfy everyone. He does what's best. If someone should question his motives, perhaps they need to be silenced."

He awaited their ruler's anger—cutting words to muzzle the intrusive woman who had no business speaking.

But none came, and the prince chided. "It would be unwise to silence tens of thousands. The masses would revolt. Lady Bethnee, it's best if ye held yer tongue in matters which don't concern ye."

At his dismissal, her eyes blazed with fury. "These matters concern our child—the king's heir apparent who will inherit the throne. Perhaps ye should nay longer provide counsel. Shortly, yer position will expire."

Baeddan held his hand between them. "Enough. Lady, ye've spoken out of turn. Whether I wanted yer condition shared was my choice and not yers. Bryce, her pregnancy may be true. She could bear my successor."

"Then why wouldn't ye marry her?"

"The proclamation has reached every corner of Baitsloam. And now with the knowledge ye've provided, it would be unwise to waiver in this decision." He shook his head. "Nay, I'll wed Belinda. I may get two heirs out of this new arrangement."

"So ye understand, *Bryce*," Bethnee degraded him by using his first name. "I most certainly have the rights of the queen."

The king didn't deny her claim, and therefore, the prince had little choice but to accept it.

Day 153
Dugout
Belinda's Home
Crow's Pass City, Baitsloam

Again, someone fidgeted above where Aedyn slept, and the bedframe's stresses brought him awake. Throughout the night, it had been a constant battle. He would doze off only to be woken by the noises and while the person tossed, he would gain no further rest.

He dressed and scaled the ladder. Not wanting to wake anyone else, he settled on the bench and carefully peered through the window's sheer curtains.

Few stirred—the predawn hour too early for most to venture outside. If he ever had a chance to escape this kingdom, the comings and goings of those around would be useful. He made a mental note to ask Bret about the area and their sleep customs.

The hinges on a bedchamber door creaked, and he shifted, letting the heavy drape fall over the flimsy material.

"Morning." Beatrice splashed water into a pot and set it on the stove. "What has ye risen this early?"

"I couldn't sleep." As he stepped inside the kitchen and sat at the table, he stretched his tired muscles.

"Did Belinda keep ye awake as well?" She arranged plates and utensils before him. "I checked on her. She's ill."

He lifted his brow. "Is it serious?"

"Nay, nothing a day of rest won't solve. I'll prepare our morning meal. Bret plans to fish today."

Aedyn wished it were possible to accompany him—anything to disrupt the many days spent inactive. In Aldersward, a day rarely passed without feeling the sun's warmth on his skin. An entire day with the old woman while she sewed, cooked, and cleaned, loomed before him.

"If you arrange a tray, I'll take it to her."

Before Aedyn entered, he tapped softly on the door and waited for her response. The sun's rays spilt through the open window. He set the tray down, lit the candles at her bedside, and then closed the heavy drapes.

"Good morning." One corner of his mouth lifted with a smile.

As he placed the tray onto Belinda's lap, she shifted upwards, propping her back against the wall, and stifled a yawn. "Good morning. Am I to dine in bed?"

He dragged a chair closer. "It's only proper I reciprocate the same care you offered me."

"Oh, but..." *I'm not ill.* Her remark trailed off and her cheeks flamed. "It's lovely but unnecessary."

From inside the back of his trousers, he pulled the book. "Bret's fishing and Beatrice sews. This affords me a purpose." He fanned the pages. "At which part did you stop reading?"

She abandoned her argument, understanding his frustration. "They entered the castle."

He located the spot, cleared his throat, and read.

The crowd parted as the pair weaved their way to meet the king, who sat on his throne. She had never attended the castle before and she trembled with fear.

As she wet her lips nervously, her lover cast his gaze on her and smiled.

"We're safe here." He advised.

She believed him—this man now dear to her heart. She couldn't remember her life before him nor imagine a life without him in the future.

His voice was husky and deep as he read the enchanting passage—pleasingly different than if the words came from her.

She drew an unsettling parallel between her feelings for Aedyn and the heroine's romance in the novel. Unconsciously she realised the characters' images were no longer faceless, but her and the Alder prince.

"The words are romantic." Her face reddened. Her unpleasant habit of speaking her thoughts out loud embarrassed her.

He studied her flushed cheeks and her delighted gaze.

Indeed, he thought as he propped his heels on the bed and relaxed his ankles against her blanket-covered feet, then turned the page.

Day 154
Bethnee's Chambers
Castle's Second Floor
Baitsloam City

When King Baeddan approached, the servant closed the door and turned into the hallway. She genuflected as he strode past and entered. Without knocking, he carried through the sitting room and into the bedchamber.

Lady Bethnee, her robe gaped wide, emerged from behind her privacy screen. She pretended to correct it as she bowed. "Sire."

He kissed her offered hand as his eyes roamed over her rounded breasts. *How long had it been since he remembered being with a woman?* He wondered. "How are ye feeling?"

From beneath the bed, she noticed her lover's boot jutting out. She stepped into the king's frame, closing the space between them, and smiled intimately. "I'm convinced I grow yer heir."

Urging his attention, her tongue dampened her lips, then she grazed them over his while playing her fingers through his hair. She curved her body against his, ensuring her peaked nipples brushed his chest and the warmth of her womanhood rubbed his thigh.

He intensified the light kiss brazenly, and he folded his arms around her waist.

Slowly she turned them and walked back towards the bed, using her foot to kick the object underneath.

He used his hands to brace himself against the mattress, forcing her to bend under the pressure, then caused her to fall onto her back.

He had ploughed her garden before, and no further harm would come from doing so again, he reasoned. Perhaps this occasion would be less painful for her. He lifted her robe and nightgown onto her stomach, exposing her pale flesh to the sunlight, then freed and stuffed his cock inside her.

Day 154
Belinda's Bedchamber
Belinda's Home
Crow's Pass City, Baitsloam

Aedyn placed the book down, then straightened and stretched. The single position held for two days had taken a toll on every cramped muscle.

Belinda watched his athletic frame work through several exercises and, realising his discomfort, she shuffled her body over and waited for him to turn. When he did, she patted the mattress.

"I'm not deathly ill. Ye can rest yer back against the wall and spread yer legs out." Her big, innocent eyes encouraged him.

He ruffled his hair with his fingers. Could she not understand a man had his limits? "No. It would be inappropriate to be in a lady's bed without marriage."

"There are so many things about our present situation which make it inappropriate. I don't wish for ye to suffer on my account. If ye must feel useful, then join me here." She suppressed a yawn and brushed her hair to her other side.

Like a fumbling virgin, he lifted the book and perched on the edge, leaving one leg hanging.

She gripped his calf and pulled it closer. "We are adults. Beatrice is in the next room, and the door's open. Come now, get comfortable."

He lifted his leg onto the bed, his thigh ached from the momentary half-on, half-off position. Determined to ignore her scent and her body's warmth beside him, he pushed his back into the wall, then raised the book, and read.

"I understand the king has rewarded ye for yer bravery—lands, and a title." She turned away, the ache in her heart too much to bear. She did not wish for him to witness her sadness.

Unsure of her sudden coldness, he nodded. "He has. And he awarded ye a husband and a cottage here at the castle. Congratulations."

"Congratulations, indeed." She didn't look back when she walked away. Her life was a long, desolate tunnel before her and she wished he had let her perish during one of the many occasions he had rescued her.

Belinda wiped a tear from her cheek and leaned into his side, resting her head on his shoulder. "It's sad."

He shifted the book to look at her. "Is it?"

She wrapped her arm through his. "Of course. She loves him and wants to be with him."

"Then why doesn't she reveal it?" He lifted his brow. "If she said it, then he would know."

Her chin lifted upward. "She did—with her body when she turned away. It's a clear sign her heart is breaking."

"Or a sign she's leaving." He chuckled.

"Nay, men should learn to communicate better." She placed her hand over his heart. "What am I telling ye now?"

"You're wondering if I'm still alive?"

"Nay, be serious." She giggled. "I'm determining if yer heart beats quicker when I'm nearby." She lifted her hand to his jaw. "Here, I'm checking if ye swallow or if yer skin tightens under my touch." She wet her lips, realising he had swallowed.

His throat worked, and when she wet her lips, the temptation was too great to ignore. Her mouth was only a few inches from his. Abandoning the book, he cupped his palm on her cheek and lowered his lips onto hers.

Her heart somersaulted as she closed her eyes. Her arm circled his neck and her fingers laced in his hair as he settled his mouth firmly onto hers.

Desire ignited through him. He shifted one arm behind her back and the fingers of his other hand trailed a path down her side.

As his tongue coaxed her mouth open, her hand slid over his shoulder.

"Tea's ready!" Beatrice called from the kitchen.

Instantly, he broke the embrace and came off the bed. Disturbed by his behaviour, he wiped his palm over his face. "I apologise."

She blushed. "Nay, it was my fault."

"When you believed me unconscious, and you explored my body—that was your fault." She reddened further, and he shook his head. "This time it was mine."

Day 155
Earl Austen's Study
Royal Estate
Coaldale Village, Aldersward

In the study, Physician Axton waited as the king read the nighttime correspondences. When finished, he organised and placed them aside.

"I've examined Achelle again. There's no change."

The king leaned back. "Could this be the illness her mother suffers from?"

He shook his head. "No. Their pupils react differently, and I'm certain your daughter ingested tonics whereas the queen had not."

"Is there nothing you can do to wake her?"

"No. If she comes through this, it will be of her body and spirit."

A knock sounded, and Adahy waved his dismissal as Earl Austen entered and sat opposite.

"I've news of one who walks through people's minds. I've requested their presence, but it will be several days before they arrive."

"Keep searching in the meantime. We must communicate with the vessel as soon as possible." The king rose as Commander Ainco appeared.

"What's the construction status?"

"Sire, fewer than seven days until we can load and depart."

He nodded as he left to witness the progress of the training men.

Day 156
Dugout
Belinda's Home
Crow's Pass City, Baitsloam

Aedyn straightened on his mattress and sipped the cold tea laced with honey. His throat burned from narrating the pages.

It was unclear what ailed Belinda, and no one offered an explanation. Occasionally, her sharp intake of breath revealed her discomfort, but it dispelled quickly.

As he had read, he caught himself rushing through the text, more interested in her reactions. Her face betrayed her every emotion and, late at night, his mind replayed his dragon dream while he integrated these new expressions.

His voice was so hoarse, that even in sleep, it broke as he called to his sister.

He settled and closed his eyes, reimagining himself and Belinda as the novel's characters, and he drifted to sleep.

Loud cries and roars sounded outside the hunting cabin as he backed Belinda against the wall. An intense lust burned in his abdomen. How he wanted to relive his dream—get lost in loving her, but he knew he couldn't and begrudgingly, he ended their embrace. And like every night since he had woken in Baitsloam, he attempted to reach his sister.

He focused, first eliminating the outside commotion, then the cabin, and finally her, before he visualised his mother's chamber. The sunlight flowed through the curtains as it played against April's conjured flowers. As they had on the day he departed, he stood with his family by her bed. One by one he removed them and settled at his mother's side.

He yelled for his sister, but she did not appear. He covered his face in a moment of self-pity. Would his eyes ever glance upon Aldersward again? He called to her through his hands.

"Aedyn?" Achelle's voice choked with sobs.

He heard her before she hurried through the doorway. He spun, crossed the space quickly, and then crushed her in his arms. Her body shuddered as he held her. Fear kept his hands on her as he crawled his palms to her cheeks.

"Where have you been? What's happened? Where's the vessel?" He inspected her tears.

Immense relief washed over her—she had located him and wanted to inform everyone.

She clutched his tunic and buried her face in his chest. "I've searched for you. We wondered if you were dead when I couldn't reach you. Where are you?"

"There's no time to explain. I'm fine and safe. You must withdraw. It's been twenty-five days. Where's Auren?"

"Twenty-five days?" She calculated in her mind. It could not be. His calculation must be wrong or the Baitsloam calendar must be different. Should she tell him about the tonic? No. She would not tolerate his disappointment now. There would be time later. "Tell me what to do."

Day 156
Prince Aedyn's Quarters
Anya's Endeavour
Baitsloam's North Sea

Auren poured ale, then joined Bennet and Asa at the smaller table.

"How was your private ceremony?" Asa asked, oblivious to the particulars.

"It happened much slower this time." Bennet winked and laughed, knowing they could not understand.

"Five nights. Are all Vaguestimber ceremonies as lengthy?" Auren wondered.

"Aye. If the couple is lucky, it does." He sipped, covering his smile as he remembered his dedication and her pleased moans. It was only that morning they had emerged fully clothed.

"We need to discuss your eldest." Asa drew the older man's attention.

He slicked his hair back from his face. "What's happened?"

He shrugged. "I'm uncertain. I've questioned Sahana repeatedly, and her only answer is *an error in judgement*, but Bowan walks with a limp caused by her."

Bennet's brows furrowed. "I'll confer with both in the morning."

"See you do." He ordered, then calmed his sudden irritation. "The prince promised her safety here and anyone who jeopardised it would be punished. I encourage you to reiterate the attitude."

"Are ye implying–" He lifted his frown to his companions.

"No, we're not implying—we don't know what transpired." Auren drank half his mug and wiped the foam from his lip. "I've decided we turn for home tomorrow. We've waited too long without communication."

"It's sensible. I would decide nay differently if I were in yer position."

"I've instructed Amos, Abner, and Ackley. They'll handle it with the morning crews." Auren raised his mug. "For Prince Aedyn—my brother, your friend—never will he be forgotten. And to our future, our home, and safe travel—may it be swift."

Day 156
Sitting Room
Belinda's Home
Crow's Pass City, Baitsloam

Aedyn rapped two fingers on Belinda's door and waited for her to answer. In the hours before dawn, she slept. Again he tried, and it opened as she secured the robe around her waist.

Her eyes, veiled with sleep, raised to consider his. "Are ye ill?"

He held his finger to his grinning mouth, shook his head, then caught her hand and pulled her out. When they reached the seclusion of the sitting room, he turned around suddenly, propelling her into his arms.

He gazed into her upturned face. "I've reached my sister. Plans for my escape will begin immediately."

Both delighted and disappointed at the same time, Belinda backed out of his hold. She remembered her own reaction when she arrived home from the castle—a wonderfully pleasant feeling. Then she imagined if her home and people were much farther away. She smiled as she perched on the bench behind her.

Her words were appropriate, yet hollow. "It's marvellous news. Congratulations."

She pondered her own emotions as he spoke. Had she thought, somehow, he would remain here indefinitely? Perhaps he would want to? Did she think they had a future here together with her married to the king, and he trapped within these walls? Her disappointment was illogical, and she chided herself.

"I confide my hope waned. I began to fear and wonder if I would ever find my way back." He sat, crushing her against his chest, and whispered. "It won't be long now."

Day 157
Princess Achelle's Bedchamber
Royal Estate
Coaldale Village, Aldersward

Achelle struggled through her mind's hallways, obscured by dense fog.
Why, she wondered. *Where had this eerie fog come from?*
She stumbled down some stairs, nearly falling, but she caught a railing and steadied herself. She brushed her hair aside as fright quickened her pulse and she swallowed the lump in her throat. Staircases, doorways, and drop-offs often shifted positions with no rhyme or reason here and ordinarily, she was able to observe it. Without sight, it was impossible to know what changes were occurring. She slid her foot forward and probed the ground. It was solid and deliberately she repeated the act with her other foot. Her hand disappeared through the drifting mist and connected with a wall. She settled her back against it, then passed her fingers over its cold surface, searching until they encountered a doorframe.

As the floor beneath her quaked, the hallway groaned and weightlessness fluttered in her stomach. Somewhere nearby, the area changed. Carefully, she probed for the door's latch, unable to see. Her hands fumbled against the handle. She cursed and kicked, but it did not budge. She raised her hands and sought to inspect them. Either her vision blurred or she trembled. She was weak and tired, but she knew it was imperative to go on. Her brother's return depended on it.

She slid down the wall and rested her head in her hands. What if she never found her way out? What was happening to her? Were her abilities waning? She took long, slow breaths, trying to steady her mind and emotions.

This is a puzzle. I only need to solve it, she rallied herself.

She crawled on her hands and knees, desperation driving her hurried movements. Her palm found no contact, and she tumbled over an edge, free-falling into the black abyss of her mind.

Astrid ran to the study, but the guards blocked her from entering. "Sire, Axton. Come quick."

Axton rushed to the fireplace and disappeared. The king brushed past the two guards and maid, then took the stairs two at a time.

The physician was already examining her when the king burst inside with Astrid on his heels.

"Her pupils are responding normally now. When I arrived, she was mumbling. She may be waking." He stepped back, allowing her father to advance.

"I'll wake her." Without the physician's approval, the king hoisted her back off the mattress.

She flailed, her arm pushed against his chest, and she mumbled. "Open, damn you!"

The king, unable to hold her struggle, let go, and dropped her backwards. Then, with the back of his hand, he struck her jaw.

Achelle's body struck the staircase and somersaulted downwards until she laid flat on her back against a hallway's cold white floor. Her body ached and her forearm throbbed as she rolled to her side. She braced both palms against the ground but fell over when a searing pain shot through her arm.

The three standing next to her bed heard the bone snap and watched a jagged cut open along her forehead as blood spilt from her nose. Red angry scrapes and nicks appeared on her exposed skin. Astrid gasped as Axton reached for a cloth and the king backed away.

The dense fog dissipated and Achelle pushed herself upward, then stumbled to a door. She turned the handle without success. She shifted sideways and thrusted her shoulder against it, then cried out in agony as she jolted her broken arm. On her second attempt, the door gave way, and she fell forward, landing on her knees.

Anguish marred her expression as tears ran down her cheeks. She writhed with pain and her eyes opened. She choked as she sobbed, "Father?"

Worried and relieved, he clasped her icy hand. "You're all right. You're going to be fine now."

The physician placed a hand on his shoulder, urging him aside. He barked orders at the maid and she scurried out to retrieve his medicine bag and supplies as he knelt beside Achelle, examining her eyes and feeling her neck.

"Do you know what day it is?" He straightened her arm.

She winced. "I don't know. Aedyn said he's been missing for twenty-five days. But I believe it's day one-hundred-and-fifty-one?"

"You've slept for almost a week. It's day one-fifty-seven, and Aedyn disappeared twenty-three days ago." Axton continued to search her body for injuries. "Aedyn said?"

She tried to sit up, but weakness plagued her, and she fell backwards. The physician held her as he stacked pillows behind her back.

"I found him well, but ready to come home. I tried to reach Auren without success."

Her mind appeared lucid, and Axton nodded to the king.

Stunned, her father sat on the bed. "Praise Jezabet."

Day 157
Sitting Room
Belinda's Home
Crow's Pass City, Baitsloam

"Ye believe yer sister will visit again tonight?" Bret accepted the mug his wife offered as he sat in the desk's chair.

Lounged in the armchair, Aedyn nodded. The excitement had fled and his full belly and exhaustion replaced it.

Beatrice disappeared into the kitchen, where Belinda finished cleaning the remnants of the midday meal.

"You should consider accompanying me. You should have your women pack."

The old man shrugged, and his voice carried. "What would we do in Aldersward? Nay, this is something to discuss and weigh."

The women came to listen.

"Discuss Aldersward?" Belinda glanced between them.

The prince eyed her. "I believe you three should come with me when I leave Baitsloam."

She shook her head. "Escape the king? Commit treason? A generous offer, but ye can't risk any more animosity between our kingdoms. It would service neither."

He ruffled his hair. "Let me worry about the politics. If they ever discovered you left, Aldersward could protect you easily."

The elderly woman folded a cloth. "This would be yer king's decision, would it not? Should ye seek permission first?"

"If it would appease you, then yes, I'll ask him. Nevertheless, we should plan for–"

A small fist pounded frantically against the exterior door.

"Lady Belinda! Please, Lady Belinda!" A panicked female called.

Bret lifted the hatch, Aedyn dived through it, and it fell shut as Belinda answered.

She recognised Brayleigh's servant—a close friend's maid—as she pushed past, forcing her way inside.

Dread crept down Belinda's spine. "What's happened?"

The girl bent at the waist, trying to calm herself. She took a few deep breaths, then straightened. "The king's soldiers took our mistress. One gave me this." She handed her a folded letter with the king's seal. "I was ordered to deliver it to ye."

She broke the seal and scanned its contents. Her face turned white, and her mind reeled, but she forced herself to appear calm. "I'll see to this. Don't fret." She hugged the girl tightly, offering her comfort, and forced a smile. "Don't worry. The king's taken her so she may be present at our wedding. Nothing untoward. Pack a bag and deliver it to me. I expect to leave in the next few days."

The words placated her and the girl breathed easier, her duty done. She walked outside and turned. "Thank ye, Lady Belinda."

As Beatrice closed the door, Belinda nodded and sat on the bench, numbness striking her body. Bret took the letter from her now shaking hands.

He scanned it. "He intends to sell her."

"I read it." She gazed at a troubled Beatrice. "It's to guarantee my cooperation. He's sending soldiers to collect me in two weeks."

"How did he know about her? And why didn't he send them to collect ye instead of Brayleigh?" Beatrice sat beside her as Bret opened the hatch, and Aedyn climbed up.

She shook her head. "While we shared an evening meal together, he asked about my life here. I mentioned Brayleigh. It never occurred to me he would use her against me." Guilt gripped her heart.

When she paused, the Alder answered the second question, towering over the women. "Quietly taking a peasant would pass relatively unnoticed." He shrugged. "Belinda wrote she was helping rebuild the community, perhaps gaining favour from his subjects. Their impending nuptials are common knowledge and his subject's discontent must have reached him. For appearances, he needs Belinda to appear happy and excited to become his queen. It's definite now. You must escape Baitsloam."

She stood and glared, her resolve cemented. "He'll sell her to a whorehouse. I can't allow it. I'll marry him willingly." She left, seeking the solace of her bedchamber.

Before he followed, Aedyn glanced at the elderly couple. Then he entered without knocking and closed the door for privacy.

Ignoring his intrusion, she stood at the window.

He approached her, staying out of the light.

"Ye warned me, and I did nothing." Her whisper quivered.

"You couldn't have known." He grabbed her shoulders, pulling her backward.

She turned, and a tear slid to her chin. She imagined how scared her friend must be and where she might be imprisoned. "I must obey him and free her."

He wiped her tears away. "He may never free her, even if you obey him."

"Regardless, I'll pray his word is true." More tears replaced the last. "Brayleigh requires my compliance."

He settled his palm on her neck and drew her against him, nestling her hair under his chin. Offering her safety, he locked his strong arms tightly around her.

Honour always had a cost. He hoped hers would not be too much to bear.

Day 158
Prince Aedyn's Bedchamber
Anya's Endeavour
Baitsloam's North Sea

Auren bolted upright, tossed aside the blankets, and reached for his boots. He did not bother with a tunic as he strode through the quarters and onto the main deck.

Through the dark night, his loud words startled everyone from their mundane watch into action. "Wake and gather everyone here immediately!"

He hurried onto the navigation deck, slapped Amos's back, and grinned, then climbed to the observation deck's railing.

Men came forward to stand below. Some carried lanterns while others lit the permanent fixtures. As a gentle glow built, Asa and Bennet remained with the women at the back of the group.

Determining most were present, he raised his hand and silenced the speculative voices.

A wide smile revealed his joyous mood. "Prince Aedyn is alive and safe! We'll return to our previous hold position and await further orders. Amos and Arturo, prepare to turn and Azariah, man the anchor deck. Bennet and Asa report to Aedyn's quarters. Gentlemen, it's going to be a fine day indeed."

When he withdrew, excitement and cheers rang out.

Day 159
Kitchen
Belinda's Home
Crow's Pass City, Baitsloam

Bret unravelled and placed the map in the table's middle so they could examine it. "Ye can't have yer craft return here. Prince Bryce will have scouts watching."

"What's this?" Aedyn reached over Belinda and pointed to a city northwest of Crow's Pass.

She felt the warmth of his arm as it brushed against her cheek, and her eyes followed its direction. "Tomlin."

The old man elaborated, "One-hundred-and-fifty miles from here and about sixty miles from the shoreline."

Aedyn rested his hand on her shoulder. "It looks promising. How many would live along this stretch?"

"Very few, maybe three farmhouses, here," he indicated where the fields intersected. "They could see the shore. If yer boat arrives at night, ye could escape from these woods or this field before anyone would reach ye."

As he thought of his sister, he nodded with a smile. "Achelle and I discovered another difference in our kingdoms. Our dates are different. Our calendar is two days behind yours. I'll arrange with my vessel to meet me there in the early morning of day one-hundred-and-sixty-six on our calendar—one-hundred-and-sixty-eight on yours. Could we reach it by then?"

Bret noted the prince's familiarity with the young woman. "To there, from the edge of Crow's Pass, it may be ninety miles. By covered wagon, we could make the entire trip. It's best if we leave the afternoon of day one-sixty-four and travel through the night."

Aedyn rubbed his hands together in excitement. "This is the plan. We depart in five days and bring only what you can carry."

Belinda turned on the bench, raising her eyes. "We'll help ye, but ye escape alone. I must save Brayleigh."

He wanted to shake her but instead glanced at the older couple, their faces void of opinion. "You can't know if your cooperation will free her." He crossed his arms. "We escape. Then I'll return with more vessels and rescue her."

Irritated by his authoritative tone, she stood. "Nay, we'll see ye off, then we'll go to the castle." She left the room, seeking her bedchamber.

For a moment, their body language conversation crossed his mind. Did she want him to follow her?

Day 160
Earl Austen's Study
Royal Estate
Coaldale Village, Aldersward

As he listened to the men, King Adahy swallowed the ale, then waved his hand, silencing them. "Prince Aedyn believes we should stay the fleet's majority and send only three to Slaysfold. He believes he can escape without us. Divide one-hundred-and-fifty men between the three crews. One will travel to Slaysfold castle and two to Larkburgh, where we'll abandon one as Lady Synnova's payment."

"Sire, perhaps the decisions are better left to our commanders." Lord Austen drank.

Adahy threaded his fingers and braced his elbows on the chair's arms. "You believe our judgement better than one who's navigated the sea, other kingdoms, and enemy attacks?" He regarded those around the study's long table. "He designed and fought for this voyage. No one thought it possible, but he's proved it. If he says the vessels should wait here, then they will."

Commander Ainco nodded his agreement. "Your Majesty, will you select which groups go?"

"No, but ensure they're more useful than my son's original group. He requires men who would strengthen his combat capabilities. Load King Sumner's vessel with trees and gifts. We will repay his kindness generously. Right now, Slaysfold is our only ally."

"They can leave as soon as tomorrow. Gentlemen?" Ainco stood, signalling the others to follow him.

Only three remained. The king stretched, then sat in an armchair before the hearth. He leaned forward and tossed a few logs on the fire, building it back up.

Leaving Earl Austen at the table alone, Axton joined him. "We should discuss Achelle."

He stared into the flames, lost in their flickering dance. "What about her? Has she manipulated her new staff?"

"No. There's no evidence of it."

He shrugged. "I'm not a physician, but she reached her brother and Auren. It suggests she's over whatever ailed her?"

"There's no recovery without effort. It's true she reaches them and reports her findings. But her body still quakes from withdrawal. She requires the tonic like she needs air to breathe. Her symptoms will worsen before she becomes better. I've witnessed individuals who killed themselves because their sane minds left."

"You think it may affect her the same?" He examined his trusted friend.

"It's a concern, yes." The physician nodded. "I know of a herbalist in Edson who successfully treats those dependent on tonics. It may be wise to send her there."

"The other conscious walker's ability is restricted to only those she knows. She'll meet the new vessel crews. Nowhere near as advanced as Achelle. Until Aedyn's out of Baitsloam, I have no alternative but to utilise her."

Day 160
Belinda's Bedchamber
Belinda's Home
Crow's Pass City, Baitsloam

On her wedding day, Baeddan paraded her through the room and she saw Brayleigh bound and held by guards. But after signing the registry, the king motioned for her friend's removal. Belinda fought to reach her, but her new husband seized her and she struggled against him until he pushed her backwards onto a bed. It was then she woke.

She sat and looked out the window, noting the bright stars in the sky. A cough sounded below, and she decided to investigate. She threaded a black ribbon through her hair and shrugged into her robe and soft slippers.

She paused on the dirt floor and transferred the candle's flame to the lantern.

"Are ye awake?" She quietly called, in case he slept.

"Yes. Come in." Aedyn's low voice invited her, not wanting to wake the others above. He lit the candles beside the mattress.

Her face revealed concern. "Ye coughed?"

"I suspect it's the moisture." He positioned his back against the wall.

"I understand. I only meant to check on ye. Good night." For an instant, she hesitated. Her eyes skimmed his naked chest, then she turned.

"I'll not sleep for a while. Should we provide each other company until we tire?" He preferred her to stay. It was lonely, exiled in the dugout at night.

She settled onto the blanket on the floor. This was a bad idea—being here, unchaperoned—especially since their kiss. Though, she reasoned, the blanket was safe as long as she was on it alone. Her mind envisioned it, like land surrounded by the sea's blue dragons. No one, including herself, would dare cross the water.

He shifted, laying his head on the mattress's end by her knees. "What should we discuss?"

"Not Brayleigh, or my marriage." She blurted, then reddened. "For tonight, I would rather forget them in hopes of further sleep. Perhaps ye can tell me about yer life as a royal."

As he studied her, his face twisted with disgust, "A mundane topic indeed."

She smiled. "The duller, the better. It'll serve our purpose."

"All right," he laced his fingers together and placed them behind his head. He closed his eyes and grinned. "Let me tell you what it was like growing up with Auren."

Day 161
Dugout
Belinda's Home
Crow's Pass City, Baitsloam

As he woke, Aedyn's head lolled to the side. He inhaled the scent of jasmine as something tickled his nose. He sought to brush it aside, but found his arm trapped. Immediately alert, he opened his eyes.

Fiery red hair covered his bare chest, and he realised the warmth against him was Belinda's face curled into his neck. She laid on her blanket with her head resting on him. Enjoying the feel of her sleeping against him, he stilled, not wanting to wake her. Slowly, he turned his head away and closed his eyes.

What must have woken him were the footsteps he heard above, then someone descended the ladder rungs.

Without entering, Beatrice's voice questioned. "Is Belinda with ye?"

He wondered what the old woman thought she would discover if she peered inside. He did not want to answer and break the enchantment, but he had little option.

"She is."

Belinda stirred.

"This is most inappropriate."

The old woman's tone reprimanded, and he responded, smiling pleasantly. "I couldn't agree more. I'm as stunned as you. Your mistress's behaviour is quite dishonourable. Come in, see for yourself."

The redhead against him stretched, and he knew the serene spell around them was about to break. He struggled to force his disappointment aside.

"Nay, I imagine her behaviour had little to do with it." She called and climbed the rungs, incapable of venturing through the doorway.

He chuckled as Belinda shifted, and her eyes fluttered open against his shoulder.

She expected the morning sun, forgetting then remembering where she was. Her head snapped back to focus on the naked flesh and realised her mouth had been moments ago pressed into his shoulder. She sat up, pretending she had not noticed.

He rolled onto his side and propped his head in his hand. A lazy smile appeared. "Good morning. Did you sleep well?"

She stood and stretched. Her face flamed with embarrassment. "Aye, yer story must have been terribly boring. I fell asleep without warning."

His grin widened. "When your face reddens like now, it's incredibly mesmerising."

As she straightened her hair and clothes, she turned away. "A decent man wouldn't bring attention to my embarrassment."

"A decent man wouldn't have led Beatrice to believe you seduced me. But if it's what she believes–"

She spun to learn if it was the truth or a lie, but the smug grin revealed no answer. "What did ye say?"

He sat up, grabbed his tunic, and popped it over his head. "I elected to preserve my honour over yours. She's like your mother and would forgive you more readily than me."

"Ye are teasing." She accused with a flustered frown as she walked out.

He continued to jest. "Go. See their faces. They should reveal all you need to know." He laughed as he pulled on his trousers.

Belinda climbed and met Bret's indifferent expression. His uncanny ability to keep his thoughts secret annoyed her as she crossed to the kitchen.

Beatrice's eyes revealed her concern but approval as she walked to where the old woman stood at the stove.

From above, she withdrew four mugs.

"Is it done then?"

Not understanding the question, Belinda turned to look at her and quietly whispered. "What?"

"The answer to yer heir problem. Was he able to solve it?"

"We didn't, he didn't–" She tucked her hair back and her face reddened as Aedyn greeted Bret in the sitting room.

"I assumed, I apologise. However, this could be Jezabet's solution. If ye haven't considered it, ye should." Beatrice turned to find the Alder standing in the doorway, and she handed him two mugs.

He raised his brow. "What things should she consider?"

"Ye may have ruined her reputation." The elderly woman easily answered, but his eyes narrowed.

He didn't need his ability to know she was lying. With a shrug, he carried the second mug to Bret.

Day 161
Dugout
Belinda's Home
Crow's Pass City, Baitsloam

Belinda found herself distracted, and her mind drifted throughout the day as she thought of the older woman's earlier remarks. Could Aedyn be the answer to providing the king an heir? Their circumstances had formed a bond between them, and whenever he touched her, she felt a new excitement build within her. Lacking knowledge of mating rituals, she wondered what coupling would feel like. The act required the part of her which bled and, from Beatrice's remarks when he had dreamt, his hips were involved, too.

A few times, while she thought of him, she realised she was smiling from the pleasant heat swelling in her midsection. She would glance to the other three, unaware of her thoughts, and then refocus her attention wholeheartedly on her sewing.

The old woman's words and her own desire fluttered her heart as she climbed into bed, waiting for the hours after midnight to seek him out.

For some time, no one stirred in the cottage, and Belinda watched as the stars grew brighter against the blackened sky.

She crept from her bed and added a dab of jasmine oil behind her earlobes. She stepped into her slippers and forewent her robe. As she rushed across the cottage and descended the ladder, her anticipation grew.

Her footsteps fell lightly on the dirt, but she said nothing when she entered and Aedyn watched her with one eye in the dim light. When she removed her shoes and lowered herself onto the mattress, he examined her body through the transparent material. She wore nothing beneath it and his body stirred with interest.

She laid her head on the pillow next to his and closed her eyes, taking a deep breath.

Before her courage was lost, her body turned to his. Her heart raced as she reached out her fingers and laid them against his neck. He swallowed. Her palm felt it, and instinctively, she knew he was awake.

She had to speak. "I woke ye."

He cleared his throat and opened his eyes, peering down into the red waves of hair on top of her head—her face averted from his gaze. "You did. The mattress shifted. Have you come because you can't sleep again?"

She shook her head. This was a mistake. She could not tell him her purpose, and her cheeks flushed at the thought.

"Nay matter the reason—I shouldn't have come." She pushed the covers aside, but her movements stopped when his hand found her hip and an arousing sensation crawled up her spine.

"Stay."

The single hoarse word he uttered against her hair raised her flesh into tiny bumps along her neck and over her shoulders.

"Do you feel it?"

Every nerve ending took on its own life. His fingers slid up her torso, then cupped her chin, forcing her gaze to his. For several seconds, neither acted nor spoke as their warm breath washed over the other.

Her heartbeat quickened. The intensity of his gaze in the dim light made it near impossible for her to breathe. "What?"

"This undeniable connection between us, whenever we're near."

The tiniest smile parted her lips. "I blame that silly novel."

"I blame you." A slight smile lifted the corner of his mouth. "And now, you must decide."

He brushed his hand against her hair, sending it back from her face.

Her innocent eyes blankly examined his. "Decide what?"

He inhaled deeply. Never had this conversation been needed, and he wondered nervously how to proceed. "How far this should go?"

His hand planted on her hip, and he kneaded her flesh through the flimsy material as she thought about how she should answer. What was she meant to say? She had no idea what was about to happen. She chided herself for her innocence as she bit into her lower lip. "I'll tell ye when to stop?"

He clenched his jaw and raised his eyes above her. Quickly, he prayed for Jezabet's strength to endure the torture he was about to bear. He smiled and slowly inched his mouth closer to hers. "You can try."

Interchangeably, his lips tugged and his tongue grazed her bottom lip. She was unsure of his actions, but trusted him. This was like no kiss she had observed before. It was delightful, and she wondered if this act was a cultural difference.

When he responded by pulling her lower body towards him, it pleased her.

He realised this would differ from anything he had experienced. Between them existed an emotional connection and within him an overwhelming instinct to protect her from life's difficulties. His mind cautioned him to be delicate and careful, so he would not frighten her.

For a moment, he stopped and pulled his face back to check her expression. "Should I stop?" The words were strange. He had never asked this question of other women. His desire intensified from this suppressive behaviour.

"Nay," her voice was a breathless whisper, but, when he bent his mouth to cover hers, she placed the tips of her fingers over his lips. He misunderstood and sucked them into his mouth. Her face reddened. "I don't know what to do."

"Trust me." He whispered. "Do whatever increases your pleasure and if I displease you, tell me." Her innocence weighed on his conscience as she nodded. "Open your mouth under mine." This time, when he settled his mouth onto hers, hers opened beneath his and he laced his tongue with hers.

He felt her palm resting against his chest. He gripped it, encouraging her fingers to press into his flesh. After several seconds, her hand acted on its own. Their other arms were trapped, and he no longer cared for their position. He wove his hand around her hair, moving it upward and out of the way. He clasped her shoulder and pushed her onto her back as he placed his naked thigh between her legs.

His tongue trailed down her jaw and onto her neck as he lifted her now free hand to his hair. Her pulse rushed, and he nibbled on the spot, using his lips to massage the cord in her neck. Granting him further access, her head turned as her fingers roamed over his shoulder.

Sharp heavenly sensations tingled through her body. Like those when she ran her own fingers lightly over her neck in private, but more powerful. These seemed forbidden, and she knew she should stop this, but she couldn't speak as his warm breath caressed her ear.

It was as though he read her thoughts when he murmured. "Should I stop?"

She let out her breath, unaware she held it. She banked these new feelings in her memory. "I think so."

He had not expected her affirmative response. As he fought to regain control, he stopped and rested his head above her shoulder. He was thankful for the fabric which separated his lips from her flesh. He lifted his upper body away and examined her. "Have I displeased you or hurt you?"

Her eyes opened, and she shook her head. Could this be a conversation a woman endured during coupling? Embarrassment flamed her cheeks.

Without meaning to, his voice begged, and his gaze narrowed. "Why then? Tell me what you feel."

"Strange, wicked, and embarrassed," she dropped her hand from his neck, realising she still kneaded it. "Is this normal?"

"Yes, you'll feel these things. We will be naked, and I'll touch the places on your body only you have touched before. I'll place my fingers between your legs and bury them inside the wetness there." His words caused images to play across his mind, and his manhood hardened. He inched his leg off her until he was sure it no longer pressed against her.

She swallowed as she imagined his fingers between her legs. The yearning within her built. But she had to know. "Do all kingdoms couple this way, even my own?"

He smiled as he realised without many animals or her mother, she had not witnessed or spoken of this to anyone. At least back home, a woman could imagine from the animal kingdom what it would be like before it happened. His sudden insight grew his confidence. "More than you would think. For every creature born on Speranza, this is how they came to be."

"I must trust yer words." She conceded and turned her head away. She waited for his lips to return to her body.

He placed his palm against her neck and guided her face back so her eyes would look at him. "Now you understand. You should relax and enjoy what you can, however your body wants. If you need to scratch my back, move, or moan, then do. Any reaction you have is acceptable and encouraging. The more you participate, the more incredible it will be. Should I stop or continue?"

Her eyes fluttered closed, "Continue," then opened to gauge his reaction. Would his expression flash with disgust over her inexperience or irritation by her many questions?

With a slyly mischievous smile, his hands found the nightgown's collar. He pulled the tie, releasing it. "We must remove this barrier." Her hands acted to intercept his, but he pushed them away. "I'll do it." He shifted his body to rest between her legs and propped his elbows against the mattress. One by one, his hands unfastened each clasp, which ran a vertical path down the material's front. His whisper invited her. "Use your hands to explore my flesh."

Her fingers coiled into his nape. He dropped his mouth onto hers and tongued it open. He pushed the fabric away from her and he silenced her protest with his drugging kisses as the cool air raised bumps over her skin. His hands travelled up her rib cage, lifted her back off the mattress, and freed her arms from the nightgown.

He ended the kiss to admire her naked body as the single candlelight played over her. Her fingers curled around his neck and urged him to return his mouth to hers. Instead, he buried his face into the side of her neck, and his breath danced over her skin. Her body quivered with excited thrills.

He was unsure where to touch her first, but he settled his hand against her waist and his fingers dug into her back as he roamed his mouth over her shoulder and collarbone. She extended her throat, inviting him to explore, and her breath hitched when he cupped his warm palm over her peaked breast.

Her body churned, and his reacted. His hips pushed into the bed as his rod sought temporary relief against the material of the nightgown beneath them.

His muscled torso pressed her into the soft mattress, and her legs opened wider as he lifted her calf, positioning it over the back of his thigh. She moaned when his mouth covered her nipple and he kneaded the other with his hand. He divided his efforts between her breasts and he traced his fingers along her leg, pushing the other wider. He tested her response by scraping his nails up her thigh, then brushed his thumb against her wetness—her back arched. His hand increased its pressure as it grazed her thigh, and he settled his thumb between her legs. He rolled the tiny nub under his abrasive skin. An uncontrolled groan escaped her, and he captured it with his mouth.

He trailed his tongue between her breasts and moved his body lower, tonguing her navel. He lifted her leg higher onto his back and then wrapped his hands around her waist. His thumbs pressed into her hipbones as he settled his mouth on the inside of her thigh.

She felt his mouth's heat against her leg and his hair brush her swollen clit. When an intense need for fulfilment rushed through her, her stomach muscles tightened. She did not know what she needed, but she needed more as she arched her hips, drawing his attention.

He isolated the button under the pressure of his open mouth.

And as he covered it, she heard herself cry out. Tiny flames ignited along her spine and, in awe, she surrendered to them, allowing them to fire through her.

He was aware her folds tried to escape as her torso wriggled, but his powerful arms held her in place as her every muscle contracted.

Euphoria claimed her body and, even if she wanted to, she could not protest when his finger slipped inside her.

Excited by her release and wanting to provide her another, he lapped his tongue against her as he pushed his finger inside. He sensed the tight muscles push against it and he massaged her opening until it relaxed and would accommodate a second.

She felt the stretch of her opening as his digits prodded. She did not understand why she ground her hips farther into the bed, but it was a delicious sensation.

He forgot his own needs and sought to deliver her complete satisfaction as her body pleaded to receive him. His fingers touched the barrier he knew existed but had never encountered, and he backed his fingers off from it as concern clouded his mind.

She arched her hips towards his fingers, wanting more of him inside her. She frowned from the removal of the pressure.

He manoeuvred his tongue inside her cavern, adding his saliva to her wetness, and he fingered her clit between his digits in a steady rhythm. She rewarded him when her thighs tightened against his ears and her hips violently jerked.

His own need heightened. He crawled up her body and fastened his mouth onto hers. As her waves subsided, he rested his erection against her.

He moved his lips to her ear, hoping she heard him through her lust and heavy breath. "Do you feel my shaft pressed against you?"

She did not want to speak. She tried to bring his mouth to hers.

He pulled back and whispered. "Do you?"

Her passion-filled eyes opened, and she nodded.

He returned his lips to her ear, breathing his words as he lowered his hand between them, slickening himself in her wetness. "Its entirety, the length and thickness, will burrow deep within your small, wet sheath. Your muscles and flesh will stretch around it. Of itself, your folded skin and tight opening will demand my completion."

She felt the warm, smooth flesh against her swollenness and she gyrated her hips. His muscles jolted at her sudden encouragement, and he clenched his jaw, fighting the instant urge to climax.

His hand travelled to the flat of her stomach, dissuading her from further movement, then used his hips to guide the tip's search for her warm centre. It slipped between her satiny pleats. He settled on her, wrapped his arms underneath her back and trailed his tongue along her neck, then slowly flexed within her.

She struggled to keep her wits about her as new sensations washed through her body. His probing felt wondrous inside her, but she wanted more. She was uncertain how to communicate it. She lifted her legs to his waist.

Her action was his undoing. He slid his hands down her spine and cupped both her ass cheeks, forcing them upward. In anticipation, he covered her lips with his, then plunged his full length into her sanctuary.

The thin barrier broke under his force, and she cried into his mouth. She felt something tear inside her as he drove himself forward. Her muscles protested by clamping tightly around him and she struggled beneath him as her fingers clawed his back.

Their coupling was primal, like nothing he had experienced. He knew he could not stop and pumped at a steady tempo, waiting for her pleasure to return. He used his mouth to tease her neck and shoulders while he kneaded her ass with his palms.

His decision was rewarded when, after a few moments, her teeth bit into his shoulder, and her ass lifted to meet his strokes, forcing his cock deeper into her silk texture.

Again, she writhed with passion, and he meant to prolong her pleasure as he pulled out his length, then pressed back inside her, increasing his pace. He couldn't take much more of the prolonged pleasure, so he ground his hilt against her clit, hoping she would reach her apex soon.

His hairy flesh ground against her button, and it began to tighten under his assault. When she felt she could no longer take it—her body let go, like weightlessness in a dream. Her body spasmed and her muscles contracted around him.

His conscience argued to pull out, but his body disobeyed, demanding the satisfaction of knowing her completely. He thrusted harder and more rapidly as their friction created heat, building against him, and he couldn't get enough. His release began, and under its severity, he pitched his hips and collapsed against her.

He dwelled on the unfamiliar sensation, enjoying it, and wishing for it to last.

As their breathing returned to normal, she pushed against his shoulder. "Ye're squishing me."

He rolled off, propped his head on his elbow, and chuckled. "My thigh is thicker than your waist." He leaned over and planted a kiss on her lips. "Did I hurt you?"

She closed her eyes. "Ye know ye did."

"Did I give you pleasure, too?" He inspected her face as it reddened, but she did not answer. He shifted onto the flat of his back and pulled her to rest against his chest.

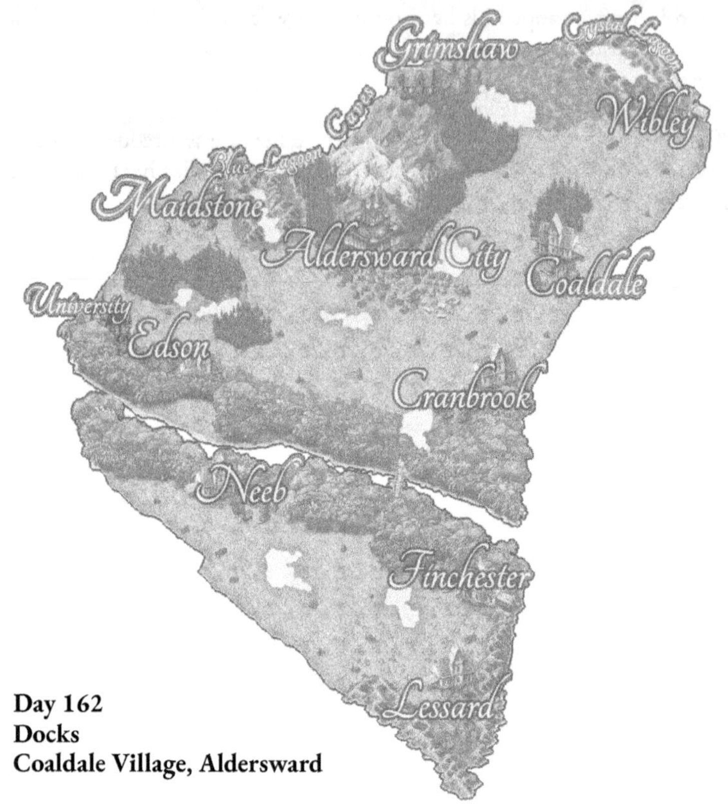

Day 162
Docks
Coaldale Village, Aldersward

Positioned in the mid-morning sky, the sun warmed those who waved the three vessels farewell. They floated gently from the dock and into the open sea. In awe, comrades, carpenters, and townsfolk watched and prayed the men aboard would return safely.

King Adahy turned and clasped Earl Austen's hand. "Thank you for your hospitality. You must attend Aedyn's wedding so I may extend you the same kindness."

Austen smiled. "I shall plan on it. Take care, good friend."

His eyes focused on the carriage, which held only his daughter, locked within. He preferred no one see her condition or allow her the opportunity to persuade another to secure more tonics.

Commander Ainco disrupted his thoughts. "Sire, unless there is need to update you before, I'll send messages on schedule. I'll continue to have the men prepared, and the crafts completed."

"That will do. My presence is no longer required, and I must return to my wife and my duties."

He strode to his carriage as his men mounted. He inhaled a breath of relief, knowing for now everything was all right.

Day 162
Dugout
Belinda's Home
Crow's Pass City, Baitsloam

Against her bed, Belinda stretched her body and discovered her movements restrained. She lifted her hand to push the covers away, but instead, touched a large, warm arm. Abruptly, she recalled where she was and what had transpired.

Aedyn's powerful arm tightened around her waist, dragged her backwards, and settled her naked ass against his groin. He burrowed his face through her hair and planted his mouth on her neck's sensitive cord.

She was unsure if he was awake or what etiquette she should use. She preferred to leave before words were spoken.

It was not to be as he whispered. "Do you suppose the noises you made last night keep Beatrice from intruding this morning?" He smiled into her neck as he nibbled her throat.

In indignation, her expression furrowed. "Impossible. I made nay noise."

He lifted his hand to her shoulder and pulled until she was flat on her back, then leaned over her. Her eyes were closed tight and her face an embarrassed amber. He slid his hand down her shoulder, skimmed her breast, and relaxed it over her abdomen. He felt her muscles stiffen under his palm.

Aedyn walked his fingers over her midriff, then clutched her side and returned his mouth to her neck. "You moaned from the intense passion created by my hands and mouth. Your body writhed against my tongue when it covered your woman's flesh, and my fingers were inside you." He felt her pulse quicken. His manhood hardened, and he pressed it against her thigh.

Above, heavy footfalls sounded.

Her pulse jumped, and she struggled against him to sit up. Modestly, she gathered the blanket over her front and tugged it off him as she stood and turned so he would not see her exposed backside.

He had no such shyness. She had taken the covers, so even if he preferred to hide his long, thickened shaft, he could not. Throwing himself back onto the mattress in frustration, he closed his eyes and sighed. At this time, he realised a repeat of their nighttime activities was unlikely.

She pointed to the single-burning candle and hissed. "Make yerself useful–"

He peered at her and smiled. "It was my intention, but you escaped the bed. If you come back–"

She shook her head. "Light the candles. I must dress and go above before they suspect anything."

He lifted the single candle and lit the others. "Your nightgown is here." He yanked it from underneath him and tossed it in her direction.

She reached for it but missed. Exasperation filled her tone. "Avert yer eyes, so I may dress."

He chuckled and turned over. "There's no part of you I haven't seen or touched."

"Regardless." She reddened as she collected the nightgown and fought her arms through the tangled sleeves. As she fastened the front, she turned her back and allowed the blanket to fall.

She slipped inside her shoes, and he rolled towards her. "Am I to understand last night did not happen? Should it be a secret?"

"Aye," her eyes searched the room.

He knew what she was seeking and grinned. "It may be difficult. You never brought your robe."

She glanced at her body and could plainly see her dark nipples and the fuzz covering her womanhood.

He laughed and rose, towering over her proudly. Then, uncaring, he strolled to his trousers and pulled them on. "I'll fetch it."

"They will know." Her face burned as he pulled on his boot.

He moved to stand before her, then hauled her into his arms and tilted her head. "In either case, they will know." His lips seized hers, and he deepened the kiss by lacing his tongue with hers. He lifted his mouth to gaze at her wet, puffy lips. "You have the look of a satisfied woman."

She wondered at his words. Had she changed? She would need to study her appearance as soon as possible.

Day 163
Castle's South Bailey, Aldersward

As King Adahy dismissed the staff who attended their arrival, he hugged Princess Annora and greeted Ammaris, then manoeuvred them away from the row of carriages.

"Accompany me to the queen's chambers and tell me what has happened while we were away." He glanced over his shoulder as Axton wrapped a thick cloak over Achelle and hooded her face.

Sheltering her from any staff who came near, the physician guided her weak body upstairs. Her bruises faded, the scrapes almost healed, but the laceration on her forehead and her broken arm remained evident.

Axton pushed open her chamber doors and ushered her inside. Her trembling body was barely aware of its movements.

He left her standing in the middle of the room and spoke quietly to her guards outside, advising them that under no circumstances should anyone enter except her father, nor was she allowed to leave. He closed the door and removed the heavy garment from her, then steered her into the bedchamber.

Her expression remained detached as she crumpled on the bed, motionless.

He searched the interior, opening every drawer, trunk, and wardrobe, riffling through to ensure there were no makeshift weapons or tonics present.

He addressed her as though her condition was natural. "Your father made many arrangements. Until you've regained some weight and strength, you'll have no visitors except him. Whenever you're attended by staff, there will be multiple. I'll check on you a few times a day as he has ordered, but I don't know what help I can offer." He looked at her, but she made no indication she was listening.

Pity stirred within him. Her naïve nature had caused her state, and now she was held without help until her brother was free.

With feigned enthusiasm, he spoke. "I'm certain you'll recover. You'll return to your previous self, and all this will seem like a bad dream. You can mark my words."

When he left and locked the door, his arms carried the few things he had found.

Again, he realised he must plead with the king. Perhaps the herbalist could come here, instead.

Day 164
Dugout
Belinda's Home
Crow's Pass City, Baitsloam

Aedyn laid on the mattress and smiled as he remembered Beatrice's knowing expression yesterday morning when he strode through the kitchen and returned with the robe in his hand. But she made no comment.

He wondered what the conversation would have been if Bret had not already left the cottage, leaving the three to find a new relationship under their current circumstances.

He cared not what the older couple thought. His only concern was to ensure Belinda had no lingering feelings of shame or embarrassment. He did not want her to withdraw from him.

He smiled widely, then leaned his back against the wall and crossed his arms as Beatrice stood next to him, stirring the pot.

"Ye've risen in good spirits." Beatrice peered at him.

"The best spirits. It's settled—you three will accompany me to Aldersward."

She shrugged with a grin. "Yer mid of night negotiation served ye well, then?"

He nodded as Belinda's door opened and when she stepped into the kitchen, his arm snaked out, pulling her against his chest. He offered her no chance to object as he covered her mouth with his. He trapped her arms between them and he exercised his lips against hers, deepening the kiss. When her fingers finally curled into his tunic, he was satisfied. He relaxed his hold and raised his mouth.

Pleased, he smiled. "Good morning."

After accepting a mug of tea, he closed the drapes over the sitting room window, then reclined on the bench. He waited for her to come in and join him. When she sought to walk past him, he captured her and pulled her down, holding her in place with his heavy shoulder. From beside him, he pulled the novel and together they stayed there most of the day, taking turns reading to each other.

All day he longed to take her hand, pull her below and leisurely torture her as she moaned beneath him, but it was not to be as the older woman stayed within hearing at all times. She played the perfect chaperon.

Belinda had not visited him last night. And, as hard as it was for him, he hadn't sought her out.

He used the many hours alone to examine his emotions. Immediately upon waking from his unconscious state, feelings had stirred for her, and he faulted her for them. She read the book out loud and tested her innocence on his body. He did not know what other things she had done to him while he slept. Though they had no deep, meaningful conversations, he cared more for her now than his time acquainted with Ammaris.

And what of—what was the name of his whore? Azalea.

Were the feelings comparable? No—Azalea was a distant memory.

He focused on her, but no lust roused, only respect, something akin to friendship.

Whatever his feelings were for Belinda, they were powerful and unfamiliar.

He thought of the novel they read, and he compared the characters' emotions to his. Could it be the same as them?

Love, he wondered. The concept was hard to fathom.

They had spent such little time together, but yet he knew. It explained his protective nature, his need to satisfy her, and his worry for her. He'd lost his detached, analytical reason anywhere she was concerned.

This was a genuine dilemma. When they arrived in Aldersward, he would have to denounce his engagement to Ammaris and marry Belinda immediately. Perhaps a swift marriage would soothe his father's rage. Better, would be to have the wedding before they arrived.

He would have to ponder this. He did not know her feelings, but was certain they would grow.

For hours, the candle burned, and then, as it choked out, his eyes closed.

Something nudged his chest, and he rolled onto his back, escaping it. He was still exhausted and once he evaded the hand, he instantly fell back to sleep.

Day 164
Dugout
Belinda's Home
Crow's Pass City, Baitsloam

Hours before, the morning meal had occurred and they would depart soon to meet his craft. They had expected him above earlier, filled with excitement, but he had not come. In the barn, Beatrice and Bret gathered belongings they wished to take with them.

As she placed her hand on his chest and shook him, Belinda worried. But he merely rolled onto his back. Had fever taken him again? She had not noticed his leg wound angry two nights before, but in honesty, she had not checked. She cursed herself for not doing so.

Frantic, she could not allow this opportunity to pass for his escape. Another time may never present. She straddled his hips and lifted his head so she could examine his face.

Try as he might, he could not ignore her weight as her thighs settled, and her natural heat burned his arousal. After two days of waiting, she had come to him. He bucked his hardened erection against her as he rolled them over and planted himself between her legs.

He opened his eyes and peered into her surprised expression. "You've come."

He buried his lips in the sensitive spot beside her ear.

For a moment, her eyes closed, savouring his wet mouth against her skin. She shook her head. "It's late morning." She stammered. "Are ye all right?"

"Tired," he whispered as his hand lightly traversed her rib cage until it cupped her breast. "I've waited countless hours in agony for you. Why have you tortured me?"

She shook her head again as her resolve waned. "We mustn't. It's nearly time to leave."

His hand glided downwards and bunched her skirt around her waist, exposing her first to the cold, then his smooth thickened staff as it probed against her heat. "It's precisely why we should. There will be no privacy for us once we board." He slipped his tip inside her warm folds.

Her breath hitched, and her pulse quickened. Using saliva, he slickened his hard length. She struggled to keep her senses, but his probing sent pleasant shivers through her spine.

"Please–" *We must leave*, she meant to beg. But he interrupted her.

His voice pleaded as he pushed deeper inside her. "Let me love you."

His words were her demise, and she lifted her lips to receive his kiss. Hungrily, she drank from him as he slid slowly in and out of her sheath. Powerful emotions made her abdomen flutter, and she raised her urgent hips.

As his mouth found hers, she surrendered. They could not be close enough and he buried his arms under her, wanting their bodies to become one. He had never known this longing and no matter how quick he moved or how hard he pushed, he could not stop his all-consuming need.

She wrapped her leg over his thigh and instinctively he knew what she wanted. He rocked his hips, meeting her protruding button with his hilt each time.

His breathing quickened as he buried his face in her neck.

Her nails dug into his back, pulling his weight more firmly onto her, and he allowed his body to relax its weight.

He whispered his ragged breath into the side of her throat. "Your moans please me. Feel me further harden and thicken within you."

Loudly, she moaned against his shoulder as she writhed against him.

It was unexpected and almost his undoing, but he concentrated. He plunged deeper as he sucked on her neck. It was unfair she wore clothes, wanting to sink his teeth into the flesh at her collarbone.

"Tell me I please you." He ran his tongue up her throat. "How do I feel inside you?" He bit her earlobe and tugged gently. "Do you want to scream?"

Louder, she moaned, and he silenced her with his mouth, then raised his head and looked into her eyes. He stopped his hips movements, but she thrust her hips upward, begging him to continue.

Her desirous eyes slit, and her mouth pouted as she sought to rock herself against him.

"I need your answers." He settled his mouth onto hers. "I'll move and you will be louder. The louder you become, the more I will please you." He drove himself inside her and she moaned. Again, he tested with his hips—this time he was assured she understood.

As her moans grew louder, he resumed the frenzied pace. Matching his every heave, she curled her hips.

She pleased him, and he rewarded her.

He slid his arms down her back and lifted her ass off the mattress, forcing himself even farther inside her.

Her breath caressed his shoulder. "Ye please me."

He stroked harder and faster as an intense moan escaped her.

"Again," he pleaded against her mouth, then buried his face in her shoulder.

She clenched her teeth and spoke as he hammered his pelvic bone against her swollen clit. "If ye reach any deeper, I may taste ye in my throat. Already ye reach above my navel." Her skin tightened—the build she recognised. Knowing its promise, she moaned. Her mind lifted, then fell. When her body thrashed beneath him, she raked her nails up his back. "*Aedyn.*"

A fresh wave of desire washed over him. Her walls gripped around his cock, then constricted like a vice.

She screamed his name as her body pulsated.

It was more than he could endure, and he launched his seed deep inside, enjoying the waves of her climax as she squeezed his shaft.

She milked him even though her orgasm had ended.

Pleased by her satisfaction, their eyes met and his chin dimpled. He flexed his hips, enjoying how her expression changed. Instantly, his desire reignited, and he wanted to watch as he gratified her again.

One of the exterior doors above crashed against the wall when it flung open. He leapt to his feet and dragged her upwards. He grabbed his trousers while she settled her skirts.

Something urgent was occurring, and she ran from the room. As Bret's boots landed on the dugout's bottom, she met him.

"Go." He ordered in a low tone, and she scrambled up the ladder.

Aedyn stalked towards him and the older man lifted a silencing finger. The trapdoor above thudded and pitched the area into darkness. The heavy chair dragged across the wooden floor as it covered the hatch. They both strained to listen.

The old woman held the dugout's door and she let it fall when the young woman climbed through it.

"They've come." Beatrice dashed to the armchair and together they pushed it over the hatch.

When many boots sounded close outside and a heavy fist pounded on the exterior, no time for questions remained. Belinda fixed a bright smile and opened it.

A dozen of the king's men lingered within her yard and her glance bounced over them, noting their formal military attire.

"Lady Belinda." The man who knocked stepped forward, took her hand, and kissed it. "The king orders us to escort ye to the castle." He lowered his voice for only her ears. "Ye come with us now. Any excuse will forfeit Brayleigh's safety."

Her eyes jumped with panic, but she nodded. "I'm ready. Please allow me a few minutes to direct my staff and finalise my trunk."

She pushed the door but his hand stayed it. "I'll wait inside while ye finish."

She invited him in with a wave of her arm, and he walked into the centre of the room, noting the thick window coverings.

"Beatrice, open the windows. My headache has left." She ordered. "Please sit. The journey will be long. Enjoy a few minutes of rest while I finish gathering my things."

The pair below listened to the women shuffle, then the loud stride of a man's boots. Belinda's words were clear, and the man settled into the large chair above the ladder. The women's footsteps retreated and Aedyn silently walked across the dirt, following them.

Beatrice rushed to the wardrobe, removed swaths of clothing, and dumped them into the empty trunk. Belinda swept everything from her dressing table into her arms and dropped the contents onto the bed, then sat as the older woman arranged the things.

Belinda reassured. "For a few days, I'll be fine without ye. Ye and Bret will take the trip we discussed. Once ye return, see to my remaining belongings, and close the house. Ye will join me as soon as possible."

When Bret joined him, Aedyn's eyes turned, and he whispered. "This is my fault. We must stop this."

"There are at least ten men above. Not to mention how many would come forward upon seeing ye. I'm too old to be of any use. Nay matter how long ye fought, ye would be outnumbered and they would execute us three for treason." He reasoned in a quiet tone.

"If I had risen earlier or if we had left before daybreak, this would not be happening." He hissed.

"Or they may have stopped the wagon and most certainly they would have discovered ye. If ye've any feelings for her or us, ye must let this happen. Once ye reach yer men and yer other boats, then ye can return and save her."

The prince knew he was right, but still rage seethed inside him. When heavy footsteps fell in her bedchamber, his jaw clenched. The trunk scratched the floor as men hoisted and carried it away. The pair followed the sounds back to the sitting room.

Beatrice draped a cloak over Belinda's shoulders as the men stalked outside, leaving only the one supervising from the armchair.

She hugged her tightly, and the young woman's body trembled as she whispered in reassurance. "We'll be with ye soon."

As a knot formed in her throat, she nodded. She had so many things to say, yet she could not. She glanced at the king's man. "I'm ready."

He walked to the door and waited, but Belinda dashed to the bench and handed the book to her.

The old woman could not watch. It was too painful and so she escaped into the kitchen.

Belinda shuffled backwards towards the exit. "Goodbye."

The man stood straighter and peered over her. "Who are ye talking to?"

"My parent's memories," she offered quietly, but continued to stare into the room as she stepped out and reached for the door handle.

The single word reached Aedyn and crushing guilt surged through him. He never intended there to be a farewell, and now he could express nothing in return.

Hysteria broke Belinda. Uncontrollable tears flowed and her stomach violently turned.

"I love ye," she shrieked as she slammed the door, then collapsed.

The thin thread of common sense holding Aedyn still snapped. He tried to push the old man whose hands held firm to the rungs behind him. He did not want to hurt Bret, but if forced, he would.

"Move," he ordered, spittle frothed from his mouth.

"Ye'll kill us all." He would be no match against the Alder's strength, he merely had to hold him off until reason prevailed.

Consumed by boiling madness, Aedyn forgot his combat skills, and pushed against him. "I'll kill you, kill them all—anyone who tries to stop me."

Bret seized his shoulders. He meant his direct tone to cool him. "Nay, ye won't. Stop this. It serves nay purpose."

Beatrice watched from the window as the man caught Belinda, then carried and placed her inside the carriage. The men mounted and the carriage wheels rolled over the gravel as they built speed. She heard the prince's angry voice sound below, and she prayed her husband could control him. She added her plump weight to the armchair, for reassurance.

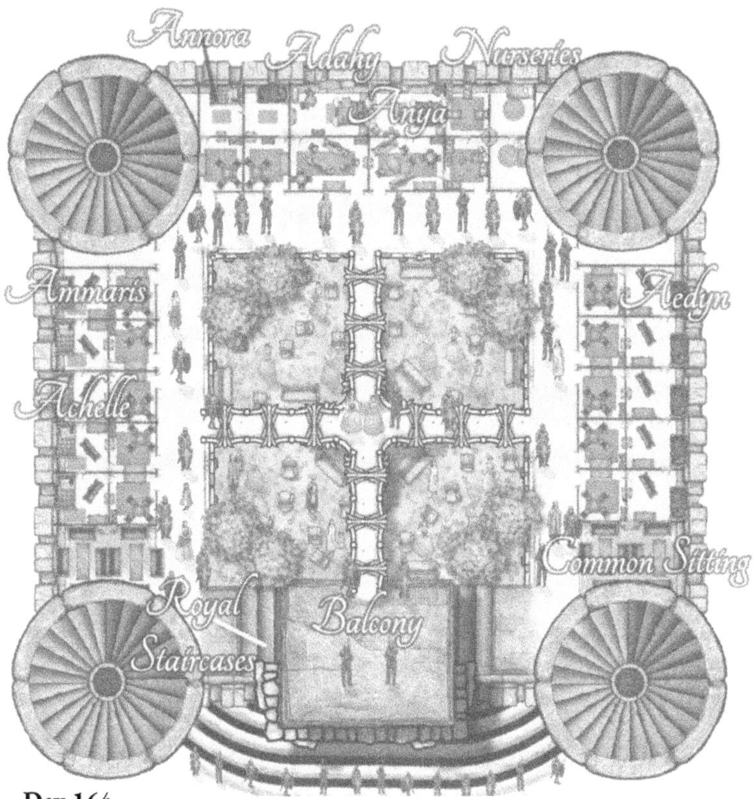

Day 164
Queen Anya's Chambers
Castle's Second Level
Near Aldersward City

The king's guards joined Annora's outside the queen's chamber as Adahy continued, and the servants genuflected when he entered. He waved his hand, sending them scurrying from the rooms.

His young daughter, dressed in an ankle-length, plain pink dress, remained motionless beside the bed. Her long brown hair with knots cascaded down her back, a sign she continued to thwart her staff with her magic, and with her family otherwise occupied, no one saw to her.

Her green eyes with gold flecks swung to him when he brushed her shoulder. "Please, I wish to spend time with your mother alone."

She placed her palm down and the pink lizard climbed from the bed, up her arm, and perched next to her face. Closing the door, Annora's maid followed her out.

As he carefully sat beside her, he examined his wife's frail, still frame. She had suffered further weight loss, and he wondered how much longer her body would endure before it abandoned its fight.

He raised her delicate hand to his mouth and kissed her wrist. He yearned to feel her caress, something as simple as her fingers on his face.

"I've created such a mess of things." He confided. "Addiction plagues our daughter, Aedyn lives among enemies, and Auren's stranded at sea, waiting to rescue him." Imagining her remarks, he listened.

He laid her hand back at her side. "Axton sent for a herbalist. It's his hope the woman will help Achelle overcome this. I've dispatched messengers to every community to identify another who can walk in others' consciousness. Until then, I have no choice but to utilise our daughter. Sometime today, Aedyn will start his journey to Auren, and within a fortnight, both will turn home."

"I love you." He stroked his fingers over her cheek. "And I'm stricken by immense guilt and grief because I cannot allow them to continue their search. This is what you would want. I feel it more strongly than anything I have before. Your body pleads with me to let you go, but I can't. For the sake of our kingdom and children, I should. I'm simply not ready for our story to end." As he gathered her into his arms and rocked their bodies in unison, a tear slipped onto his cheek.

Day 164
Sitting Room
Belinda's Home
Crow's Pass City, Baitsloam

After several minutes of quiet, a knock came from below. Beatrice pulled the chair away and her husband pushed the hatch cover upwards as he climbed through. Stress and fatigue marred his normally stoic features. She sought comfort in his arms, and he wrapped her tightly.

Still embraced, he walked her to the bench under the window and pulled her with him when he sat. They watched as Aedyn appeared above, his armour and weapons secured.

None spoke, each lost in their thoughts.

Without words or a backward glance, he strode through the kitchen to Belinda's bedchamber, where he could come to terms with her fate. He slammed the door and leaned his back against it. How could so much have happened in such a short time? It seemed like a nightmare. He prayed he would soon wake to discover her next to him.

He scanned the dishevelled and barren surroundings. The open wardrobe's hooks were void of her clothing and the bottom empty of shoes. Her dressing table lacked its normal clutter, wiped clean of the things which had their specific place. The bed summoned him closer with the promise of her smell and remembered warmth.

Without regard for the window, he crossed to it, sank, and grabbed her pillow. Hugging it to his chest, he inhaled her sweet scent. When he returned it, he spotted the tiny end of her black ribbon trapped between the wall and her bed.

He pulled it gently between his fingers and its length followed. He held the silky fabric to his nose, then wrapped it around his wrist and tied it. This would be his, a piece of her he would carry until they reunited.

A quiet knock interrupted, and Beatrice's voice reached him. "It's time." Her feet retreated.

One last time, he glanced over the room.

As he stood, something bounced from the mattress and rolled across the floor. He stooped, meaning to return it, but instead he recognised her jasmine oil and, without thinking, he secured it in the pouch at his waist, and joined Beatrice in the kitchen.

"Bret will bring the wagon close to the back door. Ye'll need to cover yer head with this and crouch, so nay one sees ye." She offered him the blanket. "I won't be travelling with ye. There's nay point now." When she handed him the book, she could not say the woman's name. "She wanted to ensure ye took this."

For several seconds, he stared at it, then seized the tattered book and stowed it inside his tunic.

His eyes held a determined stare. "I swear I'll return for her. You have my word." He embraced her and kissed her cheek. "I owe you my life."

The noise of the horses' harnesses and wagon sounded outside as he draped the blanket over his head.

Aedyn was hot, uncomfortable, and thirsty hidden inside the canvased wagon. He laid beneath a bed of old, stained blankets which were covered by stacked crates. Their insides filled with various tools and knick-knacks. On top of those, turned upside down, was a small fishing boat.

With each rut and bump the wheels rolled over, his back ached further. On the crowded, busy streets, voices and movements melded together, so he could not make out anything specific. It was only noise—irritating and deafening—which drove his mind into sensory overload. It produced a pounding throb in his temples.

His hand crept upward, and he tunnelled the blankets with his fingers to create a wrinkle large enough where he could access fresh air. His nose detected a hint of jasmine from the black ribbon tied at his wrist. He breathed deeply, attempted to block out the sounds, and prayed for sleep to relieve him.

When the wagon slowed, he woke. It was considerably quieter, but still there were horses' hooves, other wagons, and the distant murmur of conversations. Bret shifted and pulled the flap above his head open.

"Stay still. We've reached the city's edge and there's a block ahead." He took the flask and retied the opening as two of the king's men approached.

"Where are ye headed?"

Bret finished sipping. "Fishing off Tomlin's coast. What's the blockade for?"

"We're searching for those who organise against the king."

Bret laughed. "Let me ease yer mind. I'm Bret of Crow's Pass, Chamberlain to Lady Belinda of Crow's Pass, soon to be Queen Belinda of Baitsloam Kingdom.

This morning, my mistress left for the castle and instructed her servants to close her family home. As I am not required, I packed and headed out. I intend to spend tomorrow and the next day fishing. It may be a long while until I see the north coast again."

Footsteps pestled against the rocky ground, circling the wagon. The flaps at Aedyn's feet came loose and opened. He held his breath and waited. The man pulled one crate from his legs and rummaged through it, repeating the action with another.

Slowly, Aedyn exhaled when the canvas closed, and the ties refastened.

Bret watched the pair as the second man returned and nodded.

The second man spoke. "Ye're not much for organising?"

He shook his head. "Those Alder sards destroyed my cottage. Anything worth salvage is inside. Luckily, at the castle, I'll receive new housing." He reiterated his station.

The first said. "It's yer duty to report questionable activity if ye come across any on yer travels."

"Aye, I will indeed. Jezabet's blessing to ye both." He nodded and flicked the reins. The wagon lurched forward and trudged at a snail's pace.

Day 165
Prince Aedyn's Quarters
Anya's Endeavour
Baitsloam's North Sea

Men crowded around the long table and chatted amongst themselves, pouring sweet tea as they waited for Auren to emerge from the bedchamber. Sahana and Brielle sat at the smaller table, listening.

Auren entered, noting the significance of the two empty chairs at the table—Aedyn's and his own. It would soon be corrected and wondrous relief filled him, glad his reign would soon end.

He cleared his throat as he sat. "Let's begin. Where are we?"

Arturo replied, "About twelve miles east of Tomlin's shore."

Amos added. "We're organised to set course once we see tomorrow's stars and we'll arrive within distance before the mid of night."

"Perfect. Who will meet Prince Aedyn's boat?"

Asa offered. "I've chosen the six strongest men, and they've trained with Ackley in the cargo hold for the past few days. It shouldn't take more than ten or fifteen minutes to reach him."

He rubbed his head's stubble and eyed Asa, who stood behind those seated. "Six? You mean six, including you? You're our strongest."

The thought brought bile to his throat, and he swallowed it. "I hadn't planned on accompanying them, but I will." His eyes darted to Sahana and back.

He dipped his quill. "Yes, you go." He turned. "Sahana, tomorrow you and the page will clean these rooms. No one will enter but the two of you until he returns. For now, we hold our position. You're dismissed."

The men and Brielle exited while Auren wrote in the voyage's journal. Sahana gathered the used mugs, placing them in an empty crate.

"Auren?" Her voice sounded tiny to her ears, and she winced at having to initiate their conversation.

He continued to write. "Refill it, please."

Unsure of what to say, she fetched the pitcher from the table's end, returned, and poured the tea. Again, she tried, her voice a little more assertive. "The decisions you've had to make, I wouldn't wish to be you."

He was so preoccupied he had not heard her. She shrugged, giving up. She handled three more mugs and walked away. When she turned back, he was watching her.

"Did you say something?" He asked curiously. It was unlike her to speak first in any conversation.

She wet her lips and swallowed. "Yes. I've said the decisions you've made have been difficult."

He smiled, pleased she was comfortable enough to converse with him alone. "Yes, but soon to be over." He stretched his back. "Aedyn's return will be my reward."

"I wonder though..." her voice trailed off, not sure how to broach the subject.

"You wonder?" He lifted his eyebrow and relaxed backward against the chair. With any other woman, he would have finished her sentence with something sexual. "Are we friends?"

"I suppose." She nodded.

"I expected your words to be more definite. But pain knifed my heart just then. I imagine it felt much like Bowan did when you injured his leg." When shock flashed over her face, he smiled. "You see, we can discuss anything."

She took a deep breath. "I wondered about the anchor."

"What of it?" He tried to connect her thoughts on his own, but failed.

"If something happened to our rescue boat, how do you suppose we lift the anchor if Asa is lost?"

"It would take more men to operate the wheel and lever."

Her expression relaxed. "I'm relieved. I knew you would have an alternative method tested and ready."

"Yes." He nodded absently and strode past her, out into the morning's sunlight.

Before the door swung closed, she heard him bellow for Asa and she smiled.

Day 165
Coastline
East of Tomlin City, Baitsloam

Aedyn woke as the wagon travelled through branches and low bushes which rubbed against the underside and tarp. He listened. There were no noises of other horses, wagons, or carriages. He shoved the covers away from his face; the interior was dark.

He loudly cleared his throat.

"It's safe for ye to come out from under the blankets. It's after the mid of night, and we left the road to skirt the forest about four hours ago."

He sat upright. His muscles burned from the long hours without movement, but he was grateful for the reprieve from the heavy warmth. He leaned his back against the wood where the older man faced forward, driving.

Aedyn kept his voice low, as Bret had. "How long?"

"We'll reach it by the mid of morning, roughly ten hours."

"How do you think the women fair?"

He knew he meant Belinda. "He intends to wed her. I imagine it will be over before Beatrice and I get there. She's bright—she'll adapt and survive."

The prince listened to the night sounds, or more so, the absence of them. No animals or birds called to each other. Without the movement of their wagon, it would be rather eerie. Hours passed before the whipping of the brush ended, replaced by the sound of lapping waves as the wheels ran smoothly over the sand.

In the early afternoon, Bret pulled the boat out, then settled the crates back over Aedyn's body.

The prince witnessed the distressed lines around the man's mouth; his age and exhaustion taking their toll.

He climbed down. "I'll be back in a couple of hours."

He secured the flaps together, placed his fishing gear in the boat, then dragged it to the water and rowed out. As he cast his hook, he examined the boats, the men, and the few camps. Time passed and his boat drifted towards the floating barriers which forewarned men of the blue dragons beyond. He rowed to shore and secured the boat to a nearby tree, then ran a spool of wool through the woods, marking the route with the least obstacles.

In the pit of his stomach, a sick nervousness took hold as he estimated six groups would remain when the sky faded to black. He flattened his bedroll under the wagon and knocked on its bottom, letting the Alder know he would sleep now.

It took every ounce of Aedyn's self-control not to fidget during the hours as his excitement built. It helped to concentrate on footsteps and the voices of those nearby. The setting sun turned the sky orange through the wagon's tarp, and the smell of fish cooking over open flames made his stomach rumble. Soon, those around them would eat their evening meal.

The smell must have woken Bret because he lightly tapped on the wood and rolled out. He freed the back flaps and entered.

He moved about with the canvas open, preferring his activities viewed by others. He extracted two bundles, one he held low and inserted under the covers while he took the other outside, and relaxed against a wheel as he ate.

The sun would create a shadow effect on the canvas, exposing Aedyn inside to anyone who looked his way. It forced him to eat in his current position.

When dusk came, the old man scrutinised those who remained as others climbed onto their horses or drove wagons away from the shoreline. The closest fire was about three-hundred yards northwest, then another roughly four-hundred yards straight north. The closest group were four men with horses and no shelter. He assumed they had bedrolls and would sleep under the stars. The other fire had two families and tents situated around it. More were farther back.

Would the paddles cutting the water alarm and bring these people to investigate? As he strolled to the first fire, Bret's stomach twisted anxiously.

"Hello there." One man greeted when Bret entered the fire's light.

"Good evening. I wondered if ye caught anything today?"

"A fair amount," another man nodded. "I noticed ye out there. How'd ye do?"

"Not so well. " He breathed deep, urging his stomach to calm. "The night is silent here."

"The blue dragons will surface and cause an awful ruckus around the mid of night."

"What bait ye using?" Bret asked.

When he left them, he was certain they would sleep immediately. They had enjoyed enough drink that he hoped they would not investigate if they heard any noise he and Aedyn made.

Day 165
Prince Aedyn's Quarters
Anya's Endeavour
Baitsloam's North Sea

In the bedchamber, Sahana ensured every surface and belonging was clean and in proper order. When Asa came through the exterior door, she returned the empty pitcher to the bored-out hole in the sideboard's centre. She smiled at him.

He closed the door, barring them from any ears who may hear. He lessened the gap so only a few feet separated them. "It wasn't your business to speak to Auren about me."

As she shook her head, she noted his annoyed expression, and her smile dissolved. "I didn't speak to him about you. I wondered–"

He kept his voice low. "Conveniently, about an anchor which only I can lift? I didn't require your interference."

"Does it keep you from going?"

"Of course, it keeps me on the Endeavour." He snapped, then calmed himself. "It takes one of me or twelve of them to secure it. It required simple wisdom to decide."

"Which neither of you used prior to my question." Her mouth widened with smugness. "In Slaysfold, this is why most things run smooth—men leave the important decisions to women."

"We would have considered it, eventually." He muttered the words over his shoulder as he stalked out.

Her laugh followed him. "Are you certain?"

Day 166
Coastline
East of Tomlin City, Baitsloam

The fires smouldered and died. It appeared the two closest camps were asleep. Bret tapped on the wood above, then moved to the wagon's end, and untied the flaps. Aedyn's feet made no sound in the rocky sand when he carefully emerged.

Bret led him across the open rutted track and into the trees, where it was shadowed and black. The old man guided the prince's hand to the taut wool. At a sluggish pace, they started forward. Each deliberate footstep landed with caution to ensure underfoot nothing would snap, scrape, or crack.

With the toe of his boot, Aedyn tested the area, and it connected with a solid object.

Had he turned around or lost the path?

His hand travelled along the string and encountered the other's fingers waiting.

Bret lifted the younger man's hand from the string and planted it on the obstacle.

His touch met the scratchy texture of a downed tree. Its branches long decayed and fallen away, leaving only the protruding knots and jagged breaks.

He lifted his leg over, then reached out to find the elderly man, who directed his hand back to the yarn. Against the armour at his shoulder, a thick bough of leaves rubbed, and he slowed his momentum to ensure it brushed past him without noise.

The precise movements, the deliberate placements, and the complete blackness dragged the twenty-minute journey into what seemed like an hour.

Finally, when Bret broke through the woods, the Alder inhaled a deep breath and willed the anxiety from his body. Here, at least, he could see the man's shape, no longer concealed by the deep shadows of the towering foliage.

The Bait squatted against a thick piece of driftwood while Aedyn remained hidden, and together, they scanned the sea for the craft's signal—a flicker of light.

On the Endeavour, at the first sign of stars, Auren ordered all lanterns extinguished and anyone not instrumental in the rescue sent below. He stood on the anchor deck with a dozen men—all silent. The mood was tense and charged with anticipation. Their attempt must succeed—another opportunity may never occur. A matter of loyalty and honour.

Through the darkness, the vessel floated. Only the material of a single small mast captured the wind above them.

He leaned closer to Azariah. "Anything yet?"

"I see several things, but nothing in the water."

He turned to his other side. "How far?"

"Just over a mile," Arturo murmured.

He whispered to the chosen group.

Men shuffled aside as two came forward.

As the two men positioned at the railing's edge, Auren stepped closer to the man with heat seeker abilities. "We need to learn if they are there."

Azariah understood his failure would end the mission, and the burden weighed upon him. He whispered, his tone stamped with anger. "I realise what you need. Demanding me to answer will only cause me to second-guess what I do see. There's no movement yet."

Again, Auren turned. "Strengthen his ability and extinguish it as quickly as possible. A single burst of light when I tell you." He turned back to Azariah. "Watch carefully." He swung his head and ordered, "Now."

At the same time, both men on shore witnessed the brilliant flare. Bret untied the boat and pushed it off while Aedyn covered the space between the woods and the water, then hopped in.

The prince lifted the paddles and rowed in the general direction.

"He's there." Azariah scrambled down the stairs, pursued by five others. They descended the ladder and settled into the small boat at the bottom.

Aedyn knew he only needed to be in the water. Azariah would locate him. He chose this last opportunity to speak to the old man. "Tell her I'll return before the full moon and bring the entire force of Aldersward down on King Baeddan."

"I'll tell her."

"His successor will cooperate and, in turn, we will provide your kingdom with all it requires. I swear this to you." His hand sought Bret's shoulder. "You believe me, don't you?"

He responded in a solemn tone. "Aye, I believe yer intentions are honourable but there are many factors out of one's control."

"Not out of mine." Sudden determination fuelled his strokes.

After several minutes, he stopped. The sound of several paddles sliced through the water nearby, and he waited.

Through the night, Azariah whispered. "Your Highness, we're here."

Hands pulled the boats together and palms reached out to help him manoeuvre from one boat to the other. He turned back and swore. "I will return, my friend."

"May Jezabet guide ye." Bret said in final farewell before lifting the paddles.

The Alders cut the sea with fevered rows.

The only voice whispered commands, directing the men back to the Endeavour. Aedyn inhaled the security of home, the certainty of his power, and freedom from the dangerous limbo.

"The dragons are surfacing." Azariah's tone filled with fear. "Quickly, raise your paddles. Don't act or speak."

The prince controlled his instinct to turn and inspect the shore. Would they be discovered? What would happen to Bret?

Thump! The sound was dull, but the boat rocked with force as a dragon's thick digit hit against its bottom, followed by two smaller hits. When the blue dragons surfaced, the water churned. All around them, splashes echoed like miniature explosions, and the increased spray further dampened the men's bodies.

Had he come this far only to die in the last leg? Once again, he was a prisoner, but now by these creatures.

Crack! Crunch! Wood snapped and crushed behind them and they heard Bret's alarmed yell thunder through the blackness.

Though impossible to see, Aedyn turned backwards. From the camps, men's loud calls rushed to the water's edge.

The prince murmured. "We can't remain here. If the old man isn't dead, he soon will be if we're discovered."

"I'll row where I see space, but it will be tedious." Azariah lifted two paddles.

Bret had placed himself in jeopardy to aid an outsider, and death could be his reward.

Guilt riddled Aedyn and his eyes raised to the stars as he delivered a silent appeal.

On the anchor deck, Auren and the few others stood in silence after the echoing yell, unsure whose voice rang out. Regardless, they would remain until morning, if necessary, to witness their comrade's bodies wash ashore. They would not leave until certain. As each minute passed, his hope waned.

Nearly an hour passed before the small boat returned to the Endeavour, and the sole indication was the scraping of the smaller vessel against the larger. The group above bounded onto the main deck and rushed to the ladder.

Azariah boarded first. "We're unscathed, but Prince Aedyn ordered silence."

When the prince appeared, the men genuflected.

Auren clutched his adoptive brother's shoulder, but was pulled into an embrace instead—one which suppressed their overwhelming emotions. Then they hardily slapped each other's back with affection as Aedyn whispered. "Once we hoist the smaller boat, depart. I don't want to be discovered when the sun rises."

The temporary leader whispered the commands, and a few minutes later, fabric spread from the masts. The wind's direction changed and their vessel sped across the expansive water. All waited in the dark until Arturo calculated their distance to be ten miles, and Azariah confirmed he no longer detected the land.

Auren called for the lanterns to be lit and sent someone to inform those below of their success. He glanced to the last position where he'd seen Aedyn, but he was gone. His quarters' exterior door swung shut.

Aedyn lifted the lantern by the door and strode inside. Motionless, he gazed at his things and the furniture. The room felt cold and empty, as if no one had entered, like a shrine to a dead man. There were no kegs or mugs out of place and no small blankets on the backs of the four cushioned chairs. From the long, larger table, they had tidied the drawings and documents. He wandered to the other room and found much of the same, nearly everything untouched.

Absorbed in thought, he jumped at the sound of the exterior door when his best friend entered.

Auren began to apologise, but the prince waved it aside and turned back to his bedchamber, placing his palm against the frame. "We'll sleep now. There's considerable decisions to discuss and organise." Belinda's image and her final words tormented him. "The force of our retribution will be reverent." His hand slid into the dark inside after he disappeared.

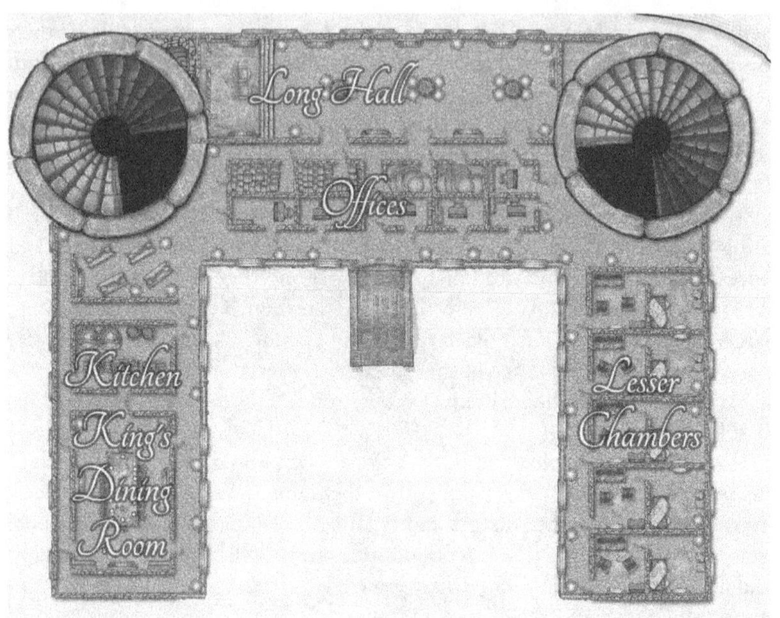

Day 166
Long Hall
Castle's Ground Floor
Baitsloam City

The bright morning light played through the windows, illuminating the pale grey walls lined with people who watched her stand in the entryway. Belinda preferred rain to match her misery. This would not be the marriage she dreamt of as a girl. At least the corseted gown's embellished, dingy blue matched her mood. The colour suitable for a queen, the dresser had explained.

She imagined her feelings were comparable to those of death-sentenced men marching to the gallows as she stepped inside. The king's secretary had reminded her to walk slowly through the hall. It was unnecessary; she wished to prolong her existence, and she urged Jezabet with every step for something or someone to intervene. But no voices came, no footsteps sounded, and no explosions happened as she reached the man who would be her husband.

Stoic and numb, she kept her eyes downcast on the stone floor. She gave no care to the king's disposition. If he killed her today, she would take comfort in the release.

The officiant gestured and a young page carried forward an elaborate silver necklace encrusted with jade stones nestled in a green velvet pillow. The king secured its heavy, bulky weight around her throat and the iciness of the shackle made her new prison final.

He steered her around the room so all could witness their union.

Twenty minutes passed before they returned to their original position.

"Our ruler gives his fealty to this woman, his bride. She becomes her majesty, Queen Belinda of Baitsloam Castle. King Baeddan, please register yer marriage."

As the king signed their names, the officiant bowed, and the interior echoed with cheers, stomping feet, and clapping hands.

When finished, he escorted her onto the rise, which held two thrones. Instruments tuned, then played as several doors swung wide and servants streamed through, carrying large food trays and refreshments. Excited by the king's generosity and the elaborate festivities, the guests were joyful—except one.

Lady Bethnee remained against the wall until tables and chairs were set throughout the room. She ordered a servant to place a small table near her and, once delivered, she sat in the shadows and viewed the young, inexperienced woman on her throne. Fury coursed through her. It should be her day, her marriage, and her crown.

She flicked her wrist, and her maid scurried away to fetch refreshments while she thought about her next plan. It was essential to protect her position as the king's mistress.

When Prince Bryce observed the woman's restrained animosity, he grinned. Despising her, he sauntered to her side.

"Lady Bethnee, share a toast to our queen and yer departure?"

"Nay, ye're mistaken. I'll go nay where and she won't remain queen for long." She rose, tilted her head aloofly, and swept past him.

Day 166
Prince Aedyn's Quarters
Anya's Endeavour
Baitsloam North Sea

Aedyn's ankles rested on the small table as he flipped through the voyage's journal. It was strange to read the words written about himself. Many passages admitted Auren's fears and doubts—a characteristic he never would have associated with his friend. He understood the anguish.

He discovered Auren's detailed encounter with Synnova, Bennet's wedding, and a speculative incident between Sahana and Bowan. A knock sounded, and the door opened.

"My Prince," Asa bowed, sweeping the floor with his hand.

He stood. "Come here, you ass." The two embraced in quick fashion. "I was reading. What's this about Sahana and Bowan?"

Asa sat. "We aren't altogether sure. Perhaps you can pry what happened from her. In any case, we advised Bowan of her position and your promise. Hopefully, his education ends it."

"Where are Auren and Bennet?"

"Auren's savouring his new freedom with Byunca on the observation deck and Bennet's educating Sahana and Brielle."

At his wrist, Aedyn's fingers rubbed the black ribbon. "Arrange refreshments and have the evening meal served here. Fetch the others, and we will plan."

Aedyn studied each as he recounted his tale, carefully leaving out his intimate relations with Belinda, but Sahana and Brielle shared a knowing glance.

Auren looked older somehow. Perhaps it was the worried lines or a slight variation in his resting expression. Still, he relished in the sight of the man who had been raised as his brother.

Bennet appeared happier than he ever remembered, much as Asa had been before this journey. He watched as his mentor doted on Brielle. The poor man did not realise she led him by his nose, but he seemingly enjoyed it.

The biggest difference was in Sahana. She no longer walked meekly with her face averted or concealed. She did not startle or flinch when someone happened past or addressed her. In their company, her mouth curved easily, and she spoke without hesitation. Pleasant weight had added itself and she looked healthier. He needed time to reacquaint himself with her scars and roaming eye.

Auren grinned, chewing a cheese cube. "Aidrik's itching to examine you. He's requested three times today. What should I tell him?"

He shrugged. "There's no need. I'm fine."

"It's quite fortunate ye found willing allies. Many would not have." The older woman settled her hand on Bennet's.

"I can only imagine Jezabet intervened. The likelihood of stumbling inside the future queen's home and her despising him more than us were slim." Everyone nodded at his remark.

Auren lifted his brow. "You spoke of vengeance last night. Has your position changed today?"

"No. I'll speak to Achelle tonight. I want the vessels sent immediately to Slaysfold. Then we'll return to Baitsloam and replace the king with another more cooperative. Afterwards, we'll offer aid so they may live better than they ever have under Baeddan."

"Aye, if King Adahy agrees, we shall follow ye." Bennet sipped from his mug.

In thought, he pulled at his bottom lip. "Perhaps I should send your family and Sahana back to Aldersward. This is no place for women, considering what will occur in Baitsloam."

Brielle said. "Do ye intend to harm our people?"

"Only those who stand between us and the king. I shall present them the opportunity to escape, but if they keep their loyalty, then yes, I imagine there will be bloodshed. Since you left, discontent developed throughout Crow's Pass, maybe even through Baitsloam. There may be no one standing between us and him."

Asa counted. "We'll reach Slaysfold Castle in five days. If our king sends the crafts tomorrow, we would be another seven days in Slaysfold before they would arrive. Six days to Baitsloam. Uncountable more, before we discover Reinshaven and linger, then return home. We could remain at sea for sixty days or greater." His mind whirled with the realisation—*will this never end?*

When the prince confirmed his calculations, Asa excused himself. No one except Sahana noticed his once merry demeanour had diminished. He no longer smiled freely and his natural enthusiasm evaded him. The drastic changes concerned her.

Day 166
Prince Aedyn's Quarters
Anya's Endeavour
Baitsloam North Sea

Aedyn struggled to force Belinda from his thoughts. His imagination tormented him with depictions of her suffering cruel abuses, while her anguished voice pleaded. They were difficult to manage, and it would be dangerous to dwell on them. No, his focus must remain on rescuing her, on his efforts.

Picturing home, he closed his eyes. Mounted and positioned on the bluff overlooking the activities in the west bailey, he drifted.

"Aedyn?" Achelle appeared.

He jumped from his stallion but lost his smile when he saw her arm. "What happened?"

"I fell. Axton believes I will recover."

She was another promise of home, and he embraced her gently, avoiding her sling. He helped her sit in the thick grass. "I'm free and have a message for Father."

She nodded and swallowed her discomfort. "He has one for you as well. You're to meet the other crafts and accompany them home in haste. There shall be no detours."

Shocked, his gaze narrowed. "What? Why? I must return to Baitsloam, then find a cure."

"Our father has promised Mother he would bring you and Auren home. He senses her surrender and wants us to accept it."

"No, no, I won't." His mind reeled.

This was their father's directive. Uncomfortably, she plucked a blade of grass and examined it while she waited for his reply.

"You once mentioned you can draw someone inside your mind? Is it possible to bring him and I together so we may speak directly?"

She shook her head. "The continuous use has weakened my ability. I'm uncertain I could pull you in, let alone both of you."

He clasped her hand. "By doing so, you may save our mother's life. Isn't she worth it?"

"Of course she is, but I'm not strong enough." Achelle glanced elsewhere as she remembered the pain from pulling April in. The dream had not lasted five minutes, yet she had suffered excruciating torture for an entire night and day. It had been years, but the memory could still conjure the agony. At the mere prospect, she shuddered.

"I believe you are. I trust you to save our mother. Please, for Auren, Annora, and I, you must try. You're her last hope." He pleaded.

His words provoked guilt within her. Still, she weighed the decision. At the encounter's conclusion, there would be no help. The physician would grant no relief and she would endure alone. She thought about the Endeavour's dead, her brother's sacrifice, and her mother, who if awake might return them to simpler, happier times—turning this past into an awful nightmare.

Readying herself for the agony she knew would come, Achelle inhaled a deep breath. "All right, but there's no guarantee this will serve. I've never brought two people together. And even if I achieve it, there's no telling how long it will last."

He smiled. "Even a minute will be worth it. What do you require of me?"

She clutched his grip stronger. "We'll lay back so you don't move and close your eyes. I'll do the rest."

She took a moment to view the sky above, then shut her eyes and concentrated. The sounds of nature faded, the wind died, and, finally, the sun's warmth vanished. Through her clothes, the cold seeped into her spine. "You can stand, but be mindful. These staircases and hallways move. I'll retrieve Father."

He straightened, glancing around. It was desolate—stark white and blackness wrestled for reign, like good and evil. She stepped from one door to the next, and an unsettling fear shrouded him. She fixed her hand on each as if she searched. On the third, she disappeared inside.

He was unaware of how long it actually took, but only a few seconds passed when she spoke behind him.

"Father, you may stand." She sat, twisted her back to the white wall, and leaned against it.

"Son," the king's eyes gleamed as they embraced. "It seems like years since we've seen each other."

"It does. We may not have much time. I must relieve Baitsloam of its present king. These communities survive with little food under a dangerous ruler who convinced them we are enemies. With the other vessels, it would end quickly. Then we'll find Reinshaven and gather healers."

The king shook his head. "No. It's over. You're to return immediately. I want you and Auren here when your mother dies. Once she's buried, we'll help the Baits."

Shocks of needling pain fired through Achelle's brain, and she shook. She drew her legs against her abdomen and unaware her body rocked.

"I can't leave these people to suffer. They healed and helped me escape. I've made commitments."

"You had no authority to make commitments. Your obligation is to our kingdom first. They'll understand our delay."

Her throat hummed, and the sound gradually built while the two men argued. They failed to notice the powerful fingers of white light snaking out around them.

"No, we'll advance with the men you've already sent."

As his son raised his voice, the king's eyes thinned. "No, I am king. I've instructed them to return after they meet with you. They will do as I have ordered, as will you. There will be no further discussion. You will maintain your present manifest and make haste."

Unable to handle the pain, her mouth opened and a long scream escaped her.

Both men charged, but before they reached her, they were driven back into their own dreams.

Through the nearly deserted halls and outside into the bailey below, loud shrieks bellowed. Like an injured animal losing a battle against another, her wails echoed. Achelle's guards heaved against the thick door as Ammaris's joined them. The other sets maintained their posts, staring in alarm across the open hallways. Ammaris, half-asleep, emerged and ran to wake the king. As she approached his door, he appeared, pushing her aside.

He fumbled with his heavy keyring as his guards accompanied him. When he reached for the handle, Axton opened it from within.

"I heard her in my chambers downstairs." He explained. "I don't understand what's happened."

The king swept past into her bedchamber, where Achelle still screamed—much louder without the door to muffle the sound.

He yelled so Axton would hear. "Aedyn and I met in her mind. Suddenly, she screamed. We tried to reach her but didn't. She's in pain. You must stop it." Concern marred his expression. He could not let her condition continue.

"Giving her something—anything—could jeopardise her further. I don't advise we risk it."

The king's hand snaked out, dragging him within an inch of his face. "You'll not leave her like this. The herbalist will arrive tomorrow. Until then, provide her with whatever she needs."

The physician knew this was a dangerous request. Still, he had no choice but to do as the king ordered. He bowed in submission and disappeared into the hearth. In a few moments, he returned and pinched her cheeks together, then rubbed a finely ground powder against her gums as her able arm fought against him.

The king paced to an armchair and sat down. "We'll remain until she wakes or is without pain. I assumed you would give her a tonic?"

"I applied it in concentrated powder form. Until she no longer resists, this will be best."

Day 168
Anchor Deck

Anya's Endeavour
Baitsloam North Sea

From high above, the afternoon sun warmed Sahana as she listened to Brielle and Bennet speak in deep conversation. She shifted her back from the railing and peered down onto the main deck. Several men practised combat exercises and more observed or accomplished menial tasks nearby. Auren exited the prince's quarters and strode to the navigation deck to see Amos.

On the observation deck, her eye found Asa standing alone, his back turned to her. They had not spoken since the night he excused himself from Aedyn's presence. Often, he remained alone, asleep, or nowhere to be found. Even when the prince requested an audience, he failed to appear. His sudden withdrawal worried her.

She clambered up the railing and excused herself, then started the journey to him, acknowledging Auren and Amos as she passed and climbed the ladder.

Asa's palms rested on the railing, and he leaned forward, looking into the vessel's wake.

Again, she used the aid of the nearby fixtures to stand.

"Asa?" She spoke and he startled, not realising her presence.

Irritated by the intrusion, he lashed out. "I'm fine. Leave me."

She shook her head. "You're not. The journey's increased length troubles you. Confide in me."

A cynical laugh escaped him. "I'm a man—a strong one. There's no place for weakness. Yet, I'm so drained and know I can no longer continue. This adventure has beaten me."

"You're here, surviving. It hasn't beaten you. You'll return to Aldersward when the prince has finished his tasks."

He shook his head. "You can't know for certain. We were to travel for twenty days, but we're nearly four times the length now. His current plan means another sixty at least, barring no other obstacles or diversions. Every day we remain is another where one or all could die. I'd rather be dead now than live in this precarious limbo."

"Don't speak like that. You must teach me how to live among your people." She waved her hand. "One day, you'll recall this time with fondness as you tell your children of your grand adventure."

Neither realised a third had joined them.

"Sahana, withdraw, please." Aedyn commanded in a quiet, hard voice.

He helped her onto the ladder's rungs. When he was certain she had gone, he walked to his friend's side, rested his buttocks against the railing, and faced Asa.

"If I hadn't overheard, would you have told me?" He asked.

"No." Asa shrugged, still watching the water. No reason existed to resist the prince's ability.

"Tell me how this ends. Do you jump overboard when no one watches?"

"I'm considering it."

"My father has ordered the additional crafts to return home and he will not dispatch more." He struggled to speak the words aloud. Once he did, there would be no taking them back. "He believes the Baits are better handled later. He wants us to return home now."

Surprise claimed Asa's expression. "Do the others know?"

"Not yet." His hand settled on the other's shoulder and he shook his head. "I did a stupid thing in Baitsloam." He turned to study the sea. "I had relations with the woman who treated me, and there were emotions. I've examined my motives for returning to Baitsloam immediately." He hesitated, took a long, deep breath, and inspected the black ribbon knotted around his wrist. "It's not to save the Baits—only her. I vowed to return, but I struggle now, seeing the weight of my decisions on everyone." He rolled his sleeve down, covering the reminder. "According to my father, my mother is ready to die."

It was time for complete honesty as he listed his decisions' consequences.

His tone thickened with guilt. "Achelle has not mentioned her toll, but I see the effects in her appearance. Even knowing this, I urged her to facilitate a meeting between my father and me. I had no qualms about manipulating her. Nor did I consider the pain she would have to endure, or the families of those who will never return. What have I done to them? Now this with you and chances are others feel similar, like Auren." He turned to face him. "If nothing else, the Slaysfold and Baitsloam rulers have demonstrated what can occur when one places his desires above his people. I will not become them. It's time to go home." He placed his arm along his friend's shoulder and feigned a smile. "Come, I'll tell the others."

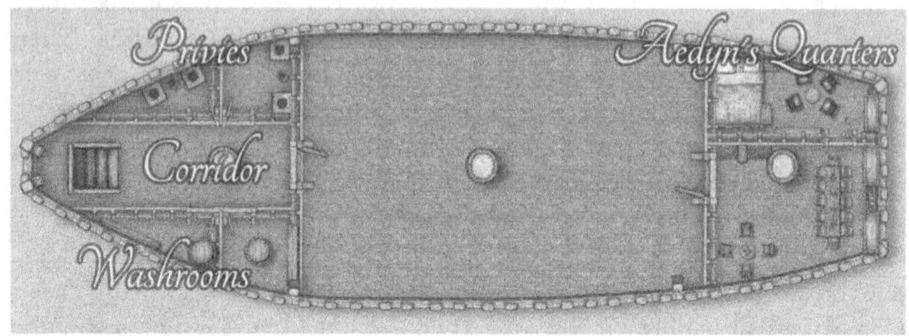

Day 169
Prince Aedyn's Quarters
Anya's Endeavour
Slaysfold's Southeast Sea

The sky darkened as Aedyn tossed on his bed. His morals warred against his emotions. Knowing what was right was far simpler than carrying it out—especially when his heart compelled him to disregard his integrity.

He brought his wrist to his nose, inhaling her scent, but it had faded. He wondered if her memory and his feelings would as well. Each time he dreamed of her, they shifted to nightmares. Her radiant face would stain with bruises, her belly would round with the king's child, and her alluring voice sounded with pleas for help.

Since the disagreement with his father, he scarcely slept.

How would Belinda change in a year or two?

He flipped onto his stomach. He pictured the east bailey and imagined training there as his wife, Ammaris, observed from the side.

Would Belinda understand?

He twisted onto his back. How had the thought snuck in? Ammaris would show her first pregnancy in winter's midst.

Would Belinda ever forgive him?

He looked to the small window, praying for Jezabet to absolve him of his guilt and feelings. When no answer came, he counted the stars and drifted to sleep.

"Aedyn?" Achelle appeared.

Aedyn relaxed in a high-backed armchair beside a hearth while he studied a pale red-haired woman sewing. He seemed unaware his sister had arrived.

"Aedyn?"

Absently, he reached for his sibling. "I'm here."

"Who's this?"

"One of the women who cared for me," he closed his eyes, willing Belinda to vanish and, when he opened them, the bench was vacant, and profound emptiness echoed through him. "Come sit. I wish to share news."

As she sat on the abandoned bench, he spoke. "Tell Father we will not travel to Slaysfold. We're coming straight home." His tone was bleak.

She understood his inability to be happy. He would return without a cure. But she was pleased he would no longer be in danger and smiled. "It will ease his worry."

He shrugged. "There's no need for you to visit so often. Let's return to our previous schedule."

"All right," she disappeared. Aware, he required time to come to terms with his failure and their mother's death.

Day 170
Prince Aedyn's Quarters
Anya's Endeavour
Slaysfold's Southeast Sea

Allowing a cool breeze to flow through the room, the exterior door stood wide. The women had complained of the heat, but now the men's teeth nearly chattered.

"Ladies, at this temperature, our manly bits will likely shrivel and fall off." Auren crossed to close the door.

"I assure you bits still work at this temperature. I recall you with a few women in Slaysfold. Did your parts drop off?" Sahana smiled, and the group laughed.

Aedyn interjected. "Auren, I thought you had grown up—matured while I was gone. I guess I was wrong."

"The essential part grew longer," Auren smirked, showing his teeth.

"I have something to show ye." Bennet unrolled a scroll and placed it between the four men. "It cannot be definite, but from where Slaysfold and Baitsloam were, I deduced with some certainty where Reinshaven could be." He pointed his finger east. "It's here—give or take a few days."

Auren surveyed the sketch while Aedyn watched Asa remove himself and join the women at the smaller table.

"It's straight south of Aldersward," Auren said in wonderment. "We'll pass by in ten days or so."

Asa ignored the men as he involved himself in the women's conversation.

Aedyn's brows furrowed with frustration—how could he let this opportunity go?

"How far from our course?" he asked.

"Perhaps three or four days," Bennet drank from his mug.

"Asa?" he demanded. "Your thoughts?"

"It's not my choice."

Auren's voice was angry. "We could save Queen Anya. How can this be a discussion?"

Asa shrugged. "If we stop, then we'll have to deliver a healer to Slaysfold, as we've promised.

Aedyn joined, sitting next to Asa. "I have no intention of prolonging our journey. I promised the men aboard we would go home and we will. But this may save our people—our queen, my mother. What are a few days? We would take the healer destined for Slaysfold to Aldersward and send her on another craft."

Asa attempted to hide his distraught tone, but failed. "It sounds as though you've already decided and there's no choice but to make myself right with it."

Sahana leaned forward, squeezing his hand. "While they fetch a healer, you can keep me company."

"Asa, instruct Captain Amos of our decision." Aedyn walked him to the door, then turned back. "I swear, no further changes. The fear he once confided has become so much greater. Until we reach Reinshaven, he will be observed at all times. Perhaps someone there can help him." He sat in his chair as the other returned.

For the first time, Auren's eyes noted Asa's worried expression. He had not realised the change and berated himself for not discovering it sooner. He vowed to alleviate his friend's discomfort.

Day 172
Queen Belinda's Chambers
Castle's Second Floor
Baitsloam City

The midday sun played off the whitewashed grey walls lined with portraits of previous queens, though none of King Baeddan's former wives were displayed. Someone had well-furnished the chambers with a wooden table and chairs, two backed benches covered in cloth and a wooden tea table. Worn bald and torn from use, animal fur layered the floor.

Belinda's thoughts centred on Aedyn.

Had he overheard her declaration? Did he feel the same? Had he escaped? Would he return for her?

She had not ventured from her chambers or seen the king since their marriage. In isolation, she existed without Beatrice or Bret, who should have arrived before now. The couple's absence and her questions fed her anxiety.

Outside, in the corridor, raised tones argued. She would have ignored them, but she recognised one voice. Twinges of delight travelled through her as she jerked open the door.

Instantly, quiet fell over those in the hallway. Her guards repositioned themselves and genuflected. Bret's hand rested on Beatrice's shoulder, drawing her back from the man she stood toe to toe with, both enraged.

Belinda applied her most authoritative tone. "Those are my staff. Why are ye blocking them?"

Bret's arm fell, and the old woman relaxed her stance with a smug smile as the man spun.

He genuflected. "Yer Majesty, Lady Bethnee ordered ye undisturbed."

The name sounded familiar, but she could not place it. "I demanded nay such thing. Allow them through and return to yer duties." She waited until he stepped aside and the pair followed her inside.

Bret locked the door as the two women hugged, greeting one another.

Belinda studied him. "What happened to him?"

"Escaped without issue. Nay one knows the Alders returned to our coast."

She shed the heavy strain of uncertainty. "Then what kept ye?"

Beatrice took her hand, pulling her to sit. "We arrived a few days ago. Ye must do something about Lady Bethnee. In yer sequestered state, she has inserted herself into yer role as queen. I finally persuaded one of the kitchen staff to allow us entry. And only because Bethnee and the king have departed were we able to reach ye."

"Departed?"

"They visit Wimlock."

"All is well for a time, then." She surveyed Bret, standing against a wall nearby. "Did Aedyn have a message for me?"

"Nay," his expression feigned indifference, but his wife's turned guilty, and until she could cover her emotions, he meant to keep Belinda's attention. "We didn't raise ye to cower and evade. Ye're queen. Ye must accept it, determine what yer future holds, and act accordingly. For months, ye knew this was yer fate and ye've wallowed long enough. The king will return in a few days."

His stern reprimand, though harsh, was needed. The old woman squeezed her hand to soften the blow.

His additional remarks didn't register. Belinda's mind numbed. *He left nay message? I meant nothing and he will not save me.* Hurt, her eyes welled and unaware, she retreated to her bedchamber, preferring the solitude.

Moving to her husband, Beatrice kept her voice low. "I'm concerned. Why must ye keep his pledge from her?"

He drew her to his side. "We're protecting her should he break his promise."

"But ye've taken the hope she had."

He rested his chin on her hair. "It's better this way. If we tell her and it doesn't eventuate, it will hurt her again. Ye must encourage her. She cannot remain in her rooms and avoid her husband. She must willingly participate in her marriage, or Baeddan will force her. If, with Jezabet's aid, she's pregnant now, then she must attend her marriage bed or risk discovery."

"I'll speak to her." She hugged him tight, troubled by what awaited Belinda.

Day 173
King Adahy's Study
Castle's Ground Level
Near Aldersward City

The windows were closed in an attempt to obscure the lingering stench of the sewage pond. Dishes burned, camouflaging it, but a hint remained. It was dark, humid, and eerily quiet. Only the snapping of dry timber in the fireplace sounded as the king read through the documents on his desk, preparing for tomorrow's disputes—another hunting claim, another proposed land joining, another exploration through the mountains behind Aldersward Castle.

Boring, but he realised it resulted from his ancestors' rule. Their punishments kept more serious and demented matters at bay. One did not dare when the consequence was maiming or death.

The page forced the heavy door wide, drawing his attention. "King Adahy, Herbalist Alvira of Edson and Physician Axton wish an audience."

"Set a pitcher and mugs, then show them in." He tidied the papers and cleared the surface, placing the stack behind him on the shelving.

He rose as the pair entered. His glance bounced from Axton to the old and hunched woman beside him. Her white and grey hair curled of its own will. When last had she washed or brushed it, he wondered.

Her dull blue eyes met his as she bent slightly, then hobbled closer.

"Sire," her raspy voice matched her age spots and uncountable wrinkles.

As Axton took position behind him, the king gestured for her to sit.

The physician cleared his throat. "Your Majesty, we've discussed Achelle's condition, and under certain terms, Herbalist Alvira has agreed to manage her."

"Which are?" The king relaxed, crossing his arms.

She answered. "King Adahy, there can be no interference from you or your physician. In her care, I make decisions alone. Your daughter will be angry, often seeming in pain, and will lash out—especially at those who love her most. You'll want to intervene and ease her discomfort. But know, if you do, this won't serve and you could lose her forever to the promises of the tonics and potions. It's imperative I know whether this will be an issue."

The king regarded Axton, and seeing him nod, he considered the woman. "You'll have my complete support and cooperation."

"I prefer two adjoined chambers. Before we relocate her, I will inspect them. No belongings will accompany her and no one will see her unless I allow it."

"While Prince Aedyn remains away, I require her to communicate with him."

"My responsibility is your daughter and her dependency. Until I determine how her ability and dependency function together, I cannot venture to say how often she may accomplish your tasks."

"Fine. My secretary will assign you rooms and staff."

Without waiting for his dismissal, the woman rose, turned her back, and hobbled out.

Day 174
Prince Aedyn's Quarters
Anya's Endeavour
Slaysfold's East Sea

Pushing his empty plate aside, Aedyn poured more ale. He turned, took the voyage's journal, quill, and ink from the cabinet, and wrote.

In Baitsloam, I hadn't noticed how much cooler it was, but it's much cooler now than Aldersward would be at the height of summer. I wear my wool coat almost continuously.

Asa, Auren, and I have spent much time together. It seems the closer to home, the better everyone's spirits.

There's a problem with my sudden decision to head for home. Our rations are depleting quickly. Some have attached nets and ropes to boat paddles and strive to catch fish. We don't know how long it'll take to secure enough fish for a meal. I've asked the cook to keep all wasted or rotten food so Apex can turn it into pots of pork and beans. Starting tomorrow evening, we'll substitute every second meal.

Sahana confided she may prefer to leave the castle to pursue her own business in a smaller village. I keep this to myself. On our vessel, she's accepted, but I'm concerned about how she may be received by my countrymen.

Bennet has initiated a class every afternoon, requiring his children to join his wife and Sahana. I believe they will adapt well.

Achelle visited last night. She seemed upset and withdrawn. I've chosen to keep our detour from those back home. There's no reason to raise hope or for her to feel my father's anger. With no explanation, she mentioned she would visit me in six days instead of three. It's most likely because my father no longer needs to know our every movement since we're obeying his command.

Day 175
Queen Belinda's Chambers
Castle's Second Floor
Baitsloam City

In the previous days, Belinda ventured from her chambers, explored her new home, and enjoyed organising the staff. It gave her courage and time to examine her new life, compiling a list of tasks to accomplish. First, she would remove Lady Bethnee from her station of power, and second, improve her favour with her husband. If she was not pregnant, then she determined she must gain her husband's affections, with the hope he would spare her.

"Belinda?"

She shook her head, ridding her thoughts. "I apologise. My mind was elsewhere. What did ye ask?"

Beatrice fastened the young woman's hair in place. "It wasn't important. What's troubling ye?"

She sighed, turning to her. "I was thinking of him. Why did he leave without a message for me? Was I nothing—just one in a string of many?"

The old woman clicked her tongue. "Don't play the martyr now. Ye used him for yer own purposes as well."

She draped her cloak over her shoulders, securing it. "But I felt for him. I don't think I could've gone through with it otherwise. He left without a word. I maintain my hope and pray he'll return to rescue me as he offered to do for Brayleigh."

"And perhaps he will. If hope eases yer pain, then hold onto it. I'm sure he felt something for ye. He offered to take us with him." The pair walked into the hallway. "What became of Brayleigh?"

"He released her, and she's home."

Commotion echoed from the courtyard below, and Belinda peered outside.

The royal entourage entered and dismounted as Baeddan handed Bethnee from the carriage, familiarity apparent. She watched the woman push her breasts upwards as she pulled her corset down, straining to brush the king's chest while she tilted her face to receive his kiss.

Belinda almost laughed at the irony. The woman wanted him, yet he'd chosen her.

Day 176
Herbalist's Chambers
Castle's Second Level
Near Aldersward City

Achelle followed Herbalist Alvira across the skyway, which linked the east and west hallways. As she clung to the stone railing, slowly walking along it, the old woman offered no kindness or help. The herbalist had provided a small amount of tonic this morning, making her limbs rubbery.

They reached the long east hall where Aedyn's chambers were, but turned right.

"Inside," Alvira pointed.

The dark room was void of furnishings. The bedchamber's doorway cast a stream of light into the through-room. Achelle's clouded, warm mind could not shake the drab, cold of her surroundings, and she walked into the bedchamber. A small bed, table, chair, and chamber pot were the only things present. The windows held no coverings, and the doorframe had no door. It was barren and dismal.

When she heard the chamber's exterior door close, and a hammer pound, she turned as the elderly woman came inside.

"It's being nailed shut. Unless I provide it, you'll communicate with no one or be given anything. This includes possessions or food."

Unable to care, Achelle sat on the bed's edge.

"Any messages you have for your father or he for you will be delivered through me. I'll continue to supply you with small doses of tonic. In turn, you'll only use your ability when I allow." Alvira understood the euphoric state the young woman felt. Often, she witnessed it in her patients while she allowed them to continue their dependency supervised.

The list of rules continued. "Consider this room a gift. If you abuse the privileges I afford you, then they will be revoked. Once your abilities are no longer required, I'll withdraw the support of the tonics." She studied the wispy woman, who said nothing in return. "I assure you there are worse things than this room. Test me, and you'll discover them."

Day 177
Prince Aedyn's Quarters
Anya's Endeavour
Aldersward's South Sea

When one by one the others excused themselves in the night's late hour, Bennet remained at the smaller table. He thumbed through the journal, then dipped the quill and wrote.

Severe winds and heavy rain have done two things.

They have diminished the men's fishing efforts. What they trapped, seaweed and a few fish, we added to the pile of decaying rations Apex turns edible. Prince Aedyn ordered a change in meal schedule. We eat Apex's pork and beans at midday and other rations in the evening. The cook divvies portions with the help of Brielle and Byunca. We try not to grumble, but we're all hungry. Sweet tea and drinkable water have run out and so we take from the sea and Ameer turns it to ale, the least potent of the available alternatives.

The wind has sped us closer to where we assume Reinshaven must lie. Arturo believes we've sailed farther than six days' distance in merely four. This lightens our spirits, especially Asa's. We've passed the point where we would head north to Aldersward.

Prince Aedyn's time in Baitsloam matured and readied him for his duty as future ruler. He spends much time among us, yet he's disengaged and his mind is often elsewhere. I see his strained expression and forced smile. It's as if he battles a war within himself and it's yet to be determined which part will prevail.

My wife and I decided we'll take a cottage on the castle grounds and our children will remain with us. This pleases me, we'll become better acquainted. Perhaps one day, after Brielle and I pass, they'll return to Baitsloam.

Sahana has claimed a place in my heart, like a daughter, and Brielle has permitted me to ask her to live with us. I'll observe how matters develop between now and Aldersward before I make a final decision.

I'm excited for Reinshaven and the promise of a healer for my friend's wife. When we present a healer, it will elate King Adahy and his daughters—and restore the castle's light-hearted atmosphere. Since Prince Aedyn's birth, this may be the most joyous and celebrated event.

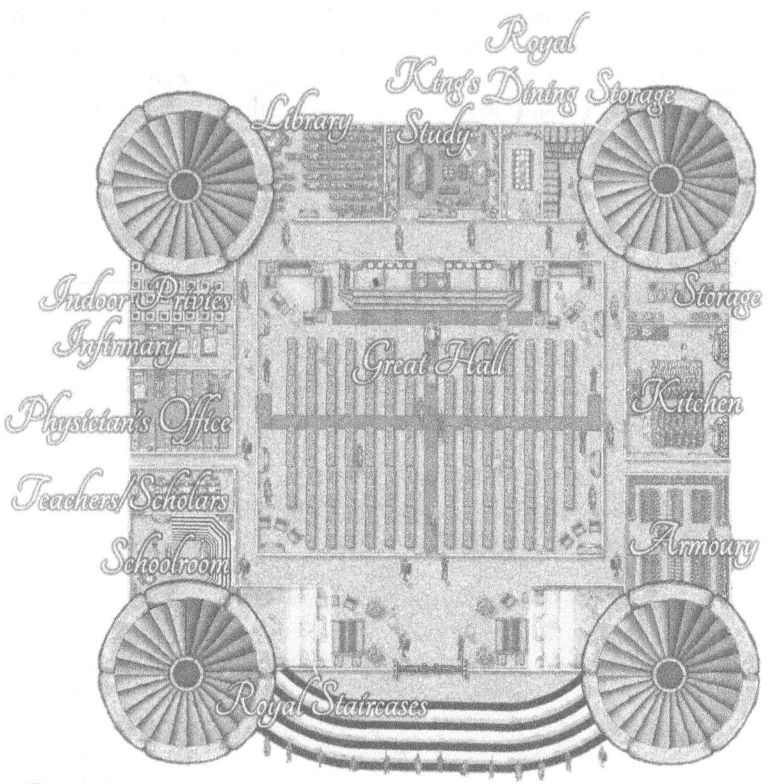

Day 182
Schoolroom
Castle's Ground Level
Near Aldersward City

The students' loyalty was no longer divided between the royal sisters. Surrounded by those who craved a place within her social circle, Annora basked in the attention. They sought to move closer, speak louder, and be more interesting than each other.

When the scholar thumped his walking stick to draw the students' attention, they hushed and sat straighter. "Addison, please come forward and give your report."

The shy girl rose from the room's rear and descended the risers. A hand snaked out, tripping her, and she tumbled down, landing on the floor with her dress bunched around her waist. As the teacher helped her up, the children laughed.

Last year, the nine-year-old lost her hair's length when it caught in the wheel of her father's wagon. It nearly reached her ears now, in an unruly mess of curls, and still the students were cruel. He worried her withdrawn silence continued to alienate her from her peers.

She fidgeted at the podium, and her voice shook. "The Reins and Reinshaven."

"Louder," a voice called, and the others snickered. The walking stick thumped, silencing them.

She cleared her throat and fixed her gaze on the pages. "In 2631 F.Y., it was the most southern kingdom and shared its borders with Clinesfurrow along the Rayanne Forest and its west border with Aldersward and Slaysfold. It was three times smaller than Aldersward but boasted fertile fields, rolling hills, and small canyons. The Reins named themselves using the letter *r*."

Someone conjured a swarm of flies and they buzzed around her as she continued, pretending not to notice.

"The Reinshaven women held healing powers. Its cost was a drain on another, not of their choosing. One could heal in Fernstake, and if the healer took too much energy, another could die, clear across our world in Vaguestimber. To the healers themselves, it caused a permanent diminishing of their hair's pigment. Many of their marriages were arranged outside of their kingdom. Their healing did not function in Tannorsbrace. Their men were noughties. They welcomed Aldersward's reign and were our first allies. In exchange for abilities, they adopted every societal change and governance our kingdom implemented.

"In 2631 F.Y., their rulers were King Ryder and Queen Tabitha. They sent Emissary Ryme to receive King Asmaud's gift at Amelia's birthday celebration. The end."

Day 184
Anchor Deck
Anya's Endeavour
Reinshaven's West Sea

Their backs welcomed the warm afternoon sun as they stood on the anchor deck, regarding the fielded land. They skirted the coast northward, searching for a settlement. The deep water and the absence of docks or fishing boats encouraged them to travel closer than they had in the past.

Bennet wrapped his arm around his wife's waist and pointed. "There. See the treetops? The enormous height leads me to believe it was once part of Rayanne Forest, which means nestled at its base should be Agerton."

Auren turned to Prince Aedyn. "What's our strategy?"

He noted Asa, who wrung his hands together. "We wait. Let's see how the Reins react. Once we're in proximity, drop the anchor. Lady Sahana, I would like a word, please." He took her agreement for granted, held her elbow, and helped her navigate the stairs.

The prince left her to seat herself as he stepped around the table, taking the high-backed middle chair, then filled two mugs.

"I wish Asa to escort me to shore, but I worry he's readied many excuses. I may require your support."

Though scared, her loyalty to her liberator was stronger. "How?"

"I've given this much consideration. If you agree to act as Emissary Sahana of Slaysfold, then the people would accept you; an advisor, of sorts. Should the circumstances allow us ashore, this is what I would ask. I'm wondering if a healer may restore him to his former self."

Her stomach rolled with unease. "I'll do whatever you ask. But you worry too much about others."

"I'm responsible for his pain. The least I should manage is support to fix it." He finished as Auren and Bennet entered and seated themselves. "What knowledge do we lack about Reinshaven?"

Bennet lifted a mug. "Before the divide, Reinshaven was yer ally and adopted whatever decisions Aldersward made. I'd like to suggest they would accept Aldersward again, but I took it for granted in Baitsloam and it cost us."

"Sahana's agreed to be my emissary, and I assume you'll continue for Baitsloam. Perhaps you should explain what expectations there will be."

Like a proud father, he smiled at her. "I'm delighted. Let's move to the other table."

Before Bennet could stand, the boat rocked as the anchor dropped. The occupants clutched the stationary objects, waiting for the heavy weight to grab bottom. When it did not, Auren and Aedyn bolted outside and raced to Asa's position.

"What's happened?" The prince demanded as he reached the top.

Asa held firm against the railing, looking down into the dark water, then back to the shore as the vessel drew closer. Roughly sixty feet separated them.

"I don't know." Asa lifted the cable easily. "The weight remains attached."

Aedyn yelled below as he seized the railing. "Alberto, change the wind's direction! Everyone brace."

The man lifted his arms and pulled them back. The vessel slowed its forward movement and the anchor finally caught, heaving bodies forward.

Auren regained his composure first. "Look at all the people."

"We're too close. Hoist the anchor and take us farther out." Fear gripped Aedyn, remembering their reception in Baitsloam.

Asa ran his hand over his face. "I can't—it's heavy and I've spent too much energy. Give me an hour and then, maybe."

He scanned the thickening shoreline. "Auren, quietly, have everyone shelter inside. I'll not endanger their lives in the meantime." He turned his gaze on the other man. "My order includes you."

"No." He stood shoulder to shoulder with him. "Should you die, your final vision will see me defending you."

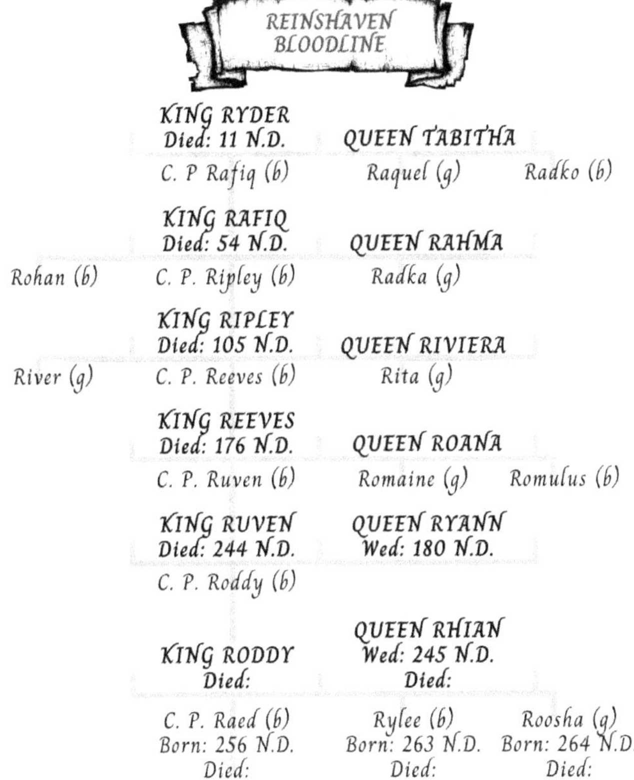

Above shows the Rein kings' bloodline. C. P. means Crowned Prince, future king. (b)/(g) indicates gender at birth.

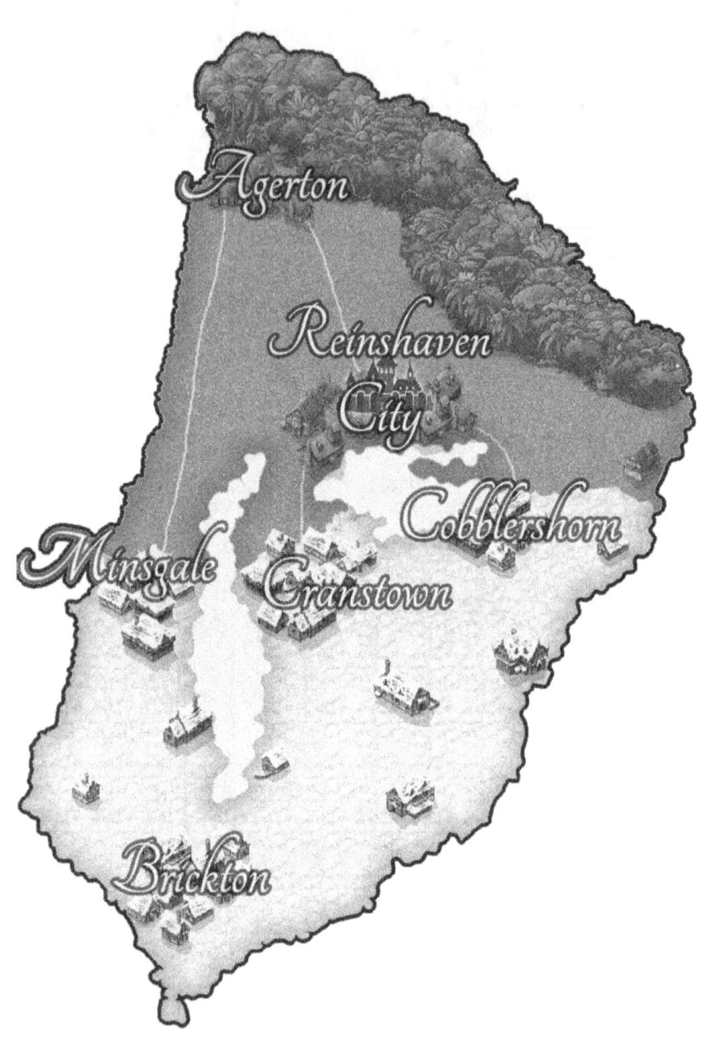

Reinshaven (285 N.D.)

Most notable features above include:
Agerton (northwest)
Rayanne Forest (north)
Character index page 405.

Day 184
Anchor Deck
Anya's Endeavour
Agerton Village, Reinshaven

In less than an hour, a crowd, like swarming locusts, blanketed the shoreline, numbering in the thousands. The innocent children sang as they darted through the people, chasing one another, full of glee. The merry adults greeted each other with friendship and joy while others produced instruments to entertain them. As if this were a celebration or festival, families carried food baskets and settled on blankets.

Asa leaned closer, so Aedyn heard. "What do you think?"

"I don't know. There are so many children."

The music stopped, voices hushed, and the crowd divided. The Reins turned from the water and genuflected as seven strolled through the narrow aisle. In the lead were two men dressed similarly, no clothes, markings, or jewellery differentiated them. Two women with black and white streaked hair walked next, followed by three who were the same age or a few years older than the Alder prince.

The first pair halted, and one cupped his mouth. "I rule Reinshaven, but Aldersward rules Speranza. Countrymen, if you haven't yet pledged your allegiance, then join me now."

The thousands yielded, like rolling waves. Never witnessing it from this height, it struck Asa with awe.

The man bellowed, "Praise Jezabet."

The crowd reiterated the sentiment.

Again, Asa leaned. "Can you use your ability from here? Would you know if he were lying?"

He shook his head. "No. We'll have to send a boat to them." The man turned, but the prince gripped his shoulder. "Let's be strategic. I'll choose the men. Inform our men they may emerge. Secure the ladder and lower a few boats."

The prince waved at the shore, and a thundering cheer erupted.

Aedyn thumbed through the journal, to the manifest, then ordered Bennet and Auren. "Have Aron lead Aldo, Austin, Alvin, Archer, and Ace to shore. Unless certain there are no ill intentions, instruct them not to land. Once Aron's confident, he can communicate our food shortage, and leave the empty boats behind. Let's see how they respond. Bennet, instruct Amari, Anthony, Ahmad, and Apollo to entertain the crowd with their abilities."

Both left, and Sahana remained at the smaller table, seemingly paralysed.

His brow lifted. "Will you be all right going ashore?"

Her stomach rolled. "I will. I'll find Asa and discuss this with him now." She draped a blanket over her head, guarding her face against onlookers.

She found him in the deserted sleeping quarters, lying in his bunk. When she reached his side, his eyes were closed. She pushed the curtain aside on her bunk and sat, then studied the worried lines on his face.

"Quit, you aren't sleeping. You snore. I seek your counsel."

"Counsel?" His head turned, opening one eye. "What for?"

His unruly hair misbehaved against the pillow, and she smiled. "Aedyn has asked me to go ashore."

The possibility excited his tone as he rolled to sit. "That's wonderful. They could heal you—make you beautiful and restore what you once were."

Pain jarred her heart and expression, but she covered it by hobbling towards the door. "Never mind, I don't need your counsel."

"What do you mean, *never mind*?" Asa straightened, placing his hands on his hips as he watched her leave.

"I'll find Bennet. This discussion is better had with him." She hid the anguish caused by his words. She lifted her chin higher as she tossed aside the blanket she had used to hide.

He combed his hair down. "I don't understand. Don't you wish to be beautiful again?"

"My idea of beauty differs from yours." She slammed the door with renewed self-worth and anger as she crossed the main deck, not caring who saw her.

When she entered, Aedyn noted her anger. It was an emotion he had not experienced from her. Her complexion was crimson, her eye scowled, her forehead frowned, and her mouth pursed in a straight line as she stood before him. He wondered what Asa had said or done and his gaze swept her clothing, searching for the man's blood.

She watched his inspection. Her anger melted, and she smiled. "I didn't kill him. Though, I could have."

"I applaud your self-control." He chuckled. "Is he coming ashore?"

"He doesn't realise it yet, but he will." She turned, selecting a smaller chair.

"If the Reins come, you may use my bedchamber." He offered.

"Thank you, but I won't hide."

Bennet appeared. "They've accepted the boats Aron left behind."

Aedyn tidied the table. "Find Auren. He needs to arrange my guard. Then tell Asa and your wife I require their presence."

Day 184
Prince Aedyn's Quarters
Anya's Endeavour
Agerton Village, Reinshaven

As the boats carrying the Reins tied against the craft, Asa scowled as he entered. His eyes encountered Sahana next to Brielle at the smaller table, but she ignored him. He huffed, not understanding her issue. Did she not prefer her suffering removed? It bothered him.

Aedyn motioned to his side. "Here."

Two guards were posted behind the prince and Auren seated on his right. Asa took the chair between Aedyn and Bennet, then poured a drink as the outer door opened.

Anik, Aedyn's page, announced. "Emissary Aron, King Roddy, and Queen Rhian of Reinshaven and their children, Prince Raed, Prince Rylee, and Princess Roosha." He stepped aside as the group entered.

No Rein guards followed. Everyone rose, except Sahana. Aedyn was the only one who did not genuflect—even Sahana attempted from her position. As the Alders straightened, the Reins yielded and remained so.

Bennet tapped Aedyn's back.

"Rise," the prince waved his hand. "King Roddy, your household may join us here or your women may join ours."

The king gestured his daughter and queen aside as he and his sons sat across from the men.

"Your Majesty, your survival was one of the many things we prayed to Jezabet for."

Bennet corrected. "It's Prince Aedyn."

"Your Highness, of course. This is my eldest son, Crowned Prince Raed."

Nearing thirty, the man dipped his head. His long hair fell across his cheek, but he kept his eyes on the Alder prince as he swept it back. "A pleasure for us all."

King Roddy placed his hand on the other's shoulder. "And this is my youngest son, Prince Rylee."

Rylee produced his hand and extended it. "I'm called the *spare heir*."

Aedyn shook his hand, noting his similar age.

Loudly, Auren chuckled. "I like it. We don't have a *spare*. We're stuck with this one."

Bennet craned his neck, silencing him. "Let me introduce those present. I'm Emissary Bennet of Baitsloam. At the smaller table—my wife Brielle and Emissary Sahana of Slaysfold," both women smiled, then whispered to the other two as he continued, "On Prince Aedyn's right, his Lead and Advisor, Auren of Maidstone and to his left, his Guard and Advisor, Asa of Lessard. Please forgive Emissary Sahana for not rising earlier and Lead Auren for making jokes at such serious times."

The king waved the explanation away. "We've brought food. There wasn't time to prepare an elaborate feast, but once word spread, many contributed, so you and your men are fed this evening."

"Let's speak plainly. There are too many titles present to trip over. We appreciate your generosity. Under the circumstances, we were unsure how you would receive us." Aedyn concentrated on the man and asked. "Do you and your people mean us harm?"

"No. Our entire kingdom will rejoice at your returned rule." The king answered.

He nodded, signalling the man's truth. "Shall we share our meal?"

"We cannot stay. We must return before dusk." The king's tone was regretful. "We wanted to assure you of our renewed loyalty and invite you to shore an hour after dawn tomorrow. I'll have a hearty meal arranged." The king rose, as did everyone present.

"Then we bid you good night until the morning." Aedyn and his men accompanied the Reins out and the royals observed in amazement the garden, levitated objects, and the man who played music using only his mouth while they walked to the ladder.

Once the small boat departed, Aedyn turned to Auren. "Your men with Augustus's will have first watch tonight."

Asa's eyes widened with apprehension. "You believe he lied?"

He shook his head. "No, he spoke true, but vigilance won't hurt."

The Alders ate, then viewed the festivities on the coast. As the sun descended on their backs, many sought extra clothing to keep the chilly night at bay. Lounged on the anchor deck, Auren and Augustus heard a thunderous trumpet sound from the woods and the Reins scattered in chaos, as if their lives depended on their speed.

Immediately, those aboard came to attention and drew their weapons, realising something was horribly wrong as their screams grew louder. The Reins rushed for any structure as Aedyn emerged from his quarters.

"What's happened?" He yelled as he climbed the stairs.

"I don't know. Something spooked them." Auren held his bow.

Pushing through those present, Azariah said, "The woods! There's something in the woods close to the shoreline. It's large and travelling fast towards them. It'll break through in a few moments."

After drawing an arrow from his back, Auren steadied himself as the men backed away. His mind quieted, and he fixated on the arrow's tip. He inhaled deeply, then held his breath. When the nearest trees swayed, he let go and as it whooshed across the distance, the beast burst through. He adjusted the trajectory slightly down and right. They had no time to inspect the animal before it collapsed.

None of the sheltered Reins witnessed his ability and as the sun disappeared, the village appeared abandoned except for the soft glows from the slatted, boarded windows.

Day 185
Queen Belinda's Chambers
Castle's Second Floor
Baitsloam City

The morning light added a refreshing reprieve to the rooms—a stark contrast to the ugly place which had known the death of the three previous queens.

Beatrice emerged from Belinda's bedchamber and spied her resting in the window seat, staring longingly out the window, oblivious to the other's presence.

After she crossed, the older woman cleared her throat and settled her palm on the woman's knee. "It's time."

Without understanding, she shook her head. "What time?"

"Ye've missed yer bleeds. Ye must seduce yer husband."

An icy shiver rushed along Belinda's spine, raising bumps on her skin. Her chin quivered. "He isn't coming?"

Offering sympathy, Beatrice squeezed her hand. "Nay and ye must form strategies to survive. Bret will make the arrangements with Baeddan's secretary, and I'll numb yer body."

Belinda nodded as her heart shattered over the finality of her loss.

Beatrice reached the hall door. "Tonight, then."

Day 185
Sleeping Quarters
Anya's Endeavour
Agerton Village, Reinshaven

Listening for those who might still sleep, Sahana rolled over. One of three men was with her, as per Aedyn's original request. She let out a long exhale, attempting to release her anxiety. Today she would act as Emissary for Slaysfold.

"Will you never speak to me again?" Asa's voice reached her through the curtain.

"I'm sleeping." She smirked and closed her eye, wishing it were true.

His voice sounded apologetic. "I misspoke yesterday. *Beautiful* was not the word I meant to use."

Her hand snaked out, dragging the curtain back so she could watch him. "What word then?"

He combed his hands through his hair. "I meant, wouldn't you like to dance like Byunca, step without pain, and see from both eyes?"

"I don't know." The thought had not occurred to her. Would she want to be who she was before? Naïve and weak of mind?

Asa raised his voice in anger. "How can this be something you ponder? They could restore your body."

"I don't know. But the decision is mine."

"Well, make it—unless you're scared?"

His words flared her irritation. She clambered to a seated position, swinging her feet off the bed. The nightgown riding above her dangling bare legs, went unnoticed, by her.

"Me? Scared? You ignorant fopdoodle, I've known the most depraved times in one's life and survived. Scared, really?"

Once again, he didn't understand and would have questioned it, but his eyes caught sight of her knees. He blushed and averted his gaze.

Witnessing his look, she growled. "You spunky cock!"

She shifted her legs back into her bunk, closed the curtain, and reached for her clothing.

Her crude tongue shocked him, but he was too indignant to remain silent. "You expose your flesh and I'm a–" he couldn't, "for noticing?" He straightened and strode for the door at the other end of the room. "If you're scared, I'm offering to escort you."

"Yes, you are. And thank you." She smiled as she tugged her dress over her head.

Day 185
Main Deck
Anya's Endeavour
Agerton Village, Reinshaven

When the boats were lowered and tied to the vessel, dawn was breaking. As they readied, loud explosions sounded in the water, and the men hurried to the seaside. A pod of humpback whales, a few miles away, threw themselves into the air and plunged back down, shooting spray upwards, high above them.

Recognising the animals, the men laughed and slapped each other's backs playfully, the momentary fear lost. The first boat commanded by Auren, excited to examine his kill from the night before, departed.

They waited for the shallowing shore, but it never came. Only a steep, jagged edge of land met the bottomless sea. Two men jumped onto the land and dragged the boat's nose onto shore, steadying it so the others could exit.

Auren strode towards the forest's edge. He expected an elephant or a rhinoceros, not the mishmash monster before him. When he stared at a lion's mouth with three rows of razor-sharp teeth and a head three times larger than any lion he had ever seen, his jaw dropped.

"Hey, what is it?" An Alder ran up to join him. "What–"

Auren's nerve endings tingled, and his skin rose. "Have you ever seen anything like it?"

The man shook his head. "A winged lion with a claw at every tip? What is this? Are we certain it's dead?"

His gaze travelled over the beast's back of hard scales, then followed their length to a thick-shelled tail, like a scorpion. "It's dead. Azariah said it lost heat shortly after I shot it. Call to the vessel and ask Bennet to come. I want to know what it is."

Mesmerised, Auren studied the frightening creature, and it seemed only a short time lapsed before Bennet spoke, coming to his side. "Ye requested me?"

He turned, eyeing the old man. "What is it?"

Bennet's eyes lit with excitement as he crouched. "My word. Incredible, it's a manticore."

Auren ran a frustrated hand over his head's stubble. "Let's suppose I don't know what a manticore is. What is it?"

"It's a beast which tormented Clinesfurrow, Davensberth, and Fernstake—the entire east coast. When the divide happened, it must have trapped one or more on the southeast side of Rayanne's Forest."

"Will there be more?"

"Likely. I've never seen one. But, in the king's library, I've read they carry both sex organs. It's conceivable they fertilise their own eggs. It's fascinating." He rubbed his chin.

"I know you meant *terrifying*."

Engrossed in the monster's corpse, they had not noticed when Prince Rylee approached. His words startled Auren.

"Who killed it?" The prince's long, dark, wavy mane spilt over his shoulder.

Auren recognised him, much like his older brother, only not as broad or muscular with brown eyes instead of green. He bowed. "Was I not meant to?"

"Many have tried but have never succeeded. We try when they are young. However, this one evaded us."

As if orchestrated, Reins flooded outside from where they sheltered and reunited or ventured closer to where the Alders disembarked. Auren joined Aedyn and Asa while they helped Sahana onto the sand.

Rylee strolled closer, hiding his compassion for the disfigured woman. Her exposed neck drew his attention. Rein women did not display their necks in public and concluded he preferred her dress.

He genuflected, and the villagers followed his lead. "I'll lead you to my father."

Rylee held Sahana's trembling arm in his and wandered slowly along the path. "Lady Sahana, I assumed it was impossible, but you look more radiant than last night."

Those who followed overheard his remark.

She smiled but continued to watch ahead for obstacles, not wanting to trip. "I wonder, does education train you to have a brilliant tongue?"

His laugh rang loudly. "No, it's a skill I taught myself."

"Perhaps others should aim to learn this skill." She ensured her voice carried.

Asa frowned, but Aedyn grinned and nudged his friend in fun.

In precise, tight lines, cottages and buildings bordered either side of the wide path, then nestled behind was another row.

"What's the purpose of the village's layout?" Bennet asked.

"In order to withstand the lengthy, cruel winters and the ferocious monsters, we reconstructed the villages to add waste trenches. We no longer use outdoor privies or pots."

"It's like Aldersward castle but available to all." Bennet surmised, impressed with the ingenuity.

"Are we in your winter now?" Aedyn asked.

Rylee peered over his shoulder. "This is the heat of summer. Our winter will freeze your breath in the air and, after only a short time, you'll no longer feel your exposed extremities. The snow will accumulate higher than the buildings. In the south, there are places blanketed in massive chunks of ice, bigger than your craft, and they never melt. Cold grips those areas all year long."

Auren scratched his head. "You mentioned *monsters,* as in plural. Are there more besides the manticore?"

"There are the vily."

Bennet educated, "Alluring, beautiful women with long hair, pointed ears, and tempting bodies. Their fingernails grow several inches long and their legs resemble tree roots, and those roots climb their torso, covering them like attire."

Auren shrugged. "They don't sound frightening."

"If you do anything to offend or interfere in their rituals, they'll kill you. We offer friendship by leaving gifts near where they live. Otherwise, it's better to maintain a healthy distance. My father will occasionally communicate with their queen. They live on the northeast side of Reinshaven. Here we are." Rylee stopped and lifted Sahana's hand to his lips, allowing them to linger a second longer than necessary.

She felt his lips brush against her skin, not the customary chaste peck she received from the Alders. She blushed and averted her gaze.

Asa severed their contact by clasping her elbow. As he settled her arm against his, he wiped the back of her hand, erasing the man's touch. "We appreciate your guidance."

After the initial shock of seeing the estate grounds, identical to the ones in Aldersward, the men walked to the cookhouse while Aedyn, Sahana, and Bennet joined the royals inside the official residence to share a meal. They discussed the manticores, vily, and the Alders' journey.

Bennet watched Raed, the king's heir, eat heartily. "Has Reinshaven gone through any other changes?"

The king spoke as he chewed, "Our religion. We no longer pray to Jezabet's son, Jordan. It's our theory he caused the destruction of our world. And we've adapted—building structures from ice and snow in the south. We lost much farmland; so to conserve what little remains, we either entomb in ice or burn our dead. These differences will require the Alder king's approval. We're eager to realign ourselves under his reign with specific concessions."

Aedyn lifted his brow. "What concessions?"

"Queen Rayanne of Aldersward was Rein and married an Alder ruler." King Roddy mentioned, as if in passing, but Raed studied his father.

"Are you suggesting a betrothal?" Aedyn's young sisters' images flashed through his mind.

The king shook his head. "Not any betrothal. Not our spare to your sister or your cousin to Raed. An arrangement between my daughter, Princess Roosha, and you would be the strongest bond we could forge."

The statement gained everyone's eyes. The princess's neck snapped upward and her mouth opened as if she would speak, but her mother's hand on her arm checked her angry outburst.

Aedyn shook his head, pleased to utilise Ammaris. "I'm already betrothed."

Roosha released a long exhale. Clearly, she had no interest in their union either.

"Did this contract happen before your journey?"

"What difference does it make?" His eyes narrowed.

The king shrugged. "I believe your king would willingly break it to form a royal union. We need not decide now. I merely hoped to propose it early in your visit so you could consider it. Should we discuss your supplies and what brings you to our kingdom?"

"Roughly, three moons ago, an illness struck a few dozen in our population and a handful in Slaysfold, including my mother, Queen Anya. We seek healers."

"How many healers?"

"With some modifications to our vessel, we could accommodate an additional fifty. Of course, those could be any who choose to accompany us to Aldersward. It's something for you to consider while we visit." He mimicked the king's sentiment as he ate the red cabbage and deer meat.

Raed handed him a dish, and Aedyn nearly dropped it when he saw the boiled potatoes. It brought to mind a sharp image of Belinda and he passed it to Sahana as if it burned his hands. He wondered how long he would ache for her.

Day 185
Queen Belinda's Chambers
Castle's Second Floor
Baitsloam City

Fog drifted through Belinda's vision and what she could see spun dizzily, the aftermath of the alcohol Beatrice had provided her. Outside, the day sounds shifted to the near nothingness of night.

The older woman suggested. "Go straight to the bed and don't speak. Let him do what he will."

Beatrice guided her to the adjoining door, then pushed it open, and glanced inside. Offering a dim path to the king's bedchamber, a single candle burned. The old woman knocked and when the entrance opened, she quickly stepped aside, cloaked by the darkness.

Belinda walked slowly, trying not to sway. Inside, a pair of formally attired guards stood on either side of the doorway. Both frozen like statues. In a corner, the large wooden habitat which housed his snakes shook from the vibration of their movements and hisses.

Neither guards nor snakes registered as she focused on her husband's naked, wrinkled body sprawled on the thickly piled bed.

His interested eyes appreciated the partially gaped nightgown—the valley between her tits and their swell exposed. He righted himself and swung his legs over the bedside, and offered his hand to her. "Join me here."

His manhood thickened as his timid young wife walked toward him. He grinned with anticipation, recalling how he had rubbed the new from his other wives.

She set her hand in his clammy one, and he drew her closer. His legs gripped her hips and his hands grabbed the globes of her chest. Her soft pink nipples rested against his palm.

She caught a whiff of his putrid body where loose skin hung from his deteriorating muscles and bones, signs of his advanced age. And when he touched her—gripped her breasts with his gnarled hands—her stomach turned, and she recoiled backwards. Even drunk, her strength easily defeated his.

She couldn't. She would rather die. Her uncoordinated feet backtracked until her spine met the solid steel chest plate of a guard.

Baeddan said nothing, yet each of the guards seized her arms. She struggled and twisted against their hold. When those actions didn't work, she tried to drop, but they held her firm between them, like an offering to their ruler.

The king stood, "I've afforded ye many days to adapt yerself to our union."

Through the alcohol-induced lethargy, Belinda's fight continued, until she witnessed his pointed erection approach, then scared, she froze.

His grip forced her chin upwards, and his sunken eyes glared into hers. His nearly toothless mouth separated their faces by a hand's width and his sour breath accosted her. "This happens one of two ways. Ye allow me to use yer body, or I force myself inside ye. Either way, yer position here depends on ye supplying a successor."

Renewed strength coursed through her and, like a crazed, cornered animal, she fought.

When he tore her nightgown wide, the row of buttons popped and slung in every direction, then pinged when they ricocheted off other objects.

Her exposed, unblemished white torso nearly glowed in the stream of brilliant light cast by the moon.

For an instant, she stilled, and waited, until he closed the gap between their bodies and attempted to handle her breasts again.

This time, she punched her legs outward together, hoping to connect with his stomach.

Instead, the guards dropped her, and she landed with a painful thud on her tailbone, but she scrambled backwards, trying to avoid the hands, seeking to capture her again.

"Aye, my bride, ye prefer the hard way, then." He snapped his fingers. "Bring her to the bed."

Though she clawed—a guard caught her hair and dragged her upwards until his other arm wrapped around the flesh of her ribs. She felt the rough texture of his fingers lock on her delicate waist.

After several strides, he tossed her face down onto the thick mattress.

No longer confined, she attempted to scramble upright and discovered a guard on either side of the bed. The second guard reached for her hands and, even though she tried to evade him, he managed to snatch her wrists. He jerked her across the covers and she screamed, tears trailed her face. Searing pain shot through her arms as he nearly ripped them from their sockets.

The entirety of her focus was set on escaping his hold. And she didn't realise her mistake until she felt the first guard's hands seize her ankles.

Her mind was intensely dizzy, and yet she shifted her neck, one way then the other, fighting for air through the thick mass of her hair. Her energy was exhausted as she tried to buck free, her frame barely lifted. She was helpless against their strength. Half-naked and on display between them. Nevermore had she felt the vulnerability of her person.

Through the huff of her breathing, and the sobs from her throat, she heard Baeddan's muffled voice, but couldn't register his words.

The cold steel of the guard's leg armour touched her exposed legs, and an uncontrolled quake went through her. The metal joints clanked and squeaked, and the material of her nightgown rode higher as his heavy weight crawled up onto her back, ensuring she was pinned by his straddle.

Bared from the waist down, the night's air chilled her to the bone.

Her captors seemed far removed from the immoral act. Each undertook the task placed upon them without emotion or much exertion. Merely restrains and instruments of the king's wishes. It was demonic.

Her weak legs thrashed when she felt the king's naked hips touch her inner thigh. His gnarled hands gripped the soft flesh of her ass and pulled, spreading her most intimate place to his gaze.

She heard him gather the phlegm in his throat, then it splattered against her anus, and he smeared it downward with the tip of his penis to her clenched entrance.

Her body shook with convulsive cries of disbelief. Though she couldn't flee, it didn't stop her body from attempting to shrink from the foreign, unwelcome touch.

With the slimy ooze of his lust and spit, his cock prodded. Like an arrow aiming for its target. Then, without warning, he drove his full length through her folds.

Attempting to eject his unwanted invasion, her muscles stiffened and her soft, delicate skin tore under the friction.

She wailed—a blood-curdling scream. Its volume certainly reached every corner of the castle.

From her back, the guard wrapped his hands over her mouth, causing her breasts to lift from the mattress into the air.

Relentlessly, the king's weapon stabbed into her and out. Each of his strokes was a new violation.

One thrust shattered her dignity.

The joints of the guard's armour pinched the skin at her sides, delivering torturous forks of anguish through her body.

Another plunge destroyed her power.

She could feel him—hunched over her. The slap of his hairy thighs. The heat of his exerted breath on her lower spine. His hands anchored to her hips for leverage as he cruelly pushed and pulled.

And so on, until all that remained was an intense shame.

Relief came when her mind and body deadened to his continued savage assault.

Belinda had no concept of how long his rape lasted or when he finished. Her wits only returned when her wounded body slid off the bed to the icy stone floor.

When her frame coiled to protect itself, every inch of her hurt and she wanted to shriek from the overwhelming pain. Her mouth opened, but the hoarseness of her throat prevented her. Instead, she bawled—tears, snot, and spittle covered her chin and chest.

Suddenly, through her cries, words tumbled out, and she seized her husband's leg. "Kill me...end me...there's nothing left..." Her mind begged Jezabet or Jordan for death—it didn't matter who the agent was.

His fist thumped the top of her head several times before her hold broke, then he lifted the length of her thick red hair, and into it, he wiped the gooey blood and fluid from his limp cock. "Return her to her room."

Day 186
Earl Ryke's Study
Royal Estate
Agerton Village, Reinshaven

In the study, Aedyn relaxed his back against the desk's chair while his gaze found the window, covered in slatted wood. Only tiny streams of light managed through. It reminded him of Belinda's dugout and the floorboards above where he had spent so much time.

A heavy hand knocked, drawing his attention and he studied Prince Raed as he bowed. A lily-white ermine clung to his back. His tunic and wool vest hung loosely over his torso, but his arms bulged with muscle against the fabric.

When he straightened, he swept his long hair back. The large curls made it appear shorter than it was as it settled against his shoulders where it buried his small pet. The stubble covering his jaw and lip was well groomed, kept at a few days' length. His poise radiated self-confidence and determination.

Aedyn gestured. "Let's adopt frank speech."

The other adjusted his clothing as he sat down. "I play no part in theatrics. What you see is who I am. I would act no different if you weren't here. But, I seek to evaluate your character. Are you what you present?" His green eyes scrutinised him.

With instant admiration, Aedyn smiled. "I believe I strive to be genuine and true to my word—although, in our kingdom and my position, it's not always achievable." His pledge to Bret played in his head. "I have no other motives but to find a healer for my mother."

Raed's brow lifted. "What do you think of my father's proposal—a union between you and my sister?"

"It was a simple, well-placed suggestion. I don't know your sister, or my betrothed, Ammaris, much better. If I must wed her to obtain a healer, then I will. Do you believe your father is serious?"

He could see the man's mind work as Raed carefully folded his hands on the desk. "I believe my father is serious, my mother is worried, and my sister is furious—all natural but expected. Our people prayed for Aldersward and no other kingdom. At our last temple, we still prayed to Jezabet. Even with Aldersward's destruction, we considered your reign."

"I can't predict how our new world will intertwine. Your kingdom's acceptance differs greatly from what we've encountered. Slaysfold has accepted our friendship but not our rule and Baitsloam, under its current ruler, accepts nothing."

"With your permission, I prefer to remain near you and offer my counsel as we study each other's character."

A fist pounded, interrupting them. Aedyn nodded his answer to Raed, then invited those waiting to enter.

The room filled quickly with a dozen Alders and Sahana. Auren's eyes travelled to the Rein prince and he would have taken the position at Prince Aedyn's side, but the monarch shook his head, staying him.

Welcoming, Aedyn smiled. "Thank you for answering my summons. We've much to cover, so as I hand out orders, you may leave."

He noted the troubled lines on his friend's expression. "Asa, discuss with Amos a dock for the Endeavour, then take your men, and build it. Amos, consider changes to the interior with your men. Gut my bedchamber and ready it with as many bunks as possible. Where the through-room's small table is, convert it into a privy and washroom. Change both existing washrooms to single sleeping quarters, then one of the current privies into a washroom."

As the pair left, he examined his list. "Angelo, Augustus, and Auren. Prince Raed will arrange a hunt and gathering of supplies in the next few days. Ready your men and have enough collected for one-hundred passengers for fourteen days' travel. Apex, consult Arvo, then reorganise the cargo hold using Aron's men. Leave behind anything unnecessary. Build more shelving if you must, and relocate Sahana's things to where the new bunks are." He dismissed them with a nod.

"Bennet and Aron, make yourself available to King Roddy. I noticed much interest in the crowd this morning when he announced our willingness to accept passengers. Sahana, be available to the queen, princess, and their ladies. Alonso, as it's decided who will accompany us, add them to the manifest, and meet each one. Go."

When they left, three remained. His gaze bounced from Raed to Aidrik. "Find out if a healer can cure Asa of his anxieties."

The door closed, and silence hung between the two princes.

The Rein's smile was genuine. "We'll get on fine together."

Day 186
Royal Estate
Agerton Village, Reinshaven

Augustus and Angelo observed as Auren took their men through the combat exercises in a fenced enclosure normally used for livestock. Reins and children gathered along the sides to watch the exhibition. In Aldersward, all the men's chests would be naked, but the brisk air here kept them clothed—except for one.

No perspiration rolled down Auren's muscular torso as he battled against his attackers. One by one, he blocked, then used the wooden sword to strike each down. He offered his hand to pull one upright as another charged from behind. Those spectating lent their presence to his energy, and he strove to provide them with the entertainment they craved.

As he entered the ring, Angelo shook his head and called for a change.

With a wide grin, Auren trotted and vaulted over the fence.

Augustus laughed and threw the waded tunic to him. "Your nipples are peaking."

"I offer the women sensual visions to occupy the frigid nights ahead." His gaze ran over the crowd, acknowledging the appreciative glances he received as he dropped the fabric over his back.

A hand clasped his shoulder, and he turned, discovering Prince Rylee. Augustus and Auren bowed.

Rylee wore a wide, mischievous smile. "My brother's assigned me to act as your guide. I thought to take you on a tour of my favourite hunting grounds this evening."

"You hunt at night?" Augustus asked.

Rylee leaned in and confided. "The long-haired, two-legged, and naked specimens prefer it."

Auren rubbed his hands together. "Let us hunt."

The lead lightly kicked the door closed with his heel. The king, opposite Aedyn, turned to see who it was.

Auren bowed and sat beside the king. "Prince Aedyn, I seek permission to take Augustus and Angelo with Prince Rylee into the village for the night?"

"Granted. Take Asa as well," Aedyn answered, knowing their purpose by his lead's excited expression.

"Your Highness, would you accompany us?"

"No, I'll remain here with Sahana and Bennet. Aidrik reported there are women who will service a man and heal him. Ensure you locate one for Asa and do not allow him to beg out of it. Arrange his healing if nothing else."

The king grinned. "And maintain a quiet tongue. Most women don't know these places exist."

"Sire, you'll have our utmost discretion," Auren smirked as he departed.

It took Aedyn ordering Asa to accompany them. Shortly before sundown, the four walked into the brothel. Rylee waved for them to join him at a table in the back.

Auren's eyes roamed over the dimly lit room filled with both men and women. No smoke, music, or naked bodies adorned the furniture. It looked like an ordinary dining room of any inn in Aldersward. He whispered as they sat. "I understood we were attending a brothel?"

As the prince pulled the mug from his mouth, he smiled. "This is a small community. It's necessary for us to disguise our establishments in plain sight. Choose a woman from any group of two or more and send her a drink. If she accepts it, she's available. If she refuses, she isn't."

"What should I do if I require a conversation beforehand?"

"Wait. Those who don't intend to spend the night will leave shortly, before dark. The manticores become more courageous at night."

Asa's eyes narrowed with anger. "Are we stuck here until morning?"

"You are if you wish to live." He shrugged. "There are worse places to be stuck. There'll be games and entertainment later." He motioned for more drinks.

They drank three ales each while they talked, joked, and shared stories. When the proprietor barred the exit, a hush fell over the room. There remained three men other than themselves and a dozen or more women with varying degrees of black and white hair.

A woman strummed an instrument, playing a soft melody as the others scanned the available men.

"First, I've duties to attend. How do I hire?" Auren asked.

"Converse, if it's what you desire. I have already chosen." The prince stood, raised his hand towards a woman, and she approached immediately. He cupped her ass in his palms and rocked their bodies to the rhythm of the music.

"What duties?" Asa studied his friend.

"I have strict instructions to find a woman suited to your tastes."

The other shook his head. "I'll wait and play cards."

Auren smiled, but his voice was stern. "You'll accompany her to a room. I won't have anyone question whether or not my duty was executed. What you do inside is your business." He walked to the closest unattached woman.

Asa sat alone for the better part of an hour before Auren returned.

The lead tossed a wooden chip down and said. "You're in room five, down the hall and on the left. I've paid for the night, and I mean to stay here for a bit to ensure you remain inside. Afterwards, the night is yours. I'll be in room six, if you should require me."

He snatched the button and stomped off in anger.

Scratched with five deep marks, Asa knocked on the room. His eyes swung to his friend, who raised his mug in salute before he entered.

When he turned, he found a woman waiting. Grey and smoke colours painted her lids, giving her eyes a seductive glow. A piercing ran through her nose, another on her bottom lip and another under it. A thin strip of white hair ran along her face, otherwise it was black.

He dropped the button into a dish and uncomfortably stammered. "I've no wish to use you."

Unbuttoning the side of her robe, she sauntered towards him, then raised onto her toes and her sweet tangy breath whispered in his ear. "No, but you've been ordered to." She dragged the material over her head, exposing her pierced breasts and navel to him.

As she settled his palm over her breast, he swallowed and his face reddened. She wrapped her fingertips around the back of his neck and pulled him towards the bed.

His legs brushed the bedside as she licked her tongue along his throat and nibbled his ear, gently tugging. She dragged his palm to her ass.

She urged his neck to bend, and she enticed his lips with hers. When his tongue ran over her piercing, she unbuckled his trousers, letting them slip to the floor.

She nudged him backwards onto the bed, running her fingernails over his frame and along his legs as sunk and fixed her heated lips over his semi-hard member.

It stiffened in her mouth, a thrilling sensation he did not have time to dwell on as her lip piercing glided up, then down his shaft. She devoured him with enthusiasm and hunger, as if this would be her last meal. Never had he known a woman's mouth to be so greedy. She sucked harder and her cheeks caved against his flesh.

His enjoyment intensified with every new movement she made.

Her hands searched the bed for his, then raised them to her hair. The added weight forced more of his length inside her.

He elevated his hips and pressed her head down, feeling the vibration of her throat against him as she hummed. Her hands returned to his stomach and rested flat above his navel.

He grinned tightly and concentrated.

Thrust.
Her hands warmed against his flesh.
His hand twisted her hair, and her lips met his pelvic bone.
Thrust.
He felt his tip bounce against the back of her throat. As his muscles constricted and his climax came, his toes curled, then stretched.

She raised her head. Her hands were fiery hot as she chanted, and his seed dripped from her chin.

He would have stopped her, but dizziness spun all his thoughts to blackness.

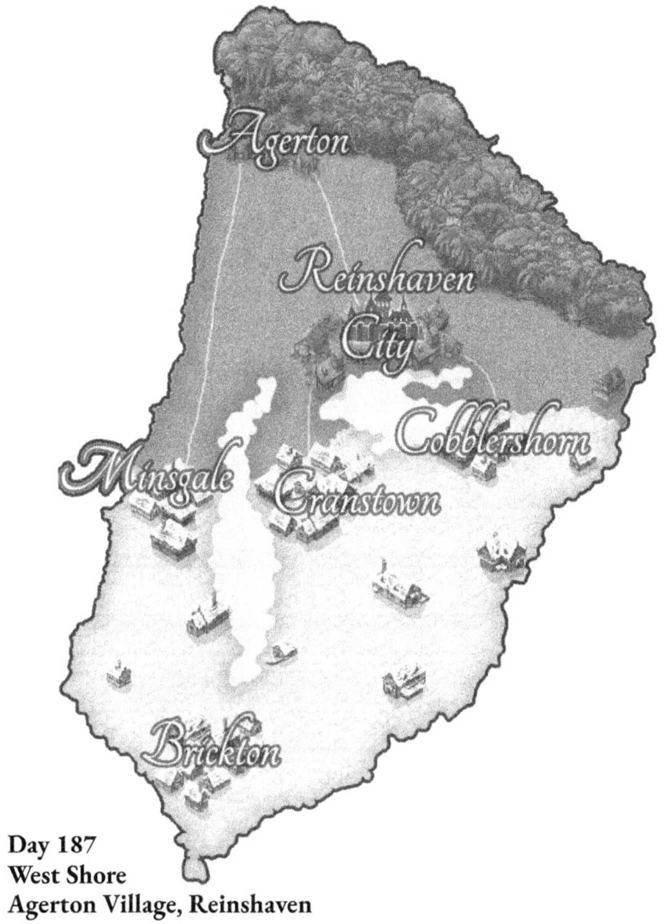

Day 187
West Shore
Agerton Village, Reinshaven

At dawn, Asa whistled as he strolled toward the shoreline to meet those building the long dock. They hammered the end of six thick tree trunks together. This morning the men would fasten the other side, then he would push it into the water and secure the end against long poles he had driven into the ground.

Somehow, he was lighter—happy, and he couldn't stop from grinning as he reached his friends.

"Prince Aedyn." Asa exaggerated his bow, then slapped his back.

"I take it my gift was well received?" He chuckled.

"It was." He recalled the woman lying next to him when he woke. She looked the same as he remembered, except for a second patch of white hair at the base of her neck.

A glow of desire coloured his cheeks, and he laughed. He felt renewed—restored.

Aedyn shared a glance with Auren, then said. "Get to task. Let's finish this today."

Asa left with a tune on his lips as the pair turned back to the estate house.

Auren draped his arm over his friend's shoulder. "I would never have known a difference between healers existed. Were you aware?"

He shook his head. "We know now. I'll speak to Alonso and inform him that Slaysfold will need two and we'll require four of each. It's at least eighteen women. Find the one who treated Asa. If she wants to come with us, she can."

Auren strode off as Aedyn continued, hardly noticing those who bowed as he passed. His mind was on his sister's impending visit. He would have no choice but to explain Reinshaven and the king's requested betrothal.

My betrothal, he amended.

He wandered to a tree in the estate's centre garden, sat, and closed his eyes. Ammaris, Belinda, Roosha, Azalea—a vision of each came to mind as he thought their names. He easily scratched the whore's name from his internal list. Their chemistry had been fun and comfortable, but neither had expectations of a continued relationship.

Ammaris, he heard himself sigh. If she took it badly, her reaction would riddle him with guilt, possibly for as long as he lived. She was innocent, selfless, and her sole intent was to please and love him.

If only I felt the same. He wondered why he was so detached from her. Could it have been because of their long acquaintance? Her existence barely registered in his world. He wondered if hurting her would be the hardest thing he ever did.

No, he shook his head—leaving Belinda and not returning for her would be the hardest thing he would ever do.

He realised an agony in his chest, a searing hurt. As the emotion intensified, his fingers found his wrist and caressed the black ribbon still tied there. He refused to consider what tortures she endured since they parted. Instead, he envisioned her excited blue eyes and laughing smile. The way her hair burned brighter against the sun's light when it spilt through the window as she sewed. Her melodic voice when she read to him. Those images diminished his suffering and brought a slight smile to his mouth. He lifted his wrist to his nose and inhaled her scent.

Women's voices approached, and he opened his eyes.

He did not need to imagine King Roddy's daughter as she walked past, trailing Queen Rhian, Sahana, and their ladies.

When Princess Roosha spoke, he noted her voice lacked the airy quality of Belinda's, which he enjoyed. She separated, approached him, then pulled on the high-collared neck of her robe as she sat, and arranged the material around her.

Silently, they inspected and measured the other. She was not Belinda. She was the same height and weight, but the similarities ended there. Her skin was not as flawless or pale. Her black and white thin hair hung limply straight and a single piercing adorned her nose.

He was unsure what had betrayed him when she spoke. "You're no prize either, Prince Aedyn."

"I beg your pardon?" Surprised, his brows lifted.

As she shook her head, her laugh sounded callous. "No, but you will beg if you accept my father's betrothal. I've no desire to wed you. The very prospect turns my stomach. I–"

"Turns your stomach? You've shattered my ego." He smiled, disregarding her childish outburst.

Her voice dripped with venom. "If you force me to marry you, then understand, on our wedding night I'll sever your man-bit and nourish whatever animal or beast is nearby. Do I make myself perfectly clear?"

"My groin shrivels at the imagery you've described. Should you succeed, I wonder, would a healer have skills to regrow or reattach it?"

She shrugged, not caring either way. "If your part was present, yes, but since I intend to make a feed out of it, there's no hope. To my dismay, you would never experience satisfaction again."

Dismissing her threats, he smiled and discovered himself fond of her direct tongue. "Yes, you sound dreadfully upset by it."

She rose. "I love another. More man than you will ever achieve. Nothing will stop our union, including a puppet prince from Aldersward." She turned on her heel and hurried to reunite with the other women as Raed passed her.

"Your Highness," he bowed, and it occurred to Aedyn that Roosha had not afforded him the respect he was due. "What did she want?"

"She used exemplary language to describe how she yearns to remove, then feed my manhood to a beast."

He grinned and withdrew his ermine from a deep pocket. "Felyx, would never."

Aedyn laughed. "No, I suspect she meant in Aldersward." He changed the subject. "I would like us to be close friends, so excuse me in advance for asking. She spoke of loving another?"

"Did she?"

He braced himself for the rage which would overwhelm the man forced to answer the question. "Does she?"

"Yes, she does—a new farmer near Snakestongue Lake. His father died when he rushed into a mine after it collapsed, about four moons ago. I found and forbade them from seeing each other anymore."

No anger surfaced—no notice of Aedyn's ability.

The man's honesty impressed him. "How would you advise me?"

Raed laughed. "Depends on whether you believe her." His voice lost its light-heartedness. "I would prefer my parents not learn of the farmer."

Day 187
Royal Estate
Agerton Village, Reinshaven

In the neatly trimmed grass, Princess Roosha with the other ladies played a game, while Sahana and Queen Rhian observed from the shade. The day was cool, and the Slay was grateful for the blanket draped across her legs. The queen poured the tea, and it felt strange for someone to serve her.

Rhian touched the woman's knee, drawing her gaze. "I've seen you wince when you move, and yet you haven't requested a healer."

"Your Majesty, I don't know if I want it." She concentrated on the fibres spread out on the ground in front of her, and used her ability. One at a time, she moved her gnarled fingers, each to command a single strand. The pieces wove intricately together like a passion-filled dance between lovers. A pale yellow basket's bottom formed and then tall, strong sides.

"Speak freely. Are you frightened?" The woman's voice was kind, not as Asa had accused.

Sahana glanced at those who ran playfully over the area. "No, but truthfully, I don't want to become who I was before. I don't wish to forget."

"There are different types of healing; physical, emotional, and mental. You could accept one without the others. Even with complete healing, you would never forget. It would merely separate you as if it were a dream."

The queen's understanding caused her throat to tighten, and she swallowed the lump. "I shall consider it."

"Please do and know each process can be performed in stages. Whenever you desire, you can start and stop." When her daughter struck the wooden ball with her mallet, the queen clapped.

Day 187
Prince Aedyn's Chamber
Royal Estate
Agerton Village, Reinshaven

After the evening meal, Aedyn filled a mug with whisky and excused himself. The candles and hearth burned, lending heat and light to the room. He drank a generous swallow, then laid down and covered his body with the heavy blankets. While he waited for his frame to warm, he closed his eyes, concentrated, and drifted.

"Aedyn?" his sister materialised, and he swung from the bed to greet her.

Carefully, he hugged her. She was narrower and trembled as he squeezed her to him, then kissed her forehead. "Six days is a long time." She lifted her face, and for the first time, he noted her sunken eyes. "What's wrong?"

She shrugged free. "It's nothing. A herbalist is caring for me."

"A herbalist? Why not Axton?"

"I don't know. You'll have to ask Father when you return." She realised she lied and discovered his abilities did not function in his dreams.

"Count on it." When she did not answer, he continued. "There's considerable to discuss. We aren't as close to home as you would expect, and we've stumbled on Reinshaven."

"Reinshaven?" She squealed with delight, embracing him.

He smiled. "They accept Aldersward as the ruling kingdom, but King Roddy wants a formal action to reunite our kingdoms. I require our father's answer tonight."

"What action?" She wondered, only half listening, still elated by his news.

"If Father agrees, I'm to marry King Roddy's daughter, Princess Roosha."

"But Ammaris?" Achelle worried about the woman who gloried in his previous message, happier than she had ever seen her.

His voice hardened. "I haven't forgotten. Have Father decide. Will you bring me his answer tonight?"

Trapped in concern, she failed to guard her words. "I'll plead to meet our father tonight but I can make no promises."

Aedyn's tone thickened with anger, and he grabbed his sister's arm, almost lifting her. "What are you hiding? What do you mean, *plead*?" He let go, realising his grip must hurt her.

"While I searched for you, I became dependent on tonics. The herbalist, assigned by Axton, is weaning me from them. As a condition, she rules my every visitor and action."

"Preposterous!" He exploded, sweeping the contents of the table onto the floor. "Bring us together in your mind. I'll see this end immediately."

She shook her head. "You don't understand—it's what must be."

Day 187
Herbalist's Chambers
Castle's Second Level
Near Aldersward City

Achelle woke, bolted upright, and yelled for the old woman.

From the room's shadows, Herbalist Alvira emerged. Her hoarse voice asked. "Does your head hurt?"

"Yes, but it isn't why I called. I must see my father tonight."

The old woman sat on the bed, holding a mug the other knew contained tonic. "I could allow it, but how would you repay me for my kindness?"

"I have nothing." Her shoulders sank. "You've taken everything from me."

"Not everything." She swirled the contents of the mug with a shake of her hand, drawing the other's eyes. "You have this. Would you trade it?"

She glanced from the tonic to the woman, then back—weighing the decision. Her head thumped, and she was uncertain if she could endure without it.

Alvira witnessed the conflict in her expression as she waited for her answer.

When Achelle finally nodded, the herbalist smiled, walked to the window, and poured the tonic onto the ground below. "I'll fetch him."

Day 187
Prince Aedyn's Chamber
Royal Estate
Agerton Village, Reinshaven

He dreamt of when he read to Belinda, relaxed on her bed. So vivid, he could smell her scent and feel her warmth against his shoulder when she rested her head. His heartbeat quickened. She laughed, and he swallowed when she touched him. It was cherished agony.

"Aedyn?" Achelle appeared. "She's beautiful. Is she Roosha?"

"No," instantly, he closed his eyes and erased her. "What was Father's answer?"

More cheerful than necessary, she responded. "First, he's elated you've located Reinshaven and the healers."

He detected the nervousness in her tone. "I'd wager."

"Well, he'll *be* happy once you return."

He lifted his brow. "What about the betrothal?"

She stammered, rephrasing their father's anger. "He suggested you decide yourself."

"Exact wording?"

She shrugged and mimicked their father. "*Again, he's defied me and never follows my directives. Why ever should he begin now? Let him decide if his own happiness is worth his mother's life.*"

"I'll consider it further, but after his anger passes, approach the subject again. There is time before King Roddy requires an answer, and we wouldn't marry until we reach Aldersward."

Day 188
Main Thoroughfare
Agerton Village, Reinshaven

In the mid-morning sun, the Alders completed their tasks, trained, or entertained themselves. It was hard to believe Reinshaven only enjoyed what they called summer for seventy days. Currently, Aldersward would be humid and scorched with heat.

As he strolled along the rutted pathway, Asa whistled through his foolish grin and his eyes admired the surroundings. A few times, he paused to shout a greeting to someone he knew or help another with a task they performed. He realised his return to the estate was taking longer than expected, but he did not care—couldn't care. He laughed out loud, feeling free.

"Emissary Sahana!" He called to the women crossing farther along the path.

When she turned, he waved and rushed towards her as the others continued.

He clasped her hand, then bowed and kissed it, lingering as he had seen Rylee do days before. "You look well."

She smiled, pulling her hand away, "As do you."

He wrapped her arm over his and steered her into the small centre garden, then helped her to sit on the stone bench. "I feel as though I have not seen you in some time."

"You mean other than in the study?"

"We never spoke, and I only attended for a few minutes. I miss our lengthy chats."

She nodded, "As do I."

"How are you treated?"

"Everyone is kind. I sleep in the royal house and have been given a maid—it's dreamlike. Sometimes I worry I'll wake, and find myself dirty and sleeping on the floor in a dark corner in Slaysfold castle."

"I assure you, this is real. Have you thought any more about being healed?"

She shrugged. "I once was a stupid girl who thought the world was wonderfully pleasant—I don't want to lose who I have become. Queen Rhian has said it could be done slowly and limited to what I want, so I may accept. I long to speak with Brielle, but she and her children remained on the vessel."

"Today, we'll guide it against the dock. If you wish, the next time I go, you can accompany me."

Day 188
Sitting Room
Royal Estate
Agerton Village, Reinshaven

Warding off the chilly evening, the two hearths blazed. Next to one, Sahana sat wrapped in blankets. The cold intensified the ache in her bones and the heat helped. Princess Roosha read a book, but Aedyn thought perhaps she pretended—instead, present to eavesdrop on the conversation. The king and queen sat together on a cushioned bench while Raed, Bennet, and he sat in high-backed, upholstered chairs.

"Why have we found you here and not at Reinshaven castle?" Aedyn set his empty mug down.

Raed answered. "Whenever travel is possible, we do. Sometimes, for months at a time, winter cold and ice storms can trap us inside."

"We will depart within a few days. Don't allow our presence to keep you."

The king joined the men. "I wanted your opinion. We would like to accompany you to Aldersward—to see our daughter married?"

Bennet left the chair, allowing the king to sit next to the Alder prince. "Ye speak of a winter so severe and cold. The sea may be impassable and could prevent yer return for nearly a year. Who will rule in yer absence?"

"And there is Princess Roosha to consider. She does not wish for our union."

Shocked, Queen Rhian dropped her sewing. "Whatever has given you the impression?"

Raed coughed.

King Roddy met his daughter's eyes, then swung his attention. "She'll do as we wish. It's a sacrifice for our kingdom." He turned to Bennet. "You've met Earl Ryke, my friend since childhood. I trust he would rule Reinshaven as I wished."

Aedyn took his mug and crossed to the side table. "I have no objections. I'll order your names added to the manifest, but I've yet to decide if a union between our families will occur."

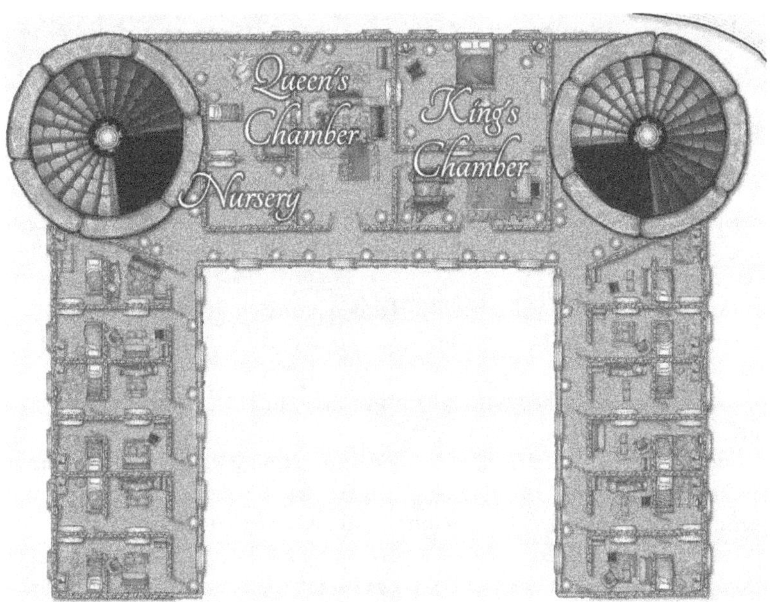

Day 189
Queen Belinda's Chambers
Castle's Second Floor
Baitsloam City

Beatrice threw back the heavy drapes covering the window. The day's brightness cast away the dark, depressing shadows. Belinda stirred when the old woman dropped her clothing at her feet.

"No matter how much I drink, the moment I'm naked, I sober, and live through every disgusting detail."

"When he dismisses us, we're escorted to our cottage and can't return until morning."

"He throws ye out, but his guards remain, watching—nay, participating. I feel their gaze on me, and I'm relieved when his repulsive body covers mine." Her muscles protested when she pushed the covers away and swung her legs over the bedside.

Hatred marred Beatrice's expression. "We should poison him."

Belinda shook her head as a knock sounded on the hallway door. Bret would answer while she stepped into her gown. Beatrice lifted it and pulled the ties closed at the back. The old woman wrapped a leaf green shawl over the queen's shoulders, hoping to hide her bruises.

From the sitting room, Bret announced, "Queen Belinda, Lady Bethnee of Pennington, wishes an audience."

She coiled her hair in a bun, then secured it with a ribbon. She paused to examine her reflection.

Why live if I imprison myself each day and am raped each night? I must improve my circumstances. But how?

Belinda emerged with her chin raised a fraction higher than she would normally carry herself.

Lady Bethnee remained seated on a bench as the other attendants bowed.

She waved her hand and walked to where her breakfast waited. She poured the steaming tea. "Bret, ask the king's secretary for his attendance." She turned to face the room. "It's most inappropriate ye visit my chambers without invitation. Leave us."

"My staff and ladies will serve me." Lady Bethnee contradicted.

Her eyes flashed with anger and she did not recognise the cackled laugh from her own throat.

"Nay, they won't." Her loud voice echoed, and it sent those within scurrying out.

She kept her gaze on the seated woman until the door's latch clicked in place.

"Ye're disrespect is quite boring and borders on pathetic. Ye'll rise and genuflect. I've woken in a hateful mood and invite ye to test me."

Lady Bethnee smiled, eased backward against the bench, and checked her fingernails. "Truly, I would, but I fear the movement would jeopardise the king's heir I carry."

"Ah, it's clear now why ye're still here." Belinda's eyes lit with laughter. "I'll try to suppress my jealousy." She perched on a bench, facing the woman. "How does yer game play out?"

Her tone was conversational. "Within a short time, I see ye dead. Then the king shall make me queen and my child will succeed him."

A light tap sounded. Neither took their eyes off of each other as it opened, and Bret announced the secretary. He came inside and she witnessed his bow from the corner of her eye, his manor uncomfortable.

Pleasantly, she purred. "Secretary Barlow, I appreciate yer presence."

"Yer Majesty, I'm humbled by yer invitation."

"It seems I've neglected my duties for far too long." She broke her stare from the older woman and concentrated a contrite expression on him. "Perhaps, could I trouble ye for a reminder of my duties?"

He looked from one to the other, then stammered. "Queen Belinda, charity to those less fortunate, direction of the castle servants, the daily running of the household, including meals and seeing to our guests."

She walked to his side, ignoring the woman's presence. "Very well. I mean to correct this. Tell me where Lady Bethnee resides?"

"Yer Grace, in the south wing."

"Who else stays there?"

"Yer Majesty, the hall is otherwise empty."

She crossed her arms and clicked her tongue, "How very lonely. Where are our other guests kept?"

"Queen Belinda, in the north wing."

"How many rooms do her staff occupy?"

"Yer Grace, there's a combination of eight staff or ladies occupying rooms."

She feigned astonishment. "So many?" She icily regarded the woman, running her gaze from her toes to her smug face. "Move Lady Bethnee to the north wing and reduce her ladies to one and her staff to two."

The other's voice was venomous. "Ye cannot do this!"

Her outburst shocked the secretary, but before he could censure her, the queen answered. "Oh my, the heir she grows makes her forgetful. Escort her to her rooms so she may make the necessary arrangements. If the extra staff haven't vacated by the evening meal, have the king's men remove them from the castle grounds. Lastly, notify everyone she's stripped of all duties. She holds nay authority and will be treated as such."

The secretary offered Bethnee his arm, and the queen's cool expression urged the woman to refuse.

She took his arm. "Ye won't get away with this. I'll see the king." She walked quickly, dragging the man beside her.

"Not before I. Secretary Barlow, have the kitchen prepare my husband's favourite meal and inform King Baeddan we'll dine together this evening."

Day 189
West Shore
Anya's Endeavour
Agerton Village, Reinshaven

Aedyn's council walked with him to the shoreline and onto the dock. Solely focused on the vessel, their supplies, and what still needed accomplishing, he ignored the people bowing around him.

When they boarded, Sahana excused herself to find Brielle, while the men crossed to his quarters where a new wall cut the room where the smaller table used to be. The men felt like giants crowded together.

"This won't do," Bennet spoke his mind. "How are we to meet and speak without being overheard?"

Inside his bedchamber, he counted twelve bunks. "I don't think there are enough beds in there. Step out, let's see the cargo hold."

As they wandered through the corridor to the stairs, he surveyed the washrooms turned into private bedchambers. They would be adequate enough. When the four landed below, the cargo hold had undergone an extensive transformation. In the centre walkway, kegs were piled two high. And, on either side, shelving secured them in place, then jutted outwards, leaving the craft's sides bare.

Apex called. "I'm back south."

"We'll wait here," Auren answered.

"We could place a table here." Asa rubbed his chin.

"Nay, it still affords nay privacy. Anyone in the hall above would hear us."

Aedyn exhaled in frustration. "Let's have another wall installed in the women's bunk, thickening it as a sound barrier. Then cut the table to accommodate four. I realised this would be tight. Asa, inform Amos of the further adjustments. The women must sleep in shifts as we do."

Apex appeared, and, hearing the conversation's end, he added. "We've taken the men's possessions and stored them under their bunks, but I may require the space. There's little room left."

"Perhaps you can steal space from the dining hall." He turned and retraced his path.

Aedyn climbed over the long table as Asa chewed the snake meat. He yanked chairs from their stationary positions, then hoisted the table, tore the legs off and carried the heavy top outside. The room seemed to breathe easier with the large, excess furniture gone.

The prince slid down the cabinet and sat with his back against it. "Sit. I require your counsel. In Aldersward, Ammaris waits, eager for our union. She brings a dowry and already has our subjects' favour. Roosha revealed her willingness to maim me if I marry her, but she brings her kingdom's allegiance. My father has left me to choose."

Bennet and Auren took the last two chairs nailed to the floor, and Asa filled four mugs of whisky.

"It's no contest, Ammaris brings little." Asa shrugged.

He closed his eyes, then blinked away Belinda's image. "I have a confession."

Bennet raised his brow. "Is it about the other woman?"

Auren accepted a mug. "What other woman? Azalea?"

The old man laughed. "It astounds me how ye've survived so long being this self-absorbed—the betrothed woman from Baitsloam."

Aedyn's lips thinned, but Auren still wore his perplexed expression. "Again I ask, what woman?"

"Yes, it's about my time in Baitsloam," he shrugged, "And about the woman. Her name was Belinda."

Bennet could see no discussion. "By now, she's likely married to King Baeddan. Yer motivation for returning to Baitsloam, was it to dethrone him for the sake of his subjects, or was it to rescue her?"

"I love her." It was not a direct answer, but it was the only one he gave.

Day 190
Anchor Deck
Anya's Endeavour
Agerton Village, Reinshaven

Exponentially, over recent days, Agerton's population had grown as news spread of the Alders' arrival. The king and his children came aboard to tour the craft with Queen Rhian to determine how much they could fit inside the cramped room the prince had offered them. Onward, Aedyn would remain on the vessel until their departure.

He stood beside Roddy on the anchor deck and behind them were his family and the prince's council. Voices carried through the crowds on the bank, and when the attendance satisfied the king, he raised his hand, silencing them.

Aedyn stepped forward as the people's bodies waved in genuflection. "At sunrise tomorrow, those of you accompanying us will board. Bring only what is necessary. More boats will come later. My secretary, Alonso, will address any questions." He pointed him out and the man waved his hand high. "It's with great honour I announce my engagement to Princess Roosha, future Queen of Aldersward."

From the vessel's decks and the shore, deafening cheers sounded. However, he still heard the expletive curse from Auren. He turned to silence him, but witnessed the young princess swoon, caught in her brother's arms.

Drawing their attention, the king stepped forward as Aedyn motioned for Raed to precede him down the stairs and through the sheltered corridor. Once there, he scooped the woman from him and unceremoniously dumped her onto the mattress in his new room. She came awake with a start as he turned, eyed her brother, and shut the door in his face.

Aedyn blocked the exit and crossed his arms while he waited for her senses to return.

When it happened, with violence in her eyes, she leapt off the bed and attacked him. Her leg shot out, thankfully connecting with his outer thigh as he shielded himself, but her small fist struck his cheek.

She shouted, "You, you cruel monster!"

He would have laughed if her intent had not been so strong. Her foot landed against his abdomen.

"I'll murder you for this. I swear."

He caught her fist as it flew towards him, and he twisted her arm.

"Your pleasure shall end on our wedding night." She reminded him of her earlier threat.

Her entire body twisted away, and he wrapped the vice of his forearm around her waist.

"Stop this." He ordered as she struggled to escape. He was no happier with their engagement than she was, but neither had choice in the matter.

She was deranged, like a vicious wolverine. She kicked her heels backwards, and her fingers reached over her head, trying to scratch his skin or pull his hair. "You can't marry me. I love another. I won't do it. I'll kill myself." With every statement, her fight weakened, and her body shuddered with defeat against him.

And the guilt within him grew—this was how things were done in the past. It was her kingdom's and her father's wish for the union, and Aedyn would do what he must, silently cursing her family for sacrificing her.

When he slackened his hold, she slipped to the floor, a bawling mess as her energy left her. Leaving her where she lay, Aedyn opened the door, then shouldered past her brother, Raed.

Day 191
Anya's Endeavour
Reinshaven's West Sea

Bennet latched the door, then sat on the floor. The washroom was the only space no one occupied, and he took advantage of it. He settled the voyage's journal in his lap and wrote.

On our journey to Aldersward, fifty-two Reins accompany us.

Prince Aedyn has accepted a marriage contract to Princess Roosha, daughter of King Roddy and Queen Rhian of Reinshaven. The wedding will occur on day two-hundred-and-eighty at Aldersward Castle.

Today, this news, combined with the realisation we're returning home, are the only redeeming happenings.

Catastrophic—several men used the word. My observation, when one adds thirty-one women into an overpopulated, inescapable prison and they share a single privy and beds, the trip is doomed.

The women waved to the crowds while the men carried their belongings inside. Apparently, Prince Aedyn's 'pack only what is necessary' should have been an itemised list. The females couldn't quarrel over who would sleep where because they could not see through the luggage stacked to the ceiling and overflowing into the reserved small meeting room.

Sahana and Brielle attempted to sneak away. I suspect they meant to hide for the remainder of our trip. Ultimately, it was Asa who thwarted their plan. But it was Prince Aedyn who tasked the pair with organising the women and stipulated every three should share one trunk. We transferred anything deemed nonessential to the dining hall. There were many tears and heated words. Auren believed, if not for the Slay warrior's presence, there would have been physical altercations. None happened, much to his disappointment. This was the word's first occurrence.

Once two trunks rested near each bunk, Princess Roosha demanded she and her ladies be provided bunks for their exclusive use. Prince Aedyn would have intervened, but Prince Raed pushed past him. He hauled her out and locked her in her parents' room. I overheard her brother say she will sleep on the floor. Asa used other words besides 'catastrophic' but there's nay need to elaborate.

Sahana and Brielle selected a few women to help Arvo in the kitchen, but in less than an hour, they took over his domain. His yell carried onto the main deck before Augustus banned them. Imagine telling a woman she is not welcome in a kitchen? It was catastrophic.

The women will have sleep-shifts of eight hours. They could not merely be assigned, and it was an irritated, tired Sahana who trimmed three pieces of wood for the women to choose from.

When it seemed the day may come to a quiet end, it occurred to them there were nay cushioned chairs and only benches on the main deck.

Could it be conceivable they should sit on the hard surfaces?

Similar criticisms and complaints were Sahana's snapping point. She called Brielle out and barred them inside. It was a long time before the women were let out, suddenly delighted to sit on the benches outside.

Captain Amos, at first, lenient of those passing over his navigation deck to the observation deck, eventually restricted anyone outside of Prince Aedyn's immediate circle.

This evening, I've yet to locate either my wife or Sahana, but they're probably pleased with the silence of the cargo hold.

At first, the Alder men considered the situation comical, but after listening to the women for hours, many of them muttered under their breath. The Alders' remarks offended the Rein men but soon they themselves were adopting colourful curses. As the day progressed, men disappeared. I do not think they have jumped overboard yet, but hide in the men's bunkroom below.

I pray Jezabet spares us all—the more immediate, the better.

An updated manifest follows.

Prince Aedyn's group:
Aedyn – by asking an exact question, the person responding cannot lie
Alan = animate dolls
Abraham = make dirty things clean
Andres = recreate music he has only heard once
Arjun = make objects glow—five minute limitation
Aryan = instantly create weapons made of wood
Anderson = ability to unlock any lock by touch
Anik – change glass into mirror (Aedyn's page)

Guard Angelo's group:
Angelo – recharge fully on two hours of sleep (Guard)
Aidrik – feel other people's pain when he touches them (Physician)
Arlo = poetry—he rhymes well
Apollo – create elaborate illusions of gardens—only lasts an hour
Aldo – unbreakable bones
Ameer – duplicate fermented drinks
Alec – change his own legs into arms
Anson – disease resistant
Bowan – communicates with frogs
Blake – communicates with squirrels

Guard Asa's group:
Asa – super-strength by consuming snake meat (Guard)
Alberto – change the wind's direction
Austin – enhanced hearing, direct line, no barriers
Alcott – conjure any fur as long as he has seen or interacted with it before
Arthur – paint an image from memory, extremely detailed, on eucalyptus paper
Albert – accelerate creating a weapon but must have all materials

Alvin – shatter stone with his scream
Azariah – heat vision
Ackley – change target's voice to another (Carpenter/Boatswain)
Amos – turns adult to infant—five minute duration (Captain)

Guard Augustus's group:
Augustus – conjure clothing from cloth (Guard)
Archer – force field for himself only
Alonso – never forgets a face—remembers names and abilities if told
Ashton – enhance another's fire ability and strengthen it
Antonio – enhanced dodging reflexes
Ari – make other people sad
Ahmad – absorbs sunlight, can exude it on command as only heat
Amos – grow his own hair quickly
Abner – barrier which prevents teleportation (Engineer/Boatswain)

Lead Auren's group:
Auren – change the trajectory of an arrow forged by his own hand (Lead)
Apex – conjure rations, pork/beans only using rotting meat/vegetables (Advisor)
Ametheus – turn wood to stone
Anthony – imitate musical instruments one at a time with his voice
Adrian – fire—create flames from his fingertips
Ace – invisibility for himself only—must be naked
Andy – move ink only on hemp paper
Abdullah – speak and understand any language
Anders – breathe underwater for ten minutes

Emissary Bennet/Aron's group:
Bennet – communicates with birds (Emissary)
Aron – instantly likeable—must make eye contact (Emissary)
Arturo – a human compass
Alexander – grow any seed by touch
Asher – change the colour of any fabric
Amir – mute any water ability, one at a time
Amari – levitate objects as big as his hand
Armando – disintegrate excrement
Ares – resistant to poisoning, will not die but gets sick
Arvo – marks target's past course (Cook)

Sahana – conjure constructs with plant fibres
Byunca – communicates with butterflies
Brielle – communicates with wolves
Randi – mental—35% used
Rani – physical—84% used
Raphaela – physical—14% used

Rava – emotional—55% used
Ravenna – mental—19% used
Ravinia – physical—20% used
Ryah – emotional—93% used
Raygan – physical—51% used
Rayla – physical—85% used
Rayne – physical—20% used
Rayven – mental—13% used
Reau – emotional—29% used
Reeva – physical—5% used
Regina – physical—80% used
Rehema – physical—43% used
Rhian – physical—98% used (Queen)
Roosha – physical—5% used (Princess)
Riverlyn – emotional—33% used
Rie – mental—61% used
Rita – physical—100% used
Raylee – physical—100% used (Slaysfold)
Raylene physical—3% used (Slaysfold)
Rayme – mental—51% used (Slaysfold)
Ruby – emotional—14% used (Slaysfold)
Rayelle – emotional—100% used (Slaysfold)
Rashida – physical—15% used (Slaysfold)
Rana – mental—88% used (Slaysfold)
Rila – emotional—24% used (Slaysfold)

Reinshaven males:
*Ryder (King), Raed (Crowned Prince), Rylee (Prince), Randolph, Raniel,
Raphael, Rashad, Rasmus, Raul, Ravi, Raylan, Raymond, Raz, Raziel, Reef,
Ramy, Randall, Reginald (Slaysfold), Rayden (Slaysfold), Rashawn (Slaysfold),
Refugio (Slaysfold), Rance (Slaysfold)*

Day 192
Main Deck
Anya's Endeavour
Reinshaven's North Sea

The women's drab-coloured clothing appeared more so by the overcast
afternoon. Large, heavy, water-filled clouds threatened to discharge. A breeze
colder than any Alder had known sent them below to add more layers to
their bodies. Enjoying the pleasant summer day, the Reins merely snickered.
Thirty-four slept while another thirty-four ate, leaving thirty-five to roam the
vessel's openness.

Men stood at various structures and positions throughout, waiting for the captain's instructions, while others trained or relaxed.

Above, on the observation deck, with their legs hung through the spindles lining the vessel's interior, Rylee, Auren, Aedyn, and Raed sat.

Auren breathed heat into his cupped hands, then pulled the blanket tighter around him. "I don't know if I shall ever be warm again."

Raed watched as his sister arrived on the main deck. She smiled when she greeted her mother and several women, then excused herself, mounting the stairs to the anchor deck. She stared into the sea as the boat sliced through the water.

The other brother spotted her as well and smiled. "Do you suppose she's still angry?"

He nodded. "I imagine. One of us should speak to her."

"I'll go," Auren slid backwards.

Aedyn laughed, grabbing the man's shoulder. "Not you."

"Right or left, Rylee?" Raed peered around the other two men, glancing at his brother.

"Definitely right."

Both men focused on their sister and when her right hand pushed her hair back, Rylee triumphantly chuckled and Raed sprung to his feet.

Those present bowed and Raed motioned for them to leave. In a serious conversation, Asa and Sahana had their heads close together and never noticed his arrival. Roosha turned, and he held her hand, drawing her to the area by the stairs, as far from the other couple as they could manage.

He re-affixed his long hair at his neck, then opened his arms. "Do you still treat me with silence?"

Roosha said nothing but accepted his invitation, burying her face under his chin. His arms drew her securely against him, offering her his comfort. As he held her, he remembered her birth. The tiny, fragile human excited him and he swore to protect her. And he had, until recently.

On one early morning, in Snakestongue Lake, it was by accident he discovered her swimming with the young farmer. Through the night, he had travelled from Cobblershorn to meet his father in Reinshaven City. He could not believe his eyes when he spotted the pair surface from the water, their bodies fully clothed.

Raed reacted, perhaps badly, now reflecting on the situation.

He vaulted from his mount and seized the young man by his tunic as he demanded her to leave.

But instead, Roosha planted herself between them and guarded the man's body, announcing they would wed.

Never had he witnessed such strong conviction as the love she professed to have—but never would anyone accept their union.

Roosha brushed her cheek against Raed's wool vest, reminding him of her presence.

He relaxed his grip, and she stayed. It pleased him.

"I'm sorry," he kissed her hair. "It isn't reasonable or fair, but it's who you were born to be. I've devoted nearly every moment to Prince Aedyn since his arrival. I'm convinced he'll be a great ruler and a pleasant husband. Please reconcile yourself to this union."

She lifted her gaze and backed away. "Would you conform if our positions were reversed? If you loved another who brought you happiness—could you marry another, a stranger?"

"I've lived your role my entire existence. My birth saw to it, same as you and Prince Aedyn. I've never loved. Perhaps I've shielded myself, realising one day I would have a marriage of alliance, like our mother and father. Do you assume he's any more happy than you are? Do you forget he was betrothed to another?"

Her laugh was cynical. "Of course he's pleased. I provide Reinshaven's allegiance to him, and he gives me what? Nothing, I desire."

He shook his head. "Regardless of your marriage, our allegiance would be his. The Aldersward ruler offers our countrymen abilities and a chance to improve our people and kingdom. You bring very little to him, if anything at all."

"Then, why?"

"Duty. In almost three-hundred years, this will be the first marriage of alliance. Scholars will write and retell it to future generations—King Aedyn and Queen Roosha. THe power couple who reunited Speranza. You'll live on as legends."

Glancing over the main deck, she walked past him. "I simply wish to love Rupert and live in a small cottage with our children—A single home for my lifetime, not a migrant like our parents. It's not an exciting existence, but it's the one I want."

He put his arms around her and drew her back to rest against him. "If it were my decision, then I would allow it, but it's not."

"Could you not argue in my favour?" Her eyes found Aedyn studying her. "A woman knows when a man is interested. He has no interest or love for me. When he looks at me—like now, I feel judged or measured, and each time, I fall short."

Raed followed her gaze, then turned her in his arms. His determined eyes searched her expression. "If you promise to accept what is and make an effort to know him, then I vow I'll do anything *reasonable* within my power to find an alternative solution. If, in the end, it's what you want."

She hugged him, and a genuine smile appeared as she pecked his cheek. It was the happiest he had seen her since he had hauled her from the water's edge—and Rupert.

Asa sat with his legs hanging through the railing gaps, and Sahana's legs were curled beneath her. Only a breath separated their heads as she spoke, and he leaned closer to listen.

She played with a fold on her dress. "After speaking to Brielle, I've made a decision. If Prince Aedyn approves, I'll learn what the healers can offer. I don't know how much or which healing I'll agree to, but there's no harm in exploring it."

His gaze travelled to their ruler across the vessel. "Why wouldn't he allow it?"

She shrugged. "These healers are for his people and King Sumner. He may find it selfish of me to even ask."

He stilled her hand with his, then left it to linger against her skin, enjoying the warm sensation. "We've known each other for a long time, him and I. There's no question; if you ask, he'll agree—even if it forced him to return for more healers. You *are* his people now. If you're worried, I can speak to him."

Feeling the glide of his fingers over hers, she smiled. "I'll seek him out, but there will be little chance for us to speak alone."

He turned his eyes to her, placed his hand on her arm, and drew her towards him. He placed a chaste kiss on her forehead. "I'll take care of it." He felt his face and ears redden. Not wanting to witness her rejection, he turned his head to observe those below.

Her face blushed, and her eye dropped to her dress where their hands laid together. She used her free hand to cover them and looked away, feigning interest elsewhere.

Day 193
North Hallway
Castle's Ground Floor
Baitsloam City

Once Belinda emerged from her room, found her husband, and begged his forgiveness over her foolish behaviour, their daytime relationship evolved.

Her eager acceptance of her role repaired the tension. They were not friendly but could share a meal, a conversation, or discuss the adjustments she made.

King Baeddan wished for her to take a set of servants and ladies for her use, implying Beatrice was too old to follow her. Hesitantly, she agreed with his assessment and thanked him.

During his favourite meal, their discussion centred on Lady Bethnee. The perfect opportunity presented itself when Barlow, the king's secretary, approached to inform; Bethnee waited to join them.

Belinda settled her hand on the king's. "We must protect yer heir. In her advanced age, pregnancies can end easily." She read the shock on his face, then shifted her eyes to the secretary. "Please advise her, her duty is nay longer needed. It's imperative she remain in her chambers and take special care of the child growing inside her. I'll have a midwife appointed to her immediately." She returned her attention to her plate and ate.

Afterwards, the pair retired to the long hall and relaxed side by side on the rise as their guests enjoyed the food and the musicians who played.

She planted a warm smile on her lips, then confided. "I should arrange a celebration. It's not every king who has two heirs coming at once." She placed a protective hand over her stomach.

Baeddan was not a stupid man, but she bet if Lady Bethnee had convinced him she was pregnant, then she knew she could do the same. She lifted her gaze, thanking Jezabet.

"Yer Grace?" The words shook her out of her thoughts.

She strolled down the long hallway, pausing to speak to several staff and guests, and she turned as the king's secretary rushed toward her, his short legs cut like scissors quickly.

He was out of breath when he bowed, taking an extra moment to inhale deeply. "Yer Grace."

"Secretary Barlow, how pleasant to see ye," she offered with a soft smile. "Please speak freely."

"Lady Bethnee has requested a formal audience with ye and the king."

Her smile widened. "Has she? How wonderful! What did King Baeddan reply?"

"He informed me she falls under yer purview."

She nodded, "Of course. I'm quite busy at present planning the celebration, hiring staff, and interviewing ladies. Did she indicate an issue?"

"She requests the leave of her rooms."

Belinda clicked her tongue. "Oh my, it won't do." She lowered her voice, ensuring discretion. "The heir could be lost. Please explain, I'll visit her as soon as I have a few moments to spare—perhaps in a few days."

He bowed, then turned and rushed in the opposite direction.

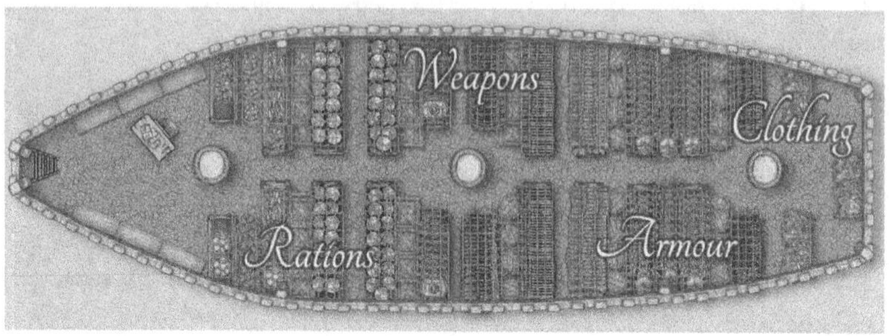

Day 195
Cargo Hold
Anya's Endeavour
Aldersward's South Sea

Sahana listened to the gentle rhythm of the sea as it lapped at the vessel's sides. From the stores in the dining hall, they collected clothing and blanketed the rocky bottom. Brielle helped her remove the layers of wraps, dresses and tunics, leaving her in a single shift, then assisted her to lie on the crudely constructed mattress.

The woman from Baitsloam stood by the ladder. Within her hand a lantern lit the dark bottom for Queen Rhian and the healers.

The nighttime could be eerie—the blacker the sky, the quieter the passengers' voices became.

Light footsteps sounded above, and four women descended. Brielle stepped aside as the queen accepted the lantern from her, then knelt next to the disfigured one.

Her manner was gentle and soothing. "Sahana, we hadn't discussed where to start, so I've brought three different healers. Could we explore your body?"

Sahana swallowed, shut her eye, and nodded.

The ties of the shift opened, exposing her scar-riddled body to the cool, damp air. Hands travelled over her torso and limbs as fingers pressed against her marred face.

Humiliated, she wanted to cry, but she buried the emotion.

After a time, the shift's edges pulled back together.

The queen threaded her fingers with hers. "I won't mislead you. In most instances, when we heal, the person's wounds are fresh. Yours have healed, but incorrectly. Some of what needs doing may cause unbearable pain for several moments before it gets better. But I promise there will be none thereafter."

When she did not respond, Brielle stepped around the kneeling women and sat on the other side. She clasped the other hand and stroked her hair. "Sahana, are ye afraid?"

Her eye scanned the faces surrounding her. "Yes, I'm frightened. But I don't know where to begin."

"Tell me about yer most cherished memory?"

She closed her eye, then inhaled deeply. "I was seven. It was a beautiful, warm spring day. My father and brother remained behind while my mother and I rode side by side, she on her tall horse and me on my pony. We travelled through the fields west of Larkburgh until we came upon Crane Lake. The surface was sparkling blue. In the sunlight, we stood naked and the warmth bathed our bodies as we waded into the cool water. It was simple and carefree—glorious." Reality faded, consumed by her memory. "She spent hours teaching me to swim. I remember weightlessly floating. I imagined it's what flying felt like. She killed a rabbit for our meal and we spent the night next to a roaring fire. In the morning, I showed her I could vault onto the pony's back. She laughed so musically, and taught me how to stand on his rump while I rode." She blinked—the pleasant euphoria vanished, replaced by an immense sadness. "That's it."

"Lovely. Ye would have trouble managing those movements with yer legs and hips as they are now. Perhaps ye should start there."

She nodded, and Rhian motioned for the healers to gather more closely around.

It would take only one to heal her, but it would take their entire strength to hold her still.

"We can give you a cloth to conceal your sounds." The queen offered, but Sahana shook her head. "Shut your eye, calm your mind, and relax. Feel the gentle waves rocking the craft." She repeated her words several times. She motioned for Bennet's wife to place her hands on the disfigured woman's shoulder. "Imagine floating in the water."

Near her legs, two women shimmied farther up her torso, setting their palms below her navel. The third parted her feet to sit between her calves.

"Breathe in."

The healer secured Sahana's ankles, then chanted soft and slow.

"Breathe out."

The chant's tempo increased—her legs grew warm, and her hips tingled.

The chant grew loud—her held limbs began to burn.

Faster. Louder.

Sahana's mouth gaped as the formerly broken bones cracked and popped free from where they had healed incorrectly.

She twisted and struggled, but the women's hands imprisoned her.

Caused by the pain, her body quaked, goose bumps rose, and her skin paled. A string of throaty, torturous moans escaped her as tears slid to her temples.

Rapidly, the healer chanted with her face skyward.

The bones in her legs and hips straighten, scraping with a grind against each other.

As her intense suffering continued—her muscles dilated, purging urine and faeces beneath her.

In her throat, a scream rose, but her shallow breath and thick saliva choked it.

Brielle's voice cooed next to her ear. "Shh, ye'll be all right, my luv. Soon, ye'll ride and swim." She stroked her hair. "Let yer tears flow. Soon, ye'll dance. Ye're so strong and brave. Shh."

She concentrated on the words—on the voice. She angled her sweat and tear soaked face to the soothing sound.

Bennet's wife leaned her forehead against hers.

Sahana's moans and cries stopped as they stared into each other's eyes.

Brielle's palm stroked her cheek, and wept for what the other suffered.

Day 195
King's Dining Room
Castle's Ground Floor
Baitsloam City

Disinterested in the tasty meal, Belinda pushed the eel and carrots over her plate. Her stomach flopped queasily. As if she had swallowed a fly and it buzzed around her insides. The feeling did not last long, but happened often. She reached for her mug.

"Ye don't like yer food?" The king's eyes narrowed.

She lowered her drink. "I'm fine, merely queasy."

"It could be the babe. Lady Bethnee complained about sickness." As he spoke, he chewed, sending tiny pieces down his front and through the air. He ripped another piece of the eel and shoved it inside his greedy mouth.

She pushed her plate away. "I should ensure she's all right. When was this?"

Unimportant, he shrugged, "A few days before we married."

"Perhaps, now, because I'm pregnant, she should wed. The dismay we bring each other could bring harm to the heirs. Do ye not wish to reward her?"

He swallowed and gulped his wine. "Our marriage flourishes, but still ye don't welcome me into yer chamber."

She hid her disgust by feigning a smile and lifted her mug. "The night act is strange and something I'll learn to endure."

"Lady Bethnee never endured my mounting. She opened her body willingly for me."

Suddenly, her mouth sweat, wanting to vomit from the image her mind painted, but she took a large drink instead and stood. "Then more reason to reward her. I'm certain a title and holdings would entice any man to accept her and yer child."

She bowed, then turned to leave, but his words stopped her. "Nay—the child will be ours. When it's born, its mouth will suckle from yer tits. Every day after, it shall only want for ye. Ye'll care and raise it as ours. She may marry, but my heirs will remain here, together."

Day 198
Main Deck
Anya's Endeavour
Aldersward's South Sea

If it were anyone other than Queen Rhian, Aedyn would have refused. She presented a convincing argument—everyone required a respite from the monotonous wait, and so, the women's disposition would improve.

His leadership team begged him to test her theory.

As he watched the party from the observation deck, men conversed around him. Soft music drifted upwards, illusions of bright exquisite gardens decorated every surface while lanterns bordered the entire perimeter and around the largest mast.

Auren whacked his back, drawing his attention. "It's not as nice as the spread I arranged for Bennet's wedding."

He cocked his eyebrow. "It's a shame I was otherwise occupied and couldn't attend."

Auren laughed. "You can no longer use your time in Baitsloam to cause me guilt, brother. I believe you enjoyed yourself."

Asa rested his ass against the railing, faced the pair, and kept his voice low. "Keep your eyes on Bowan."

He searched the crowd. "The last thing I want to do is execute Bennet's son before we even reach Aldersward."

King Roddy settled his hand on his shoulder. "Prince Aedyn, perhaps you can encourage our races to mingle by dancing with Roosha."

Raed offered. "She claims she'll make an effort."

He pushed away from the railing and left to fulfil his duty. Several followed behind him.

Gathered at their quarter's entrance, the women conversed. As the ladies noted his presence, they bowed and withdrew, leaving Roosha standing alone.

He scowled as he dipped his head slightly and, when she genuflected, he studied her hair's intricate design. The centre was black with white strands lining it and tiny wisps hung and framed her face. When she straightened, he flashed her a devilish half-smile.

He kissed her hand and stepped closer, whispering, "For a time, let's pretend."

He guided her to the clear area below the anchor deck.

When Aedyn placed a hand on her waist, leaving a proper amount of distance between them, Anthony's throat opened and a new song played. It took several steps before she predicted his and could raise her gaze.

She wondered what his remark had meant.

Pretend—*they were in love? Were elsewhere? Were other people?*

Whatever the meaning, his expression charmingly softened with an incredible smile, but still he looked through her.

It was easy for him to imagine her as Belinda. She was almost the same height, same build. He only had to envision fewer, form-fitting clothes, paler skin, and bright, flaming hair. His grip on her waist certainly enjoyed the similarities as his gentle fingers kneaded her flesh through the material.

Forcing him back to reality, she landed her heel on his foot.

His puzzled gaze met hers—angry. His hand stilled, loosening his hold. Then he averted his face to watch the other couples who had joined them.

Rylee and his partner stopped, bowing as they stepped back to allow Queen Rhian and her ladies to emerge from the privy corridor.

He and Auren mimicked the show of respect.

Before Aedyn straightened, his friend sharply inhaled. "Sard me."

Instantly, he discovered the cause. It took a good length for him to recognise the alluring, provocative woman—and only then by the circlet in her hair.

Rylee recovered first. Forgetting his current partner, he presented his hand and drew Sahana from the group as they filed out. He pulled her into his arms after raising her hand.

Her graceful body glided through the steps as the pair danced across the open space. The Alders hushed, turning to watch. Gone was her bow-legged hobble and her contorted, hunched spine. Her nose was no longer mashed into her skull and her mutilated useless eye had returned to its proper place.

When Rylee separated Sahana from the other women, an abrupt weakness struck Asa's knees, and he steadied himself against the observation deck's railing.

The cool night air caressed her naked, long, delicate arms, the rounded globes of her breasts and her flat, smooth abdomen. He glanced over the black corset with crisscrossed ties constructed to force her breasts upward. It created an open valley for a pendant to rest, and it sucked the breath from his lungs.

Suddenly parched, he leaned forward and wet his lips as his pulse raced. Her body's transformation was miraculous, but what attracted his attention most was the exquisite beauty of her radiant face. He swore she was created in the likeness of a goddess, perhaps Jezabet's wife. While she conversed with her dancing partner, her aligned oval eyes sparkled with pleasure and mystery. Her small nose protruded straight between her eyes and a defined bow separated it from her full, inviting lips. It was as if someone had painted the perfect masterpiece, then animated her—her body, her movements, and her pleasant demeanour.

As her partner turned her, he spotted the tattoo on her tailbone, peeking from beneath the long, sheer black skirts resting below her navel. His stomach burned and his muscles clenched when he witnessed the man's fingers on the soft contour of her hip.

Her spontaneous and whimsical laugh made him turn away. This was the outcome he had encouraged her to, yet he could not help but yearn for the woman he had known.

Sahana laughed when Rylee spun her loose and into Bennet's waiting arms. Her hair brushed against his shoulder, and he studied her as disappointment flitted across her excited expression.

"How do ye feel?" Fatherly pride thickened his voice.

"Free, finally." Her excitement returned, widening her smile. "My body no longer aches. It's as if those years were a dream."

He nodded in understanding. "Another awaits yer company."

"Asa?" She peered over her shoulder.

"Auren," Bennet let her go, sending her in his direction.

He caught her hand and kissed it, "My Lady."

She scanned the area as he guided her to the melody. "Where is he?"

He tsked, tightening his eyes in jest, "A harsh jab to my fragile ego if you already seek to replace me."

She laughed. "Your ego will survive a few jabs."

The slow music ended, and a fast one began. Couples flocked onto the floor. He would have taken her through the dance, but she backed away.

"Perhaps later." She bowed, then left Auren standing alone.

A waving hand caught her attention, and she mounted the steps to the navigation deck.

"Lady Sahana, your beauty is breath-taking." Captain Amos praised.

With a giggle, she bowed. "Thank you, kind sir. I'm searching for Asa. Have you seen him?"

"Not for a while. Earlier, he was above on the observation deck. He may still be there." He smiled.

She climbed quickly, her new movements amazed her.

When she reached the top, two Alders waited to descend. One helped her to stand, then followed the other down, leaving her and Asa alone.

His back leaned against the mast and his arms crossed over his chest as he watched the Endeavour's wake. He appeared not to notice her presence, and she studied him.

He was not manly handsome like Auren or mysteriously beautiful like Aedyn. Nonetheless, she was drawn to him. The excitement in his eyes, his goofy, easy grin, and the softness of his features melded to form a youthfully handsome man. Her hands had touched his solid chest and arms and she'd seen with her eye the strength of his ability. In his voice, she heard the warmth when he spoke to her and once, she had felt his lips on her forehead.

He turned, and caught in her inspection, she blushed.

As she walked toward him, he pushed himself upright. He greeted her, then returned his back to the mast and his eyes to the wake.

His easy dismissal somewhat hurt her. She smiled, seductively innocent, then blocked his view. "I thought you would dance with me?"

His own behaviour infuriated him. He should be happy for her, delighted, not...jealous? It could not be.

She was a free woman. Free to experience her race's customs and beliefs. No matter his feelings, she deserved happiness, and he had no right to diminish it.

He smiled. "Rylee was closer, more eager, and a much better dancer than I."

She stepped closer and offered her hand. "But I wish to dance with you."

She was close. A single scar ran through her eyebrow and eyelid, a small trace of her former self.

He wanted to pass his fingers over it, but instead, he accepted her hand and laughed nervously. "We did not dance so well together before, remember?"

Ensuring the appropriate gap, he stiffly framed his arm and placed his other on her hip, then led her through the steps. He grinned, softening his hold as they moved in unison. He turned her outward, and she giggled as she returned—except she took an extra half-turn and found her buttocks firmly embedded against his groin. Intent on shifting her out, his hand planted on her hip, but her fingers threaded his, holding them to the bare flesh of her side.

With the arm he still held, she lowered it and folded his forearm against her waist, then she raised those fingers to his neck, laying her back against his chest.

His glance met the fullness of her breasts, and his heartbeat raced when he smelled her familiar scent. His hands acted on their own, kneading the naked flesh of her stomach and his lips nuzzled into her hair.

"Sahana," he stammered awkwardly. His trousers tightened, and he shifted his stance.

She pulled her hair aside, exposed her neck, and wiggled her hips against his, encouraging him.

He dipped his mouth to her ear. His voice was hoarse. "We must stop. Anyone could see us."

She turned against him, ensuring he felt every warm, soft detail of her body drag along his, then lifted her gaze. "Does my appearance please you?"

He set her away, then walked to the railing, his back to her. "I recall our first conversation. You wanted to wait for your marriage bed."

She followed. "It became clear immediately after the assault no one would ever touch me. Things happen in an instant to change one's entire world. I was naïve to think otherwise."

"I've touched you before." Looking into the water, he shrugged. "And I would have touched you again."

Her voice was decisive and blunt, guaranteeing no misinterpretation. "I'm asking you to touch me now."

When he turned, her stance was proud and self-assured, reminding him she was a Slay. He wanted to and because of her beliefs, he could. But two thoughts checked him. How much had she healed and how much had it changed her? Whether or not it was accurate—he was looking at a complete stranger. Asa would not use her like a common whore.

Frustrated, he raked his fingers through his hair. "Aedyn has requested I depart at Lessard and guide a tour of our kingdom for anyone who wants to go. If you should–"

She interrupted. "I'll accompany you."

Day 199
Bethnee's Chambers
Castle's Second Floor
Baitsloam City

A fine-boned corset, covered in intricate beading, showcased Belinda's pleasing curves and the long flowing skirts swished around her lengthy legs as her ladies followed her. Small amounts of colour tinted her lips, making them a shade darker than the beautiful hairstyle embedded with white flowers for a crown. A thick, wide band wrapped her neck while fringes of beads danced along her collarbone.

With arrogance, her chin lifted higher as she walked. Her ladies mimicked the movements. When she reached the west hall, the king's men bowed, hiding their appreciation.

"Open it."

The two men shared a glance, then one removed the wooden bar. "Yer Majesty. Should ye be announced?"

Her laugh was melodic as she waved them away. "This is my home. There should be nay expectation of privacy." She pushed by and walked inside.

At the sound, Lady Bethnee turned from the window. Belinda waited. One... two... three beats—the woman and her staff genuflected.

Belinda smiled. "Ye look well, pregnancy suits ye. Have ye gained a single ounce?"

Her voice dripped with hatred. "Queen Belinda, ye needed eight women to accompany ye? Are ye so frightened of me?"

She snapped her fingers and everyone present fled. "I thought ye would appreciate our company."

As the queen sat down, Bethnee walked past the small desk to a side table and poured two mugs. "Let me pour ye a drink."

She accepted the mug and lifted it to her lips, but then lowered it without drinking. "Have ye learnt nothing from yer solitude?"

"I've learnt yer beauty is only skin deep."

Belinda shook her head and fingered the mug's rim. "I once was so beautiful and happy. But I've chosen to adapt and learn, mainly from yer example." She laughed. "Are ye pregnant? For myself, I hope ye're not. Though the king has deemed it my duty, I don't know if I can nurse two infants at once."

The older woman's eyes leapt. "I will nurse my child."

She sat forward and placed the drink down. "Nay, ye're mistaken. *Will?* Unless the king or I allow it, ye'll do nothing. And as we speak, the king's putting a generous and lucrative dowry together for ye." Her voice turned serenely sincere. "I've wholeheartedly endorsed yer pregnancy and accepted the duty of mother. Once yer babe comes, we'll be rid of ye—perhaps Clayview or Irondale, the farther the better." She smiled as she pushed herself up, then reached for the mug, holding it out. "Care to taste?"

Bethnee pushed the queen's hand aside. "I have my own."

She walked to the door and pulled it open. "Ye'll stay here, have yer babe, and I'll raise him. Ye'll be forgotten." She turned to eye the other woman. "If ye should require anything, send me word. If ye cross me or mean to contact my husband, ye'll find accommodation in the dungeons."

Day 201
Dining Hall
Anya's Endeavour
Aldersward's South Sea

When the small group entered and barred the door from intrusion, it was late, nearly the mid of night. Sahana and Brielle withdrew the candles from the lanterns they carried to light others fixated on the walls, casting away the shadows.

From the kitchen, Asa emerged, bringing a crate filled with mugs while Auren set a keg on the table and seated himself beside the prince.

As Asa poured and distributed the sweet tea, the others joined them.

Aedyn smiled. "Do you hear?"

Sahana dragged her hair over her shoulder and whispered. "I hear nothing."

He laughed, "Exactly. I've longed for silence for many days." He cleared his throat. "This could be our last private exchange. I wanted the opportunity to thank you and celebrate our success." He raised his glass, and they drank. "Asa, how many will disembark at Lessard?"

He pulled the list from his pocket. "So far, nineteen—King Roddy and Queen Rhian with their staff, Amos, Ackley, Abner, and Sahana."

Bennet touched his wife's arm. "My family will accompany ye. It'll allow me the opportunity to prepare for their arrival and lend myself to Aedyn."

Auren laughed. "I cannot wait. The first thing I'll do is spend an evening in unwedded bliss. Just imagine, all the women who missed my attention—the streets must run with their sorrowful tears."

Bennet smiled. "I'd rather not."

"Prince Rylee will escort the Reins bound for Slaysfold. And I've requested him to deliver a message to King Sumner. I want Sumner to approach Baitsloam, inform King Baeddan of my wedding, and extend an invitation. Maybe he will encounter better success."

Beside him, Bennet felt Sahana stiffen, and he gripped her hand. "When they come, Sumner will have nay recourse. He'll not wage war against Aldersward over ye. Regardless of the brutal warriors he possesses—Adler magics and numbers outweigh any attempt he would consider."

The prince nodded. "You're under our protection. He must accept it."

Day 203
Anchor Deck
Anya's Endeavour
Lessard Village, Aldersward

In the early afternoon, a lone mast propelled the vessel along the rocky grey shoreline and as their countrymen spotted them, they waved, then raced off to spread the news. By the time the craft docked in the bay, a substantial crowd had gathered, cheering their return. It was much the same fanfare as when they had left, only more impromptu and less organised.

Once they set the planked bridge, the men who lived in Lessard disembarked and met their families—a joyous, teary reunion.

Sahana watched when Asa went ashore.

As fast as he could push past the slower men, he strode the long dock and when his feet hit the sand, a pair of young women rushed towards him. He opened his arms, and they hurled themselves into his firm embrace. His face snapped back and forth between them, kissing their hair.

A rush of jealousy plagued Sahana.

Who are those clingy women? She wondered.

At the centre of the main deck, Aedyn spoke to the leadership team. "Augustus, secure wagons to escort Asa's party to the estate house. Aron, see to the accommodation and staffing arrangements there. Angelo, seek messengers to deliver letters to the dead men's families. Auren, hire retired guards to accompany the Rein royals if they wish to wander today." The prince raised his hand, silencing those who milled about the decks. "Those of you disembarking here, collect your things and say your goodbyes. You will leave soon. Those bound for Coaldale—we'll remain here tonight. If you decide to explore Lessard, return before first light or we'll leave without you."

A flurry of activity followed.

Day 203
Earl Adisa's Study
Royal Estate
Lessard Village, Aldersward

From the incessant noise of the Endeavour, the night calls of birds, insects, and animals were a welcome change. Aedyn took advantage of the vacant room, reclining in the desk chair as he savoured his whisky. The taste and burning sensation were a definitive indication he was home.

He opened the voyage's journal and wrote.

Our story feels like the start of an old jest; a legendary lover, a gentle guard, an ancient academic, and a predestined prince walked into a kingdom—or kingdoms. One, seemingly friendly, where women rule their men and sex is currency. Another an enemy who mistreats his subjects and where betrothals mean murder. And last, an allied kingdom who reinstated our rule and tied my fate to Princess Roosha of Reinshaven.

Today, this journey ends at Lessard. Lord Adisa has not returned from Aldersward castle yet. I've situated Guard Asa's party and he'll make the travel arrangements.

We successfully procured healers, and without those accompanying me, I would have failed. With this knowledge in mind, I write my final entry.

For Boat Builder Amos, Carpenter Ackley, and their households, I will offer residence in Coaldale as Lead Architects for subsequent fleets or modifications on the current fleet.

For Guard Angelo, Guard Augustus, and Engineer Abner, I will award permanent command on other vessels, conducting routine trips between the kingdoms.

Physician Aidrik may join the scholars in Edson or become an Aldersward emissary.

Guard Asa and Lead Auren will be released from service with lands and titles so they may seek whatever life they desire.

Within the castle's court, I will offer Emissary Aron a position, and beside Emissary Bennet, they will train our new emissaries.

On the rest, we'll bestow with a yearly stipend, a small reminder of our gratitude.

I've developed an appreciation for my father's rule and the sacrifices he and my mother may have made. I've learnt the importance of my position and how careless decisions may affect our race.

From our new discoveries and relationships, I wonder how our world will change.

Day 205
Docks
Coaldale Village, Aldersward

To earn an extra profit, vendors set up crude stalls to peddle their wares and services as the masses roamed the area. A woman poured flavouring into water, added a stick, and then with a touch instantly froze and handed it to a young child. From a barrel, hundreds of soapy bubbles rose as a teenage boy gaped his mouth in rapid succession.

As Prince Aedyn strode off the dock those nearby genuflected. He realised—because they would station the vessels here—Coaldale would grow.

He met Commander Ainco, who waited for him. "Are any vessels equipped and ready to depart?"

He nodded. "It'll take the day's remainder to finish loading, but they could leave tonight."

"Very well, make the arrangements. Prince Rylee, Azariah, thirteen Reins, and seven from the Endeavour will accompany the craft."

Aedyn's eyes tracked Ainco as he left, then settled on Auren, who waved goodbye.

He mounted a horse and kicked its flanks. Dust settled behind him.

Too many fresh guards, assigned by the commander, stood around Aedyn. After his time in Reinshaven, their presence felt restrictive.

The setting sun's colours painted the sky. It was stifling hot and muggy as Prince Rylee watched the others file onto the new vessel. Everything was special here. The sounds of the animals, birds, and insects were strange—nothing like the quieter calls in Reinshaven. The smells of the slight breeze were stronger. His excitement increased with the promise of adventure.

Heavy footsteps landed on the dock, and Rylee turned.

Raed hugged his brother. "You'll behave and act appropriately?" He grinned, letting go.

"As you would," he matched his brother's light-hearted nature.

Raed draped his arm around him, walking them to the planked bridge. "I wish you luck. I hope you discover fulfilment wherever you settle."

Rylee laughed. "I request you be more careful than I. Your spare possesses no interest in returning to Reinshaven." Seriously, he added. "Take care of our parents and sister. See to Roosha's happiness."

They hugged again. Rylee boarded, remained at the railing, and the brothers stared at each other while the planks withdrew and the mast's fabric opened, propelling the craft slowly forward.

Auren expected cheers from the welcoming men and the women would shriek excitedly, fighting one another to service him first. Perhaps one would even swoon with pleasure.

His anticipation grew the closer he rode, and it was the mid of night when he arrived at Den's Mercantile, ceremoniously barging through the door.

Men barely looked up from their cards as half-naked women caressed and encouraged them. The music sounding from a woman's throat did not cease, and the barmaid ignored his entrance.

Only a single baritone voice called out. "Hail Prince Aedyn's fainting goat."

The room's occupants erupted in laughter as, astonished, Auren sat at an empty table.

He expected the numerous women to surround him but none came and he passed his hand over his stubbly head.

The owner approached, and Auren addressed him with a friendly smile. "It's good to be back."

The man lifted his brow. "I told you, regardless of your station, you're no longer welcome here."

He leaned forward, his elbows on the table. "Muckspout, what do you mean, *no longer welcome*? Was I drunk? I don't remember this conversation."

"After Prince Aedyn departed on his journey–"

Confusion marred Auren's expression. "Are you mad? I accompanied Prince Aedyn." He rolled his sleeve, exposing the burned scar on his wrist. "While a captive in Baitsloam, I received this."

The man lowered his voice. "Your cowardice was a point of contention, and I have lost many patrons. My whores refused your new morbid desires and grotesque nature. At least one moon has passed since I barred and advised you to take Lady Azalea and find another brothel–"

Instantly enraged, his jaw clenched. "Where is Azalea?"

Fright clouded the proprietor's eyes, and he stammered. "He looked like you. And, Y-y-you took her and left."

Red coloured his vision as he tossed the table over and seized the man's neck, driving him upward and into a wall.

Auren couldn't muster a word—beyond articulation.

Everyone present scrambled to the walls, knowing better than to intervene with the prince's lead guard.

Strangling the man wasn't enough. And after releasing the breathing man; pent, violent energy exploded from Auren's body.

He overturned tables. Liquid-filled mugs and pitchers smashed against the floor as cards softly flitted downwards. Scantily clad women screamed.

He kicked and launched the wood chairs through the air. Scared women dodged and raced for the stairs, or sought shelter behind the male patrons as objects, turned weapons, flung past them.

He tore an arrow from his back and shot it at the hearth, but before it struck its mark, his eyes steered it through the room. Behind the bar, it punctured through several kegs, and the large containers became fountains. Their delicious fluids sprayed and covered every dry surface.

He shouted to those still inside. "I don't know who he was. I am Lead Auren of Maidstone—Prince Aedyn's Lead. There's fifty thousand gold for anyone who brings me information about my sister!"

With his hand, he caught the arrow as he stomped out and left the establishment silent and in ruins.

Day 206
Main Thoroughfare
Aldersward City

The jubilant crowds' deafening applause, stomping, and shouts of elated sentiments nearly drowned out the fanfare of music which welcomed them home. As the Endeavour's party travelled through the heavily lined lane, flowers and mementoes of gratitude rained down around them.

Auren, his expression angry, cantered his horse, settling next to Aedyn who rode with Bennet and Raed.

Aedyn laughed. "Not as missed by women as you thought?"

He clenched his jaw. "We must speak."

Hearing the significance, the prince lost his humour. He leaned closer and dropped his volume. "Can it keep until things settle?"

"If I have permission to utilise fifty of the king's men."

Aedyn's brow raised. "Of course?"

"Then it will keep." Auren flattened his torso against his horse as he jolted its sides. It launched into a furious gallop, knocking spectators out of his path.

Day 206
Castle's South Bailey
Near Aldersward City

The trip through the city took more hours than Prince Aedyn wished—slowed by the carriages filled with the females, and many more heavy wagons than when they had left.

Word of their impending arrival had spread, and the south bailey swarmed with those in residence when he called for the halt at the bottom of the wide, enormous staircase which led to the castle.

To accept charge of the animals and relieve the riders, stablemen hurried forward.

Though observed, the moment was personal. And astounded, Aedyn spun about, appreciating every detail with new a perspective. This was home—his devoted subjects and his beloved family. The dedication of countless ancestors—their perseverance, their actions—equipped him with the foundation he would need to rule and lend himself to his kingdom's future.

Never had he known such profound insight and satisfaction.

Again, those gathered bowed towards the stairs. Aedyn turned, witnessed his father and Annora come to the landing, and with eager speed, he jogged to them.

He raised his sister high above his head and whirled her around, then hugged her. She was taller, more beautiful—more grown than he remembered. *Jezabet, how he'd missed her.* No longer would Annora be the young girl who hid from her nightmares in his bedchamber. It was bittersweet.

And he hugged his father in a strong, unreserved embrace, then met his gaze with admiration. "It's good to see you."

"And I you," with his large hands, the king patted his back and watched the people climb from the carriages below. "Where is she?"

He shifted. "Second last carriage, she's standing beside her brother Prince Raed, the Crowned Prince. Where's Achelle?"

"In her room. You can visit her later." The king then warmly greeted his friend Bennet, who guided him to meet the Rein royalty.

By the castle's wide entrance, Ammaris lingered. Her hair pinned and flowed down her back. When her eyes spotted Aedyn, her mouth split in a generous, loving smile. No one existed but him. It felt as if she hadn't been whole until this moment. Excessive speed carried her as she ran and threw herself against him, encircling his neck with her arms. His scent, the contour of his body, and the steady beat of his heart reassured her of his survival. It was impossible, yet true. She loved him with more depth than ever possible. And, as one, in the past, who had never needed anything—she needed him with the desperate thirst of a drought-suffering man.

Shock brought his arms around her, but quickly he corrected the mistake. He tugged her hands free, then dropped his own to his sides when he stepped back.

"Lady Ammaris, you look well." He offered, clasped her elbow, and steered her to the west bailey garden, out of sight. Without a backward glance, he lifted his hand, signalling their guards to stay back as he led her to the fountain, then sat next to her on its bench.

Her palm cupped his jaw, and she whispered as she edged closer. "I've missed you so very much. The arrangements for our wedding are complete. My gown hangs in my chamber."

Aedyn witnessed the euphoric happiness in her person, burning brighter than the sun, and immeasurable guilt weighted him.

His hand joined hers, then he dragged it down, and returned it to her side.

For a silent moment, he prayed for Jezabet to bestow his merciful compassion on her; then for their god's guidance in his words.

She, of all, was an innocent victim.

The hard pit of his stomach knotted and twisted, threatening to heave. *Dear god, save her.*

Incapable of facing her, he walked a few paces away.

Clouds rolled in, gathering overhead as the sky darkened.

No, he decided, *she deserves more than my back.*

A sudden nervousness wrung her hands, and she came to her feet. "Aedyn, what is it?"

He stepped toward her. "I brought healers."

Puzzled, she nodded. "Of course. I'm so proud of you."

From above, fat raindrops dropped and landed loudly against the greenery.

He shook his head, his expression grim. "We've negotiated an alliance with Reinshaven, and difficult choices were made. They affect our betrothal."

Without further explanation, she understood and stopped listening.

Disbelief reeled her mind. Her every thought included him and his happiness. He and the promise he had made were her entire world.

Was this rage? She wondered. The burn in her chest and loud quick heartbeat. She was numb, yet her blood boiled.

A cold torrential downpour soaked them.

She lost control. Her hand arched across his cheek and lightning clapped across the sky.

From the docile woman, he had not expected the burst of violence. But he understood and deserved it. His men would have pressed forward, but he stopped them, not taking his eyes from her face.

Realising her action, she crumpled to the ground. As fast as the rain began, it dissipated, turning into a drizzle, misting the air.

The last thing he could offer her was privacy to grieve.

He reached their guards as Auren arrived. "Did you obtain the men you required?"

"They've been dispatched."

Aedyn nodded, then grimly angled back to glance at her. "Good. Remain here with two others. Ensure no one intrudes before she's recovered. I'll seek atonement when she's ready."

Day 206
Prince Raed's Chambers
Castle's Second Level
Near Aldersward City

After dismissing his page, Prince Raed stripped, sunk into the tub's cool reprieve, and relaxed. Into the empty room, he sighed and leaned his head against the wall, savouring the peaceful quiet.

On its haunches, his ermine, white with pink ears and black eyes, peered over the side into the water. His paw played, splashing the man.

His deep voice demanded, "Away, Felyx. Leave me."

The small creature obeyed, investigating its new environment.

His mind blissfully empty, Raed dozed off.

Through the wall behind him, a female melodic sound like humming stirred him from his slumber, before it turned to quiet, pleasant singing.

Though subdued, it grew louder and its haunting beauty addictive.

The lyrics gripped his heart.

"Their bodies danced across the lakeshore, like no other existed as the rain pour–" Interrupted, he heard her surprise, but still he waited—wanted to hear more. "Oh!"

It was not a girly shriek like his sister would have made.

"Who are you?" She purred, perhaps addressing a small child.

Achelle rested on the windowsill, singing to pass the time. Her progress spurted, and she was stronger today. A few good days, one terrible, then it repeated in a similar pattern. She glanced around the barren room.

Tonight, Alvira promised to reward her with a personal possession. She wondered what it would be.

It seemed like her day of birth, even though it would be something she previously owned. Now free of the sling, she stretched her arm.

"Oh!" An animal slinking through the small hole surprised her. It was foreign—a long body with a tiny, cute face. It neared her position, stood on its back legs, and examined her with interest.

"Who are you?" Unthreatened, she smiled. "What's your name?"

She squatted on her knees, wanting a closer look, then sat next to the hole with her back pressed against the wall.

She heard water splash behind her, and a man's deep voice called out.

"Felyx? Where are you?"

As if it could understand her, she spoke. "I think someone's calling you." But it made no movement, and she placed her mouth by the opening. "Are you searching for a small white animal?"

He twisted and saw the hole. "I am."

"It's here with me."

Unexplainably, he craved her voice. "Who are you?"

"Prince Aedyn's sister."

Raed nodded. "We met earlier. You're Annora."

"No." She giggled in a splendid falsetto, and the air left his lungs—the sound, the sweetest he'd ever heard. "I'm Princess Achelle."

He searched his memory for an image of her. "The dream-walker? Your brother speaks fondly of you. How is it no one introduced us when I arrived?"

"I didn't attend. Is he well?"

"He is."

"And you are?"

"Prince Raed of Reinshaven."

"A pleasure, Your Highness," she answered as the small creature left. "Your beast returns. Enjoy Aldersward, Prince Raed."

It was as if the gods had sung his name in flawless worship.

He had no reason to detain her further, and yet he wished for one—just another moment. Even if only to hear her to recite alphabet.

Immediately, he missed the connection he had felt.

Hearing the bells chime, she crossed to her bed and waited for the herbalist to bring her meal.

Day 206
Great Hall
Castle's Ground Level
Near Aldersward City

From twelve long tables, each with enough space to seat one-hundred, bright glowing orbs lifted to the ceiling, illuminating the dim room as a plethora of serving staff raced about to place the hurriedly prepared dishes. Typically, only the centre six tables were used, but because of the prince's return, the meal would gather many more.

A single man stood on a platform, high above the rise, and with the blow of his breath, he cooled the muggy interior.

All had dressed for the occasion. Women wore beautiful elaborate gowns with long sleeves and skirts which grazed the floor. Men, removed of their hats, their beards and, or, moustaches groomed perfectly, wore long embroidered tunics, and immaculately clean trousers.

As was customary, the first dozen chairs of each table were reserved. When nearly all settled, the king's steward announced each one who came through the west door.

The prince stood beside his father's throne when Auren entered from the north door behind the rise.

Aedyn's pleasant expression remained as he acknowledged those arriving with a nod or a gesture. "Ammaris?"

Auren crossed his arms. "Once she calmed, I escorted her through the back staircase, then called for her staff."

He kept his voice low as Roosha and Raed mounted the rise. "When she's ready, I'll speak to her again and make any arrangements she wishes. For as much as I didn't wish for our union, I realise she did." He eyed the royal siblings, then muttered. "Propriety be damned. I wished to wake my mother immediately, but the kingdoms' reunion takes precedence. We'll wake her in the morning." He turned to the princess, took her arm in his, and held her at his side.

"May I take leave afterwards?"

The prince eyed his troubled friend. "You needn't ask. I trust your judgement."

Auren bowed before he backed into the shadows.

Aedyn received a proud nod of approval from his father as the king rose.

The lively, crowded room fell silent when he raised his hand and cleared his throat. "Our vessel, Anya's Endeavour, returned successful. We pray to Jezabet for those who perished and their families. Prince Aedyn's determination will see our Queen healed. We celebrate tonight—our renewed relationships with Slaysfold and Reinshaven. King Sumner's and Lady Synnova's generosity proved instrumental. King Roddy's and Queen Rhian's cooperation humbles our kingdom. It's under these newfound circumstances, we proceed forward. For this purpose, I have dissolved Prince Aedyn's previous betrothal. On day two-hundred-eighty, he will wed Princess Roosha of Reinshaven, reviving the relationship between our kingdoms. Praise Jezabet's name for the achievements and discoveries he granted us."

The occupants cheered. Aedyn whispered to Roosha, and, feigning happiness, they stepped forward.

Day 207
South Hallway
Castle's Ground Level
Near Aldersward City

Servants utilised their abilities to clean and complete the necessary tasks. As Aedyn and Auren walked from the great hall, the morning light played through the hallways and windows. The prince studied the silent man. His features were coiled in anger and his appearance unkempt, as if he had not slept. Whatever the issue, dread crept Aedyn's spine.

He whispered, but even so, his voice carried. "Is it something we can discuss now?"

Auren's glance darted, noting there were too many around. "I've had images created of the woman who frequented Den's Mercantile. I've dispersed the men you allowed to search for her."

"You suspect foul play?" His eyes flashed and brow lifted, otherwise calm.

"Yes. I intend to join the search. I'm uncertain when I'll return."

Aedyn nodded as the pair strode to his mother's chambers. At the hallway's end, his guards stopped, typical when the royal family congregated together.

While Annora held the king's hand, Achelle nestled against his side.

It took a few moments for greetings, their first private encounter.

Aedyn unwrapped the cloth-covered tablet from Slaysfold and presented it to his father.

"They gave it to you?"

"With Aedyn's orchestration," Auren offered.

The king studied the blackened tablet, running his fingers over the etched words and symbols. "It looks similar to ours, maybe identical."

A guard announced the three Rein healers. The atmosphere turned formal. Everyone stood as the healers genuflected.

"How do you know which method of healing to use?" King Adahy questioned.

The oldest cleared her throat. "We don't until we each try. If she suffers from something mental, then only a specific healer's magic will function. If I tried, and there's nothing emotionally wrong with her, nothing will happen."

Auren lifted the water pouch from Annora's waist as she asked. "Will it hurt?"

"Because she sleeps, it is uncertain."

Achelle hugged herself. "Can we watch?"

"As long as no one interferes."

From the bedchamber's doorway, Physician Axton spoke. "She's this way."

Everyone shuffled inside. On the far side of the bed, Auren stood with Annora, his hands on her upper arms as Stinger hopped from her shoulder onto his and back. Between Aedyn and Bennet, on a bench at the bed's foot, Achelle sat, and the king dropped into a bulky corner chair.

The oldest healer sat on the bed's edge. She lifted the queen's hand onto her lap and cupped her face. Through the room, her slow words drifted, then repeated and as she repeated, they grew louder and faster.

Fascinated, the Alders watched, mesmerised by the woman who turned her face upward, seeming to draw energy from above.

When she stopped and shook her head, the prince realised he held his breath and exhaled. He wrapped his arm around his younger sister and placed a reassuring kiss in her hair. He glanced at his father, who sat forward then back, nervousness moving his body. Annora turned into Auren's body, and he hugged her.

A second healer replaced her. The volume and pace were the same, though the words differed. To the ceiling, she lifted her chin, but then it violently pitched downward, sinking to her chest as if an invisible hand held it. Her voice echoed and the speed of her chant became inaudible, one word tumbling over the next.

From her hair roots, the black pigment stripped downward along the straight length. Behind it, a magnificent white rushed to replace it. And after its entirety changed, her tone hoarsened and slowed into nothingness. Drained of its energy, her body shook as she cradled her head with her hands.

With bated breath, the family stared at the unconscious.

Wake up, wake up, wake up, Aedyn urged his mother. This must work—if it didn't, all their sacrifices had been for nought.

The other two healers approached the third.

Achelle looked to the window. *Jezabet, if you should return my mother, I shall never ask for anything again.*

Held by their support, the spent healer took a chair beside the door.

Men didn't cry, and though he tried, Auren couldn't prevent the tear which slid down his face. How he loved her—more than anyone. *Mother, I need you.*

Bennet observed the fingers on the queen's right hand twitch, and he stood and took a single step closer.

Then when Aedyn and Achelle noted the lift of her hand, they joined him as their mother's fingers fluttered to her cheek.

Auren tapped Annora's back. She looked up, seeing his wide smile. The young girl spun and raced to her mother's side.

As she rubbed her face and stretched, Queen Anya's eyes flickered open.

Annora threw herself onto her mother's stomach in a tight embrace while confusion darkened the queen's expression.

Anya's weak voice cracked. "Why are you here?"

At her words, Achelle rushed to her side, sat, and grasped her hand. "You were ill. We've missed you so much."

Aedyn and his friend embraced, both smiling.

"Adahy?" She wanted her husband.

"He's here." The prince turned to include the king, whose head was tucked to his chest.

"The chanting put him to sleep," Auren laughed and crossed to wake him with a shoulder shake. "Come along, old man, your wife awaits you."

The tablet slipped from the king's hand and fell to the floor.

Instantly, Auren realised something was wrong, and he shook him with both hands. "Axton!"

In the opposite corner, to allow privacy, the physician stood. He rushed to assist when summoned.

The concerned voice brought Aedyn to stand before his father as Auren stepped aside so Axton could examine him.

The pair blocked the women's view as the physician pushed his head back.

No colour animated his skin, no movement lifted his chest, and no expression held his face.

Immediately, the prince recognised his father's death. He spun and captured the white-haired healer, lifting her from the ground, then accused. "Did you know he would die?"

The woman cried out. "No. In nearly three-hundred years, no one has passed from our healing."

"You mean no one in Reinshaven. I assure you people here suddenly die in this manner frequently." He dropped her and returned to his father.

Hearing the exchange, Queen Anya scrambled upward. She screamed and flung herself toward her husband, but Auren caught her. She fought him, but he held fast as she sobbed.

Bennet offered the frightened daughters his comfort.

"Guards," Auren bellowed, and as twenty entered, their heavy footsteps stomped on the stone floors. "The king is dead."

At his words, eerily, time seemed to slow. Only the sisters' quiet whimpers sounded as all froze, each lost in shock and grief.

After an eternity, Bennet turned the siblings into each other's arms. In his time, he had witnessed similar ends. He dropped to his knees and proclaimed. "Long be King Aedyn's reign!"

As the words sunk in, Aedyn turned to find nearly everyone in a knelt position. The large bell hung above the castle's centre rang in long, sad tones—signalling a significant death.

He quietly instructed. "Take my father to his room."

Everyone stepped aside, allowing Adahy's personal guards to come forward and perform their last duty for their ruler.

When the guards lifted him, Aedyn stooped to take the tablet and simultaneously a single dribble of blood fell from Adahy's mouth. It landed, ran across the tablet, and in its wake turned a brilliant gold. In an instant, it dissipated.

The split-second—trickery of his mind or a foretoken? He couldn't be certain.

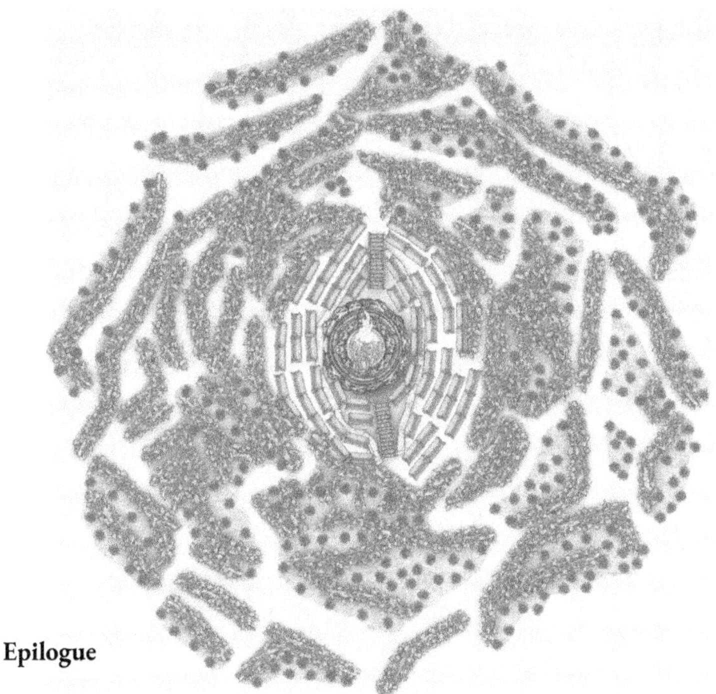

Epilogue

**Day 209
Dotato Temple
Aldersward City**

When King Aedyn's carriage stopped outside the temple, it was the mid of night. Aedyn's head and frame were cloaked. A wide band of guards surrounded the perimeter—shoulder to shoulder—ensuring no one would enter.

Auren opened the carriage door and ushered him inside through the maze of oddly skewed walls. Once they entered, Aedyn pulled the tie, and the cloak slid down, exposing his naked upper body. The large fire pit burned blue and white, sending flames flickering high above them. He climbed the stairs to where Bennet stood next to their kingdom's highest priest.

While beads of nervous perspiration slid down his body, he stretched his muscles, and the firelight danced over his damp skin. He dropped to his knees beside a large cubed stone, and Auren came forward, tying his arms to the straps secured beneath it, ensuring Aedyn was trapped.

Bennet held a thick, weighty volume open as the priest took a fine blade and knelt next to Aedyn. He dipped its tiny tip inside a small jar, then made precise, thin cuts on his back.

From the flames, Bennet lifted a long-handled ladle filled with hot coals and ashes, then offered it to the other. The man used the knife's blade to scoop the ash out and pressed them firmly inside the cuts.

Aedyn gritted his teeth and counted the process's repeats, losing track somewhere in the fourth hundred. He wanted to fight, not because of the countless tiny cuts—he could endure those. It was the ash. When applied, they seemed to travel through his veins to every extremity. His entire body burned as though it were on fire.

When the ordeal was over, Auren untied his wrists, and helped him stand.

Exhausted, he leaned against his friend, and in a hoarse voice, tested his ability. "Tell me brother, was Synnova pleased by your sexual expertise?"

Thankful he could lie, Auren smiled. Aedyn no longer held his truth ability, replaced by the ruler's bestowal magic. "No, no, she wasn't." He clamped his mouth shut.

Aedyn closed his eyes. His mind clouded with confusion as he gave into the dizzying blackness.

...Until Book II

Here's what to expect:
Will Auren find Azalea?
Why does Aedyn's ability still work?
Who's loyalty will betray Aedyn and Aldersward?
Why did the tablet turn gold?
What happens to Belinda when she births an Alder child?
Pre-order now.
www.friendswithpensauthorgroup.com
Releases June 6th, 2023.

You can reference (in order of appearance) when you forget:
How a character looks
What their ability is
How they fit in the story
Who employs them
Most notable attribute

Abigail (Abby) - **origin:** Edson, **age:** 15, **description:** 5'1", 65 pounds, slight, undeveloped, **hair:** flat, thin, chestnut, straight to waist, **face:** oval-shaped jawline, wide and long forehead, small eyes and mouth, laugh lines, jutted chin, **scars:** Jezabet's brand upper right hip, **skin:** olive, **magic:** change hair colour, **one word:** submissive, **relationship(s): parent:** Ashley, **best friend:** Annora

Abrahin - **title:** King Of Aldersward in 442 F.Y. **accomplishment:** delivered the gold tablets to the races, **scars:** Jezabet's brand upper chest, magic insignia tattoo on back

Achelle - **title:** Princess of Aldersward Kingdom, **age:** 18, **description:** 5'9", 140 pounds, flat stomach, ample breast, high curved ass, **hair:** halfway down back, thick dark brown, straight with subtle wave, no bangs, **eyes:** green with thick lashes, **face:** square-shaped jawline, high cheekbones, pouty lip, eyebrows are thicker at nose then thin and arch at ends, **skin:** olive, flawless, **scars:** pea-sized circular scar on forehead, Jezabet's brand outer left hip, **magic:** walk and communicate in others' dreams, **one word:** naïve, **relationship(s): best friend:** April, **love interest:** Augustus, **parents:** Adahy and Anya, **siblings:** Aedyn, Auren (adopted), Annora

Adahy - **title:** King of Aldersward Kingdom, **age:** 78, **description:** 6'1", 260 pounds, some muscle, some fat, **hair:** grey curls, unruly long beard, moustache, thick hair on chest, **eyes:** faded blue, thick lashes, **face:** oval-shaped jawline, thick eyebrows arch at ends, **skin:** olive, leathery, aged, **scars:** magic insignia tattooed on back, Jezabet's brand back of calf, right leg, **magic:** bestow magic on *noughties*, **one word:** passionate, **relationship(s): best friend:** Austen, **wife:** Anya, **children:** Aedyn, Achelle, Annora, Auren (adopted)

Adam - title: Earl of Grimshaw, King's Council, **scars:** Jezabet's brand bottom left foot, **employer:** King's Council, **services:** King Adahy

Adesh - title: Master of Lessard, **age:** 18, **scars:** Jezabet's brand right shoulder, **one word**: gullible, **relationship(s): parent:** Adisa

Adisa - title: Earl of Lessard, King's Council, **scars:** Jezabet's brand right shoulder, **one word**: entitled, **employer:** King's Council, **services:** King Adahy, **relationship(s): children:** Adesh

Aedyn - title: Crowned Prince of Aldersward Kingdom, **age:** 23, **description:** 6'3", 200 pounds, toned, **hair:** unruly jet black, cut at nape, covers 2/3 of ears, falls forward and haphazardly parts right, short sideburns above earlobe, **eyes:** bright blue, thick lashes, **face:** square-shaped jawline, high cheekbones, pouty lip, slight cleft in chin, thick eyebrows, arch at ends, dimple with smile/half smile, **skin:** olive, flawless, tight, **scars:** snake bite right wrist, Jezabet's brand left side under arm rib cage, **magic:** Ask the right question no one can lie, **one word:** self-reliant, **relationship(s): betrothed:** Ammaris, **mistress:** Azalea, **parents:** Adahy and Anya, **siblings:** Auren (adopted), Achelle, Annora

Ahsan - title: Secretary of Edson, King's Secretary, **scars:** Jezabet's brand upper chest, **magic:** voice projection **one word:** busy, **employer:** King's Council, **services:** King Adahy

Ainco - title: Commander of Finchester, King's Council, **scars:** Jezabet's brand upper chest, **one word:** loyal, **employer:** King's Council, **services:** King Adahy

Alvira - title: Herbalist of Edson, **scars:** Jezabet's brand right forearm, **one word:** strict, **employer:** Physician Axton, King's Council, **services:** Princess Achelle

Ammaris - origin: Wibley, **age:** 18, **description:** 5'8", 140 pounds, thin, defined collarbone and neck, **hair:** shoulder-length, chestnut brown with soft curls, no bangs, pinned back, **eyes:** blue with thin lashes, **face:** heart-shaped jawline, high cheekbones, small thin lips, eyebrows are thicker at nose then thin and arch at ends, **skin:** olive, but pale, **scars:** Jezabet's brand curve of lower spine, **magic:** doesn't know yet, **one word:** selfless, **relationship(s): betrothed:** Prince Aedyn

Anik - title: Page of Aldersward Castle, **scars:** Jezabet's brand left side under arm ribcage, **magic:** change glass into mirror, **one word:** eager, **employer:** Lead Auren, King's Council **services:** Prince Aedyn

Annora - title: Princess of Aldersward Kingdom, **age:** 15, **description:** 5', 90 pounds, undeveloped, average, **hair:** shoulder-length, dark brown with sand colour highlights, very loose curls, no bangs, **eyes:** green eyes with gold flecks, thick lashes, **face:** diamond-shaped jawline, high cheekbones, pouty lip, eyebrows are thicker at nose then thin and arch at ends, **skin:** olive, pretty, 2 small (ant-sized) moles right side, 1 right of my nostril and other near my lip, **scars:** Jezabet's brand outer right hip, **magic:** combined voice and touch, convince anyone a lie is truth, **one word:** important, **relationship(s): best

friend: Abigail, **parents:** Adahy and Anya, **siblings:** Aedyn, Auren (adopted), Achelle

Anya - **title:** Queen of Aldersward Kingdom, **age:** 57, **description:** 5'7", 140 pounds, average, **hair:** halfway down back, gentle waves, faded brown with flecks of grey, no bangs, **eyes:** green, thinner lashes, **face:** diamond-shaped jawline, thinner eyebrows which curve with eye, **skin:** olive, flawless, but pale—due to illness, **scars:** long blade slice on upper right arm, Jezabet's brand back right shoulder, **magic:** consume written word through touch, **one word:** approachable, **relationship(s): best friend:** Ashley, **husband:** Adahy, **children:** Aedyn, Auren (adopted), Achelle, Annora

April - **origin:** Aldersward Castle, **age:** 18, **scars:** Jezabet's brand right calf, **magic:** garden illusions, **one word**: happy, **relationship(s): best friend:** Achelle

Asa - **title:** Guard of Lessard, **age:** 25, **description:** 5'11", 180 pounds, average, **hair:** unruly light brown, cut at nape, frames ears, no facial hair, **eyes:** blue, thin short lashes, **face:** oblong-shaped jawline, goofy grin, buck teeth, smallish ears, straight eyebrows, **skin:** olive, soft, **scars:** Jezabet's brand right shoulder, **magic:** super strength after ingesting snake flesh, **one word:** jovial, **employer:** Lead Auren, King's Council, **services:** Prince Aedyn, **relationship(s): best friend:** Auren

Ashley - **title:** Maid of Edson, **scars:** Jezabet's brand left shoulder, **magic:** animate small wooden objects, **one word:** loyal, **employer:** Queen Anya, King's Council, **services:** Aldersward Castle, **relationship(s): children:** Abigail

Astor - **title:** Earl of Edson, King's Council, **scars:** Jezabet's brand centre chest, **employer:** King's Council, **services:** King Adahy

Astrid - **title:** Maid of Aldersward Castle, **scars:** Jezabet's brand nape of neck, **magic:** boil water instantly, **one word:** obedient, **employer:** Queen Anya, King's Council, **services:** Princess Achelle

Athan - **title:** Earl of Maidstone, King's Council, **scars:** Jezabet's brand navel, **employer:** King's Council, **services:** King Adahy

Augustus - **title:** Guard of Edson, **age:** 25, **description:** 6', 180 pounds, thin, **hair:** waist-length thick straight mousy brown, no facial hair, **face:** oval-shaped jawline, large pointy nose, thin mouth, straight thin eyebrows, **skin:** olive, **scars:** Jezabet's brand left shoulder, **magic:** conjure clothing, **one word:** honourable, **employer:** King's Council, **services:** King Adahy

Auren - **title:** Lead of Maidstone, **age:** 23, **description:** 6'2", 200 pounds, very muscular, visible without flexing, veins protrude in arms, hands, legs, and neck, **hair:** stubbly short dark brown hair, five o'clock shadow of beard and moustache, **eyes:** piercing brown, thick eyebrows that arch on ends, thick lashes, **face:** square-shaped jawline, high cheekbones, thin lip, thick middle-arched eyebrows, eagle-like nose, **skin:** olive, tough, tight, **scars:** scar (quarter circle) under left eye, bite mark on left shoulder, two 2 inch claw marks on right peck, one 4 inch claw mark on left top two abs, starting in the centre of chest and running diagonally to side, Tattoo of a wolf on right peck just below the collarbone, Jezabet's brand left abdomen, below navel, pants cover it, **magic:** change the trajectory of an arrow he forged, **one word:** gorgeous, **employer:** King's Council, **services:** Prince Aedyn, **relationship(s): sister:** Azalea, **adopted parents:** Adahy and Anya, **adopted siblings:** Aedyn, Achelle, Annora

Austen - title: Earl of Coaldale, King's Council, **scars:** Jezabet's brand right forearm, **employer:** King's Council, **services:** King Adahy

Authos - title: Earl of Neeb, King's Council, **scars:** Jezabet's brand left ribs, **employer:** King's Council, **services:** King Adahy

Avin - title: Earl of Wibley, King's Council, **scars:** Jezabet's brand left shoulder, **employer:** King's Council, **services:** King Adahy

Axton - title: Lead Physician of Aldersward Castle, King's Physician, **scars:** Jezabet's brand lower left calf, **magic:** teleport through hearths, **one word:** honest, **employer:** King's Council, **services:** royal family, oversees kingdom's physicians

Ayrton - title: Earl of Finchester, King's Council, **scars:** Jezabet's brand back of left hand, **employer:** King's Council, **services:** King Adahy

Azalea - origin: Maidstone, **age:** 22, **description:** 5'7", 150 pounds, ample curves, **hair:** ass-length, dark brown, curly, thick eyebrows, **eyes:** bright, deep brown, long lashes, **face:** triangle-shaped jawline, overbite, large smile, deep laugh lines, **skin:** olive, beauty mark, left eyelid, **scars:** Jezabet's brand right ankle, ears pierced, **magic:** turn things transparent, one way, **one word:** survivor, **relationship(s): husband:** Leathersmith Daley (deceased), **companion:** Prince Aedyn, **siblings:** Lead Auren

Azrael - title: Earl of Cranbrook, King's Council, **scars:** Jezabet's brand left leg, **employer:** King's Council, **services:** King Adahy

Bennet - title: Emissary of Crow's Pass, King Adahy's Advisor, Lead Instructor, **age:** 797, **description:** 5'10", 190 pounds, muscle is turning to fat, but not unpleasant and is easily hidden, **hair:** nape-length brown and grey, widow's peaks, slicked back and curly, peppered moustache and short kept beard, **eyes:** brown, thin lashes, **face:** oblong-shaped jawline, goofy grin, buck teeth, smallish ears, thin grey eyebrows, **skin:** iridescent, leathery, aged, **scars:** tattooed bands on triceps, **magic:** communicate with birds, **one word:** fatherly, **employer:** King's Council, **services:** royal family, castle's children, **relationship(s): wife:** Brielle, **children:** Bowan, Blake, Byunca, **best friend:** Adahy

Stop here if you haven't reached Chapter Eight.

Sabeen - title: Baron, **location:** Ravenwick, **age:** 65, **description:** 5'8", 170 pounds, thick muscled arms, tapered waist, **hair:** grey short hair, bushy eyebrows and moustache, **eyes:** baggy, green, squinty, **face:** permanent scowl, heart-shaped jawline, big nose, thick lips, bushy eyebrows, thin lashes, **skin:** white, leathery, deep wrinkles in forehead, **magic:** conjure from wood, **one word:** coward, **relationship(s): siblings:** Stew, Sheena, **sister-in-law:** Sydni, **nephew:** Sumner, **niece:** Synnova, **wife:** Saya

Sahana - origin: Larkburgh, **age:** 25, **description:** 5'9", but 5'3" after beating, 100 pounds, average, **hair:** nearly white blonde, long, matted, straight, no bangs, **eyes:** crystal blue, one pushed higher than other, **face:** triangle-shaped jawline, mashed nose, flattened into face, thick arched brows, thick lashes, **skin:** white, dirty, **scars:** face, legs, arms, hands, feet, torso, right face scar, deep and jagged, runs from eyebrow through eye then down cheek, tribal tattoo on my lower spine, **magic:** conjure from plant fibres, **one word:** timid, **relationship(s): parents:** deceased, **siblings:** deceased, **best friend:** Sydni

Sandra - title: servant, **location:** Larkburgh, **employer:** Baroness Synnova, **services:** Baroness Synnova

Sarrell - title: Baron, **location:** Larkburgh, **age:** 45, **one word:** smug, **relationship(s): wife:** Synnova (3rd wife), **brother-in-law:** Sumner, **mother-in-law:** Sydni

Saya - title: Baroness, **location:** Ravenwick, **age:** 55, **one word:** ashamed, **relationship(s): husband:** Sabeen, **sister-in-law:** Sydni

Sheena - title: Baroness, **location:** Wrenswater, **age:** 72, **description:** 5'6", 150 pounds, **hair:** grey straight bob to bottom of ears with bangs, **eyes:** blue, **face:** circle-shaped jawline, high cheekbones, nose drops straight down from forehead, full lips, thin defined arched eyebrows, thin lashes, **skin:** white, few wrinkles, **scars:** red tattoo from bottom lip to under chin, nostril ring piercing, **magic:** conjure from iron, **one word:** happy, **relationship(s): siblings:** Stew, Sabeen, **sister-in-law:** Sydni, **nephew:** Sumner, **niece:** Synnova, **husband:** deceased

Sile - title: Princess, **location:** Slaysfold City, **age:** 7, **relationship(s): parents:** Sumner and Sofia, **grandparents:** Saul (deceased) and Sydni, **siblings:** Svara, Solara, Sorcha

Sofia - title: Queen, **location:** Slaysfold City, **age:** 40, **description:** 5'4", 370 pounds, very large, **hair:** light brown, long fuzzy curls, cloth weaved through it, no bangs, **eyes:** green, hooded, **face:** oblong-shaped jawline, multiple chins, big nose, thin eyebrows, thin lashes, big mouth, buck teeth, **skin:** white, **scars:** long gash right arm, several small scars in various locations, **magic:** conjure from gold, **one word:** breath-taking, **relationship(s): husband:** Sumner, **children:** Svara, Solara, Sile, Sorcha

Solara - title: Princess, **location:** Slaysfold City, **age:** 10, **relationship(s): parents:** Sumner and Sofia, **grandparents:** Saul (deceased) and Sydni, **siblings:** Svara, Sile, Sorcha

Sorcha - title: Princess, **location:** Slaysfold City, **age:** 1, **relationship(s): parents:** Sumner and Sofia, **grandparents:** Saul (deceased) and Sydni, **siblings:** Svara, Solara, Sile

Stew - title: Baron, **location:** Hawkerton, **age:** 67, **description:** 5'8", 200 pounds, thick muscled arms, tapered waist, **hair:** shoulder length grey hair, long goatee beard with thin moustache, **eyes:** green, squinty, **face:** permanent smile, round cheeks, circle-shaped jawline, big nose, thin lips, thin eyebrows, thin lashes, **skin:** white with red undertone, deep wrinkles around eyes and mouth, **scars:** tattoo on right hand, **magic:** conjure from plant fibres, **one word:** easy-going, **relationship(s): siblings:** Sabeen, Sheena, **sister-in-law:** Sydni, **nephew:** Sumner, **niece:** Synnova, **children:** Sandi

Sumner - title: King, **location:** Slaysfold City, **age:** 49, **description:** 5'5", 130 pounds, skinny, **hair:** wide widow's peaks, short slicked back, patchy goatee, **eyes:** baggy, bright blue, squinty, **face:** heart-shaped jawline, pointy nose, thin lips, thin eyebrows, thin lashes, **skin:** white, **scars:** tattoo eagle on chest, knife slice on back, **magic:** conjure from wood, **one word:** hard, **relationship(s): parents:** Sydni and Saul (deceased), **wife:** Sofia, **children:** Svara, Solara, Sile, Sorcha

Svara - title: Princess, **location:** Slaysfold City, **age:** 13, **relationship(s): parents:** Sumner and Sofia, **grandparents:** Saul (deceased) and Sydni, **siblings:** Solara, Sile, Sorcha

Sydni - title: none, **location:** Slaysfold Castle, **age:** 62, **description:** 5'9", 160 pounds, still has pleasant curves, **hair:** jet black curly hair, breast length, **eyes:** deep blue, **face:** diamond-shaped jawline, high cheekbones, eagle-like nose, small mouth, full lips, very thin defined arched eyebrows, heavy lashes, **skin:** white, a few age wrinkles around mouth and eyes, mole on right cheek, **scars:** tribal tattoo on left shoulder and travels 8 inches down arm, **magic:** conjure from wood, **one word:** toughened, **relationship(s): husband:** Saul (deceased), **children:** Sumner, Synnova

Synnova - title: Baroness, **location:** Larkburgh, **age:** 44, **description:** 5'6", 150 pounds, beautiful breasts, curvy ass, **hair:** long brown with cornrows on top, rest flowing over my circlet, no bangs, **eyes:** icy blue, **face:** heart-shaped jawline, high cheekbones, hooked nose, thin lips, thin defined arched eyebrows, heavy lashes, **skin:** white, flawless, tight, **scars:** tribal tattoo lower spine, **magic:** conjure from stone, **one word:** fierce, **relationship(s): parents:** Sydni and Saul (deceased), **siblings:** Sumner, **husband:** Sarrell (3rd wife)

Stop here if you haven't reached Chapter Fourteen.

Baeddan - title: King of Baitsloam Kingdom, **age**: 815, **description**: 5'11", 165 pounds, skinny, ailing, **hair**: shoulder-length grey curls, neat short beard, bushy moustache, **eyes**: sinister brown, thin lashes, **face**: oval-shaped jawline, thick eyebrows arch at ends, **skin**: iridescent, leathery and wrinkled, **scars**: tattoo on back of family tree, including dead wives, **magic**: communicate with snakes, **one word**: dictator, **relationship(s): wife**: Valencia (deceased), Basanti (deceased), Begum (deceased), **siblings**: Bryce, **courting**: Belinda, Bethnee

Barlow - title: Secretary of Garsbend, King's Secretary, **one word**: frantic, **employer**: King Baeddan, **services**: King Baeddan

Basanti - title: Queen of Baitsloam Kingdom, **age**: deceased, sudden unexplained, **relationship(s): husband**: Baeddan (2nd wife)

Beatrice - title: Chambermaid of Crow's Pass, **age**: 637, **magic**: communicates with scorpions, **one word**: happy, **employer**: King Baeddan, **services**: Lady Belinda, **relationship(s): husband**: Bret, **children**: Belinda (adopted)

Begum - title: Queen of Baitsloam Kingdom, **age**: deceased, murdered, **relationship(s): husband**: Baeddan (3rd wife)

Belinda - origin: Crow's Pass, **age**: 192, **description**: 5'10", 150 pounds, tiny waist, big breasts, round hips, long legs, **hair**: knee-length red with orange and yellow highlights, wavy curls, no bangs, ear always covered, **eyes**: big bright blue, sparse lashes, **face**: oval-shaped jawline, high cheekbones, small mouth, thick eyebrows, arch at middle, **skin**: iridescent, soft, and can burn and freckle, **scars**: ear piercings, **magic**: communicate with animals (species unknown), **one word**: self-reliant, **relationship(s): betrothed**: King Baeddan, **best friend**: Brayleigh, **parents**: deceased, Beatrice and Bret (adopted)

Bennet - title: Emissary of Crow's Pass, King Adahy's Advisor, Lead Instructor, **age**: 797, **description**: 5'10", 190 pounds, muscle is turning to fat, but not unpleasant and is easily hidden, **hair**: nape-length brown and grey, widow's peaks, slicked back and curly, peppered moustache and short kept beard, **eyes**: brown, thin lashes, **face**: oblong-shaped jawline, goofy grin, buck teeth, smallish ears, thin grey eyebrows, **skin**: iridescent, leathery, aged, **scars**: tattooed bands on triceps, **magic**: communicate with birds, **one word**: fatherly, **employer**: King's Council, **services**: royal family, castle's children, **relationship(s): wife**: Brielle, **children**: Bowan, Blake, Byunca, **best friend**: Adahy

Bethnee - origin: Pennington, **age**: 639, **description**: generous curves, **hair**: shoulder-length thick silver straight, **face**: diamond-shaped jawline, **skin**: iridescent, weathered, wrinkled, **one word**: ambitious, **relationship(s): potential husband**: Baeddan

Blake - origin: Crow's Pass, **age**: 297, **description**: 5'7", 130 pounds, very skinny, hair: shoulder-length straight light brown, **face**: heart-shaped jawline, upturned nose, thin straight eyebrows, thin mouth, **skin**: very pale, iridescent, **magic**: communicate with squirrels, **one word**: sweet, **relationship(s): parents**: Bennet, Brielle, **siblings**: Byunca, Bowan

Bowan - origin: Crow's Pass, **age:** 301, **description:** 5'9", 180 pounds, average, **hair:** blonde centre braid, shaved sides, short red beard, **face:** oval-shaped jawline, hooked nose, patchy thin eyebrows, large mouth, **skin:** very pale, iridescent, **scars:** tattooed lightning bolts from eyes, left ear pierced, **magic:** communicate with frogs, **one word:** destructive, **relationship(s): parents:** Bennet, Brielle, **siblings:** Byunca, Blake

Bradley - title: Commander of Crow's Pass, **age:** 546, **one word:** loyal, **employer:** King Baeddan, **services:** Prince Bryce

Brayleigh - origin: Crow's Pass, **age:** 192, **magic:** communicates with animals (species unknown), **one word:** pleasant, **relationship(s): best friend:** Belinda

Bret - title: Chamberlain of Crow's Pass, **age:** 640, **magic:** communicates with foxes, **one word:** reserved, **employer:** King Baeddan, **services:** Lady Belinda, **relationship(s): wife:** Beatrice, **children:** Belinda (adopted)

Brielle - origin: Crow's Pass, **age:** 750, **description:** 5'9", 160 pounds, curvy, **hair:** blonde and white, mid back-length straight, **face:** oblong-shaped jawline, button nose, thin straight eyebrows, large mouth, **skin:** very pale, iridescent, **magic:** communicates with wolves, **one word:** strong, **relationship(s): husband:** Bennet, **children:** Bowan, Blake, Byunca

Bryce - title: Prince of Baitsloam Kingdom, Duke of Crow's Pass, next in succession, **age:** 780, **description:** 6', 190 pounds, average, **hair:** short peppered, **skin:** very pale, iridescent, **magic:** communicates with cats, **one word:** opportunistic, **relationship(s): brother:** Baeddan

Byunca - origin: Crow's Pass, **age:** 289, **description:** 5'9", 150 pounds, average, **hair:** mid back-length straight wheat coloured, **face:** oblong-shaped jawline, button nose, beautiful defined eyebrows, curved midway, thin mouth, **skin:** very pale, iridescent, **magic:** communicates with butterflies, **one word:** agreeable, **relationship(s): parents:** Bennet, Brielle, **siblings:** Blake, Bowan

Valencia - title: Queen of Baitsloam Kingdom, **age:** deceased, natural causes, **relationship(s): husband:** Baeddan (1st wife)

Stop here if you haven't reached Chapter Thirty-Four.

Raed - title: Crowned Prince of Reinshaven Kingdom, **age:** 29, **description:** 6', 195 pounds, broad frame, defined muscular, **hair:** long to shoulder blades, brown wavy, very trimmed beard and moustache, **eyes:** deep green, hooded, mysterious, **face:** diamond-shaped jawline, high cheekbones, pouty lip, thick eyebrows, long lashes, **skin:** white, smooth, tight, **scars:** left eyebrow corner, bite on left forearm, **magic:** noughty, **one word:** analytical, **relationship(s): parents:** Roddy and Rhian, **siblings:** Rylee, Roosha

Raquel - title: Countess of Agerton, **age:** 73, **magic:** mental healer, **one word**: pleasant, **employer:** King's Council, **services:** King Roddy, **relationship(s): husband:** Ryke, **best friend:** Rhian

Rhian - title: Queen of Reinshaven Kingdom, **age:** 78, **description:** 5'8", 155 pounds, flat stomach, ample breast, high curved ass, **hair:** waist-length, mostly silver, tied loosely at middle back, **eyes:** brown with thick lashes, **face:** triangle-shaped jawline, high cheekbones, thin lips, small mouth, thin non-existent eyebrows, **skin:** white, age-spotted, weathered, wrinkled, **scars:** semi-circle on my knee, **magic:** physical healer, **one word:** kind, **relationship(s): best friend:** Raquel, **husband:** Roddy, **children:** Raed, Rylee, Roosha

Roddy - title: King of Reinshaven Kingdom, **age**: 85, **description:** 5'11", 190 pounds, well fed, comfortable, **hair:** white well-kept hair, no bangs, thick moustache, thick short beard, **eyes:** brown, thin lashes, **face:** oval-shaped, under eye bags, heavy laugh lines, wide mouth, **skin:** white, age-spotted, weathered, wrinkled, **scars:** knife scar on right hand, **magic:** noughty, **one word:** kind, **relationship(s): best friend:** Ryke, **wife:** Rhian, **children:** Raed, Rylee, Roosha

Roosha - title: Princess of Reinshaven Kingdom, **age:** 21, **description:** 5'9", 150 pounds, broad frame, defined muscular, **hair:** slight wave, long to shoulder blades, black with silver layer underneath, **eyes:** green, **face:** circle-shaped jawline, average cheekbones, small mouth, thick lashes, thin brows, **skin:** white, flawless, **scars:** septum piercing, **magic:** physical healer, **one word:** quick-tempered, **relationship(s): parents:** Roddy and Rhian, **siblings:** Raed, Rylee

Rupert - title: Farmer of Cobblestone, **age:** 25, **magic:** noughty, **one word**: hardworking, **employer:** self, **services:** Cobblestone, **relationship(s): love interest:** Roosha

Ryke - title: Earl of Agerton, King's Council **age:** 82, **magic:** noughty, **one word**: loyal, **employer:** King's Council, **services:** King Roddy, **relationship(s): wife:** Raquel, **best friend:** Roddy

Rylee - title: Prince of Reinshaven Kingdom, **age:** 22, **description:** 5'11", 160 pounds, not skinny, not muscular, **hair:** long to shoulder blades, wavy and almost black, very short goatee and stubbly moustache, **eyes:** light brown, hooded, **face:** oval-shaped jawline, high cheekbones, thick eyebrows, long lashes, **skin:** white, a few blemishes, **magic:** noughty, **one word:** adventurous, **relationship(s): parents:** Roddy and Rhian, **siblings:** Raed, Roosha

442 years   Unification War
1F.Y.-2631 F.Y.   Peace
2631 F.Y.   The event/Amelia's Birthday
1-285N.D.   All other kingdoms are lost

N.D.

187-285 Aedyn/Achelle dream-walk - found Reinshaven
Chapter Thirty-Seven
190-285 Aedyn announces Reinshaven departure and betrothal
191-285 Bennet journals - women complicate the vessel (manifest)
Chapter Thirty-Eight
195-285 Sahana healed
198-285 Sahana's healing revealed
Chapter Thirty-Nine
203-285 Vessel reaches Lessard
205-285 Vessel reaches Coaldale - Rylee goes to Slaysfold
205-285 Auren discovers Azalea missing (doppelgänger)
206-285 Aedyn/Ammaris broken betrothal
206-285 Adahy announces Aedyn/Princess Roosha's betrothal
207-285 Queen Anya's healed
Epilogue
209-285 Aedyn's insignia/ability still works

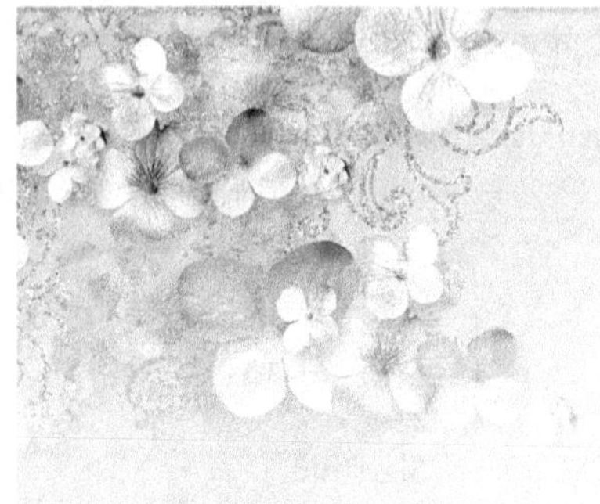

I want to thank all who helped, supported and pushed me forward on this journey.

My husband, **Derrick**, and daughter, **Kat**, who withstood the long hours of silence in our home, and many takeout meals.

Ashley Hempel, my friend, who read every line of this project, including my series bible, more times than I can count. She could probably quote any scene word for word, but never once faltered in her support. She pushed me every day through doubt and worry. Without her, I'm not sure I would have continued.

Jodi Malloy, my friend, who listened to countless hours of book talk, even though this isn't her preferred genre.

Jennifer Bailey, my friend, who steered me back into this genre, and stood by me through nearly two years of this project. I am forever grateful.

Aubrey Spivey, *Aubrey Spivey Editorial Services*, for her polish on my work. Her developmental notes added to the magic of this project.

Keylin Rivers, *Fantasy Book Cover Design*, for her patience during my indecision and numerous changes. The cover is gorgeous, and I can't wait to work with you again.

Chelsea Mongird, *Atticus Resources*, for helping and finding quick solutions for my support issues.

Starlet Montgomery, *Personal Assistant*, for your incredible generosity, wisdom, and dedication to an unknown author. Thank you for putting up with my crazy ideas.

Rachel Lithgow, Bart Baker, Jordan Barnes, Deanna Roy, Celeste Barclay, RJ Gray, Julie Kenner, Suzi Katz, Jessa York, Ellie Masters, Bianca D'Arc, Fatima Fayez, and everyone in the *Writers on the Storm, The Author Conference*, and *New Hollywood* groups on the Clubhouse Social Audio app. All of them, friends and colleagues, whose wisdom, guidance, and support were immeasurable.

From my heart to yours,
Thank you.
Marlayna

I'm just Marlayna.

Private. Writer. Giver of feels.

I use pen names. Several: *Aaryanna Abbott, Annora Adams*, and *Achelle Ashby*. The pictures on my website and social media (including Marlayna's), aren't real people. They are AI generated slices of my personality. I'm not attempting to be dishonest. I don't like or share my appearance, and I appreciate my readers' compassion.

About me...

I sing well. With music, I'm not picky. I can appreciate all genres—belting them out at the top of my lungs as I drive through town.

I love downunder TV shows. The longer the series, the better. *Offspring. A Place to Call Home. McLeod's Daughters.* A warning: they will tear your heart out.

I'm a *Buffy* fanatic. Watch the series every year from start to finish. I can tell you which episode by only hearing a single line.

I'm the coolest mom—still playing video games, smack talking with the young'uns through my headset. *CoD* and *Witcher* are my favourites. Beware, my language can get quite spicy.

I love to read and have an extensive library in my basement—there's no room for it elsewhere. They are unapologetically smutty romances. Don't like—don't look.

I enjoy thrift shopping—especially books. I mean, hours and hours to find a single book. That's my idea of an incredible day.

Little bits: veggies over candy, vacuums over jewellery, and water over any beverage.

Want to hang out with me or learn more about my books? Join my VIP reader group on Facebook. It's where I am the most social :)

https://www.facebook.com/groups/fwpvip